THE PEACEABLE KINGDOM

JAN DE HARTOG

THE
PEACEABLE
KINGDOM

An American Saga

New York Atheneum 1972

m+l

1000
g

C. 3

M ANY WRITERS HAVE DEDICATED BOOKS TO THEIR WIVES; few of them can have done so with more justification. Not only did mine sustain me with her faith in what I was doing, suffer my tantrums, bear my periods of gloom, share my moments of exultation; she did most of the historical research, made up a card file of over three thousand items, corrected two successive versions with painstaking thoroughness, and somehow managed at the same time to run a household, rear two children and emerge for committee meetings as if she had actually been looking forward to them. Yet all this does not touch upon the essence of her contribution to this book.

Some years ago, when both of us were involved in a concern called "Friends Meeting for Sufferings of Vietnamese Children," a gathering of its members took place one night in Arch Street Meeting House, Philadephia. I was sitting in the back of the room, listening to the minutes being read by Marjorie, who was one of three women on the facing bench. I know not what triggered it—a word, a sound, a passing thought—but suddenly the three women in the lamplight seemed to embody that intangible movement called The Religious Society of Friends. Suddenly, it no longer seemed a quaint coincidence that in the adjoining room was a glass case containing William Penn's first treaty with the Delaware Indians, that underneath the floor of the building in which we were gathered lay the graves of hundreds of Friends who had died nursing the sick during an epidemic of yellow fever, two centuries ago. It was as if, behind those three, the vast and numinous presence manifested itself of all the generations of anonymous Quaker women that had gone before, whose lives had been dedicated to the same things: war orphans, abandoned children, refugee camps—all the sufferings of the helpless and the innocent.

It was an extraordinary experience, and without it I might not have undertaken the writing of this book. For that night I was moved, in one of those moments of rashness to which writers are prone, to erect a monument to those generations of women, who transmitted the love of God through their lives, rather than their words. Now that this tome finally lies before me, I cannot let it go forth without planting on it, as a flag, the name of one of them, a far better Quaker than I, without whom this book would not be there—neither, I suspect, would I.

So, here goes *The Peaceable Kingdom,* dedicated to MARJORIE MEIN DE HARTOG, wife and friend, with love and admiration.

J. de H.

Florida, Summer 1971

Although based on events that took place and people who lived, THE PEACEABLE KINGDOM *is fiction. To emphasize this, I have changed all names; this was impossible only for the founders of the Society of Friends, George Fox and Margaret Fell, and some of their companions. I have also taken liberties with the layout of Lancaster Castle, in order to bring home to the reader the unmitigated horror of the place in the seventeenth century. In short, I have used the novelist's prerogative of being inspired by historical facts rather than governed by them.*

As to the dialogue: I have tried to avoid glaring anachronisms, but, aside from the use of the second person singular, I decided that the syntax and manner of speech of the period would seem quaint and thereby intrusive in the story.

CONTENTS

PART ONE

THE CHILDREN
OF
THE LIGHT

Lancashire, England, 1652-1653

BOOK ONE

(1652)

CHAPTER ONE

THE horsemen were first seen crossing the quicksands of Morecambe Bay by Harry Martin and Boniface Baker, stableboys
of Swarthmoor Hall. It was the first really warm day after Saint
Swithin's; the grooms, the gardeners, even Mr. Woodhouse, the
steward, had turned in for a nap after the noonday meal, all so
drowsy with the unaccustomed heat that nobody had thought to set
the boys a task. They made the most of the occasion by sneaking
out in their stockinged feet, clogs in hand, running swiftly and silently
along the walls of the courtyard, past the pigeons clustered together
in the shade, too hot to flutter or even to coo. They risked the
birch, on top of whatever other punishment might be meted out to
them for playing truant, by running across the forbidden rose garden
with Mistress Fell's opulent flower beds into the orchard, where they
loped like young dogs through the hip-high grass strewn with daisies
to the high arch of the entrance gate, and out onto the deserted fells.

They started by looking for cockchafers, the June bugs that were
worth a fortune if properly trained to pull little carts or run little
treadmills that watered miniature gardens; they were one of the main
attractions of every village fair. The boys gamboled in the bracken,
oblivious of the rapidly gathering thunderclouds that began to reach
out over the fells from the mountains in the north. There were plenty
of cockchafers about, flitting with rattling wings from shrub to shrub,
but this early in the year they were still too nimble to be caught. So
the boys started to look for birds' nests, especially those of the
yaffingale, for if the chicks were lifted and fed for a few weeks with
small bugs and then blinded with a red-hot needle, they would start
to sing and could be sold in the market. They were not worth a brace
of trained cockchafers, but they might bring in two groats apiece,
more if they were hawked from door to door of the manor house
kitchens in the neighborhood. But that was risky because of the
gossiping that went on among the cooks; sooner or later Will Hartford,
the head groom, or Mr. Woodhouse would be sure to hear of it
and then the fat would be in the fire.

There were no birds' nests either, however; or if there were, they
were well hidden. All the boys could raise were a few larks that
started to flutter around them, anxiously chattering, to lead them away
from their nests; but there were no yaffingales at all.

It was Harry Martin who first spotted the horsemen: two small
dots that had detached themselves from the dark bluffs on the other
side of the estuary and were now approaching across the sands.
"Bonny!" he cried. "Look, over there! Look!"

Boniface Baker looked, but he saw nothing; the whiteness of the sands in the fierce slanting sunlight blinded him. "What is it?"

"Over there! Below Holker Hall!"

Bonny shielded his eyes with his hand and gazed into the distance; after a moment he saw them too: two horsemen, small and lost in the immense expanse of the sands, following the brogs of the bridle path that wound its way between the sinkholes and the patches of quicksand, from which no horse or man could ever extricate himself. He leaped to his feet. "But they'll never make it!"

"Of course they won't. Look! The tide has already turned!"

So it had. Lonely Chapel Island, where in the old days the monks had tolled a bell and said masses for the souls of travelers who had perished in the quicksands, was already surrounded by the sea. The incoming tide raced across the sands faster than a galloping horse, and the strangers faced certain death in the onrushing waters unless they turned back at once and rode as fast as they could to the bluffs of Cark. If they tarried only a few minutes longer, they would be doomed; the sands were soft in the center of the estuary and would slow down their pace; the swirling tide would overtake them and sweep their horses off their feet; the moment the brogs that marked the path were submerged they would end up in one of the pits of quicksand and be drawn under.

Fascinated by the spectacle of two men riding to their death, the boys stood motionless in the bracken; then, for the first time, they heard the rumble of the approaching storm.

"Look at the weather," Harry Martin said.

Bonny looked. The peak of Old Man Coniston in the distance had already vanished in the clouds; lightning flashed in the blackness; the wind dragged a slanting curtain of rain across the fells toward Ulverston; even as they looked they saw the shadow reach the town and extinguish the spark of the weathercock atop the church tower. It would not be long before the storm reached them; if they wanted to be home before it hit, they would have to run for it.

But the distant horsemen had failed to turn around; they continued to ride unsuspectingly into the deathtrap of the shimmering sands. They could not see it from where they were, but the boys, hearts racing with excitement, saw the swift ripple of silver water slide inexorably toward them. "Somebody should go and tell the Colonel!" Bonny said. "Maybe somebody could signal them from the tower."

"Too late. They are done for."

"But we can't just stand here and watch! We should do something!"

"We should be on our way home," Harry said, "and fast! Come on!"

But Bonny did not move. He gazed at the two little horsemen innocently cantering toward their end; they had almost reached the soft sands and the first slithering tongues of water were lapping at their horses' feet. They were close enough now that he could distinguish the color of the horses: one brown, one white; one of the men wore a white hat, stark in the sunlight. But not for much longer, for from the north, almost as fast as the water, the black shadow of the thunderstorm came racing toward them with the slanting curtain of rain.

"Come on, Bonny! They'll be missing us at the Hall! Hurry, please!"

"Tell thee what," Boniface said, suddenly determined. "Go thou to the Hall, I'll go and tell the Colonel." He turned away and began to run in the direction of the town.

"Don't, Bonny!" Harry shouted after him. "It's too late!" But his friend was out of earshot now, or refused to listen; he went on running, jumping over clumps of bracken, frightening the browsing sheep, while in the distance forked lightning flashed in the ink-black sky and the low, angry rumble of thunder growled. It was a crack-brained thing to do; a child could see that the men could not be rescued now, it was too late, they had gone too far, not even a boat could reach them in time. Will Hartford would be furious when he found out the boys had played truant; the dramatic news of the drowning horsemen might have diverted his attention, but with Bonny Baker gone there was certain to be terrible trouble. Harry Martin spat angrily at the back of his treacherous friend leaping in the distance; then he started to run as fast as his legs could carry him toward the Hall. The sharp sunlight, about to be extinguished by the storm, flashed in the windows of the west wing; a wisp of smoke rose from one of the chimneys; Cook was starting the kitchen fire for supper.

* * *

The house of Colonel Best, the coroner, lay on the outskirts of town, a small manor built of ship's timbers and red brick in a walled garden. Bonny Baker, panting, stumbling, reached the gate just as the first heavy drops of rain thudded into the dust of the road. In a last spurt of strength he sprinted down the garden path, pelted by rain; he hit the closed bottom half of the kitchen door with a bang, one of his clogs slipped from his hand and fell inside on the flagstones with a loud clatter. It startled "Monsoor" Bonne-charme, the Colonel's cook, who stood cutting up something at the table, his back to the door. He jumped around, brandishing a foot-long carving knife, and cried in a high-pitched cantankerous voice, "*Sacré nom!* You are crazy, no? You want me to run myself through, no? *Sacré gosse!*"

But Bonny knew Monsoor well enough to be no longer frightened by his French explosions; he panted, "Monsoor, Monsoor, please, please, the Colonel! The Colonel must come! Two men, two horse-men . . ." He could not catch his breath.

Kathryn, Mrs. Best's buxom maid, who had bustled in when she heard the noise, asked, "What's going on here? What's the matter with thee, boy?"

"Two horsemen on the sands . . ." Bonny panted. "They're in

the soft part now, they'll never get out. The Colonel must help them, somebody must help them, or they'll drown . . ."

"Ah! *Sacré nom de putain!*" Monsoor cried, shaking his carving knife at the ceiling. "There go my lobsters for tonight! That's the fishmongers from Cark! Ah! *Misère! Miséricorde!* What a country!"

"No, sir, no, sir, no, Monsoor!" Bonny cried. "It isn't the fishmongers, sir, it's strangers, two strangers. People who live here know better than to ride out across the sands with the tide coming in."

But Monsoor Bonnecharme refused to be consoled. He threw his carving knife among the pewter dishes on the table with a clatter, slapped his skull with alarming force and shouted, "There they go! My lobsters! What am I going to give them for supper tonight, what, *bon Dieu de bon Dieu?*"

"Oh, come," Kathryn said with obvious disgust. "Two people are choking to death in the quicksands and all you can think of is lobsters! Bonny—"

"Well, *sacré nom de putain de Bretagne!*" Monsoor shrieked, getting into his stride. "Who, in the name of the smoking Trinity, will think about lobsters if I do not? If I were not squeezing my life's blood out of my *entrailles* to feed them, *Monsieur le Colonel et Madame* would have to subsist on peeg's trotteurs, feesh and cheeps, shepherd's pee!"

"Oh, for mercy's sake!" Kathryn cried, turning her back on him. "Wait here, boy, I'll go and tell *Madame!*" In the doorway she turned around and said, "Don't go away, now. The Colonel may want to speak to thee."

"*Voilà!*" Monsoor cried triumphantly, pointing at the door through which she had vanished. "*Le Colonel,* he want to speak to thee!" He mimicked her, cattily. "She does not say 'Poor boy, stay in the warm kitchen until the rain stops,' no, no! I am *un monstre* because I worry about her supper instead of praying for two fools drowning in the sand, while she would send a child, drenched by the rain, exhausted from running, back into the storm without turning a hair on her—her *cul de guenon!*" He took a deep breath to continue, but a rapping on the ceiling overhead cut him short. "*Sacré nom,*" he whispered. "*Madame . . . !*"

The thunder crashed much closer; a whirlwind lashed the windowpanes with rain. As Monsoor Bonnecharme rushed toward the door to close it, a huge man with matted hair and a beard dripping with water appeared in the opening. He glanced about him before holding up a big dead hare.

"*Monsieur* McHair!" the cook cried, a shout of joy. "Angel, messenger from heaven, Gabriel! How did you know my lobsters were drowning?"

"Good day to thee, Monsoor, my friend," the man growled, with a grin of rotted teeth. "How about inviting me in for a bowl of soup?"

"Come in, come in," the cook whispered, opening the door, "but be quiet and do not show this glorious beast! I'll stick him in a bucket! Come, come," he urged, letting the giant in and closing the top door, locking out the rain. "Hush!" He pointed at the ceiling. "She is upstairs, listening. Do not speak about thees . . ." He took the big limp hare from the poacher and kissed its dead cold nose. *"Ah, mon petit chou! Mon petit joujou!"*

The giant grinned and winked at Boniface; obviously, he had never seen a man kiss a dead hare before either.

Boniface smiled at him a little wanly, for an astonished sadness had been growing within him ever since he arrived. Nobody seemed to give thought to the two little horsemen who must now be struggling for their lives in the ice-cold swirling waters of Morecambe Bay. He could almost hear them shouting for help, faint desperate voices in the wind; then lightning flashed behind the windows and a terrific thunderclap crashed nearby.

Monsoor Bonnecharme closed his eyes, folded his hands with the dead animal in his arms and mumbled rapidly, *"Douce vierge pleine de grâce, protégez-nous,"* before taking the lid off a bucket by the stove and dumping the hare into it, head first.

* * *

"What on earth is going on below?" Henrietta Best asked irritably when her maid entered. She hated thunderstorms, they set her nerves on edge.

"One of the stableboys from the Hall, *Madame,*" the girl answered. "He came to tell the Colonel that two horsemen seem to be caught by the tide."

"In this weather? What does he expect the Colonel to do about it? Who sent him, anyhow?"

"I think he saw them himself, *Madame,* and just came running to tell the Colonel. He's too young to know that he could have saved himself the trouble."

Henrietta Best shot her a glance in the steel mirror. "How touching," she said, and continued fussing with her wig. She had begun to ask herself of late whether the girl was impertinent or merely artless. "Has anybody told the Colonel?"

"I don't believe so, *Madame.*"

"Well, why don't you? We don't want that little boy to have run all the way for nothing, do we?"

As in her mirror she saw the girl turn to go, she asked, "What was Bonbon shouting about?"

"Oh, I don't know, *Madame.* Something about lobsters."

"I thought I heard the words '*cul de guenon.*' What does that have to do with lobsters?"

"I really couldn't say, *Madame,*" the girl answered stiffly. "I don't speak his language."

"They mean 'fat buttocks of a female baboon,'" Henrietta Best explained, observing her in the mirror. "I hope you are not picking a quarrel with him again?"

The girl mumbled, "No, *Madame*," and hurried out of the room, her composure shattered.

"And, Kathryn!" Henrietta Best called after her. "When you're through warning the Colonel, tell Bonbon to come up here. I want to talk to him." There was no reply.

Silly to needle that girl. She was an excellent maid; rather than poking fun at her bulk one should be grateful for it, as it lessened the chances of her being carried off by some yokel to breed little Puritans in one of those dank, smelly cottages on the fells. Really, with an overweight maid and a *pédéraste* for a cook, she should count her blessings rather than take out on them her nervous irritation induced by the weather. Poor Bonbon; what a swath a true Frenchman could have cut in this sanctimonious town of strait-laced females, every single one of them desperate to leap into the hay with a shriek of perdition, wringing her hands in prayer while being mounted. Thank God dear Bonbon was the way he was; next thing you knew, one of his paramours would have had him up for witchcraft or blasphemy or for having closed a pact with the devil, never because she had been raped, of course. Oh, no, never rape; in this blessed corner of these blessed isles we all pretend that babies are hatched out of eggs, pink eggs for girls and blue eggs for boys, not torn screaming from our guts *intra faeces et urinam*. Like Jeannot, in that cellar in the straw, with all those men watching . . . She shivered. Not again, not that.

She threw the comb angrily at the aging woman in the mirror; it clattered down among the little bottles and the jars. What in the name of sanity was she wearing this idiotic wig for? Look at it: lace, velvet bows, silk ribbons; and all that just to sit opposite her dear nincompoop at table and hear him grind on about grouse or horses or the plight of the weavers since the Civil War, messily masticating one of Bonbon's exquisite delicacies, washing it down with draughts of claret with which he rinsed his mouth, while the little man hovered pathetically behind him, on tenterhooks with the artist's desperate need for praise or even a sign of awareness that something had been created.

Another colossal thunderclap crashed into the foaming trees outside the window; she closed her eyes and covered her ears with her hands, her elbows on her dressing table. Don't be foolish, she told herself, don't be foolish; it is only thunder. It almost worked; then she remembered that this was what she had said to the children when the guns started firing.

She tried to extricate herself from the past; she must not allow herself to think any further, she mustn't, she mustn't . . . Then she remembered, with a feeling of liberation, the two men lost in the quicksands, the message brought by a boy. Boy! She sat up sharply. To be thankful that Bonbon could cause no trouble with women was one thing, to furnish him with young boys another. She got up briskly and strode toward the door, damask rustling, out of danger now, and came face to face with her husband in the doorway.

"Well, m'dear," he said, buttoning his coat, "I had better go and start the search for the bodies of those poor wretches. It's a deuced nuisance just before supper, and in this weather . . ." He tried to look pained, but it was obvious that he would enjoy it immensely.

"Here," she said, "give me thy sash."

"Sash? Oh—of course."

He handed her the wide orange ribbon with tassels that he had hung around his neck when he started to button his coat; she lifted her skirts and knelt in front of him to tie it around his corpulent waist. Just then Bonbon came running up the stairs and appeared behind his master. *"Monsieur le Colonel* is not going out?!" His voice sounded reproachful, like a lover's.

"Of course I am!" Her husband stiffened irritably.

"Stand still," she said.

Bonbon began a long jeremiad about spoiled dishes and wine that had just been decanted; her husband muttered, "Oh, for mercy's sake! Send that screaming parrot away."

"Ça va, Bonbon. Monsieur le Colonel sera de retour dans une demi-heure." It was not true, of course; once he left the house he would be away a great deal longer than half an hour; apart from riding to hounds, the stag hunt and the occasional hanging, he had nothing by way of entertainment, poor dear, except his ghoulish duties.

"Forgive me," he said as Bonbon, huffed, clattered down the stairs in his plopping slippers. "I just can't stand the creature. Must be his nature, I suppose."

"Stand still." She tied a neat feminine bow in his sash of office. The thunder rumbled and rain lashed the windowpanes, bringing reminiscences of other sashes she had tied, and untied.

Then a child's voice screamed shrilly in the kitchen.

* * *

Colonel William Best wondered what the devil it was this time; there could be no other household in bleeding Lancashire so addicted to screams, tantrums, flying into snits or taking umbrage. He was about to stamp angrily downstairs and tell that hysterical bunch of good-for-nothings what he thought of them when he happened to look down and saw his wife's face. She stared at him with eyes full of horror; in one second she had aged ten years. He was torn between staying with her and going downstairs; then she leaped to her feet and rushed out of the room, breaking her own spell or being drawn into its vortex, he did not know which. He followed her, no longer angry but deeply worried.

The past year it had seemed as if at last they had managed to erase her past; she had seemed gay, carefree, loving. But, obviously, she had been unable to exorcise her ghosts; all it needed to throw the poor soul back into the torments of hell was the scream of a child. As he clumped down the stairs in his heavy riding boots, sideways because of his spurs, his anger returned with a vengeance.

Whoever the idiot was that had caused his wife's distress, he would
pay for it, as would that castrated poodle and that shrieking wench.

The first one he saw as he entered the kitchen was the damned
poacher. This was the limit! He had given orders not to buy any
more game from that brigand, for the sake of sweet peace with
John Sawrey, yet here he was again!

And there was the boy, obviously the one who had brought the
message, as white as a sheet; in the doorway stood two strangers
dripping with rain and disheveled by the storm, one with a white
hat which he had not bothered to remove.

"Well?" he inquired gruffly. "Did you find the bodies?"

Then the boy spoke up. "No, sir," he said in a high-pitched,
frightened voice. "There are no bodies! Those are the men I saw . . ."

"Don't talk bloody nonsense! Nobody can cross the sands at incoming tide, not even if his horse has wings."

"The boy speaks the truth, friend," the stranger with the white
hat said. "We crossed the sands, our horses swimming part of the
way."

"Nonsense!" the Colonel repeated, angered by the man's presumption. "I was born in this town, my father was coroner of this county
before me; never has any man who set out from Cark after the turn
of the tide reached this shore alive. It is impossible."

"I can well believe it," the stranger said. "But we were in the
power of the Lord."

His wife must have sensed his outrage, for suddenly he felt the
coolness of her hand upon his and he heard her say, "You are
drenched, gentlemen; won't you come in and partake of a meal
and dry your clothes in front of the fire? Surely you're not planning
to travel on tonight?"

"We are bound for Swarthmoor Hall," the stranger said, courteously
enough but still without doffing his hat or addressing her correctly.

"Are you expected there tonight?"

"No."

"In that case, you had better stay here until morning, and so had
thee, dear boy," she added, turning to Bonny. "Bonbon, take care
of these gentlemen. And now, if you will excuse me . . ." She
pressed her husband's hand and he had no choice but to proffer
his arm to escort her back upstairs.

But she did not want to go back upstairs; she steered him across
the hall to that small withdrawing room in the far corner, where they
were wont to drink a glass of muscatel before supper. As they walked
he felt her hand trembling on his arm; the screech of that idiot
boy must have upset her deeply. He closed the door behind them
and led her to a chair; as he turned to pour out the wine, he said,
in an effort to divert her attention, "I thought I'd made it clear that
I did not want any more game to be brought to this house by John
McHair! Didst thou not inform thy French creampuff of my wishes?"

But she was not listening; she only became aware of his presence
when he handed her the heavy glass. She smiled to thank him, but

did not speak. She took the glass and held it close to her bosom as if she were sheltering it, like a kitten. He was about to say something soothing when she said, "Whatever brought that man here, it was an ill wind."

"What man?"

"That fanatic. The one with the white hat."

"Why? What hast thou against him, other than that he has no manners and is an obvious liar?"

"Oh, no, he is no liar," she said with a wistful smile. "He crossed those sands, all right."

"But, dear heart, it is not possible! The tide runs too strong, and once the brogs are washed under, no man can find his way through the quicksands. Not even those who have lived here all their lives."

She shrugged her shoulders with feminine disdain for the laws of nature. "Oh, his horse must have swum or something, I don't know," she said wearily. "All I know is that he is a bird of ill omen."

"Now, what makes thee say that?"

She looked at him with an odd expression in her eyes. It was not fear, it was not despair, it was as if she had dropped a mask and now was looking at him as her true self, the Douce Tété he had met and married in Paris thirteen years before. "Because he looked at me with love," she answered.

The words were so unexpected, their impact so stunning, that he stood looking at her, mouth open, for several moments before rage overwhelmed him. "Well, God spare my soul!" he cried, slamming the glass down on the table. "I'll go and throw the swine out of my house right now!"

"No!" She seized his sash and stopped him in his tracks, making him feel ridiculous. "That's not what I meant! Not that kind of love!"

His anger collapsed; he felt suddenly embarrassed and ill at ease. For thirteen years they had never mentioned the conditions under which they had met; they had avoided the subject so skillfully that by now it was as if it had concerned two different people. "Then what dost thou mean?"

"He looked at me the way the . . . the saints used to look," she replied. "With divine love."

He wanted her to don that mask again, more for her sake than his own. But he had to know. "What dost thou mean?"

"Indiscriminate, impersonal love," she replied, with that wistful smile again that distressed him more than anything else. "Love for its own sake, not mine."

Obviously, she thought of the past all the time, it was an obsession, a kind of mania. He closed his eyes and wished, more fervently than he had wished anything for a long time, that he could help her forget, help her free herself of the fetters he had thought she had shaken off. But this was a cross she would have to bear for the rest of her days. What had happened in that little town in

France twenty-four years before still dominated her life. "I can have him thrown out of the county," he said unconvincingly.

"That would be the worst thing thou couldst do. People like that thrive on persecution."

"Who is he, for sweet Christ's sake? How dost thou know all this?" His anger returned; it was a different anger now, the anger of powerlessness. What had they done to God to have this man foisted upon them at this point, so late in their lives?

She shrugged her shoulders. "I don't know who he is, I only know what he is: a saint. I mean someone who is drunk with God."

"I don't understand."

"Thou must have met them thyself in the courtroom or in thy travels. It doesn't matter what church they belong to, whether they are Papists or Protestants or Independents, they are all exactly alike. Their eyes shine with love; they are obsessed with mercy and salvation; they hear voices nobody else hears, see visions only they can see; they believe that they have been sent by God to change the world. But all they do is set people at each other's throats, separate parents from children, husbands from wives. They want everyone they meet to desert those they love, drop whatever they are doing, give up all they possess and follow God, which means following *them*. It always ends in violence and horror and death, but that does not matter to them. They would feel rejected by God unless they were imprisoned or tortured or burned at the stake or hanged from a meat hook or had their tongues ripped out or their genitals torn off . . ." She covered her face with her hands.

He could not allow this; whatever happened, he had to stop her from being drawn back into that dark unknown horror in her past. He went to her and put his hand on her shoulder with tenderness. He wanted to speak, but did not know what to say. Some of his concern, his love must have been evident, for suddenly she grabbed his hand and covered it with kisses and whispered, "Oh, Will, Will, Will, my love; hold me, please, please hold me . . ."

He held her, while distant laughter rang out in the kitchen.

"Where wert thou born, friend Boniface?" the stranger asked the next morning, as the horse they were riding turned onto the fells.

"I don't know, sir," Bonny answered happily. "I suppose somewhere around these parts, Lancaster way."

"Surely thy parents must have told thee?"

"I never knew my parents, sir."

It seemed a dream: the horse, the warm presence of the stranger behind him, the birds, the sunrise, the rolling fells, the white clouds of summer in the high blue sky. It made his heart swell with pride and happiness; never before had anyone betrayed such interest in him. It took the menace out of the gloomy Hall ahead. All night he had tossed and turned in the straw of the loft over Colonel Best's stables; he had wakened not knowing where he was, and had become afraid when he remembered. He did not dare think of what Will Hartford would do to him when he got home; ten strokes of the birch were the least he could expect. But, sitting in front of the powerful stranger astride his white horse, all fear dissipated. He was safe; compared to the miracle of riding across the sands against the incoming tide, to protect a stableboy from being beaten by the head groom was nothing.

"Ah, thou art an orphan?"

"No, sir," he replied. "I am a foundling."

"Then who gave thee thy name?" the stranger inquired. "Did someone write it on a piece of paper, by chance, and pin it to thy swaddling clothes?"

"No, sir, it was given to me by the women in the foundling house in Kendal. I was found on the stoop in a little basket, early in the morning."

"Ah?"

"Somebody banged on the door and opened it and shoved in the basket, calling, 'Baker!' The mother told me she was the one who said, 'I'm going to call him Boniface, he has a bonny face.'" He grinned and tried to look up at the stranger, but he could not twist his neck that far.

"And who put thee to work at the Hall?" the voice behind him insisted. "Justice Fell is an important man in these parts. It is quite an honor."

"I know, sir," Boniface said eagerly. "I was very lucky. I was playing outside when a coach-and-four came down the street; I saw that the cap of one of the wheels had come off, and I ran after it, shouting; I had to run quite a way before they heard me. Then the coachman stopped and got down and looked; if they had gone on a little longer, the wheel would have come off. Then somebody opened the door of the carriage, a man in a big hat with an ostrich feather; he wanted to give me a groat, but I didn't take it, because we had been taught never to take money for doing a kindness. Then he said, 'How would you like to work as a stableboy at my house?' I said, 'I would love to, sir, but I would have to ask the house mother and she may not know who you are.' And he said, 'Tell the house mother that Chief Justice Thomas Fell of Swarthmoor Hall wants to see her and thee tomorrow morning.' Then he pulled the door shut, they drove off and I went back to the house and told the mother. We went the next day. I was lucky I got his name straight."

"Well, Boniface," the stranger said earnestly, "what dost thou think made thee run after that coach to warn them about the wheel?"

Boniface thought. "The same thing that made me run to the Colonel's house to tell him about you, sir, I suppose."

"Even more so, for by doing that thou risked punishment. So, what made thee run through that thunderstorm and risk being punished?"

"I don't know, sir. I just couldn't watch you and your friend ride into the quicksands without doing something about it."

"Thy friend could."

It was true what the stranger said, yet it did not seem fair to Harry Martin. "If I'd known you were going to perform a miracle, sir, I wouldn't have run either."

"It wasn't I who performed the miracle, friend Bonny. It was the Lord in whose power we were."

"Yes, sir," he said obediently.

"That has little meaning for thee, has it?"

The question startled him. It was as if the stranger, apart from the power to do miracles, could read his thoughts.

"Dost thou know the Lord, friend Bonny?"

He had heard about the Lord all his life, prayed to Him every night, but know Him? He was about to say something evasive when he remembered that his thoughts would be read anyhow. "No, sir," he said.

"That is strange, for a boy who has been in His power twice in a lifetime."

"I . . . ?"

"It was He who made thee run after that carriage. It was He who made thee warn the coroner, knowing thou wouldst be punished."

He thought about it, gazing at the Hall across the meadows. He could discern the lattice on the windows now; something white moved in the shade of the trees that sheltered the house. It must be one of the young ladies; none of the servants wore white.

"Well?"

"But I didn't see anything, sir. I didn't hear any voices either. I just saw you and ran."

"But what prompted thee to run?"

"I don't know, sir. Something—something inside me."

"Aha!" the stranger cried. "Where dost thou think God lives? In the sky?"

He wasn't sure he liked this turn in the conversation. He would rather talk about himself.

"That's where thou art wrong," the stranger continued. "He lives within thee, friend Boniface. Within everyone."

"Have you done many miracles?" Bonny asked, to change the subject.

"Not I, remember? Man performs miracles only when he is in the power of the Lord. It may happen to anyone, it may happen to thee. His power is within thee; He is there, in all His glory: all light, all joy. He is the power that creates and rejoices in His creation. What He radiates, above all else, is joy."

Bonny felt the joy radiate from the man behind him. Suddenly he was overcome by the desire to shout, to sing. He had never felt this way before; he had never dreamed that anything to do with church could be gay. "Yes, sir," he said.

"Hast thou ever prayed?"

"Yes, sir."

"Don't call me 'sir.' Thou and I are children of the Light, we are brothers. Call me George, and address me with 'thou' instead of 'you.'"

He could hardly contain that shout. He whispered, "Yes, George."

"Hast thou ever really prayed? Hast thou ever not asked for anything, but just opened the gates of thy soul, to let that of God within thee fly forth?"

Boniface shook his head.

"Dost thou feel like doing so now? Go on, friend Bonny! Sing, whisper, shout; pray, little friend, pray!"

So it came about that John Foster the shepherd, tending his flock outside Swarthmoor Hall, was startled by a high-pitched child's shriek which flushed a lark from its nest and sent it, twittering and warbling, straight up into the sky. He saw a white horse canter by, on its back a man with a white hat and in front of him one of the stableboys from the Hall. He thought the child was being abducted and that the shriek he had heard had been a cry for help; but when the boy spotted him, he waved and shouted, "Top of the morning to ye, John Foster!"

He did not return the greeting. He gazed after them, mouth open, leaning on his staff, as the horse thundered through the bracken, clods flying, down into the glen. There, small and white, it forged the stream, silver flashing in the sun, and cantered across the rutted road, raising a cloud of dust before it vanished through the gate.

* * *

A few hours later that morning the same shepherd, from his vantage point on the high fell opposite the Hall, saw another cloud of dust rising on the road from Ulverston. Soon a small carriage drawn by two black horses appeared around the bend; he recognized it even at that distance. It was the coach-and-pair from the Hall, bringing Mistress Fell back from her weekly visit to the market. Every Friday morning, come rain or shine, he watched her leave and return. He had known her ever since she was a little girl, a beautiful child, golden-haired, picking flowers; one time the maid had brought her to him to ask if Miss Margaret might stroke the little black lamb. He had stood outside the church when she came out, radiant and beautiful in her wedding gown, by the side of the judge old enough to be her father. Now, twenty years later, she was still a strikingly beautiful woman, but with a flaring temper, as he had occasion to witness whenever his herd happened to block the way as Mistress Fell in her coach-and-pair came careening down the road, horses snorting, foam flying; she had at times told him to move along so forcefully that he had still been shaking in his boots hours later.

Margaret Fell did not see John Foster as her carriage lurched and bounced down the lane to the Hall. Despite last night's thunderstorm, dust swirled around the coach in clouds, obscuring the view; only as the horses slowed down and entered the gateway did the dust subside. From the thinning cloud emerged a black-cloaked shape with a floppy hat, like a scarecrow; she recognized Priest Lampitt and rapped on the little window in the roof. The coach stopped joltingly; she opened the door. To her amazement, the priest did not stop to pay his respects; he strode past, his very back expressing wrath. Something had upset him; maybe young George had plagued him again with questions about Adam's navel or Cain's wife. She was happy the boy was showing some mischief at last after ten years of impersonating his father, but he should not tease priests as part of his growing up. She signaled Will Hartford, who was peering at her through the little window in the roof, to drive on; as the carriage rolled up the driveway, lurching and creaking, she told the maid on the opposite seat to hold on to the basket containing the bottles of sack and the jar of stewed Morocco plums which she had bought on the spur of the moment, prompted by an intuition that her husband was on his way home. If he did not come home, she would give the plums to the priest, to smooth over Adam's navel.

As always on market day, Will Hartford drove the coach around to the kitchen entrance. There another odd thing happened: Cook did not come running out for the groceries. Will Hartford opened the carriage door and helped her down the wobbly steps; she looked around and saw that the yard was empty. No servant girls scouring crocks at the back of the house, no stableboys to take over the reins of the horses; only the pigeons, strutting and cooing on the cobbles, and Cassandra the cat, washing herself on the kitchen steps.

"Where is everybody?" she asked.

Will Hartford bellowed obligingly, "Henderson! Harry! Bonny! What's going on here?"

The kitchen door opened and Henderson, the henchwoman, came flip-flopping down the steps in her house mules, startling the cat. "Forgive me, ma'am, forgive me," she breathed, in a fluster. "We were all in the kitchen, listening to the preacher. We did not hear the carriage."

"But I saw him leave minutes ago!"

"Oh, not that preacher, ma'am! The new one! He performed a miracle last night by crossing the sands against the tide, and he ' brought Bonny home this morning, and when Thomas Woodhouse wanted to scold the boy for staying out all night, he explained that he had been in the power of the Lord when he ran to warn the coroner and—"

"For mercy's sake, woman!" Margaret Fell cried. "Stop snattering and help Mary with the shopping!" She gathered her skirts and ran up the steps; at the door she turned around. "Mind those plums in the basket!" She swept into the kitchen, sending several shapes scurrying in the gloom; those nearest the door were unable to escape. "What is going on here, may I ask?"

Normally, the servants would have responded with apprehension; this time their reaction was sluggish, almost sullen. "Beg pardon, ma'am," Thomas Woodhouse said, from the center of the group.

"We have been listening to a soul-stirring sermon from Preacher George. The love of the Lord was over us all." He put his hand on the shoulder of Bonny the stableboy, standing beside him; the child looked flushed, as if he had knocked back the remainder of his master's stirrup cup.

Her anger flared. It was amusing to receive itinerant preachers in the house, they provided a diversion from the dreary routine, but if they started to stir up the servants, they were going to be shown the door. "Where is this holy man?" she asked.

"Ann Traylor showed him into the garden to await your coming, ma'am," the steward replied with a dignity that did not improve her mood.

She felt tempted to send them all about their business with an angry command, but there was something challenging in their attitude, as if they were daring her. The love of the Lord indeed! She turned away and walked through the dark passage to the main house.

In the drawing room she ran into another gathering, in front of the empty hearth: her six daughters, Ann Traylor the governess, Will Caton the tutor, and Mabby the skivvy, all huddled together in excited conversation. Her appearance surprised them, but they too seemed oddly unperturbed. Isabel, the eleven-year-old, always the first to climb a tree, cried excitedly, "Mother, Mother! You have missed something! A new preacher and Priest Lampitt got into a fight, and the priest lost!"

"Don't be ridiculous, Izzy," Meg, the oldest, said sternly. "Thou talkest as if they had come to blows."

"Well, they jolly nearly did!" Isabel's hair was hanging over her forehead again and the lenses of her lopsided spectacles were grubby as usual; she had to look over them to see. "I really thought he was going to hit him!"

"Who was?"

"Priest Lampitt!"

Then five-year-old Mary piped up, in one of her rare forays from the world in which she lived, "Do you know what he said, Mother? He told the priest that God was in his belly."

"That God *was* his belly," Meg corrected.

So that was why Priest Lampitt had left in such a huff! At least it had not been George, let's be grateful for small mercies. "And where is this fisticuffer?" she asked.

"In the garden, ma'am," Ann Traylor replied, respectfully, but not sufficiently so.

They were all watching her. They sensed her anger and were eagerly awaiting the next act of the drama. Well, they were going to be disappointed. She would not give the troublemaker an opportunity to taunt her. She had dealt with his kind before; nothing doused their zest more effectively than regal politeness.

"All right," she said briskly. "You have had enough excitement for one morning. Mabby, go and help Henderson unload the groceries. Ann, take the girls to the orchard to gather daisies."

"Oh, Mother!" Isabel protested. "We have daisies coming out of our ears!"

"That will be enough from thee, young woman! If thou art not content playing in the orchard, go and put thy closet in order. Methinks that was last done months ago." She turned away and crossed the hall to the bright open door to the garden.

On the bench by the rose garden a fair-haired man was sitting, head bent as if in prayer, a white hat on the seat beside him. Her steps crunched on the gravel as she walked toward him; he heard it and looked up.

He did not rise to greet her, let alone bow or make a leg; he just stared at her. He was younger than she had expected, poor, ill-kempt, unwashed: a traveling student, trying to find board and keep for a few weeks, as did scores of others every summer.

"Whom have I the pleasure of welcoming to Swarthmoor Hall?" The courtesy did not come readily in the face of his boorish behavior.

His eyes went on searching hers. They were blue, like a sailor's, and of an odd shape, rather slanted. "I am George Fox," he said. "May the Lord, infinite ocean of light and love, bless thee and awaken thee, Margaret Fell."

The ludicrous presumption that he was in a position to dispense such a grandiloquent blessing made her bristle. "Who directed you here, sir?"

He looked at her with unsettling intensity and answered, "The Lord."

"I see. Do you perchance have a letter of introduction?"

"Yes," he said.

The insolence of his reply made her want to call Thomas Woodhouse and have him thrown off the premises. But his eyes kept her from doing so. There was no impertinence in them; he seemed absorbed by what he saw, heedless of the impression he made. "Last night my companion and I crossed the sands," he said. "We are strangers here, we did not know they were dangerous. When we reached Ulverston we were welcomed by a crowd of people who told us that we were the only men in living memory to set out from Cark on the incoming tide and reach Ulverston alive. Now, who dost thou think guided our horses safely through the quicksands, if it was not the Lord?"

If he spoke the truth, he should be congratulated on a stroke of exceptional good fortune. Attempts to cross the sands on the incoming tide had proved so consistently disastrous that a monastery had thrived on the proceeds for three hundred years, saying yearly masses for the dead at a fixed fee. Obviously, her servants had needed no further proof of his claim that he was an emissary from the Almighty. "Have you any idea, sir, why the Lord chose to send you hither at such expense?"

"No," he replied. "Hast thou?"

She had had enough. "No. I am at a loss why He should single us out for a visitation by a boorish stranger who presumes to inform my priest that God is in his belly and incites my servants to insolence.

I am afraid I cannot consider you to be God-sent, sir, merely because you failed to drown on your way here." She made a gesture toward the house. "You know the way out, I believe."

He smiled. "I am sorry I gave the impression of boorishness, Margaret Fell. The fact that I failed to rise and bow is part of my testimony."

She knew that if she wanted him to leave she should be firm now and not let herself be drawn into an argument. But she could not resist asking, "And what would your testimony be?"

"All men and all women have that of God in them, which will respond when appealed to by that of God in myself. For me to bow or doff my hat would be to deny that of God in thee. I would be honoring thee not as a unique, irreplaceable person who has never been on earth before and never will be again, but as a symbol, wife of Judge Thomas Fell, mistress of Swarthmoor Hall."

"And on what, pray, do you base your authority to pronounce all this?"

He looked at her with utter serenity. He was unlike other preachers; as a matter of fact, he was unlike any other man she knew.

"Why don't we share a moment of silence before I answer that question? Let us ask the Lord to reveal why He chose to send me to Swarthmoor Hall. Come."

The last thing she wanted to do was kneel beside this unsettling young man with the whole house watching them. But to put him in his place was one thing, to turn down a call to prayer another. She doubted that God would use these means to communicate His wishes to her, but you never knew. She compromised by sitting down beside him. "When did the notion to come here first strike you, Mr. Fox?"

"Two weeks ago in Derby jail."

A jailbird! This was serious. She wondered how she could prevail on one of the children to go and alert Thomas Woodhouse without arousing the man's suspicion. "Is that so? What put you there, may I ask?"

"Blasphemy."

"Who was the justice who sentenced you?"

"Gervase Bennett. I am afraid I made things worse for myself by calling him Jerry."

"You don't say?" she said blandly. She knew all the judges; among them Sir Gervase was the last to take kindly to impertinence from a prisoner in the dock. This should have been obvious to the most obtuse miscreant; the fact that this odd young man had so blithely brought about his own doom seemed, somehow, reassuring. "What in the world made you do such a foolish thing? What is the point of insulting a judge about to sentence you?"

"I was not insulting him. I was trying to reach that of God in him, hidden behind all those barriers."

"Which barriers?"

"A powdered wig, a scarlet robe, a woolsack."

"But those are symbols of his office!"

"They turned him into a symbol too. As he sat there looking down on me, he did not hold himself personally accountable for his judgments. To Justice Gervase Bennett, goodness, kindness, compassion, regard for a prisoner's humanity had no place in his decisions; he could hang a human being without compunction. Jerry would never dream of doing such a thing; he would be unable to do it. For me to have accepted the symbol would have meant to betray that of God within him. So I called him Jerry and told him that the day would come when he too would quake in the presence of the Lord."

"How interesting. And what was his reaction?"

"He said, 'Take the quaker away!' The name 'quaker' stuck; all Children of the Light are now called 'quakers.' But he could not undo what I had done to him."

"What was that?"

"I had set him free." He corrected himself. "No, not I. Like a chick breaking out of an egg, he pierced his shell himself, from within. After that there was no going back."

"How do you know all this?"

"He told me."

She managed to hide her bewilderment. "When?"

"Later, in Derby jail. He had me put in the foulest cell, to break my spirit. But the more I was brutalized, the brighter the Light within me began to shine, the more I felt free . . ."

The things he was saying were outrageous. Free from what? Duty? Social conventions? He was free the way a bird in the sky was free. What would have become of her, had she renounced all laws and restrictions of society at his age? How old could he be? Twenty-five, twenty-six? Suddenly she seemed to catch an inarticulate, sensuous whiff of the freedom he was describing. She was thirty-eight; an old woman in the eyes of society. She accepted that her life was over for the simple reason that everybody said it was. Yet an entire lifetime still seemed ahead of her. . . .

She gazed at his manly, almost noble face. That was it! He must be the younger son of a nobleman. He had never known what it was to be socially inferior; that explained his supreme self-confidence. For a young lord not to remove his hat and to call a baronet Jerry was not rebellion.

"What do your parents have to say about all this?" she asked.

He fell silent in the midst of a sentence. It had been uncivil of her to show she had not been listening, but it did not seem to upset him. "In the beginning they were disturbed," he said, "but now they have accepted my mission."

"Who is your father, Mr. Fox?"

"He is a weaver."

A weaver! This boy had no business behaving as if he were her equal. "I am sorry I interrupted you. Is there anything else you feel you must tell me before luncheon?" She realized too late this meant a meal before she could show him the door.

"I should like to finish telling this one incident, as it brought about the convincement of the warden of Derby jail. So, I watched from my cell window as they dragged the screaming woman across the courtyard toward the gallows. She struggled; they struck her, but she would not be silent. When they reached the ladder to the scaffold, she managed to hang on to one of the rungs, screaming. One of the henchmen climbed onto the scaffold from the back and pulled her up; the other one pushed. They managed to drag her to the gallows and to put the noose around her neck. She began to cry for her mother, for someone called 'Harry,' for Jesus, whom she begged to come and save her. Hanging on to the bars of my cell window, I watched, in agony; then the power of the Lord came over me."

She stared at him, frowning. "What do you mean?"

"I cannot describe it. A tremendous strength arose in me, but it was not mine. It burst forth from me like . . . like . . . I don't know how to describe it."

"Try."

"An immense feeling of mercy, not for the woman, but for the men who were about to hang her. *They* were about to fall into damnation, not she. I wanted to stop them, but the only way I could reach them was with my voice. That of God within me burst forth in one word, *'Stop!'* It flashed across the courtyard like an arrow, pierced the wall behind which that of God in the men lay buried, fused with it, and the power of the Lord tore them asunder."

"How?"

"They tried for half an hour, but they did not have the power to hang that woman. In the end they had to take her back to her cell. That same night the warden, who had been there, came to see me. We talked and prayed and worshiped; the next day he moved into my cell."

"The warden of Derby jail?!"

"He did his work during the day, but slept in my cell. We talked for hours every evening; he stayed until I was released, nine months later."

She gazed at him incredulously. But she had sensed his power when he shouted *"Stop!"* She too would have been incapable of acting against his will. It was disturbing, but intriguing; part of her would love to find herself reduced to helpless submission to a man's sovereignty. Because her husband was rarely home, she had been a leader all her married life; even as a child it had not been she who obeyed, but everyone else, including her father, God rest his soul. What luxury it would be to let someone else take the lead for a while.

"Shall we go in to luncheon?" She rose.

He held her back by putting a hand on her arm, not forcefully; the thought simply did not enter his head that she might refuse to do his bidding. "Before we go in, let us have a moment of worship."

"Here?"

"Why not? 'Where two or three are gathered together in My name, there I am, in the midst of them.' Nowhere did Christ say that this miracle could take place only in certain buildings, at certain hours, under the supervision of hireling priests. Let us worship God where He is: here."

She had recovered. "I am sorry, Mr. Fox, but I do prefer to worship in the proper place."

"In thy steeplehouse, on First Days only?"

"The least our heavenly Father may expect from us is courtesy, wouldn't you think?"

He looked at her with benign amusement. He really was insufferable. "Dear Margaret, dost thou realize that the God thou servest has been created by thee, after thy own image: a stern, benevolent administrator in an office in the sky?"

She could see now why he had been condemned to prison for blasphemy. "Where else, pray, would you allow me to situate my Creator?"

"Within thyself."

"Pardon?"

"Part of thee, yet not thine."

"I see. Like my stomach. Priest Lampitt's belly."

"Not like thy stomach. He is a spirit; He cannot be defined. But if thou seekest an analogy, He is more like thy unborn children."

"I *beg* your pardon?"

"Part of thee, yet not thine; future human beings whose identity is still in the mind of God. Shall we worship?"

She rose, deeply offended. "I am sorry, I do not feel disposed to join in a blasphemous adoration of my intestines."

His face darkened. "That, Margaret, was blasphemous! Do not rile at the spirit of the Eternal thy humanity allows thee to carry!"

"I am not riling at the Eternal, Mr. Fox! I am riling at *you,* at your —your impudence! I'll thank you to leave my house, now!"

He smiled, unruffled. "Come. Thou art, in thy heart, yearning for the experience."

"Which experience, for God's sake?!"

"The experience of the presence of God. Come, sit with me. Be still; listen to the voice of God within thee. Thou wilt hear Him, thou wilt feel Him rise within thee, if only thou wilt set Him free."

His obvious sincerity made her hesitate; then she decided she would give him this one chance. She sat down again. "Now, then. What am I supposed to do?"

"Relax thy body as well as thy mind. Put thy feet together, like this. Settle thy body comfortably, so it will have no cause for restlessness. Put thy hands in thy lap."

She found herself obeying his instructions.

"Now put thy mind at rest. Close out all thoughts."

She tried, and discovered that she had no thoughts, only awareness: of his presence beside her, the bees buzzing among the flowers, the scent of roses.

"Be still," he whispered, as if in reverence, "silence the small thoughts that babble in thy mind. Be still! Wait upon the Lord . . ."

His faith in his own brand of magic was so persuasive that she closed her eyes and lifted her face, trying to eradicate her awareness of the world around her. The bright sunlight shone red through her eyelids. Impish little thoughts danced through her mind. 'My unborn children! How dare he! Are my born children still watching?' She managed to banish them, until there was nothing except the red sunlight in her eyes. She lowered her head to close out even that.

In the darkness, slow-moving, luminous shapes advanced on her as her eyes recovered from the light. Pink blotches, opening up as they approached. Pink flowers, exposing round red seeds. She folded her hands tightly, tried to concentrate; suddenly she recognized the red round seeds: Morocco plums! Henderson must have assumed they were meant for luncheon for everybody! She must get up at once and tell her that they were very expensive and intended for the judge.

She opened her eyes and glanced at him. He was sitting, head lifted, eyes open, gazing at the clouds. There was something very young about him. She cleared her throat and smoothed her skirt; he looked at her as if he had been miles away. "I'm sorry, Mr. Fox," she said, "I'm afraid I'm no good at this." She rose. "Now may I invite you to our table, before you travel on?"

"Do not feel discouraged, Margaret," he said. "It takes time. Before that of God can rise within thee, thou must accept thyself as thou art."

"Quite. Now shall we partake of some sustenance?"

He rose at last. She was a little disappointed to find that he was shorter than she. She led the way to the hall, worrying about the comments the children might make at table. How could she explain the scene to them? 'We joined in a brief supplication of our Lord for the safe return of your father . . .' What on earth made her want to lie? What was there to be secretive about?

As they entered the cool, dark house, she wondered why she should have such an odd feeling of guilt.

As they entered the dining hall where her daughters, the tutor, her son George and Thomas Woodhouse were waiting for them, she met the young man's companion for the first time. His name was Richard Hubberthorne; a frail young man, simply dressed, obviously of even humbler background. He too omitted to remove his hat, but it seemed to make him uncomfortable.

She was getting tired of the pious offensiveness of the pair; her young son George, obviously, felt more strongly. He swept his plumed hat, which he must have put on especially for the visitors, made a leg and said proudly, "Gentlemen, your humble servant."

Fox said, "God bless thee, friend." The other said nothing, but just stood there, all hat.

"This is my son, Master George Fell," she said lightly. "George, these two gentlemen are on their way north and will do us the honor of sharing our table before they continue on their way."

Fox, impervious to innuendo, made matters worse by smiling down upon the boy and saying, "George, eh? How old art thou?"

"Thirteen, sir," George answered, his nostrils sharpening. "Thank you, sir, for your kind interest. Mother, may I have the honor?" He executed another bow and sweep, a little less successfully this time, and offered his arm to guide her to the head of the table.

"Thank thee, George," she said gratefully, hoping to smooth his ruffled feathers.

He led her to her chair, bowed again, bowed to his sister Isabel, who snickered, and sat down, outraged adolescence personified. She thought of asking him to say grace in the absence of his father, but that would constitute an insult to her visitors, who as men of God, be it self-styled, should be granted that privilege. "Will you do us the honor of speaking the blessing, Mr. Fox?" she asked.

George Fox looked about him questioningly. "Are thy servants not to join us?"

She felt the un-Christian impulse to slap his face, but the sight of her children, waiting on the edge of their seats for the sparks to fly, restrained her. "I am sorry, Mr. Fox, that is not the custom in this house. I am sure that Thomas Woodhouse, our steward, will be happy to conduct you to the kitchen, should you so desire, after the meal." She folded her hands and closed her eyes as a pointed invitation to him to get on with it.

Instead of the time-hallowed words, she heard him say, "Let us join hands and wait upon the Lord." She opened her eyes and saw he was holding out his hand to her. Reluctantly she put her right hand in his, her left in that of his companion on her other side. The children followed their example, young George consenting only after she had given him an ominous look. She waited with mounting impatience for the unfortunate young man to speak, but he said nothing. He just sat there, eyes closed, holding her hand; the other was being held by the horny paw of the creature on her left. They sat like this for an inordinately long time. She expected the children to become restless, but they seemed to quieten down instead; there came a moment of absolute stillness that had about it an unexpected sense of tenderness and peace. She could have sat like this a while longer when he said, "Amen," and released her hand. His companion followed suit; Isabel released her pent-up giggles in a clumsy pretense of blowing her nose. She would have to have a word with that young woman.

Yet it was as if irritation and hostility had been swept from the atmosphere; the rest of the meal was pleasant. Only afterward, when she offered her guests a glass of sherry in the hall, did the awkwardness return. They refused the wine, barely consented to listen to the girls sing a madrigal, "The Andalusian Merchant," which they were rehearsing for their father's return; then Fox rose and said, "I would be happy now if thy steward would guide me to the kitchen."

She had suggested it herself, so all she could do was smile and nod to Thomas Woodhouse. The moment they were gone, the children burst out chattering like an aviary; she silenced them and expounded the principles of hospitality and good manners.

"And what does one do in the face of deliberate rudeness?" young George asked. He was nursing his grievance with dark voluptuousness, like his father, who sometimes would brood for days as a result of some slight, real or imaginary.

"Their use of 'thou' does not imply disrespect," she replied carefully. "It is an expression of their religious convictions."

Meg asked, "How?" So she found herself forced to expound Fox's subversive theories. The children went on pressing her with questions; in the end she lost her temper and cried irritably, "Why don't you ask our guests?"

They did just that. The moment George Fox came back after whatever he had been up to in the kitchen, Isabel tackled him as if he were a new tree to climb; before long he was holding forth at the children the way he had held forth at their mother in the garden. She had planned to make it plain that she expected him and his friend to be on their way before nightfall, but she could hardly interrupt this discussion without being ungracious. By the time he began to lose his audience it was too late for him and his companion to arrive at the next manor at an acceptable hour; as a result, she had to invite them to supper as well.

That night, when the candles were lit and the children were about to bid them good night, Fox sprang the suggestion that the servants join them for an hour of worship. This was customary only at Christmastime, when the symbolical meaning of the occasion was so obvious that it could not possibly put ideas into their heads. But as he had obviously been up to no good in the servants' quarters earlier that day, she thought it might be an effective antidote if she allowed it, as a sort of spiritual fire drill.

So they all gathered in the candlelight in the drawing room, every soul who lived under the roof of the House of Swarthmoor. At Christmas they usually sang a carol together, so she asked for a hymn; Fox answered that true worship did not need hymns, although anyone among them who might feel moved to sing during the next hour should feel free to do so. Their worship would be silent; anyone present could pray, speak, or whatever the Spirit might lead them to do, on condition that each ministry was brief and was followed by a long period of silence. "Now, let us wait upon the Lord."

He sat down. The poor servants did not know what to do; to lower their humble posteriors onto their master's furniture was, despite all dreams of equality, an emotional impossibility. Most of them followed the example of Henderson, the henchwoman, who, with the intelligence that had secured her position for her, sat down on the floor. Only Ann Traylor, the governess, and Mabby, the skivvy, sat down on chairs—the Traylor girl because she had delusions of grandeur, Mabby because she was too stupid to know better.

The gathering fell silent. It was a restless silence; poor Will Caton was plagued by a bout of extraordinarily loud stomach rumbles. The gurglings and barkings reverberated preposterously in the silence, making him scarlet with embarrassment; his hands, folded in prayer, went white at the knuckles, his eyeballs rolled behind his closed eyelids in an agony of mortification, until he looked like a bullfrog about to have a fit. Isabel started shaking with suppressed laughter that finally erupted snottily through her nose.

Suddenly, George Fox spoke. His voice was quiet, without the theatrical solemnity considered fitting by other priests. "Listening to the sounds of our friend's digestion brings the thought that these must have been the first sounds the newborn Jesus heard as He lay, blind and bewildered, in the manger among the cattle."

Had any of the preachers who had preceded him over the years said this, it would have sounded ludicrous, but the image of the newborn infant, blind and bewildered, was placed among them with such evocative power that Will Caton could go on gurgling and burbling without causing any further hilarity; his stomach rumbles were magically transformed into ministry.

Suddenly a high-pitched voice yammered, "Oh, God! Jesus! Dear God! Forgive me that I sit here thinking those sinful things! Forgive me, Christ Jesus, sweet Jesus! I want to pray to Thee, I—I—we must—I—I must sing! I must sing! Jesus, I—'*Heavenly Father, Holy Ghost, Precious Savior and Thy Host . . .*'" It was Mabby, the scullery maid, shaking like a leaf, swaying on her feet, bawling her head off.

Margaret looked about her; to her astonishment, none of her children seemed to be fighting giggles. They all sat quietly, either with their eyes demurely downcast or watching Mabby with fascination; none of them seemed outraged by her disgraceful exhibition. She sang the entire hymn from beginning to end; then she sat down, quivering like a jelly.

What had brought about this strange outburst? All they were doing was to sit in total silence, like people waiting for the mail coach. Yet there was tension among them, an excitement that seemed to feed on some insubstantial fuel drawn from their very souls. Was it their souls? Mabby's behavior had been anything but soulful. Then a new voice intruded upon her thoughts; this time it was Henderson, of all people.

"When I was a little girl, my mother used to sing a ditty in the kitchen," the henchwoman said in a soft, dreamlike tone that had nothing to do with prayer or devotion. "It ran: 'Lord, temper with tranquility our manifold activity, and let me do my work for Thee in silence and simplicity.'" There was a pause; the woman sat, eyes tightly closed, hands folded, as if she were formulating some thought; but she said no more.

How was it possible that the servants spoke so freely, without waiting for the family to speak first? How right, Margaret thought, her husband had been when he said that Cromwell was stirring up more than a religious revolution. It had never occurred to her that a time might come when she would sit in her own drawing room listening to a couple of wenches sounding off like drunkards. Her family suddenly seemed an apprehensive minority; the balance must be redressed somehow. It was ludicrous to leave the speaking to the servants.

She did not give anyone else the chance to continue this perilous parlor game. "Heavenly Father! We are grateful for the inspiration Thou hast granted us tonight. But, even as with earthly food, Thy heavenly fare can only be digested if we know when to rise from table in humble gratitude, lest our hunger turn into gluttony. So we thank Thee for the presence of Thy servants George Hubberthorne and Richard Fox, whom we shall sorely miss tomorrow. Let us now return with gratitude to our daily lives inspired, as we were reminded tonight, by the desire to do our work for Thee in silence and simplicity. For the sake of Thy Son, Jesus Christ, Amen." She rose, smiling seraphically; but again Fox held out his hands, forcing all those present, servants and children alike, to form a circle.

Despite this last effort at subversion, her speech had had a sobering effect. The servants, back in reality, retired after mumbling their thanks to her with a bow or curtsy. When the last of them was gone she said, smiling, "Thomas Woodhouse, pray show the guests to their quarters for the night. Sleep well, gentlemen."

After that, even Fox could not think of a device to linger. Before following the steward, he looked at her with those eyes full of awareness and said, "Be watchful, friend Margaret; the day of the Lord cometh as a thief in the night."

An hour later she made the rounds of the children's rooms, let the cat into the servants' quarters for the night and carried the little pug with her to her bedchamber, as was her custom when her husband was away. She was about to blow out the candle on the landing when a voice called softly from the shadows, "Mother?"

It was young George. He emerged from the children's wing like a miniature replica of his father, complete with spurred boots, little sword, velvet breeches and plumed hat. He looked as if he were about to go hunting.

"Why art thou not undressed?" she asked. She tried hard not to treat him as a child, but when he marched about the house at dead of night fully dressed with his hat on, it was hard to do otherwise.

"When are those men going away?"

"What is that to thee?"

"In the absence of my father," he said pompously, "it is my duty to see to it that nobody opportunes my mother, my sisters or any members of this household."

"Opportunes? What dost thou mean?"

"I do not think Father would approve of what went on here tonight."

"What? Thou meanst the prayer meeting?"

He stretched to his full height, which was not very high as yet, and clutched the handle of his sword. "If that was a prayer meeting," he said loftily, "then I am a volcano."

It would have rekindled her hopes for his originality had she not known that Will Caton had spent the day discussing earthquakes and their origins.

"I think it's bedtime for volcanoes," she said, casting to the wind her decision to do the right thing by him. She added insult to injury by pulling his hat over his nose, turning him around and slapping his buttocks. "If there's any protesting to be done in this house, it will be I who do it, not my children. Good night."

He stood still, trying to express defiance, but his fragile moment of virility had run its course. "Thou hadst better run, for I'm going to blow out the candle," she added. When he did not move, she did. He would have to find his way back in the dark.

She entered her room, closed the door behind her and listened at the crack. She had handled him ineptly, but whenever they challenged her authority she instantly forgot that she was dealing with children. That very morning she had caught herself crying at five-year-old Mary, "Oh, don't be childish!" With a mixture of regret and relief she heard his shuffling steps go down the landing. At least it saved her from trying to explain to the child something she did not understand herself. Why did she feel so unsure of herself in the face of that young preacher? He seemed different from the others, but was he just another demagogue or a true man of God? How could one know? For the second time that day she wished that her husband were home. He would know, his understanding of human nature was prodigious. Maybe the fact that she had bought those Morocco plums was indeed an omen. He might be back this very night; the tide would turn at midnight and there would be a full moon.

She undressed modestly, with her back to the steel mirror, and put on her nightgown. Then she took it off again and put on the one with the silk ribbons and the matching cap; if he indeed came in at dead of night, the sight of her should be pleasing. She knelt by the side of the bed, mumbled her evening prayer; then she raised her gown, showing the whiteness of shapely calves, and climbed into bed.

The moment she settled down in the pillows the little dog jumped onto the bed and settled on her feet. "Oh, for Peter's sake, Mongol!" she cried. "Go back to thy basket!" The pug peered at her over the soft embankment of the eiderdown like a frog from a pond. "Get off, little monster!" She tried giving him a sharp kick from below, but it was not possible through two blankets and an eiderdown. Mongol, snorting asthmatically through his fashionably short snout, collapsed and curled up in the hollow between her feet.

She sighed, took the Bible from the bedside table, opened it at random and read some chapter, thinking at the same time about the curtains of the bed of the two youngest girls that should be lined against the summer sunlight or they would be waking up too early. She was pleasantly conscious of the warmth of the little dog between her feet, the fragrance of pomandered oranges from the bed linen and the drowsiness that crept over her while the solemn admonitions of the Prophet Amos reverberated harmlessly in her somnolent mind. Finally she closed the book, put it back on the bedside table, snuffed the candle and stretched her limbs luxuriously under the sheets. The memory of the candle flame roamed inside her closed eyelids, then darkness slowly doused it. Ah, the delight of drifting off to sleep, sprawled wide in the warm bed, alone . . . A small feeling of guilt raised its drowsy head that she should enjoy her husband's absence; she tried to formulate a loving prayer for his safekeeping, but did not finish it. She was asleep, asleep, lovely, lovely sleep.

Amidst the twilit flittings of a meaningless summer dream a door slowly opened. She must be half awake, for she knew she was lying in bed, arms and legs flung out, only there was no door at the foot of the bed. Yet the wall opened, blinding sunlight blazed forth, and she became aware of a man standing in the lighted doorway, gazing at her; the sun behind him was too bright for her to see his features. She was about to cry out, "Dear heart!" and open her arms for her husband when it penetrated to her that it was not he. The intruder's hair was fair, his shoulders were powerful. He stood gazing at her, legs planted apart, and suddenly she realized who it was. Seeing him there filled her with the frantic desire to wake up; she tried to gather her limbs, but felt, with terror, that she was paralyzed by a dead weight on her feet. He slowly advanced on her, wading ashore from an ocean of light. She cried, "What do you want?!"

He stood still at the foot of the bed, gazed down on her and said, *"I have come to confound the priests."* The blasphemy gave her the strength to recoil; she was awakened by the yapping of the dog, in a tangle of sheets, her gown twisted around her waist. She lay half out of the bed, clutching the curtain; Mongol, snorting and slobbering, rummaged behind her.

The dream had been so vivid, his presence so real, that she stumbled toward the window, groping for the reality of her house, her children, her husband, God. Moonlight slanted through the slatted shutters; she opened them and stood, eyes closed, letting the coolness of the night wash over her.

She looked at the sky, the stars glittering coldly in infinity. She felt like praying, but her words would be lost in the immensity of the night. No tender concern for a fallen sparrow emanated from the icy stars, the bottomless void; all she could sense out there was an awesome, impersonal indifference—the indifference of unimaginable vastness for her unimaginable smallness.

Suddenly she was moved to whisper at the night, "God? God, look at me. It's Maggie . . ." She turned away as she realized what the stars saw, if they could be bothered: an old woman in a window, asking God to call her Maggie.

She lit the candle, climbed back into bed, pushed Mongol over the edge, took her Bible and opened it once more.

"For your souls know perfectly that the Day of the Lord so cometh as a thief in the night. For when they shall say, 'peace and safety,'

then sudden destruction cometh upon them, as travail upon a woman with child, and they shall not escape."

She raised her eyes and looked at the wall, where the door had been.

CHAPTER TWO

T HE next morning, as they broke their fast, Margaret Fell invited
George Fox and his companion to accompany the family to church.
He replied that he must do whatever the Lord might require of him,
took leave of her and walked out into the garden.

It was a warm sunny morning; the birds were singing, all nature
seemed to be awakening. The orchard looked inviting; he waded through
the high grass, still wet with dew, and sat down underneath an apple
tree, out of sight from the house. Dew was everywhere; all about him
bees were drying their wings with busy buzzing; a finch caroled in the
branches, making a joyful noise unto the Lord.

Leaning against the tree, head back, eyes closed, wrists resting on his
knees, he let all tribulations, all trivialities of daily life drop away from
him until there was nothing but the present, nothing but stillness, in
which he waited, passively, for that of God to rise within him. As a
youth he had prayed, pleaded, beseeched God to manifest Himself; only
in prison had he learned how to let God use him as an instrument, avail
Himself of his thoughts by directing them. That was the secret: utter
passiveness, which could only be achieved by complete surrender of the
will. Mysteriously, that state of complete surrender manifested itself by
a sudden feeling of power, a surging joy, that always preceded the indefinable but unmistakable presence of God.

Again, that morning, it happened, but not until the last preoccupation
with himself had been relinquished: the wish for understanding, for a
glimpse, however fleeting, of the purpose of his coming to Swarthmoor
Hall. Once he had let go of even that and said, "Thy will be done,
Thine only," the Light within suddenly dawned with growing radiance,
like a sunrise. He felt the Power fill his soul, his mind; in joy and awe
he waited for the first thought to rise, for the voice to whisper, which
would be his own, yet not his alone. Thy will be done. Thine. Thine
only.

The bees buzzed. The finch above him rustled and left. The melodious
wingbeat of a flight of pigeons whisked overhead. The scent of dew
evaporating in the sun became stronger. Beyond the orchard, out on the
fells, a lark began its jubilant ascent. God's Spirit was upon the land;
all of nature was singing His praises. But no thoughts emanated from
the center of the stillness; no leading came to him from the depth of his
soul, only a feeling of power, and peace. Then, out of nowhere, came
an image. A spire. A word: steeplehouse.

He waited, but no other images, no other words came out of the stillness. Steeplehouse. That was all. He sat there for a while longer, in silent adoration of the Presence. Then, filled with light and love, he rose.

body had left yet; he was the first worshiper to arrive at Ulverston church. He tethered his horse to the fence, went into the graveyard and stood among the tombstones in prayer, an alien figure in shepherd's clothes and a white hat. No one on his way into the church could fail to see him, and although he looked lost to the world, he saw them. He saw the priest arrive from the vicarage across the graveyard. He saw Margaret Fell arrive with her children in two coaches, the little boy trailing them on his pony. He saw a four-in-hand roll up with high-stepping horses and, inside, a portly man and a woman wearing a high, modish wig with a little dog on a pillow on her lap. As she glanced at him he recognized her as the wife of the coroner in whose stable he had slept after crossing the sands. He saw Richard Hubberthorne arrive on his patient old mare, which he tethered to the fence next to his own.

When the last of the worshipers had entered he remained behind, alone among the tombstones. Inside, an organ struck a deep and mournful chord; the congregation started to sing, *"Here in Thy house, O Lord of Hosts . . ."*

After a last prayer: *"Thine only, Thine only,"* he slowly went into the steeplehouse.

*   *   *

Like everybody else in the church, Henrietta Best had been waiting for George Fox to come in. The rumor that he made a practice of interrupting services had been all over the town. When he did, she was struck by the perfect timing of his entrance.

He had been standing in the graveyard like a prima donna in the wings, waiting for the congregation to sing its first hymn in order that his entrance would be savored and his appearance drunk in by the enraptured audience. What was it Delange had cried in the theatre room of the Louvre? "Never rush onto the stage, please! When you enter, be it *côté jardin* or *côté cour,* always stand still for a few seconds so the spectators may take in your appearance before the action starts. Now, will you do that over again, *chère?"*

Unconsciously, she trembled with apprehension. She became aware of it through the shivering of the little dog on the pillow on her lap; she always communicated her moods to Froufrou before she was aware of them herself. While the hymn, somewhat raggedly, was bawled to its conclusion by the preoccupied congregation, she did what Delange had wanted from the audience: she took in Fox's appearance. Two days earlier in her kitchen she had hardly looked at him, so upset had she been by the child's scream; now she could observe him at her ease. His appearance, carefully calculated to arouse disapproval, was that of a shepherd, complete with floppy hat. She wondered whether the people in this Godforsaken town knew of the fashion for shepherds that had swept the French court about a decade ago; tired of war and heroics, fashion had turned away from the knight errant and the *chevalier* to a symbol of more peaceable yearnings. By the time she had left Paris even the most notorious rakes, who would duel at the drop of a rose, came to the park in the misty morning garbed in the disguise of the harmless shepherd, floppy hat, leather breeches, homespun cloak and all, exactly like the man who now stood in the aisle facing the pulpit, fixing Priest Lampitt with the baleful stare of his hypnotic eyes. Strange, that this should happen again; she wondered if twenty-eight years ago she would have been smitten with this one too. It was hardly likely, so obvious were the histrionics.

The hymn over, Priest Lampitt, his voice trembling slightly, his face a little more drawn than usual, spoke a prayer, for which the man in the aisle conspicuously removed his hat, thus—like any consummate actor—using the speech of his antagonist to draw the more attention to himself. After the "Amen," a passage was read from the Scriptures. *"Come to Me and I will give you sustenance. Come to Me and I will give you bread."*

The congregation coughed, shuffled, settled down; just as poor Lampitt took breath for the start of his sermon, the stranger in the aisle queried, "Is this a sermon for hireling priests only?"

The commotion among the congregation was not one of surprise, but of excitement. All heads craned in his direction, all attention was drawn away from the poor, talentless man in the pulpit. What an opening! And what a magnificent voice! Despite her detestation of all he stood for, Henrietta felt a twinge of admiration that only great artists of the theatre could provoke. It was the cue for Priest Lampitt, but he bungled it; he just stood there, pin-eyed and paralyzed. The man in the aisle timed the exact moment to resume speaking. "If not, friend Lampitt, what nonsense art thou talking! The only ones who receive bread and sustenance from the words of the Lord are those who use them to make a living!" Not what he said, although it was outrageous enough, but the way he said it hit her and the rest of the audience in the solar plexus. His voice, deep and stirring, achieved what the dreary tootling of the church organ had failed to do: it created an atmosphere of drama and brought about a heightened awareness. If she read the play right, there should now be an effort by some minor character to bar the hero's way, if only to enhance the sense of drama by turning the audience from spectators into participants.

Sure enough, there came a crowing voice, thin and pedantic in the taut silence: "Take that man away!" It was Junior Justice Sawrey, pompous little fool. He fitted the role perfectly—it almost looked as if he were in league with the actor. Everybody in town disliked him heartily; even those who might have vacillated would now feel irresistibly drawn toward the man in the aisle.

Then a woman's voice cried out, quite close, "Let him be! He has a right to speak!"

It was Mistress Fell. She had risen in the squire's pew near the pulpit and made a commanding figure in her costly gown, showing to their full advantage her statuesque body and the swanlike grace of her aristocratic neck. Of course, the man was her guest and Lampitt in her pay; in the absence of her husband, she could not let little Sawrey rule the roost.

The priest, more eager to please the wife of the Lord Chief Justice than a junior judge, replied, "He may speak. And let me remind you, dear brethren in Christ, that we must not let ourselves be led astray by personalities or emotions, but at all times turn to the Scriptures for guidance." It was a muddled effort to re-establish his authority by identifying himself, somewhat obscurely, with the Lord; the man in the aisle gave short shrift to him by latching on to his words.

"It is not the Scriptures which give guidance, but the Holy Spirit which inspired them! I say unto you that the same Holy Spirit that once inspired those who wrote down the words of God still inspires us today! If the Scriptures are indeed God's words spoken to man, then He is still speaking to us today! But do you hear Him? Your worship is but the repetition of other men's words; you do not listen to the Spirit speaking within yourselves. For He *is* speaking, right now! Not to Christianity, or the Independent Church, or the congregation of Ulverston, but to each of you individually, man, woman, child, priest, here, now. Yes! His voice speaks in the heart of everyone here, *now,* and the voice says, 'Christ says this, Paul says that, but what dost *thou* say?'" He pointed at the mistress of Swarthmoor Hall, who sat looking down on him from the high pew of honor with a haughty stare. He kept pointing at her, heightening the tension to an almost unbearable degree, then he cried, "Thieves! We are all thieves! We have taken the Scriptures in words and know nothing of them within ourselves! But it is written: there will be a shepherd, and the sheep shall follow him, for they will know his voice!"

Aha, Henrietta Best thought, there we have it, the old recipe. For a few minutes, swept along by his power and his consummate skill, the idea of throwing the responsibility for listening to a speaking God back at each individual of the congregation had seemed magnificent; but now there had to be a shepherd, and guess who it would be. Of course the sheep would follow him, for they knew his voice; only, it was the voice of the devil, of communal madness, of the dark desire locked up in all men for death and destruction. That was the conclusion she had come to twenty-four years ago.

She looked at the congregation, letting the words of the glorious voice roll off her. Bowled over by the great actor, unmistakably, were the women. The men sat glowering at him with sullen anger; the women's faces expressed a fascination that ran from wary interest to rank rapture. She glanced at the mistress of the House of Swarthmoor and noticed that she was no exception. The man's assault had been concentrated on her; there she sat, eyes bright, lips parted, cheeks flushed, to all the world a tender soul deeply moved by a spiritual message. To all the world except to one who had been married to someone like him. When Henrietta herself had been in the throes of spiritual rapture, it had never occurred to her that what she felt might have less to do with God, Christ or the Holy Ghost than with a magnificent male's overwhelming masculinity. At that time she had not possessed the experience that life was to impart to her later; yet, though she had come to know every aspect of carnal passion in all its

delirious frenzy, she had never quite understood the mysterious relationship between saintliness and lust. What gave this irresistible
seductiveness to sanctity? Why did a woman respond to passionate
spirituality in a man more rapturously and recklessly than to any of
the more obvious attributes? Flattery and flowers, compliments and
gallantries, chivalry and courage were like chaff before the whirlwind of true spirituality. Look at the Fell woman: spellbound, bewitched by that indomitable male drunk with God. What made an
astute, imperious person like her respond to the man's blatant virility
with the instinctive desire to conquer him? Was it the challenge to
take on God? Was that what had happened in Paradise? 'I'll make him
love me, not above all other women, that is easy; I will take on God,
who makes him radiate with love and shine with passion, who fills
him with that breathtaking power, now wasted on stupid people in
stuffy churches!'

Could it be that after all these years she was witnessing the same
gruesome story starting all over again? No, no, not in this country.
What had been possible in France could not happen here. This was
England: insular, dull, but with a basic decency that rendered im-
possible excesses of cruelty, obscenity and destruction like the Night of
St. Bartholomew, the fall of La Couvertoirade.

It all came flooding back—a wave of blackness and death. She
nudged her husband and rose, handing him the pillow with Froufrou,
overwhelmed by the irresistible urge to flee.

Despite the pillow with its frantic little occupant, Colonel Best
managed to help her out of the pew, down the aisle, past the roaring
saint, into the open where the air was pure and the birds were singing in the trees of the graveyard.

*   *   *

The sudden commotion in the Best pew settled something for Margaret Fell. In her outrage at their protest against the young prophet,
she suddenly knew what she had to do.

Until that moment she had let the man's power wash over her, almost sensuously, moved by the sheer beauty of it. He stood among the
dun-colored, shock-eyed creatures of Ulverston like a young god, visitor from another world. Power, courage, freshness did not adequately
sum up the essence of his impact. He seemed to be the only human
being in that church who was really alive. There was no doubt left in
her mind: he *was* a man of God.

When Henrietta Best rose in protest and the unprepossessing couple
banged and clunked down the aisle with their impossible little dog,
she made up her mind. George Fox needed protection, now that the
second most influential man in Ulverston had turned his back on him.
She would provide it.

Priest Lampitt spoke the closing prayer as if it had been he who had
been holding forth for the past hour instead of the broad-shouldered
youth flushed with passion, eyes shining with the glory of the Lord.

She rose; all waited respectfully for her to move down the aisle. In full view of everyone she took young Fox by the arm and said, "I want a word with thee, friend George. Let us go outside." She knew that this would set tongues wagging furiously, but she was sure now of what she must do. She had seven children to send into the world. Now, doubt had been sown in her soul as to the validity of the values she was imparting to them; they should not inherit a faith that had been shaken. It would take courage, but she must rise to the challenge of her doubt.

She did not wait for Lampitt, even though out of the corner of her eye she could see him trying to reach the door before she did. She led George Fox out into the graveyard and faced him with determination.

"Friend George, I have decided to give thy message a try. Tell me what to do, and I will do it. Thou wilt have to stay on to instruct me and my family, but that, I presume, is thy wish."

He gazed at her with the look of utter perspicacity that had unnerved her during their first meeting. "Thou dost not need me, friend Margaret. All thou needest to receive God is to be truthful toward thyself."

"Do not tell me what I need, George Fox," she said with the voice that no one ever contradicted. "I desire for thee to stay at Swarthmoor Hall until my family and myself shall be—what dost thou call it?—convinced."

"Thou art convinced, Margaret," he said calmly. "Now put thy convincement into practice."

She realized, with incredulous amazement, that he was about to turn his back on her and leave her standing there like any other persistent female. "George!" she said with an urgency that she had not intended. "I am sorry. I—I wish thee to stay because I need thee. We need thee! Thou canst not do this to—to people, arouse them, disturb them, put them at odds with the world they live in, and then turn away and leave them!"

"As I told thee, it is not I but God—"

"God, fiddlesticks!" she cried, realizing too late that this was hardly the language of a convert. "I am prepared to treat my servants as equals, to allow them to address me as 'thou.' We will hold meeting for worship every evening. I will instruct my children in the principles of thy persuasion. But in order to do so, I must know what those principles are!"

The way he looked at her made her realize, with a sinking feeling, that she had used exactly the same tone to him she used when she haggled with tradespeople.

"My principles, Margaret? Thou knowest them by now. Gather together with thy family and thy servants in His name, and He will be there, in the midst of you."

People were coming out of the church. She was aware of how she must look to them: angry, pleading. "But *how* do I put them into practice?" she asked with an edge of exasperation.

She saw from his expression that, despite his apparent involvement with her, he was utterly remote. "The practice is simple," he said. "Mind the Light." Then he turned away and walked toward the gate. It had sounded like a farewell, and she was convinced that was how he had meant it. But she knew that he would be back.

On the way home in her carriage, while the girls chatted excitedly about the adventurous morning and young George bobbed behind them on his pony, she wondered at her own certainty.

"Mother, do you know what he meant by 'the inward light'?"

She looked at Isabel's innocent face. "I think so," she said. "But before I tell thee: there is a new rule in the family. From now on you children shall address me as 'thou.' So will the servants, to whom we shall not refer as servants any longer. From now on we shall talk about friend Ann and friend—whatever Henderson's first name is. That goes for everyone, even Mabby."

"But why?" Meg asked, alarmed.

"Because we are starting out, as a family, on a search for truth."

* * *

Oh, the embarrassment, the shame of it all! Young George Fell, roaming the downs on Faggot a week later, was anguished. The household, the one stable element in his life, was in chaos. To have all the servants calling him "thou" again for the first time since he was breeched, and meeting for worship every evening with everybody free to jump up and bellow as the spirit moved them was bad enough. But the night before Mabby had "ministered" again, this time in response to Thomas Woodhouse, who had carried on in gory detail about Jesus' crucifixion and terrible suffering. Suddenly Mabby had leaped to her feet, eyes rolling, writhing and undulating in crazy contortions, screaming that she wanted to share Jesus' suffering, be nailed to the cross like Him, be stuck by spears and bleed to death like her beautiful, beautiful Savior. She began to foam at the mouth and to pull at her bodice, shrieking that clothes were an abomination, that all of them should rip off their garments and throw themselves on the floor, ready for the spears to pierce them. It looked as if she were about to do so, but Henderson put an arm around her and guided her, slobbering about Jesus, blood and spears, back to the kitchen.

At dead of night George was awakened by screams and shrieks in the courtyard. He stumbled to the window, stubbing his toe, but forgot the pain when he saw what was happening in the courtyard. The moon was full; in its light two white bodies were dancing and twirling. He did not recognize them at first, but as they pranced, hooting and squealing, toward his window he recognized Mabby and Harry Martin the stableboy. Neither of them had a stitch on, Harry as hairless as a slug, Mabby with bouncing breasts of surprising size, her hair loose, waving her arms as if she were about to take off and fly. She shrieked about Jesus, blood, the Cross, beseeched somebody, anybody, to pierce her with a spear; Harry Martin bellowed about Jesus too, but without much variation. Suddenly he crashed into her and both of them tumbled to the ground; there they lay, wrestling and thrashing, trying to strangle each other. The courtyard filled with running shapes in nightclothes and loose breeches; someone threw a bucket of water over them; others pulled them apart and dragged them away, Mabby screaming and struggling, Harry Martin yelping like a dog as Will Hartford kicked him.

That had been last night; this morning, as George rode on the fells, Justice Sawrey had stopped him, with the ever present hulk of the constable in the distance. He had tried to pass with a mere greeting, but the judge had called, "Stop!" and, as he drew up alongside him, "Listen, boy. Your mother's friend has been causing trouble in Dalton, Aldringham, Dendron, Ramside Chapel. Now I have learned that he's on his way back here! Do you know that after what happened at your house last night your mother could be accused of witchcraft?"

It seemed impossible that anyone outside the household could know of the goings-on in the courtyard; Judge Sawrey was an awful man, and obviously out to make trouble. What would Father have done? Could he ride out and find him? Send a messenger? God, dear God, what could he do?

Never before had he been faced with a decision of such magnitude in such utter loneliness. If only there were someone, an uncle, a friend, someone who would take over the responsibility! The only one he could think of was Chief Justice Cartwright, whom his father visited regularly when he was home, but he lived miles away in Gleaston. It had to be someone in the neighborhood, someone he knew personally, who knew him . . .

* * *

Colonel Best was in the process of being shaved by Bonbon, a daily ritual which started by his lying down in his shirtsleeves on the leather couch in his study while the eunuch put his tools at the ready: a bowl of hot water, razor, razor strop, lotions, soap scented with rose petals, towels. He grunted ungraciously, "All right, get on with it," but once he lay on his back on that couch, eyes closed, and the smarmy little man began his ministrations, he was like an opium addict sensuously relishing the ritual. The creature began by covering his face with a steaming hot towel, which, after resting on his bristles for a while, was gently removed, as a sculptor uncovers the first clay mold of a head. Then the feminine, caressing hands applied oil smelling of boudoirs, followed by another steaming towel, hotter than the first, and finally the lather that was brushed on with the voluptuous softness of an houri's caresses. As he lay there, his face buried in warm, scented foam, his body more sated and relaxed than in the afterglow of love, he heard the surreptitious squeaking of the razor stroking the strop. Then the delicate fingers of the creature gently pushed up his right sideburn to stretch the skin on his jaw, the harem voice whispered, "All right, *patron?*" and he grunted unpleasantly, to make up for his involuntary grin of well-being. The razor stroked down, softer than the tongue of the tenderest of women, and the voice asked, "Does eet pull, *patron?*"

He growled, "No, you idiot! Stop blathering and get on with it!" The steel, working so gently that he could barely feel it as it caressed his cheeks, started replacing the heat of the lather with the coolness of naked skin. Bonbon did a meticulous job, nipping even the furtive little hairs high on his cheekbones and underneath his Adam's apple; then, with the sound of two small perspiring bodies in the raptures of love, he slapped his obscene little hands with yet another secret ointment, an oil that smelled of leather and horses and wenches in the hay, the two lascivious flippers started to massage his face and he felt as if he were awakening from a depressing dream of old age and regret to the vigor of the youth he had once been, the dashing British rake abroad with the unwrinkled face that had dazzled a thousand wenches, full, sensuous lips and no bags under the once mischievous eyes that now had grown mournful and morose, like those of a bloodhound with nothing to trace. He was waiting for the third hot towel, when Thomas Fell's son was announced by Kathryn, the maid. He growled, "Go away. Too early. Let him wait."

"He says it's very urgent, sir," the maid insisted, damn her hairy haunches.

He ripped the towel off his face, cried, "I said, let him wait!" and was about to throw it at her head when he saw the boy standing in the doorway, in a green velvet suit, hip boots with silver buckles, a miniature sword at his side.

He looked like some rich woman's plaything, but his face was hauntingly like his father's when he took off his plumed hat and swept it, mumbling, "Your Honor, your obedient servant." The Colonel threw the towel at Bonbon instead, who was ogling the succulent little visitor with the hooded eyes of a lizard.

"*Mais, patron,*" the creature cried in his castrato tenor, "won't you let me feenish while the little *monsieur* states his business?"

"Get out!" he cried, grateful for the chance to vent his irritation. "Take thy mess away!"

"*Mais, patron!* Your *foulard* . . . your *plastron* . . .*"

"I'll put them on myself!" He relished this display of virility, although it was a poor substitute for the rejuvenating ritual of the third towel. "Now get out! Sit down, George Fell, there, take that chair. Forgive this domestic *brouhaha.*" He had intended to put the boy at ease, but he caught Bonbon's insolent mutter, "*Brouhaha, pardon . . . !*" which gave him the gratifying opportunity to kick him out of the room. Like a wily old mongrel bitch, the ninny squealed before his boot made contact, flitted out the door, emitting little shrieks of panic, but without spilling a single drop from the basin or leaving anything behind. He could hear him ululating as he leap-frogged through the drawing room, obviously to ensure that his mistress would notice the commotion and later call her husband to task for brutalizing so delicate and sensitive a person. He slammed the door on all pederasts and wenches and on the hope of getting shaved that day; then he turned to the boy, standing pale and insecure in front of the chair he had indicated. "Sit down, sit down," he repeated, going to the sideboard in the corner. "How about a glass of sack, to start the day?"

"Thank you, sir." The boy was not accustomed to drinking sack at nine o'clock in the morning; when handed the glass, he accepted it as if it were a little live animal. He looked as if he had not slept for days.

"I trust your gracious mother and sisters are doing well?"

If he had intended to postpone getting down to business, it had been the wrong question. Suddenly the boy blurted out, "No, sir, no, not at all, sir, not at all! That's why I'm here, sir, I did not know where to turn—I mean, you as a friend of my father's—I mean, in his absence I must try and take his place . . ."

"Of course, of course," he said with a smile, while his shrewd eyes observed the boy with fascination. He had heard rumors about hysterical goings-on at the Hall since that traveling preacher's visit, but had not paid much attention. "I'll be glad to advise you, if I can," he said, "though I am sure that your father's place is most satisfactorily manned by you during his absence."

At this, the boy recovered some of his composure; he even made a move as if to sip his wine, but thought better of it. "I would not have op—importuned you, sir, if I hadn't been warned that—that the man has been causing trouble in Dalton and Aldringham and that he is on his way back here and that his converts may be accused of . . ."

"Of what?"

The boy cast a sidelong glance at the door, then he took a deep breath and said, "Of—of witchcraft, sir."

"Who said that?" He tried to keep up the tone of casual banter, but, suddenly, this was serious.

"Justice Sawrey, sir."

"When?"

"This morning. We met out riding on the fells." He added apologetically, "I—I would not have bothered you with this, sir, but the fact that you and Mistress Best walked out of the service led me to believe . . ."

"Quite, quite," he said. "I'm glad you told me. But tell me a little more . . . What made Mr. Sawrey conclude that your gracious mother might be considered a convert?"

"Mother is very taken with what Fox said, sir; we now have prayer meetings with the servants every evening, and—and the servants seem a lot less respectful, sir."

How young the boy was, yet how gallant! Best had no particular liking for Thomas Fell; the man had always seemed to him slightly inhuman. It was as if in the son he was suddenly given a glimpse of the true character of the father, sensitive and decent.

"The word 'witchcraft'—is that what Justice Sawrey actually said?"

"Yes, sir."

"Any idea why?"

"After—after what happened last night, I gather, sir . . ."

"What did happen?"

"Er—one of the maids and a stableboy danced in the yard—er—without—*in natura,* sir. I cannot understand how, but Justice Sawrey seems to have got wind of it."

His first reaction was to send the boy home with some vague fatherly advice and wash his hands of the whole affair. But a neighbor's family was being threatened; there came a moment when all must stand up for one another or the violence that was sweeping the country would make short shrift of them. He must try to stop Sawrey before he could do any more mischief.

He managed to reassure the boy but committed the error of saying, "Don't drink that wine if you don't feel like it," which of course made him gulp down the rest in one straight draught as if it were lemonade. By the time he rose to leave, young Fell was swaggering with self-confidence. He nearly knocked himself off his feet with the sweep of his hat, mounted his pony only after three lurching tries and rode off like a djinn, hoofs clattering, his hat bouncing on his back.

A quarter hour later Colonel William Best rode out himself, accompanied by his groom.

*   *   *

When her husband returned, Henrietta Best saw by the way he dismounted that something had upset him. Coming up the flagstone path to the door, he looked haggard and gray; when he embraced her, his cheek to hers, she realized it was because he had not been shaved. "I have to talk to thee," he said, "come." He led her to the small withdrawing room, closed the door behind him and stayed there for a moment, listening for footsteps in the corridor. Then he said in a hushed voice, "Thomas Fell's family is in trouble."

"Ah?" It did not surprise her, after the way the woman had looked in church. "Why?"

He told her about the boy's meeting with John Sawrey. "I went to make the rounds of the neighbors this morning. As it turned out, they had already had visits from Sawrey and Lampitt, who had, so they said, reliable information that the man is on his way back to Ulverston to complete the subversion of the household of Justice Fell before his return from the Welsh Circuit. Lampitt's role in all this is clear, the man made him look like a fool. But Sawrey is not interested in Fox. He has his eye on Thomas Fell's place on the bench; now, obviously, he has the bee in his bonnet that he can achieve his end by discrediting Fell's wife. Under the guise of wanting to protect her, of course."

"What do the neighbors say about all this?"

"They have no plan of action yet, but should Fox come back and disrupt another church service, he is going to be dealt with by them."

"Thrown out?"

"Let us hope that is all they will do. Sawrey is using the word witch-craft in connection with Mistress Fell."

"O douce vierge . . . !"

She turned to the window and looked at the road through the lush green of the linden tree. In the distance the small red roofs of Ulverston looked a picture of security in the dell of the forbidding fells. But she knew how small, peaceful villages could explode into murderous insanity, as if they were inhabited not by honest simple folk but by an alien inhuman breed obsessed by lust for torture, rape, murder, obscene mutilation.

"What will Mistress Fell do now?"

"Thou art a woman. What wouldst thou do?"

There was a small black figure on the road now, trudging wearily in the heat, carrying a staff and a sack on his back. Nobody dangerous or alarming; but then, few of them were; most of them lived God-fearing lives, loving their families, going to church, until suddenly an evil demon within them was sparked into life and those same people would, in one nightmarish hour, change into . . . She must stop this. "I think she will probably be quite forceful in her efforts to protect her saint," she said. "She may even come between them, should they start to manhandle him."

"I'm afraid that's exactly what Sawrey wants her to do."

"I don't believe that they would dare lay hands on her, though. Not the squires."

He said carefully, "I am not so sure. I had the feeling that the fanatic and the Fell woman's adulation of him are the symbol of something else now, something that has been rankling inside us all ever since the King was murdered. It's completely irrational. It was the Puritans who did that, yet it looks as if their rage will vent itself not on Lampitt and Sawrey, who are both Puritan creatures, but on the man who challenges them. As I listened to Rutledge, I went on asking myself: How is it possible that sane, civilized men . . ."

Suddenly she knew what she had to do. "What if I went to warn her?"

He remained silent for so long that she turned to look at him and was struck by the expression on his face. He looked gray and drawn, his eyes full of old men's anguish. "What if I dispatch my groom to warn Fox?" he suggested. "We'll send word to the man to change his itinerary . . ."

"There is not the slightest chance of it," she said. "It would only whet his appetite; people like him thrive on persecution. No, I'll go to see her, and after that, we leave. I don't wish to be around when all this comes to a head."

He blurted out, "Thou must not go to her!"

"Why not?"

"I cannot agree to anything that—that might hurt thee!"

She went to him, looked into his anguished eyes so full of tenderness and melancholy, kissed the tip of his nose and said, "Thank thee, old friend." She touched his stubbly cheek. "Now thou hadst better be shaved. I'll call him."

She rustled to the door and went to call for Bonbon and for her coach, feeling strong and confident and utterly secure.

The groom drove her to the Hall in the coach-and-pair, which was less conspicuous than the four-in-hand. She even left her maid behind, but she did take Froufrou on his tasseled pillow, in a symbolic gesture of protection.

On her arrival at the Hall she had expected to be ushered into the withdrawing chamber of the lady of the house, where they would have their intimate conversation, after which she would leave as unobtrusively as she had come. But she had forgotten about the seven children; the moment she arrived her coach was surrounded by breathless girls in white dresses. She stepped down daintily and was considerably shaken, as was Froufrou, when another girl dropped at her feet from a tree, losing a pair of spectacles as she sprawled in the gravel. The others helped in the search for them, which diverted their attention, but the son of the house came out, in full gentleman's regalia, to greet her effusively with bow, leg and hat. When he finally conducted her to his mother, she had the feeling of being observed from every window.

As she followed the boy across the cool, vaulted hall she heard to her dismay that the girls were following her. Despite the religious ecstasies in which they reportedly indulged, they seemed desperate for entertainment. The woman was in the garden, at the far end of a gravel path, on her knees, clipping roses. The wide pocket of her apron full of pink and red blooms made her look pregnant with flowers as she rose to greet her visitor. Her reception was distinctly chilly, she even seemed reluctant to ask her children to leave. When they had gone she asked, without inviting her to sit down, "And what can I do for you, *Madame?*"

Henrietta frowned. Why this hostility? Ah, of course. Her leaving the church in the middle of the man's harangue. "First of all, I would like to assure you that we did not leave the church the other day as an expression of disapproval," she said. "I became indisposed and my husband had no choice but to take me home."

The other eyed her without tenderness. "If it is your intention to discuss the rumors that we all have lost our heads here," she said stiffly, "I am grateful for your kindness, but I cannot see why any of this should concern anyone outside my family." It was as close to an invitation to leave as a civilized hostess could come.

"I'm afraid it's not quite as simple as that," Henrietta said matter-of-factly. "You are in danger of physical harm. I am not talking about your evangelical friend, but about enemies of your husband who are conspiring to destroy him through you." She did not wait for the invitation, but sat down on a nearby bench, facing the roses.

The woman was obviously of two minds as to how to react to this bluntness; after a moment's hesitation she said, "Would you be kind enough to talk in particulars rather than generalities?" With her apron full of roses and a lock of her hair loose, she looked strikingly handsome for her age—passionate and yet innocent, a combination irresistible to any unscrupulous male.

"Mr. Lampitt and Justice Sawrey are making the rounds of the manor houses of the neighborhood, drumming up support to throw your friend out of church this coming Sunday."

"Nonsense," the woman said with impatience. "Mr. Fox is away."

"My dear," Henrietta said, with the quiet authority of the older woman, "let's stop snapping at each other and talk sense. There are, as you must be aware, certain people who would like nothing better than to embarrass and maybe even unseat your husband by discrediting you."

"But how?" the other cried irritably. *"How* could they?"

"For one thing, the goings-on here at the Hall last night."

"Which?!"

"Well, the—er—pentecostal extravaganza, maids and grooms dancing *à la Bacchante . . ."*

"Oh! For mercy's sake!" The woman sounded exasperated, but sat down beside her, the mass of roses on her lap. Their fragrance, heady and voluptuous, enveloped them. "Surely nobody is hoping to unseat my husband because of my servants dancing round the Maypole?"

"What I am talking about, *Madame,* most urgently, is your friendship with this young man Fox. That is how they will try to get at you. You see, Mr. Fox gave quite a performance last Sunday, which you should try to see from the point of view of the squires of the neighborhood. Not only did he bruise their pride by holding forth at them without their invitation; not only are his ideas radical and even subversive; above all, he is powerfully male. No woman, young or old, could remain entirely unresponsive. This is exactly—"

The woman bristled. "Are you by any chance, *Madame,* including me?"

Her heart sank. The very violence of the reaction meant that she had touched a live nerve. *"Voyons,* Mistress Fell," she said, smiling, "you cannot tell me that you have remained unaware of his, how shall I say, professional virility as he stood there raising the roof, bringing every single woman to heel and ignoring the menfolk? To the squires, this man—"

But the woman was outraged. She sprang to her feet, spilling roses. "That is enough!" she cried, eyes flashing, her anger formidable and preposterous among the flowers. "I will not listen to another word! I fully respect each person's private affairs, wherever she comes from or whatever her reputation may be, but in this case I must insist that you do not judge me by your own standards!"

It was a slap in her face, but Henrietta gritted her teeth. It was obvious from the woman's indignation that, despite her seven children, she was still inexperienced. Her outrage was sincere, her innocence frighteningly real. "Dear friend," she said, stroking Froufrou, who had started to tremble, "I do not wish to meddle in your affairs either. But I must make you understand the choice before you. Think for a moment of your children. I once had two children of my own, so I speak from experience . . ."

The woman, totally oblivious, gave her a look of utter contempt and said, "I am sure you do, *Madame*. I am well aware of your reputation."

She sat for a moment speechless, hurt beyond words at the very moment she had been about to make the supreme sacrifice of confiding in this miserable creature and thereby living through it all again. She rose and retorted, at her worst, "In that case, *Madame,* let me be completely frank. There is nothing more exciting to a passionate woman than a true prophet, but let me tell you that as lovers they are terribly disappointing, certainly not worth the price we are expected to pay for the privilege of bedding with St. Paul."

Before the other had been able to close her mouth, she swept down the path, across the dark hall and out the door, to break down and sob in the privacy of her coach, with Froufrou on her lap greedily licking the salt of her tears as they dripped onto his little satin pillow.

"Oh, Jeannot, Christine . . . Tonton, Titi, *mes chéries, mes petits choux* . . ."

The coach lurched, knocking her wig sideways; a few straggly locks of gray hair fell across her forehead. But she was beyond shame and humiliation. She was, as she had been ever since that radiant morning twenty-four years before, a sorrowing mother going through the torments of hell.

*   *   *

The moment she saw Mistress Best vanish down the garden path, Margaret Fell felt ashamed of herself.

That very morning, despite the superstition that to see a spider before noon was a bad omen, she had placed a glass over one of the hairy beasts, slid the marker from her Bible underneath it and carried it outside; now, not an hour later, she had treated a fellow human being so cruelly that the woman had left sobbing. As she sat there with her apron full of roses, it seemed the worst thing she had done since George Fox had come into her life.

But how sordid! The woman was obviously incapable of understanding it; two weeks ago she herself would have been hard put to understand. Then George had still seemed to be an unstable dreamer, with his notion of God as "an infinite ocean of light and love." Now she knew exactly what he meant. She experienced it all day. She moved through the house on winged feet, flying up the stairs, singing as she sorted out the linen, smiling at spiders, kissing Mongol, being angelic with the children. George had nothing to do with this; she felt for him what she had felt for her dear father. A deep fondness, that was

all. But it was a pity that Thomas might be disturbed on his return by
rumors, distortions. Perhaps she should go to meet him; wait for him
in the inn in Lancaster where he always stayed. But no, her place was
here, especially now. Without her, her little flock might fall apart.

Worrisome as the situation had seemed for a moment, her feeling of
security soon returned. Even so, when she was about to drift off to sleep
that night, she arrived at a decision. She would not go to church come
Sunday, but leave George to God.

* * *

Both his followers and his enemies rejoiced when they saw George
Fox loom in the shadows under the organ as it played the prelude to
the opening hymn of the evening service. This time he was accompanied by more than a dozen disciples, townfolk converted by
his first sermon, who had been waiting outside the church for his
arrival.

The only representative of Swarthmoor Hall was George Fell,
alone in the squire's pew. He had never before had it entirely to himself; it was an unnerving experience to face the curious glances of all
those people alone. Never before had he seen the church so
crowded; throngs of people stood pressed together on the tombstones
behind the benches; when the hymn started, the massive sound of all
those voices sent a shiver down his spine, for it was beautiful and
grandiose. He had never felt so important, invested with such authority, for he sat there as the sole representative of the House of
Swarthmoor, only son of Thomas Fell, Lord Chief Justice of the Duchy
of Lancaster. If Fox were once again to interfere with a divine service
ordained by his father, it would depend on him alone, in splendid
isolation in the family pew, as to how the populace would react. It
filled him with giddy pride and buttock-tightening apprehension; he no
longer regretted having taken his mother at her word when she said
that every member of the family was free to go to church if he
wished. What a story to tell his father! How proud he would be of
his son, representing him in such a dignified manner! He did not deign
to look at Fox, he did not deign to look at anyone; he sat staring ahead
of him in his blue velvet suit with starched ruff and cuffs, a miniature
replica of his father on the bench.

When the singing ceased, a hush fell over the congregation. Even
those women who had been staring at the young boy in the Swarthmoor pew now turned their heads and watched the dissenter in the
shadows, waiting for him to speak. Fox let the silence deepen until
there was no whisper, no shuffle, not the rustle of a prayerbook left;
then he slowly came down the aisle toward the pulpit, where Priest
Lampitt, pale and unhappy, stood waiting. But when he was about to
speak, his way was barred by Justice Sawrey, who today had taken a
seat on the aisle. "Stop!" Sawrey cried. "You will be allowed to speak
only if you speak according to the Scriptures!" The words seemed to

convey a permission, but the tone in which they were spoken belied it. Obviously, the squires had charged the judge with using that formula before anything was done to silence the man.

Fox looked down upon Sawrey with a rueful expression, as if he were commiserating with him in this degrading situation; then he said, "Of course I will, friend John. As thou wilt remember, that is my point."

The judge went scarlet with rage; he said, through clenched teeth, "At least take your hat off in church, you blasphemer!"

Fox's tone was conciliatory when he answered, "I am sorry, friend John. I only take off my hat when I speak to the Almighty God in prayer."

For some reason this reply, peaceable as it was, enraged the judge beyond endurance. "Stop him!" he cried, his voice now shrill with fury. "Throw him out! Show him what kind of men live here in Ulverston!"

For a moment nobody moved. Had Fox insulted the priest, they would have sprung at him without a qualm; all he had done was to insult an individual who did not himself quite belong. For a moment it seemed as if Fox would win the day; then Mistress Best's little dog suddenly began to yap hysterically, and a voice yelled, "Come on, men! Let's show His Honor who we are!" It was John McHair the poacher; his self-interest was so blatant that only the ruffians in the congregation rose in response. They threw themselves upon Fox with raucous shouts and a rumbling of boots, and began beating him with their fists. Somebody cried, "Stop that! Not in church!" But it was as if with the first blows the pent-up rage of the men in the congregation had been unleashed after all, against their better judgment. It was no longer only the ruffians who were beating and kicking Fox, almost every man in the church seemed to have joined them.

Young George saw Colonel Best give a note to his groom, who took it to Justice Sawrey. The judge, who had been egging on the assailants, read the note and started to shout, "Not in church! Not in church! Take him outside!" It took some doing, but he managed to fight his way into the mob until he reached John McHair, to whom he shouted something; it resulted in the poacher dragging Fox through the mob to the door of the church, where the constable and his henchmen stood waiting, ready to grab him. As they started to beat on him with their staves, Judge Sawrey shouted, "Throw him out of the town! See to it that he never sets foot here again!"

"Don't worry, Your Honor!" John McHair yelled. "I'll break the bugger's back meself, with this!" He showed the gnarled stick he always carried whenever George spied him hanging around Sawrey's park at dusk.

"Good man!" the judge cried. "The God of our fathers is with you!"

It seemed an inappropriate remark for a man who, as everyone knew, was only a fisherman's son: but George Fell, spellbound in the family pew, felt a wild, unbridled response. Suddenly he rose to join them.

*   *   *

Boniface Baker had been waiting outside the church, as it had been too crowded for him to get in. He had heard the commotion inside with growing alarm; then, to his incredulous horror, he saw John McHair the poacher drag George Fox out the door and throw him down the steps, where the constable's men started to whack his cringing body with their rods so cruelly that Bonny heard himself shriek, "No, no! Stop that! Stop!" and rushed to his friend's aid.

He tried to stop the constable by grabbing his arm, but he was thrust aside, squawking, without the man even noticing him. Then a mob came pouring out of the church: people he knew well, who suddenly seemed transformed into something terrifyingly different, animals, shrieking, with wide staring eyes. They all threw themselves upon the prostrate body of that wonderful, kind man, his friend; he forgot how small he was, how weak; he began to fight his way through the flailing fists and the kicking boots toward his friend while the raving mob shrieked all around him.

He was unable to reach him. He stumbled, fell, was kicked, shoved; it was as if he had fallen in the midst of a herd of stampeding cattle. Nobody noticed him; those who caught a fleeting glimpse of him thought that he was trying to add his own feeble kicks. He was trampled upon, but something drove him on, stronger than pain and fear; he *must* get to him, he *must,* he had to shield that poor battered body from those blows, those boots that went on kicking, kicking, as the surging mass of men slowly dragged George Fox toward the open fells.

He had just about given up hope of getting to his friend when he heard the high, terrified whinny of a pony, the shriek of a boy. The mob faltered; in that moment he managed, agile as a ferret, to worm his way toward George Fox and grab his leg. Then, with a shriek of fury, the kicks and blows started all over again; this time he was part of the body they were battering.

*   *   *

George Fell ran to his pony tethered to the railing outside. In the distance, toward the fells, he saw the mob, arms flailing, their shouts a fierce, bestial roar that was terrifying and yet irresistible. He leaped into the saddle, dug his spurs into Faggot's flanks and raced after them, the pony's little hoofs clattering on the cobbles.

He overtook them at the edge of the town, where they all seemed to be piled on top of one another on the narrow bridge across the sewer ditch. As he approached and reined in his pony, he discovered that they were no longer beating up Fox alone; they had begun to fight among themselves. People who had come to church to hear him and who were trying to stop the violence were being knocked down;

several had had their heads broken and blood was running down their faces. Their screams as they were thrown into the ditch were so chilling that he dug his spurs into Faggot's flanks again and lashed the pony with his whip.

But he heard someone cry, "There he is! The witch's son! Get him, get him!" They threw themselves upon him, shrieking; for a moment it seemed as if Faggot would escape them, then the sharp little hoofs slithered on the cobbles. Whinnying with a human sound of agony, the pony crashed to the ground.

He screamed in terror, "Mother! Mother! Help, Mother!" He was grabbed by cruel, hurting hands, lifted above the heads shouting hatred and derision, and hurled into the ditch. There he lay in the stinking sludge, gasping, choking, feeling the cold slime seep through his clothes and drag him down until only his head, open-mouthed, with terror-stricken eyes, remained above the surface, floating disembodied on the white ruff, while all around him moaning people were wallowing in the sludge, choking in the pestilential stench of the excretions of Ulverston, his father's town.

* * *

After they had dragged him across the bridge, the mob fell upon George Fox anew with stakes and clubs and continued to beat him until he fell to the ground, dazed and broken. Yet, even as he was bludgeoned and dragged along, there was within him a mounting exultation that grew until he knew: He is here, I am in His love.

At that moment the power of the Lord sprang through him. He stood up, stretched out his arms and cried in a loud, joyous voice, "Strike again, beloved friends! Here are my arms! Here is my other cheek!"

His tormentors backed away for a moment in bewilderment. Pain and fear had dropped away from him like a cloak; only a heavy weight attached to his leg still tried to drag him down. Then the huge bearded man who had grabbed him in the church cried, "Strike again, Quaker? Hast had none but soft blows until now? Faith, then: I'll strike thee in earnest this time!" He bore down on his outstretched hand with a staff so cruelly that pain shot, white hot, through his arm into his chest, knocking his breath away. He staggered under the blow: all that was mortal in him cried out in agony; then the power of the Lord sprang through his arm, his hand, and all pain ceased. Christ, that battered, bruised Man of sorrows who had stumbled and cried out on the road to Golgotha, rose within him in utter tenderness. He held out his hand, closed it, opened it again; then he slowly raised his arms in a gesture of blessing and said, "May the peace and the love of the living God be with you all, Amen." As he spoke, the weight on his leg finally dropped away.

He looked about him at the multitude, so full of love for them that tears blurred his eyes. A soldier made his way toward him, sword drawn, and said, "I will protect you, sir, for you are a man!"

But he said, "Sheath thy sword, friend, throw it from thee and live in the spirit that removes the occasion for all wars."

Then he walked back into the town; the crowd around him grew as he went. He climbed the pump in the market place, and, from there, gave the most powerful sermon of his life.

* * *

When Bonny Baker woke up he did not know where he was. All around him people were moaning and crying, "Help . . . help! Please, somebody! Help, please . . ." He was overcome by fear and wanted to flee, but the moment he moved he shrieked with pain and fell back, panting. But he had saved him, he had saved his friend! The memory of that triumph was for a moment stronger than the pain that held him pinned down. He managed to raise himself on one elbow, saw all around him people lying in the dust, some stirring, some moaning. He could not see what was going on across the bridge, but he heard voices, horses; then a filthy body came crawling out of the sewer ditch and stumbled in his direction. He recognized Master George Fell, covered with slime, bleeding from a cut on his face, lurching drunkenly as if sleepwalking.

"Master George . . . help . . . help!" His voice was too feeble; pain shot through his body again and he fell back, fainting.

As he regained consciousness, people were standing around him. Someone bent down, touched his shoulder and called, "Bonny? Bonny, boy? Art thou hurt?" It was Mr. Woodhouse; he burst into tears. "Hush, easy, me boy," Mr. Woodhouse said. He felt hands grope under his body, trying to lift him. The pain was so excruciating that he gave a wild scream of anguish.

"It's his thigh," he heard Mr. Woodhouse say, with echoes, as if he were lying at the bottom of a well. "Easy, I think it's broken." The hands tightened their grip on his tortured body; as they began to lift him, he opened his eyes wide, saw the face of Mr. Woodhouse in the sky and cried, "I did a miracle! Mr. Woodhouse, I did a miracle!"

Mr. Woodhouse looked down on him in a way he had never looked before, and said, "I know, laddie, I know. Now let me take thee home."

Pain overwhelmed him; he spiraled back into oblivion.

* * *

The first intimation of what had happened came to Margaret Fell when Will Hartford, the head groom, rushed in to tell her that Master George's pony had just come home alone, so shy and nervous that he feared the little animal must have had a terrible fright. He suggested that he go out on the fells to look for Master George, as he must have been thrown; maybe the pony had been attacked by a ram, the mating season for the sheep having started.

She knew at once that it had not been a ram. She ordered Will

Hartford to prepare the two-in-hand and called to Ann Traylor to get their cloaks and accompany her. She was about to step into the coach when Will Hartford cried, "Madam, look!" She saw her son stagger into the courtyard, filthy, covered with mud, whimpering her name.

She rushed toward him, knelt in front of him, pressed his shivering, stinking body against her; the stench from his clothes and his hair was horrible. He trembled uncontrollably; his breath came in heaving gasps; all she could do was lead him indoors, dirty as he was, kissing his grimy face, whispering, "Sweeting, sweeting, don't cry, I'm here, I'm here, don't worry, thou art home, thou art safe now . . ."

She bathed him and put him to bed herself. Before he finally fell asleep, all he said was, "They hurt me. They hurt me terribly . . ."

Her first impulse was to flee with her family. The town had obviously taken leave of its senses; after assaulting a defenseless child, God only knew what they might do. She should pack her family into the traveling coach and go to her aunt in Great Urswick, or, better still, to Judge Cartwright in Gleaston, her husband's mentor. Certainly he would be better equipped to protect them than Aunt Clara, who had nothing with which to shield them from a rabid mob but a doddering gardener and a foul-mouthed cockatoo.

But what about George Fox? If this was what they had done to a child, what had they done to him? If she had not been so selfish, thinking only of her own security, she would have been in church this morning; she could have prevented the whole thing by the sheer weight of her authority.

For a moment she thought of leaving everybody in the Hall to fend for themselves while she went to look for George; then there was a knock at the door and Thomas Woodhouse came in to ask if he might take Will Hartford and Harry Martin along to look for the servants who had not returned: Henderson, little Mabby and Bonny Baker. She gave them leave to go; as Thomas went to the door, she added, "Please look for George Fox." Then, as an afterthought, "bring along any others who may be in need of help and shelter." Thomas said, "Very well, Madam," and left; neither of them realized that they had returned to their old relationship.

She was totally unprepared for what followed. When, an hour later, the first of the injured were brought in, she was stunned by the magnitude of the disaster. Among them was Bonny Baker, unconscious, horribly bruised, moaning as the men put him down on the settee in the hall. She was told he had a broken thigh and instantly sent Harry Martin for the apothecary. It was fortunate she did so; Bonny Baker was only the first of many, all of them bleeding, beaten, terrified out of their wits; all of them begging her to protect them, to save them from the fury of the hellions in town.

It was her worst moment; she was dumfounded, incredulous and very much afraid. Then the mounting chaos of all those wounded people, crazed with fear or limp with shock, forced her to face reality.

The old Margaret, mistress of Swarthmoor Hall, took over from muddle-headed Maggie and her wild-eyed fancies. She began, with calm determination, to turn the house into an infirmary, ordered mattresses to be brought down from all the beds in the house, bed linen torn up for bandages, hot water, towels, camomile tea, wine; she ransacked the household to succor the victims of her folly, or spiritual awakening, or whatever it had been. But whatever it turned out to have been in the end, she knew that her world would never be the same again, and that for the House of Swarthmoor the years of the locust had started.

* * *

When Henrietta Best stood on the threshold of the Hall and stared at the scene with horrified eyes, she almost turned and fled. Everywhere, among the furniture, along the walls, in front of the hearth, on the landing of the second floor, injured people lay on mattresses, settees, rows of pillows, pads of folded blankets. Among them moved the servants of the Hall, washing their wounds, bandaging them, supporting them as they sipped from china cups and pewter goblets. It was all so reminiscent of La Couvertoirade after the Cardinal's troops had made their first assault on the town, that she was overcome by the urge to run back to the coach; then she heard a child's voice calling, "Mama!"

A little girl, no more than five years old, stumbled toward her mother with a pitcher of water almost too heavy for her. The sight gave her back the notion which had moved her to come: that here was a chance, at last, to give a posthumous sense to the calvary of her own children. She had to grasp it quickly, before the flesh became weak; she hurried past the beds, ignored the hands stretched out to her in supplication, and found Mistress Fell bent over a small boy who was being examined by the apothecary. Despite her protests, she managed to steer her into an empty little room, off the hall. There, in the semi-darkness, she confronted the woman with what lay in wait for her if she did not come to her senses, now! She told her about the saint she had married because of his spiritual passion; how they had been forced to flee from persecution, leaving all their worldly goods behind; how they had gone into hiding, five hundred Huguenots in the little town of La Couvertoirade, in an effort to escape from the mercenaries of Cardinal Richelieu; how, after a siege of five nightmarish weeks, the enraged soldiers had finally breached the walls and massacred every single man, raped every woman, and as for her children . . .

She could not say it. She covered her face with her hands, tried to force herself to speak, but she could not. She felt the arm of the woman around her shoulders, calm, self-assured, and she was about to shriek in anguish when she felt that someone else had entered the room. The arm around her shoulders was taken away; she knew who it was before she heard the woman cry, "George!"

She looked up. Fox stood in the doorway, mud-streaked, his clothes in tatters; a power and a light shone about him that were irresistible to any woman, old or young, married or widowed, virgin or harlot. It mattered not what he called himself, Paul, Savonarola, Calvin, Rohan, he was always the same and always would be; he was the monster that had devoured her children.

"Art thou hurt?" the woman asked, the voice of all the women who had ever loved a saint and suffered for the rest of their lives.

"I was," he answered, "but the power of the Lord was over me, and my wounds were healed by a miracle. So I guided my enemies back to the market place and the power of God thundered among them."

"A miracle?"

Henrietta cried out, "Yes! He performs miracles! He heals the sick, he raises the dead, he cures broken limbs, drives out madness! But to what purpose? What good does it do? I can tell you what it will do! I have known him, I married him, I bore his children! Do you know what will happen to your children if you don't cut yourself loose from this monster now, *now,* while there is still time?" The woman tried to hush her; she knew that she was losing control, but she cried, "They will break down the walls, they will tear your children from your arms, they will grab them by their ankles, and while they shriek your name they will smash their heads against the wall! And while you scream their life away, you will be raped, in the blood from their skulls, the pulp of their brains!"

For a motionless moment she hovered on the brink of a precipice of unspeakable horror, death itself. Then Fox opened his arms and said, "Friend . . ." He said it with such tenderness and infinite understanding that she broke down. His strong, sheltering arms guided her to a chair, where she collapsed in defeat and disgust. She had fallen for that irresistible siren's voice again, for the chilling, impersonal love of the saint.

She felt a hand on her shoulder and looked up. Margaret Fell stood in front of her, holding out a bandage. She gazed at the woman, aghast, for she was asking her to take up her life again where it had been twenty-four years before. Then she heard her name. There stood her husband, in the doorway. Stretching out her arms toward him, she cried, *"Chéri, chéri!* Take me away, take me away! *Je te supplie!"*

He led her away, gently, from what she knew had been her moment of truth.

*   *   *

The sight of the wounded had sobered George Fox; the outburst of the deranged woman deeply distressed him. He went back into the hall and bent over the stableboy with his chalk white face, his leg crudely bandaged with two croquet mallets for splints. He heard him say, "George, I saved thee, George, didn't I, George, I saved thee?" He put his hand on the boy's brow in a gesture of tenderness, overwhelmed by doubt.

An hour ago he had known ecstasy as the power of the Lord healed

his hand and enabled him to deliver his message of hope and love
to his tormentors. Now, looking down upon the child who had tried
to protect him from the mob, he knew a moment of total despair.
Again he heard the voice of that woman, saw the images it had evoked.

"The apothecary says he cannot cure me," the boy said, "but he
can't do miracles like thee, George, can he?"

At the sight of that face, radiant with confidence and adoration,
he stretched out his hand toward the child and beseeched the infinite
ocean of light and love to bestow upon him the blessing of being
whole again, without pain and fear, to restore his broken limb. But
even as he prayed he sensed that his plea would go unanswered.
The power of the Lord had been withdrawn from him. He was torn
with pity for the child who saw his simple trust abused. 'My God,' he
prayed, 'why hast Thou forsaken me?' He opened his eyes. "Friend
Bonny, the Lord says: Not yet."

The child looked at him, perplexed.

"Don't ask me why. God speaks through me only at times. All I
can give thee at this moment is my gratitude for what thou hast done,
and my pride at being thy friend."

The joy and expectation on the boy's face, furrowed with pain,
slowly dimmed. Then he whispered, "Yes, George."

He could stand it no longer. He turned away to go outside, but a
hand on his arm held him back. It was Margaret Fell; he had not
realized she was standing beside him. "George? Art thou all right?"

"Yes," he said. He walked away, past the litters, out into the night.

A pale half moon seemed to move breathlessly through racing
clouds. He stood in the darkness, praying, when a voice called him
softly.

"Quaker?"

He looked around, but saw no one. The voice had seemed to come
from overhead, but above him there was nothing but the moon, the
scudding clouds.

"Quaker? Come over here."

Now the voice seemed to come from the dark orchard.

"Where art thou?"

"Here." The dark shape of a man stepped out of the shadows of the
orchard into the light of the moon. It was the man who had struck
him. "Show me thy hand, Quaker," he said quietly.

He lifted his arm. The man took his hand and squeezed it, hard.
There was no response; the man seemed to stand dumfounded; then
he said, "Show me the other."

He obeyed. The man squeezed that hand too; it was as sound as
the other. Then he said calmly, "Hold out the other again."

"Why?"

"I am going to break it."

He had often been threatened with violence; that of God within
him had always rallied in response. Now there seemed to be nothing
within him, only a dark, despairing void. He saw the man lift his

staff for the blow and cried, "Not again! This time thou wouldst break it!"

"Why? Because there are not enough people around? Thou wilt not perform a miracle for just me?"

"It was not I who performed the miracle, it was God! And His power has left me."

"Never mind thy fancy talk," the man said, lifting his stick. "Give me thy hand."

"I told thee, thou wilt break it this time!" But he lifted his hand.

The man lowered his stick. "Thou really wouldst have me strike thee again?"

"Yes."

"Why?"

"That may be the way in which God wishes to punish me."

"For what?"

"For the suffering I have caused."

"Suffering?"

"All those people in there. That poor child with the broken leg."

"Art thou mad?" the man cried angrily. "That was not thy doing! I struck them! I struck *thee!* What is thy game?"

"It is no game! God brought me here; I unleashed all this violence in the belief that I was in His power. Now He has drawn away from me, I see only suffering, destruction. I came out here to wrestle with the angel, like . . ." He fell silent. Perhaps this was the angel. It was as if, in the darkness, something had changed. Jacob! The angel had touched him, and he had limped for the rest of his life.

He lifted his hand once more, this time with eagerness. "Strike it!" he cried. "Break it! Bestow upon me the mark of Jacob, in the name of the Lord!"

For a moment the man stood speechless; then he said vehemently, "No, Quaker! Go and find thyself another angel!" He threw his stick away; it rustled briefly in the branches of a tree. "The devil take thy tricks!" he cried. "I wish I'd never set eyes on thee! Let Justice Sawrey do his own dirty work from now on!" Suddenly he pleaded, "I believe thee. I believe in thy miracle, I won't doubt again; now let me go!"

"But thou must understand," he urged, with great joy, "it was not *my* miracle, it was God's! I am nothing! We all are vessels for His love, tools for His power. If it pleases Him to draw away from me, I can do nothing! I tried, but I could not even help a child with a broken thighbone!"

"Which child?"

"A stableboy."

"Is he in there?"

"Yes . . ."

"Take me to him."

"Thou?"

"I have set bones before. I had a dog once that broke his thigh in a trap. I set the bone; we walked the woods together for years."

For a moment he hesitated, then he said, "Very well. I'll take thee to him." They went back into the house together.

So it came about that John McHair the poacher set Bonny Baker's broken thigh. He stayed on to help the women carry pitchers of water and kettles of soup from the kitchen; when, later that night, all those present gathered in meeting for worship, he was among them.

During the silence George Fox thought about Jacob. The angel had touched the hollow of his thigh; he had limped for the rest of his life. Then it came to him what had really happened: the sign of Jacob had been bestowed not upon him, but upon a stableboy, and as a result a wolf had entered the Peaceable Kingdom.

He looked at the poacher, across from him. There he sat, his eyes bemused in his hirsute face. *The wolf shall dwell with the lamb, and the leopard shall lie down with the kid, and the calf and the young lion together, and a little child shall lead them.*

Suddenly, there it was again: the indefinable, unmistakable presence of God.

CHAPTER THREE

THE virgin stretch of silver beach, bared by the tide, lay shimmering in the sun; the three horsemen who had appeared on the crest of the bluffs paused for a moment before starting their descent. Obviously, they were a master and his two underlings, there could be no mistaking the authoritative aloofness of the man in the center, on the white Arab mare. He was the slightest of the three; his traveling clothes, covered with dust, were not conspicuously different from those of the others, but his elaborate wig distinguished him as a gentleman. Feeling the cool breeze from the estuary, he removed the wig and tossed it to the man on his right, who caught it deftly. He suddenly looked old, with his short-cropped gray hair, a Roman general surveying the sands before crossing them.

He sat for a moment, eyes closed, with a blissful expression on his face, savoring the freshness of the sea breeze after their long, dusty ride; his nervous, hot horse stirred below him with a tinkling of chains and a creaking of leather. "Ah," he said. "It's good to be home!" Then, as if catching himself in a moment of untoward emotion, he opened his eyes, his face took on its disdainful expression again and he said, "All right, let's proceed. The tide is favorable."

As the horsemen began to descend the steep slope of the fell, a bird flew screeching from the bracken; the grit kicked up by the horses' hoofs rustled among the leaves. The wind that had blown fresh and clean on the top of the bluff subsided; the miasmic scent of primeval creation enveloped them, the stench of myriad sea creatures dying, of algae rotting in the sun, turning into fertile soil for future generations. Often, as a young man, had Thomas Fell galloped across these sands with his heart in his mouth, in a mad race with the onrushing tide, wondering if this time he had left it too late, chilled by the sudden terror of an untimely, stupid end to his promising career. It had taken him years before he had begun to enjoy the sands, to savor their timeless beauty. So it was with some irritation that he heard the creaking of a saddle approach from behind. If only Sam Pruitt, with his petulant babble, would leave him alone! "Yes, what is it?" he snapped.

But it was not Sam Pruitt, it was Charles, his groom, who had been riding a respectful distance behind him but who at the sight of the small band of horsemen approaching from the other shore drew ahead to protect his master. It was a symbolic gesture, but he executed it with pride and solemnity. He rode toward the riders in the distance, a small concentration of multi-legged life cantering in thin air like a mirage, gossamer cloaks flying.

"Is that Priest Lampitt, Your Lordship?" a voice asked on his other side. This time it was Sam Pruitt.

"I could not say."

"They seem to be in a hurry, don't they?"

He did not reply, it would only encourage the man.

"I wonder whether they are coming to meet us?" Sam always talked about "us," like a midwife.

"Why not ride ahead and find out?"

The clerk hesitated; then he spurred his horse. As he overtook Charles Cotten, the latter turned in his saddle, looking hurt; Thomas Fell gave him a wave of the hand to reassure him that no offense was meant. Ah! What a bore servants were! He watched the small figure of his clerk join the distant horsemen. They all milled together for a moment, then Sam came cantering back, ahead of the others. They were now close enough for him to recognize some faces: Priest Lampitt, John Sawrey, Rutledge. Indeed, it looked like a delegation; he called to Charles for his wig and put it back on. The panting horse of his clerk drew up beside him.

"Your Lordship!" Sam Pruitt cried. "Something has happened at the Hall! Something concerning your family! It seems that your wife, your household . . ." His voice was drowned out by the rumble of hoofs as the others joined them.

As always, at the hint of any calamity, Thomas Fell froze. At the first agonized outcry of his sensibilities, a drawbridge was pulled up between him and reality, achieving an instant inaccessibility that enabled him to meet catastrophe with equanimity. As they drew up around him, he welcomed the flustered squires on their foam-splattered horses with aloofness. Lampitt, doffing his hat respectfully, cried, "Your Lordship! We have grave news concerning your family! Her Ladyship, your daughters, even your servants have succumbed to witchcraft!"

Despite his detachment, Thomas Fell was relieved. At least no one was dead.

"I'm afraid the good priest is right," a high, pedantic voice continued. It was John Sawrey. "During your absence Mistress Fell gave hospitality to a vagrant called George Fox, who proceeded to bring herself and your entire household under his spell. Not only did the man interrupt a church service with profanities in which he was, I am grieved to say, supported by your good wife; day before yesterday he turned up in church again and this time caused a riot which resulted in injuries and broken limbs among the population. I am sorry to have to report that Mistress Fell has seen fit to give the man sanctuary; he resides as of this moment at your house. We look upon you as the highest authority in the county, and also presumably in your household, to put matters right without delay."

The word "presumably" filled Thomas Fell with fury. Until that moment he had been confused and worried, despite his detachment; now he recovered his wits with a vengeance. God's fish! How dare he, the bloody little upstart! "Am I to conclude that you gentlemen have turned up in such numbers to tell me how to run my household?" he asked, knowing it was unwise, but Sawrey's insult had stung him to the quick.

"No, Thomas Fell!" a deep voice grumbled close by. "Of course not!" It was Rutledge, his closest neighbor, a man with a heart of gold but the brains of one of his mastiffs. "We just thought we would warn you about the situation before you reached home, so you would be fully prepared."

"I see. Thank you. Now," he continued, turning to the priest, "would you be so kind as to justify the word 'witchcraft'?"

"Well, Your Lordship, the actions and attitudes of your good wife . . ."

"Do you realize, sir, that a charge of witchcraft is a serious matter? Are you going to stand by it or was it spoken in the heat of excitement?" Without waiting for a reply, he turned to Sawrey. "I take it that you support the accusation?"

Sawrey, though his face showed no sign of it, realized the implications of that question. Despite his ludicrous struggle for high life, he was an astute lawyer, as quick-witted as they came. "I apologize in behalf of Priest Lampitt for that unfortunate word," he said. "It was indeed spoken in haste." He turned to the priest. "I am sure Mr. Lampitt will be eager to apologize; he obviously does not realize the implications." He said it affably enough, but there could be no doubting the urgency of his tone.

Lampitt responded at once. "Forgive me, Your Lordship," he said, doffing his unsavory black hat again. "I apologize. Indeed, I spoke in haste, in—in my eagerness to impress upon you the seriousness of the situation."

"Exactly how serious is it? Did anybody die?"

"No, Your Lordship."

"Any damage to property? Any cattle killed?"

"No."

"I'm afraid it's more serious than that," Sawrey's cool voice interceded, obviously aware that his distinguished colleague was demolishing the witness. "No doubt at the instigation of the blasphemer, your good wife has ordained that there shall be no distinction in rank or intimacy between her family and the servants. Every night there is a heathenish gathering of a highly emotional nature, during which the servants are encouraged to hold forth at their fancy; a few nights ago scenes of shocking lechery took place in the courtyard."

"What would constitute shocking lechery, Mr. Sawrey?"

"Members of your staff danced naked in the moonlight and ended on the ground in communal fornication."

"How do you know this? Were you there?"

"I have the eyewitness reports of impeccable witnesses."

"Members of my household?"

"Indeed."

"Who presumably are also under the spell of this satanic gentleman, whatever his name is?"

"Decidedly not. They are among the few who resisted the blandishments of the blasphemer. Their testimony is above suspicion."

"Whose suspicion? Your own?"

The little man eyed him coldly. "Indeed, sir."

"In that case, I demand that you present me with a warrant, duly sworn, against Margaret Fell, spouse of Thomas Fell of Swarthmoor Hall."

"Warrant?" The face of the damned pipsqueak began to show some emotion at last.

"I will then instantly swear out a complaint of slander against yourself and anybody else here who feels that what happens in the courtyard of my house at dead of night concerns him sufficiently to put my family in prison." It was, of course, theatrical bluff; but Sawrey was the only one among them to realize it.

"Come, come, Fell, that's not what we intended," Simon Rutledge protested in his mastiff's bark.

Then Rutherford piped up, "Look, dear friend," he said in his gentleman farmer's voice, "the whole business has been blown out of proportion. What we are worried about is the sudden footing of equality on which your servants and your family seem to be. It has begun to infect our own households. Damn it all, this morning my wife told me that our kitchen wench had tried to call her 'thou,' and when I went to berate her she started to rant about his man Fox. He is just one of those rabble-rousers we have seen off and on since the revolution, but it is your good wife's support that makes him a threat to the community. That is why we're here. He *did* cause a riot in which people were injured and the innocent suffered. So, don't let's bandy about any big words like witchcraft, let's settle this as neighbors, among ourselves. That is all. It it not, gentlemen?" He looked about him. The others muttered in agreement; their relief was obvious. That left Sawrey and the miserable Lampitt.

"Thank you. As we proceed, will someone be so kind as to acquaint me with the facts, now that we have all vented our emotions?"

"Maybe I, as their shepherd, am best qualified to do so," Lampitt said unctuously, eager to undo the damage.

"No, thank you, sir," he said. "I do not want to hear any more about blasphemy. I want to hear the facts about the rebellion in our households. Thank you." With that, he turned to Rutherford. "Tell me more about your good wife's problems," he said with cold relish.

They started forward across the sands to Ulverston.

*   *   *

While the sober-minded Rutherford gave his account of the happenings at the Hall, William Best watched Fell with relief. The man really knew how to rise to the challenge. But how was he going to handle the wider situation? What could be done to defuse the bomb that threatened to destroy their community? How could that devil Fox be spirited away before he had a chance to do more mischief? How could that impetuous woman be induced to take up life again as if nothing had happened?

He did not get a chance for a word with Fell until after Rutledge and Rutherford had branched off. The moment they were gone, he drew up alongside his colleague and asked, "Did my groom manage to find you yesterday?"

"Ah, Best. No, I haven't seen him."

"I don't understand it—I sent him to meet you yesterday morning with a message warning you about this. I need not tell you that I find the whole affair extremely painful. Whatever happens, I am at your disposal."

"Thank you."

From the way the dark eyes sized him up, he knew that, to Fell, his solicitude was suspect. There was nothing he could do about it, at least for the present.

He rode home alone, deep in thought, and found, to his relief, that his wife had recovered sufficiently to welcome him. She looked happy and relaxed; it was a miracle how she had managed to rally. He was overcome by admiration.

They went to her little withdrawing room, where he poured out two glasses of muscatel. Maybe it was the relief he felt at her recovery, but as he told her what had happened the whole thing seemed to be reduced to its right proportions. A storm in a teacup.

"Poor Mistress Fell," he said. "Sawrey told him about those servants cavorting in the courtyard without a stitch on. God knows where he got hold of it; it must be all over town now. He even added a detail the boy did not mention: it seems the whole thing ended in communal fornication. H'm." He took a sip of his wine.

"For a man in his situation, there is only one way of handling it," she said thoughtfully.

"What would that be?"

"Get her with child."

"What an extraordinary thing to say."

She smiled. "To understand that, *chéri,* thou wouldst have to be a woman."

"Well," he bantered, "that, I'm afraid, is one thing I cannot do for thee."

She laughed. "Thank God for that." In the silence that followed, there was a knock on the door.

"Come in!"

It was Kathryn, the maid. It would be only a cold supper this evening, she announced. Bonbon had taken to bed with a migraine.

It was most inconsiderate of him, but they met the emergency with determination. There is nothing more effective for removing the remains of a crisis than the emergence of a new one.

* * *

The moment she heard that her husband was climbing the bluff, Margaret Fell rushed upstairs to the window of their bedchamber. It had become a tradition over the years: each time he came home from the circuit she would stand there and watch him, and on his way to the house he would look up and wave; that would be their first contact.

She was so sure of the rightness of what she had done that she did not doubt he would understand, even though, she had been told, some of the neighbors had gone to meet him, obviously to make trouble.

There was a clatter of hoofs and suddenly he was there, looking tired and travel-stained. She watched as he dismounted and Harry Martin the stableboy came running to take the horse and welcome his master. But the boy did not doff his hat; Thomas, with an angry blow, knocked it off his head.

It was so unlike him that she suddenly felt afraid. She closed her eyes and prayed for strength, for divine assistance; when she opened them again she saw Thomas stride across the drive without looking up at the window and vanish from sight. He had never done this before; she waited, with nervous twinges in her stomach, for his steps to come down the passage. But they did not come. She was prepared for his anger; not for his not coming at all. Was he talking to someone? She had to know. She gathered her skirts, went to the landing and peered down into the hall. He was not there.

She started down the stairs; then, through the window on the half-way landing she saw him: in the garden, sitting on the bench where she and George had sat. He must be so furious that he did not trust himself to face her.

Well, that was ridiculous! She started down the stairs to go to him, explain . . . Then she faltered and stopped. Perhaps someone else should speak to him first. But who? Only George had the power to confront him in one of those moods; but George had left early that morning and would not be back until nightfall. Whom else could she send, capable of braving the awesome fury in which he sat there, waiting for his first victim? Yet he looked terribly lonely, sitting there, terribly hurt. What a homecoming, poor man! Maybe someone should go there and love him, just love him. She could not do it; one of the children? Who? Mary was the only one who had never been intimidated by him, and he had never failed to respond to her. The little wretch! She might be only five, but she had the wiles of a woman.

She went to the playroom and found the children huddled there around Ann Traylor, the way they did when there was a bad thunderstorm. All seemed subdued except Mary, who sat alone in a corner, tearing a sheet of paper into little pieces, which she stuffed into the pocket of her pinafore.

"What on earth art thou doing?"

The child looked up. Her large blue eyes were remote. "I am making something."

She wanted to tell her to take that mess out of her pocket before going to see her father, but decided to let it pass. "Father is in the garden, on the bench by the roses. I think he is waiting for thee."

The little girl said calmly, "I will go when I have finished my prize." It was her private word for "surprise."

She went on tearing up paper until Margaret was about to scream. Only when the whole sheet was gone did she spring to her feet and skip out of the room.

* * *

Thomas Fell had fled into the garden because he did not trust himself. He detested conjugal scenes; to have confronted his wife at that moment would have resulted in a flaming quarrel. The times she had plunged headlong into some sudden passionate concern, setting the whole household by its ears! When they still lived in London, there had been a soup kitchen for the poor, a school for orphans, a whole slough of harebrained enterprises; after their return to Swarthmoor she had press-ganged the villagers into a choir that sounded like feeding time in the Colosseum, and when the Puritan revolution had pronounced choirs to be relics of Popish idolatry she had changed it blithely into a "madrigal society." Oh! The commotion, the heartburn she had caused, over and over again, with her insufferable willfulness! The cleaning up of the graveyard and the church, every able soul scrubbing tombstones; and those gargantuan Christmas parties for the villagers, turning the Hall into a madhouse of milling humanity munching Christmas pudding and rubbing hard sauce into his ancestral chairs! His father, God rest his soul, a notorious wencher in his day, had cried when he heard that his son was planning to marry Margaret, eighteen years his junior, so pure, so shy, so delicate, "Delicate?! I may not know the gal too well, but I can tell thee this much: marry her, and she'll keep thee running out of breath for the rest of thy life! Delicate? God strike me vitals! A battering ram in petticoats!"

At the time, he had listened to the old man's tirade with condescension, but how the words had rung in his ears later! Now, damn it, she had done it again. Here he was, after three grueling months on the circuit, looking forward to a warm welcome and a few happy, peaceable months at home, and what did he find? A commotion that had sent a delegation of his neighbors to meet him on the sands! Oh! If only he were not so incurably civilized! This time he should really take her across his knees and spank the daylights out of her! By God, this time . . .

He caught a movement out of the corner of his eye, turned and saw his daughter Mary coming down the garden path, followed by a cat and a dog. The sight of her filled him with tenderness, but the dog seemed to symbolize the chaos that had struck his home. It was the stable dog, a filthy old bitch that had never been allowed in the house, let alone the garden. Yet there the mongrel came, breathless with obesity, her tits, elongated by perpetual maternity, brushing the gravel. The three stopped in front of him and the child said, without a greeting, as if they had interrupted their conversation only moments before, "Close your eyes."

"Why?"

"I have a prize for you. Close your eyes."

He closed his eyes. There was a small rustling sound; some insects settled on his hands.

"Open your eyes."

He opened them. His hands were covered with small bits of paper; so were his lap, his shoulders and his hair. More scraps of paper came fluttering down, handfuls of them, which she tossed at him from her apron pocket, as if she were sowing. She went on covering him with bits of paper until there were none left, then she looked at him with satisfaction and said, "There."

"What is the meaning of that, pray?"

"It is snow."

"I see."

"I made it for you. Nobody else knew."

He saw himself as he sat there: a furious man covered with bits of paper.

"I have something to show you," she said. "Look." She came close and opened her mouth in front of his nose. It was small and vulnerable, with the pink innocence of childhood. "Do you see it?"

"What?"

"My new tooth, in the back. Look." She opened her mouth wider. He peered inside; there was indeed a small white speck on the left side of the lower jaw.

She closed her mouth. "Did you see it?"

"I did."

"I kept it a secret. Somebody else may have seen it, though, without me wanting to. She may have peeked in my mouth when I called her."

"Who?"

She pointed at the cat. "Here, tell me if you can see it." She brought her face close to his and called, "Cassie! Cassie!" opening her mouth wide.

"Yes," he said. "If thou didst call her that close, she has seen it."

"I do not think *she* did, though." She pointed at the old mongrel panting in the sun. "Look." She called, "Mimi! Mimi! Mimi!" barely parting her lips. The mongrel, with the ingrained sense of guilt that went with her lowly station, laid her ears flat and licked her nose in preventive ingratiation.

"Thou art right," he said. "She can't have."

"I'll show her now." She knelt, took the wary old dog's head between her hands and said, "A-a-a-h. A-a-a-h." The abused animal rolled over in abject surrender. She said, "She saw it," got up and came back to him. She gazed into his eyes from close quarters, one after the other. Then she asked, "Shall I tell you about the mouse?"

"Last time it was in the attic, visiting the bats."

"Now," she said, "it is dead."

"Ah?"

"While you were gone it went dead and was buried, But it got bored and got up again, and then it decided to go on the circuit. The mouse circuit, with a little coach, and when it came to Lancaster . . ."

It became a long, rambling story which she obviously made up as she went along. She leaned against his knee; her small white hands moved gracefully against the red background of the roses while she drew him, with feminine subtlety, into her world.

Seen from that world, Margaret's latest outrage was hilarious. She had gone through many bizarre phases, but never a conversion. He should go inside and find out what the devil it was all about.

* * *

Margaret Fell watched them from the window of the upstairs landing, delighted to see little Mary break through his brooding anger. When they came in, hand in hand, she faced him with brave composure; the sight of the bits of paper on his wig and shoulders made her feel like laughing. He gave her a withering look and strode, without a word, into the hall, where the girls were waiting for him with trepidation. It was obviously not the right moment for them to sing the madrigal they had rehearsed, so, behaving as if nothing had happened, she kept the conversation on a harmless level by inducing them to chat incoherently about their various activities during his absence. He listened to them as he would to a long-winded witness; he had never been particularly close to the other girls. He asked after young George; when she told him that he was in bed after a fall from his horse, he asked, "Nothing serious, I hope?"

"No, no, more shock than anything else. But I am sure he would love to see thee."

"Anon. Now shall you and I go and have a word together? It would appear to be overdue."

Oh dear, oh dear. "You" was always a sure sign of exasperation.

"Yes," she said, in the refined voice she affected whenever she began to feel unsure of herself. "That would seem a splendid idea."

"Would you kindly accompany me to the study?"

She took the arm he proffered and let herself be guided to his study, feeling like a lamb being led to slaughter. She fully expected him to fling her inside, once they were out of sight and earshot of the children; she almost hoped he would. If only he would burst out of this impeccable courtesy and raise the roof! It would clear the air like a thunderstorm, the whole thing would end in embraces and contrition, after which everybody would at last be able to relax.

He opened the door and bowed to let her enter; as she did so, she almost expected to feel his boot, for he looked cross-eyed with fury. But no; he closed the door quietly. She turned to face him. He looked like the headmaster of a school, about to berate a pupil; his insufferable superiority got the better of her. "Wouldst thou do me the courtesy of treating me like an adult, please?" she asked.

If it had been her intention to goad him into meeting her on her own terms, she failed. He eyed her with distaste. "A what?"

"Pardon?"

"I can scarce believe that an adult would commit the follies thou hast seen fit to indulge in during my absence."

"What follies, pray?" She could not help joining him in his ridiculous formality.

He said coldly, "Before thou regalest me with thy version of thy latest extravagance, let me tell thee that thou very nearly hadst a warrant sworn against thee for witchcraft. And that danger is by no means over."

"Witchcraft? By whom?"

"By all our neighbors."

"On what basis, for heaven's sake?"

"From what I understand, there have been incidents that might well be parlayed into manifestations of witchcraft by a malevolent adversary."

"Mention one. Just *one!*"

"What about the Walpurgis Night that took place in the courtyard recently?"

"What art thou talking about?!"

"The night when the servants found occasion to prance naked in the moonlight, ending up in wholesale fornication."

She cried indignantly, "Who told thee that wicked story?!"

He stared at her. "It is not true?"

"Of course not! What dost thou take me for?! All it was was Mabby the skivvy and Harry Martin the stableboy losing their heads! In religious ecstasy!"

"Were they naked?"

"I think it's more important—"

"Were they naked?"

"Yes! But they did not—well—they did *not.*"

"Art thou sure?"

"Of course I'm sure! Thomas Woodhouse was there and he threw wa—" Too late.

"He threw water. I see."

"But the whole story is pure fabrication! And it was the only time! It . . . Oh! What's the use?"

"Quite." His voice was so maddeningly urbane that she turned away in exasperation.

"Why start demeaning the whole thing straightaway with—with this?" she cried. "Why not let me tell thee what really happened? What happened to *me?*"

"I am most interested," he said frostily. "Pray do so." He went behind his desk and sat down the way he did on the bench, to lean back and gaze at her with detachment. She felt outraged and at the same time helpless, as must those who faced him from the dock.

"A few weeks ago," she started, her voice trembling slightly, "a young itinerant preacher came to visit the Hall. His name was George Fox . . ."

* * *

As she continued to tell her story, Thomas Fell's attention wandered from her words. He had never seen her quite like this before. She was a passionate woman who had never made a secret of her emotions, it was part of her charm; but this time there was something disturbing in her passion. On previous occasions, the soup kitchen, the tombstones, there had been joyous, happy excitement; this time there was an element of desperation in her that alarmed him profoundly. He felt his anger subside. He loved the woman; to see her in such torment filled him with concern.

As her story rambled on, he tried to define what he sensed in her and came to the conclusion it was fear. Could it be that she had released a demon she could not control? "Er—forgive me, my dear, where *is* Mr. Fox? Somewhere in the house?"

She looked at him, disoriented. "Oh? . . . Oh, no, no. He'll be back tonight. He has so looked forward to thy coming."

"I am surprised, considering how he has wrecked my household."

"Oh, Thomas, please!" Suddenly she was pleading, leaning across the desk, desperate, tormented. *"Please* don't, *please* don't fight him, *please* . . . I . . . Can't thou see? I—I'm involved . . ."

He looked at her eyes. They were limpid, gray, beautiful. "Don't worry," he said. "I'll take him seriously."

"Oh, yes, please, please . . . thou wilt understand if thou wilt only *listen* to him!" He wondered whether she knew how distraught she looked at that moment. "He is a remarkable man," she went on, "full of love and understanding. Give him a chance to explain himself. To *be* himself. Don't crush him—please, please?"

He smiled. "From what I have heard, he would be a hard man to crush."

"Oh, that's where thou art wrong! That's where everybody is wrong! He is so sensitive, so . . . well, thou wilt see for thyself. Now shall we join the children?" She patted her hair nervously.

"Of course." He rose.

"I haven't told thee half . . ."

"I trust we'll have occasion to return to the subject."

He went to the door and opened it for her. She hesitated, her face anxious, her eyes searching. It would have been the moment for him to take her in his arms, but he could not do it. Before he let himself be led astray by tenderness, he must know what she was so afraid of.

Arm in arm, they returned to the drawing room.

* * *

"The Andalusian Merchant that returns
Laden with cochineal and china dishes
Reports in Spain how fiercely Fogo burns
In an ocean full of flying fishes . . ."

The high, innocent voices of the six girls blended in exquisite counter-point. Thomas Fell sat listening, eyes closed.

"These things are wondrous, yet more wondrous I,
Whose heart with fear doth freeze,
With love doth fry."

The last chord, entrancingly spiced with a dissonance in the youngest of the voices, drifted, *largo sostenuto,* into silence. He sighed, opened his eyes and said, "Charming, charming. Children, I must compliment you. That was beautiful." Aware of their discomfort, he wondered whether his praise had not been warm enough; then he realized that they were looking not at him but at the door behind him. He turned around and saw a young man in a shepherd's smock surveying the scene with a smile of indulgence. Margaret said, "Thomas, meet George Fox . . ."

Before he could rise, the young man intoned, "God bless thee, Thomas Fell, awaken thee and set thee free."

His first impulse was to cut the pompous ass down to size; his wife's anguished expectancy stopped him from doing so. He rose. "It would seem, Mr. Fox, that a discussion between us in in order. Would you care to accompany me to my study?"

The young man made an incongruous gesture, as if the house were his own. "By all means."

In the study Sam Pruitt sat writing at the desk. "Sam, wouldst thou mind?"

"Oh . . . Certainly, Your Lordship . . ." The clerk rose in a fluster, collected his papers, dropped his spectacles, retrieved them, then, bowing to his master, he let himself out, his arm full of documents.

"Pray be seated." He indicated the chair in front of his desk. "May I offer you a glass of sack?"

"No, thank thee, Thomas Fell." The youth sat down.

There was no point in losing his temper. "I gather your ministry has made a deep impression on my family, Mr. Fox, especially on my good wife. She took pains to explain to me the nature of your message, but I'm afraid that I did not get the essence. Would you mind giving me a concise definition of it, if you can?"

The youth's pale blue eyes searched his. Where had he seen those eyes before? The same deceptively ingenuous personality?

"What transformed Margaret Fell's life was the truth. It has done so to a great many other people."

He sighed. "Mr. Fox, I hope you will forgive me, but as a judge I have become suspicious of the word 'truth.' In my experience, there are many versions of it."

The youth smiled. "That may be so in a court of justice, but in the eyes of the Lord there is only one truth—namely, that every man carries the divine within him, and that it is our destiny to follow its leadings."

The arrogant presumption! "How do you determine whether your leadings are divine, Mr. Fox? Are you implying that you are in touch with the Almighty?"

"I did receive a call from God," he said simply.

"When was that?"

"As a young man."

"You are not exactly on the brink of decrepitude."

"I was nineteen."

"What form did the call take?"

Again the youth's eyes searched his with that familiar intensity. Where the devil . . . ? "How much didst thou see of the war, Thomas?"

"In the way of actual combat? I was a Member of Parliament at the time."

"Didst thou ever hear of the battle of Penny Drayton?"

"Can't say I did. Where is that?"

"A hamlet in Leicestershire, where I lived. When I was nineteen, there was a battle nearby, a small one, no more than a skirmish. On the King's side, fifty or sixty dragoons. On that of the Roundheads, a few hundred men on foot, armed with pitchforks and flails and axes and a few muskets. I watched them march through the village, carrying banners saying, *'The Lord is with us.'* They were blessed by our priest, told to smite the chariots of Pharaoh and marched on, singing, *'O God, our rock in ages past.'* I was absolutely certain that the banners were right, that God was on our side, that this was a holy war."

"You joined them?"

"I marched with them, carrying a pitchfork. I heard our enemies before seeing them. They were singing the same hymn."

"Are you going to tell me that you received the call when you discovered that both parties in a war always claim to represent the divine wrath?"

The youth ignored the question. "The Roundheads were massacred. I fled with the survivors, hunted down by the dragoons as if we were hogs. Only at nightfall did the women of the village dare to go and look for their husbands and their sons; I went with them. We had to be very careful, the dragoons were camped nearby in the woods, singing around a big fire; they were drunk. There was a full moon, we could see the bodies clearly. Some were still alive. One of the women found her son and began to wail. A guard heard her; suddenly there he was, on his horse, with a lance. The women fled, I hid in a copse. I saw him seek out the wounded and gore them with his lance, cursing them. He went all around the battlefield, sinking his lance into any body that moved. He finally got off his horse, a few paces from where I was hiding. He talked to the horse as he rubbed it down, tenderly. I could not understand it; he had just killed at least a dozen people with his lance; their screams still haunted me. Then I realized that to him the horse was a person, but that those people had not been human like himself, but Roundheads. Things."

"Yes, Mr. Fox, war is a gruesome business. Especially civil war."

The youth contemplated him thoughtfully. "Every war is a civil war, Thomas. That is what I discovered that night. I asked myself, 'How could men do such things to one another and believe themselves ordained by God?' If indeed God had willed us to do battle, He must have willed the others to do battle as well. What *was* His will? What was the truth? I had to find out. Suddenly, it was a matter of life and death.

"So I went on a pilgrimage to ask priests, doctors of divinity. Some said it was a punishment for our wickedness, that God had ordained both parties to destroy one another in His wrath. Others, that we must smite the Popish idolaters as the children of Israel smote the Hittites. 'But what about God's love?' I asked them. 'What about His mercy?' God said, 'Thou shalt not kill.' Did He mean: 'except Hittites, Egyptians, Philistines, Cavaliers, Roundheads, the Irish'? Is there no absolute law? I became a pest to them, a fool who would not let them be. I was told to have myself bled, to take up smoking tobacco, to get married, to join the army, anything, as long as I left them alone."

"I can well believe it." How young, how adolescent! These questions were natural for a callow youth; to go on agonizing over them after the age of discretion was infantile. Maybe that was the secret of the success of all prophets: they asked the adolescent questions that had never been resolved and lay buried in each man's heart until he found the courage to exhume them and face them for what they were: proofs of life's absurdity, the acceptance of which was the door to maturity.

"One morning," the youth continued, "after I had returned home in desperation, I wandered into my father's orchard. I was at the end of my tether. I wanted to believe, I wanted the questioning voice within me to be still, to leave me in peace, but it would not, it went on and on, urging me not to take anyone's answer unless it spoke to my condition. I even considered the possibility that I might be mad. Suddenly I heard a voice, *'There is one, namely Christ Jesus, who will speak to thy condition.'* It stunned me. I asked, 'Who is there? Who is that? Who spoke to me?' There was nothing, only the trees."

"Was it literally a voice?"

"I thought so at the time. I know now that it was the voice of that of God in me."

"If I understand you rightly, you carry within you an element that is part of you, yet not you?"

"Exactly."

"And that is what you presume to be God?"

"It *is* God. The Bible says so. John One, verse nine. *'The Light that lighteth every man who cometh into the world.'* Every man, not 'except Philistines, Hittites or Popish idolaters.' And that is the essence of my message: we all carry the divine within us, and there is only one, Christ Jesus, who will speak to our condition. But we must receive His words direct, not via interpreters, and live up to them in all their simplicity. If He says: do not kill, then do not kill. If He says: love thine enemies, then love them, without exception. If He says: where two or three are gathered together in My name, there I am in the midst of them, then take Him at His word, literally. If He says—"

"Mr. Fox, excuse me: you have so far failed to give me any justification for your acts. Did the divine in you induce you to uproot people's lives, destroy their domestic peace, estrange them from those they love and who love them? Surely, the great command is, 'I tell ye to love one another'?"

"Thomas, thy anger makes thee blind. Look. Here I am, like thyself: unique, irreplaceable, never been on earth before, never to be again. Come, try to understand me by identifying with me. Let us approach our conflict after the manner of friends, not adversaries."

"Mr. Fox, I am as well disposed toward you as is humanly possible, but you have not settled the argument. You *are* destroying the peace of people's homes in flagrant contradiction of the precepts of the Sermon on the Mount, which you exhort us to take literally. It is your hypocrisy I take exception to, not your eccentricity."

"Thomas, I—"

"You say you received a call. What call? To incite people to interrupt church services, be branded as blasphemers, beaten up, flung into prison? To bewilder and bedevil housewives who have nothing to defend themselves with except their generous hearts?"

"I activate that of God in them. What God leads them to do—"

"Come now, come now, Mr. Fox! You cannot go about the country inciting people to riot and, if they do, disclaim all responsibility!"

"Thomas, each man, each woman is unique; their reaction to the arousal of that of God within them is different in every case. It is not my mission to tell people how to react. On the contrary—I encourage every individual to react to that of God within him in his own manner."

"Mr. Fox, I cannot let you get away with that. How many unique, irreplaceable ways are there in which to divest oneself of the clergy? It is hypocrisy to say, 'I tell people that the man in the pulpit in their church is an interloper, but what they do as a result is up to that of God in them.'"

The imperturbable young man smiled. "I told thee, Thomas, the only way to get to the truth is by approaching one another after the manner of friends. Come, let us enter into silence together for a while. Just sit quietly, allowing that of God to rise within us."

"I'm sorry, Mr. Fox. I cannot see what purpose it would serve, other than to let you off the hook."

"As that of God in thee and that of God in me are essentially the same, by allowing both to rise to the surface we would find unity in the truth."

The man's self-confidence was overwhelming. Then he remembered— of course! "By the way," he said, "I don't know whether anyone else has told you this, but you remind me of Oliver Cromwell."

"Ah?" Suddenly the youth's serenity, which was obviously nothing but supreme indifference to what anybody else might say, changed to personal interest. It was the final proof: most reminiscent of Oliver Cromwell in the young man was his reaction to the information that he was like Oliver Cromwell.

"Yes," Thomas continued, "at one time I knew him well. He too was a man of great persuasion. He too thought himself divinely inspired. He too managed, by his sincerity and emotional power, to convince people, myself included. He convinced me that God had spoken to him, that I should abdicate my own responsibility and follow him, that he had been entrusted with the truth. Before I knew it, I was party to a murder, facing the King not as a warrior, but as his executioner. There he was: a frail old man with a thin, scraggy neck. And I, in my religious rapture, was about to help condemn him to be beheaded. Do you wonder I have mistrusted religious rapture ever since?"

The young man observed him with benevolent detachment, exactly as Cromwell used to look when confronted with an irrefutable argument. "How many people hast thou condemned to death as a judge, Thomas?"

"Come, come, Mr. Fox, that is unworthy of you. The people I condemned to death were sentenced according to law; what Cromwell requested of us was to suspend the law in favor of his private divine guidance. Alas, Mr. Fox: according to Oliver Cromwell, the King had to be killed for truth's sake. Those were his very words."

"Oliver Cromwell was in error. God is a spirit of love; truth can never lead to violence, only to unity."

"I am glad to hear that. I hope you will remind yourself of it in the future. There has been a great deal of violence as a result of your proclaiming your truth."

"I may provoke violence in those who are confronted by the truth; I myself—"

"I see. To provoke someone else to violence is not violence, is that it?"

"Jesus said—"

"Mr. Fox, you are *not* Jesus! You are, by your own definition, unique, irreplaceable, never seen on earth before and, God willing, never to be seen again! So do not hide behind quotations from the Bible!"

"Thomas, thy pronouncements are based on law, mine on the Scriptures."

Thomas Fell slumped back in his chair. It was hopeless. There was no way of rattling the man. Like Oliver Cromwell, he was a bull in a china shop; the only way to get rid of him would be to foist him upon some other unfortunate community. It might not be a charitable solution; it was the only one. He had to be spirited away somehow, or he would wreak a havoc from which the town would never recover. "Mr. Fox, it might be more constructive for us to discuss the immediate future. What are your plans, sir?"

"That is not for me to decide."

"It's up to God, I presume?"

"Indeed."

Lord Shorwell, erstwhile Master of Requests at the King's Court and now Cromwell's confidant, had remarked, "The thing to remember about the Protector is that whenever he mentions God he means himself."

"What makes you people so sure that it is *you* who have been singled out to implement God's will?" he asked in exasperation.

"Thomas, we are all God's implements. How else wouldst thou have Him execute His will, if not through us? Through the beasts in the field? The trees, the mountains, the rivers? The mission of man is to act out God's will; there is no other living creature He could use for that purpose. The same goes for God's love: He is unable to communicate His love to us directly; that He did through His son Christ Jesus, and by Him through ourselves. This is the essence of my message, Thomas: that in order to transmit His love to those in need, all Christ has is us."

He had had enough. He rose. "Shall we rejoin the ladies?" He went to the door. "Sir—after you."

Margaret seemed relieved at their appearance, as if she had expected only one of them to emerge.

* * *

Something about undressing in each other's presence makes frosty formality seem ludicrous. Thomas Fell was sitting on the edge of the bed, pulling off his hose, Margaret, on the other side, was putting on her slippers, when suddenly the whole thing became ridiculous. "Well?" she asked. "Did he explain his message to thee?"

Thomas deposited one stocking by his side. "Indeed." He rose. "Would my nightshirt be wrapped around the warming pan?" He pulled back the counterpane.

"There is no warming pan in the month of May, sweeting."

He fluffed his pillow instead. What could she do to break this icy deadlock? Suddenly she was overcome by weary despair. With every minute that passed they drifted further apart; soon he would be out of reach. "Thomas," she pleaded, "please, *please* . . ."

He looked at her, it seemed, with a beginning of concern. "I'm sorry to appear noncommittal about our conversation." He said it in that impossible formal tone, but she sensed that she had unlocked a door. "It was rather disturbing, I must confess."

"I'm not surprised!" she gushed. "He does upset people, before they really know him! But I assure thee . . ."

He walked away to the tallboy, opened a drawer and started to rummage in it.

She felt her tenuous hold on him slipping again. "What art thou looking for?"

"My nightcap."

"It's here, love!" In her eagerness she jumped onto the bed, crawled across it on her knees, fetched the nightcap from his bedside table and held it out to him. "Here . . ."

"Thank thee." He took it and put it on his head; she got under the covers and held them open for him.

"Thank thee." He got in and lay down by her side. Then he said, "Blast, we've forgotten our prayers. Or hast thou given up prayers?"

"Oh, Thomas!" Impulsively she turned over and threw her arm and her knee across him. "Please . . ."

Reluctantly he put his arm around her and she rested her head on his shoulder. "Forgive me," he said, "but I'm unable to appreciate Mr. Fox's message. Oliver Cromwell spoiled him for me."

"Cromwell?" She lifted her head to look at him. "Don't tell me there is a likeness in thy eyes?"

"Very much so."

"Thomas!" She sat up, outraged. He lay staring at the ceiling, avoiding her eyes. "But they are *totally* unlike each other! Cromwell is a—a bully! A bigoted, narrow-minded bully! George is warm and loving and understanding and—and—he has compassion for people!"

"Margaret, I must insist that thou dost not try to impose thy own dream on me. The situation is too serious for that."

"But I—"

"This is not a matter of a soup kitchen, or a park for old people. Those concerns were as frenetic at their height, but they were harmless. They may have induced people to exasperation, never to violence." Suddenly his eyes confronted her. "Yes, violence. If thou insists on sponsoring that man, thou wilt end by destroying thy family, this house, this town. Thou wilt destroy all that we have built together these twenty years with such pains, such gentleness."

"But, dear heart! He *is* gentle! He is all—"

"Margaret, come to thy senses! Look about thee! What has he done? Set people who have been living in peace together for a lifetime at each other's throats! He caused a delegation to ride out to meet me to plead for peace. He made me strike a child because it refused to take off its hat, something I have not done since I was a stupid youth. Considering all that, dost thou not agree that, however gentle Mr. Fox may pretend to be, his acts, or the acts to which he inspires others, are the reverse? Cromwell too spoke of nothing but peace; as a result we had the bloodiest civil war this country has ever known, and the murder of a King. We can only expect more violence if the man stays."

"Oh, Thomas, Thomas! What can I do to make thee *see?* What can I say? Oh, damn Cromwell, damn, damn Cromwell! He has nothing to do with George, nothing! They are the opposite of one another!"

"All right, Margaret. Tell me what thou wouldst have me do."

She looked up, surprised.

"I am serious. I want to know thy wishes."

"But thou art planning to send him away . . ."

"I doubt whether Mr. Fox can be sent away. It will take more than gentle persuasion to prevail upon him to bestow the blessings of his presence elsewhere."

"Oh, Thomas, *please!*" she pleaded. "Stop slapping his face with every word thou sayest! Please, *please,* listen to me, look at me, love me . . ."

"Dearest, if I did not love thee, I would not be in the state I'm in. I am troubled about thee, Margaret. Thou art stricken by a lunacy, a madness. Canst thou not see this man is a deadly danger? That he threatens everything we have? The very substance of our lives?"

"No, Thomas, no! Art thou so afraid to believe? Afraid of what will happen to thee once thou dost accept his message? I know, I was afraid myself. I—I still am."

He looked at her, his concern now evident. "I thought so. What art thou afraid of?"

"Of—of losing thee."

"Nonsense. Thou hast me, right here. I want to help thee."

"But a moment ago—"

"A moment ago I said that unless Mr. Fox goes we are headed for disaster. Don't tell me that his message is valid only as long as he is around?"

She looked at his wise eyes with a feeling of awakening. Was he right? Was she really convinced, or did George's presence . . .

"Sweeting," his patient voice continued, "why dost thou not tell me in thy own words what it is he has convinced thee of? Maybe that is the way to find out what this is all about. Come, lie down, put thy head on my shoulder and tell me. Just tell me."

She lay down, with a sigh. It was all so difficult, so confused. "But that is what I tried to do before."

"I know. But this afternoon I was not ready for it. I still had to recover from what turned out to be quite a homecoming."

"Oh, I know, I know! I worried about that all along, all along!"

"Hush . . ." His hand stroked her hair, soothingly. "Just tell me. The same thing, all over again."

She took a deep breath. "Oh, Thomas, I love thee so . . ." It was not what she had intended to say.

"I love thee. Now tell me."

"Well . . . what it boils down to *is* love. We all have a great capacity for love within us. That is, really, what he calls 'that of God.'" It was strange; some of the meaning seemed to have gone out of the words. Maybe just because she was tired. She remembered the magic effect of lying like this, her head on his shoulder; it always made her feel instantly drowsy, even if she had lain down in a state of tension. The moment her head rested on his shoulder and her knee lay across him, her thoughts seemed to liquefy until they oozed imperceptibly into sleep.

"Tom?"

"Yes, love?" His voice was a tremor in his chest.

"Dear Tom . . ."

There she went, oh dear, oh dear, sliding into sleep.

* * *

As he heard her breath come regularly, he relaxed. It was almost as if she were under a spell of some sort. He had never known her so divorced from reality, so disoriented. Poor, poor woman; what could he do to help her? Obviously, the man had some hold on her, whatever it might be. He had to be removed from the scene. But it would have to be done subtly. Subtly: this was where he knew he lacked talent. It demanded a quirk of the mind that he did not possess. Few did, as a matter of fact; he knew only two men who possessed it. One was Lord Shorwell. In his case it amounted to genius. The other was old Justice Cartwright, who indulged in subtlety almost as a parlor game. Perhaps he should pay Cartwright a visit.

It did not distress him to discover that he needed help. He was secure enough in his authority never to hesitate to seek advice. Old Cartwright would know how to coax the bull out of the china shop without the young monster realizing what was happening. He would go to see him first thing the next morning.

He fell asleep in the peace of postponement.

* * *

In the attic over the stables, George Fox lay staring at the square of night in the little window overhead. A few stars quivered in the darkness; somewhere under the eaves swallows rummaged in their nests.

"God . . ." he thought, slowly, hypnotically, "God . . ." The stillness of the Presence enveloped him until he was adrift, floating on the infinite ocean of light and love. "God, lead me. Lead me . . ."

But although God was all about him, numinous, vibrant, an unearthly peace, no sense of direction came from the stillness. All that came to him, out of the depth of his soul, were the words "Not yet." He had to stay where he was. Go on waiting upon the Lord, every day, until the command would come, softly, a whisper in the night.

It filled him with the peace of acceptance; yet he felt a small sadness. He would have liked to give these good people some respite, to stop churning up their lives. He knew that his continued presence would create havoc, for by now he had ceased to be a person to the town and become a symbol. They would burden him with all their sins, all their fears, despair, guilt, and end by sending him out into the desert straddled by their demons, laden with their terrors, their damnation. For the first time in Swarthmoor Hall he felt a quaver of fear. What would they do to him, in the end?

Suddenly he found himself praying, "Father, if it be possible, let this cup pass from me."

There was no answer, either from within himself or from the silence of the night. The sense of the Presence receded, leaving only the small cold stars, the secretive rustle of the swallows under the eaves, the growing fear in the pit of his stomach.

CHAPTER FOUR

STRANGE, Thomas Fell thought, how the relationship between teacher and student never really changes even if the student eventually surpasses his erstwhile master in their profession. The moment he faced Justice Moses Cartwright he instantly reverted to the student who had looked up at the old judge with the mixture of awe and rebellion peculiar to their relationship. Even now, whenever he was uncertain about a case, he would occasionally catch himself impersonating Moses Cartwright on the bench. He would put on his eyeglasses, rummage owlishly among his papers, look at the prisoner in the dock and say, in the colloquial tone that never failed to impress, "Well now, what am I going to do with thee? What would thy decision be if thou wert in my place today? I can tell thee what thou wouldst do: thou wouldst put on the black cap and sentence the prisoner to be hanged by the neck until dead. That is exactly the type of justice thou didst mete out to thy victim when thou tookest the law into thy own hands." Yet the device never quite came off. He was not Justice Cartwright, whose homilies camouflaged one of the most incisive minds on the bench and to whom the practice of law was a science rather than a social function. Like his brother Aaron, the biologist, Moses Cartwright had never married or engaged in any of the human frailties that brought about humility, portal to compassion. He was brilliant, resourceful, and if there was in the jurisprudence as far back as the Domesday Book an obscure precedent to justify a sentence, he could be counted upon to unearth it. Even after sixty years on the bench he was never haunted by doubt, let alone remorse, as he looked back on the long trail of gallows from each of which a human being had briefly danced in the sky at his instigation. He had never considered himself to be anything but a link in a chain of causes and effects forged out of pure logic. Putting logic into practice involved, for some reason, the colloquial homilies with which he presented his findings; their rank hypocrisy was never apparent to anyone in the courtroom.

At the first sight of those beaming blue eyes, that hearty, ruddy face creased with wrinkles of merriment, Thomas instantly fell prone again to the delusion that his old master was warmhearted, humane, all-forgiving, the ideal father. "Come in, come in, me boy! This is a wonderful surprise! Mary! Bring more bread! A mug of ale for His Lordship!"

"I broke my fast, thank you, sir," Thomas said, handing over the reins to Charles Cotten. "But maybe my man would appreciate it."

"By all means!" the old man cried genially to the groom. "Go round to the kitchen, lad! Help thyself to anything thou fanciest, bread, beef, wenches . . ." He winked bawdily; maybe his performance as a human being was so convincing because of his own implicit belief in it. He was so devoid of normal feelings that he had no standard by which to judge his own humanity, just as a person devoid of a sense of humor can think of himself, in all sincerity, as a wit. He seemed unchanged since the last time they had met; so did his brother, who stuck his head out of the door of his laboratory when they entered the hall and retracted it, like a turtle, the moment he saw them. All that had aged was the house and the servants; the housekeeper white-haired now and thinner, the furniture somewhat threadbare, as were the curtains.

"And what brings me the pleasure of thy visit, dear boy?" the old man inquired, pulling out a chair for him at the breakfast table, which looked unappetizing. "I hear thou hast been appointed Vice Chancellor of the County Palatine! Congratulations, me boy, congratulations; I have reason to be proud of thee."

"Moses!" a cantankerous voice screeched in the passage. "Was it thou who covered up the tank with my tadpoles?"

The old justice looked at his pupil with an amused expression. "I haven't touched thy tadpoles for thirty-five years! I haven't even been inside thy smelly workshop since last Christmas!"

"Well, somebody did!" the voice snarled, closer. "Three of them are floating in the scum, before I even touched their tails!" He loomed, skeletal, in the doorway, clad in a shapeless smock.

"Say good morning to our good friend Thomas Fell," his brother said amiably. "Come and join us."

"Thomas Fell? I thought he was Lester Peacock." Aaron came to the table and sat down, stretching out a clawlike hand toward a basket of clapbread.

"Lester Peacock! Lester Peacock was five foot three, stuttered and, what's more, he's dead. Thou wert at his funeral."

"Oh, well," Aaron muttered, grabbing a bun. "We are all the same to the worms."

"Well," the old justice said, dismissing him. "What can I do for thee? Another of thy tricky cases?"

Thomas smiled. "This time I am in a real quandary. Let me explain . . ."

He proceeded to present the facts as economically as possible, the way he had been taught by the uncompromising old man who sat listening with his craggy face frozen in a meaningless smile of bonhomie while his little eyes observed him with unnerving detachment. The brother, as in the past, did his best to be a nuisance by emptying the basket of clapbread, munching noisily, muttering.

"Interesting," the old justice said finally, with the smile he affected when faced with a challenging problem or a succulent dish. "I have heard about this Fox. Persuasive fellow. So, all thou wantst to achieve is to remove him from the scene?"

"Yes."

"No conviction?"

"No."

"First thing would be to prevent his creating another disturbance in church."

"How?"

The old man smiled. "Suggest he hold his Sunday services in thy house."

"I beg your pardon?"

"No surer means of keeping a preacher away from someone else's sermons than giving him a congregation of his own. If thou wert to stipulate an hour that coincides with the church service, it would ensure the peace, at least for the next few weeks."

"I am sure it would. But—"

"Listen!" the old man frowned. "Didst thou come for my advice or to listen to the sound of thy own voice? Make up thy mind!"

"Forgive me. Please proceed."

"All right, then. It goes without saying that thou shalt not attend those meetings thyself. Thou and thy son will attend church and sit in the family pew. Thus thy priest's self-importance will be gratified in a manner under thy control." There came the spectacles, which served only as an attribute of humanity. "Next thy priest and as many clerics from neighboring towns as possible must be prevailed upon to lodge a complaint of blasphemy against Fox. The complaint will be presented to thee, and thou wilt put it on the docket of the next Assizes. Thou wilt decide, however, that this is a case for the clergy. By law, only the church is competent to rule on what constitutes blasphemy; but the verdict must be supported by two secular justices presiding over the proceedings. One of the two, *ex officio,* being thyself. Who is second justice this session?"

"William Best."

"Where does he stand in this matter?"

"He was part of the delegation that rode out to meet me. He said, only to keep himself informed."

"Dost thou believe him?"

"Yes."

"Sawrey and the priest consider him to be one of their own?"

"I gather so."

"Then he will be the man to suggest to the priest that he take up contact with his colleagues regarding the complaint against Fox, especially with Dr. Marshall of Kendal, a pompous idiot who will instantly make himself their spokesman. He is sufficiently intemperate in his reactions to hang himself, on condition he is given plenty of rope. The beauty of this solution is that he will consider himself to be in the enviable position of both plaintiff and prosecutor. Thou wilt be able to sink the whole thing without a trace."

"Explain, sir."

"An ecclesiastical trial is jurisprudence upside down. As presiding judge, thou canst rule out all facts and force them to limit themselves to opinions. There were, in the past, certain acts that constituted blasphemy, like pissing on a saint or defecating on the altar, but those have been removed from the books by the revolution, at least *de facto*. So thou canst rule 'opinions only' from the start; they will be tying themselves into knots before the day is over. Let them and Fox fire opinions at each other until they are black in the face, then declare thyself incompetent and send the whole thing on to appeal, or, if they are sufficiently at a loss for thee to get away with it, declare the man innocent and kick him out into the street. My guess is that the mob will make short shrift of him there, if I know Dr. Marshall. He may be Balaam's ass, but he preaches a mean sermon; he knows how to make the rabble's blood boil. So, thou wouldst be rid of Fox without having had a hand in his execution."

"I remember the precedent," Thomas said dryly.

"Which precedent?"

"Pontius Pilate."

"As a judge: what wouldst thou have done in his place? Roman law—"

He had to head the old man off or he would ramble on for hours; Pontius Pilate was one of his favorite subjects. "What about Sawrey?"

"Ah, Sawrey!" The old man grinned admiringly. "Don't underestimate him! Brilliant barrister. He'd go far, if only he weren't such a snob. But that's neither here nor there. Sawrey cannot take part in the proceedings of an ecclesiastical court other than in an advisory capacity, but, of course, thou shouldst keep him away altogether. If he starts feeding instructions to ministers from the floor, he may blow the whole scheme to kingdom come."

"To keep him away is not going to be easy."

"Wouldst thou consult me if it were? Would I be sitting here beating my brains out if it were? The priests must be made to launch their complaint as fast as possible, before Sawrey makes it a civilian case in which the prisoner in the dock might be Mr. Fox but the real defendants would be thyself and thy family. Let me tell thee, my young friend, if I were to judge that case, I would not envy thee."

"I had better go and see Best. This begins to look serious."

"That, dear boy, is my point! Make no mistake, the moment this becomes a civilian case it is lost, *a priori*."

"How so?"

Justice Cartwright raised his eyebrows in exaggerated astonishment; he was enjoying himself hugely. "How so? This man is a Quaker! Even I, in this Godforsaken rathole, know that Quakers refuse to swear the oath! Or has that little item escaped thy attention?"

"I'm afraid it has."

"Very well, I'll spell it out for thee. In an ecclesiastical court the presiding judge can rule that no oath is necessary, on the grounds that witnesses will be required not to relate facts but state opinions. No man need swear an oath as to his opinions. They change. They may change during the trial itself."

"I'm sorry, but in this instance I cannot agree."

"Thou asked for my opinion, right? Of course thy ruling will be hotly

contested, but it can be settled only in appeal. Unless Sawrey is there
to instruct them, none of the clergy will know *that* much about the
legal implications."

"Suppose all this were enacted as you suggested, in what way would
it remove Fox from the scene, ruling out the possibility of his being
lynched by the mob? What is there to stop him coming back to Ulverston, once the verdict is under appeal?"

"Ah!" The old man lifted his finger as if he were about to produce
the card up his sleeve. "The removal of Mr. Fox will be the easiest
part of the operation. There is no preacher in this country who does
not dream of becoming the gray eminence behind the throne. Right?"

"I'll take your word for it."

"Imagine thyself as one of those imposters, traipsing around the
countryside, bellowing the glad tidings at yokels, having thy buttocks
bared at every opportunity and beaten black and blue. What drives
thee, if not lust for power? What power was there to be reaped in
Ulverston? The answer is easy: Swarthmoor Hall, home of Lord Chief
Justice Fell, Vice Chancellor of the County Palatine. Good going, for a
country bumpkin. But give him a whiff of Cromwell and he'll streak
after him like a greyhound. What is thy relationship with Cromwell
nowadays? Art thou in a position to give Fox a letter of introduction
to him?"

"Hardly."

"Dost thou know anyone in his entourage who might arrange an
audience?"

"Yes."

"Very well. Tell Fox at a judicious moment—on the way to the trial,
for instance—that if he behaves himself, answers concisely without stirring up everybody, his case will be appealed and he will be free to go
to London, where thou hast arranged an audience with the Protector
for him." The old man beamed.

"But I am no admirer of Fox, and he knows it. Why should I suddenly be overcome by the desire to arrange an audience for him?"

"To get him away from thy wife!" a mocking voice said, surprisingly.

Thomas turned around. He had forgotten about the brother.

"How old is that Fox?" the scarecrow asked.

"Twenty-eight, thereabouts. Why?"

"And thy wife?"

"Er—thirty-eight."

"So there." Aaron stuck his finger in the sugar bowl. "Religious
conversion! Ha! If I were thee, I would go and assert my marital
rights forthwith. And never mind *his* fancy schemes!"

"Aaron!" his brother cried sternly, "take thyself and thy under-
graduate jokes to thy laboratory, where they belong!"

"Joke?" Aaron asked, licking his finger and dipping it in the sugar
pot again. "I should say it is. All French farces depend on it."

"That's enough!" the judge snapped. "Stop thy nonsense! Back to thy
room!"

With baffling meekness Aaron rose to his feet and went to the door. There he turned. "Babes in the wood, both of you!" He darted out.

Justice Cartwright and his pupil shared a moment of self-consciousness; then the old man growled, "He may have something there. He can be an infernal nuisance, but there is no better judge of women than he, believe it or not. I could never cope with the wenches in this house; he wraps them around his little finger."

All Thomas could do was nod. For as he sat there making polite conversation and sipping tea from a grimy cup, he was overcome by a sudden doubt. Could there be something to the old man's words? Ludicrous as the suggestion had been, he suddenly found himself obsessed with the jealous rage of the cuckold.

He knew that Margaret was the last person to harbor adulterous desires, yet he raced home, thundering through the bracken on his cruelly driven horse, ruthless and single-minded. When he arrived at the Hall, boots and breeches covered with mud, he strode into the house bent on violence. He was met by his son George, who nervously asked, "Father? Could I speak to you, please?"

"Where is thy mother?"

"I—I don't know, sir . . ."

He tramped across the hall, spurs jangling, and looked about him, whip in hand.

"Thomas?"

There she was, on the landing, caught in a slanting sheaf of sunlight. He ran up the stairs, three steps at a time; when he reached her he grabbed her hand. He saw a look of alarm on her face; it gave him a malevolent satisfaction. He led her, without a word, to the bedchamber.

"What is the matter?" she asked, bewildered. "What happened? What dost thou want of me?"

He pushed her inside and slammed the door shut behind him. She looked at him open-mouthed, her eyes round with incomprehension. He threw down his whip and took her in his arms.

"Thomas! What on earth—"

He closed her lips with a kiss. For a moment she struggled, but it was only her surprise, the momentum of her preoccupation with the household. In the middle of a moan of protest, he felt her respond with a shiver of surrender that moved him to do something he had never done before: he lifted her bodily and carried her to the bed.

There, in a rustling tangle of skirts and petticoats, he took her with a passion that at last enabled him to express what he had been unable to put into words since his return.

*   *   *

For the rest of that day Margaret Fell lived only partially in reality. Although she resumed her household duties with the customary briskness, inwardly she continued to savor the raptures of love. She seemed to float through her household routine with slow, sensuous movements, weightless as a fish, filled with a sense of utter well-being. It had been a long time since they had made love like this; never before had he subjugated her so brusquely, almost brutally, which for some reason had evoked in her a most passionate response.

The fullness of love stayed with her all day. When time for evening worship came, her husband retired to his study, but she saw that he left his door ajar. She tried to center down; instead of sliding into a deeper level of silence, however, she continued to plane in the sensuous contentment in which she had lived all afternoon. Eyes closed, seemingly steeped in pious contemplation, she relived the glorious experience, savoring it from the moment he had lifted her in his arms and carried her to the bed, sweeping her off her feet as Leda must have been when she was overwhelmed by the swan . . .

She sat up sharply and looked about her, hoping to find the way back into the communal meditation by observing the others. They all seemed wrapped up in their own worlds; George, face lifted, as if he were listening; Will Caton beaming like the cat that had swallowed the cream. Was he thinking about that of God within him? A likely story. About Meg, of course. And Meg? Inscrutable face, very willful, domineering like her mother. And Ann Traylor, the little red-haired devil? Beautiful child, straining at the leash. If God . . .

"Almighty Father, creator of heaven and earth, sower of stars, caster of suns . . ." George, larger than life in the candlelight, had risen in prayer; he had taken off his hat, which he did only when addressing God. A stirring sight; what power, what vitality! *"I'm sorry to disenchant you, but as lovers they are a terrible disappointment."* As she watched him, Mistress Best's words sounded ludicrous. Just look at him quaking in the presence of the Lord, not like an intimidated coward but like Moses facing the burning bush. A terrible disappointment? He? If he were ever to take his eyes off that of God in a woman, heaven help . . . She recoiled. This could not be she! This was that of the devil in her! She folded her hands and beseeched God to deliver her from evil; as she closed her eyes tightly, pink shapes began to drift toward her again from the darkness, as they had that first time in the garden: only this time they were definitely not Morocco plums.

She opened her eyes and found herself looking at John McHair. Unlike the others, he sat with his eyes open, brooding. He looked very gloomy; he must be worried about something. Gazing at him, she began to share his gloom. She must take herself in hand! If she could not think of pious things, she should concentrate on something positive, constructive. What, for instance, could she do for her husband by way of a treat to welcome him home? Before they went to bed she would serve him the Morocco plums.

She remembered the plums late that night, after they had made love again, this time very tenderly. She had already snuffed the candle flame; she would give them to him for breakfast.

As she was about to fall asleep, she felt an odd apprehension; for some reason, she was suddenly afraid of what she might dream. When she awoke at first light, it took her a worried moment or two before she recaptured a dream: swans gliding on black water, the reflection of a church spire, a joyous peal of bells that scattered pigeons from the belfry: a silent white explosion in a radiant blue sky. Thank God, perfectly innocuous.

She felt on top of the world, and her bliss was complete when, during breakfast, Thomas suggested casually that the Quakers of Ulverston meet at the Hall for worship. She could not believe her ears. "Tom! Thou wicked . . ." The rest was lost in kisses.

At the earliest opportunity she ran to tell George the news. His reaction was disappointing; his eyes searched hers with suspicion. "Was this thy idea, or his?"

"Why? I swear—I mean, it was his! Not a hair on my head ever thought of the possibility!"

He smiled; it was not a happy smile.

"What is the matter?"

"I wonder what thy husband has in mind."

"In mind? Dost thou not trust him?"

"I trust that of God in him," he replied, "but very little else."

She turned away, hurt and intrigued. As she walked to the kitchen to confer with Henderson about the day's activities, she wondered whether George was jealous.

"Well, Henderson, what is the program for today?"

The henchwoman told her, respectfully, with a hint of resignation, knowing her mistress would substitute for it a program of her own. She had done so every day for the past twenty years.

* * *

It was with a sense of relief that Colonel Best saw Thomas Fell and his young son arrive at the church. He had worried about this morning's service; like everyone else, he expected Fox to return. He had prayed, without confidence, that the troublemaker might be kept away; if the town were to recover, a few weeks' respite was essential. He wondered about the other members of the family; Fell must have prevailed upon his wife to keep the madman at home, away from the church.

The change in mood brought about by Thomas Fell's arrival was amazing; it seemed as if everyone present heaved a sigh of relief. Even Lampitt must be relieved by the return of the old days of obedience and security that, in a moment of aberration, he had helped to put in jeopardy.

It came as a surprise to Best when Fell accosted him after the service, in the throng of people in the doorway. There were many ears around eager to catch every word; a man of Fell's astuteness would not have chosen this moment unless he wanted the town to hear what he was saying.

"Good morning, Colonel, good morning, *Madame* . . ." He bowed courteously to Henrietta. "I would like to have a few words with you, my good friend. Would it be convenient if I came by tonight after supper?"

"But of course. You'll be most welcome." Best hoped his surprise was not too obvious.

"It is my feeling that we should not let matters rest as they are," Fell continued with a wintry smile. "Until tonight, then. *Adieu, Madame;* good day, Best." On his way out he shook hands warmly with the priest, who also, Best suspected, had trouble hiding his surprise.

In the carriage on their way home, he discovered that his wife too had seen through Fell's public demonstration; but then, she was a woman of experience in palace intrigues. "That is one of the shrewdest men I have ever met," she said. "I do not believe that he wishes thee harm, but I would watch my step. He'll have Sawrey and Lampitt hang themselves without their knowing it until after they have jumped."

"I wish him luck."

"Yes," she sighed, "so, God knows, do I."

*   *   *

When Fell turned up that evening, Henrietta Best's estimation of him was confirmed. After the usual courtesies, when the second glass of wine had been poured, he explained his plan. It was deceptively simple. If friend Best would suggest to Lampitt that he get in touch with his colleagues in the neighboring parishes, especially Dr. Herbert Marshall, they might, as ecclesiastical authorities in the country, issue a writ of blasphemy against Fox and his companion. The writ should then be presented to him, Fell, for inclusion in the upcoming Quarterly Assizes. Lampitt should be urged to register his charge as soon as possible, before someone else in town, notably Sawrey, made it a civilian case.

"I don't think Sawrey would do that," her husband said.

"Why not?"

"I had occasion to pass a note to him that Sunday, pointing out that he was throwing himself open to a charge of assault within consecrated walls."

"What was his reaction?"

"He instantly ordered the man removed from the church and handed over to the constable outside."

"By which time he had already compromised himself?"

"Indeed."

Fell took a thoughtful sip of wine. "In other words, you might put it to him that we made this an ecclesiastical case in order to avoid a counter-charge from the defendant against him."

Her husband smiled at Fell's astuteness.

"As far as I can see," she said, troubled by their smugness, "you gentlemen are caught between the devil and the deep blue sea. If your verdict were to go against Fox and he were put in prison, it would make a martyr of him. If he were acquitted, he would remain a nuisance. In my experience, his kind of nuisance never diminishes, only increases."

"Ah?" Fell was courteous rather than encouraging.

But she was not going to be silenced. She surprised herself; to disregard obvious hints was unlike her. But she had a stake in this matter; she wanted Fox spirited away, forever. "You must realize," she continued, "that men like he need conflict, even though they know the conflict will eventually end in their crucifixion." She looked from one to the other. "I need not spell out what the consequences would be, were Fox to choose our town for his Golgotha."

Thomas Fell watched the candle flame's reflection in his wine. "Would it not be rather a humble setting for that momentous event?"

"Not unless he were offered a better location."

"Would that not be decided by his receiving a communication from the Almighty?"

"God rarely communicates directly even with His favorite children," she replied. "Even personal friends of the Almighty like Mr. Fox are forced to decide what His wishes are by interpreting signs or events."

Thomas Fell pursed his lips. "Let us hope Mr. Fox will find a worthier stage for his catharsis than Ulverston."

"That will depend on his antagonist in the final scene," she said.

Suddenly, Thomas Fell dropped all pretense. He looked at her for the first time with a natural smile; it transformed him into a beguilingly impish man. "Are you by any chance suggesting that I give him a letter of introduction to Oliver Cromwell, Madame?"

She was taken aback for a moment; then she answered, "You must forgive my presumption."

"There is no need for forgiveness," he said, rising. "On the contrary, we will need more of your presumption before the case is closed. Would you do us the favor of attending the trial?"

"It will be a pleasure." He bowed over her outstretched hand, then went with her husband toward the door, where he turned and bowed once more.

When her husband came back to the little drawing room, she said, "Well, well! Thou hast never invited me to a trial!"

"H'm," he said, dourly, pouring himself another glass. "That means he will have to invite his own wife, too."

"Well, why not?" She had to admit that had not occurred to her.

"He should not make a social occasion of this." He took a gulp and rinsed his mouth with it. "I may be able to sell Sawrey the idea of the ecclesiastical court, but I doubt whether I can keep him away from the trial if all the *beau monde* of Ulverston is going there."

"*Voyons, mon chou!* Thou canst hardly call Mistress Fell and myself a social prize!"

"A bunch of overconfident clerics is one thing," he grumbled on, "but a court of clergy masterminded by John Sawrey? No, thank thee. I would rather meet him in a civilian trial. Using those priests as his mouthpiece will free him of the risk of being charged with assault."

"But there must be a means of keeping him away!"

"How? Obviously, we have to think of a way. I'm afraid I'm not very good at that kind of thing."

She went to him and kissed him. "Dear heart, stop being humble. Be thy old self again, for just the once: bold, dashing—then come and love me."

With a flick of her fan at his nose, she turned away and left him gazing after her with mournful tenderness.

*   *   *

He got another bottle from the cupboard, sat down in his chair and put his boots on the table. He poured himself another glass of the sweet liquid and slurped it pensively. Sawrey was indeed the kingpin of the whole scheme. Only if they could keep him away would they have a chance. Was there some lure he could use, to trick the canny little runt away?

Maybe it was the wine, maybe his wife's confidence in him had been infectious; before he reached the end of the bottle he had hit upon the solution. It was ridiculously simple, and if his estimate of John Sawrey was right, it could not fail to work. He looked at the clock; the servants might have gone to bed, but he pulled the bell cord all the same. After a few minutes there was a knock on the door and Kathryn the maid entered.

"Is Bonbon still about?" he asked.

She looked surprised. "Yes, sir, I think so . . ."

"Tell him I want to see him."

The maid's surprise turned into astonishment. "You want to be shaved now, sir?"

"Don't be foolish!" he exclaimed, irritably: "None of thy business why, I just want to talk to him."

"Very good, sir . . ." She shuffled away, closing the door behind her. He finished the bottle, grunting.

*   *   *

Louis Bonnecharme was trimming his eyebrows in front of his mirror, by candlelight, when his door was opened and a cantankerous voice cried, "All right, Monsoor! He wants to see you in the withdrawing room," making him jump and stab himself between the eyes with the tweezers.

He hissed with rage at the fat cow's contemptuous disregard for his privacy. *"Oh, la vache!"* he cried at her. "Why do you not knock? Have you no *chasteté,* to burst into a man's chambers like *un sacré éléphant?"*

He expected her to retaliate in kind—indeed, he wanted her to; he needed a throat-scalding row for his *crise de nerfs,* but she saw how the land lay. She said, "Since when are you a man?" and hastily closed the door; the tweezers he threw at her bounced off the door with a preposterous little tinkle. Nobody had the art of needling him down to such a fine point as that waddling ton of female blubber. But for *Madame,* he would have gone back to the sweetest country in the world ten years ago—*à vrai dire,* he would never have left it! But here he was,

aging eunuch lost in hell, victim of stupid instinct—for he had long
since decided that his sacrificial loyalty to La Douce Tété could only
be explained as blind instinct. Until she caught him in her net he
had been a free man, happy, with a glorious future before him.
Everybody in the kitchens of the Court had known that Louis Bonnecharme, assistant *patissier* to the great chef Turlupin was heading
for the top; whenever there was some special occasion, requesting tiny
delicate *bouchées* or *canapés* or *petits fours* that would melt in the
mouth, he was called for. He knew exactly what to provide when
a courtier or one of the foreign envoys was planning a *tête-à-tête*. In
every gallant adventure it was the *hors-d'oeuvres* that set the tone;
his persuaded even the most jaded old *roué* to feign delicate sensitivity.
In his more reckless moments, when he strolled through the servants'
gardens dreaming impossible dreams, he knew there must be some
pastry, some beguiling little delicacy which would almost blush when
uncovered by the silver dome of the tray, that would in its effect upon
the mood of the players be more subtle than champagne. At times
he would slap his forehead and curse under his breath at the coarse-
ness of some of the courtiers whose boorish brusqueness would have
embarrassed a bull. The dalliance of love was enhanced in rapture
according to the delicacy with which the senses were titillated—all
the senses, not just one. Everything should be brought into play:
music, perfume, artful endearments, sumptuous surroundings, the intimacy of insufficient candles and, to crown it all, the most delicate
tactile sensation of touch and taste attainable: the little *pouf-poufs*
concocted by that magician Louis Bonnecharme, *patissier du Roi*.

His big opportunity came when Chef Turlupin recommended him to
his brother, the great buffoon who, together with Gaultier-Garguille,
provided the farces after the tragedies staged at the Théâtre de l'Hôtel
de Bourgogne. Had it been up to the rabble in the flea pit, those
tragedies would have been discontinued long ago; it was the rich and the
privileged who kept them going, for they were the ideal cover for
leisurely lovemaking in the darkness of the private boxes, which all
seemed to become devoid of occupants the moment the tragedies
started. When finally the buffoons came tumbling onto the proscenium
and the first roar of laughter rattled the rafters, the pale little moons
of faces would pop up again in the dark cavities of the *loges,* and the
evening of passionate sport would terminate in cleansing, childlike
merriment.

He became the head of the kitchens of the theatre, caterer to the
rich, the noble and the spoiled cavorting in those boxes. Soon he found
himself the darling of the *cocottes,* and he was well on his way to a
return to the royal kitchens with enough culinary laurels to unseat his
benefactor, Chef Turlupin himself, when he was caught in the net of a
nobody, a little amateur from the provinces, who entered her box for
the first time with the trembling terror of a virgin sold to a sultan. As
he brought in the first tray of pastries, she looked at him with such
despair, such haunting sadness, that he was unable to put her out of his

mind and went to see her when the show was over and her *patron* had left.

She sat on the couch in the *loge,* her head in her hands, a picture of loneliness and defeat among the debris: a half-empty tray, wilting flowers, candles dripping their last, her hair disheveled, her dress open, her provincial little fan on the floor. Something happened to him as he saw her sitting there, something he had never really been able to understand. For she deflected the rising young star from its proud climb and turned the future Chef Patissier at the Royal Court first into her confidant, later into her manager. When he first met her she was an insecure, inhibited dilettante; he created a new personality for her as completely as he created his pastry. He instantly recognized the value of her tragic background; she was a young Huguenot widow whose husband and children had been massacred somewhere in the Camargue. He knew that her fey, doelike temerity might, with the right partner, suddenly flare up into a brief, frenzied spasm of passion that would leave her faint and limp but that would give the most sated rake the almost forgotten sensation of defloration. He discreetly mentioned her exotic attractions to a few gentlemen of his choice; as a result she was before long set up in her own little *salon* by one of the richest merchants in the city, so cultured and tactful that he never appeared unannounced.

Bonbon himself became her major-domo and turned her, as "La Douce Tété," into one of the most successful courtesans of Paris. She had the secret of youth, a magic innocence that somehow remained unsullied for a decade, during which most of the influential men of court and city discreetly visited her *salon* to praise his pastry and to press a *louis d'or* into his hand when discreetly ushered out. Her youth, her tragic fragility seemed to last forever, untouched by time; they remained untarnished until Colonel William Best, one of those coarse, *louche* Englishmen, with middle-aged rapaciousness grabbed her all to himself. She succumbed not to the man's blandishments, but to some *bourgeois* ideal she had of marriage, which proved she was at heart no more than a little *midinette* despite her airs. Bonbon tried to appeal to her reason, but she allowed herself to be carried off, like a Sabine maiden, to a Godforsaken outpost of barbarians called Lancashire, a boundless, desolate place with ice-cold, dank houses peopled with provincial boors and bug-eyed females, rank with body odor, whose breath was rancid with haggis and rotting teeth. Convinced that she had fallen victim to a temporary aberration and that she would soon need him to help her return to Paris, he went with her. But something catastrophic happened: before his very eyes he saw her succumb to the one enemy he could not keep at bay: the moment she set foot in England, as if the spell of the fairy that had protected her had been unable to cross water, she fell prey to old age. In one year she aged ten. Horrified, he saw her go flaccid and pouchy, lose her fragility, the dark beauty of despair; he saw her turn into what, in her heart of hearts, she must always have wanted to be: a dowdy, complacent matron. She was content, there could be no doubt about it, but it was a depressing, pedestrian contentment; the incomparable swan of La Couvertoirade sang its last song on the bleak hills of Lancashire and a jolly, waddling duck rose from its ashes.

The same could be said of himself. Tempter of royal tastes, who had catered to the most refined palates of the most civilized city in the world, he suddenly found himself condemned to dish up steak and kidney pud, shepherd's pie and boiled haddock. Instead of being the undisputed ruler of a household of seventeen servants, he now had to battle in the kitchen with one spiteful, fat maid and scrape every morning the bristles of the hated jowls of his new master, insulted by curses, degraded by taunts about his virility, reduced to a cringing jester.

He sighed and rubbed his eyes and buttoned his coat, bent down toward the mirror to smooth his eyebrows and pat his hair into place for that brute, who would not even look at him and who probably wanted nothing more than a tankard of ale, to be ruined by heating it up with a hot poker. Didn't the man realize that the fires in the kitchen were banked at this hour of the night? His hatred for the conqueror rose like bile to his gullet as he groped his way down the dark stairs, uttering little shrieks of fright as he stumbled, splashing hot candle grease onto his hand. His knock was answered by the usual growl, which even after all these years made his hackles rise; he opened the door and found the Colonel lolling in a chair, his boots on the table, a bottle on the floor, an empty goblet in his hand. Especially late at night, something seemed to compel the man to behave as if he were a soldier of a conquering army that had requisitioned his own house.

"Listen," he said as if it were nine o'clock in the morning, "the hare we have had lately; did you get it from that poacher?"

O douce vierge! Was that why he had been dragged out of bed at dead of night? *"Non, non, mon Colonel!* You forbade me! I would not dream—"

"Oh, don't give me that nonsense!" the boor cried, lifting his filthy boots off the table. "I know you have been buying game off him. All I want to say is: I liked it. I liked it very much. You understand?"

He did not, but said, "Er—*oui, mon Colonel.*"

"Well, send a messenger to tell him I want more game. Every day. And I don't care what game it is. Is that clear?"

"But, *mon Colonel!* Game every day! One hare will last—"

"I don't want it to!" the bully cried, with total disregard for the realities of the kitchen. "I don't want bloody hares to last a bloody week! I want fresh game every day, and I want it from that man, and that's final! And I want to be told what he brings in, the moment he delivers it!"

The whole thing was a mystery, but at least he had not been ordered to go down on hands and knees in front of the kitchen stove to heat up a poker for his ale. "Very good, *mon Colonel,*" he said. "Will that be all?"

"Yes."

"Good night, *mon Colonel.*" When he was about to close the door, the voice called after him, "By the way, there is no need to tell *Madame!*"

He looked around, his eyes narrowed in sudden suspicion. But he was careful to hide it. "Very good, *mon Colonel.* Good night."

While slowly climbing the stairs, on his way back to his room, he wondered about it. Why should the Colonel suddenly reverse his own order not to buy any more game from McHair under any circumstances, to demand game every day, without respite, until they all had hoofs and furry ears? Why had he insisted on being told what the poacher delivered? And why not tell *Madame?*

If it had not been for that last remark, he would not have smelled a rat. It was completely unrealistic; of course *Madame* would find out. But why try to keep it from her? What was he up to? Whatever the boor was plotting, he had suddenly, after thirteen years, given his implacable enemy power over him. Bonbon did not yet know what it amounted to, but of one thing he was certain: it was power that at a given moment might—who knew?—prove sufficient to destroy him.

Ah! To take the sweet, befuddled duck back to *la douce France,* to the meadows where the swan had thrived! No man could give her back her youth, but they could, together, drift down the Seine in summer, with all of Paris mirrored in the sky, and remember the days when they were young and the key to heaven seemed to be made of *patisserie.*

He looked at his haggard face in the mirror, whispered, "Ah, *mon pauvre ami!*" and blew out the candle. There was no curtain; he found his bed by moonlight.

* * *

John McHair was a bewildered, unhappy man. Ever since the night of the riot he had tried to resume his normal life, but without success. Something essential to his prowess as a hunter seemed to have been impaired.

He roamed the woods in Justice Sawrey's park no longer as the uncontested king of the forest; his power seemed to have been eroded by some indefinable corruption from within. He no longer felt part of nature, of the animal world in which for as long as he could remember he had been at home, completely sure of himself. Not that he now considered killing animals for a living to be wrong, he simply was no longer interested in killing as such, not even as part of the inexorable pattern of life in the wild. He could not understand why, but for the first time in his life he found himself thinking about an honest job as he ghosted silently along the trail on his nightly beat, a marauder in the twilight. An honest job! What job? All he could possibly do in the tame, airless society of the town was to be a butcher; but he could not slaughter helpless tethered animals that he had not hunted and forced to surrender by his skill and the power of his will.

What else was there? A laborer, like his father, a serf who would die of exhaustion to be tossed into a pauper's grave? Never. He would never fit into the boot-licking, back-biting community of lackeys to the rich. To hunt for his food, to live with the trees, the birds, the clouds, the rain, the running hare, the dancing rabbit, that was his destiny; he could not conceive of any other. He simply could not live without the woods, the fells at dusk, the secretive, rustling night, the blue glory of the dawn. But it was as if nature itself had started to expel him, as if he were overcome by some elemental weakness that made him falter at the moment of the kill. It was the spell of that bloody Quaker, those crazy women, that insane sense of brotherhood which left him with his eyes full of tears and his heart full of love for everybody. Like a bout of drunkenness, that's what it was: the effect of one jug of ale on a man was the same as that of sixteen hundred years of Christianity; only this eerie drunkenness did not evaporate after a good night's sleep. He seemed unable to shake off that treacherous weakness, the sentimental reverence for all life which made the motionless hare, paralyzed by the power of his will, suddenly take heart and dart away in a sinuous, life-saving bound instead of waiting meekly for the blow. At the crucial moment, when the slow upward curve of his stick reached the point where it would suddenly in one vicious flash strike and kill, his concentration would be distracted for a split second as for the first time in his life he became aware of the resignation in the unblinking eye held helplessly in his gaze. To become aware of his prey as an individual, even if only for a split second, was enough to set it free.

It made no sense. Whatever it was that rose between him and his prey at the moment of truth, allowing it to escape, condemned him to death by starvation, for it simply meant that he could no longer hunt, and to hunt was his life. He tried, instead of clubbing his prey to death, hunting with snare and trap, although it made detection by the judge's gamekeepers much more likely. But it did not work; he could not kill by subterfuge, he had never been able to. He thought of telling Monsoor that he was going away for a while, but he would be mad to alienate so good a customer, or so he felt during the day. During the day everything seemed normal; the moment the twilight settled and the first bats began to swoop from the belfry of the church and the ancient call of the hunt drew him to the forest, that weakness, that spell would creep over him again. It gave him the unnerving sensation that something lay waiting for him in the darkness, to pounce and kill as he had killed so many times himself when he was still the undisputed king of the wild. Like his own victims, he seemed doomed to be felled by some killer, waiting for him in the night, who was not crippled by this eerie weakness.

If only he knew what it was, he would be able to defend himself! He wanted to escape, he wanted to shake it off, but he was powerless until he discovered why that hesitancy went on paralyzing him at the moment of the kill. Why, why, why?

* * *

The trouble about pretense between husband and wife, Henrietta Best thought, is that it interrupts all communication between them. She was sure her husband was nursing some unsavory scheme in the back of his head. If they had not, for weeks now, pretended that her embarrassing outburst in Swarthmoor Hall had not taken place, she would have asked him outright; but because of their well-intentioned dissimulation the gossamer threads of intuition that linked long-married couples had begun to snap. She could no longer be sure if indeed something was going on or whether the strain of pretense was beginning to tell.

One morning, as she protested to Bonbon about the unending dreary procession of game at supper, she discovered that this was according to her husband's instructions and she became sure that William Best, aged fifty-six, was indulging in subterfuge, with the transparent wiliness of a boy of twelve. How idiotic of him to think that she would not notice Bonbon's sudden transformation from a master chef, whose hallmark had always been variation, into a dull-witted purveyor of hare and venison *ad nauseam!* What was her husband up to? She did not know, but she was worried. To persuade the clergy of the surrounding counties to sign a warrant for blasphemy against George Fox was risky enough; but while she felt fairly confident that Thomas Fell and he would be able to handle the situation, she felt intensely alarmed at the discovery that her dear spouse was hatching some plot of his own. He was not the plotting kind; what made him a poor conspirator was the quality that had once saved her. There always came a moment when, suddenly and unexpectedly, he fell victim to his own humanity. He could scheme and plot like the worst of them; then, like an arrow from the dark, pity, mercy, compassion or whatever it was struck him between the shoulderblades and spoiled everything. That was well and good and she loved him for it, but in the process he was likely to stir up a lot of complications. Now an ancient wifely instinct told her that something of this nature was going on again.

No matter what, she had to find out. She decided to ask him outright, choosing an appropriate moment, for men were ticklish creatures. Sweet reasonableness reigned supreme until some casual word, a stifled yawn, some innocent curtness caused by preoccupation would trigger an outburst of resentment pent up inside them. Despite her experience, this always paralyzed her, as if she saw an avalanche cascading down on her, incredulous that it could have been brought about by an innocent sneeze.

The best moment of the day was during the half hour before supper when they took their *apéritif* in her little withdrawing room. That evening she stopped him as he moved to get up for their drinks. "No, sweeting, let me do it this time," she said. "Thou art so comfortable right now." She had learned that to ask a man not to bestir himself because he looked tired would have the opposite result; "tired," in the male vocabulary, stood either for "old," in which case he would feel bound to prove his youthful vigor, or for "sickening for something," which would make him so worried for the next few hours that intelligent conversation was out of the question.

He fell for the lure, and gratefully accepted the brimming glass she handed him. *"Parbleu!* That's very full, my heart!" He spilled some, luckily on the floor and not on his breeches.

"I'm sorry." She smiled and kissed his forehead. "I'll put the decanter beside thee." She hoped she was not overdoing it. "How is the Fox affair going?" she asked, settling in her chair opposite him.

"So far, so good," he replied, swallowing a draught. "Fell should have received the warrant by now."

"Who swore the warrant?"

"Dr. Marshall." He chuckled. "All according to plan. Clever fellow, our friend Fell."

"How many ministers joined?"

"Thirty-eight."

"When will the trial be?"

"Next week."

"And Sawrey?" she asked. "How has he been taking all this?"

"According to plan, according to plan." He took another mouthful of wine and disposed of it noisily. Something told her that she had touched upon his secret.

She waited until he had swallowed his next mouthful, then she asked, without any effort at dissimulation, "Art thou perchance planning to keep Sawrey away from the trial by handing him that poacher?"

"Huh? What's that?"

"Bonbon told me thou hast ordered him to buy game every day and to keep thee informed of what he buys. The only reason for that can be that thou art planning to keep Sawrey away from the trial by handing him the poacher he has been trying to catch red-handed for years, at a moment that suits thee."

"But—but how—" he stuttered.

"Come, come, dear heart," she said. "Sawrey wants the poacher. I have learned enough about judicial procedures to know that all he needs is to have the man delivered to him with some marked game by way of proof."

"But why should I do such a thing?"

"Sawrey would be so eager to get even with John McHair that his attention would be distracted, at least for a while. By the time he began to suspect trickery, thou and *ton petit camarade* Mr. Fell would have acquitted Fox and spirited him out of the duchy. Am I not right, *mon chou?"*

He frowned; then he grunted, "Never mind. Don't bother thy head about these matters."

She had no particular fondness for the poacher, but it seemed barbaric to use any human being as if he were cattle. "Why?" she asked. "Why risk the life of an innocent man?"

His frown became a scowl, not a very convincing one. "Nonsense! He's a poacher."

"Why risk the life of an innocent poacher?"

"What flummery!" he exclaimed angrily. "The man won't be hanged for simple poaching! Not any longer."

"I would not put it beyond little Sawrey."

"Don't fear; if he were to kill that man for poaching on his own land, it would mean the end of his days on the bench. Fell would see to that, or I, for that matter. No, the worst that can happen is that McHair gets a couple of years in prison; and that he richly deserves."

She did not take his determination at face value. To trick a man into committing a crime only to denounce him at the judicious moment was too callous for him. There would come a point when he would suddenly weaken and make things worse than they were to begin with. "Why do it?" she asked. "Why compromise thyself in this way?"

"I am not compromising myself." He slurped his wine irritably.

"Dear heart, Sawrey is vindictive, suspicious and has nothing to lose. If he finds out about this, he will never forgive thee. Why risk a dirty little man's undying hatred for so small a matter?"

"Small matter? I want to make sure that Fox leaves the district after the trial and never returns! That is no small matter! That concerns the sanity and the peace of this town! So—this is the last I want to hear of it." He smiled grimly. "We shall go on having jugged hare for supper for some time yet."

She knew that further protest was pointless. He was not a complicated man; his shifts of mood were simple and basic. Any further effort to shake his resolve would be sneezing in the mountains. She wondered for a moment whether she could warn the poacher that he was being readied for slaughter, but this was one of those occasions when a wife had to remain loyal to her husband, regardless of her convictions. She could not do this to William; he was sure to find out and her betrayal would be mortifying to him, not worth the price. What was more, she of all people was not the one to throw the first stone.

CHAPTER FIVE

THE small party from Ulverston on its way to Lancaster was half-way across the sands. It was a sunny day, Morecambe Bay glistened in the distance between sand and sky like a ripple of silver. The odor of shellfish bared by the tide was pungent in the still, hot sank into the spongy banks of seaweed. air; the horses, soaked with sweat, stepped nervously as their hoofs

There were a dozen people in the party: Judges Fell and Best with their grooms and scribes, George Fox and, in the center of the procession, Henrietta Best and Margaret Fell, each sheltered from the rays of the sun by a brightly colored canopy, and their respective maids.

As they approached the other shore, Judge Fell asked George Fox to fall back with him to discuss the coming trial. George obeyed with reluctance; he did not fear the trial, but he had a growing sense of uneasiness. He knew enough about the way the law was administered to realize that things could be arranged beforehand; Justice Bennett himself had suggested during his year in Derby jail that if he were to ask for a new trial and confine himself to a short list of prearranged statements, his sentence would be reversed.

The moment they were out of earshot George said, "Friend Thomas, I do not wish to discuss the trial." He felt a great relief and smiled at the man by his side in a spirit of conciliation.

Thomas Fell's eyes were as uncommunicative as beads of glass. "Very well. I merely want you to realize that in a case like this, where the questioning is conducted by the plaintiffs, it will be their purpose to trick you into further evidence of blasphemy. I will have to intervene each time that happens. Is that clear?"

"Yes."

They rode for a while in silence. There seemed to be nothing left to say, yet the judge made no move to join the others. "By the way," he said at last, "the more I think about it, the more convinced I am that it's time you carried your message to more receptive ears. I mean Oliver Cromwell."

"That is easier said than done."

"That is why I brought it up. I could give you a letter of introduction to someone at court who would take you straight to the Protector."

Well! At last the cards were on the table. He was astonished at the crudeness of the scheme. It was obvious now that the trial had been arranged by Fell and Best; the whole scheme was such an insult to the essence of his mission that he was about to say, 'Thank thee, friend,

I will meet Cromwell when the Lord's time comes.' But the thought struck him: might God not use the schemes of sinful men to achieve His will? He still had not found the answer to why the Lord had sent him to Swarthmoor. Could it be that He wanted him to go to Cromwell, and that the shortest way led through the machinations of Fell and Best? For the first time since he had arrived in this bewildering place he saw a possible purpose to his coming. He decided to go to London and confront Cromwell in the power of the Lord. "Thank thee, Thomas," he said, "I will."

As he said it, he was filled with a motion of love toward the man. "Do not let it concern thee," he added kindly. "We are all at His mercy. If He counts the hairs on our heads, He must be aware of the schemes and the plots we hatch underneath them. Our consolation is that, whether we know it or not, we hatch them at His prompting."

To him it was utterly obvious, but he had the feeling that the man by his side did not begin to know what he meant. Maybe one had to be guided safely across these very sands against the tide before one could accept one's utter dependence on the currents and the tides of the infinite ocean of light and love, which was both our origin and our destination.

* * *

The morning of the trial was sweltering. Lancaster Castle loomed, massive and forbidding, above the low roofs of the town; the square in front of it was filled with a milling crowd, as if there were a fair in progress. Vendors of hot chestnuts, ale, paper fans, pamphlets hawked their wares in shrill voices; the crowd was so tightly packed that some people had climbed onto the base of the statue of St. George that had been beheaded during the revolution because of its halo. The excitement mounted when, with angry cries of the guards, a narrow furrow opened in the crowd to allow a sedan chair to pass, carried by two men. By its side strode two justices in full robes and wigs, instantly identified as Lord Chief Justice Thomas Fell and Colonel William Best, presiding judges at the trial. The chaise was carried not to the steps of the courtroom, but into the gateway of the castle, the entrance to the prison. The iron grilles opened and closed; its passenger descended, to vanish into the warden's office. A shriek of fury arose from the crowd outside the gates. They spat, shook fists, bellowed curses, for the chaise had contained not the judges' ladies, as everyone had assumed, but the blasphemer George Fox, who by this stratagem had been protected from the fury of the mob. Judging from the invective his appearance caused, the measure had been a wise one; the temper of the people in the square, incited by the clergy, was such that had the accused appeared in public he might well have been lynched right then and there, as Father Herringdon and Father Finster had been at the height of the Civil War. When finally the doors to the courtroom were opened and the people poured in, there turned out to be not enough room for them all, although it was the largest courtroom in the duchy. Many had to be content with standing on the steps outside or in the square, where they would have to rely on messages relayed from the doorway to follow the proceedings.

The violence in the air was such that when a second chaise arrived, this time at the steps to the courtroom, people shouted and screamed, the pamphlet vendors shook their fists at the pale, startled faces inside; it needed three guards with halberds to make room for the door to be opened. Two women stepped down and began to make their way up the steps; the fact that they had been party to the deception made them objects of rage and derision. Heads bent, close together as if to seek each other's protection, they hurried, stumbling, up the steps. They were booed, spat at, cursed; just before they vanished inside the courtroom one of them was struck on the back by a cabbage. It sent the armed guards charging down the steps. Suddenly from inside the courtroom came the sound of a trumpet. In the silence it created, a solemn voice chanted, "Oyez, oyez, all rise . . ."

The trial of George Fox for blasphemy was in progress.

Thomas Fell, slumped in the high-backed bench, sweltering in his wig and his robe, looked about the courtroom as Dr. Herbert Marshall, spokesman for the ministers, made his first long-winded presentation. The hall was packed; the forty ministers sat huddled together like a flock of crows on one side of the dais; Fox faced them in the dock opposite. The heat lay over them all like a pall, stifling, even though the windows were open. Hot sunlight streamed in through the high windows, flies flitted through the dancing sheaves of dust. The shrill cries of the pamphleteers, still vending their leaflets in the square, added to the atmosphere of tension; the hatred in those voices was unmistakable.

Strange, Thomas Fell reflected, that a trial for blasphemy should generate such excitement among the rabble. Were these people really concerned about the things to be discussed here—freedom of interpretation of the Scriptures, the relationship between God and man, the authority of the church? Most of the spectators, if questioned on these matters, would answer with garbled nonsense. No, they had come for the cockfight, the clash of violent emotions; yet it was they who would ultimately decide the fate of the man in the dock. The true judges were not Best and himself, but the rabble in the court, the screaming vendors outside.

The night before, in his rooms at the inn, he had studied a report on Fox's past activities that Sam Pruitt had drawn up for him with his usual painstaking thoroughness; twenty pages of copperplate handwriting telling of incident after incident where the man in the dock had been attacked, manhandled, set upon by infuriated villagers incited by their priests. In the great Minster at York, Fox had been thrown down the steps when he tried to deliver his message. At Warmsworth, people had assaulted him, thrashed him with staves, thrown clods and stones at him, the priest himself had laid violent hands on him. At Tickhill, as soon as he began to speak in the church, the entire congregation had fallen upon him fiercely, the minister had struck him on the head with his Bible so that it gushed blood. He had fled, staggering, into the street, where the people had knocked him down, kicked him, thrown him over a hedge, dragged him through a house and back into the street, stoning and beating him as they went. In Walney Island, a man had come into the meeting with a cocked pistol, asked for George Fox, and when Fox stepped up to him through the fleeing crowd, the man had pressed the trigger, but the pistol had not gone off. The next morning a mob of villagers with staves, clubs and fishing poles had fallen upon Fox, as they believed he had bewitched one of their townsmen, who now called himself a Quaker. The mob, led by the man's wife, had beaten Fox and dragged him toward the sea, where the priest exhorted them to throw him in and drown him. They had knocked him down on the beach, stunned him with volleys of stones; the man he had converted had shielded him with his own body, while the man's wife tried to smash her husband's skull with rocks. The man had finally succeeded in dragging Fox into a boat; the mob had stoned them from the shore until they were out of reach. When Fox landed on the mainland, another crowd was waiting for him with pitchforks, flails and staves; they grabbed him, flung him into a cart, took him to the churchyard, where they intended to put him to death, but he managed to escape. No wonder that Priest Lampitt had found forty colleagues ready to sign the warrant; so far, the clergy had been unable to stop the impetus of the Quaker movement by persecution. Judging by the atmosphere in the courtroom and the town, were Fox to stay in these parts, he would be put to death sooner or later in the atrocious manner these savages reserved for witches.

What was it that drove the man? Useless question. Fell had asked himself that many times in connection with Oliver Cromwell, and the only answer he had found was: obsession. Like Cromwell, Fox was obsessed by a demon that drove him on with the momentum of a spinning top; no man could foretell how many decent people he would drag along with him in his headlong rush toward some violent, blood-soaked Golgotha. How little we know about the forces that propel us, Fell reflected, how thin our veneer of culture, reason and common sense! Take Herbert Marshall, Doctor of Divinity, a not very intelligent but sensible man, more a politician than a cleric. In connection with George Fox he behaved in a totally irrational fashion, letting his judgment be clouded by passion, submitting accusations that a child could tell him would be thrown out of court as ridiculous. Why? What made a man of stature and learning put himself in a position where he could not help but look like a fool? Was he, like Fell himself, driven to distraction by the instinctive knowledge that if Fox were to be allowed to continue he would cause untold suffering, misery, disruption? What godliness was there in driving simple, uneducated people like that couple in Walney Island to the point where the wife tried to brain her husband? What "eternal truth" was worth this foundering of two decent people into savagery?

He should not allow Marshall to degrade himself to a point where for the sake of his prestige among the mob he had to destroy Fox rather than let him get away. The arguments should be kept at an esoteric theological level, far over the heads of the crowd in the hall.

The charges against George Fox, as read by Marshall in questions of one sentence, sounded like the ravings of a madman. "Did the prisoner dissuade men from reading the Scriptures, telling them it was carnal? Does the prisoner affirm that he has stated that both baptism and the Lord's Supper are unlawful? Does the prisoner affirm that he is equal with God? Does the prisoner affirm that God teaches deceit? That the Scriptures are anti-Christ? That he is the judge of the world?"

The preposterous list, read by the normally reasonable Dr. Marshall, sounded tragic. But the ignorant rabble in the courtroom catcalled, whistled, shouted; a raucous voice yelled from the back of the hall, "Give him to us! Give us the blasphemer!" It took more than a minute before the sergeant-at-arms could restore order.

"If there are any more demonstrations in this court, I will have it cleared!" Fell said frostily. "Will the defendant please rise and present his answers to these charges?"

George Fox rose, but before he could speak, the shrill voice of Dr. Marshall, taut with rage, interrupted, "Does not the prisoner have to take the oath?"

This was the moment old Justice Cartwright had foreseen. "Considering the nature of this trial," Fell answered carefully, "and in view of the fact that the defendant is asked merely to state his opinions, not to relate facts, it is the judgment of this court that no oath is necessary."

"I protest!" Marshall cried. The ministers behind him conferred in angry commotion; again a hubbub rose in the courtroom which had to be subdued by the sergeant-at-arms.

"I repeat that I cannot tolerate any interruptions!" Fell said sternly. "As to you, Dr. Marshall, you know as well as I do that your protest will have to be lodged in the proper manner with a higher court, after the trial. At this point the ruling of the presiding judge has power of law." He turned toward the accused waiting in the dock. "George Fox, pray present your answers to these charges precisely and directly, without digression. Number one. Do you adjudge the Scriptures to be carnal?"

The man in the dock waited, with calm assurance, until the excitement in the courtroom had died down and a hush fell, in which the cries of the vendors outside sounded like the shrieks of distant peacocks. "No, I do not. As to my dissuading men from reading the Scriptures—"

Fell interrupted him sharply. "Answer only my question, Mr. Fox! I did not ask what you may or may not have *done,* I asked for your *opinion.* Whether you do or do not persuade others is not the issue; it is your views that are at stake."

"But, Your Lordship!" Marshall protested. "On that basis, the whole trial—"

"Dr. Marshall," Fell said in his most glacial manner, "the same goes for you, sir. You have presented your charges, now it is the turn of the accused to either refute or substantiate them. You will be given a chance to cross-examine him later."

"But, Your Lordship! My charge was that he *did* persuade others—"

"Dr. Marshall!" he cried, leaving no doubt as to his exasperation, "already you are both plaintiff and prosecutor! Would you usurp the role of judge as well?"

"No, sir, no, Your Lordship, but—"

"In that case, please remember that the purpose of this trial is for you and your colleagues to prove blasphemy as defined by law, to the satisfaction of this court. At no point will the defendant's actions be admitted in evidence. Now, Mr. Fox: the Scriptures, in your opinion, are not carnal. What exactly do you mean?"

"I believe that everyone should read the Scriptures," Fox said, obviously chafing at the bit as impatiently as his opponent. "I have never tried to convince anyone that—"

"Mr. Fox!" he snapped angrily, "either you obey the rulings of this court or I will hold you in contempt! We are *not* interested in what you tried to *do!* We are concerned with what you *think.*"

"But, Your Lordship—!" Marshall wailed.

"Dr. Marshall! One more intervention from you and I will declare a mistrial!"

Marshall and his cronies went into an angry huddle; the courtroom hummed with excitement. "Silence in court!" the sergeant-at-arms bellowed, at Fell's signal. "Silence in court!" Of course the ministers had reason to be flustered; good thing Sawrey was not here. He could have prompted them as to how to challenge the court's argument. "Mr. Fox, proceed," Fell said when order had been restored.

"As to the Scriptures being carnal," the young man continued with blithe self-assurance, "the letter of them is. The letter always is. The letter kills, the spirit is eternal. So I judge it to be the hireling priests who are making the Scriptures carnal, by making a trade of them . . ."

This, of course, set the ministers honking like geese; the courtroom exploded in boos, catcalls, obscenities, bellowed threats; the guards had to subdue several hotheads who made for the dock to assault the blasphemer; they were bundled out with a great deal of commotion. The sergeant-at-arms hammered and hammered with his halberd on the floor, his stentorian voice became hoarse with strain. Finally, a semblance of order was reimposed upon the unruly mob.

Fell addressed the defendant. "Mr. Fox, this is the last time I will let you deviate from the substance of a question. I need not remind you again of the alternative; but, for your information: we can sentence you, *ad hoc,* to a public whipping, two days and two nights in the stocks and a maximum of two years in prison for contempt of court, and we will not hesitate to avail ourselves of that power." Without soliciting the young man's reaction, he continued, "Second question, and confine yourself to answering its substance. Do you consider yourself to be equal with God?"

"No, but I consider that I have that of God essentially in me, that

God is part of me, as He is of you and everyone else in this courtroom, hireling priests included."

Again the ministers protested, but the mob was sufficiently interested in what Fox was saying for Fell to let them protest.

"This is not something I invented," Fox continued. "This is what the Scriptures say—"

"Blasphemy!" one of the ministers cried. The sergeant-at-arms, at Fell's sign, sought him out.

Fell continued. "Third question. Do you consider both baptism and the Lord's Supper unlawful? Begin with baptism."

"Ah," the prisoner replied, as if he were broaching a favorite subject, "the sprinkling of infants! Nowhere do the Scriptures speak of it as a sacrament . . ."

He droned on, safely caught in the rut of theology. Thomas Fell could relax; this was better. Somnolence, that was what was needed; soporific involutions about sacraments and their Biblical justification. What for a moment had threatened to be a clash of emotions had, thanks to his dogged efforts at impersonating Justice Cartwright, ended up in the dry sands of exegesis. He glanced at the bench for distinguished visitors, where his wife and Mistress Best were sitting, heavily guarded by halberd-toting creatures of Warden Farragut's. Margaret looked frightened and upset. No wonder, poor woman; he had seen from the passage on his way to the courtroom how she had been treated by the mob and how some miscreant had thrown refuse at her. The savages! What a calamitous notion that they should be able to govern themselves, that England should be handed over to this rabble and their vicious, self-serving priests. As the trial droned on, he yearned for an age when demagogues like Cromwell and this execrable youth would be treated for what they were: lunatics loose in the street with a weapon deadlier than a cannon, mowing down the innocent in the name of a barbaric god.

* * *

That same morning, in the small, airless courtroom in Ulverston, another trial was in progress: that of John McHair accused of poaching, Justice John Sawrey presiding.

The few spectators on the uncomfortable benches sat fanning themselves with their hats, creating with their slow, hypnotic waving an atmosphere of torpor. Everyone was overcome by somnolence, even the prisoner in the dock, who stood swaying on his feet, eyes glazed, his face slack with drowsiness.

The only one alert and bright-eyed was the witness on the stand, Colonel Best's French cook, whom John Sawrey was in the process of questioning. The evidence against the prisoner was overwhelming; all that was needed now was a concise statement by the witness that John McHair had delivered game to the kitchen of Colonel William Best, stating it to be provender from the parklands of John Sawrey,

Esquire, Simon Rutledge, Esquire, and others, lands on which hunting, trapping and snaring of game was prohibited by law.

"Let me go into this a little further," Sawrey said. "You stated that on the morning of the seventeenth the prisoner brought in two hares and one partridge which he told you had been snared in the Rutledge parklands?"

"Yes, *Monsieur le Juge,*" the old eunuch replied ingratiatingly, "many times."

"What do you mean, many times? Did he state this more than once that morning?"

"No, no, *Monsieur le Juge.* Not just that morning." The beady eyes looked at him brightly.

"You mean: you had been aware for some time that the game you bought from the prisoner had been criminally obtained?"

"Yes, *Monsieur.*" There was an expression of relief on the witness' face. What was the matter with the man?

"How long have you been conversant with the fact that the game you bought was criminally obtained?"

"Oh, many months, *Monsieur.*"

"You mean to say you were aware all that time of the fact that the prisoner was a poacher, and yet you went on buying his wares?"

"Yes, *Monsieur!*" The man seemed definitely pleased with this line of questioning, despite the fact that he was busy implicating himself. It did not make sense.

"Do you realize that your being aware of the origin of the game and continuing to buy it makes you an accomplice after the fact?"

"Oh, yes, *Monsieur!*" The creature was positively beaming now. "But it was not I, *Monsieur!* I am only a servant following instructions."

Sawrey instantly drew back, irritated. The old buzzard wanted to embarrass William Best, his master. Vicious old frog—he would take care of him. "Nonsense!" he said sharply. "Whether you are servant or master is immaterial. Whoever may have paid for the game, your master reported the crime as soon as he became aware of it."

"Oh, but he did not, *Monsieur le Juge!*" The old freak fixed him again with his beady, eager eyes; there could be no doubt that he was urging him to probe further.

"What do you mean?"

"I was told to buy game from John McHair every day, and to keep my master informed of what I bought, even though we all knew that it had been poached."

It was a nasty little dilemma, and Sawrey turned to the clerk, saying, "Strike his last reply and my question as immaterial." He looked at the witness with distaste and was about to question him further when it came to him: the sudden, heart-stopping realization *why* the man on the witness stand had been given that order by his master. It took a few moments before he grasped the extent to which he had been hoodwinked; he felt the blood drain from his face as he saw, clearly and in detail, the bait he had swallowed. The sudden denunciation of John McHair was part of a plan to keep him away from Lancaster.

Almost absent-mindedly he sentenced the prisoner John McHair to one year in prison—a ridiculously light sentence, but his main compulsion at that moment was to regurgitate the bait; the sentence was a slap in the faces of Fell and Best, who had thought that they could hoodwink him with impunity.

The trial ended with a sudden change of pace from glassy-eyed torpor to undecorous urgency. Sawrey rushed out of court with unbecoming speed, ripped off his gown and wig in chambers and threw them on a chair; thus far, he had always treated the credentials of his office with reverence. He slapped on his own wig and his hat, slung his cloak around his shoulders, ran to the stall in the courtyard where his horse was waiting. He threw himself into the saddle, galloped home, flung a few things into a bag, told his wife that he had to go to Lancaster to take part in a trial and that he would not be back for several days; then he raced off in the direction of the sands.

The tide was out, but about to turn, he could make the bluff of Cark comfortably; to cross from there to Lancaster, however, would be risky. But he was obsessed by only one thought: to get to that courtroom, to throw a cudgel into their unholy work, to snatch the prize from under the noses of his contemptuous peers. Despite the risk, he pushed on to Lancaster across the treacherous sands, his fury unabated; he clattered into the darkening streets of the city that evening and dismounted, trembling with fatigue, in the courtyard of the inn where his doxy was lodged. He hurried upstairs and opened the door to find her bedded down with another man.

Incoherent with fury, he slammed the door on the sheepish couple, stamped downstairs, snarled at the innkeeper to cancel the room and present the month's bill to the gentleman in residence; then he stumbled into the dark courtyard, where the stable groom had already unsaddled his horse. He ordered him to saddle up again and rode out into the night, slumping in weariness, to find rooms elsewhere.

That was not easy; most inns near the castle were occupied by the ministers and their supporters; only the Boar and Stag had rooms available, but he discovered in time that Fell and Best were lodging there. Sick with fatigue, he finally bedded down in a flea-ridden tavern on the outskirts of town, where carousing went on downstairs until the small hours. Sweating, itching, he tossed and turned on the lumpy mattress, unable to sleep, shaken by the sudden turn his life seemed to have taken. His fears gradually lost all perspective; when dawn broke he was convinced that even his betrayal by that faithless harlot was part of the plot. He decided, in his mad anguish, not to go to court at all, but to hide his shame by riding back to Ulverston and holing up abjectly in the home that was not his but his wife's.

With the sun his spirits rose. His self-pity made way for determination. He told the groom to keep his horse stabled, and walked to the castle, mingling with the crowd. He brushed aside the vendors in the square and tried to enter the courtroom, worming his way through the tightly packed throng on the steps. When he was turned away from the doors, he identified himself to the guards and was led to the distinguished visitors' bench. There he found himself seated next to the Mistresses Fell and Best, which honed his fury.

Once he was recognized by Lampitt and the other priests, he decided that, after all, it was better this way. He could intervene in the proceedings only by feeding suggestions to Dr. Marshall. Now, should Marshall receive a note from him, he would read it instead of putting it aside in amateurish self-confidence.

Fell, as presiding judge, was the first to enter, followed by Best. Sawrey saw Fell's glance roam through the court, pass his bench and then, with unmistakable surprise, return to him. Fell whispered to Best, Best glanced in his direction; there could be no mistaking the concern his presence caused them. It was balm for his bruised pride. He felt suddenly confident that he could still frustrate their scheme, which it must seem to them had already succeeded.

At Fell's request, Dr. Marshall rose to begin his cross-examination.

* * *

John Sawrey's arrival deeply alarmed Margaret Fell. Until that moment she had bravely assumed that all was well, despite the terrible hatred of the people in the court and those outside. She had gazed upon George with growing admiration and confidence as he stood there, noble, young, unafraid, radiant with gentleness and love, never losing his patience under the hateful probing of those miserable priests who almost drooled with venom every time they as much as looked at him. Now, suddenly, all that had changed. Sawrey had bowed to her politely enough; why had she such a feeling of danger? She put her hand on her breast to calm the racing of her heart and turned away from him toward Henrietta Best as if to seek the security of her presence.

As she listened to the questioning of George Fox by Dr. Marshall, however, she could not see how Sawrey could exert any influence at this late stage. The trial was almost over; the ministers, in the assumption that their cause was irrefutable, no longer put any limit to their odious ardor. She heard Thomas' calm, authoritive voice ask, "Is it true, Dr. Marshall, that some of you have stated you would do away with George Fox, should you have the opportunity?" and there came Dr. Marshall's reply, spoken in a high, shrill voice, "Indeed, Your Lordship! Many of my friends and colleagues here have stated that, could they only lay hands on the blasphemer, they would be tempted to remove him from the face of the earth!"

The audience cheered and somewhere somebody booed. She watched Sawrey from the corner of her eye and saw that he was staring fixedly at the bench.

"We would do so," Dr. Marshall's voice shrieked, "for the sake of Christ's church! For the honor of God!"

The cheering doubled in force; but even she, with her limited experience, realized that the statement was self-incriminating; he must have done his own case irreparable harm. The night before, Thomas had explained to her at length how punishment for blasphemy was carefully circumscribed by the law and did not include the death penalty. There certainly was no provision under the law by which the clergy could execute at will people with whose opinions they did not agree. All their charges had been answered in a reasonable fashion by George, who had never lost his temper, never been immoderate, never used any but loving and understanding words, and he had substantiated every utterance by quotations from the Scriptures. Surely there was no case of blasphemy here? The only charge that could be brought was by Priest Lampitt for creating a nuisance in church.

She looked at her husband, stern and aloof in his high-backed chair, a figure of majesty in powdered wig and scarlet robe. Despite his lack of sympathy for George, he must have noticed that there was about the young man's concept of the relationship between God and man a breadth of vision that contrasted painfully with that of the ministers. Even to Thomas it must be obvious that George's version was closer to the message of Christ, certainly in compassion.

"We have one final question to ask of the accused," Dr. Marshall cried, "and thereafter we shall rest our case. For we are confident, My Lords, that the blasphemer's answer will be self-explanatory toward the totality of our charges." He turned toward George, waiting calmly in the dock. "Do you deny that you, George Fox, plead for the equality of heathens and Christians before the Lord?"

A hush fell over the audience that left no doubt as to the drama of the moment. She saw a look of worry cross her husband's face and he bent sideways to whisper something to Colonel Best without looking at him. Best's face seemed to darken, he nodded, and both of them, she thought, glanced at the man beside her. She had forgotten about Sawrey for a moment; now she was reminded of his presence as of something odious, menacing.

"In Titus Two, eleven," George's powerful voice replied, "Paul writes, *'For the grace of God that bringeth salvation hath appeared to all men.'* So it behooves us to respect and love all men, Negroes, Indians, Moslems or members of other Christian sects, as our equals before the Lord."

"I appeal to the judges!" Marshall cried triumphantly. "This rests our case! Herewith it is proven that George Fox is the anti-Christ!"

There were cheers and shouts; they frightened her, so vicious were they and so full of hatred. All the time she was aware of the unemotional presence of the man by her side, whose eyes never seemed to leave the judges on the bench. Thomas signaled the sergeant-at-arms; when he proved unable to restore order, Thomas himself rose. Instantly the courtroom fell silent. The Lord Chief Justice was about to announce the verdict.

"Having taken careful note of the arguments of the learned gentlemen," he began, in a solemn voice that sent a shiver of awe down her spine, "this court cannot arrive at any conclusion under the law, or as reasonable and just men, other than that the statements of opinion presented by the accused George Fox do not constitute blasphemy according to the definition provided by the law."

A commotion started in the hall; she realized that there was going to be trouble.

"During the trial," Thomas continued calmly, deaf to the rising protest, "not a single proof of blasphemy has been presented to the satisfaction of this court. What we have witnessed, and witnessed with interest, was a dispute between theologians about the interpretation of the Scriptures. At no point during his testimony has the accused expressed any doubt as to the divine inspiration of said Scriptures, neither has he voiced refusal to accept Christ Jesus as the Son of God. It is these two points . . ." The commotion in the hall was now such that he was barely audible. The sergeant-at-arms rapped his halberd angrily, quiet returned. "It is these two points," Thomas repeated, "that are singled out by law as the touchstones of blasphemy. Consequently, the accused is acquitted of the charge, and free to go as he pleases." He sat down, and the hall exploded.

"I protest!" Dr. Marshall shouted over the tumult. "I want to make it abundantly clear . . ." Nobody knew what he wanted to make clear; pandemonium drowned his cries. She heaved a sigh of relief; the fury of the people around her was terrifying, but George was safe, Thomas would see to it that he did not fall into the hands of this rabble. Suddenly she became aware that the man beside her had come to life. He was talking to one of the guards behind their bench, handed him a piece of paper; the man saluted respectfully and took it to the sergeant-at-arms. She was not the only one to notice the exchange; other people in the courtroom began to realize that something was going on. The sergeant-at-arms handed the note to Dr. Marshall, who read it, then looked at their bench with a frown. She saw John Sawrey nod, a smile on his face. Marshall rose.

The courtroom became quiet. In the silence Marshall said, suddenly calm and composed, "I will at this point, in behalf of the ministers, inform the judge against the accused George Fox and demand that the court make out a warrant for his arrest."

Suddenly the silence was profound. She looked with a qualm of fear at Thomas. He sat there unruffled, undisturbed, but when he replied she heard, knowing him so well, that the statement had come as a surprise to him. "The court rejects the demand, as plaintiffs have failed to present sufficient evidence to justify it."

Once again the courtroom exploded in violent protestations; this time it was Marshall himself who silenced the mob by holding up his hands. "The ministers . . ." he cried, and as silence returned, he repeated, "the ministers will petition the Council of State against George Fox. Therefore we insist that the accused be held in custody until such day as said Council shall have reached its decision."

She saw Marshall glance in their direction; again the little judge beside her nodded.

"The court cannot comply with that request," her husband answered calmly, "as the evidence presented and recorded does not warrant impeding the freedom of the accused for any period of time."

"In that case"—she saw Marshall glance at the note—"the ministers demand that George Fox be released only on bail. Estate for estate."

Again there was a commotion in the hall. From the way Thomas conferred with Best she concluded that this must be a legitimate request; but who would undertake to stand bail with his entire estate for George Fox, however much he might deplore the behavior of the priests? Oh, if only she had her own fortune! She would not have hesitated a second! There was more whispered conversation between Thomas and Best, then Thomas signaled the sergeant-at-arms, who rapped his halberd on the floor. When the courtroom was quiet, Thomas' measured voice announced, "Bail, estate for estate, has been presented for the accused to the satisfaction of this court."

This time the commotion was one of outrage.

"Will both the plaintiff and the accused please approach the bench?" Thomas called.

Obviously, the ministers were as taken aback as she was. Who could it be? Who had been the wonderful, saintly person to put his estate on the line for penniless George? He would have to be a man of substance for the ministers to be satisfied with the amount his estate represented. Then, in the midst of her rejoicing, she saw Sawrey start to scribble furiously and beckon the guard again. He handed the man the note, it was taken to the sergeant-at-arms, who gave it to Dr. Marshall. Marshall read it, rose and lifted his arms; the sergeant rapped his halberd, and order returned.

"In accordance with the law," Marshall read from his paper, "the plaintiffs demand that the identity of the guarantor be revealed by the court, so they may judge whether bail as presented is sufficient."

It became so silent that the shrill cries of the vendors outside became audible again. "The name of the guarantor," Thomas replied impersonally, "is Colonel William Best."

Impulsively she put her hand on that of the woman beside her. There was again a commotion in the hall, but this time it was subdued, almost overawed; everybody realized what they were witnessing: an honorable man putting every penny he owned in jeopardy. They must be as flabbergasted as she was—Mistress Best too, by the look of her.

"In that case," Marshall read with a triumphant note in his voice, "the plaintiffs cannot accept this bail as adequate. They demand that it be extended to body for body."

Henrietta Best grabbed her arm and whispered, "Oh, no!" Margaret sat there, suddenly outraged. "Body for body" meant that, should Fox fail to surrender, Colonel Best would have to go to prison in his stead. The demand was so unfair, so spiteful, that she could not help herself: she threw all caution to the wind, turned on Sawrey and said with intense emotion, "Oh! You evil little man!" She regretted it at once, at least the word "little."

But she made not the slightest impression on John Sawrey. He sat there smiling benignly, totally unruffled, the only person in the court-room who seemed completely at ease.

She looked at the bench and saw from her husband's face that he had no choice: he would have to put George in jail. Then Colonel Best rose and said something. She could not hear what, but she felt from the way his wife gripped her arm that it must be dramatic.

At the sight of him standing there, a hush fell over the courtroom. "May I ask my learned colleague to repeat his statement?" Thomas asked, calmly enough, but it seemed to her that he was pleading with Best with his eyes.

Colonel Best, in a voice that sounded almost casual, said, "I will stand bail for the accused, estate for estate and body for body."

In a stunned silence, he calmly sat down.

"May I request the parties to approach the bench, please?" her husband asked dispassionately.

The mob in the courtroom recovered from its astonishment; the noise that arose sounded like the buzzing of a giant hive. Margaret looked again at Sawrey; there could be no doubt he was as stunned by the outcome as the rest of them.

"Oh, dear Henrietta! How—how marvelous!" she cried, turning to Mistress Best. The woman put her face in her hands and burst into tears; Margaret consoled her, lovingly, with a feeling of joy.

*   *   *

Like everyone else, Thomas Fell had been taken completely by surprise by Best's quixotic self-sacrifice; it was not until they were dis-robing in chambers, after the trial, that he was able to have a private word with the man. "What in the world made you do that, dear friend?"

"Oh—er—I wanted to safeguard the sanity of the town," Best replied, taking off his wig and handing it to his groom, who deposited it in its box.

"But surely the consequences for you personally could be serious!"

"Only if those clerics pursue their petition. That, I am sure, they won't do."

He had a point there. To see this case through high court would be a costly business. Even so, it was an incredibly rash act for a cautious man like Best.

"Come, dear friend, we have been in this from the beginning, and I think we owe each other a modicum of honesty, don't you? May I not know the true reason?"

Best looked at him balefully.

"I do not ask out of idle curiosity, I assure you." He smiled. "As head of the judiciary, I cannot maintain a judge if I doubt the man's reason."

Best glanced at his groom, who took the hint and left. He looked haggard without his wig, and much older. The moment the door closed, he said, "On condition that it shall remain between us: I did it for my wife. She had a grievous experience in her younger years. Her first

husband and her children were massacred by the soldiers of Cardinal
Richelieu." It obviously pained him to speak about it.

Thomas Fell hated putting him through this, but he had no choice.
"Forgive me, dear friend. I realize this must be painful to you, but you
will understand—"

"Of course, of course." Best was quite amiable about it. "Fox brought
back those memories to her. She is a highly emotional woman, and I
began to fear for her sanity." He smiled almost apologetically. "As a
man of honor and—er—affection, I had no choice."

"But Fox would have gone to prison! Out of harm's way, as far as
your wife is concerned!"

"We agreed, you and I, that as long as he was imprisoned here in
Lancaster neither she nor the town would have come to rest. Wasn't
that the reason for the way we set up this trial? If not, we might as
well have saved ourselves the trouble and sentenced him to prison
ourselves . . ."

There was a knock on the door, and Fell cried with relief, "Yes!
Come in!"

It was George Fox, accompanied by Warden Farragut in a state of
alarm. "Your Lordship," the warden said urgently, "I cannot allow the
accused, I mean this gentleman, to leave the castle under the present
conditions. There is a mob outside waiting for him, and they're up to
no good. I do not have enough guards to provide protection."

"As I told thee, dear friend, the Lord—" George Fox began in his
insufferable way, but Thomas Fell had had enough.

"Mr. Fox," he said sharply, "we are responsible for your security,
and we do not intend to abdicate that responsibility, not even to the
Almighty, I regret to say. Mr. Farragut!"

"Yes, Your Lordship?"

"Have you a room in the castle where Mr. Fox can stay overnight?"

"Well . . ." The warden obviously did not like the idea.

"What about the provost's quarters? Is anyone lodging there right
now? Who is provost this sitting?"

"Justice Somerset, Your Lordship."

"Well, he lives here in Lancaster. So, put the gentleman in the southeast tower. Tomorrow morning at daybreak . . ."

The door suddenly burst open and there were Margaret and Henrietta
Best in a state of delighted excitement. They threw themselves upon
their husbands with keening cries; it was startling and incongruous, like
being attacked by swans.

"Just a moment, just a moment, dear heart!" From the corner of his
eye Thomas Fell saw that Best was also trying to calm his spouse, who
seemed to be sobbing on his shoulder. What a ludicrous spectacle!
"Mr. Farragut!"

"Yes, Your Lordship."

"Tomorrow morning, at first light, lead the gentleman through the
passage at the bottom of the dungeons to the guardhouse in the fields.
It is still open, I presume?"

"I think so, Your Lordship; but it has not been used for a long time."

"I should hope not. Your horse is stabled at the Three Swans, Mr. Fox, is it not?"

George Fox nodded moodily. "I am not happy——" he began.

"Very well, Mr. Farragut," Thomas Fell continued, cutting him short, "arrange for the horse to be fetched and fed and watered. Then, at first light, lead this gentleman out through the passage, and that will be where your responsibility ends." He turned to Fox. "After that, Mr. Fox, I cannot offer you any further protection, and I must urge you to make your way to London without tarrying."

"Friend Thomas——"

"Mr. Fox, I will not discuss the matter! You shall remove yourself from this county forthwith, and if I find you making any further trouble within my jurisdiction, I'll clap you in prison for disturbance of the peace. Is that clear?"

"London?" Margaret asked.

"As to thee, dear heart," he said tersely, "next time be gracious enough to knock before bursting into the judges' chambers. Now, will everybody please vacate these premises and give the justices an opportunity to change?"

George Fox acquiesced. He strode out; Margaret went after him. It was the moment when Thomas Fell realized the wisdom of William Best's decision.

* * *

"George!" Margaret Fell cried, a cry of anguish. Gathering her skirts, she ran after his receding figure, down the echoing corridor. "George!"

This time he turned around. Breathlessly she faced him. "Is it true?! Art thou going to London?!"

She saw it pained him. Was it because of the warden or because he hated to be accosted like this?

"I am indeed."

"But why?"

"To labor with Oliver Cromwell."

The coldness, the rejection in his voice! Suddenly she found herself in the throes of an anguish that struck her almost as a physical pain. "Why didst thou not tell me?!" she cried. "Was it thy idea? Was it my husband's . . . ?"

"Margaret," he said with a terseness she had never heard before, "control thyself. I would not go if it were not the will of the Lord."

Suddenly her anguish turned into fury. "I don't know about the will of the Lord!" she snapped. "But thou certainly art obeying the will of my husband!"

His face darkened; the warden stood open-mouthed, fascinated by the scene. It brought her to her senses; she must not make a spectacle of herself, accosting him as if she were a mistress he was about to desert. "It's not for myself I speak," she said, recovering her composure, "but for all those in my house and in Ulverston whom thou hast set on the road to convincement and whom thou must not desert, not yet! Before going to London, thou must make sure that thy new congregation is firmly anchored in the faith." She spoke formally, vividly aware of the warden's interest.

"I will return in God's time," George said. He had said it before; now it struck her as insufferably pedantic and wily.

"I see," she said. "He comes in handy at times, doesn't He?" She turned away, her stomach sinking at the audacity of that remark. She must get hold of herself, she thought as she hurried back to the chambers. She should not allow herself to express these excessive emotions. But ever since she had been struck in the back by that piece of trash on the courtroom steps she had seemed to live on the brink of a scream; never before had she allowed herself to make such a scene, other than with her husband. And that warden!

She set her jaw, patted her hair into place, straightened her bodice and opened the door. Her husband was waiting. Henrietta Best looked tear-streaked but radiant; William Best still had his arm around her shoulders, a touching scene. "Well?" Margaret asked curtly. "Art thou ready?"

Thomas raised his eyebrows at her tone. Oh, the insufferable self-assurance of that man! Suddenly all her misery, anger and bewilderment balled together into resentment against her husband. The coward! The devious, conniving coward! Wait till she got him home!

In the chaise on the way to the inn, with Henrietta Best opposite her in the swaying contraption, her resentment hardened as the whole nefarious scheme became clear to her at last. Of course Thomas had engineered it all, from the beginning: the trial, the letter to Cromwell, the—no! Even the permission for the Quakers to meet at the Hall? Could that have been part of a preconceived plan too? And she had been so overwhelmed by that gesture! Oh! The blackguard, the hypocrite!

She could not wait to confront him, but—pox on it!—first they had to sup with the Bests in the noisy taproom of the Boar and Stag. Wines, venison, sweetbreads, Drambuie, mocha; it looked as though Thomas were feasting the other couple out of sheer contrariness, knowing that she was chafing to be rid of them. He chatted away, witty, urbane; normally, she would have reveled in his high spirits; now she felt like slapping his face. Look at him! The schemer, the saltimbanco! And that dear, happy couple, billing and cooing like moon-sick adolescents! It was so touching she could vomit.

She barely managed to swallow a bite. Thomas did not appear to notice, let alone care. So she ate nothing, and sat there with eyes like cocked pistols, virtually foaming at the mouth, choking in speechless fury while he went on stringing one fatuous anecdote after another, all of which she had heard fifty times before. He waved his hands in the candlelight, making the couple of geese laugh and titter, as if he

were conducting them like Master Purcell the King's Musick. Oh! The
coward!

Finally, they rose to retire. By that time there was not a soul left
in the taproom except a pair of elderly topers lolling like bloodhounds
over their tankards. The couples wished each other a profuse good
night outside the Bests' door; when at last the lovers had vanished
inside, undoubtedly to indulge in some geriatric bundling, Thomas had
the effrontery to proffer his arm with a rakish smile, as if about to
seduce her. If the footman had not been there with the candelabrum
to light their way, she would have kicked his shins; as it was, she
responded with a smile of her own, put her little hand on his manly
arm and let herself be guided to their bedchamber with the meekness
of a dove. Her maid was waiting for her in the room; she dismissed
the girl with a smile. The moment they were alone she confronted him,
eyes blazing. "Well! That was a successful conspiracy, wasn't it, my
canny friend?!"

"Pardon?"

Look at him! The innocence, the astonishment! "Don't stand there
as if thou hadst been struck in the butt by an arrow!" She was barely
able to keep her voice down. "Thou knowest full well what I'm talking
about! What a cowardly thing, what a miserable, sneaky . . . For a
grown man! The Vice Chancellor of the County Palatine! Ugh! I
would have expected that kind of trickery from a London whore! *Bah!"*
She realized she was shouting; to regain control, she turned away and
started to undress.

"Dear heart, much as I admire thy performance, would it be possible to inform me what it's all about?"

She swung around to face him. Look at him! The smugness! "Thomas
Fell," she said with quavering calm, "we have had conflicts before, we
have often stood facing each other without much love in our hearts,
but never, *never* have I despised thee! Yes! I despise thee! Bah!
Ugh!" She turned away again. Really, she should try to control herself. Hands trembling, she continued to unbutton her pestilential gown.

"Look, sweeting." His calm, reasonable voice was insufferable. "I
understand that thou art distressed by the tensions of the past two days.
But let us try to discuss it in an adult, rational manner. Now. What
exactly dost thou object to with such ravishing vehemence?"

His mocking suaveness undid her good resolutions; at the sight of his
smile, his gloating triumph, she threw herself on him and battered his
chest with her fists, crying, "Swine, swine, swine! Devious, treacherous,
cowardly *swine!"* It was not what she had wanted to do, it was
despicable in someone who called herself a child of the Light. What
was worse, it prompted him to take her in his arms and try to subdue
her frenzy with a kiss. That made her spit with rage. "Let me go! Let
me *go,* I say! *Let me go!"* When he refused, she stamped her heel on
his gouty toe, as hard as she could.

"Ouch!" There he went, the gloating gander, dancing around clutching his foot, crying, "That was vile!"

"Pray remember we are lodged in a public inn," she said, suddenly calm and reasonable, but in her heart deeply ashamed. What a vicious thing to have done! But, God help her, he had only himself to blame! First to trick her, then to think he could subdue her with his charms! She turned to the mirror, finished unbuttoning her gown, stepped out of it and crossed to the armoire to put it away. He was sitting on the edge of the bed, holding his foot. Oh, what a treacherous thing for her to have done! Suddenly she felt like rushing to him to help take off his boot, which must hurt him terribly; but she checked herself; first she must know what had happened.

"Well?" she asked, closing the armoire. "Art thou ready to discuss this calmly and reasonably now?"

He did not rise to the bait, but looked at her with a marked lack of tenderness. Well, he would get over it. And he *had* deserved it, richly!

"The whole affair, I gather, was cooked up from the beginning. Warrant, trial, his trip to London . . ."

"Rather."

She had not expected that. "Thou dost not sound at all ashamed."

"My dear, good woman . . ."

Oh, it was going to be one of those speeches. She turned away.

"Let's get one thing straight before we continue this charming *tête-à-tête:* if I had not 'cooked this up,' thy saintly young friend would by now have been quartered, disemboweled and had his limbs thrown to the dogs. Not to mention what would have happened to our family and the town of Ulverston."

"I never heard such nonsense in my life! The—"

"Now, that's enough!" he roared with sudden, heart-flipping anger. "I am sick of thy irresponsible extravagances! All our married life, so help me, thou hast managed to create a seasonal frenzy, but this time thou hast gone too far! Look at the violence of the mob in the square; damn it, thou hast been struck by a dead cat thyself!"

"It was not a dead cat. It was a cabbage."

"Oh! Merciful Christ!" He rose, forgetting his toe. "Ouch!" There he went again, poor man, dancing with his foot in his hand. She could not stand it any longer; she was terribly, terribly sorry.

"Here—let me help thee out of thy boot."

He looked as if he wanted to kick her with it, then he surrendered, slumped onto the bed, stuck out his leg, let her grab hold of the boot and start tugging. He winced and moaned; at last, with a jerk that made him squeal, it came off. She dropped it, knelt in front of him and took his poor foot in her hands. "I'm so sorry," she said with sincere contrition.

"Gently!" he moaned. "Don't touch it!"

"Oh, excuse me . . ."

"I'm afraid this will need an apothecary. Pray bring me that little footstool. Then go and call the footman. See if he can find me someone prepared to bind it up at this hour."

"Oh, for heaven's sake! I told thee I was sorry! No need to make a whole masque of it!" But she went to fetch the stool and helped him rest his heel on it, on a pillow. "Now, is that better?"

He looked at her with the same chilling remoteness she had seen in George's face when she pleaded with him to stay. She was overcome by a sudden sense of loneliness. "Couldst thou not have told me?" she asked. "Couldst thou not have trusted me?"

"No."

"Why not? I would have understood. To do all this behind my back . . ."

"I am sorry, dear heart, I do not feel well. Wouldst thou be kind enough to call the footman? I'm in great pain."

She knew he was exploiting his miserable toe to make her feel contrite, but the sense of loneliness was so frightening that she threw all her accumulated knowledge of the laws of marital combat to the winds and collapsed beside him, her head on the counterpane. Her hands sought his; she held on to him tightly, desperately, as she wept.

But he did not respond. He let her sob her heart out while gazing down upon her, no doubt, with his Chief Justice's eyes. She let go of his hands, wiped her tears and looked up. Yes, there he sat: as cold and indifferent as the stars.

"What if I help thee get into bed?" she asked. "I'll bind up thy foot myself with a towel. Try to let it come to rest first, before having it bound up by an apothecary and being immobilized for days."

"I'm afraid I have no choice."

"*Truly* I'm sorry! I *told* thee I'm sorry! But I didn't think I stamped on it that hard—"

"Margaret, Margaret!" he said in a fatherly tone. "What am I going to do with thee, once I'm gone?"

"Gone where?" She looked at him, wide-eyed.

"Where dost think? My next circuit."

"When?"

"As soon as I am able to move with this cursed foot. I'll have to stay here until it dies down."

Much as she loathed the idea of his leaving, she was not going to plead with yet another man to stay.

"Don't fret," she said, rising. "I'll look after myself." She put on a robe and went to the door. There she picked up the candelabrum and asked, "Now, art thou sure about the apothecary?"

"Rather."

She wished she could start all over again, come in and face him, this time reasonably, without anger. But if there was one thing life had taught her, it was not to cry over spilled milk. "Very well," she said and left, despising him for hiding behind his toe.

On her way to the stairs she passed the Bests' door and was overcome by envy.

*　　*　　*

"We should talk things out more freely," Henrietta Best whispered in the darkness, her head on her husband's shoulder, ensconced in his arm in the unfamiliar bed. "Communicate with each other. I knew about that business with John McHair and Sawrey long before we spoke about it, and by then I had become, well, bitter. . . . *Enfin* . . ." Had she still not given up trying to change the man? Did she still not realize that he was incurably English? She might as well try to persuade a penguin to fly. And why change him? Why complain about the fact that he grew older, was uncommunicative, rinsed his mouth with wine, was full of puerile subterfuge one moment and awesome courage the next? Oh, that man, that dear, heroic man! Never since saving her from the clutches of prostitution had he made such a sacrifice of love, shown so incontestably what she meant to him. *"Oh, chéri chéri,"* she whispered, "forgive me, I don't really mean all that. I love thee as thou art. *Je t'aime, mon petit pompom. Je t'adore . . ."* She listened, waiting for his response, but all she heard was a slow, soft snoring.

Ah, well, poor dear, he must be exhausted after all those emotions. Fancy, giving away his entire estate, his freedom, for her sake, so she might be free of the ghosts of the past. Did he not realize that what had really freed her, however, was the heartbreaking tenderness of the sacrifice? Who cared whether they lost their estate, their money, their luxuries? She did not even care should the second condition of the bail be invoked, if he ended up in prison, for she would go to prison with him. Oh, yes, she would. Up to now the mere word "prison" had filled her with—no, no; not even now. She could not think of it. She must never think of it again. There were things that could not be remembered, even in this utter security, this bliss.

"William?" she whispered. *"Guillaume? Mon amour?* I love thee."

There was no response. With a sigh she settled down, and was coaxed into drowsiness by his snoring. As she was about to fall asleep she thought: 'Blind, that's what I have been. Everybody has been ranting about saints for weeks, myself included, and all that time, God help me, I had one right by my side. That is to say, if a saint is a person transfigured by love.'

*   *   *

At dead of night George Fox was shaken awake and a voice whispered urgently, "Come on, fellow! It's time to go!"

He opened his eyes and saw in the translucent darkness the silhouette of a man he did not recognize. For a moment, disoriented by sleep, he was at a loss, then he recognized the small, triangular room, the lumpy bed, the narrow, slotted window. He was in a tower of Lancaster Castle, the provost's quarters. The man must be a guard, it was time to leave. "All right, friend," he said, "just a few moments and I'll be ready."

Unselfconsciously he knelt by the side of the bed on which he had lain down, it seemed, only a few hours before, fully dressed. As always, before setting out for a new voyage, he felt the need to invoke the Presence, however briefly, and entrust himself to His loving care.

But the man behind him would not wait. "Come on, fellow," he said, touching him again, his voice impatient. "Do that once thou art in the open. My orders are to get thee out of here as fast as I can. Hurry up. All is ready."

With a sigh he rose and followed the man out toward the narrow stairway, which was dark and unfamiliar. "Why no light?" he asked.

"Hush!" the voice whispered below him. "They are out there in the square, waiting for thee. Now hold thy tongue or we'll set the pigeons off and they'll know we are on our way down."

A crowd still out there? He could not believe it. Mob violence was like a straw fire: it flared, fiercely and frighteningly, to die down as quickly as it had been enflamed. The whole thing was suspect, this business of having to creep out before dawn through a secret passage, fleeing for his life. He was convinced that Thomas Fell wanted to make absolutely sure he left the county. The people out there, if there were any, might well be Fell's creatures; he would not put that beyond him. Maybe the whole business about the letter to Cromwell had been a hoax. But no, that part of it was genuine. Fell had told him he would send the letter care of the inn at Bentham. The fact that he had not given it to him here but planted it well outside the county was proof that he was sincere.

"Careful!" the voice whispered. "Here's a high step, then we're in the corridor. Feel it?"

With his foot he felt a threshold in the darkness and stepped over it. The footfall of the other, walking away, echoed in a hollow vault. Gradually he began to discern the man's silhouette in the darkness, tinged with the first hint of the dawn behind a row of high, mullioned windows. Finally, a door opened and there was a light. He entered the same little office where he had arrived from the chaise. It was lit by a candle on a desk, behind which sat a small man with a beaked nose whom he had not seen before.

"Ah, there you are!" The man smiled unpleasantly. "Ready to weasel out, eh?"

"Is the gate down below open?" the guard asked.

George looked around and saw the guard's face for the first time, a cavernous face with a scowl of derision.

"Yes," the man behind the desk said. "Here, light a lantern, thou wilt need it." He shoved the candlestick toward the edge of the desk and revealed that he was a hunchback.

"Thank you, warden." The guard lit a lantern with the candle.

"Well, good luck," the hunchback said with another unpleasant smile. "Don't get caught down there. We are overcrowded as it is."

George felt like giving a loving retort, but the guard would not let him. "Come along, fellow! We haven't got all morning. Lively, now!" He went to a glass door. Before opening it, he turned around and added, "Just walk across behind me, without looking around. Don't run, for they'll be watching us through the gate. For all they know, this is a changing of the guard. Take that white hat off, though; it stands out a mile."

George felt his stubbornness aroused, but there was be no point in taking a stand now. The whole thing had gone too far; all he could do was obey orders and let himself be taken out as fast as possible. He took off his hat.

"Hide it under thy cloak."

He did so.

"That'll do," the guard said. "All set? Let's go." He opened the door.

They entered a dark cave which George recognized as the gateway. To his surprise, he realized that there were indeed people in the square beyond the gates. As they set out to cross the cave toward a flickering torch, he heard a murmur of voices. Someone called, "Hey! What have you done with the blasphemer?" The guard did not reply; they strode quickly across. Underneath the torch stood another guard, armed with a halberd, a key ring dangling from his belt. Without a word, the man pulled open a low, arched door on squealing hinges. "Come along," the guide urged. Stooping, they entered a deeper darkness.

George found himself on a stone landing with a black pit in the center. As the guard with the lantern began to descend into it, he realized it was a stairway, presumably to the dungeons. Suddenly he was struck by an unexpected apprehension. He thought it was the stench that came from below, but it was something else, an evil in the air. He knew prisons; entering one never failed to strike him with a qualm of revulsion, but never before had he felt it so strongly; and this time he was not even entering as a prisoner. The only words he could find for the evil that seemed to swirl around him as he followed the guide down into the echoing well, steadying himself on the wall dripping with moisture, were those of St. Paul. *"For we wrestle not against flesh and blood, but against principalities, against powers, against the rulers of the darkness of this world, against spiritual wickedness in the air."* They reached a landing, from which a number of dark passages led in all directions; then his blood froze. From the dark, gaping mouths of the passages came a sound he had never heard before, a hooting, bellowing, shrieking chorus of hatred that, unmistakably, was directed at them. He asked, startled, "What is that?"

"That?" the guard replied, his cavernous face twisted in a scowl of contempt. "That's the beasts we keep locked up in here." He yelled into one of the dark passages, "Shut up, you rabble! Shut up or I'll rip your bloody eyeballs out!" The disembodied voices went berserk and he turned away with a satisfied grin. The rumble of the avalanche of hatred was amplified a hundredfold by echoes. Curses, shrieks, catcalls; the din was deafening. As they continued their descent, quiet seemed to return; but when they reached the next landing the same thing happened. The voices of invisible prisoners shrieked, hooted, booed, bellowed, screamed invective and obscenities, a chorus of shackled fury so ferocious, so insane with hatred, that George wanted to rush headlong down those stairs, away from the unspeakable evil.

But he checked himself, forcing himself to think, 'People, they are people. They are men like thyself. Each one of those men has that of

God within him, like thee. It should be thy duty to go in there and minister to them.' 'But no,' he told himself, 'no, that is not possible! I must go to London, to meet the Protector. God wills it.'

The call within him became unmistakable when, on the third landing, the chorus of the damned again assailed them in insane fury. *"George,"* the small still voice within him urged, *"George, go in there. I want to reach them with My love, but I cannot do so without thee, George. All I have is thee."*

So real was the despair of that of God within him that tears came to his eyes, but he could not do it, he could not, he lacked the strength. *"But I will be with thee, George! I will be with thee!"* the voice urged within him, smaller now, as if drawing away. But he could not do it, he could not; he was afraid.

He continued down the spiral staircase, haunted by remorse. There were four landings; then they finally reached the entrance to what must be the underground passage. As he stood facing a last choice, there came the most terrifying sound of all: a high-pitched, desperate shrieking, accompanied by a rhythmic clanging. It snuffed out the last spark of his courage. "For God's sake . . ."

The guard laughed. "Those are our lunatics. That's how they sing, slamming their chains against the bars. Pretty, isn't it?" He opened a gate in the darkness. "Well, fellow, here goes. Half a mile and thou art as free as a bird. Here, take the lantern, give it to the man in the guardhouse. He'll get it back to me. Don't break thy neck, there are rocks about."

"Can I get lost anywhere?"

"No, it's dead straight. Half a mile and thou wilt come upon a flight of steps up to a hatch door; just knock and somebody will open."

George took the lantern and set out.

"Good luck, fellow!" the guard shouted after him, with echoes. "Whatever thou dost, don't come back!"

As George penetrated into the narrow tunnel, stumbling over stones, startled by rats, the din behind him gradually died away. At last he reached a flight of stone steps, covered with dust that tasted bitter on his tongue as he raised it with his boots. He was coughing as he banged on the hatch door above him. It was pulled upward instantly and there stood Charles Cotten, Justice Thomas Fell's groom, grinning at him.

"Well, welcome! How didst thou like being buried alive?"

George's sense of failure was so overwhelming that he could not bring himself to answer. Finally, he emerged into the open and found his horse peaceably grazing in a meadow outside a small building. The young day looked precious and pure. Dew was on the grass, mist was rising from a brook; beyond, like a promise, lay the fells, still hazy with the night. After the dungeons they looked inexpressibly beautiful; the sense of beatitude they exuded sharpened his despair. Looking at that blessed world, he felt as if he were sharing a reward he had not earned.

"He's been watered and fed," the groom said behind him. "So, on thy way. Don't let 'em catch up with thee."

He walked toward his horse, mounted and gazed for a moment at the glory of the dawning day. Then he said, "May the Lord, in His mercy, forgive us all."

He clicked his tongue, tugged the reins and went down the bridle path onto the fells, toward the hills on the horizon.

* * *

John Sawrey had risen well before daybreak. He slunk out of the inn, leaving the money for his lodging on the counter; he roused the night groom and had him saddle his horse. Toward midday, after a strenuous ride, he finally reached the brogs to Cark and discovered that the tide was coming in. So deep was his depression that he considered riding out onto the sands all the same, despite the certainty of being engulfed by the quicksands, but no, he would not give Fell and Best that satisfaction.

Even so, he could not dawdle around here for hours, waiting for the tide to turn; he would run the risk of Fell and Best catching up with him. So he continued along the bridle path at the edge of the bluffs, planning to stay on it until the tide turned. That might take him as far north as Arnside, but he did not care. He needed solitude, time to lick his wounds.

As he rode into a world of increasing solitude and wildness, his depression lessened. He had merely missed a shortcut to his goal. Sooner or later he would unseat Thomas Fell and take his place as Lord Chief Justice. In order to achieve that, he would need, above all, a cool head; his worst enemy was this rage, this feeling of inferiority. What rankled most was their concept of him as an upstart, an interloper, a "little" interloper. Damn the woman! To call him "an evil man" had not hurt; on the contrary, it expressed some sort of respect. But "little"! Suddenly his rage erupted all over again, expressing itself in another of those puerile daydreams: this time he was chasing that arrogant, voluptuous female across the fells, subjugating her in the bracken and leaving her bruised and broken, to be dragged to prison by the constable, the only friend he had in the world.

The thought of the constable brought him back to reality. What was he going to say to him? He might be able to make his wife believe that the whole affair had been a victory; the constable was another matter. He was a slow-witted, slow-moving brute who must already have been bewildered, in a dumb, brooding way, by the ridiculous sentence given the poacher. The devil should have been hanged, that's what he deserved. But to do so now would merely aggravate the situation. Fell would be after him like a demon; the execution of a prisoner without due process could cost him his position, just the chance they were waiting for. No, he would have to keep the brute alive. But he would make him suffer! What about branding him with a "P" on his forehead? No good. With his broken nose and his rotted teeth, a scar on his forehead would not disfigure him more than he was already. No, he needed a punishment that would keep him from ever poaching again. Cut off his hand? Yes, that would do it. But on what grounds? The trial was closed, the sentence recorded; the brute would have to commit another crime to justify a more severe penalty. And there he was, locked up in a cell, out of harm's way for a year.

He came upon a gorge that forced him to go down to the beach and up the bluffs again on the other side. As his horse cautiously pussyfooted down the steep path, he became aware for the first time of the world around him: the sands, the seagulls, the clouds, the rippling water silver in the sun. He sniffed the pungent stench of seaweed; the smell brought back his childhood: the little island, the cottage on the cliffs, small lair of security he had shared with his mother, a puppy dog and a cat. What had been the name of the little dog? It was so long ago, so far . . .

As if the name of that animal, long dead and gone, were the key to a lost paradise, he was overcome by a sudden yearning for that state of innocence, that sunlit cove of tenderness. What demon had drawn him away from that world, compelled him to start clawing his way up in the teeming rabbit warren of petty bureaucracy toward some illusory pinnacle of power? Was it ambition? Lust for power? He had always seen it that way and accepted it as such, but as he descended toward the beach he was struck by the suspicion that it was something else, something irrational, some sick compulsion that would not be satisfied even if he were one day to usurp Thomas Fell's place, but would drive him on toward some dark haze on the horizon, some chimeral goal.

For a moment he was afraid. Why not be content with what he possessed? A good wife, land, esteem, power . . . But what about the faithless harlot who had made a fool of him? She was the first woman in his life who had done so, yet she had been the last he would have suspected; she had been young and plump and poor, a virgin when he took her. The thought of her tipped the scales. The worthless whore! The slut! God knew how long she had been clutching louts between her thighs at his expense, in the bed he was paying for! 'That little man,' she must have thought, 'let's stick some horns on his head.' Suddenly it all seemed part of one stinging insult: the faithless wench, the poacher, Best standing bail. The only one at his mercy was the poacher.

As he climbed the bluffs again and continued his ride, he deliberated as to how he could wreak his revenge on that hairy, repulsive body.

CHAPTER SIX

WHEN Bonny Baker learned that George Fox had left for London, he was heartbroken. During all the weeks he had been lying on his cot under the eaves of the stable loft, gazing at the rivers and the lakes in the pine boards overhead, watching flies, listening to the cooing of the pigeons in the gutter, George had come to see him only once.

Bonny had been delighted to see his friend stoop in through the low doorway, but George had been different, subdued, without much to say, watching him with moody eyes, without his usual jolliness. Finally he had mumbled a rambling prayer full of the words "love" and "truth" and left after a cautious handshake. Obviously, George had been ashamed because he had tried a miracle and failed. How silly of him! Of course, it would have been nice if that leg could have been cured without pain and these endless dreary days in bed, but that was not George's fault. All that counted was his friendship; now he was gone, and he had not even said goodbye.

Without Ann Traylor, Bonny would have felt like dying of misery. She turned up unexpectedly that same evening when it was almost dark, ducking into his little room with a candle and a parcel under her arm. At first he thought she had come to fetch something, maybe Harry Martin's mattress. But she had come just to see him; the parcel under her arm turned out to be books. "Bonny, my lad," she said, matter-of-fact and rather stern, "it is time thou didst use this idleness. Thou hast learned how to read in the orphanage, hast thou not?"

He had, but the thought of getting back to it was depressing. "All right," she said briskly, "I'll come every evening from now on and give thee a lesson. It will be late, but thou hast all day to sleep." She pulled up a stool by the side of his bed, sat down and opened a book. "Let's see how much thou rememberest. Here, read this: *'Adam ate the apple that Eve . . .'* What does it say?"

"Eve—Eve peeled for him," he invented.

She looked at him disapprovingly, but her green eyes were not cross at all. *"Picked* for him! Don't guess! Read what it says, not what thou thinkest it says. Next line. *'Adam . . .'* Well?"

"*'Adam*—something *Eve . . .'* "

"Spell it! What is the first letter?"

"W."

"And the next?"

"E . . . D . . . wedded! *'Adam wedded Eve.'* "

"See? Thou canst read, if only thou tryest. *'Adam wedded Eve, and—'* What does the rest say?"

"D-E . . ."

"No. Thou hast just read D. Look, is that the same letter? No. So?"

"B?"

"Right! *'Adam wedded Eve and b*—'"

"Beg—begat! *'Adam wedded Eve and begat.'*"

"Good! And what did he beget? A—"

"Abel and C-A . . . and Cain. *'Adam wedded Eve and begat Abel and Cain.'*" He began to enjoy the lesson.

She returned every evening and the lessons broke the tedium, but she could not dispel the dull indifference that lay over him like a pall after George's departure. He brooded about it until he finally decided that rather than being embarrassed about the failed miracle, George blamed him for it. One night he blurted it all out to Ann Traylor.

She looked at him with a frown. "Well, of all the sniveling, self-pitying notions! Thou shouldst be ashamed of thyself, Boniface Baker! George Fox is a godly man, such an idea would never enter his head!"

"Then why didn't he come to say goodbye to me? Why did he look so stern that one time he was here?"

"Because he is a man," Ann answered. "Some men are good at healing people, but few of them are any good at visiting the sick. That is why I am here and not Harry Martin or Thomas Woodhouse. I did not even ask them, for they would have behaved like George Fox. Something about a sick person makes a man uncomfortable and eager to get away. It does not mean they don't like thee. It simply means they are not perfect."

"I want George to be perfect," he said sulkily.

"Don't talk nonsense," she snapped, opening the book. "Nobody is perfect except Jesus, and even He had moments we don't talk about."

"When?"

"Never mind. Fourteenth lesson: *'When Noah*—'"

He wanted to hear about Jesus' moments; it sounded much more interesting. "What did He do that was not perfect?"

But Ann was not to be drawn. "We are reading about Noah, and either we go on reading about Noah or I close this book and go away. What shall it be?"

Glumly he read, "*'When Noah had completed the ark, the beasts of the field . . .'*" Gloom settled over him again, like a cloud.

There were times when he hated Ann and her bossiness, but after a while he became rather fond of her, especially of the little red curls that peeked from under her bonnet at the nape of her neck and the secret mischief in her eyes; they seemed to give away that she was nicer than she pretended to be. She was very inquisitive; she always wanted to know exactly what he had had to eat, how much water he had drunk, whether he had washed his face before going to sleep; but she smelled nice.

It shook him when one night she came in, green eyes blazing, and cried, "Oh! I can't *wait* to get out of this place!"

The idea of her leaving upset him. He looked at her with anguish as she dragged up her little stool with an angry rumble on the floorboards and sat down beside him. She held out her hand and snapped, "All right! Where is it?"

"Where is what?"

"Thy exercise book! Don't tell me thou hast been lying here all day doing nothing!"

She was so angry that tears came to his eyes. "What's the matter? Have I done something wrong?"

She looked at him fiercely; for a moment he thought she would smack him, then her face softened and she said in a different tone, "Of course not. It has nothing to do with thee." Suddenly she bent over and kissed his cheek. He sat there, mouth open, gaping at her. She laughed. "Don't look as though I had thrown thee in the brook! Hast thou never had a kiss from a girl before?"

He shook his head, his hand on his cheek.

"Well, there's thy first. Now where's that exercise book?"

He took it from under his pillow and gave it to her. When she opened it, he asked, "What's the matter, Ann?"

"Nothing." Her face clouded over again. "They've come back, that's all."

"The judge and the mistress?"

"No, only she. He is off again. And George Fox is on his way to London, so that'll probably be the last we'll see of *him.*"

"Oh . . ."

She looked up sharply. "Don't tell me thou art going into convulsions too!"

"I?"

"Thou shouldst hear the wailing and gnashing of teeth in the kitchen! *Oh George, oh George!*" She mimicked them angrily. "As if they had lost a lover! And Mistress Fell moping around with a face like a basset hound! Ugh! All that over a vain, pompous jawbox!"

"Who?"

"George Fox, who else?! Well, all I can say is: good riddance! But I seem to be the only one. The lot of them are slavering on each other's shoulders, keening like the Welsh. Next thing thou knowest, they'll put ashes on their heads! And why? Don't ask *me!*" She flicked the pages of the book angrily.

"I'm sorry," he said. He was; but he was not as sad as he would have expected.

"Sorry? Tell me why!" She fixed him with her angry green eyes. "Explain to me why everybody acts as if they had lost a lover!"

"I don't know," he said, "but he was a nice man. I liked him."

"Why didst thou like him? Tell me."

"Why art thou so angry with me?"

"I am not angry with thee. I'm curious, that's all."

"Well, he—he's nice."

"Nice. After what he did to thy leg? After his coming to see thee only once?"

"He did not break my leg. And thou didst tell me thyself why he did not come to see me."

"I? What on earth did I say?"

"That he was a man, so he did not enjoy coming to see the sick."

"Did I say that? Yes, I suppose I did. Well, let's get on with the lesson. What hast thou done since yesterday?"

"He made everybody very happy for a while," he said.

"Oh, yes, for a while! But thou shouldst see them now! Thou shouldst see that poor woman!"

"Which poor woman?"

"Never mind. Is this all thou hast done?"

"I'm sure not everybody is carrying on that way. What about Harry Martin, for instance?"

"Oh, that one!" Her contempt was startling. "He's the only one who got something out of the visit of St. George. He got Mabby."

"Got Mabby? Are they betrothed?"

"Betrothed!" She looked at him as if she thought he needed a haircut. Then, quick as a flash, she bent over and kissed him on the cheek once more, this time the other one. Again it was all over before he realized it. He blushed, furious with himself for doing so. She said, "Bonny, thou art the only innocent in this Hall."

He did not like that. It sounded as if she were talking to a child, and he did not feel like a child at that moment.

She looked at him sternly. "What hast thou written this exercise with? A tar brush?"

For the first time since the lessons had started he saw through her sternness. It was nonsense, really. He gave her a grin and said, "Yes."

She raised her eyebrows; for a moment she looked as if she were about to make a sharp retort. Then, surprisingly, she burst into giggles and hid her face in her hands. "Oh," she said, giggling, "they make me so *mad!*"

"I like thee mad."

"Ha! My good boy, thou hast never seem me *really* mad. Believe me!"

Yesterday he would have been impressed; now he wished his leg were better.

"It's that they call it *religion!*" she cried, shaking her fists. "That *she* calls it religion! The whole thing is *disgusting!* That's what *I* think!"

"Who is 'she'?"

She turned on him. "Dost thou call it religion too?"

"What?"

"Thy friendship, or whatever it is, for George Fox?"

He looked at her. Her bonnet was askew, her hair tousled with anger. It was as if, without realizing it, she was shedding a disguise. "How old art thou, Ann?" he asked.

She looked surprised. "Seventeen. Why?"

"I am twelve."

"So?"

"So nothing. I just am."

"Oh, what am I *bothering* for!" She turned to the exercise book again.

"Tell me honestly. What is it they call religion? Who is 'she'?"

"Never thee mind!"

"George talked to me about religion once, on his horse while we were riding home from Colonel Best's. I was afraid, for I was sure that Mr. Woodhouse or Will Hartford would beat me. He made me feel, well, different. He talked about God and . . . well, that was different too."

"Wilt thou ever finish a sentence so a person can understand?"

He grinned. Her cap had been shoved up another inch; she was getting younger all the time, a friend, not someone for whose sake he washed and learned lessons.

"Well? Thou dost not wail and whinny and yammer 'I'll never experience the presence of God again!' Or dost thou?"

He shrugged his shoulders. "I suppose not," he said musingly. "I never experienced God again, not after that time on his horse. But I don't care. I don't particularly want to. I'm happy the way I am."

"I'm glad to hear it!"

"As long as thou art here."

She raised her eyebrows. "Aha! I spoke too soon!"

"Ann," he said seriously. "Thou art not planning to leave, art thou?"

Her face went blank with amazement. "How didst thou know?"

His heart sank. "Art thou?"

"If things get any worse around here, I certainly will."

"How, worse? I haven't been downstairs for weeks."

"I wouldn't mind so much if only they would be honest with themselves!" she cried, flaring up again. "What makes me so sick is the dishonesty, the pretense of it all! Why not say frankly that they like it for its own sake? Why call it religion?"

"What do they like?"

"Calling everybody thee and thou! Calling the mistress *Margaret!* Refusing to doff their hats for priests, constables, squires! Just—just letting it rip, the way Mabby did! Yoo hoo! Off with my clothes, stark naked in the moonlight, setting all the men jumping like rabbits! Thy friend Harry Martin: before you could say Jack Robinson, there he was without a stitch, galloping after her, ready to—well, never mind. Anyway, that's what I mean! Do it, but don't call it religion! *That's* blasphemous! Yes, blasphemous. I wish they had locked him up, white hat and all. For, judging by the results, that's all his message amounted to: Let's raise the devil! And why? Because we love it! I'd love it too, damn it. I like mischief as much as the next one, but I know that isn't God! If it is . . ." Suddenly she crossed herself.

"Ann!" he said, astounded. "Art thou a Papist?"

"Why dost thou ask such a fool thing?"

"Because thou didst cross thyself."

"Oh, stop it! It's just—just a sign against the hex. Think of thy lesson!" She turned to the book again.

"Ann . . ."

"Well?"

"Thou wouldst not want to do that, wouldst thou?"

"What?"

"Take all thy clothes off in front of—of everyone?"

She looked at him stonily. "Boniface Baker, thou knowest very well I was not talking about *myself*. I was talking about Mabby."

"Ann?"

"Now what?"

"Don't go away."

He saw her eyes change as she looked at him. "I'm sorry," she said. "I shouldn't have said that."

"But if it's true . . ."

"It isn't true! I just said it because I was angry. Where would I go? I'm like thee, I'll never get out of this place. I've got nobody. But a person can dream, can't she?"

"Why shouldn't we get out?"

"Where wouldst thou go? None of the houses here will take thee in unless thou hast a letter of recommendation. And Thomas Woodhouse is not going to give that to thee, just like that. Ha! That's where his religion would stop in a hurry."

"Art thou an orphan?"

"Yes."

"A foundling?"

"Sometimes I wish I had been."

"Why?"

"My father was a drunkard. Now can we get on with the lesson?"

"Maybe mine was too. I don't know."

"Dost thou want a lesson tonight or no?"

"No."

"All right!" She snapped the exercise book shut. "In that case I bid thee good night." She rose.

"Ann!"

Her eyes, as she looked down on him, were green and fiery. Her cap now sat on the back of her head.

"Wilt thou have meeting with me?"

"Pardon?"

"Those times we all sat in a circle and said nothing, I liked that. Can't we do that, the two of us, just for a little while?"

Her face was suddenly soft and amazed. "What a strange boy thou art."

"Why? Are they no longer doing it?"

"Oh, yes . . ." She sat down again and folded her hands in her lap. Then she gave him a sharp glance. "Thou art not fooling me, art thou?"

"Why?" He looked at her, troubled.

"All right. Here goes. Meeting." She closed her eyes and bent her head.

He watched her. He did not know why she had made him feel like having meeting. It was as it had been that time with George on the horse: a great joy growing inside him until he wanted to shout.

He closed his eyes and folded his hands and thought, 'Goodbye, George. Thou wert my friend, I will never forget thee.' Then all became still within him.

* * *

"Well, John, how are we doing in there?"

Startled, John McHair turned away from the little barred window through which he had been gazing at the square of blue sky, all that was left to him of the woods, the animals, the wind in the treetops, the whispering rain at night. "Aye?" he asked, blinded by the daylight, not recognizing the man entering his cell.

"Thou must have been wondering why I let thee off so lightly."

God's mercy! It was Justice Sawrey! "Aye, sir," he replied meekly, suddenly afraid. What did he want?

"Well, let me explain," the little justice said affably. "Thank you, Constable. I would like a word with the prisoner in private, please."

The constable, huge and menacing, grumbled and went out, his boots rustling in the straw. He closed the iron-clad door behind him and disappeared. Justice Sawrey locked it with a key, which he put in his waistcoat pocket. There was something reassuring about him, and John McHair's apprehension lessened. He had never felt any hostility toward the little man; it made sense, in the world of the forest, that a captured marauder took his punishment without protest, it was part of life. The sentence he had received had indeed been lenient, considering that he had poached the man's own game.

"Thou knowest me well enough to realize that it is not my custom to go easy on proven criminals."

No, Justice Sawrey had the reputation of being severe in his verdicts, almost vicious. "Aye, sir," he said.

"Thou must have realized that there was more to it, that there would be a condition. Hasn't thou?"

The fear came back. What was the man up to? "Aye, sir," he said.

"Well, it's very simple." The justice opened up the seat-stick he carried and sat down, draping his cloak over it. "I want to pick thy brains."

"'Scuse me, sir?" It sounded terrifying, he felt his cheeks go cold.

"To get from thee all thou knowest about trapping game. How to spot them, how to approach them, which snares to use . . . I gather that thou usest a club or a stick to brain the animals."

"Aye, sir. Yes, sir, that's true . . ." He felt relieved.

"To be able to do that, thou must approach them very closely. How the devil dost thou manage that?"

"Oh . . . well . . . it's—it's easy sir. I—er—I mean, it needs a lot of practice, but once you've got the knack of it, it's easy."

"Well, tell me about it. How dost thou start? Where dost thou pick up the first scent of, say, a doe? Begin at the beginning."

"Well, sir, I . . . I'm in the woods all the time, sir, so I always know where the animals are."

"Nonsense! How canst thou possibly know where every animal is all the time? Now, don't start telling me fancy stories, man, because if thou art trying to pull the wool over my eyes . . ."

"No, sir! No, sir! I—I'm serious, sir! I mean it, I mean it!" He was profuse in his protests, for he wanted to do what the man asked as honestly as he could. "See, sir, after you have lived in the woods for a while, I mean really lived, not just as a visitor, you realize that every animal has its daily run. A doe, as you say, will always be more or less in the same spot at a certain time, day or night. I mean sun time, sir, not clock time."

"Why should an animal do that?"

"Well, sir, that's just the way it is, sir. Animals are like that. You can see it with a farmer's horse, sir. Once it has made a certain run a few times, it will find the way itself. I don't know why, sir, but that's the way it is, sir. Believe me, sir, I'm not telling you a story."

"All right. I accept that. Then what?"

He could not understand it. Why did the judge want to know all this? Never mind why; he had better do as he was asked. He didn't mind talking about it; it was a poor substitute for freedom, but to talk about the woods and the animals aroused a deep, dormant craving within him. "Well, sir, you see, sir, in order to trap an animal, you yourself have to become part of the forest, have your own run, so to speak. Every animal knows at all times where the others are; the moment there is a change in the routine, they know there is something wrong. That's how the alert runs through the forest, sir. Even if you are as silent as a shadow, sir, and a little rabbit on its run sees you and hides, then five minutes later it is not in the place where it should have been, and the owl in the tree where it should have been knows that something is amiss and it will hoot, and the whole forest will know there's danger. What you have to do is make yourself part of the daily run, so they expect you at a certain hour in a certain spot. It takes a long time, sir, three or four months, before they accept you as part of their life, sir. But once they do that, they don't hide any more as long as you turn up in the same spot at the same time every day, every night. See, sir?"

The little judge looked at him through narrowed eyes. "Fascinating," he said. He put his hand in his waistcoat pocket, brought out a small silver box, put a pinch of snuff on the back of his hand and inhaled it. "Go on." He put the little box back in his pocket.

"Well, sir, once you have singled out a doe, you begin to draw a little closer each day to her run, without shying her, sir. The moment you are close enough to catch her eye—"

The judge sneezed, startling him. "Excuse me. Thou wert saying?"

"Catch her eye, sir."

"Then what?"

"Then, that's it, sir."

"What dost thou mean, that's it? Dost thou club it?"

"Oh, no, sir, no, sir! Not for a long while yet! No, the moment you catch her eye, that's when it begins, sir."

"What begins?" The judge peered at him like a squirrel.

"Well, you're a man, sir, and she's only a doe, and that's what you have to remember, sir. There comes a moment that the doe knows you are a man, and that you are going to kill her, and that you will come closer every day, until you are close enough to do it."

"I've never heard such nonsense!" the judge exclaimed irritably. "I told thee, don't give me any cock-and-bull stories!"

"I swear to you, sir, I swear to you, that's the way it's done, sir! That's the way I do it!" It seemed terribly important that he convince the man. How could he bring it home to him that this really was the way it happened?

"All right," the judge said, relenting. "Let's begin with the start of the day. Thou art in the forest. Right? Thou art waking up, right?"

"Aye, sir, aye, sir . . ."

"Tell me what happens. Where dost thou sleep? How dost thou wake up?"

"Well, sir, the last six months or so I have been sleeping, er—in, er—in your park, sir, under a gorse bush on a little hillock south of the large meadow. You know where I mean?"

"By the track to the watering pond?"

"Aye, sir, aye, sir! That's where. Now, on your way to the watering pond, if you look to your right, sir, just where it turns for the last time, you will see three gorse bushes, two small and one large, in the shape of a dog, sir, a poodle . . ."

He went on and on, more detailed and vivid as he imagined himself back in that world where, until a week ago, he had ruled over all creatures that rustled, ran, flew and flitted in the forest. He savored it, but it was like heady wine; finally, he was flushed with the freedom, the rapture of life itself.

The judge rose to leave, snapped shut his seat-stick and took the key from his pocket. "Well, John, that was very instructive. But we have only scratched the surface," he said. "I want to know much more. I'll be back tomorrow night, then we can talk for as long as we like." He went to the door, his buckled shoes glinting in the faint light of the window. He stuck the key in the lock; as he was about to open the door, he turned around. "I want to know everything there is to know about poaching," he said. "If thou canst not teach me thy trade, I will have to think about correcting thy punishment." On that ominous note, he left.

John gazed at the closed door, frowning, trying to think. Then he turned around and wandered back to the window, to breathe the clean air and stare at the patch of sky that suddenly looked infinitely precious, taunting. To talk about freedom had been wonderful while it lasted, but it left him restless and disturbed. It had undermined the only condition on which life in prison was possible: acceptance. He knew he could live through the next year locked up in this cage in perpetual twilight by turning himself into a dormant body of unstirring life, asleep, like the trees in the snow-covered forest. That's what he had done, settled down in hibernation. Now that somnolent sense of security was disturbed. To talk about the forest, to go over each day in such detail had stirred up an intense yearning, an anguish that was well-nigh unbearable.

He turned away from the window and started to walk, from door to wall, wall to door, door to wall. It was suicide for a hibernating animal to stir before the spring. A tree that was tricked into budding prematurely by a freakish warm spell was bound to suffer terribly. Suddenly he found himself wishing that the judge would not come back.

His restlessness grew worse when, later, it started to rain outside. He stood with his back to the wall underneath the little window, gray now with low-hanging cloud, and listened to the whispering rain. Voices, small voices, whispering. "Come, John, come, John, come, John."

Oh, Jesus God! He panicked. He began to pace up and down again, faster, faster, he broke into a run, bouncing himself off the wall and the door at every turn; in the end, he crashed into the straw, weak with giddiness. This was insane, he had only a year to go, by breaking prison he would condemn himself to the life of a fugitive for the rest of his days; he would never be really free again, never live happily among the animals again in his glens, his fells, his woods. He would forever be afraid of men; his happiness, his very zest for life would be hollowed out by the knowledge that, in the end, he was bound to be captured. No! Whatever he did, he must not let himself fall under the spell of that dream of freedom, for it was death. "Jesus God," he prayed, "tell that man to leave me alone!"

Outside the little window the rain went on whispering his name.

* * *

From her bedchamber Margaret Fell watched the rain. It came down steadily, monotonously; it might last for days, maybe weeks. It seemed to add to the bleakness in which she had awakened that morning after her first night home. At first it had seemed to be just a reaction, an understandable weariness after the emotions of the past week. But now, with the rain, it seemed to have settled down, like autumn itself. It always started like this: rain, rain, rain, rain, days, nights, weeks of it; then the sky would be swept clean by a gale, become green and bright and cold, and the leaves would fall, and the fells turn dark and the gales of winter come howling across the ocean. After that, life would be frozen solid for months, even the daylight would freeze until, at dead of winter, the day would be no more than a melancholy dusk; if there were clouds, life would be lived by candlelight all day. She did not know why, but this year she could not face it. The very thought that from now on it would get darker and darker, drearier and drearier, bleaker and bleaker . . . She should turn away from that window, occupy herself with the household, but a weary lassitude kept her where she was, gazing out at the rain.

Why this sense of emptiness, listlessness? Was it the thought that it would be two months before Thomas came back? Of course not; she might as well confess it to herself. It was George. She had foreseen that life without him would seem bleak for a while; she had not foreseen that it would hit her this hard. It now seemed as if his mere presence had sharpened the keenness of her senses, enhanced her enjoyment of life. Never had a summer seemed richer, the colors of the garden and the sky more vivid; never before had she felt she could carry with ease not only her household and the estate but all the woes of the world with a feeling of effortless power, the way a bird must feel as it soared in the sky.

That was it: now he was gone, she felt locked up, trapped. For a moment she felt the mad impulse to order her carriage and go after him, become one of his traveling followers until she was strong enough to stand on her own feet. For a moment the idea seemed glorious, it filled her with a rush of hope and eagerness, with life. But she smiled wryly at the rain. Imagine! Her children, the servants, the household, the whole estate depended on her. She had always accepted that without giving it a second thought; it was her life, the purpose for which she lived. Now the fact that she was essential to the well-being of so many people filled her with rebellion. She could not desert them, much as she might yearn to; she was caught. She had solicited their fealty. She had purposely made them dependent on her; it had seemed the only way to fill her life with meaning, especially during the months when Thomas was away. Now, here she was: shackled by her own chains. Oh, that rain! If only she could go riding on the fells; their vast solitude always seemed to replenish her vigor. But riding in the rain was unspeakably dreary. She could smell her cloak getting soaked; she could feel the cold drops wriggle down her back as they always did, however tightly she bundled up. And what was there to look at she had not seen a thousand times? For God's sake! She had to snap out of this before she went crazy with her own morbid gloom!

She walked to the door and suddenly saw him walk away again, down that corridor in the castle. The thought that he might never return gave her a qualm of panic. It could not be! It was impossible! She would be unable to bear it! Was it because of her that he had left? Again she asked herself that question. Maybe she had indeed brought this upon herself, by the way she had run after him like a beheaded chicken. If she had given him the impression that she was just another of those females who went running after him, shrieking, the moment he tried to get away, then chances were she would never set eyes on him again. God only knew what drove that crazy man. That was the one condition for his returning: he would do so only if told to do so by God. How? How could she prevail upon God to do so? How would he know it was God? Did he hear His voice? *"Be still, allow that of God to rise within thee and to guide thy thoughts."* What exactly was it that rose within him and guided his thoughts? What *was* "that of God"? All summer long she had bandied those words about, convinced that their meaning was absolutely clear to her; now she discovered that she did not have the foggiest idea. *'Part of thee, yet not thine.'* *'I see, like my stomach, Priest Lampitt's belly.'* *'No, like thy unborn children.'* How outraged she had been! To say a thing like that to a woman, a lady, whom he had met only minutes before . . . She wished she had asked him to explain himself more fully. That of God. What was it? An invention of his? A fact? There had been moments during meeting, though not nearly as many as she had tried to make herself believe, when she had felt something rise within her, something indefinable that had indeed guided her thoughts. But was it God? George Fox said so. Damn George Fox. Damn, damn, damn George Fox! Damn!

But her methodical mind forced her to probe further. Whatever that of God was in his case, it obviously responded to stimuli from the outside, as when he had shouted "Stop!" at the executioners about to hang that girl in Derby jail, or when he had decided to go and meet Cromwell at her husband's instigation. How could she make that of God in him whisper, *George, go back to Swarthmoor?* That was what God would have to say: *Go back, George, go back to thy helpless children, abandoned by their father!*

Father. Maybe that was the key. Young as he was, he was their spiritual father, it was his duty to return to his children when he heard them cry in anguish and fear. Father. He was a wayward father.

An hour later she was sitting at the table in the big hall, paper and ink before her, surrounded by all the members of her family and her household, whom she had summoned. "Friends," she said, "I called you because we are going to send a letter to George Fox. We must prevail upon him to return, before he gets to London."

Instead of the joyful enthusiasm she had expected, all they did was nod or grunt dispiritedly. Only Mabby cried, "Oh, yes, ma'am, I mean Margaret, yes, ma'am! Yes, Margaret! Oh, please, *please* make him come back!"

She eyed the child coldly. "This is not because of his person," she said. "It is because we are not yet steadfast in the faith. We are in need of more guidance. The moment he has given that to us and turned us from—from whatever it is we are now into true Children of the Light, he will be free to go wherever he pleases. So, if any of you have any suggestions, I'll be happy to include them. This is a draft of what I propose we write."

Nobody spoke.

"Our dear father in the Lord," she read, *"for though we have ten thousand instructors in Christ, yet we have only one father, for thou hast begotten us through the gospel, eternal praise be to our Lord. We, thy babes, gathered together in the power of the spirit, do thirst and languish after thee, and challenge the right that we have in thee."*

As she read, she felt a growing certainty. This was it; he would be unable to resist this call. He might even have left them for a while on purpose. He might at this very moment be waiting for the confirmation that the change he had brought about in them had been a true one, not a passing fancy. Well, she had told him in terms that would leave no doubt.

"Oh, thou bread of life, without which our souls will starve! Oh, give us thy bread and take pity on us, whom thou hast nursed up with the breasts of consolation! Our only desire is to see thee again, that we may be refreshed and established, and have life more abundantly. Do not let the beastly powers which keep us in bondage separate thy bodily presence from us; we would rejoice to see thy kingly power triumph over them. Oh, our dear nursing father, we hope thou wilt not leave us comfortless but wilt come again; though sorrow be for a time, let joy come in the morning! Oh, our life, we hope to see thee again, that our joy may be full! For in thy presence is fullness of joy, and where thou dwellest is pleasure forevermore."

As she looked about her at their faces, she saw that she had begun to speak for them. She resumed her reading with confidence. *"Oh, thou fountain of eternal life, our souls thirst after thee! For in thee alone is our life and peace; without thee we have no peace! Our souls are refreshed by seeing thee, and our life is preserved by thee, oh, thou father of eternal felicity . . ."*

She was suddenly filled again with a burning ardor for God and His truth. She felt that, should it ever be demanded of her, she would lay down her life for God. She thought of adding this, but decided against it. This was too personal. The letter had to be signed by them all to be effective.

She did so first, then Thomas Woodhouse, Ann Traylor, Henderson, Will Caton; the rest of the servants merely made a cross. The children each added a postscript at her prompting; Mary was allowed to make a print with her little hand. She wrote on her behalf: *"Oh, my dear father, when wilt thou come?"* She looked at the letter with satisfaction, checking that everyone had signed. The only one missing was young George. She was sure he had been there; as she looked up, she saw him slink out surreptitiously. The little monkey! She was about to call him back, but decided this was enough. George Fox must be aware of the boy's feelings toward him; to find him pleading for his return as his spiritual father might cause a frown. "You may go," she said. "Except thee, Thomas."

Dutifully, Thomas Woodhouse stayed behind while the others trooped out with some alacrity. Obviously, they were freshened by hope and eager to get back to their tasks. "Here," she said, sealing the letter, "take this to the posthouse thyself. Make certain it will leave on the night coach. And pre-pay the charge; he may be temporarily out of funds."

"Yes, ma'am."

Only after he had gone did it occur to her that he had dropped the "Margaret" again. Well, it would all come back the moment George returned. She was absolutely certain he would and felt full of zest and determination again. He would come back, some instinct told her so. Or maybe it was not instinct but indeed that of God. Perhaps this way she would discover what it was at last.

"Ann!" she called, as she saw the girl flit past on the landing above her. "Where art thou going?"

The little hoyden stopped in her tracks and looked down. With those green cat's eyes and that flaming red hair she was a handsome baggage, but much too pert for her station. A brief return to normalcy would do her no harm at all.

"I'm on my way to see Bonny Baker, ma'am."

Bonny Baker! She had left him out! She should have thought of him; George felt guilty about him, of that she was certain. "What is thy business with Bonny Baker?"

"I am teaching him to read and write while he has to keep to his bed. He has nothing else to do."

"Very charitable. But not now. I want the summer curtains in the children's rooms taken down. We haven't sorted their winter clothes yet. They will have to be aired, to get rid of the camphor."

"Yes, ma'am."

"There is plenty to do before we set out on missions of Christian charity. Start with the curtains."

"Yes, ma'am."

Ah! What joy, to be alive again! She ran up the stairs, two steps at a time. In the passage between the children's rooms Ann Traylor's ghost evaporated. Bonny Baker, indeed! She would have Cook send him a dish of calf's-foot jelly. And a picture-book. She might even go to see him herself, one of these nights. He was, after all, a member of the Swarthmoor Meeting.

With gratitude she felt the loving-kindness that had blessed her in the early days of her convincement return to her. She felt full of tenderness again, even toward spiders. She went to her room to look for one, to set it free in the rain.

*   *   *

There he was, at last! John McHair sprang to his feet, rushed to the door and pressed his head against the bars of the little window, trying to peer into the corridor, listening breathlessly. The candle flame in the lantern outside the door danced and smoked; the shadows of its little cage twitched on the wall. Water dripped somewhere, melodious in the silence. But there were no footsteps. No light came swinging down the passage. He was not coming. He was not coming!

Moaning, he turned around and started his lonely pendulum walk again, from door to wall, wall to door, door to wall. How utterly bewildering it all was to a man who wished no more than to be left in peace! He wanted no more from life for the next year than the somnolent security of hibernation; if only the damned judge had left him alone instead of arousing in him that unbearable yearning for freedom, for life! Why was he being treated this way? What did the judge really want of him? Why had he come back every single night now for over a week, to sit there on his seat-stick, probing, asking questions, making him go through every minute of every day, over and over and over again, until his head was spinning and his throat dry and his eyes burned with desperation? He had become dependent on the man's visits like a drunkard on his daily tankards of ale, and now, suddenly, he stayed away. Why? Why?

Crazily, he tried to talk to himself, the way he had talked to the judge, to say aloud the things that haunted him, the yearnings that had been stirred up by those questions. But without the judge he was nothing but a jabbering fool.

He could not stand it! He could not stand being cooped up here any longer! His senses had been awakened to the world outside once more; he could not bear the captivity! He must get out, he must! He still knew that it made no sense; but something inside him, some instinct, had turned upon itself. It compelled him to nurture the mad dream of knocking down the judge, grabbing the key from his pocket, opening the door and bursting into the boundless space of freedom. During the evenings the judge was the only man around the prison; he had said so himself. He had brandished that key every night. And now, God damn him, he stayed away. Maybe he would never come back. Maybe he had done all this on purpose, just to make him suffer, like a chained dog, for eleven interminable months! Oh, Jesus God! He could not stand it! He could not stand it!

Faster and faster he paced, up and down his cell. He broke into a run, bounced off the wall at every turn. In the end, exhausted, giddy, he crashed into the straw once more.

While still roaming the sunlit fells, the dappled woods, he had never realized that the condition of all living things in that magic forest, except himself, was a permanent state of terror. It was the state in which he now lay there, groaning, in the straw, in the stench of his own excrement. This was hell, anything was better than this, anything, anything. Hush! Was that him . . . ?

Again he leaped to his feet, rushed to the door, peered through the little window, listened, his heart pounding in his throat.

But there was nothing, only the dancing shadows, the dripping water, softly singing his name.

*   *   *

The two letters, one from Judge Fell, one from his wife, reached George Fox at the same time. Farmers and laborers from all around were gathering in the muddy yard of the house; before meeting started he wanted to read them in privacy. He took them with him to the haystack where he was to sleep that night.

He opened the one from Margaret Fell first, and read it slowly. Fleeting patches of sunlight chased the shadows of clouds across the fields as he sat reading, his white hat by his side, his hair whisked about in the wind that swept down from the fells and across the fields, where the wheat billowed like the sea.

He had received a goodly number of rapturous letters from women over the years, never one so passionate and at the same time oddly innocent as this one. He had come to know her well during the weeks they had spent in proximity; this letter was just like her: strong, impetuous, generous and tender, with a startling frankness. He gazed at the wild chase of light and shadow on the wind-swept wheat; from the courtyard came the whinnying of horses, restless with the turmoil in the air; high overhead, screeching thinly, a flock of seagulls was blown about the sky.

Her letter, he thought, could never have been written by a woman of humble origins. Her very exuberance of expression had something imperious about it, a contempt for what other people might think that belied the very thing she wished to convey: her utter dependence on his spiritual guidance. Margaret Fell would never be dependent on any man; the beguiling thing was that she herself had no idea of this. As far as she knew, she could not live another day without him, spiritual father, guide, shepherd, bread of life, breasts of consolation, whatever else she had called him in her determination to have him come back at once. He had always thought of true feminality as dependence on a sovereign male, yet she was the most feminine woman he had ever met. No one had ever filled him with such admiration and irritation, such delight and exasperation. Did she also excite him carnally?

He did not evade the question, he had long since found peace with his natural self and accepted it. If God had furnished him with an instinctive response to women like every other man's, there could be no basic evil in it; the evil began when the law was broken, if only in his heart. To suppress his awareness of Margaret Fell as a woman would imply that he was unable to refrain from breaking the law unless he went through life with his eyes and his ears closed. Margaret Fell attracted him greatly. She had done so from the beginning. But the essential element she generated within him was joy, making other women seem joyless in comparison, especially in spiritual ecstasy.

He read her letter again. The passionate lines, like herself, radiated joy, despite the plea they intended to convey. How he would love to heed her bidding and turn around right now, head back for those treacherous sands he had crossed in God's power, that somber house aflutter with children in white dresses, the excitement of her presence, the fullness of their meetings for worship. But there was the other letter.

He knew what it contained before he broke the seal. It was indeed an introduction to a Lord Shorwell, who was requested to take him forthwith to Oliver Cromwell. It was exactly what Judge Fell had promised, yet it filled him with dismay. The cautiously worded, dispassionate letter seemed cold, calculating. Reading it made him feel tainted with lovelessness, a pawn in a game, a symbol, not a man.

Suddenly he was no longer sure of God's intention. The way that had seemed to open with the first mention of this letter on the way to Lancaster seemed to close again. He had no clear leading as to what he should do next. All he could do was wait upon the Lord.

He rose and went to join the crowd in the farmyard, putting the letters in his coat pocket as he went. The crowd was small, which was no wonder considering the blustering weather; they were nearly blown off their feet, especially the women, whose voluminous skirts, ballooning in the wind, tugged behind them. The meeting turned out to be entirely silent; no one could have made himself heard above the whistling and hooting of the wind. It was one of those rare meetings that seemed dull and dead. That was the only drawback of spontaneity: on rare occasions the Presence did not manifest itself and the expectant crowd was gradually reduced to a haphazard group of people waiting for something that never materialized. Maybe the letters prevented him from centering down; he found he could not banish them from his thoughts, especially hers. Its passionate lines went spiraling through his mind like the dust whisked about the yard by the wind.

After meeting broke, a number of people came to talk to him, mainly women. It seemed as if the demands on him would never end; but finally the last one, a voluble widow, released him and he fled into the hayrick, where he supped on cheese and ale. The wind died down at sunset and the rain started. He listened to its gushing, secure in his dry little shelter of light and warmth. After he had blown out the lantern, he lay on his back in the darkness, thinking of her. Suddenly he knew: Beware. Thy self-assurance may prove hollow, should she ever be allowed to assail it. She is tempestuous, and noble—that may be thy downfall. Despite thy sincere desire to see in people only that of God, thou art pleased that letter was written by the wife of a Lord Chief Justice. From this even the armor of God will not protect thee, for the devil is within. He can do no harm as long as thou knowest where he is at all times and exposest him to the light when he attacks thee. But to consciously go and challenge the devil in *her* would bring about that the two would fuse, as surely as that of God in thee fused with that of God in the hangmen in Derby. As it did then, it would unleash the ocean, only this time not the ocean of light and love, but that of death and darkness. So—away with thee! Away to London!

It pained him, for the moment all this was in the open his body and his heart ached for her, ferociously. But he began to formulate in his mind the letter that he would send her on the morrow. A loving letter; yet it should leave no doubt. Away, away—London was safer, despite the plague.

*   *   *

Yes! There he was! This time there he was! At last!
John McHair saw the light of the lantern approach, heard the foot-

steps echoing in the corridor. The key tinkled, scraped in the lock; the door squeaked open and there stood Judge Sawrey, the light from the lantern on his legs. He closed the door, put the key in his waist-coat pocket—the moment had come. John McHair found himself pray-ing to God, the God of the Quakers. "God, God of Fox, help me, help me . . ."

The judge put the lantern on the floor, opened his seat-stick, sat down and said, "Well, friend John, I thought I'd come to see thee one more time. Tomorrow I am leaving for a long journey."

Yes! This was the moment, the last moment! He stretched out his hand. "Give me the key," he said hoarsely.

An odd look crossed the judge's face. "My good man, thou must be mad! Is this my reward for coming to see thee in thy affliction?"

Something about those words seemed to convey a warning; but it had been too long. With a bellow of despair he threw himself upon the judge, knocked him down, ripped his waistcoat as he pulled out the key, sprang to the door, stabbed the key into the lock, pulled it open. For one moment he thought he was free; then he saw the constable and three men waiting outside, their swords drawn. He threw himself upon them, roaring.

He fought for his life; it took a long time before, finally, he was overpowered and dragged back into his cell. He heard the constable ask, "Are you hurt, sir?" and the judge answer, "No, I'm not. Are you men all right?" Then the constable asked, "What shall we do to him?"

Somebody kicked him, and he opened his eyes. There, looking down on him, was the judge.

"That was very foolish of thee, John," he said. "With the powers invested in me I can now order thy execution for assault and jail-break. But because of the detailed information thou hast given me these past weeks, I will show mercy." He smiled. Somehow, that smile was terrifying.

John stammered, "No, no . . ." in the sudden knowledge that whatever was about to happen would be worse than death.

"These men have been witnesses to thy assault upon my person," the judge continued. "They would kill thee; I want them to under-stand the reason for my mercy." He turned to the constable. "For striking me with his right hand in an effort to escape, cut it off by the wrist."

He screamed in horror; he fought like a demon, he nearly managed to throw off the men who clung to him with the tenacity of hounds bringing down a stag. But they threw him on his back on the floor, pinned his arms down by kneeling on them; a sword flashed in the lantern light and, shrieking, he felt his wrist being severed.

He fell into darkness, worse than death; the men did something to the stump; had he known it was to prevent his bleeding to death, he would have torn off the bandage. "God, God, Quaker God," he whispered, "mercy . . . mercy . . ."

But, like the dying fawn, the broken hare, he received no answer from the great indifference.

* * *

Margaret Fell was the first to hear the postman's horn because she had been waiting for it every day. She rushed to the window and saw him cantering toward the house on his pony, his yellow-and-green uniform bobbing among the bracken brown with autumn; sunlight sparked in his horn. She had to force herself to stay where she was, not to run downstairs.

He was entering the gate now, on his way to the kitchen door, where Thomas Woodhouse or anyone else around would take the letter and—oh, no! It might be addressed to all of them, considering that all of them had signed hers! They might tear it open without waiting for her! She ran out of the room and swept into the kitchen just as the postman appeared at the door.

"Good morning, Mistress Fell! I have a letter for you from, let me see, Yorkshire way."

What business was it of his? "Thank thee, Master Floris." She took the letter, said to Thomas Woodhouse, "Pay our friend his due," and walked out of the kitchen. In the hall she broke into a run, stormed up the stairs, ran into her bedchamber, slammed the door and, leaning with her back against it, broke the seal. The paper shook in her hands.

"Dear and tender and loving sister in the Truth of God. My tender love in the Truth of God to thee and all the rest of thy family in the Truth. Walk in the Truth of God, and in that which keeps you pure to God; and the everlasting God of power and Truth keep you to Himself in His Truth to Whom be praises and glory forever. The Lord doth show much of His Love and His power here amongst us, to Him be praise forever, to the confounding of the deceit for the simple One's sake and making His power known and thy words are fulfilled. I can say little of coming over. Thy loving friend, G.F."

She gazed at the letter, stunned. Then she read it again, certain she must have misunderstood. His language was not easy; there were so many "truths" in it and one line did not seem to make sense. But when she returned to the casual little sentence at the end, it penetrated to her at last. He was not coming. That was what the letter said: I am not coming. The rest was pious balderdash.

She was overwhelmed by a terrible, heartbreaking grief. No! It was not true! She should read it again, slowly and lovingly, trying to hear his voice as she read. *"Dear and tender and loving sister in the Truth of God . . . ."* Well now, wasn't that exactly what it said: dear and tender and loving? Didn't he call her "sister," wasn't "in the Truth of God" just one of those phrases he always used, dear boy? Of course it was. Just because she was disappointed that he was not coming straightaway, there was no point in overlooking his shy and tender declaration of—what? *"My tender love in the Truth of God to thee and all the rest of thy family in the Truth . . . ."* There: he sent his tender love to her, and of course he mentioned the rest of the

family, she had made them all sign the letter . . . Oh! What was the
point of fooling herself? He was not coming! Those words were just a
mealy-mouthed, cowardly effort to—no, no! She should not allow
herself to think like that! She must read on, without that terrible disappointment distorting every word!

*"Walk in the Truth of God, and in that which keeps you pure to
God; and the everlasting God of power and Truth keep you to Himself in His Truth—"* Balderdash! Bloody, boring balderdash! She
felt tears running down her face as she shook the letter with both
fists. She tried to suppress her rage; it was the fury of a child who had
always had her own way.

He was not coming. It was obvious why not: *"The Lord doth show
much of His love and His power here amongst us."* He was off and
running again, stirring people up, filling them with passion and light,
saving their souls and wrecking their lives. *"To Him be praise forever,
to the confounding of the deceit for the simple One's sake and making
His power known and thy words are fulfilled."* Now, what the devil
did that mean? "The confounding of the deceit for the simple One's
sake" obviously was a fancy way of saying, 'I'm ripping up another
church and goading its minister to make his congregation realize that
he is a fake and a windbag, whose God is in his belly—' No, whose
God *is* his belly.

She sat down at her dresser and rested her head in her hands, overcome by nausea and giddiness. She took a deep breath in an effort
to get the weight off her chest; when she opened her eyes, she was met
by the stare of a haggard woman looking like a beaten dog. Was this
what "walking in the Truth of God" had done to her? Of course not.
It had nothing to do with God. It had to do with a thirty-eight-
year-old woman and a twenty-eight-year-old youth.

She tried to brush the thought aside, but she had better face the
truth. She had fallen in love with a youth ten years younger than she,
after twenty years of marriage and seven children. She was not the
first to whom this had happened; it must, God knew, be common
enough: the subject of countless tales of gossip among women cooped
up in their manor houses all over the countryside, tittering and giggling
behind their fans.

So, she was a woman scorned. At last proud Maggie had made a
fool of herself. It had been innocence, embarrassing inexperience. She
had been cooped up all her life; despite her seven children, her true
passion had never been aroused because it had never been challenged
by anyone other than her urbane, courteous husband. Who would
have dared trifle with the wife of Justice Fell? It had taken a revolution, the disruption of the church, the murder of a king to produce a
male who dared break into the castle and awaken the sleeping beauty.
A nobody, a weaver's son who had refused to recognize established
power, rank and authority. In a way, he had been as innocent as she;
his impudence had presented itself to him as prophetic fervor, eagerness to obey the will of God. *"Let us kneel together and ask the Lord
why He brought me to Swarthmoor Hall."* How innocent, how self-con-

fidently chaste! And she had been as innocent, as chaste . . . But what about the way she had thought of him after her passionate reunion with her husband on his return?

Oh! How sordid! She hid her face in her hands. She could not accept it, she could not. "Oh, George, George!" she whispered into her cupped hands, secretly, as if the speaking of his name would make it a consummated sin. But it was no sin! She had not known what she was doing, neither had he, she was certain of it! Poor boy, he must have been filled with alarm by her letter. No wonder he had replied with this jabbering little note, in which the word "truth" was brandished six times, like a frying pan at a charging cow!

She suddenly burst into giggles. She had a fair idea of her own power once she cut loose; he must have run for his life, backward. *To the confounding of the deceit for the simple One's sake and making His power known and thy words are fulfilled.*" Incoherent goosegobble from a thoroughly rattled swain who had provoked more than he had bargained for. *"I can say little of coming over."* Well, dear boy, if I were in thy shoes and given the choice between going to see Oliver Cromwell or a reproachful old woman . . .

"Oh, George, George!" Her fragile composure caved in; she sobbed, her head on her arms, among the bottles, the potions, the pathetic paraphernalia with which she had tried to cling to youth. "God, have mercy on me! Save me, save me . . . !" But she had lost God. All her life she had been happy with the fatherly God of daily prayers and Sunday sermon, then George had brought her a new One, a living One, radiant with love, only to—

She became aware that someone was knocking on her door. She wanted to cry "Go away!" but that would set the household buzzing. She hastily dried her eyes, slapped some powder on her tear-streaked face, brushed her hair back; then she took up a comb and started to arrange it. "Come in!"

The door squeaked. "Shall I make the bed?"

"Yes, Mabby, of course."

She was aware of the fascinated interest of the silly little thing, who started to rummage behind her. At least it was not Henderson or Ann Traylor. Even if Mabby did sense something amiss, she was too stupid to put her finger on it.

"Was that a letter from George Fox, ma'am?"

"Letter? Oh, yes. A letter from Mr. Fox. Indeed."

"I wonder if he knows about John McHair."

"John McHair?" She tried to bite back the tears as she was suddenly overwhelmed by the emptiness of the life she was condemned to live from now on.

"Didn't you know? Justice Sawrey had his hand lopped off."

"What didst thou say?"

Mabby stood, flushed and beaming, behind the bed. "Justice Sawrey had John McHair's hand lopped off!"

"Who said so?"

"The constable told Will Hartford this morning at the smithy."

"Why, for God's sake?!"

"I don't know, ma'am." She sounded alarmed by the vehemence she had provoked. "I think he tried to escape . . ."

Margaret stared at the child; then she said, "Go and tell Thomas Woodhouse to come here at once!" That poor, inarticulate man who had sat opposite her in meeting with such a bewildered, mournful face! What a monstrous thing to do! She must go and see him at once. She could not just let him lie there in that dirty prison cell, she must do something . . .

Thomas Woodhouse arrived.

"Thomas! Is it true about John McHair?"

"Yes, I'm afraid so."

"Did they—did he lose his hand?"

"He did."

"How *is* he? Hast thou any idea?"

"No—all I know is what they did to him."

"Very well, tell Will Hartford to bring out the two-in-hand, ask Henderson to get from the cellar the jar of Morocco plums I bought a while ago, tell Ann Traylor to get ready to come with me. I am going to the prison."

His face went blank with amazement. "Prison?" Then he recovered. "No, Margaret Fell! That is out of the question! If thou wishest John McHair to have those plums, I'll take them to him; for thee to go is not possible!"

"Why not?"

"Prison is no place for a woman, not even if she were to go there as an act of charity."

"Charity?" she cried. "A man who sat with us in meeting, who set our own Bonny Baker's leg? For me to go to him in concern after he has been willfully mutilated, thou callest *charity?*"

Thomas Woodhouse looked at her with dignity. "Margaret," he said, "I maintain: thou must not go there thyself. No woman should go. For one thing, thou wouldst not be allowed to see him."

"Oh, all right, then. What about a man bringing a letter? Surely they will admit a man. Or a boy? How about Harry Martin?"

Thomas Woodhouse shrugged his shoulders. "I don't know," he said. "In that case, Bonny Baker would be better."

"Why? He is still as feeble as a reed!"

"If thou art planning to send John McHair a letter, someone will have to read it to him. Harry Martin can't read either."

"All right. Tell Bonny Baker to come and fetch the letter in a few minutes. Or Ann Traylor."

After Thomas Woodhouse left she sat down at her dresser, pushed aside the bottles and jars and wrote: *"Dear John McHair."* That sounded impersonal. Dear John? Too familiar. *"Dear and Tender and Loving Brother in the Truth of God. My tenderest love to thee in thy cruel affliction. I cannot tell thee how my heart goes out to thee. What must hurt thee most, I know, is the thought that he for whose*

*sake thou art now tormented has deserted thee and left thee to rot in
loneliness and despair . . ."*

Her pen raced across the paper. Blurting out all her misery, loneliness and despair, she wrote to the illiterate poacher as she would
have written to a sister. Only when she was done did it occur to her
that John McHair would find it completely bewildering. He was in
prison not because he was a Quaker, but a poacher. He was mourning
the loss not of George Fox, but of his hand.

As she sat there in doubt, she became aware that she was not alone.
She turned and found Ann Traylor standing behind her, looking at
her with knowledgeable eyes. All she could do was fold the letter, hand
it to her and say, "Give this to Bonny Baker and tell him to deliver
it to John McHair in person. Did Henderson get that jar of plums out
of the cellar?"

"Yes." Ann Traylor took the letter.

The image of the poor man lying there with only a stump where
his hand had been was harrowing. There must be something else
she could give him, other than those plums and that incoherent letter.
Something that would convey to him her identification with his
suffering. He was in a dungeon underneath the courthouse. It must
be dark and damp and cold. Some candles? Something to combat
the dampness? What about that pair of mittens sent to her husband
by Aunt Agatha for his last birthday? "Just a moment," she said,
and went to look for them in his chest of drawers.

There they were: just the kind of thing a maidenly aunt with
failing eyesight would knit for her nephew during lonely winter evenings. But they were right for John McHair. Only as she was about
to give them to Ann did she realize that, instead of conveying identification, they would stress to what extent the poor man had been a
pretext for her letter. He needed only one mitten now, not a
pair. What she should do was to send him one mitten and something
else to put over his stump, which must be cold and very tender. A
sock? It would serve, but seemed depressing. Wait! Another of Aunt
Agatha's stained-glass offerings: a bonnet for Mary when she was a
baby. "Ann, that little red bonnet my husband's aunt knitted for Mary
some years ago—where did we put it?"

"In Mary's chest, with her doll's clothes."

"Get it. It's just the thing to go with this mitten for John McHair."

The girl looked at her quizzically.

"I am making up a parcel for him, and I want to put in these
mittens, but he has only one hand now. The bonnet would be just
the thing for his stump."

"What about the tassel?"

"Oh, we can cut that off. But why should we? Leave it on! It
may look a little foolish, but why not? He's not dead! I don't want
to commiserate with him; I want him to feel hopeful. Yes! We
must somehow cheer up that man cast out in darkness. As a child,
what I liked best about Christmas was the silly presents, the gewgaws
in my stocking. Let's get a box and put in lots of things, nonsense

things—here . . ." She went back to her husband's chest of drawers. "Some underclothing. And here: some gay kerchiefs to blow his nose in, or just to look at. Does he smoke tobacco?"

"I don't know."

"He's probably not allowed to smoke in prison. Would he be allowed to make tea? No, of course not. I know!" She went to her dresser. "Some toilet water. I know it is not meant for a man, but I am sure he would love to smell something nice right now. Hold out thy apron, let's put it all in there. Now, what else can we give him? Canst thou think of anything?"

The girl looked at her with a faint smile. There was no way of knowing whether it expressed condescension or amusement, and she did not care. She had a life to live, a house to run, children to shelter, even though George had taken with him all her joy, her hope, even her God.

* * *

Boniface Baker was resting on his cot in the loft when suddenly Ann came in, early for once, and handed him a folded piece of paper. "Here," she said, "read this aloud."

"What is it?"

"Never mind, read it. Loudly and clearly."

"But why? What *is* it?"

She sighed. "Oh, wilt thou do as I say? Open that letter and read it aloud to me! If thou canst not do it properly, they'll have to send someone else."

"Ann," he said quietly, "I want to know why."

As she had begun to do of late, she sighed and gave in. "Oh, all right! It's a letter Mistress Fell has written to John McHair, in prison. She wants thee to take it to him; he cannot read, and thou wilt have to read it to him. So, go ahead and let me hear if thou canst do that."

"But I can't walk all that way!"

"Thou art not going to walk! Thou art going to be taken there in the coach-and-pair, and I'll come with thee to see to it that thou dost not fall on thy snoot. So, read! They are screaming for thee downstairs."

He unfolded the letter and read, *"Dear and Tender and Loving Brother in the Truth of God. My tenderest love to thee in thy cruel af-af . . ."*

"Affliction."

"What is that?"

"Never mind! Say it: affliction. Affliction."

". . . affliction. I cannot tell thee how my heart goes out to thee. What must hurt . . ."

The door to the loft was thrown open rudely and a voice hollered, "Bonny! Where the devil—" It was Will Hartford, big and angry, stooping under the eaves. "What art thou doing here?"

"Art thou by any chance addressing me?" Ann retorted.

"Who else? Come on, boy! I'm waiting!"

"He will be ready in a moment, once I have made sure he can fulfill his mission."

"Ah, da-dee-da . . . !" Will mimicked her unpleasantly. "I'm so sorry, ma'am! Forgive me for intruding, ma'am! Make sure his britches are buttoned, ma'am, before he—" He ducked as a book came fluttering at his head.

"Get out!" Ann screamed with skin-tingling fury. "Get out, thou foulmouthed bully!"

"La-dee-da!" Will taunted, behind the closed door. "I'll go and tell the steward that His Lordship isn't garbed yet, but will descend anon."

"Do that!" she screamed. "And then drown thyself!"

"Ann," Bonny said soothingly. "Don't be angry. It's just his way."

"He's a brute! A vile brute!" She spat, chest heaving.

"Hand me my breeches."

She threw them at him. "Now, don't let thyself be bullied into going if thy leg hurts on the stairs. Dost thou hear me?"

"I hear thee."

Standing up, his leg hurt. He put his foot down gingerly and tried his weight on it.

"Well?" Suddenly, there she was, her arm around him.

"I think I'm all right. Let me try . . ."

"Now, take it easy, Bonny, take it easy! If it hurts on those stairs, tell me honestly. I'd rather go myself than let them use thee this way. Religion!"

'Hush," he said. "Let me try by myself."

Painfully he hobbled toward the door. As he started down the narrow steps, Ann hovered over him like an anxious mother hen. At the bottom of the stairs Will Hartford was waiting.

"Well, well, there's His Lordship!"

"Hold thy tongue, thou big oaf! How is it, Bonny? Dost thou think—"

"Never mind what he thinks, let's go!" Will Hartford took him by the shoulder. He winced; before he knew what was happening, Ann was upon the man, claws out.

"Don't touch him!" she shrieked. "If thou touchest that boy, I'll scratch thy eyes out!"

"All right, all right . . ." Will Hartford, despite his size, backed away from Ann's fury. Outside the stables, the coach-and-pair was waiting. Ann helped him up and was climbing in beside him when suddenly Thomas Woodhouse was there. "What dost thou think thou art doing?"

"I am going to accompany him to the prison," she said defiantly.

"Come out of there!"

"Mr. Woodhouse, I happen to be the governess in this house, not a maid. I am not under thy orders."

"Oh, yes, thou art. Come out of there. I will not have any woman from this house turn up at the prison, I don't care who she is."

"I am not taking any orders from thee!"

"No nonsense," Thomas Woodhouse said, holding out his hand. "I would not allow Mistress Fell to go and I'm not going to take any arguments from thee. Come out of there."

For once, she obeyed. The mention of Mistress Fell had done it. It seemed incredible, but at that moment Mr. Woodhouse looked as if he had indeed told Mistress Fell to come out of there and been obeyed.

"Hartford, accompany the boy and see to it that he comes to no harm."

"Aye," answered the man, climbing up into the driver's seat. "I'll keep an eye on him from up here."

The leather seat was very soft; Bonny's thigh hurt when he sank into it farther than he had expected. He winced.

"Bonny!" Ann looked at him anxiously through the open door. "Art thou sure—"

"Oh, come away, lass!" Mr. Woodhouse cried impatiently. "The boy's going to be all right! Come on!" He slammed the door.

Bonny heard Will Hartford clack his tongue and flap the reins, and there he went, as if drifting on a cloud. He had never been inside any of the carriages; neither had Harry. Will Hartford always cleaned them himself. He saw the buildings around the courtyard float past and was overawed by a feeling of luxury and importance. But when the coach started to lurch and sway on the road, his thigh began to hurt. He grabbed the strap by the window and tried to hold on to it, lifting his thigh off the seat, but the stabs became so violent that he cried out to Will Hartford to slow down. Will did not hear him; all he could see of Will was his shadow moving to and fro across the little window in the roof, each time the carriage pitched into a pothole and bounced back. It was torture; he hoped the bumps would get less once they got to town. But the cobblestones turned out to be worse; he had been able to brace himself more or less against the lurches and the bounces, but the cobbles caused the whole coach to shudder and he wailed in agony.

At last the coach halted. Will Hartford opened the door; Bonny nearly fell out of it. It took him several moments of standing still, eyes closed, clinging to Will Hartford's arm, before he could put his weight on his sore leg and limp painfully to the door of the courthouse. Will Hartford carried the box of gifts and explained the purpose of their visit to the constable's men at the door. At first they did not want to let them in. Then the constable himself appeared, and Will Hartford had to tell the whole story all over again.

The constable said, "Justice Sawrey has ordered that the prisoner be treated leniently, so the boy may come in to take him the message. But thou must wait here, my man."

"All right," Will Hartford said. "Now, art thou sure thou canst walk alone, Bonny?"

"Oh, yes," he answered, for the delay had helped him recover somewhat.

"He may need help on the stairs," Will Hartford said to the constable, "he favors his left leg. Maybe someone can carry this box for him, he might drop it on those stone steps."

"Ah, thou knowest the inside of our jail from experience, I gather," the constable said.

"No, but I never knew any steps down into a dungeon that were carpeted," Will Hartford replied. Obviously, he and the constable did not like each other much.

"All right, lad, come in." The constable held out his hand. "I'll take thee down myself. Give me that box." To Will Hartford he added, "He won't be long. The prisoner is only allowed visitors for five minutes at a time." Then he took Bonny by the shoulder and began to guide him down the steps, into the darkness.

The first thing Bonny noticed as he descended, cautiously, was a stench that was vaguely familiar; it became stronger as they ventured farther into the world below. It was too dark for him to see where he was going; then they reached a landing, where the constable lit a lantern before going on. "Take it easy, lad," he said. "Down here it's damp, the steps may be slippery. Does it pain thee much?"

"Not too much, sir," he replied politely. "As long as I'm careful not to put my weight on my leg."

"Was it thy ankle?"

"No, sir, my thigh." The stench was becoming stronger.

"Thy thigh? That must have been difficult to set. Did Master Phelps do it?"

"No, sir, *he* did . . ." He gestured with his head toward the darkness into which they descended.

"John McHair? Thou art telling me a fancy story!"

"No, sir, no, sir! He did it. He had once set the thighbone of a dog."

"Well!" The constable sniggered. "That would make him quite an expert! Let's hope it won't set thee barking! Now, watch out here, me lad. Careful! This next step has a hole in it. Right. Now turn to thy left . . . I'm not going too fast, am I? Is all well?"

"Yes, sir—thank you, sir . . ." But all was not well at all; he felt like throwing up, so sickening had the stench become. He had met it once before when Apple, the old piebald mare, had lain wheezing in the stable, dying with lung rot. It suddenly came back to him: the heaving, laboring breath full of squeals and rattles, the terror in the huge, moist eye as it caught the light of the lantern, the ghastly grin of yellow teeth, and that horrible, putrid stench, as if she lay already rotting in her grave with only her head still clinging to life. "It would have been best had the mistress allowed me to put her out of her suffering when her agony started," Will Hartford had said as he stood looking down upon poor old Apple's glistening eye and its mute, uncomprehending terror. "Mercy from a distance can be a cruel thing."

Those words rang in Bonny's memory as he caught his first glimpse of a motionless, prostrate body in the straw, in the feeble light of the constable's lantern after he had opened the door.

"Hey there! John! John McHair! Wake up, man! Here's a visitor for thee!"

Straw rustled; the body stirred, but did not turn toward them. It lay there so still and buried that Bonny could not make out where the head was and where the feet.

"Come on!" the constable shouted, and he nudged the body with his foot. "Come on, bestir thyself! Is this the way to welcome a messenger from the Hall?"

The body moaned; then something seemed to sit up in the straw, something small, a mannikin. The lantern light swung closer, and Bonny stifled a scream. It was the stump of an arm, swollen, filthy, oozing from a huge running sore. The stench was so overwhelming that he stood there swaying, giddy and faint.

"Come on, lad, brace up!" the constable said. "Let's leave this box with him so he can open it when it suits him. He is obviously not going to wake up in thy honor."

"But—but I have to read to him, sir. I have to read the letter . . ."

"Whose letter?"

"Mistress Fell's, sir. She wrote him a letter, and I promised I would read it to him in person."

The constable hesitated; then he kicked the body viciously and shouted, "Come, get up, thou sack of filth! A great lady went to the trouble to write thee a letter, and thou canst not even be bothered to wake up! Come on, up! Up!" Again the boot kicked the body, sending a small puff of chaff whirling in the lantern light.

The body moved. It rolled over heavily, and Bonny saw with amazement and revulsion that the head was where he had thought the legs to be. It was barely recognizable as human, so thickly had straw and blood matted its hair and beard; from that tangled bush he was suddenly, breathtakingly, fixed by the baleful stare of old Apple's terrified, dying eye. So hallucinating was the resemblance that he would have turned and run if the constable had not held on to his arm.

"Come on, lad, let's get this over with. Where is thy letter? Read it to him. Come, I haven't got all day!"

"Yes, sir, yes, sir . . ." His hand trembled as he reached inside his doublet. He pulled out the letter and opened it; without looking at the staring eye, he read, *"Dear and Tender and Loving Brother in the Truth of God. My tenderest love to thee in thy cruel affliction. I cannot tell thee how my heart goes out to thee . . ."*

He read all three pages of it, without mistakes; when he was through, he still did not dare look at the body in the straw, but asked the constable, "Was that all right, sir?"

The constable stood looking at him with an absent-minded expression, as if he had not been listening. "What was that, lad?"

"Did I do all right, sir?" he repeated foolishly, still not daring to look back at that horrible eye.

"Oh, yes—yes, thou didst well, lad. Who taught thee to read so well?"

"The house mother in the foundling house in Kendal, sir, and Ann Traylor . . ."

The constable said, "Oh, yes, of course. Now, do we leave the box, or dost thou want to open it up for him?"

Bonny did not, but Mistress Fell was sure to question him in detail; he could not tell her that he had been too fainthearted to complete his mission. "I think we must open it, sir," he answered. "There are little notes with the presents and I have been told to read them to him." He noticed how they were talking about the body as if it were a dumb animal like Apple, as if the real John McHair had nothing to do with that filthy bundle of rags, that ghoulish stump, that horrible eye.

"Well, let's get on with it." The constable squatted by its side and opened the lid. The first thing he brought out was a bundle of underclothing; he detached the note that was pinned to it and reached it up to Bonny. "All right, read it."

"This is a change of underclothing for thee, dear friend," Bonny read. *"Please send thy dirty linen back with Bonny Baker so we may launder it for thee and keep thee supplied with clean linen every week during thy confinement."*

The constable looked up at him open-mouthed and back at the bundle in the lantern light. "Underclothing? Drawers for a poacher? And clean ones every week?"

"That's what the mistress said, sir."

"Well, I must say . . ." The constable put the bundle down gingerly, as if it were fragile. "What's next?"

It was a picture-book with Biblical scenes that Bonny remembered bringing into the house once from the lawn, where one of the young ladies had left it. He had not dared to open it at the time; it had looked very expensive. He pulled out the note that protruded from its pages and read, *"This book may help thee, dear John, to while away the empty hours and maybe inspire some reflections on what others went through for the sake of their faith."*

The constable gazed at the book, astounded, opened it cautiously to look at some of the colored pictures, then put it in the straw beside the bundle of underclothing with the same reverence. The next present was a pack of candles; but before Bonny had been able to read the note attached, the constable said importantly, "He can't have those. Candles are not allowed in prison." He tossed the package back into the box and pulled out another one: a small bundle of dried heather.

The note that went with it read, *"May the scent of this bracken remind thee, dear friend, of thy beloved fells and assure thee that when the day comes in which thou canst roam them once more in freedom thou wilt find many loving friends waiting for thee."* The constable was about to put it down with the rest when suddenly the straw rustled and the body rose on an elbow. A grimy hand reached out in the lantern light and a voice, cracked and broken, whispered: "Give to me . . ."

The constable placed the small posy of heather in the hand. Although Bonny did not want to look, he could not help himself. He saw the hand lift the little bouquet of heather to the dirty nose that stuck out of the matted hair, and heard deep, wheezing inhalations.

"Come on, come on," the constable urged, "let's get this over with! What's this?"

One by one, Bonny read the notes that went with the rest of the presents: a comb, a bottle of toilet water, a bag of sweetmeats, a roll of gaily colored kerchiefs, and, finally, one mitten and a little red bonnet. The message attached to them ran, *"Dearly beloved friend, the cold weather is coming and in our concern to bring thee comfort and a token of our loving thoughts, please find here a mitten for thy left hand and one woolen muff for thy right arm. May all this convey to thee what need not be put into words among children of the Light."*

To his surprise and embarrassment, Bonny saw tears running into the filthy beard. Yet, somehow, the eyes were no longer those of a dying mare, but those of a man awakening.

"Well!" the constable said, getting to his feet. "That was the nicest parcel I ever saw sent to a prisoner in my time. Any message for the lady, McHair?"

The eyes looked from one to the other, then the voice said, "Dove . . . Tell her she is the dove . . ."

"The dove," the constable said. "Whatever that may mean." He picked up the lantern again and took Bonny by the arm. As they walked down the corridor, the prisoner's voice called after them, "The letter! Give me my letter!"

"But thou canst not read, man!" the constable called back.

"My letter," the voice pleaded, "give me my letter!"

"All right," the constable grunted, "give it here, laddie." He took the letter from Bonny. "And let's have those candles too, so the poor brute can see it, at least."

When he rejoined the waiting boy and took his arm again, he muttered, "Women!" as if with that one word he put it all behind him.

* * *

Alone, squatting in the straw by the light of a candle the constable had lit for him, John McHair surveyed the objects surrounding him, touching each one in turn the way he used to touch the first furry buds of the willow in spring. The comb, the bottle of toilet water, the sweetmeats, the kerchiefs, the underclothing, the picture-book, the jar of plums. He picked up the sprig of bracken, inhaled its fragrance of freedom and summer, then turned to the greatest miracle of all, the mitten and the little red sock. That those friends, those loving friends, had sent him a mitten for his hand and a sock for his stump was proof of their concern for *him,* John McHair, dear, beloved friend John. Who said the loss of his hand was the loss of his life? He picked up the mitten, then the little sock, and suddenly he felt as if life were only beginning. A new life, fuller than before, for not only had he been given back his old self, there seemed to be more of him, not less.

He wanted to pray, a prayer of thanks to God; but he could not think of any words, only sounds: the wind in the trees, the whisper of the rain, the great swelling sound of the forest awakening in a summer dawn.

* * *

Margaret Fell was in her bedchamber, reading in the gray light of the evening, when Bonny Baker came to report on his visit to John McHair. He described in his boyish voice how he had found the man; he told her of the effect of her gifts; he gave her the message he had been given, *"The dove. Tell her she is the dove."*

It was quite touching, but the gloom in which she had sat there prevailed. Bonny left her sitting in the window seat, gazing at the rain, the Bible on her lap.

In her misery, she had turned to it again; it had always helped her in the past. But this time, as she read the marvelous story of our Savior, she discovered to her horror that George had spoiled even that. Reading about Christ, how He had spoken and acted, she was struck by a haunting similarity to George himself. Instead of a spirit of love and compassion, ethereal, almost disembodied, she found a swarthy George roaming the hills of Galilee, a rabble-rouser who invoked·the ire of the priests by saying he was the son of God. George said the same thing, angering the priests, who maintained that the only child of God was Jesus, only Jesus was perfection. But was He? On the one hand, she saw Him much more clearly: a swarthy George; on the other, she suddenly discovered traits in the ethereal spirit of pure love that gave Him a shocking humanity, even maleness. His destroying with heavenly fire that innocent little fig tree, for instance, only because it happened to have no fruit available at the moment of His passing—exactly what George would have done. And the poor farmer who owned the herd of Gadarene swine! She saw him rub his hands the night before, saying to his wife, "Well, a couple more weeks and they will be ready for market! I've never seen 'em as fat and slick as they are this time! They should fetch a good price!" How stunned the poor people must have been the next day when they were told that a passing saint had cured the village idiot by casting the evil spirits into their herd of swine, which had proceeded to hurl themselves over the cliff, the lot of them. In effect, it was the farmer who had paid for the miracle. Should he not have been consulted? Or at least thanked afterward by the saint who had dashed all the man's hopes by this demonstration

of his divine powers? Exactly what George would have done! That
was what he had been doing all along: miracles, convincements, rapture, and there was John McHair bleeding in the straw, mutilated
for life, Bonny with his broken thigh. And where was the saint at
this moment? Somewhere, on his horse, on his way to see the Protector.
And why? Because God told him. Which God? Which God, for heaven's
sake?!

This was what bewildered her to the point of desperation: there
did not seem to be any consistency in the Scriptures when it came
to the nature of God. One moment He smote entire cities, babies
and all; the next, Jesus described Him as a merciful Father, fount
of love, light of the world. What about the other miracles Jesus
had wrought in the name of His merciful Father? In her present
state of desolation it seemed to her that most of them were executed
almost petulantly, the only purpose being to convince the spectators
that He was indeed the Son of God. What about the thousands of
sick people, for instance, who had come limping, crawling and staggering
to the wayside so they might touch the hem of His garment as
He passed and be cured? Only a few of them, picked at random,
had received the benefit of His miraculous powers. What about the
other thousands, all those sad, crippled creatures racked by pain,
beset by the terror of death, who had failed to catch the bridal
bouquet of salvation tossed by the Son of Man? Exactly like George!
It was cruel to convert people only to leave them bewildered, like
John McHair, herself, all the others in the house, in town. The
miserable prophet! He had ridden off not only with her heart, her
peace, her God, but with her Savior as well, leaving her bereft,
utterly alone.

She could face it no longer. She must tear herself away, occupy
herself with the evening meal, the children, anything to force her
eyes away from that precipice of despair. She managed to rally
and go downstairs; but that night, during meeting, the thoughts about
George came back. He had turned out to be imperfect, weak, selfish
—like the rest of them. Yet his power had been real. He had conveyed to her, to all of them, a real awareness of the presence of
God. Now here they were, abandoned. How many others were there
like them, all over England? This was only one town; there must be
hundreds of John McHairs languishing in prison in George's wake.
In her mind's eye she saw the straw, the bloodied bandage, the
joy of the man who had just received a beautiful present, and suddenly
she found herself thinking: If I could do it for John McHair, why
not for those others left behind and forgotten? There must be hundreds—

Suddenly a mysterious energy seemed to sweep through her, forcing
her to her feet. "Friends," she said, "you know that I wrote John
McHair a letter and sent him a few tokens of our concern. You
heard from Bonny the effect this had on him. George Fox has affected
the lives of many others like him. How many are there at this
moment in the same condition as John McHair? Imprisoned, betrayed,

beyond reach . . ." She hesitated, was it right to talk about practical things in ministry? But that energy swept her along. "I want to write to other Meetings, asking for the names of Friends in prison. I want to know details about each one of them, so I may send them a personal letter. We could even send them each a parcel with gifts, food, clothes, anything to alleviate their loneliness, their despair. If all of us join forces, we may be able to send them more than just one. We may be able to send one regularly, say, every month. This way we would, with divine assistance, give sense to George Fox's visit to Swarthmoor Hall. He said in his ministry: nothing that happens to us is senseless. If we want to discover a sense in his passing our way, it seems we will have to provide it ourselves."

She opened her eyes and looked about her, disoriented, for the mysterious energy had left her. She found herself, bewildered, committed to something she had not had a chance to think about. Suddenly full of doubt, she was about to sit down when someone in the circle rose and came toward her, arms outstretched. To her astonishment, she saw it was Ann Traylor. The girl embraced her and said, "God bless thee, Margaret Fell." Then she went back to her seat.

Hours later she finally found herself in her bedchamber. The mood in the house had changed completely; gone were the despondency, the sense of abandonment; everyone had responded to her idea with a zest and an inventiveness that were surprising. It had been decided that those people in town who sympathized with them would be approached for contributions, in money or in kind. She herself would do the writing, but if the number of Friends in prison was anywhere near what she thought it might be, she would need help. It looked, in fact, like the beginning of an organized church, rather than a haphazard band of people interrupting sermons, refusing to remove their hats, challenging authority and ending up in jail.

Her enthusiasm was such that she undressed quickly, eager to kneel by the bed and thank God for His goodness. But as she knelt there, the words that came to her seemed hollow, meaningless, flat. Instead of sinking into silence, she became conscious of the asthmatic breathing of Mongol, the pug, which had again sneaked onto the bed. What a thought for someone who had just been blessed by a Revelation! Come, she told herself, be still, silence thy thoughts, even the small babbling ones, and wait for that of God to rise within thee.

What rose was the thought: *'What is Thomas going to say when he finds his house turned into a mailing station?'* And then, *'It will serve him right.'* This was shocking! This was not the way . . . There came another thought. *'What will George think when his movement is being taken away from him? It will serve him right too.'*

Aghast, she opened her eyes, to be met by the vacant stare of the pug. Had she, in heavenly inspiration, quaking from head to foot as the storm of the Presence swept through her, been doing nothing but cooking up a device for revenge?

She got up and wandered over to the window, opening the curtains to gaze out at the night; but all she could see were black wet windowpanes full of squiggling raindrops. She sat down at her dresser. Look at that face! She closed her eyes. There was the silence again. Once it had been full of light, joy, certainty, love . . . *'If anything will bring him back, this will.'*

Oh, my God! The eyes that stared at her in the mirror were wide with horror. Was this the truth? Was the whole plan no more than a trick to get George back? If so, she should go downstairs, call them together to tell them it had all been a mistake! But what would she say? 'Friends, I have discovered that it was not that of God in me, but that of the devil'? The confusion, the bewilderment! Not now. She should not think about it now. Tomorrow it would all become clear.

She went to bed and kicked at Mongol through the covers. "Off! Get off the bed, thou pop-eyed—" That was unfair. To stumble upon the truth about herself and kick the dog for it? No wonder he didn't trust her. Nobody should trust her. Least of all she herself. *'Take his church away from him and he'll come running . . .'*

Well, whatever it was, it was true. Once his converts, now scattered over the prisons of England, were drawn into one organized body, he could not help becoming their captive. His church would become his cage, and she would have the key.

Again she covered her face with her hands, in shame. She was worthless, a conniving bitch. Poor John McHair! She was about to do to hundreds of others exactly what she had done to him: write a letter addressed to him, but directed at a fleeing horseman heading for the hills, cloak fluttering. Yet John McHair did not seem to have minded; whatever her motives had been, there could be no doubt as to the effect. Was it immaterial whether she did it as a saint or as a sinner, as long as she did it? Did God, whoever or whatever or wherever He was, really avail Himself of people like her to do His work? It was a ray of hope.

She wetted her fingers and reached out to snuff the candle flame. In the darkness she heard Mongol sigh and felt him settle down in the hollow between her legs. 'Oh, Thomas, Thomas!' she thought theatrically. 'Why hast thou deserted me?' Well, that was easy: because she had ground her heel on his gouty foot. What a thing for a convert to have done! But don't let's start all that over again.

She turned on her side, shoving Mongol out of his nest as she did so, and composed herself for sleep. She was just drifting off when, out of nowhere, she heard George's voice. *"It takes time for Him to reach thee. First, thou must accept thyself as thou art."* He had been standing in the sunlight, the bank of red roses behind him.

Well, she finally knew herself as she really was. But should she accept that? Should she not throw herself upon the mercy of Christ, now that she knew she *really* was a miserable sinner? Or should she say: "All right, Maggie, thou art a bitch; now get on with those letters"?

She slid out of bed, knelt down and prayed, "God, here I am. Thou knowest me for what I am. Even so, perhaps Thou canst use me. I cannot promise that I will be able to change, though. Is that acceptable to Thee? It will have to be, for that seems to be the way of it. Both Thou and I had better accept me as I am, and hope for the best. Amen."

It did not give her a sense of liberation, but peacefulness of a sort; at least they knew now where they stood. No one need know except God and she and, possibly, Thomas. Suddenly she had the uncomfortable feeling that Thomas knew already. Yet he loved her. She was not sure of anybody else, but Tom loved her all right.

She got to her feet, lit the candle again, put on her robe and went to her dresser. There she lit the candles by the mirror, fetched her inkwell, quill and paper, pushed aside the pots and jars and started to draft a letter to the Meetings.

"Dear Friends, this Meeting has a concern about those who find themselves imprisoned for Truth's sake . . ."

She wrote and rewrote it, while Mongol watched her from his foxhole in the counterpane. Finally, she signed it: *"Margaret Fell, Meeting for the alleviation of the suffering of Friends in prison."* That was too cumbersome. *Meeting for the sufferings of prisoners?*

She tried it several ways and ended up with: *"Margaret Fell, recording clerk; Meeting for Sufferings."*

CHAPTER SEVEN

HENRIETTA Best did not know what prompted her to go and see Margaret Fell again, but the moment the thought struck her, she decided to act upon it. She did not stop to consider that more than a month had gone by since Fox's departure; all she thought about was how she herself would feel at the realization that the man she loved was gone forever. There was no doubt in her mind that Margaret Fell had fallen in love with him; a woman could fool herself about her relationship with a man only as long as he was around. The moment he had left, she would drop all pretense, and no wonder; at that moment her heart would break and the awful, awful sickness begin: the agony, the hopeless yearning with every fiber of her body, every nerve, for his presence, his touch; her every waking thought, her every dream would be centered on him in unbearable, self-inflicted torture. It was the most harrowing torment to which women were prone, and it made no difference how old they were, how wise, how rich, how well schooled in the control of their emotions. To see a woman in that anguish made every other woman want to sneak away and leave her to lick her own wounds, knowing that for this torment there was no solace, no cure. The only remedy was time.

In the carriage, on her way to the Hall, Henrietta knew that even if the house were filled with gloom, her happiness would be a match for it. She would be able to give the poor woman something any other reasonably cautious female would hesitate to give: tenderness and compassion. Who knew? Margaret Fell might welcome a shoulder to cry on, a chance to let go at last.

It came as a shock to find the Hall a beehive of activity, and its mistress, instead of steeped in misery, preoccupied with preparations for what seemed to be a huge, unseasonable Christmas party. Long tables in the main hall were covered with a multitude of small objects in the process of being wrapped; every servant, it seemed, was taking part in the frenzied activity, as well as the entire family. Everybody was sorting out gifts, consulting lists, wrapping parcels; the air was spiced with the scent of sealing wax and smoking candles; instead of gloom and despondency, the mood was one of joy and anticipation.

When Margaret Fell caught sight of her, she dropped what she was doing and came to welcome her, rather effusively, as if she had noticed her visitor's self-conscious discomfort. This was not at all what Henrietta had had in mind; before she knew what had happened, she found herself wrapping parcels with the rest of them. Somebody told her the recipients would be prisoners, but the first present she wrapped seemed a strange choice for someone in a dungeon: a small brass kaleidoscope, the worse for wear, which must have belonged to a series of children before being discarded. Puzzled by its incongruity, she sneaked a look through it, to see if it perhaps contained a secret message; but all she saw was colored stars and diamonds, fascinating only to someone under the age of five. She lowered the toy self-consciously when she heard Margaret Fell's voice beside her. "Ah, yes, the kaleidoscope! Let me see . . ." She consulted a list. "This is going to Herbert Meiklejohn, in York prison. Now, where is the note to go with it?" She searched among a sheaf of papers she carried in her hand; Henrietta looked at her flushed cheeks, her youthful beauty. There was about her a tenderness and a joy which, coupled with this frantic activity, stirred up some vague memory from long ago.

"Here it is!" She handed Henrietta a piece of paper. "If you will, please put it with the present. Maybe the best thing would be to wrap it around the kaleidoscope, don't you think? I don't want him to miss it."

"Good idea," Henrietta said lamely.

The other noticed her bewilderment. "I'm so sorry to put you to work like this," she said, again rather effusively. "You must wonder what this is all about!"

"I gather that you are planning to surprise some prisoners of your church. I didn't realize that they put children in prison too for this."

"Children?"

"Well—this kaleidoscope, isn't it going to a child?"

"Herbert Meiklejohn? Good heavens, no. He is professor of astronomy at Oxford. That's why I chose it for him." She brushed a strand of hair off her forehead; suddenly she looked tired. Dark rings showed around her eyes; under the flush on her cheeks was a hint of pallor.

"Aren't you doing too much?" Henrietta asked impulsively. "You look exhausted."

"Oh, no, no!" She tried to hide it with a forced smile. "Just a little queasy, that's all. Why don't you and I sit down in my room over there for a moment? I haven't even asked you yet what gives me the pleasure of your visit. You must think me uncivil indeed."

"Not at all. Shall we go there now?"

"One second." She put an apologetic hand on Henrietta's arm. "I'll be right back, let me just . . ." She did not finish; off she went to one of her daughters, messily stuffing a string of sausages into what seemed to be a sock.

Henrietta could not resist sneaking a look at the note to the professor of astronomy. *"Dear Friend Herbert,"* it ran. *"We thought this simple toy might give thee the opportunity to explain to thy fellow inmates, or even thy jailer, some of the principles of thy scientific work, in so far as it concerns the refraction of light and the colors of the spectrum. Thou might find this a suitable way of introducing a discussion about the Light in ourselves, and the joy of answering that of God in one another. Let us know, dear Friend, any special wishes and desires; we will comply with them if we can. Let me assure thee, dear John, of our loving thoughts and constant prayers for thee, as thou art carrying our burden with such courage and loving power. Thy Friend, Margaret Fell, Recording Clerk, Meeting for Sufferings."* It was a sweet letter, so obviously sincere that, hiding it behind her reticule, Henrietta discreetly changed "John" into "Herbert."

She had finished wrapping the parcel when Margaret Fell beckoned to her from a door in the far corner which led to a small, untidy withdrawing room. A desk by the window was strewn with papers, a tea set and incongruous knickknacks, obviously awaiting their designation as gifts. The autumn light, streaming in through the narrow window, was bright with the clearness of winter; it made the woman look even more exhausted. She must be taxing her strength to the utmost; it seemed a Herculean task.

"How many prisoners are you sending parcels to, Mistress Fell?"

Margaret Fell laughed. "Thus far, sixty-eight, but that covers only part of the country. We haven't received the list from the Midlands yet, or from Wales. Would you like some mint tea? I'll send for some fresh . . ."

"No, thank you. Do you intend to send presents to all of your co-religionists in prison?"

"Oh, yes. We intend to send each of them a parcel every month, if we can, and I hope to write them a letter every week."

"But you can't possibly! Sixty letters a week, as well as all those parcels?"

The woman laughed, but it did not sound convincing. She looked desperately tired; there was about her a translucent quality that was disturbing. Henrietta felt a great sympathy for her, for she sensed, underneath it all, the heartbreaking grief and loneliness that she had expected. The young man had been in his twenties, Margaret Fell must be well into her thirties; a classic situation. The gallantry of her trying to fight it with work was very moving.

"Why?" she asked.

"Pardon?"

"Why are you doing all this?"

The other gave her a quick look. "Oh, I discovered by chance how much it means to a prisoner if he feels that someone in the outside world is aware of him and cares about him." She smiled. "Believe it or not, it was you who decided me. That night we had all those injured people here, you said something that has stayed with me ever since."

Despite her sympathy, Henrietta stiffened. She had managed to push that memory aside and did not want to be reminded of it.

Margaret Fell must have noticed her discomfort, for she added hastily, "Forgive me, I don't mean to distress you. But do you recall saying to me, 'He performs miracles—to what end?' I was shocked at the time; I have since discovered that you were right. It would all be pointless unless someone else gives the people he touched a sense of continuity, of constancy . . . I am trying to convince them that he meant what he said when he spoke about—about his loving them." She walked to the window. Although her back was turned, she could not hide the tears in her voice. "That is what they need, love. Oh, they need it so badly! Those poor, poor people, sinking into loneliness, doubt, despair . . ." She turned away from the window; the light showed all her secrets. "I am determined not to let that happen," she said. "And I can do it, because I am a woman."

Henrietta was deeply moved. But something in the woman's eyes, the sheen on her hair, an intangible element about her bemused her. Then suddenly it all fell into place: radiant tenderness, frantic activity, queasiness, that peculiar, translucent pallor . . . "Shouldn't you slow down a little?" she asked gently. "For one who is with child, you are doing far too much."

A look of utter astonishment crossed the other's face. Then she said, "Oh, no . . . !"

"Forgive me, I must be imagining things." Could it be that Fox was the father? Was that why she was so distressed? No; not with that inveterate innocence. The pregnancy must be the result of the sudden increase in marital passion that always accompanied the early stages of adulterous infatuation. Strange how women's most personal experiences followed such common patterns.

Margaret Fell had sunk down in the chair at her desk. "Oh, Lord . . ." she said wearily. "Of course, that's what it is! How could I be so stupid? One would think I should know by now . . ." She looked with stunned despair at the papers on her desk, the knickknacks awaiting a destination. "How am I going to—" She did not finish. She set her jaw. "Well, I had better start organizing things differently."

Henrietta said calmly, "You are not going to organize anything right now. You are going to stay where you are. Look, all you need is a few women like myself who have time on their hands and are prepared to help you out for a while, writing those letters for you . . ."

"Letters?" She had not quite recovered from the shock. "No, I must write those letters myself."

"Well, perhaps sign them yourself, but I don't think it is a good idea for you to try and write sixty-eight or more a week, even if you were not with child. If you take on too many of them, you are bound to get mixed up."

"What do you mean?"

"The letter you wrote to go with the kaleidoscope. I'm sure Professor Meiklejohn will love every word of it, but you start by calling him Herbert and end up calling him John."

As if this were the last straw, the poor woman looked at her with dull despair. "Well, I'll have to do that one again, won't I?"

"No, you won't. I changed it for you. Maybe I should write the whole thing over again. All you'll have to do is sign. But what you need right now," she said, getting to her feet, "is some nourishing broth. I'll go and see your cook."

The woman rose heavily and went with her to the door. Henrietta Best put an arm around her shoulders. "Look," she said, "one child under your heart, seven under your roof, sixty-eight in prison? *Voyons, soyez raisonnable."*

For a moment it seemed as if Margaret Fell would continue, crazily, to shoulder the world and all its woes alone; then she surrendered to that sheltering arm.

Henrietta Best put the mistress of Swarthmoor Hall to bed for a nap, arranged for a light meal to be sent up in an hour; then she tackled the chaos downstairs. She recruited a girl called Ann to help her with the correspondence and proceeded to write her first letter. To her dismay, it turned out to be flippant, despite her earnest intentions. *Enfin,* she decided with realistic resignation, it may have little to do with Quakerism, or whatever it is called this time, but perhaps I can make them laugh.

Twenty-eight years before, as a proud young convert, the idea would have shocked her; now she thought differently. As she had come to know from bitter experience, saintliness was impervious to suffering and oppression; it might, conceivably, be vulnerable to laughter. She was going to try it, with a sense of vocation, for anyone clinging to saintliness who could possibly rid himself of it was crazy *comme la lune.* It seemed an unsuitable way of resuming life as a convert, but this was what God had finally made of her, after many trials and errors, and if He did not like the final product, *zut!*

"Dear and beloved Friend Edward Harrow. Believe it or not; this muffler is for you." She mumbled, *"Merde!* 'Thee'!" crumpled the sheet into a ball and started again. *"Dear and beloved Friend Edward Harrow . . ."* A limping boy brought in lighted candles; she remembered his coming to her house during that thunderstorm with the news that two men were drowning in the quicksands. It reminded her of her dear, unsuspecting husband. The news of her new activity, when it got to him, would be quite a shock; it might not be a bad idea to have it brought to him by this child.

She told the boy to go to her house with a note for Colonel Best. The haughty girl called Ann intervened. "He can't do that, ma'am; he still limps."

"Never you mind, *chère,"* she replied with calm authority. "He will be taken there and back in my coach. It is waiting outside."

She felt in complete control, on top of the world, yet deep inside her was a small, cold fear.

* * *

Until the boy from the Hall delivered his wife's note, Colonel Best had assumed that she was delayed and would merely be late for dinner. But even the few scribbled lines were enough to arouse his anxiety. Something about the note did not sound right; it had a false

flippancy that conveyed something quite different. It read like a note
sent by a prisoner, innocuous to anyone except a close relative to
whom it conveyed a secret, frantic call for help.

When finally she came home, late that night, she managed, however, to convince him that he had worried needlessly. As she told it,
gay and excited, she had finally found something to divert her during
her leisure hours. The idea of sending letters and parcels to all
Quakers in prison sounded harebrained, but this might indeed be a
way to put her mind off other things. She almost convinced him; but
that night he was awakened by her dreaming aloud. It obviously was
not a pleasant dream, and her mumbled words were French.

It revived all his earlier suspicions. After he had gently shaken her
awake and she had drifted off again into sleep, her head on his shoulder, he lay worrying, staring at the ceiling. Of course his first feeling of apprehension had been right; by becoming involved once again
in a religious movement, in people being hurt and molested and sent
to prison, she had succumbed to the tidal pull of the past. It was almost as if she had been so terrified of a precipice that she now had
thrown herself over it out of sheer desperation. She was the last person
to write to religious fanatics in prison. Perhaps he should take her
abroad, or visit Margaret Fell himself and explain to her why his wife
should not be allowed to do this; or they could enlarge the garden,
as they had been discussing of late; anything to give her something
else to do. But none of it would work. She had at last been claimed
by her *alter ego,* Henriette de Coligny, who had collapsed into temporary insanity when her children were brained in front of her eyes
and had awakened, after weeks of aimless wandering, as a shabby
little cocotte, "La Douce Tété." He lay there, frantically searching for
a means to protect her from the demons of her past, but there was no
way out now his own love had failed.

At breakfast the next morning she asked casually, "By the way—
dost thou remember thou asked me, a month or so ago, what Thomas
Fell should do to bring his wife to her senses?"

"Why, yes . . . get her with child."

She laughed. "Well, he did. That really is the reason why she needs
help."

He muttered some remark, but his mind was racing. Suddenly he
had the answer to his prayer.

That morning, on the pretext that he had to go and look at a horse
Simon Rutledge had told him about, he rode off to the town of Kendal
without his groom. In Kendal was a foundling house of which he was
one of the regents; it was full of infants waiting for childless couples
to pick them up and rear them as their own. To get her with child!
It was his only hope; at their age this could only be achieved by
giving her a little foundling to mother.

He set out with a sense of purpose and relief; but as he cantered
down the winding trail across the fells, the somber landscape, already
touched by winter, got the better of his cheerful self-confidence. How
would she accept a strange child? He did not really know how vivid

was her memory of her own children and whether the cure might not be worse than the disease. The more he thought about it, the more certain he became that if he were to present her with a little orphan himself she would almost certainly turn it down. But what if the child were found on her doorstep? This would seem an act of God; chances were that she might at least consent to keep it until the formalities of putting it into a foundling house were over, and he could see to it that those formalities took a long time.

The joyous self-confidence with which he had set out did not return, however. Alone on the melancholy moors underneath the stormy sky, his thoughts centered on the child itself. What would it be like? It was not as if he were on his way to pick a lap dog for her, although he felt no compunction about asking the matron of the foundling house for the pick of the litter. A child was a human being—at least, it would be, before too long; how could he be certain that he was not bringing a born scoundrel or a future harlot into his house? Despite the fact that he was one of the regents of the Kendal home, he did not know much about the inmates. In some cases, a child's background could be established on the basis of the clothes it was wearing when found or a little note pinned to the basket; sometimes the mother was a woman of good breeding who had been forced to abandon a child of love; Moses had been a foundling of noble birth. But even if it were such a child, what about the responsibility? He was fifty-six, his wife fifty-two; it was realistic to expect that in another ten or fifteen years he would be gone, and though his wife might be around awhile longer, the child was certain to lose its parents at a tender age. Of course he would leave it well provided for, but was that enough? Lofty as his motives might be, he could not rid himself of the uneasy notion that, somehow, he was about to commit an unpardonable sin against another human being. He frowned, disturbed by this trend of his thoughts; it almost seemed, despite his hearty dislike of the man, that Fox the Quaker had infected him with some of his high-flown notions. One phrase in particular, which at the time he had merely registered as another of the Quaker's aphorisms, came back to him, *"Never use a man as a means, only as a goal."* Here was a clear instance of a man being used as a means; he was not on his way to Kendal to save a child but to save his wife.

But this was ridiculous; even though the child was not his primary concern, whoever he was to pick from the litter could call himself fortunate. The difference between being reared as a pauper, a ward of the church, or as the only son of Colonel William Best with an assured future was enough to justify the deed, even if the child would in all probability be orphaned once more before reaching maturity. But what about himself? To put it bluntly, he was about to mess up his life, the few years of it that were left to him. At his age he had a right to peace, privacy, a pleasant, calm existence without the noise, the untidiness and the constant upsets that went with small children. To put a cuckoo into his nest, of his own free will, was sheer folly.

As he rode on through Kendal forest, the increasing wind hissed and foamed in the shedding trees, sending whirling at him from the ghostly woods diapers, infant's colic, whooping cough, vomit on the carpet, snot on his chair, bat ears, inward squint, buck teeth, midnight screams, porridge flung across the room, piercing whistles. It was madness to solicit all that voluntarily and turn the peace and comfort of his declining years into purgatory, with death his only hope of liberation. His fears grew into panic, but when he reined his horse to turn around and head home, he could not do it. He had no choice. Unless he made this last, supreme effort to avert the destiny that awaited her, she would continue on the road to Golgotha, the ghastly catharsis of having herself crucified in expiation of her sins, which were the sins of the world, the Cardinal's, everybody's except her own. If ever there had been an innocent woman, victim of fate, it was La Douce Tété. He had no alternative; he had to do it, he had to—God have mercy on his frightened, elderly soul.

He arrived at the foundling house at noontime; the matron received him in her little office, amidst the racket of clanging pails, clattering dishes and banging spoons that echoed in a nearby hall where the children must be having luncheon. She was a thinly smiling, genteel spinster of indeterminate age who spoke in hushed, awed tones as if God were listening in an adjoining office. He was surprised by her reaction to the information that he was ready to bestow upon one of her unfortunate children the blessings of his name, rank, riches and privileges, as well as the comforts of his luxurious home. She proved incomprehensibly reluctant; then, suddenly, he remembered that when she had first appeared in front of the Board of Regents a year ago to be considered for the post, he had voted against her. She had seemed to him sanctimonious and as cold as a fish, but the others had felt differently. Somehow she must have learned of his antagonism; this was her opportunity to get even. He said tartly, "Madam, may I remind you that the purpose of this institution is to place children with families, rather than perpetuate the financial burden each of them represents to those who pay for you and your charitable enterprise?"

The matron pursed her lips. Her smile survived, but only as a ghost of its former self. "I regret to have to say this, Colonel," she said slowly and clearly, as if to make sure that God in the office next door would hear every word, "but I have not only a responsibility toward the regents, I have a responsibility toward the children and, through the children, to our Lord. May I remind you of the words of Jesus Christ, St. Matthew, twenty-fifth chapter, *'Inasmuch as ye have done it unto one of the least of these my brethren, ye have done to Me'?"*

"If I understand you rightly," he retorted in his most glacial judicial manner, "to lodge one of the least of these as a ward with my wife and myself would, in your opinion, be frowned upon by Christ. What are you surmising we want this child for, Madam? As a servant? To feed it gin and keep it small, so it may serve *hors-d'oeuvres* at our orgies without being able to see into the bed?" It was an image that, he realized too late, would do more harm than good; she must wonder at what time in the past he had acquired this knowledge about midgets in brothels. To judge by her beady eyes, it would provide ample food for spinsterish daydreams. Board or no board, he would see to it that she was replaced as soon as possible by someone more realistic about the chances her foundlings had to make good in life. All she was doing, in effect, was to confirm his first impression of her.

"My dear Colonel," she replied, with the humble superiority his unfortunate outburst had handed her on a platter, "I am convinced, of course, that any child you and Mistress Best would choose to make your own should be grateful for the honor. However, speaking plainly, I do not think it wise on your part to consider adopting a child of tender age. We do have a few older boys here that might be considered. One, a handsome little fellow, ten years old; another—"

"I do not want a ten-year-old handsome fellow!" he cried, exasperated. "I want a child no older than a few weeks or a month, and I am not prepared to discuss it any further! I demand a clear and straightforward answer, Madam, to a clear and straightforward question: are you going to assist me in the choice of such a child, or are you going to force me to propose your dismissal to the Board of Regents?"

Her hands, folded in genteel prayer on her desk, went white at the knuckles. "Put in those terms," she replied, slowly and clearly for the benefit of God, "you leave me no choice."

He rose. "Well," he said with the kindness of the victor, "now shall we look at the children, please?"

She stared at him with undisguised loathing; so obvious were her feelings that he found himself hoping she and John Sawrey would never get together; in the hands of an adroit schemer like him, her version of this little scene might be a powerful weapon. But he was beyond pussyfooting caution; his battle had been fought on the way here, on the barren fells and in the haunted forest; no argument this female might present could equal in severity the ones he had presented and disposed of himself.

She rose stiffly to her feet and with demonstrative obedience preceded him out of the office and down the hall. They crossed a high vaulted room where a score or so of toddlers were imbibing porridge from wooden bowls by the fistful, or having it spooned into them by buxom wenches, who rose respectfully as he passed. A few of the children stopped masticating porridge to gape at him, mouths open; the spectacle was so disenchanting that he found himself thinking, with callous humor, how much more effective the matron would have been had she, instead of raising his hackles, taken him straight into this room and left him there to contemplate his future at his ease.

They climbed dark, echoing stairs, crossed a landing and entered a ward full of identical cribs, each of them filled with a squalling homunculus purple in the face with apoplectic fury, trampling, waving puny fists. He was ready to concede that his idea was not only impractical but suicidal; one month with a banshee like that in his house, throwing a fit every hour and smelling like a dung cart, and he would be ready to shoot himself. But after the way he had thrown his weight around in the office and blackmailed the matron into submission, the only way out of his self-applied noose was to pick one of them at random, have it trussed and bundled so that it could not leap out of his arms and break its neck on the way to Ulverston, and return it after a few days with a curt little note informing her that this particular foundling was not satisfactory and that they were looking elsewhere for a child. He forgot about picking the best of the litter and asked the woman, "Which one would you recommend?"

She turned to a huge female squatting on a footstool who, with bovine casualness, was busy feeding two of the little monsters at her huge, heavily veined breasts. "The Colonel is looking for a child," she said, her voice raised to make herself heard above the din. "Which ones are ready to go?"

The woman looked at him with the same gaping curiosity as the toddlers downstairs. The two piglets sucking her breasts grunted and smacked with passionate determination. "Boy or girl?" she asked.

"Colonel?" The smile of the matron had come back to life; if Lazarus had risen with the same self-satisfaction, someone in the crowd would without doubt have slapped him back into his grave.

"It doesn't really matter," he said gruffly; then, as an afterthought, he added, "Maybe a little boy . . ."

"What about little Billy, over in the corner?" the wet-nurse ventured. "He has been fed and changed; and he's a bonnie little fellow. Needs lots of lovin', though. I would like to see him find a home; I can't give him what he needs, not with all the others screaming their little heads off."

"What didst thou say he needs?" the matron asked, with obvious relish.

"As I said, ma'am, lots of loving. Lots of hugs, kisses, tickles, coos and the like, somebody to tell him fifty times a day how beautiful he is, and how strong and lovable—and then hug and kiss and slap and tickle him all over again."

The matron turned on him with sanctimonious sweetness and said, "Well, Colonel, wouldn't that be something for you?"

"I am glad to see that you—er—have come round," he said, in a vain effort to turn defeat into victory. "Let me have a look at the—uh—little fellow."

The huge woman pinched the noses of the two piglets until they released her and gasped for air; it sounded like the uncorking of two bottles. Deprived of their meal, the outraged infants burst into a leather-lunged protest; he backed away involuntarily, realizing too late that the matron observed his every move with ill-concealed enjoyment. The fat woman put the two screaming, struggling homunculi into their cribs; then she waddled to the far corner and beckoned him. He joined her and looked down on a glum little face with big, dark eyes ruefully gazing at the ceiling. The tiny body outlined underneath the blanket seemed puny; the whole child seemed puny, with the exception of an enormous shock of jet-black hair coming to a point above its head.

"See?" the fat woman asked, turning down the blanket, revealing a bloated little belly and two little bow legs as thin as matchsticks. "He's the only one who doesn't yell along with the others; he's a wise little fellow, is little Billy. Come on, Billy, come on, coo coo, coo coo coo!" She picked up the tiny creature; judging by the jerky movement of his little arms, it startled him considerably. She made him sit up against her shoulder, surreptitiously arranging his diaper so as to hide his wormlike little legs, smoothed down the preposterous point of hair and tickled him under the chin. "Come on, Billy Boy, come on now, give us a little smile?" Billy Boy was not in the mood to smile; he looked at the stranger glumly and without enthusiasm. But at least he was quiet; if he could be counted on to remain quiet during the four hours to Ulverston, he would take him.

The matron asked in honeyed tones, "Maybe the Colonel would like to hold him for a moment?"

Without hesitation, the wet-nurse put the infant in his arms. He was startled by its lack of weight and by the rancid, milky smell that emanated from it; it might as well have been a little dog or indeed a piglet, but for the dark, earnest eyes observing him with unnerving reservations.

"Is this little boy to your satisfaction?" the matron asked.

Like an insecure adolescent, he was too concerned with his poise to realize fully the finality of his words when he answered, "Certainly, he will do splendidly," and handed the child back to the wet-nurse.

The matron took him down to her office, where he had to sign the required statement that the infant child Billy Monday, of unknown parentage, found on the steps of the Kendal foundling house on the morning of the fourteenth of September in the year of our Lord sixteen hundred fifty-two at the estimated age of three days, was as of this date handed over into his care, and that he accepted all the duties and obligations as described by law for a child's guardian. Meanwhile the infant was swaddled by the wet-nurse into a tight little bundle ready for transportation, and he was given a comforter to stick in the child's mouth should it start to scream. The wet-nurse was the one who handed the child up to him after he had hoisted himself arthritically into the saddle. He took the bundle from her and put it awkwardly in the crook of his left arm, convinced that he could not keep this up for more than a few minutes. He was eager to get away from the matron's pious smirk and the small crowd of urchins that had gathered around them, drinking in the fascinating spectacle of a rich old man in modish clothes setting out on horseback with a foundling. His nervousness must have communicated itself to his horse, normally docile and placid, for the moment he spurred her she started to prance skittishly, frightened by the scraping noise made by her hoofs on the cobblestones. He clutched the baby frantically to prevent himself from dropping it before they had even started; the child began to howl with fright, like a tomcat on the prowl. The wet-nurse cried,

"Give him the comforter, good sir! The comforter!" She obviously did not grasp the fact that a man had only two hands, and that to keep the horse from bolting he needed a tight hold on the reins. So he clattered, shied and skidded down the street, clutching the squalling bundle; the frantic screams of the child and the panicky clatter of his horse's hoofs echoed between the houses.

When finally he reached the open field outside the town, out of sight of the slack-jawed people of Kendal, he was exhausted and desperate. The child still screamed with high, piercing shrieks, each of them ending in a strangulated gurgle that made him fear for its life. Once he had the horse under control he stopped by the wayside for a moment, pulled the comforter out of the pocket of his coat and stuck it in the gaping mouth of the little creature, which at that moment looked, with its tightly closed eyes and its huge red orifice, like some ghoulish unknown fish gasping its last. He felt the insane temptation to throw the fish back into the sea and to flee, lashing his horse; but the comforter worked. The little monster clamped his toothless jaws on it the moment it touched his tongue; from then on, his entire attention was concentrated on sucking it frantically, making the same grunting, wheezing noises the two piglets had made at the woman's huge, veined breasts.

By the time they reached the forest, the child had fallen asleep, the comforter in its mouth. The wind increased; the swirling leaves rising in his path like dancing ghosts set his horse prancing all over the place again. He entered the writhing, hissing wood with a prayer.

He would be unable to relax sufficiently to think straight before he got home, and maybe that was a blessing in disguise. He had no wish to contemplate the future or regret the past, or to reflect on how little time it had taken him to become a father and ruin his life.

* * *

When Bonbon first heard the high, thin cries outside the kitchen, he thought it was a cats' tryst. Then the thought struck him that maybe a fox or a badger had got hold of *Madame*'s little dog, in which case there would be the devil to pay. He opened the top half of the door and peered myopically into the twilit garden. The cries had ceased; he called anxiously, "Froufrou? . . . *Viens! Viens, cocotte!* . . . Froufrou?" Suddenly there were footsteps and someone came up the garden path; only as the vague shape stepped into the light did he recognize the master. *"Ah! Bonsoir, mon Colonel!"* he exclaimed ingratiatingly; but the boor barely acknowledged his greeting. Bonbon opened the lower half of the door for him, wondering what was the matter with the man, he looked so flustered and shifty. "Shall I call Benjamin to put your horse away, *mon Colonel?"*

"No, thank you. I've already done that. Is *Madame* home yet?"

"Non, mon Colonel. But she will come any moment."

"All right. Bring me some cheese and mustard in the little drawing room. And tell her she can find me there when she comes."

"Very well, *mon Colonel.*"

There could be no doubt: the man had been up to no good. The fact that he had ridden off alone that morning had been unusual enough; for him to unsaddle and stable his horse himself made the whole thing highly suspect. What had the old *satyre* been up to, to feel the need for all this subterfuge? Did he have a wench somewhere? Most probably. But then why put his horse away himself? It could hardly be expected to be smelling of perfume, even if he had bedded down in a *partouse* with a brace of wenches doused with cheap *odeur*. Had he been out plotting with the Quakers? In that case, Justice Sawrey would be interested to hear about it.

There were ways of finding out these things; he would have a good look at the old goat's clothes when they came down to be pressed and a good sniff at his drawers. Sooner or later he would know; it all added to the foothold of power, so propitiously started with the business about the poacher. Ever since the trial, the vision of himself and La Douce Tété going back to France together to spend their old age in fond remembrance of the past had changed from a cranky pipe dream into a distinct possibility, as long as he did not let himself be tricked into hasty action and possessed the patience to bide his time, like a cat dozing beside a mousehole in the knowledge that, sooner or later, the little villain has to come out.

He took a plate of cheese to the little drawing room, where he knew the old *imbécile* would be slouching in his chair, boots on the table, guzzling wine; he was halfway across the hall when he heard excited voices at the front door. It was thrown open and there were those strange, high-pitched cries again, as of a little animal in terror or pain, and there was *Madame* stumbling into the house with eyes like saucers, her wig awry, carrying a bundle, crying, "William! Kathryn! Quick!" and, seeing him, "Bonbon! Go and fetch the master, quickly! Call Kathryn! Somebody put a child under our hedge! He may be dying!"

He stood, mouth open, thunderstruck, but there were those cries again, they clearly came from the bundle she carried in her arms. There could be no mistake; she had picked up a child.

The next few minutes were so chaotic that Bonbon did not get a chance to think. *Madame* cried orders at him for warm milk, a blanket, brandy, towels, a sugar pot; Kathryn came wheezing and jellying down the stairs and contributed squeals to the confusion before hopping toward the screaming little bundle in her mistress' arms like an overweight toad. In her turn, she started shouting orders at him for milk, hot water, brandy, towels; then the master came out of the drawing room, bellowing, "What in the name of sanity is going on here?" A natural reaction for a man who had been imbibing restorative wine after a gallant adventure which, at his age, must have left him cross-eyed with exertion; but although the sound was right, and the words were, too, he shot a shifty glance at Bonbon, standing there with the plate of cheese, watching him like a lynx.

Despite the confusion, the sudden frenzied activity, Bonbon realized with a giddying sense of satisfaction that of course it was the Colonel

who had put the child on the doorstep! That was why he had unsaddled and stabled his horse himself! As he went for milk, brandy,
spoon, towel, boiled water, prepared a washing basin   all the thousand
and one things the women went on shrieking for while fussing over the
child—Bonbon asked himself: why? Why had the man done it? Who
was the child? Why had he arranged it so his wife would be the one to
find it? There could be only one solution: the child was his own little
bastard, the outcome of a dalliance with some girl, not in Ulverston
but half a day's ride away; he was trying to smuggle it into his house as
a foundling!

At that thought, Bonbon, with a sudden sense of alarm, stopped
what he was doing. If she were to keep it, if she were to accept the
child as a foundling and fall for the preposterous lure out of over-age
motherly instinct, that would be the end of the dream of taking her
back to France and spending their last years together. Whatever happened, he must prevent this; but it would need all his wiles, patience
and nerve. All of a sudden, he found himself fighting for his life.

He managed to suppress the trembling of his knees, ignore the
pounding of his heart and the sick, dry taste of panic; he kept his wits
sufficiently about him to snatch the milk off the stove before it boiled
over. He was about to go back to the hall with a tray piled high when
the kitchen door was thrown open and Kathryn banged in, carrying
Madame's little dog. "Here," she said gruffly, "you take this hopeless
animal; the mere sight of the baby sends it into a fit." She put the
little dog, whimpering piteously, on the kitchen table, then snarled,
"Give here! This is a woman's job! Stay in the kitchen and keep that
dog quiet. There is enough fuss as it is!" grabbed his tray and breezed
out of the kitchen, back to the hall.

He slammed the door behind her, glowered at it, fists clenched, hissing, *"Serpent! Suceuse de sang! Sale vache vénérique!"* He turned to
the table, shaking like a leaf, and found little Froufrou standing there,
trembling, eyes bulging with terror, whimpering with a voice that
sounded more human than the shrieks of the child. Although he had
never liked the little bitch, he now took the quivering body in his
arms, patted her modishly coiffed, brainless little head and whispered,
"Tais-toi, tais-toi, mon petit chouchou . . . We'll get home, don't you
worry. We'll get home, somehow, soon."

He gave her what was left of the baby's milk on a saucer, in front of
the stove. He coaxed her, with coos and kissing noises, until she drank;
but it did not cure her trembling. She lapped at the milk apathetically,
looked up at him with those big round eyes as if in abject apology,
staggered a few steps and vomited on the floor.

The tiny beast's action seemed to sum up the outrageousness of what
had happened that night. It suddenly seemed impossible to let it go on
one minute longer; whatever the Colonel's purpose might be in foisting
an infant on his poor wife with such despicable subterfuge, he should
not be allowed to get away with it, not one second longer.

Without giving himself time to think, obsessed only by the notion
that he had to save her life and his own, now, *now,* he rushed out of

the kitchen, leaving everything as it was: the vomit on the floor, the mess on the table, the little dog whimpering in front of the stove. He burst into the hall, no longer master of himself, and shrieked, insane with hatred, *"He* did it! *He* put the child under the hedge! *He* brought it here on his horse! I saw him! I saw him! It's his bastard! It's *his,* it's *his!"*

For a moment they all stood still, as if petrified: *Madame* bent over the yowling baby, the *Colonel* stopped in mid-stride on his way to the child with a towel.

The first thought that came to Bonbon out of that eerie moment of stillness was: 'Take it back, God, dear God, let me take it back!' He knew with sudden, chilling lucidity that it had been wrong to do this, that instead of saving her and himself for that dream of shared old age in France, their France, he had in one split second of madness sealed his own doom.

So strong was that certainty, so irrefutable the knowledge, that he could not bear it. With a cry, half sob, half wail, like the last cry of a soldier gored by a sword, he turned around and ran back to the kitchen, out the door and, wildly, into the night.

* * *

Henrietta Best's first reaction was one of icy calm. "Thou hadst better go after him," she said to Kathryn, who stood gaping at the door through which the mad old man had vanished. When the maid seemed about to protest, Henrietta added, with an edge to her voice that carried a warning, "Don't worry about the child, I am perfectly able to take care of it. Go and do as I tell thee." Then she turned to her husband, who was still standing where Bonbon's shrieked denunciation had stopped him. One look at his face and she knew that it was true: he had put it under the hedge himself. Her first thought was, 'Don't panic, don't panic,' for she was overwhelmed by a sickening fear: a younger woman, a son—her whole world of love and tenderness had been a delusion. The child on the table screamed, screamed; she suddenly could stand it no longer and went to pick it up, without really knowing what she intended to do with it: put it outside, or hand it to him, or shake it and scream, "Shut up! Shut up!" But the moment she lifted it, its smallness, its pathetic vulnerability were so heartbreaking that she took it in her arms and cradled it, kissing its little face, whispering, *"Allons, allons, ne t'en fais pas . . . ne t'en fais pas . . . Allons, t'es beau . . . T'es un grand gosse . . ."*

She heard her husband behind her say, with awkward self-consciousness, "Here—take this. They gave me this to stick in its mouth. It's the only thing that works . . ." But as if the little mite understood every word of her silly French baby-talk, it fell silent and opened its eyes for the first time since its arrival, to find out who was holding it.

It gave her back her composure, and she turned around to face her husband. Her eye was caught by his hand, dangling by his side, holding the comforter; she noticed it was trembling. How shattered he must

be, a sad old man caught up in his own pathetic folly. She was overcome by pity and the sudden desire to help him. "Well," she said, with
a self-confidence that was not really her own but had been given her
by the baby, "I suppose we had better have a little talk, hadn't we?
Shall we go to my room?"

He looked at her with the face she knew so well, the hangdog face
of a little boy found with his hand in the honey jar, and it made her
feel infinitely sad that this was what life had done to him, who only
yesterday had been so bold, so dashing, such a wonderful, vital man.
Then he said, with an odd, searching look in his eyes, "Thou dost not
by chance believe that it is mine, dost thou?"

"Well—whose is it?"

"God knows. A foundling. I picked him up this afternoon in Kendal."

"He is not thy child?"

"Don't be ridiculous! He is nobody's."

"*Mais*—I do not understand . . ."

"I put him out there in the hope that thou wouldst be moved to make
him thine."

"But why?"

"To keep thee from throwing thyself off the cliff! It was a desperate measure, but I considered it to be a desperate situation."

She gazed at him uncomprehendingly. "Cliff?"

"I thought I had set thee free by banishing that madman!" he
cried, with a sudden vehemence that made her press the baby closer to
her. "I did not expect thee of thy own volition to throw thyself into
the pit of the past!"

"Pit . . . ?"

Her lack of comprehension exasperated him; he glared at her and
shouted, "By joining that madwoman on the hill! After all that went
before! I thought I had managed to exorcise those ghosts, to bring thee
back to life! But that foul knave who poisoned the town and turned
Tom Fell's entire household into a bunch of raving maniacs has managed to get hold of thee too!" He threw down the comforter. "That
devil's bastard! I should have let the priests hang him! Instead of
which, God help me, I not only risked my money and my liberty, but
got myself an infant to boot!" He slammed his forehead with frightening force, hurting himself in his powerless fury. "If I had him here,
I would disembowel the swine! Throttle him in his own bloody guts!
If I had him here I would—I would—"

She managed to interject quickly, because of the baby, "*Mais, mon
cher,* thou dost not have him here! Thou hast me here, and I love
thee, and I am all right, I swear to thee I am all right."

"Oh, I know thee!" he cried, refusing to listen in his rage. "I've been
married to thee for thirteen years! And now, after thirteen years, here
comes a charlatan, a blasphemous scoundrel—"

"*Chéri,* thou art distressing thyself foolishly," she said, trying to calm
both him and the child. But the child did not need calming, it did not
seem at all disturbed by his shouts or his fury. It lay in her arms

contentedly, asleep, she thought; but as she glanced down she saw two dark eyes contemplating her from below, solemnly.

"Oh, what's the use?" he cried. "It's all spoiled, thanks to that gelded toad! I'll take the child back to Kendal tomorrow. Let's put it in a basket and go to bed."

"*Mon cher,*" she said with tenderness, "we will go to my room and talk things over. Yes?" He grunted. "Before we go, let me tell thee that thou art the most wonderful, most gallant, most loving husband any woman could wish herself." He started to move toward the door. "I mean it," she continued, following him, carrying the child. "I don't know any man who would have done this, just to save his wife from—from a danger which he considered to be very real, even though I must confess to thee it is not—not any more."

He stood still, looked at her quizzically, then he opened the door. She passed him to enter the little room where they had spent so many hours, happy and sad ones, in the intimacy of their childless marriage. She wondered, as she sat down cautiously with the baby, how long it was since a child had been in this room.

He closed the door. "I wish I could believe that," he said.

"It is true! I can write those letters and help send those parcels without being bothered by the past. I have always known that I would have to come to terms with it someday. To hush it up as if it had never happened, as we did for so many years, just kept it right below the surface, to fly at my throat at the slightest provocation. Like that boy screaming in the kitchen. I didn't know it, but I was not really alive. I don't mean, *chéri,* that our life and our love haven't been real to me, of course they have. But by refusing to face the past, I stopped my life from going forward. I don't know how to put it, but writing those letters to those people in prison has set me free."

"Free?"

"Yes, free. Until yesterday my first husband and . . . and my children seemed to have died in vain. I could not think of them, because there was no way in which their suffering and their death could possibly make any sense." It was the first time she had mentioned her children, apart from the desperate night when she had screamed at George Fox. She clutched the baby tightly; the feel of that little body somehow gave her a sense of security, after twenty-four years of pretending her children had never existed.

He went to the cupboard and poured himself a glass of wine.

"It is thou, really, who gave me the strength to face the past," she said impulsively. "The knowledge of thy love for me made me dare do it."

He shook his head, took a draught of his wine and rinsed his mouth.

"What wouldst thou have done, had we decided to keep the child?" she asked casually.

"Oh, I don't know," he replied morosely. "Gone hunting, taken up horse-breeding . . . I would have found something to do."

"But, *mon cher!*" She laughed. "A baby in the house would not turn thee into a widower! We would have taken a wet-nurse, and another maid for the child, although I am sure Kathryn would be able to cope perfectly. Just the thing she has needed, poor old maid. I have been worrying about her these last months. She is getting terribly moody; a bit of a problem, really."

"Well, I mean: hunting and horse-breeding until he would be old enough to join me." He swallowed the rest of his wine.

"What would have troubled me is the child himself," she confessed.

"In what way?"

"The fact that he counts for so little in all this. As a person, I mean. We have been rather high-handed about him, haven't we?"

"I have been troubled by that myself. Something Fox said during the trial, believe it or not."

The baby seemed to be getting sleepy at last, maybe because she was gently rocking him. "Did they give him a name?"

"Who?"

"Him. They must have called him something in the home?"

"Oh, Billy. Billy Monday—the day he was found. They must be hard put to find names for the little brutes."

"Billy . . ." She looked at the drowsy little face. The dark, probing eyes were closed now; it gave him a look of trust and innocence.

"Dear heart," her husband said suddenly, "if that is what thou art considering, we had better talk about it."

She looked up, nonplussed. "What?"

"Keeping the child."

"Oh, *bon Dieu!*" she exclaimed, suddenly nervous. She needed time to think, to weigh the consequences, before being pinned down to such an irrevocable decision.

"Well?"

"I don't know! Let us not discuss it. Not yet."

He looked at her, hid his nose in his glass again; then he said, "By the way, there is one thing I should mention. We cannot keep Bonbon, in any event."

She had expected this, ever since poor Bonbon's hysterical accusation. It was another situation, like the baby, that she wanted to approach at her ease, alone. "Can't we wait?" she asked.

"I'm afraid not. Not because of myself, although after what happened tonight I am not looking forward to having his razor on my throat tomorrow morning."

"But where could he go, at his age?"

"Don't worry. I will see to it that he has no financial worries. But he cannot stay with us, after this. For his own sake. He will be much happier in France, among his own people."

"But he has no people of his own!" she pleaded, overwhelmed by melancholy at the thought of the poor, warped old man all by himself in Paris. "All he has is me!"

He looked at her with tenderness and understanding. "No, my dear, he does not have thee any longer. I don't know what did it, but the ghost of La Douce Tété has been laid to rest today. Maybe even that of Henriette de Coligny."

"But then, who am I?" she cried.

"Henrietta Best, wife of William Best," he answered calmly. "Mother of William Best the second, if thou so desirest."

Tears welled into her eyes and she quickly bent over the sleeping child. "God," she said, "how difficult life is! How confusing!"

But she did not stop rocking him. He lay there, asleep, peaceful and secure, mysteriously reassured.

CHAPTER EIGHT

W ELL, what do we do?" Henrietta Best asked calmly. "I don't know," Margaret Fell replied. "I honestly don't know." She walked, heavy with child, over to the window. It was a bright, almost blinding day; the sunlight's reflection from the snow outside made the little office seem lighter than at any other time. How peaceful the frozen garden looked, how pristine! Suddenly the child within her gave a violent series of kicks; she sat down clumsily on the window seat.

"Margaret . . ." Henrietta Best was by her side in a flash. "Art thou all right?"

"Oh, yes, quite all right . . ." She smiled, it could not look very convincing. "Our little friend is rather restless this morning. Oh! These last months are always the most difficult; nine is about two too many."

"Think of the elephant," Henrietta Best said. "She has to carry her young for a year, and it has a trunk as well as four legs."

"Well, by the feel of it, that's what I'm about to give birth to." There was a silence, in which she gazed into the garden, her mind a blank.

"Well?" Henrietta's persistent voice asked, behind her. "What do we do? We have to do *something.*"

"Yes, I suppose so." She sighed. Infernal mess, that's what it was. "Honestly, I think only George can answer those questions. I can be vague and generally pious in my letters, thou canst be jolly and down to earth, but when it comes to theology . . ."

"Where is he? Didst thou ask him to come?"

"I have asked him to come several times," she replied dispassionately. "For some reason, the young man prefers to ignore our pleas."

"But isn't he curious as to what we're doing? He must realize by now that—well, that we are providing him with an organization."

"Maybe that's the trouble," she said. "Maybe he doesn't want an organization. Maybe all he wants is to hop about like a grasshopper, bringing people to the Light, or whatever he calls it, and letting them fend for themselves."

"In that case, he may find himself overtaken by the monster he has created."

Margaret smiled. "The monster being me?"

Henrietta Best gave her a knowing look. "Thou must admit that without thee there would be no monster."

"Well . . ." She did not like this turn in the conversation. "For lack of a word from George, we'll have to make up our own Quakerism as we go along. Where is the first letter?"

Henrietta Best looked at the sheaf of papers she had brought in. "This is from a young soldier in prison in Newcastle for refusal to bear arms. His family has raked together the money to buy a replacement. He asks whether it is all right to let someone else bear arms for him, or whether this is against the peace testimony. He also shares a cell with members of other sects, to a total of fifteen, which he lists as Lollards, Anabaptists, Muggletonians, Sabbatarians, Ranters and Fifth Monarchy men, whatever *that* may mean. He has shared the contents of his parcel with them and also thy letter. Now they all want to know more about the children of the Light: what they stand for, what their dogmas and principles are. But, frankly, I think the operative question is the last one: what must they do to become eligible for a monthly parcel? Why not tell them to 'mind the Light' and send each of them a pair of socks?"

"That would scarcely be sufficient."

"Oh, I don't know. I found that theological differences become rather blunted in prison. In my case . . ." She did not finish.

Obviously, she still could not talk about it, poor woman. It was really wonderful, the way she had taken this on. Her little boy must give her the strength; ever since that foundling had arrived she seemed to have acquired another dimension. "Well, dear Henrietta, if thou dost feel that thou canst answer those questions satisfactorily, do so."

"Is that really all right? For me to start laying about me with theology?"

"Why not? We are all in this together."

"Certainement. But, my dear, I am not a Quaker. I'm not even religious. I'm just an attender, helping out until thy little elephant is born."

"Well, I'll be content to let thee answer whatever thou seest fit. What's the next one?"

"Let me see . . . Ah, yes. This one is a little tricky, I would say. It is not from a prisoner but from the woman clerk of a newly formed Meeting in Little Rostock. Do we know where Little Rostock is?"

"Isn't it somewhere in County Durham?"

"I wouldn't know. Anyhow, she writes: *'Some women members have run into notions after George Fox left. Some have taken to running through the streets, hair loose, breasts bared, shouting exhortations. Others talk in unknown tongues to priests and magistrates. One of the women stripped off her clothes, smeared herself with excrement and ran into church during a sermon, shouting that God wanted them to smell for themselves the corruption of their souls.'* That sounds like quite a circus, doesn't it?"

"Oh dear, oh dear—that's what Mabby did."

"Pardon?"

"What does she want of me? What can I do?"

"Oh, I don't know. She obviously had to unburden herself to someone. I don't blame her."

"What wouldst thou say?"

"I?" Henrietta Best smiled. *"Paul says this, Peter says that, but what dost thou say?* All right. What would I say? It's a bit late to douse her with water."

"That's what we did."

"Pardon?"

"That's what Thomas Woodhouse did when Mabby and Harry Martin were up to the same sort of thing in the courtyard."

"And did it work?"

"They were children. Someone could take them by the ear and bring them to their senses. I'm afraid that the women running through the streets with their breasts bared, as well as our smelly Friend, are beyond the reach of authority."

"Even their husbands'?"

"Perhaps."

"Thou art right. They wouldn't have started running in the first place had their emotional needs been satisfied."

Margaret frowned. "The only person to help them would be George himself. But that he is not prepared to do. He's probably miles away from there by now."

There was a silence, with an edge of discomfort.

"Well," Henrietta Best said, "why not send this letter on to him? Let him deal with it, for a change. And let us inform the clerk that we have done so. That would take care of it, at least for the time being."

"I suppose so . . ." A sense of despondency had settled over her. It was more than one of the frequent changes of mood that went with her condition. There was a deeper cause: even her appropriating his religious movement had not prevailed upon him to come back.

"Here is another one that I think thou shouldst know about," Henrietta Best resumed. "It's from one Obadiah Foot, clerk of a Meeting in Yorkshire. *'Dear Friend. Two young men in our Meeting, inspired by a miraculous healing performed by George Fox here during his recent visit, held up the burial of a dead relative in order that they might minister to the corpse, exhorting it to get up and walk. After three days, the ministry being unsuccessful, the body was forcibly removed by the sheriff because it had become offensive. The Meeting is desirous to know what steps to take, if any, should a similar occasion arise. What miraculous powers can be expected of us, children of the Light? Some among us feel that the young men in question ran into notions; others that the sheriff lacked faith. Please advise us. Thine in love, Obadiah Foot.'"*

"Oh dear, oh dear . . ." She tried to rise, but her belly seemed to weigh a ton. And the child was quiet just now, maybe she had better keep it that way.

"Can I get thee anything?" Henrietta asked, concerned.

"No, thank thee. I'm all right. Oh, I really don't know. Just put it aside. I'll think about it. Are there many more?"

"Yes, quite a stack. But I can answer most of them. There are just a few that thou wilt have to see."

"Well, let's have one more; then maybe we could have some tea."

"Eh bien, let me see . . . Here. This is a real challenge. A Friend in Liverpool jail by the name of Harry Moore. He does not mention his age; my guess is that he is very young. His question is as follows. *'My jailer often lays violent hands on my person, but the Light tells me to approach him in a spirit of love. The only way in which I can show love is by embracing him each time he comes into the cell.'* "

"Oh, no!"

"Listen! *'The jailer rebuked me more violently each time and he has now stated that if I do this filthy thing once more he will crown me with the pan of soup. I am prepared to suffer this and to steadfastly continue my testimony. But what if he were to end by killing me? Would I have turned him into a murderer? Would his fall from grace weigh upon my soul?'* "

"That is ridiculous!" Margaret exclaimed.

"Apart from that, what do we say to the boy?"

She sighed, her head in her hands. "I don't know, Henrietta, I honestly don't know. What wouldst thou suggest?"

"Truly?"

"Yes, please: what *wouldst* thou say?"

"My answer," Henrietta Best replied matter-of-factly, "would be: 'Thou art in error, beloved Friend, when calling this a motion of love. It is a motion of brittleness'—this I find a useful word. 'Whatever anyone may say, thou shouldst not do unto others as thou wouldst have them do unto thee before having made certain that your tastes are the same.' "

Margaret frowned. "George would hit the ceiling if he were to read that."

"Eh bien! Isn't it time he did? Let me write that and send George Fox a copy. My guess is he'll descend upon this house like a bolt from heaven." She paused. "Would that not please thee?"

"Yes, but—"

"All right, I'll take care of it. Shall I ask for tea now?"

"But I'm not sure—"

"Of course thou art sure. This is ridiculous, Margaret. Thou art not a theologian, neither am I. We are women, moved in our emotional way by other people's suffering. That is the only concept of Quakerism I will accept. I have no time, no patience and certainly no taste for men trying to raise the dead, frustrated women smearing themselves with excrement or youths kissing their jailers. That is not religion to me. Nor, I am sure, to any real saint, for that matter."

"Is there such a thing as a real saint?"

"Probably. But, in my experience at least, there is one quality they all share: they have a sense of humor. I would even say they are mischievous. The one thing that betrays the false saint is self-importance, the incapacity to laugh at himself. Then, of course, there is the ultimate test: what do they do? Not what do they say; what do they *do?* And that's a question I will leave thee to answer for thyself in the case of our feathered friend."

"Who's that?" she asked primly.

Henrietta broke into a smile. *"Voyons donc!"* She sat down beside her and put an arm around her shoulders. "He is, *ma chère,* a superb specimen. But there is only one person he can ever truly love: himself."

"That is not so!"

"No, thou art right: and mankind." Henrietta's motherly hug made Margaret almost burst into tears; that was the damnable thing about pregnancy: one was always so emotional. "When is thy husband due back?"

"He should be here for my laying in. But not before, I suppose."

"Well, that's not long now."

"Henrietta . . ." She held her back as she was about to rise. "Yes, *ma chère?"*

"Do not send that letter, please."

The older woman gave her a searching look. "Dost thou not want him brought hither?"

"Not by those means. Not by ridiculing the Sermon on the Mount. It seems so—so unworthy. And it would really hurt him, deeply."

Henrietta smiled. *"Ma pauvre amie,* thou art too delicate. Thou art not dealing with a delicate man. People like him do not react to delicate hints, only to red rags."

"That is why. That letter is a red rag and nothing more."

"I do not agree." Henrietta rose and went to the door. Halfway, she turned around. "Margaret, I do not say this readily, but I have been in prison myself. There is one thing we owe those people: the truth. The truth is not always what they want to hear, but to be evasive or fanciful with them is to exploit their misery for our own emotional satisfaction. And one thing George Fox said makes good sense to me: never use a man as a means, always as an end. That is what we should tell our kissing Quaker."

"Well, tell him that. But not the other thing."

"In that case: write the letter thyself. If I do it, I should be allowed to tell that boy the truth as I see it. At least, my advice will be based on experience."

She left. Margaret stared morosely out at the snow. Why not allow her to write that? She was right, it might indeed bring George back. So why not?

Maybe it was the pregnancy, but something had changed. She no longer wanted him at all costs. Whether it was the burden of a new life or something else, she found herself stricken with an in- articulate, indiscriminate gentleness. It was as if that of God in her were about her all the time. That of God. *'No, no, not like thy stomach, more like thy unborn children.'*

She wished it were true! If only that of God were as self-assertive as the little wrestler in her belly! Like most things George said, it was true enough; but somehow it seemed to lack experience. It had an element of abstraction, of theory. Yet, look at Henrietta Best! Would she have changed from a frightened recluse into this charming, forceful woman without having been touched by George in passing? He had done the same to all of them: awakened them and set them free.

Maybe she should allow Henrietta to mind her own inner Light. But in that case she had better warn her to seek refuge on top of the cupboard the moment he came charging down upon them, maddened by the red rag. Poor George, how simple his life would be without women!

Suddenly she did not trust this amused resignation of hers. Pregnant or not, she was the same old Maggie who had captured the judge, doubled his estate, ruled the town of Ulverston, chased George Fox over the hill. Should she let someone else wave that red rag for her?

'Oh, Maggie, Maggie,' she thought wearily. 'What slyness art thou up to now?'

* * *

George Fox received the packet of letters in Liverpool when he touched base at The Mermaid on arrival. A note from Margaret Fell went with it.

"Dear Heart, I am sorry to burden thee with this errand, but wouldst thou hand these to the warden of Liverpool jail to be distributed to the Friends imprisoned there for Truth's sake? I would rather they be handed to him by thee than trust the postillion. Art thou well? Let us hear from thee when thou canst find the time. Our labors are richly blessed: over one hundred letters every two weeks, and the same amount of parcels every other month. We are doing our best to interpret to those in prison the essence of thy message, realizing all along that we are but pale moons reflecting the light of thy sun. Keep warm, the winter here is severe. We often pray for thee and think of thee always as we gather in front of the big fire in the hall to have meeting twice a day. Thou art sorely missed, especially by thy old friend: M.F."

He read through the letters that evening, lying on his bed in the inn. He had been vaguely unhappy about the women's frenetic correspondence for some time. The few letters he had seen seemed faithful enough to the truth, yet there had been an element of housewifely pragmatism in them that seemed to reduce the fierce glory of the Presence to something prosaic, almost pedestrian. To be in prison for truth's sake was a witness, a testimony, not an affliction like a cold or the flux. Yet they wrote to their correspondents almost as if it were; especially that Frenchwoman, whose letters were full of practical advice on how to avoid constipation, how important regular hours of sleep were, especially in the perpetual dusk of the dungeons, if they wanted to safeguard their sanity. Was sanity that important? Was it not God's will that His children should turn their suffering into a blinding beacon for all the world to see? He had been in prison himself; he had never been troubled by such things. What had bothered him was not constipation or lack of sleep but how to keep the awareness of the Presence alive, how to nourish the inner Light with prayers and meditation.

Reading this new batch of correspondence from the busybodies in Swarthmoor Hall did nothing to lift his spirits, which had been low ever since his visit to London. The encounter with Cromwell had gone well; his arrival had obviously been planned by the Lord, for just at that time the accusation had been planted in Cromwell's ear that the Quakers had formed a secret alliance with the Cavaliers and were planning an armed insurrection. He had been able to dispel that fable at once; the audience had been very successful altogether. When they parted Cromwell had said, with tears in his eyes, "Come again to my house, for if thou and I were but an hour in a day together we should be nearer one to the other." Stirring words, and he did not doubt that, had it been up to Cromwell, they would have done just that. But it had proved impossible to get to him without going through Lord Shorwell, the Master of Requests, who was of a different breed. He was charming, effusive, chatting about his good friend Fell, but after that one visit, despite the tears in Cromwell's eyes, he had been terribly busy each day, unable to receive George Fox, who had written a note in the end, asking Friend Oliver to take that watchdog away from his door. But he had never received a reply; Lord Shorwell obviously took care of written requests also. He had considered gatecrashing, but the Light had not guided him that far. Morosely, he had hovered around London for weeks, despite the plague; then he had given up and taken to the road again.

But something of the fire, the zest had gone out of him. It was probably temporary; it might have to do with the winter, which was particularly harsh this year and had frozen not only the roads and the rivers but also, it appeared, the zeal of the children of the Light. There had been a new dubiousness among Friends, a questioning spirit that had not been there before. In earlier days the fire, the enthusiasm, the ecstasy whenever the power of the Lord thundered among them had swept people off their feet, caused them to witness loudly, regardless of the consequences. Now a spirit of caution had arisen; he could not be sure, but he suspected that the women in Swarthmoor had something to do with it. There could be no doubt that their operation ran smoothly; there was not a Friend in prison anywhere in the land who did not, in a surprisingly short time after his incarceration, receive his first parcel of socks, muffler, candles, weevil-proof biscuits, a Bible, a list of do's and don't's for prisoners, a jar of prunes against constipation and a letter exhorting him to be steadfast in the truth and to organize silent meetings with the inmates of his cell forthwith, as this would fortify and inspire all, especially himself. The letter contained a phrase that summed up the attitude of the women: *"It is a well-known fact that the person most likely to survive the hardships of being adrift in an open boat on the high seas is the one who appoints himself its captain."* Now, what kind of spirit was that? Who told those women that survival was the primary goal of a man incarcerated for his beliefs? It was a spirit of pragmatism, of denying that of God in favor of a daily bowel movement and feet without chilblains. And where had the women garnered the questionable information about shipboard life? It smacked of a housewife's musings by the fire, imagining herself at sea.

He read through the new batch of letters, dropping them on the coverlet as he finished them; suddenly he came upon something that made him rear up in fury.

He did not even stay the night; he set out for Ulverston at once.

It took a night and a day before he arrived at Swarthmoor, at ten o'clock in the morning, after a hair-raising race with the incoming tide.

He entered the hall in the power of the Lord, giddy with exhaustion, as if he had set foot ashore after a stormy crossing of the Irish Sea. When he saw the long tables covered with boxes, the rows of women making up packages, he felt like overturning those tables and chasing the women just as Christ had chased the money-changers from the temple. He had come unannounced, and they welcomed him with cries of surprise and elation. But he brushed them aside and asked grimly, "Where is Margaret Fell?"

She was in her little office, writing at her desk. On the floor sat Ann Traylor, playing with a little black-haired boy; on the window seat sat the Frenchwoman, reading. She was the first to see him. *"Mon Dieu!* Look who's here!" she cried in a tone that was in marked contrast with the squeals of delight with which the others had welcomed him.

Margaret Fell turned around and peered at the doorway over her spectacles. At the sight of him she hastily took them off and put them under some papers. "George!" It was gratifying to see her imperiousness wither in his presence. It was not he, it was not he; as a man he would be utterly powerless to do anything; it was the Lord in whose love and power he spoke.

"Good day to thee, Margaret Fell," he said sternly. "I must have a serious discourse with thee. I am disturbed to find that thou and thy household seem to have run into notions."

She looked at him as if she could not believe her ears. "Notions?"

"Close the door and I will tell thee." Ann Traylor did so, then retired to a corner of the room with the child instead of leaving, as he would have preferred her to do. "Let me begin with the cause for my return," he said, taking a letter from his breast pocket. "This is a letter sent by Henrietta Best to a Friend imprisoned in Liverpool." He read slowly, his voice charged with indignation, *"'As to thy question whether to continue embracing thy jailer: do not do unto others as thou*

*wouldst have them do unto thee unless thou art sure that your tastes
are the same.'"* He turned to the woman on the window seat. "Was
this written by thee, Henrietta Best?"

The woman, whom he last remembered as breaking down in sobs
with her head on his shoulder, looked at him coldly. "Why, yes."

"Who authorized thee to rewrite the Scriptures?"

"But, George . . ." Margaret started.

The woman in the window silenced her with a gesture. "Am I to
understand, George Fox, that thou considerest it better to affront a
man by embracing him than to identify with him and seek another
way to express one's feelings?"

"That is not the issue. It is the terms in which thou hast couched
thy advice. It is . . ." He restrained himself. "It is not consistent with
the approach to conflict after the manner of the children of the Light."

"I do not understand."

"To ridicule the Sermon on the Mount is an insult to the honor of
God, a betrayal of the spirit of Christ."

She looked at him with defiance. "Friend, I have been listening to
that kind of talk for a lifetime, without ever understanding what the
words meant. Tell me: what should I have told him to do?"

"He should do as God tells him, mind his inner Light! If the Light
tells him to go on embracing that jailer, he must do so."

"And if the jailer goes on knocking him down, he must persevere
until the day he is struck dead and turns his jailer into a murderer?"

"If that is what the Light within tells him! There are hardened
hearts that cannot be convinced; John Sawrey, for instance. They are
beyond saving, that of God within them is beyond liberating. In the
end they are punished by God."

"How canst thou know that?"

"It is important to me to know these things. I have kept record of
them."

The woman in the window gazed at him with astonishment. "Thou
keepest a record of thy enemies as they are punished?"

"Indeed I do," he retorted angrily. "I call it the Book of Rewards."

"How are they punished?"

"According to God's will. By disease, by violence, by accidents."

"So if John Sawrey were to be struck by a falling roof tile, thou
wouldst enter it in thy book of rewards?"

"Yes."

She said, *"Charmant!"* Then she rose and left the room.

He turned to Margaret Fell. "Do not let this distress thee, dear
friend. She will return to grace. But she should write no more letters
to our prisoners." He suddenly felt weary, his legs trembled with
fatigue; no wonder, after that ride. He went to the window where the
woman had been sitting and lowered himself onto the seat.

"And what would be a sign of her return to grace?" Margaret asked.
"When she starts a book of rewards of her own?"

It seemed she too had taken offense at that information. He turned
to the maid in the corner. "Forgive me, Ann," he said. "I would like

a word with Margaret Fell in private." The girl scowled at him. It made him feel very tired.

Margaret said, "Pray take little William back to Henrietta Best, Ann; I will be out in a minute." She got up and went to the door to open it for the girl. He saw to his surprise that she was heavy with child. She came back to her desk and said, "Dear George. Forgive me for snapping at thee. I love thee for what thou art, as thou art."

There was in her tenderness an element of female superiority that irked him. "Aside from all that," he said, "art thou going to stop thy friend writing any more letters? She must no longer be allowed to represent our movement."

"What exactly is our movement? Before we decide who our representatives are, we must know who we are. What are our goals, our—"

"But, my dear woman!" he exclaimed. "I have formulated that many times!"

"I know. In thy answers to the ministers at the Lancaster trial, for instance. But what those people in prison want is not a theological debate. They want something simple, straightforward, that they can explain to others in everyday words. Really, what they need is guidelines."

"Guidelines?"

"Let me give thee an example. Two young Friends tried to revive a dead man by praying over him in the power of the Lord. They kept it up for three days and three nights."

"I have done so myself, several times."

"But they did not succeed. After three days the body had to be removed because it became offensive."

"They might have succeeded had they been allowed to stay with it longer."

"George," she said patiently, "I don't think it matters whether they might or might not have succeeded. What matters is that they tried to emulate thee. All they gleaned from thy message was thy power to perform miracles."

"Thou knowest it is not I who perform miracles, it is the Lord, through me."

"But is this the essence of thy message? That if God wills it and if the moment is right, man may suspend the laws of nature? I cannot see how the restoration of thy hand, thy crossing the sands against the tide, even thy stopping the henchmen in Derby jail from hanging that girl is in any way essential to thy message. That of God in us should be expressed in our daily conduct, not in isolated acts that suspend the laws of nature. That was why Henrietta Best was so shocked when she learned of thy Book of Rewards. The God of love, whom I always understood to be thine, would send me to the aid of a man struck by lightning, whoever he might be and whatever he might have done, rather than consider it heavenly justice and cross his name off a list."

"Isn't it rather that thou dost not really believe in miracles?"

"Oh, I believe in them all right. I am sure the power of the Lord can pick up a mountain and dump it somewhere else. But to what purpose? What about the innocent people on its slopes, the terrified little animals? What could be the *purpose?*"

"To show that the kingdom of God consists not of words, but of power."

"But the whole of the universe is a demonstration of that power! There is no need for God to go on flexing His muscles!"

He looked at her musingly, then he asked, "Dost thou know of a place called Pendle Hill?"

"Why?"

"A few nights before I came to see thee for the first time, I passed that way. I was moved by the Lord to climb it; when I came to the top and looked about me I saw that the valley and the moors were filled with people, one vast mass of people as far as the eye could reach, and I heard a voice say, *'There is a great people to be gathered.'* It convinced me that as long as we do not impose our concept of God on each other but labor together in tolerance and love, a great people will be gathered, who will live together in perfect harmony, like the animals of the peaceable kingdom described by Isaiah."

"But the Sawreys of this world would not let them! Canst thou not see that this notion, beautiful as it is, is impractical?"

He looked at her with an odd expression, as if he were gazing at something beyond her. "Believe me," he said. "It will come to pass."

She looked at him for a moment in silence. Then she said, taking up the quill, "Now this is something people in prison will understand. Tell me again, and I will write it down."

He repeated it slowly. Outside, in the wintry sunlight, pigeons alighted on the window sill.

* * *

They spent the rest of that morning and all afternoon closeted in her office. Ann Traylor brought them some food on a tray; neither of them touched it. Margaret realized how exhausted she was only when, at the end of the day, a sudden faintness overcame her as she went to the door. She knew it had to do with her condition, but it alarmed him profoundly. As he stood there, supporting her, he cried in anguish: "Henrietta! Ann Traylor! Help! Margaret Fell is not well!"

Ann Traylor came rushing in, reassured the frantic man and took over. When at last Margaret lay gazing at the comforting shadows of the candlelight on the ceiling of the fourposter, she felt drained of all strength. She had managed to remain objective and detached all day, without allowing her own femininity to surface; now she felt all that suppressed emotion overwhelm her. She closed her eyes in prayer for strength, protection; after a moment there was a rustle and she heard a soft scratching sound. She opened her eyes and saw Ann

Traylor, in a chair by her bedside, writing in an exercise book by the light of the candle.

"Ann? What art thou doing?"

The girl looked up. "I am correcting Bonny Baker's lesson."

She gazed at the girl in the candlelight, her strong young face, her bright, gentle eyes. Another one transformed by George's passing; only a few months ago she had been proud, headstrong and utterly self-centered. "How is he faring?" she asked. "Tell me."

The girl's voice did so, cheerfully.

* * *

Ann Traylor babbled on about Bonny Baker as softly and monotonously as she could until, with a feeling of relief, she saw that her mistress had fallen asleep.

It had been a narrow escape, for what she had been writing had nothing to do with Bonny's lessons. As she sat there by the bedside, she had, on the spur of the moment, appropriated his exercise book to use as a diary. *"I hope she is asleep at last, poor woman. How is it possible that one person can make another suffer such agonies without noticing it? And that while he is holding forth about 'love' and 'tenderness' and 'answering that of God in everyone.' Considering the way he has treated Bonny and Margaret Fell, all I can say is—well, let me be charitable. The one who really stood up to him today was Mistress Best, bless her . . ."* Ann looked up to make certain that the poor, exhausted woman was indeed asleep; then she continued, *"I must confess: the sooner I get out of here, the better. If it weren't for M.F., I would have gone long ago. But she is so vulnerable, so trusting and generous, to leave her now would be to sneak away from the battlefield. Only, it is not my battle. I desire no part of it. I do not wish to end up in prison or the pillory for something I do not believe in. The only thing I believe in, as far as the present upheaval is concerned, is what Margaret Fell is doing: helping the poor people who, bewitched by Fox's rantings, find themselves in prison. It was such a spontaneous and wonderful thing to do that I became involved in it myself; now here I am, hanging on when I should be on my way. What way, whither? I do not know; all I know is: I desire a normal life, a simple, loving husband without fancy phrases who will be gentle and kind, a cottage with a small piece of land, some chickens, a cat, a dog; I desire children, four or five of them, who, when I am old and afraid of being alone . . ."*

The quill scribbled on, with small, busy scratchings. As the stillness deepened, surreptitious noises of the night began in the house. Floorboards squeaked, mice began to rustle behind the wainscoting, while Margaret Fell drifted deeper into the dreamless sleep of exhaustion, and Ann Traylor, aged seventeen, wrote the first entry in her diary.

BOOK TWO

(1653)

CHAPTER ONE

T HE nasty little pamphlet even looked dirty, compared to the spring day outside the study window, open to the garden. Pigeons were strutting and cooing in the first warm sunlight, a scent of honeysuckle and young grass was wafted into the room where Henrietta Best sat reading the scurrilous pages, aware that Thomas Fell was watching her intently.

"Well," she said lightly, "he doesn't exactly mince words, does he? I rather like his definition of us; it has a poetic flavor."

"Pardon?"

She read aloud from the first page of the pamphlet, " *'The evil Quakers, lurking in the hills of Lancashire like butterflies.'* I like the butterflies lurking."

"Pardon me?" He obviously was in no mood for levity.

"I think that's exactly what we are: charming, harmless and ephemeral."

"Ah?" He brightened; she had pierced his massive gloom at last. "Are you serious?"

"Serious about what?"

"About this—this whole thing being ephemeral?"

So that was why he had invited her to join him in his study so secretively, the day after his arrival from the circuit! He wanted to be told it was all a passing fancy which had about run its course. "I did not mean that," she said.

"Well, I . . ." He paused, searching for words, but could not bring himself to pronounce judgment on his wife, not even in the privacy of his own study. He looked exhausted, poor man, and no wonder. Constantly on the move, living in a string of inns all over the country, beset by anxiety about his wife and her young saint . . . She hoped he would not touch upon that subject.

"I do not believe that a single person in this house has any idea of the seriousness of the situation!" he exclaimed with startling vehemence.

"Ah?" It seemed the polite sound to make.

"This pamphlet is proof that Swarthmoor Hall has now been identified as the headquarters of the Quaker movement, and that is disastrous. Cromwell is about to issue a proclamation; I have information as to its contents. It laments the un-Christian disturbance of church services by Quakers. It requires that all such disorderly practices shall stop; those who do not comply shall be considered disturbers of the peace; constables and judges are to proceed against them accordingly. Do you realize what that means?"

"Well—yes, I suppose so." She did not, but his alarm began to communicate itself to her.

"It means that unless you women stop meddling in a movement that has now run out of hand, you will, all of you, find yourselves in prison. Now, is that worth the candle? Please, *Madame,* please try to dissuade her from continuing her present activities! Find her something else to do. For God's sake, find her something else!" He started to pace up and down, his hands behind his back, nervously clasping and unclasping them. She had never seen him in such a state of agitation. "Let her raise lambs, let her start a home for foundlings . . ." He stopped abruptly and turned to her. "I'm sorry, I did not mean to be disparaging about your son."

"I understand," she said blandly. "But I'm afraid that it is a little more complicated than just finding her another diversion." She was treading on dangerous ground, she would have to watch her step.

He shot her a glance that, maybe because of her own apprehension, looked unnervingly knowledgeable. "Would you care to elaborate on that, *Madame?*"

"Your wife has found a field for her undeniable talent for organization."

"You mean, it is she who has made the movement respectable?"

It was an odd way of phrasing it, but she supposed she understood what he meant. "If by 'respectable' you mean institutionalized, yes. It was she who drew up the discipline that has now begun to pull the movement into shape. It's a remarkable document; I wonder whether you would be interested?" It was an indiscretion on her part, but she did not like the intensity with which he watched her. Anything to avoid awkward questions about his wife and young Fox. "The whole discipline is still under discussion," she said, picking up her writing box, which she had put by the side of her chair. "But I happen to have a copy of her first draft." She opened the box and took out a sheet of paper, which she held out to him. "I hope you'll be able to read my handwriting."

"Thank you." He bowed before accepting the document. "You are very kind."

"Pas du tout." She smiled, snapped the lock on her box and rose to leave. "You'll see what the attraction is to your wife. She is a very intelligent woman."

"You think so?" He asked it as if it were the last word to be applied to his spouse. As in the case of most *cocus,* the woman he claimed as his own was only half the woman. "May I call on you again?" He opened the door for her. There was something touching about his eagerness.

"Mais oui," she said, smiling. "It will be my pleasure. I'm very fond of her, you know."

"I know," he said. "So, indeed, am I." It was a stoic understatement, yet it sounded oddly pompous.

She swished away, trying not to make it look like flight. The hall was dark and chilly, the radiant day outside seemed to beckon. She put down her writing box and walked out into the garden.

Margaret Fell and baby were sitting underneath one of the old trees flushed with the tender green of spring. The nanny and the wet-nurse were squatting by her in the grass; all were laughing at the chortlings of the infant waving its little fists in its mother's face, which loomed above it like a flower of pure love. As Henrietta watched, unseen, she knew a short, unedifying moment of envy. How young she herself had been, how full of love, when her firstborn . . .

She shook off the ghosts of the past and walked on toward the sunken garden, where she had last seen Ann Traylor playing with little Will among the rosebushes.

*   *   *

As Thomas Fell scanned his wife's draft for a church discipline for the people called Quakers, he realized with a sinking feeling that this was the last, damning item in the case against the religious fanatics. Until recently Cromwell had considered the "Children of the Light" a harmless nuisance; the proclamation was a reversal of that opinion, and the reason was that the Quakers had changed from a haphazard collection of innocuous hotheads into an organized, centrally controlled movement. As Thomas scanned the clauses of the discipline, there could be no doubt who was the author. There might be others involved, there no doubt were, but the main culprit for turning the Quaker movement from a harmless irritant into a threat to the established order was his wife. He recognized her in almost every clause.

He sighed, pushed back his chair and walked over to the open window, flushing the pigeons as he approached. There she sat, surrounded by maids, the baby in her lap, a picture of domestic happiness. She had no idea of the danger, no notion of the fate that would befall her if she did not sever all connection with the doomed movement at once. Within a few days John Sawrey would receive the proclamation and the accompanying instructions to sheriffs and judges. It would give him the weapon he must have been seeking. Last time they had been able to thwart Sawrey's scheme, this time there was no hope of doing so. Whether Margaret were the wife of the Vice Chancellor or of the lowest sheepherder on the fells, there was no difference before the law.

He must stop her before it was too late. But how? How could he convince the deluded woman that she was heading for prison, and that in prison she would die? She had no idea of the reality of what she had been dealing with as a pastime all winter. She had been writing hundreds of letters to prisoners but had never seen the inside of a prison in her life. The malevolent pamphleteer had indeed furnished the perfect definition of her and her women: "butterflies."

What could he do to save her? He weighed various possibilities in his mind and concluded that the best way would be to let her see with her own eyes what was in store for her if she did not desist: to show her a prison, the worst prison he could find.

Well, that was not difficult. There was no worse hellhole in all of England than the dungeons of Lancaster Castle.

* * *

Thomas Fell had not often visited the dungeons himself; unlike other judges, he derived no satisfaction from viewing those he had sentenced in their misery. To walk down those dark, dank corridors again, to smell that unforgettable stench, to hear the rabid shrieks of the insane—it was a harrowing experience. His belief in the justice of imprisonment was unshaken, but it repelled him as would the sights in a slaughterhouse. It took a coarser nature than his to view with equanimity the disintegration of human beings, as did the warden who guided them on their tour. A pleasant enough man upstairs in the sunlight, a deeply disturbing, almost salacious monster of vengeance once he descended into the purgatory of which he was the guardian.

From the moment they entered, Margaret impressed her husband by the way she retained her composure although he knew she must be profoundly disturbed by what she saw. The girl Traylor was obviously made of lesser steel than his wife; Margaret seemed to be more concerned about the distress of her young companion than about the horrors the warden showed them with such ill-concealed satisfaction. She gazed with apparent unconcern at the grimy, diseased miscreants squatting in the straw or sprawling in the stone bunks hewn out of the rock; had it not been for the pallor of her face, he would have thought she was unmoved.

Her poise finally cracked, however, when they reached the lowest level and she saw the madwomen in their cage, drooling, shrieking, dragging their chains, stumbling toward the bars at their passing and stretching out clawlike hands to grab her cloak. She stepped back with an involuntary gasp; he saw her eyes glisten as she stared at the women. When they reached the cell of the children at the far end of the passage, with the shrieks and howls of the insane still ringing in their ears, she made an involuntary gesture of horror at the sight of five or six little creatures huddled together in the filthy straw, their faces gaunt and grimy, their eyes glinting in the lantern light like rats'. He explained to her in a calm, unemotional voice that these urchins were vagrants, abandoned or orphaned, of the sort who roamed all of England's towns in packs and had to be eradicated if the citizenry were to live in peace. He told her about burglaries, muggings, armed robberies these creatures had committed, one of them even was a convicted murderer; but she was not listening to him. She gazed at the ratlike dwarfs with a compassion that, though misguided, was deeply moving. He concluded from the manner in which she clutched his hand that she must be almost at the end of her tether; he was loath to expose her to the worst, but he must if the experience was to have its desired effect. He turned to the warden and said, "Now let us see the rest."

The warden, who knew what he meant, as it had all been arranged beforehand, said with conspiratorial glee, "Certainly, Your Lordship. We left 'em for your pleasure. This way, please, ma'am." He led the small procession back along the corridor, past the cages with the shrieking lunatics, the clawing hands; they climbed the spiral stone staircase.

As they went, Margaret asked her husband in a whisper, "Are there any Quakers imprisoned here?"

He had expected the question and answered, "There are indeed, but they are all in solitary confinement."

"Why?"

"These are the new instructions from London."

The warden opened the door to the courtyard. "This way, please, ma'am." She stepped outside.

This time she gasped at what she saw. The Traylor girl cried, "Oh, no!" and hid her face on her mistress' shoulder. Margaret put her arms around her and stared, her face a mask, at the gruesome sight.

Despite the fact that these three children must have deserved their fate, to see them hanging there, their faces distorted, blue tongues stuck out, their thin, scraggy necks ghoulishly elongated, was harrowing. The frailty of their small bodies, making the nooses look coarse and heavy, grated on even Thomas' sensibilities as they slowly turned in the perpetual draft from the dungeons below that circled the courtyard. He looked at his wife, expecting a mute plea to be led away. She was staring at the sight, the sobbing girl in her arms, but her face was set, her eyes clear. For the first time that morning he felt he had lost contact with her. Then, slowly, she turned toward him; something in her eyes made him realize, with a feeling of disaster, that he had achieved the opposite of what he hoped for.

"Didst thou know about this, Thomas?" she asked. Her voice was casual, without emotion.

"Well, yes . . ." How could he undo the damage? "I thought it necessary to show thee this. Forgive me if I have gone too far. But this is reality, my dear. I cannot change it by hiding it from thee."

She looked at him in a way that made him go cold. It was the first time she had set eyes upon a dark part of his life that he had always hidden from her. "Didst thou condemn these children?"

"No." He steeled himself for the question he knew must come.

"Hast thou ever condemned children to this?"

He knew that on his answer their future depended. But he could not gainsay the truth. He nodded; he did not trust himself to speak.

The look she gave him was one not of condemnation but somehow of farewell. At his silent request, the warden guided them out of the courtyard, back to their carriage waiting in the sun. The day was warm; the headless statue of St. George and the benches surrounding it were covered with twittering young birds; it was as if nature conspired to make the image of the dead children even more monstrous. After they had bidden goodbye to the warden and thanked him for his courtesy, they sat mutely in the carriage as it rattled down the cobbled streets of Lancaster on its way home. Margaret had her arms around the

Traylor girl, who was still distraught. Her face was calm, almost serene; her eyes expressed no horror, no distress, no emotion at all. His attempts to start a conversation met with no response. He stared out the window of the coach at the lurching landscape for the full nine hours of their journey home. Even when the horses were changed, they did not leave the coach, but waited in silence for the journey to be resumed.

Toward the end, as they approached Ulverston and the girl slept at last, he could bear it no longer. "Dear heart," he said, with a despair that he could not hide despite his effort to sound calm and reasonable. "Thou must not hold me responsible as a person for decisions I am forced to make as a judge."

She looked at him with an expression he had never seen before and said, "I am sorry. I cannot make that distinction."

"But thou must!" he urged. "I have sworn to uphold the law, I am bound by jurisprudence! Dost thou think I enjoy condemning children to death? It's my duty!"

"I suppose it is," she said, after a silence.

There was nothing left to say. They arrived home in silence. She did not sup with the family, but retired for the night. He wanted to follow her, plead with her, try desperately to make her see reason. But he knew that only time would, perhaps, bring them back together. Alone in his study, he tried to articulate what had happened. What decisions had she arrived at, behind that calm façade?

Late that night he entered their bedchamber, on tiptoe so as not to wake her, and found the fourposter bed empty. For a moment he thought she had gone into the garden, that he would find her sitting in the dark on the bench near the roses, praying or weeping. But when he emerged on the landing, there was Thomas Woodhouse. "Margaret Fell asked me to tell thee, Thomas Fell, that she had to leave. She hopes to be back tomorrow."

The shock was such that he was about to inquire further, but he checked himself. To discuss his wife's comings and goings with a servant was more than his pride could bear.

"Thank thee, Woodhouse. Good night."

He turned his back on the man and allowed his feelings to show only when he stood staring at the empty bed. Where had she gone? Wherever Fox was, that's where. My God—what had he driven her to do with her life?

He undressed in the candlelight. When he lay on his back, gazing at the ceiling, he realized it was the first night in twenty years he spent in that bed alone. He asked himself why he had not saddled his horse and followed her.

It was a rhetorical question. Even had he stormed off on horseback at dead of night, even had he known where she was heading, no mortal man could keep her from her appointment in Samarra.

* * *

The coach from Swarthmoor arrived in Windermere toward day-break after traveling all night along the steep, winding mountain roads. Ann Traylor, sick from the constant lurching and pitching of the carriage, was beyond caring. At the beginning of the journey she had worried about her mistress, who sat opposite her, her face a mask, staring at the ghostly landscape; but soon this headlong rush toward George Fox began to appear senseless, a desperate dash into nothing. Who could undo the sight they had seen? What words could relieve them of that horror, of the confusion and despair that resulted from it? Certainly not George Fox with his notions; to see poor Margaret Fell rush to him for solace in her terrible distress was tragic. But no one could stop her, no one could reach her through the wall beyond which she seemed to have retired. Never before had Ann known her in such a frozen state of despondency; her heart went out toward the woman. But as the night progressed and she herself became weary and unwell, she too withdrew within herself, nursing her own hurt and doubt. What haunted her, even more than the horrendous image of the hanged children, were the faces of those locked up in the cellar at the end of the corridor with the shrieking lunatics. What was to become of them? Were they to be hanged too? Oh, God! How was it possible that human beings could be so cruel! Was there no one to look after those children? What had happened to their parents, their mothers? Underlying those agonized questions was a doubt she barely dared face: how could God permit the horror they had seen? Was He indeed a God of love?

It was this doubt that threw her into confusion. Had she all her life believed in a fantasy, had she every night since childhood prayed to a mockery, a priests' invention? Sick and bewildered, by the time the coach slowed down and the hoofbeat of the horses and the rattle of the wheels began to echo between the houses of a sleeping village, all she longed for was a room at the inn, a bed, the forgetfulness of sleep. The pale light of dawning had turned the coach windows into bleak squares. "Is this the inn?" she asked.

Margaret Fell did not reply. Will Hartford climbed down from the driver's seat and opened the door; when he stood there shivering and blue in the early light, she said, "Go and find George Fox. Tell him to come down at once. Tell him it is urgent."

Will Hartford closed the door again, muttering, "Yes, ma'am."

"Are we going to stay here?" Ann asked, to break the oppressive silence.

Margaret Fell looked at her as if from a distance. Finally, she said, "I don't think so. I want a word with George Fox; after that we'll return to Swarthmoor."

"Oh."

They sat in gloomy silence, each with her own thoughts, until footsteps came hurrying toward them through the gateway of the inn.

The door of the carriage was opened and there, in leather breeches, cloak and white hat, was George Fox. Before he had been able to speak, Margaret Fell said, "Step in, please." Then, to Will Hartford, "Drive to the lake. Somewhere away from houses or people. There leave us awhile."

Will Hartford said, "Yes, ma'am," and closed the door.

George Fox was large and dark in the small space of the coach. He said nothing, but seemed to exude tranquility as they were driven down the empty, hollow streets with their echoing façades to the sudden, spacious silence of the meadows outside the town. There, close to the banks of the lake that lay glinting in the dawn, the carriage halted. "Please leave us for a moment, Ann," Margaret Fell said. "We won't be long."

She almost said 'Yes, ma'am' like Will Hartford; it was as if all her dreams of freedom had evaporated. "Very well," she said wearily; George Fox opened the carriage door for her.

Outside she found Will Hartford waiting. The horses, tired and drowsy, stood steaming in the cold air. From the surface of the lake, smooth and dull like ice, spirals of mist were rising. They walked away from the carriage, down a path along the water's edge; their footfalls seemed dulled by the softness of the fog that reached out around them from the water. They walked until they reached a wooden bench facing the lake; there they sat down side by side and looked back at the silhouette of the coach with its small, glinting windows. It stood in the mist as if it were floating; the steam from the horses rose like smoke.

"She should have given me a chance to rub them down," Will Hartford said.

*   *   *

Maybe it was the fact that he had been awakened at such an uncongenial hour, but as George Fox sat listening in the pale light of the dawn to the distraught, almost demented woman opposite him, he was suddenly overcome by anger. He had been convincing people of her class and upbringing for years, apparently with success; now he realized that all his message, his miracles, his power of the Lord had meant to them was a new fad, another remedy for rural boredom. Look at her! She had been sending parcels and letters to people in prisons all over the country; she had been organizing the spiritual movement he had started and tried to turn it into an institutionalized church; now it turned out all that had been a fantasy, a mere notion. At the first confrontation with reality in the form of three hanged children, at a glimpse of what people like her husband and his friend Best had been up to in the so-called "execution of their duty," her newfound faith collapsed. There she sat, crying to have her God restored to her; instead of filling him with pity and compassion, she filled him with fury. She was not a soul in spiritual torment but an upper-class woman outraged by reality after her first horrified glimpse of it. She had dragged him out of bed, demanding he tame it instantly, make it go away, cover that horrendous ocean of darkness and death with his private invention: the infinite ocean of light and love. What did she take him for? How dare she demand that he deliver her from such sights in order that she might return, her authority restored, to her room full of parcels, like a child to a doll's house? Well, it was high time she woke up to the reality of her pastime: the world of the damned, of the lunatics howling in their cages, the world where the heads of the hanged were boiled in the basement to keep Oxford and Cambridge supplied with skulls. "What dost thou want of me, Margaret?" he asked, interrupting her, as he could no longer contain himself. "My help to return to thy comfortable world? Thy comfortable notion of God?"

She looked at him, harrowed, not understanding his harshness. But he was not to be deterred. She had to confront reality at last. "Thy own husband has hanged those children, Margaret, or others like them, and through him thou hast. Thou art as guilty of the fate of those children as thou art of the fate of the cow whose meat thou eatest. Permissiveness is complicity."

"George!" Her face was pitiful, her eyes heartbreaking.

But he had to do it, for her sake as well as his. "I am sorry, Margaret. I will not restore thy ignorance to thee. Thou shalt face the truth alone. Thou shalt turn away from it alone, or confront it alone. This is *thy* moment of truth. Not mine."

"Isn't it?" Her reaction became, as could be expected, hostile; she now eyed him coldly in the gray light. But her face was that of a woman dying.

Sympathy for her suffering churned within him, but he suppressed it. "Do not assail me, Margaret. There is no real solace in blaming others for thy awakening, only false comfort."

"My awakening?" She had recovered her composure and now sat opposite him as the woman he had met in the garden a year before. "I think the time has come, George, to tell thee exactly what happened when thou didst break into my sheltered world."

"Margaret, believe me: to blame others is—"

"I'm not blaming thee, George. But the time has come for thee to face reality also. Thou didst change my life with thy message of that of God in everyone, thy concept of God as pure love, but thou didst not convince me by thy words."

"Does it matter? As long—"

"I *experienced* that love, George; it overwhelmed me. During the months that followed I was steeped in that love, filled with it, I radiated joy and happiness and fulfillment, like a flame. I took it to be rapture of the Divine, communication with the spirit of love, with God."

"Well?"

"It wasn't. It was love, but not divine. It was carnal love, for a man. For thee."

"Well? It was not my intention." He said it coldly.

She looked at him, eyes blazing. "Of course not! It was I! My body! My aging body, yearning for one more rapture before my dotage, fell in love with thee! With all of thee, George: thy youth, thy maleness,

thy hair, thy eyes, thy lips, thy hands; even thy spiritual exaltation
or whatever it was made me love thee, not like a convert, but like
a woman! Dost thou understand? Had I faced the truth that first day,
I would have thought: *Here* is a man whom I desire to hold me in his
arms, to drive me to ecstasy, to put me with child!"

Her confession shook him. This was not what he had foreseen when
he berated her a moment ago. This was dangerous, for he realized
that her violent frankness aroused him, with breathtaking intensity.

"I have not come to ask for sympathy!" she cried. "I have not
come to beg for a consummation of my passion, either! I have come to
call thee to judgment! Look: three hanged children. Look: six more,
in a cage, waiting to be hanged. What has that of God in thee to say
for itself? Either *prove* to me, now, the existence of thy God of love,
or be damned to hell for the suffering, the pain, the confusion, the
despair thou hast inflicted upon me and thousands of others like me!"

"But, my dear Margaret—"

"No! Not thy dear Margaret! Forget about me! Here: six children,
locked in a cage, about to be hanged. Now answer me, without
evasion, without fancy rhetoric: *Where is the love of God?*"

"Ask Him," he replied calmly. "Let us go into meeting."

"No! None of thy tricks! *Thou* shalt answer me, not thy self-
fabricated, silent spirit!"

Suddenly he could take no more. She sat there radiating such power,
such elemental femininity that he felt the compulsion to take her in
his arms, right here, in this coach, to drown her doubts and his in
rapture. He closed his eyes and prayed. "God, help us!"

Even as he whispered those words, a stillness came over him, a
tranquility that seemed to remove from him the terror of damnation,
temptation itself. He opened his eyes and looked at her. "Margaret,"
he said, "I cannot prove to thee the existence of the God of love.
Nobody can do that for thee; only thou canst, thyself."

She wanted to assail him again, but he said, in the power of the Lord,
"Stop crying for proof of God's love! Prove it thyself!" Then he
added in a gentler tone, "How else dost thou think He can manifest
His love? Through nature? Through the trees, the clouds, the beasts
in the field, the stars? No, only through beings capable of doing so:
ourselves. In the case of those children in the cage, about to be hanged,
it is *thou* He touched. All He has to reach those children is *thee!*"

For a moment she sat motionless. Then she slumped forward, her
face in her hands, and sobbed.

*   *   *

The coach returned to Swarthmoor in late afternoon. As it drew up
in front of the house, it was met by her husband, stern and forbidding.
The moment she stepped out of the carriage, he hurried toward her.
"Where on earth—?"

She silenced him with a perfunctory kiss. "Not here, Thomas. Let's go upstairs. I have to change, I must get out of these clothes. I feel as if I had been sleeping in them."

"Well, hast thou not?" he asked bitterly.

"Hardly."

She swept past him, embraced the children who waited uncertainly in the hall, told them she would be right back and ran up the stairs to her bedchamber. Mongol welcomed her, squatting on the coverlet of the fourposter, with hoarse, raucous yapping. She put him down with a slap, and heard the door close behind her. There was Thomas, his face white with anger.

"I know, I know," she said. "I should have told thee I was going, but I thought it better this way. Thou dost not mind if I change while we talk?"

"Where hast thou been?"

She looked at him, his chalk-white face, his tight-lipped fury. "I went to see George Fox, in Windermere," she replied calmly. "Wouldst thou be so kind?" She turned her back on him; it took a few moments, then she felt his fumbling fingers start to undo the row of buttons down the back of her gown.

"Why, for heaven's sake?" he cried.

"There was something I wanted to ask him."

"About those hanged children?"

"Those children in the corridor near the lunatics. The ones that have not been hanged yet." She turned around and faced him. "I must be frank with thee," she said. "I am going back to Lancaster tomorrow, to concern myself with those children."

He said nothing. He just stood staring at her with those dark, fierce eyes. It made her turn away and go toward her dresser. She stepped out of her gown and sat down to take the combs out of her hair. She saw him in the mirror.

"Thou art mad." He said it without emotion, as a statement of fact.

"Probably." She took out her combs and shook her hair. It felt lovely after that long night. If only she could forget about it all and sleep. She would think about it on the morrow.

"Why go back there? What canst thou possibly achieve?"

She saw him come toward her in the mirror. "I cannot do otherwise."

"That is nonsense."

"No, Thomas. Whatever it is, it is real."

"Very well." His voice was urbane once more. "Let us look at it dispassionately for a moment, if we can. Thou dost not mind my putting thee a few questions?"

"As my husband, or as Chief Justice Fell?"

"As thy devil's advocate. Thou dost not realize, I presume, that thou art playing with fire."

She turned around to face him. "Oh, dear Tom!" she said impulsively. "I'm so terribly sorry . . ."

He did not respond. "Let's keep that until later, shall we? First let us scrutinize thy decision and see what it entails."

She suddenly knew that this was serious. She must decide whether to tell him the truth; but where would it lead them? She took up her brush, turned her back on him and said, "I am not sure I like this." She started to brush her hair, but did not lose sight of him in the mirror. He must be a merciless interrogator on the bench. She had never seen him so fierce and tense; he was a different man.

"When didst thou make the decision to return to Lancaster Castle?"

"This morning."

"Where?"

"In the coach, on the bank of Windermere Lake."

"Who was with thee?"

"George Fox."

"Thou wert alone with him?"

"Yes."

"Where were the others?"

She put down the brush carefully and turned around. "Dear Thomas, art thou sure this is what thou wantst?"

"Indeed. I think it is past time."

She decided to tell him the truth. "I had sent the others away."

"Why?"

"I wanted to talk to George Fox alone."

"About what?"

"I wanted him to tell me . . ." She paused.

"What?"

She looked at him, puzzled. This ferret-like insistence was not like him. Behind the unemotional voice, the unrelenting eyes, there was an anger that made him want to hurt himself, like a child. He must be terribly distressed. "Tom, love—"

"Margaret," he said coldly, "I want the truth."

She realized that the impulse to shelter him had been her desire to avoid a confrontation. "Very well." She turned away and took up her brush again, but she no longer sought him in the mirror. She wanted to reduce him to a voice.

"What happened in that coach?"

"I asked him how a God of love could allow what I had seen, those children."

"And?"

"He gave me the answer."

"Then what?"

She found his face in the mirror again. "Thou art not interested in his answer?"

"No."

"Why not?"

"I want to know what happened, not the answer to a theological question."

"But it wasn't a theological question!"

"It wasn't?"

She started to brush her hair again. This was going to be difficult. "So what happened?"

"His answer moved me deeply, and I—I burst into tears."

"Why?"

"Oh, for God's sake!" She slammed the brush down, suddenly un-nerved. "Canst thou not understand?" She covered her face with her hands, knowing it to be a dramatic gesture, somehow hoping he would see through it.

* * *

The way she sat there, her long fair hair around her bare shoulders, her breasts half uncovered by the low-cut bodice, she was the most desirable woman he had ever seen. "Look, dear heart," he said, "I am not enjoying this. I would prefer to spare my sensibilities and conserve my peace of mind. But if thou shouldst indeed return to Lancaster Castle to occupy thyself with those children, it would mean that sooner or later thou wouldst end up in those dungeons thyself, not as an angel of mercy but as a prisoner. Thy only hope now is absolute honesty with thyself. I will permit thee to go if thou must, but only if thou dost not deceive thyself as to thy motives."

"What matter my motives if I help those children?!" she cried. "What is it to them whether they are saved by a saint or by a— a . . ."

"Well?"

For a moment she gazed at him. Then she said with a sigh, "Very well. Ask me."

"Ask thee what?"

She tossed back her hair and took up her brush again. "I am not his mistress," she said to the mirror.

"I am glad to hear it."

"But it is not for want of trying."

He stiffened. All that was weak and vulnerable in him cried out to him to stop this torture. But he had to know, not for his own sake, for hers. "Thou wouldst if thou wert given the chance?"

"I was given the chance this morning in the coach. There came a moment when I knew he was ready to take me in his arms. Had I thrown myself at him, we would have become lovers then and there. But something stopped me."

He wanted to ask, 'The thought of me, perhaps?' But he checked himself in time. "What stopped thee?"

"His answer to my question. That may sound like an evasion to thee, but it is the truth. His answer to my question was—well, stagger-ing."

"What did he say?"

"He told me to stop crying for proof of the existence of a God of love. 'How can He transmit His love to those children,' he said, 'if it isn't through thee? It is *thou* He touched. All He has to reach those children is *thee.'*"

"He said something similar to me that first night. I thought it a pretty hackneyed thought, frankly. Why did it—"

"I don't know! God, I don't know!" she cried with sudden vehemence. "It—it just . . . To me it meant, at that moment . . . Oh, I don't know!"

"Was that the reason why thou didst not throw thyself at him?"

"I know it makes no sense, but when he said that, I—I just collapsed, and wept. Finally, I called Ann Traylor and Will Hartford and took him back to his inn, and that was that. We changed horses and came home in the coach. All the way home I sat thinking, the head of the girl on my lap; she was exhausted, poor child. I could not make out what had happened. But what it amounts to is that I have to go back to those children."

"Because of what he said?"

"Because what he said is true. In the case of those children in the dungeon, all God has is me. I don't know why that should be so, but I believe it, therefore I must go."

"And what if it were false?"

She smiled. "That is a risk I must take." Turning toward the mirror again, she shook her hair back and began to tie it with a ribbon. It was red velvet and looked exquisite. Somehow the preposterousness of her decision seemed to be summed up in that ribbon.

"Dear God!" he cried. "How can I make thee understand thou art flirting with death?" It was uncharacteristically dramatic, but he was stricken with an awful, sickening sense of finality. She was going to do it, she was really going to do it, and she did not realize what it meant at all; she never would, until it was too late.

"I am not playing, Tom," she said earnestly. "Whatever I may be doing, I am not playing." She rose and went to the wardrobe. In her silk petticoats she looked an image of sheltered elegance, ignorant of all that was brutal and obscene and cruel, all that was Lancaster Castle.

"Dost thou realize that those children are living on the lowest level, a hundred feet under the ground? That they relieve themselves in the straw they sleep in? That they have vermin, scurvy, mange? That they are murderers, thieves, as close to being animals as any human being can be?"

"That is why I must go," she said, looking thoughtfully at the row of gowns.

"What about thy own children?" he cried, his self-control crumbling. "Who is going to look after them while their mother flounces about in prison?"

She gave him a swift glance, then she took out the cornflower-blue robe he had given her after the baby's birth. She laid it on the bed and stepped out of her petticoats. "There are plenty of people here to look after the children for a while," she said.

He wanted to take her by the shoulders, shake her, take her in his arms the way he had done on his return from Gleaston when he had been aflame with jealousy of young Fox. But it would mean desertion on his part in the hour of her greatest need. Or was he exaggerating the whole affair? Was this merely another of her impulses, which would run its course as long as he did not bar her way?

"Well—all this seems pretty final, doesn't it?" he said with an effort at sardonic resignation.

"Final?" she asked, stepping into her robe. "To me it feels like a beginning. For the first time in my life I have the feeling I am free."

"And so thou puttest thyself in prison."

She smiled and began to button her robe from the bottom up, slowly covering all that intimate beauty.

In a last effort to save her from herself he went toward her, took her by the shoulders and said, "Look, dear heart, of course thou art right. I too am deeply distressed that the law imposes such an inhuman penalty on children. But face it, we are not living in the ideal society yet! We are trying to make it so, for our children and our children's children. I am yearning for the day when this will no longer be necessary, when people will look back on the gallows in •Lancaster Castle and say . . ."

She looked in his eyes with a strange new tenderness. "Tom, love, doesn't thou see? That time is *now.*"

"But, sweeting—"

"The moment thy conscience tells thee something is wrong, that is the time to stop it."

"Oh, Margaret . . . !"

He tried to escape, but she held on to him. "That is why I must go! I must!"

"To do what?!"

"To endure with those children what they are enduring. To bring to them the physical presence of one who cares. To bring their plight, by the fact of my presence, to the attention of those in power. It is the only way to save them."

"But, dearest!" he cried. "Thou *canst* not save them! Please, *please* understand that!"

"Why not?" She smiled at him, as remote as the moon.

"Because they will not permit it!"

"Who?"

"The magistrates! The regents! The warden! Everybody!"

"Thou art the highest judicial authority in the county. Even though the regents and the rest may not understand what I am trying to do, they would accommodate me for thy sake, wouldn't they?"

He was overcome by weariness. He freed himself of her arms, went to the bed and slumped down on it. "Very well," he sighed. "Exactly what art thou planning to do with those children?"

While she told him, he lay gazing at the ceiling, listening not to her words but to the sound of her moving about the room. For some reason the sound, at that moment, was melancholy and precious. Gradually he began to listen to her unworldly dream. Schoolbooks, toys, singing lessons, lifting those children out of their darkness into a state of humanity. She obviously had no idea what kind of children they were. She could not conceive, from her sheltered life, that children, even small children, could be monsters of cruelty and savagery. One of the children with whom she so airily proposed to occupy herself was a murderer, despite his tender age. A foul-mouthed little monster, the warden had told him later, worse than a rabid badger, who had brained his adoptive father with a poker. The boy's age, if he remembered rightly, was eleven.

"Very well, dear heart," he said, interrupting her. "All this sounds very noble. But what thou hast in mind should go on indefinitely if it were to have any effect. Supposing I were able to get thee in there, how long dost thou plan to stay in Lancaster?"

"Oh, I don't know." He heard from her tone that she had not even thought about it. "The Lord will provide."

"In that case," he replied, "the Lord will have to provide in one month's time. That is all I am prepared to give thee: thirty days. After that, whatever the state those children are in, whatever thy success, I demand that thou returnest to thy family."

"But, Tom—"

"I'm sorry, dear heart, but that is final. One month, or nothing." He did not tell her that one month was the limit he could take leave of his duties, to watch over her. He could not possibly let her confront the horrendous world of the dungeons alone. "Thou wilt need a woman to accompany thee. A maid, a companion."

"Oh—I suppose Ann Traylor. She's a strong, practical girl."

If he detested anything at that moment, it was strong, practical girls. "Very well. Who's going to look after the household while thou art gone?"

"Henderson."

"I shall not be here either, dear heart, and I am not going to leave our household in the hands of Henderson."

"Well, what about Mistress Best?"

"She has a household of her own!"

"I'm sure she would love to do it, the moment she knows the reason. Would she be acceptable to thee, master?"

He ignored the taunt. "There are a few things thou shouldst know about Lancaster prison. It is run by two wardens, a day warden and his assistant, who serves at night. Under them are the turnkeys. Then there are the housekeeper and her husband, who provide the food and keep the dungeons clean, or at least they are supposed to. They pay the prison for the privilege, so I need not tell thee that they extort from the prisoners every penny they can sweat out of them. It's a barbaric system, but one of those things that have become a tradition. Those who cannot pay are starved and neglected and put in the worst part of the prison. The children are put on the lowest level because they have no money to pay the housekeeper. The lunatics don't have the sense to know they should."

"Don't they have relatives to look after them?"

"No. If they had, they wouldn't be there. The titular head of the whole operation is a man called the provost. It is not a permanent office, it rotates among the judges of the district for one session each, three months at a time. They are supposed to reside in the castle during their tenure, but few of them do. It depends on who is provost during this Hilary session, whether the prison staff will cooperate with thee or not."

"Why shouldn't they?"

"Because, dear heart, the prison is riddled with corruption. God only knows what goes on in those dungeons, especially at night. To be a turnkey in Lancaster Castle is a horrible job and the men are paid very little. Why do they do it? I have never gone into that question, but I'm afraid the answer is: because they like it. What exactly they like about it nobody is in a position to know because nobody ever goes in there. It is a world that belongs to the housekeeper and the turnkeys, not even the warden, who sits in his office in the gateway and rarely goes down. Thou hast no idea what kind of hellhole thou art proposing to invade."

She looked at him with kindness. He knew that face; she was listening to indulge him, but her mind was made up and no man could change it, least of all himself. Her harebrained concern would have to run its course; all he could do was be around to protect her, should the need arise. "Well," he said, "I think I'll go down to my study for a moment before supper. Wouldst thou care to join me for a glass of sack?"

"No, dear heart. I had better occupy myself with the children. I told them I would be right back; that was an hour ago."

"Very well. I'll see thee anon."

He went to his study, poured himself a double Drambuie, on which he choked; then he slumped in his chair behind his desk, found Sam Pruitt's ledger on it, was about to toss it aside with an oath when he checked himself and began to leaf through it. Sam kept meticulous track not only of his own appointments but also of the movements of the judges in his jurisdiction.

During Hilary the provost of Lancaster prison was John Sawrey.

CHAPTER TWO

WARDEN Farragut was a youngish, rather florid man who, once he was away from the oppressive shadow of Lord Chief Justice Thomas Fell, turned out to be quite a one for the ladies. He received the two women in his office in the gateway with profuse courtesy; he even ordered his assistant to unburden them of the baskets they were carrying. They were chatting amiably and Ann Traylor was expecting him to ask the turnkey to guide her and Margaret Fell to the children when suddenly his face darkened as the man showed him something he had dug out of one of the baskets. A doll.

"Toys, Madam?" the warden asked, his face hostile.

"Why not?" Margaret Fell seemed as taken aback as Ann was herself.

"Forgive me, Madam, but I am forced to reconsider your involvement with those children. Your approach is not one to which I could subscribe."

Margaret Fell frowned; Ann knew her well enough to realize that the man was in for a surprising experience. Her mistress hated to be thwarted under any circumstances; she had prepared this expedition to the children in prison with such determination that she was not likely to let herself be frustrated at the last moment. "Would you care to explain why?" she asked coldly.

The warden turned the doll over and contemplated it with somber mien. "These children, Madam, are criminals. They are in prison to be punished for their misdeeds. To teach them to read and write is one thing, to pamper them with toys is out of the question."

"In that case, we shall take out the toys."

But the warden was not mollified. "No, Madam; I will have to discuss this with my superiors."

"Your superiors?" Margaret Fell stuck out her chin, a gesture that Ann Traylor had come to know well. "This visit was arranged by my husband, who happens to be your superior. Is that not so?"

The warden smiled. "Ah, if it were only your husband, Madam! But there are others whom I have to consider."

"And who might they be?"

The warden fell back into his role of charming host. "May I suggest you go back to your inn, Madam, just for today, and return tomorrow morning? I am sorry to cause you this inconvenience, but under the circumstances I am not authorized to admit you."

"Which circumstances, for heaven's sake?!" Margaret Fell's eyes flashed; if the warden knew what was good for him, he would now stop his procrastination.

But he did not relent. "I regret, Madam, but I cannot change the rules established by the regents of this prison. I am in their employ, Madam."

Margaret Fell rose briskly. "Who are the regents? Where do they live? I'll go and see them at once."

The warden, who had risen also, looked at the imperious woman with forbearance. To Ann Traylor there was something odd in his attitude, something she could not put her finger on. "Madam, I assume it is your intention to help those children?"

"I thought I made that plain."

"In that case, may I give you a piece of advice? Do not stir up any more official awareness of your concern than is strictly necessary. For the moment, only your husband and I know of your worthy intentions. It would be my advice to leave things as they are. Believe me, it is your only hope of achieving your goal."

Margaret Fell looked at the man musingly. She was obviously weighing a decision in her mind. "Very well," she said, finally. "I confess that I fail to understand what the fuss is about, but if this is what we have to contend with, so be it. We shall be back tomorrow morning. I trust there will be no further delays."

"I cannot see why there should be, Madam." The warden bowed, unable to hide his relief. "Good day, Madam, young lady. Until tomorrow: Godspeed."

Without returning his greeting, Margaret Fell swept out of the office, leaving it to Ann to carry the baskets. They were heavy: schoolbooks, Bibles, writing materials, toys; the snooping jailer had not dug deep enough to discover the sweetmeats.

Outside, in the bright sunshine, Margaret Fell's face looked flushed with anger. "Here, give me that," she said, taking her basket. "I'm of a mind to send a message to my husband. But perhaps it is best not to make too much of it. We'll see what happens tomorrow." She hooked her arm through the handle of the basket and marched back to the inn, half a step ahead of her young companion, who thought it best to remain unobtrusive under the circumstances.

At the inn, where they had taken rooms that were simpler than those to which the wife of Chief Justice Fell was accustomed but on which she had insisted, Margaret Fell seemed to have overcome her anger. "It's a stupid business," she said, putting down her basket on the table. "I suppose, like all little men, he feels he has to act the *grand seigneur,* lest we underestimate his importance. Well, what shall we do for the rest of the day?"

"We could seek out the Friends in these parts," Ann suggested.

Margaret Fell frowned. "No. After what happened this morning, that would not be a good idea. I don't know exactly what it is, but something about this business makes me, well, wonder." She picked up her shawl again. "Let's go for a walk," she said. "We haven't been out in the air for days."

That was nonsense. They had been traipsing about the town for three days running, buying the articles considered suitable for the

education of illiterate children. But Ann knew her mistress well enough
not to demur; obediently she followed her down the narrow stairs to
the courtyard and out into the street. What she would have liked to do
was to stay upstairs, to write in her diary in the privacy of her room,
but she accompanied her mistress for a stroll through the town to the
bluffs. There they sat down, to gaze at the blinding sunlit bay. It was
a warm spring day, the birds were out, there was a whiff of blooming
heather in the air. Margaret Fell talked a lot, but Ann did not really
listen; she was yearning to get back to her diary.

It was not until late that night, after their sober evening meal, when
they had finally retired to their rooms, that she was given the chance
to confront her bewildering emotions. She had to be careful; Margaret
Fell might turn up any time, unannounced. She lit a candle and put it
on the small table, facing the door; then she fetched her inkwell, quill
and the exercise book. She put her left hand inside it, ready to flip
back the pages to Bonny Baker's exercises at the slightest sound.

"*Today I discovered that I am a fraud,*" she wrote. "*A week ago
I was moved to tears by the sight of those sad, lost children huddled
in the straw, their eyes glistening in the lantern light; now here I am:
wondering how I can avoid going to their aid. What is this fear whenever I think of the dungeons? That corridor with the mad people?
Those clawlike hands, reaching for me? The stench, the screams, the
ghastly atmosphere of that horrible place? I do not know. Reason
assures me that there is no danger to me personally. But something,
some premonition or I know not what, conspires to send me into a
panic the moment I approach the castle. This morning, when the
warden turned us back, I felt like embracing the man out of sheer
gratitude. Afterwards, during our walk, I felt deeply ashamed. Tonight . . .*" She flipped back the pages and stared at the door. It had
been a false alarm; but it made her sufficiently uneasy to close the book
and put inkwell and quill away. She took the candle to the bedside
table and undressed. Before climbing into bed, she knelt down, her
head on the counterpane. She tried to plead with God to forgive her,
to fill her with fortitude and determination. But the words would not
come; there was only the image of that dark gateway, and it filled
her with a fear the like of which she had never known.

* * *

The next morning the warden again received them wreathed in
smiles; but the moment she set eyes on him Margaret Fell knew that
he was not going to admit them. And indeed, with effusive courtesy
he informed Mistress Fell that, to his chagrin, the regents considered
it unwise to admit ladies of her social status and costly attire into the
presence of the prisoners, who were all of humble origin and would
inevitably be aroused to ire by someone like her appearing among
them. So, though he regretted it deeply, he had to refuse them admission.

To challenge him Margaret said, "If that is indeed the reason, then surely my companion will pass muster. No one in his senses could describe her as a representative of affluence."

Before the man had been able to counter this, poor Ann went deathly pale and turned to her with eyes filled with horror. "Oh, I pray you, no!" she pleaded. "Do not do that! I could not, I could not possibly go in there alone!"

"Very well, very well." The child's reaction took her aback; she had had no idea that the prison held such terror for her. "May I ask whose idea this was, Mr. Farragut?"

"Beg pardon, ma'am?" The warden looked almost pathetically shifty.

"Come, come," she said, giving him her most captivating smile. "I'm not going to make life difficult for you. I understand that you have to follow orders, and I know that this is a real embarrassment, if not a sorrow to you."

The man heaved a discreet sigh of relief. "I'm so glad you take that attitude, Mistress Fell. I really am grieved by this arbitrary—" He realized too late that he had already said too much.

"I think it will make things a great deal easier if you tell me who is behind all this," she continued. "As you know, my husband has given orders that we are to be admitted; it would be wise if I could offer him proof that this procrastination is not of your making."

He eyed her warily. "I could not possibly do so, Madam," he said with a demureness that raised her hopes. "All it will take on your husband's part is to raise the matter with Justice Sawrey."

So it was little John Sawrey. "Well," she said cheerfully. "I am afraid we'll have to wait another day, won't we? I'll make it a point to turn up in the morning in the humblest of gowns. Good day to you, sir." She bestowed a ravishing smile upon him. "I hope to find you in good health tomorrow morning, please God. Come, Ann." Taking the child by the arm, she left the office with what she hoped was a convincing show of cheerful compliance.

Thoughts about Sawrey preoccupied her during their walk back to the inn; it was only when they were back in their rooms that she remembered the poor, terrified girl.

"I'm sorry I made that hasty suggestion, dear Ann. Of course, I wouldn't dream of letting thee go in there by thyself."

But Ann had had a chance to recover. "Oh, not at all," she said. "I just thought it a bad idea to allow them to separate us."

"Of course."

Obviously, the girl did not want to discuss it; she must be ashamed of her fears. But why should she be? After all, she was only eighteen years old; that first visit to the prison must have made a deep impression on her. "I wonder what Mr. Sawrey will think of next," Margaret said, to change the subject. "I intend to give in to his whims until he runs out of excuses."

She spent the rest of the day shopping for a gown that would be inconspicuous. Only the third dressmaker she visited had something to offer: a modest rather somber dark brown bodice and skirt with matching capulet, obviously intended as a first replacement for widow's weeds. It did not quite fit her, but it would do, although it exposed her feet rather uncomfortably. It was in this uncompromising outfit that she turned up for her third effort to penetrate the fastness of Lancaster Castle the next morning.

Again the warden, waiting for them, was courtesy personified. This time he appeared genuinely embarrassed when he told them that he could not admit them this day either, as there was a rapist loose in the castle. They had been unable to catch the man; it might be one of the inmates, possibly from the debtors' section. There had been two attacks upon women in the corridors the night before; he did not dare risk their being assaulted.

As excuses went, it was one of the better ones, even though Margaret was convinced it was a fabrication. "I am moved by your concern, Mr. Farragut," she said charmingly. "I will not go against your wishes. I trust you will catch the miscreant before tomorrow morning."

"Ah!" The warden spread his hands. "We do our best, Madam. But we have over a hundred inmates . . ."

"Quite. In the meantime, should you be honored by a visit from Justice Sawrey, would you kindly give him a message on my behalf?"

"Oh . . . well . . . I'm not sure I will see him . . ." Obviously, he had not expected this.

"Just a casual greeting," she said lightly. "We have a mutual friend called John McHair, who wishes to be remembered. Would you be so kind? John McHair. Not a difficult name to remember, is it?"

"No, indeed." The warden watched her with wariness. "It will be a pleasure, Madam."

"Thank you so much. Good day to you, gentlemen, and I hope to see you tomorrow in good health, *sans* rapist. Yes?" Without waiting for their reply, she took Ann Traylor's arm and left the office, image of charming unconcern.

Back at the inn, she was sorry. This was not the way in which, as a child of the Light, she was supposed to approach conflict. To intimidate Sawrey with a veiled threat was the very reverse of what George would have wanted her to do. She should have gone for that of God in the little judge—whatever that meant. Anyhow, it was too late. Sawrey had probably been close by and overheard their conversation.

That night, before she fell asleep, it occurred to her that this latest excuse might well have been valid. She should be very careful not to fall prey to her own imagination.

Imagination or not: when they turned up the next morning, they were admitted.

* * *

When the warden said, "Yes, ladies—this time the road is clear," Ann Traylor, who had expected they would be turned back again, went numb with terror. She tried desperately to emulate Margaret Fell as they crossed the gateway toward the door that led into the dungeons and made an effort to stride as calmly as she, with the same quiet determination; but when the jailer with the lantern turned the key in the heavy low door and pulled it open, she could not help herself, she clutched Margaret Fell's arm at the first whiff of the cadaverous stench that met them.

They stepped inside; the dank, clammy cellar air enveloped them. Staring down into the dark well of the staircase, Ann began to tremble. She could do nothing about it; she stood shivering like a leaf. Margaret Fell put her hand on hers and said, "Careful now! As I remember it, these steps are very slippery." It was not what she said but the way she said it that brought Ann a momentary comfort sufficient to enable her to make a first step down. The eerie black pit with its wet stone walls, cold to the touch and slimy, seemed filled with the accumulated pain and madness of two centuries of torture. Or was it three centuries? The warden had told them the history of the dungeons that first time; all she remembered from his discourse was that the maze of levels and passages had been dug as a silver mine in Roman times, and that the deepest level was a hundred feet down. That was where the children were. That was where they were going. She wondered how she was going to make it.

The lantern light sent eerie glimmerings wheeling on the wet, circular wall. It felt as if she were lowered into a mass grave full of people buried alive. The stench became fouler as they descended, a reek of mold and things rotting, of excrement and vomit and—

A hooting of many voices, amplified by echoes into one howl of derision, took both women completely by surprise. They had reached the first cavernous landing; dark passages branched out from it, from which the awful howl of hatred came. The jailer shouted, "Shut up, you buggers! Shut up, damn you, you filthy swine!" Then, realizing he was guardian-guide to the wife of the Lord Chief Justice, he mumbled, "Beg pardon, ma'am, but that's the only language they understand. Animals, the lot of them. Filthy, vicious animals."

Margaret Fell said nothing. When they continued on their way, down the flight of steps into the black pit, she gripped Ann's arm firmly, as if to give her support. But this time her hand trembled too; curiously, it gave Ann a sense of comfort.

On the next landing the same thing happened: boos, shrieks, clamorings, whistles, all milled together by the echoes of the corridors into a subterranean howl, as if some colossal monster were lurking in the bowels of the earth. But some of its menace seemed to have gone; Ann no longer felt the sickening fear that something would burst out of those black, gaping mouths. Terrifying as the sound might be, it was obviously that of helpless hatred, caged and chained.

The chill seemed to deepen as they descended. The stench became more stifling. The atmosphere had nothing left reminiscent of the open, of freedom. It was as if they inhaled some of the horror of the dungeons each time they breathed. There was a draft in the pit; Ann remembered the warden telling them about chimneys or air ducts. It made her clutch her basket and hold on more tightly to Margaret Fell's arm as she became giddy with the slow spiral of their descent.

The descent seemed endless, much longer than last time. Suddenly, about halfway down, the dull stupor that had gradually taken the place of Ann's fear was shattered as, with a high-pitched, witchlike shriek, a huge black object came plummeting down upon them from above. She cried out and threw herself against the wall; Margaret Fell pressed her against her with a wild grip of fright. The black object plunged past into the blackness below; all she had been able to make out was that it had wheels. A rope, taut and quivering, which had not been there before, seemed to be reeling it down from the mouth of the pit above.

"Ah, yes," the jailer said, unperturbed. "That was Mistress Fraley's cart. She's the housekeeper. She and her hubby are changing the straw on five. It's hauled up and down by a pulley."

"I see," Margaret Fell said. "How interesting. Shall we go on?"

As they continued their way down, the dungeons became quieter. No more howls taunted them from the dark, gaping tunnels. Yet the feeling of hatred directed at them was as strong as ever, despite the silence. It was as if the subterranean animal living in those deeper caves was too weak, too sick to give voice to its rage. It was almost with a feeling of relief that Ann heard, toward the end of their descent, a shrill shrieking from below. It grew in volume as they continued; when finally they found themselves at the bottom and followed the jailer and his lantern into a passage, she realized that it was the lunatics. The yells and curses of the poor, demented creatures became deafening; there were those ghoulish claws again, reaching out toward them, trying to grab them as they passed. In the twilight of the cage the madwomen barked and howled, swore blood-curdling curses, slammed their chains against the bars. When at last they entered the children's cell after a rattling of keys and a squealing of rusty hinges, Ann heard the gate close behind her with a feeling of relief. While the jailer was explaining to Margaret Fell how to let herself out, she looked at the children cowering in the lantern light. There were six of them, all staring at her, their eyes glistening in their dirty faces with an inhuman, ratlike intensity. She had been deeply moved when she had first seen them; this time, perhaps because of her fear, she was repelled by their rags, their grime, the scales on their faces, their snotty, openmouthed moronity. How was it possible? Only a week ago she had stood staring at these same children with tears running down her face; in the coach on the way to Windermere she had wept at the memory of their pathetic misery; now she felt only disgust. It all seemed incongruous, a terrible mistake.

Margaret Fell approached them. "Well, children, my name is Margaret, my young friend here is Ann, and we have come to take care of you. Now, let us see. Whom have we got here? What's thy name, child?"

The little girl she addressed stared at her, slack-jawed, snot glistening on her upper lip, slowly scratching her chest through her rags.

Ann's feeling that it was all a mistake deepened. To her horror, she felt her admiration for her mistress falter at a sudden, unsettling doubt. What if it were no more than a rich lady's fancy? What gave her the idea that these children could be reached by gentleness, concern, love? Least of all by the genteel, forced cheerfulness with which Margaret Fell proceeded to try and coax them out of their gawking passivity. Only one among them seemed to possess a shimmer of intelligence: a one-eyed boy in a filthy green overcoat, much too large for him, who stood leaning against the wall and stared at them with a contemptuous sneer. He was the only one whose ankles were chained together.

When the children refused to be charmed into any form of communication, Margaret Fell began to unpack her basket. She produced Bibles, hornbooks, slates, pencils, chalk, all of which she spread out on the straw in front of the gaping little creatures. Ann knew her heart should be wrung with pity for them, but they were so far removed from any children she had known that she could not bring herself to consider them as such. She could not even tell them apart, except for the one girl and the one-eyed boy. The other four seemed completely identical in their filthy anonymity. They came to life only when Margaret Fell produced the forbidden sweetmeats. The moment she held out one toward the girl, they all pounced on it with one terrifying lunge; before she knew what had happened they were fighting, screaming, clawing, biting, kicking, rolling in the straw, trying to grab the comfit from one another; the little girl cowered, bawling, in a corner; the one-eyed boy in the green overcoat stared at them with contempt. Margaret Fell grabbed the lantern, as the rolling mass of arms and legs threatened to overturn it; if the straw caught fire, they would all be burned to death. Ann found herself praying fervently that God might prevail upon her mistress to let the children take what they wanted, and to open the door so the two of them might get out, back to the daylight, the world of the living.

But Mistress Fell was not ready to abandon anything. With a feeling of desperation, Ann watched her determined, ladylike effort to bring the children under control. It was ludicrous; no wonder the warden had done his best to dissuade them, this could only end in disaster for all concerned. Ann felt completely discouraged, but somehow Margaret Fell managed to keep the litter of animals from tearing each other to pieces. She lined them up in a row, gave them a book, a slate and a pencil each, and started her first lesson.

"*A—apple*. See that, children? Let's try and write that on our slates. *A* for *apple* . . ."

Ann, leaning against the bars of the cage, closed her eyes. It was obvious that the children were not going to obey. They were not going to do anything. They were not even listening; all of them were gazing with those bright, ratlike eyes at the baskets. Any moment now they would throw themselves upon them, dig in them until they had found the sweetmeats and roll fighting in the straw again until the comfits were lost or eaten. The madwomen down the corridor ululated, called,

"Dearie? Dearie? Dearie, dearie?" One shouted a filthy suggestion; the mad voices all shrieked with laughter. Ann's stomach turned at the thought of what might happen to her if she ever were to find herself within reach of those claws; she was certain the obscene catcalls were directed at her. But there was Margaret Fell, now trying, of all things, to teach those wretched little creatures "The Andalusian Merchant," a six-part madrigal so complicated that it had taken her own daughters three weeks to get it right. When she started to sing in her refined, cultured soprano she set the insane women screaming with doubled fury, rattling their cage, slamming their chains against the bars until the din drowned her dainty singing.

For the rest of the day Ann squatted in the straw that reeked of excrement and urine, deafened by shrieks, stared at contemptuously by the ghoulish boy in the corner, until, finally, Margaret Fell decided that it was enough. She gathered the slates, pencils, schoolbooks, Bibles and put them back in the baskets.

"All right, children," she said in that cheery, ridiculous voice, "for a first day this went very well indeed. We will be back tomorrow, and I'm sure it won't be long before we are used to each other and can start learning something. It's *learning* that's going to be your way back to the world, children! The moment you know how to read—"

"Oh, shit!"

She looked up sharply. The boy in the corner grinned, his solitary eye leering at her with satisfaction.

"That was not very nice," Margaret Fell said calmly.

"Shit shit shit! Stinking whore!" the boy said deliberately.

It did not make the slightest impression on the mistress of Swarthmoor Hall. "That is a sorry vocabulary, my young friend," she said quietly. "I hope we'll put some different words into thy head."

"Shit," the boy said. "Ballocks. Filthy bitch."

Margaret Fell turned away. Her face was set in the haughty, firm-lipped indifference she always showed whenever one of her children or servants aroused her displeasure. "Let's go, Ann," she said. "Please hold the lantern while I unlock the door."

"Shit, shit," the boy said, behind them. "Arse rot."

Margaret Fell produced the key from her bodice, stuck her hand through the bars and fumbled with the lock. Ann wondered whether her mistress was aware of the danger; she herself watched the children tensely as she held up the lantern, prepared to see them lunge for freedom the moment the door was opened. But, to her surprise, not one of them made a move when hinges squealed and the gate swung inward; it seemed the opening of the door of their dungeon no longer meant freedom to them. It was the one moment in which she felt a twinge of pity for the alien creatures squatting in the straw, gaping at her as she slipped out of their world into the passage. Margaret Fell turned the key, put it back in her bodice and headed for the well of the stairs.

It was a marvelous moment, so full of inexpressible relief that Ann felt as if she had been freed of a crushing load; she did not even mind the demented shrieks of the madwomen, whom they set screaming in their cage like damned souls in hell. Then, as they passed the first of the narrow passages that branched off the corridor, it happened.

A faceless man in a cloak, a hat pulled over his eyes, sprang into the lantern light. Ann was so stunned by his sudden appearance that she did not realize what was happening; then he grabbed her, pulled her toward him with cruel force and she screamed in terror when she felt his hands grab her bodice, tear it, grope for her breast. She dropped the lantern; in the sudden darkness she fought, scratched, bit, kicked, struggled. She felt his hands on her naked body, she knew what he was about to do, with a last shriek of anguish she tried to tear herself free, without avail. But as she sagged in his arms in limp surrender, on the brink of unconsciousness, his grip suddenly slackened. His breath left her neck; she saw, unfocused, a figure behind him in a faint light, slamming something bulky on his head, his back, until finally he let go and fled. She slumped to the ground, heard Margaret Fell's voice say, "Ann! Dear heart, Ann!" She felt her arms around her, and fainted.

*   *   *

After beating off the girl's assailant with her basket, Margaret Fell was panic-stricken. The jailer finally came running to her assistance with another lantern, and when the girl regained consciousness, she helped him guide her upstairs. The poor child looked pitiful. Margaret felt overcome by guilt. Physically, nothing irrevocable had happened to the girl, thank God, but emotionally? It was all her fault, it seemed to underscore the recklessness of the whole ill-considered undertaking.

When they approached the warden's office, she saw a male figure in a cloak and a black hat emerge and make off at the sight of them. It struck her momentarily as strange; in the warden's office, as they settled Ann in a chair, her eye was caught by something on the floor in front of the desk. It was a brightly colored sweetmeat. When she had lambasted the man with her basket, she had showered him with its contents; he had dropped the comfit from his cloak.

It instantly restored her self-confidence; the fact that the assault had been part of Sawrey's campaign filled her with a new determination. She should get Ann to the inn as quickly as possible, but it was important that she should talk to the warden first. She said to him, "I would like a word with you in private, please."

Surprised but courteous, he requested his turnkey to leave them alone for a moment; when the man had left, she confronted him. "Friend," she said, "the attack on this child was made by one of thy creatures. I'm not going to pursue the matter, but I am distressed. For her sake and that of the children, but especially for thy own sake, Friend."

"But Madam . . ." He was trying to recover his aplomb.

"I must warn thee that by thy actions thou art putting thyself in the power of evil. It is a choice, dear Friend; the choice is thine."

"Madam," the warden said bravely, "I have my orders."

She looked at his fleshy face. He was corruptible, and therefore approachable. Sawrey himself was beyond her reach, immured in his own cold ferocity. "Pray, tell thy superiors that we will be back to-morrow."

He sighed. "Madam," he said kindly, "have you not understood yet that your presence is not wanted in this prison? I admire your motives. I admire your tenacity. But you cannot win this battle. Your husband is here only rarely. He may be the highest authority in the judiciary, this prison is not under his control. There are others, determined that you shall not interfere with the prisoners."

She hesitated, then the compulsion became too strong. "What's thy name?" she asked.

"Pardon?"

"Thy first name."

Bewildered, he answered, "Hyman."

"Friend Hyman," she said, feeling as if she were impersonating George Fox, "thou hast, like all of us, that of God in thee. If it tells thee that something is wrong, thou canst not make it right by thinking, 'It is not I who does it, it is the warden of Lancaster prison.' Thou canst hide from God behind thy office as little as I can hide behind my own. I am a mother, and a magistrate's wife. I should be looking after my own children, I should not embarrass my husband, I should not act against the wishes of the regents—"

"Or the church?"

She looked at him, startled.

He glanced at the door. "Madam, let me warn you. Do not address anyone else in this prison as you just addressed me. Your husband's position will not protect you. On the contrary."

Impulsively she said, "Thank thee, Friend. Or should I say, thank you, sir?"

He smiled self-consciously. "In the privacy of my office, Madam, I should be honored if you would address me as Hyman."

"Thank thee, Friend Hyman."

She went to Ann, slumped in the chair as pale as a sheet. "I'll take thee home now. Come, dear."

She helped the girl to her feet; the warden helped guide her out of the office, down the steps and out the gate. She wanted to call for a sedan chair to carry them to the inn, but the fresh air seemed to do the child good. When they arrived at their lodgings after a slow, careful walk, Ann had recovered, but still clung to her with frightened intensity.

Even in the privacy of their rooms the poor child refused to let go of her. Kind words, soothing admonitions made no difference; the only thing that seemed to give the girl solace was the comfort of her closeness. So, after they had bathed and changed, she decided to go to bed although it was still early, and to take the child with her, as she would one of her own daughters. Only when she lay in bed, the girl pressed tightly against her, did she discover how exhausted she was herself. The moment her head touched the pillow, drowsiness overwhelmed her.

On the brink of sleep she realized she had not had a chance to think about the children. She obviously had not yet found a way to communicate with them. The one-eyed boy and his obscene language did not distress her much; despite his efforts to appear grown-up and cynical, he obviously was no more than a terrified child. The words were sheer bravado, as the hysterical giggles had been with which her own girls used to collapse at the word "buttocks" when they were little. Poor boy, if only she could reach him! But maybe, in order to do that, she should love him first.

The idea woke her up for a moment from her drowsy slide into sleep. Love? Could she force herself to love that sad, one-eyed urchin, so filthy, so sick, so full of hate?

"Hush, baby, hush," she muttered sleepily to the girl in her arms. When she realized that the child was asleep, she fell asleep herself.

* * *

The night Ann Traylor spent in Margaret Fell's bed was one of pure bliss. She was pursued by nightmares, but each time she woke up, heart pounding, there was the warm, placid body of her mistress, the peaceable rhythm of her breathing. In her half-sleep Ann felt happy and secure; she almost began to enjoy those nightmares. For, despite the reality of their terror, she never quite lost the awareness that she would wake up in the bliss of utter security. It was all behind her now; after this there could be no question of their continuing their efforts.

But she discovered the next morning, to her shocked amazement, that her mistress was returning to the prison. It meant, of course, that she would have to go with her. It filled her with a sense of outrage, of betrayal. The tenderness and the love she felt for the woman must be totally unrequited; all Margaret Fell thought about was those infernal children. Whether her companion had to go through the terrors of hell as a result not only did not interest her, it did not even occur to her.

But as it turned out, Margaret Fell did not expect Ann to accompany her. She expected her to stay at the inn and rest; it was ridiculous to risk, for a second time, an experience like that. But by then Ann's feeling of shock had turned into hostility. For some reason, it prompted her to say, "Of course I'll come. I cannot possibly let thee go alone. If thou canst go back in there, so can I."

She could not understand why she made this foolish suggestion. Everything in her cried out in raw terror at the thought of having to descend into that darkness again. But she could not help herself; something stronger than she demanded that she accompany her mistress, a spirit of rebellion, almost of revenge. But when they set out once again with their refilled baskets for Lancaster Castle she realized that what compelled her to hang on to her mistress was weakness: she could not let go of the security the presence of the woman gave her; she would have felt utterly bereft without her. It was a sort of enslavement; she wanted to stay behind, but discovered she could not. If only she had gone on noble considerations! But no: here she went, trotting at the leash of her own feebleness. It was shameful; as a result her hostility increased toward Margaret Fell and everything she stood for: Quakerism, selflessness, those children, who, as any sane person could see, were beyond saving.

They were met in the gateway by the turnkey, who must have been waiting for them. He said he had orders to escort them to the children's cell; when they were ready to leave, the ladies should blow a whistle he gave them and he would come to escort them back. Ann, hating everyone and despising herself, again descended into the nether world of Lancaster Castle. Despite the jailer's presence, the moment she set foot on the stone steps she was certain it would happen again. At last the key rattled in the lock, the rusty hinges squealed and she found herself facing those ghoulish children once more. She could not help it, she felt a frightening hatred for them. She sat down in the straw with her back against the grille to watch Margaret Fell's hopeless efforts at turning those little sewer rats into human beings. When Margaret struck up "The Andalusian Merchant" in that genteel, refined soprano of hers, Ann closed her eyes. Again, all the woman achieved was to set the lunatics shrieking. The children uttered not a sound.

Then silence fell. It fell so brusquely and was so ominous that Ann knew, even before she turned around, that someone had arrived whom everybody feared, even the wretches next door. In the light of a lantern, politely held high by the warden, stood Justice John Sawrey, small and smiling.

"Good morning, Mistress Fell," he said in his high, effeminate voice. "I have come to see how you are getting along. Open up." The last words were snapped at the warden, who hastily obliged. Ann moved aside; the gate swung inward on its squealing hinges.

Margaret Fell, normally not given to gestures of humility, rose to her feet. "Oh, I pray you," the little man said with a smile. "Don't let me interrupt. Pray continue."

Margaret Fell ignored his request and faced him fearlessly. "Yes, Mr. Sawrey? What is it you wish?"

"I simply wanted to ascertain for myself that everything is as you wish it, Madam," Sawrey said. "Is there anything I can do to make your task easier?"

"No, thank you." Her politeness was, somehow, crushing.

"In any case, your task will be somewhat lighter as from the first Saturday of next month," the little man said in the same pleasant tone. "On that date you will have one child less to concern you." He pointed at the one-eyed boy. "He will be hanged that morning."

Margaret Fell's mouth fell open; to her own surprise, Ann reacted with coldness. She saw at once that Sawrey had come to announce, as part of his campaign, that Margaret Fell's meddlesome intervention had hastened along the child's doom. Instead of saving the children as she had set out to do, all she had achieved was to advance the execution date of one of them.

Justice Sawrey made a bow and a sweep, scraped his leg in the straw and left. The boy remained motionless, leaning against the wall, his face frozen in a snarl.

Margaret Fell turned toward him. "Child . . ."

"Shit," he said. "Shit. Shit. Shit to thee."

But the woman would not heed the warning. She went toward him, wading through the straw, stretched out her arms, perhaps expecting him to collapse on her shoulder. At her approach, his snarl became a hiss. "Piss on thee!" he hissed. "Stinking whore! Ballocks! Ballocks!"

Much as she detested him, Ann felt a twinge of sympathy.

"I—I am so terribly sorry . . ." Margaret Fell said foolishly.

Ann knew what would happen, and it came: a sharp, chilling smack. The boy had no recourse but to slap her face.

For a moment all remained silent; Ann waited for the shrill throb of the whistle.

But she was mistaken. "All right, children," Margaret Fell said, turning away, taut but controlled. "Let us try again. *'The Andalusian Merchant that returns, laden with cochineal and china dishes . . .'"* There came her refined drawing-room soprano, followed by the first scream of a madwoman in the neighboring cell. Moments later the corridor was echoing with shrieks, catcalls, the rattling of doors, the clanging of chains slammed against iron bars. It was as if Sawrey had never been; the only change was that Margaret Fell's left cheek was bright red.

The indomitable woman stayed in the dungeon all day. She achieved nothing other than to turn herself into the laughingstock of the prison. For when they were finally guided back to freedom by the turnkey and climbed the endless steps, a sound pursued them from the dark mouths of corridors on every landing. *"The Andalusian Merchant! . . . The Andalusian Merchant! . . ."* It seemed as if all the damned souls in hell were howling in derision at the woman fleeing up the stairs.

Outside in the daylight, Margaret Fell looked as if she had seen a ghost. Ann could not help but feel an inexpressible relief. This was the end; no sane person would set foot in that prison again after what they had wrought.

They supped in silence. Margaret Fell did not touch her food. There was no sharing of her bed; Ann retired to her room alone. Facing the door, her left hand inside the book, she wrote, *"Well, today brought the end of the ordeal. The one-eyed boy is to be hanged."*

She did not continue. There was a restlessness in her, she could not concentrate. She went to the window for a breath of air.

The night was full of stars; the black silhouette of the castle towered among them. The Milky Way, unimaginably far, unimaginably vast, shimmered mysteriously.

It was as if she began to discern in the world-large whorls of the Milky Way a face, a shape. She saw for a moment, fleetingly, a man slowly coming toward her. She caught, like a whiff of blossoms, a brief intimation of future raptures, ecstasies, riches, glory . . .

Yet, even as she was touched by that premonition of happiness, she felt a sense of loss. How wonderful it would have been to be a saint.

*   *   *

Next door Margaret Fell was pacing up and down in her room, going through agonies of guilt, a torment of doubt. It was inconceivable, unimaginable, but had John Sawrey decided to hang that poor boy only to thwart her? It could not be! Sawrey was a vicious man, but there were limits to what a judge could do! Yet she had no doubt he had made his announcement only to force her to give up her efforts in behalf of the children. Was he right? Was there any point in her going on?

Not only her reason seemed to persuade her to desist, all that was delicate and fainthearted in her cried out for solace, for deliverance, as she paced back and forth, fighting her tears. Suddenly she had such a sense of confinement that she snuffed the candle and opened the window.

The night outside, its radiant immensity, was a comfort at first; then she remembered standing like this the night after George's arrival at Swarthmoor Hall, when a sense of minuteness had induced her to whisper, "God? Look at me: it's me, Maggie . . ." She remembered the dream: the door opening at the foot of her bed, the young god wading toward her from the ocean of light.

Had it all been the moon-sick fancy of an aging woman? "Oh, God," she whispered, closing her eyes, "God, God . . ." Then, suddenly, there was the indomitable challenge again. *'All He has is thee.'*

She gazed at the sky. It was madness to presume that she, fly-speck on a planet among the millions of stars, should be a representative of the God who had conceived the Milky Way, the swarms of suns spinning in the darkness of the void. *All He has is thee.* The presumption of it! The heresy! Who was this boy, this uneducated weaver's son, to proclaim that it was not man who needed God, but God who needed man? *All He has is thee.* Preposterous! Blasphemous! Never before had she known such yearning for the security of dogma, the sheltering arms of the church; but, alas, all those considerations conspired only to keep her away from the boy about to be hanged. She understood why he had struck her, or thought she did; but even if she did not, some inexorable pull drew her to that lonely child pressed against the wall, facing with his one suppurating eye the terror of death, alone. She had to go back to him, she had to.

That night she barely slept. Each time she was about to slide into sleep, there was that poor child, pressed against the wall, snarling at her, as white as a sheet. "Oh, God, God, God of love, Jesus, His loving Son: mercy, mercy!" She whispered the prayer each time she woke from her uneasy sleep, but there was no answer, no heavenly certitude came to her. She was left with nothing but her own personal tenderness.

At an earlier hour than usual, she found herself with Ann in front of the desk in the little office in the gateway, facing the warden. He heard her out, his eyes expressionless, his face set. "Mistress Fell," he said at last, "the boy will be hanged whether you persist in your efforts or not. He was condemned to death, after a proper trial, by Justice Sawrey. The matter of pardon was never even discussed because in his case a petition for clemency was bound to be rejected."

"Why? What has he done?"

"He is a murderer," the warden said coldly. "A particularly vicious one. He was an orphan adopted by Ebenezer Jones, Burgomaster of Cark. You may have heard of the case. Mayor Jones was a wealthy, highly respected merchant known for his charity. He chose the boy because of his intelligence, and was murdered for his pains. God, in His wisdom which passeth all understanding, had seen fit to make him choose a monster."

"Nonsense!" she cried. "No child is a monster! Something must have happened. Didn't the boy say *why* he did it? What evidence was there that he did it at all?"

"Oh, he did it, all right," the warden said. "He never bothered to deny it. He smashed his father's skull with a poker, in the man's study, one night after supper."

"But why? There must have been a reason!"

The warden looked at her wearily; she sensed his exasperation. "It may be difficult for you to accept, Madam, but there are creatures in this world who do not deserve the word 'human.' The boy is a monster of viciousness and depravity, and I wholeheartedly agree with Justice Sawrey's verdict."

"But his eye? What happened to his eye?"

"That, Madam, was struck out in the fight." The warden picked up his quill again.

"So my appealing for a pardon would make no difference to his fate?"

"I'm afraid not." He hesitated, then added, "But it might affect yours, Madam."

"Mine?"

He glanced at the door. "Mayor Jones had many friends in this town. So has Mistress Jones, and she is a very temperamental lady; Welsh, you know. Your interference has already raised her hackles. She is, understandably enough, adamant that the boy gets his deserts. You, a wife yourself, will appreciate that."

"I certainly do not!" she said angrily; but she felt a doubt even as she said it. How could she know what a woman felt who saw her husband murdered by a child she loved?

"Believe me, Madam, for you to make an official appeal on behalf of the boy would not only be ineffectual, it would be most unwise."

She rose. "Thank thee for thy kind concern, Hyman." She did not wait for him to rise and bow; she turned and left.

The jailer escorted them down to the bottom level and let them into the children's cell. Intuition told her to ignore the boy, who instantly got up and went back to the wall to stand there, scowling. She resumed her efforts to make the children sing; the moment she raised her voice, the madwomen began to shriek again. But she persevered, while the boy glowered at her, mouthing foul words whenever he caught her looking in his direction. This child was not a monster; there must have been a reason for his attack on his adoptive father. But his guilt or innocence seemed unimportant. All she cared about was how to comfort him.

But how to comfort a person who knew he was going to be hanged, and this a boy only eleven years old? What was it like to know that in less than a month's time you would be no more? It was unimaginable. How could she reach him? He would have no part of her commiseration. But she did not want to commiserate with him; what she wanted was to take him in her arms, as she would one of her own children, transmit to him something she could not put into words.

But she could not bring herself to do it. Before she blew her whistle that night to call the jailer, she went to the boy and said matter-of-factly, "I will be with thee when—when it happens."

He glared at her with chilling hatred. "Go bugger thyself."

She turned away.

On the way back to the inn it occurred to her that maybe it was not enough to tell a child that she would be there, as if her presence were a precious gift. She should try and save his life, ask for a pardon. She knew enough about the judicial process to realize that if she were to write to the Lord Justices in London, her petition would not be considered until months later, long after the boy was dead. She should write to Cromwell himself.

That night, after supper, she wrote the letter. She decided to go for that of God in Cromwell without paying heed to the proper form of address. So she wrote, *"Dear heart! As the father of thy people, I come to plead with thee for one of thy youngest children . . ."*

It became a long letter; she finished it just before the candle gave out. The problem was how to dispatch it so it would get to him in time. Perhaps the warden would dispatch it for her, if he could do so without compromising himself.

She knelt at the side of her bed. "Dear God, please, please be with him tonight, give him comfort . . ."

She stopped. She had prayed with utter sincerity, but all it achieved was to comfort herself. There was only one answer to that prayer: *'All He has is thee.'* If she wanted God to be with that boy, she should be there herself. There was no other way: she must move in with the children.

*   *   *

The next morning, Ann Traylor's instant reaction was: No! Enough is enough! Let her move in alone! She tried desperately to think of an excuse for not joining in this latest extravagance; Margaret Fell forestalled her by stating that she intended to spend the nights in prison alone. When Ann protested, she ordered her not to be foolish, and to stay at the inn.

So Ann accompanied her mistress to the prison with, as a beckoning promise at the end of the day, the vision of having the rooms at the inn entirely to herself. She would sup alone, write in her diary undisturbed, be free to do whatever she wished. It was a vision of such delight that the day passed slowly. The children were apathetic and snotty and filthy and unresponsive as always; the one-eyed boy stood against the wall, glowering at them, muttering obscenities; her mistress persevered with the lessons and with her efforts to make them sing the madrigal which had made them the laughingstock of the prison. The very notion of laughter in a place like this was ludicrous, but the moment Margaret Fell raised her genteel soprano to lead the children in "The Andalusian Merchant," all the invisible prisoners in the dungeons roared with laughter, magnified by the well of the stairs as by a colossal speaking-trumpet. Everybody knew the song by now; lewd versions of it were shouted at them from the passages when they were spotted on the landings. The only ones in the prison unable to catch the tune were the children; all they did was gape, mouths open, eyes as dull as pewter, at the elegant lady squatting in the straw, caroling *"These things are wondrous, yet more wondrous I, whose heart with fear doth freeze, with love doth fry."* The words themselves were a mockery in the presence of a child having an attack of diarrhea in a corner, of another lying sick in one of the cavities hewn out in the wall, of a boy about to be hanged. But Margaret Fell did not seem to be aware of anything incongruous; her determination seemed part of the indomitable arrogance of the English gentry: to the mistress of Swarthmoor Hall, who had never been thwarted in any whim which caught her fancy, it was inconceivable that her ministrations to the poor should be rejected and doomed to failure.

To Ann, as she leaned against the bars of the cell, the mere thought of what would happen to the one-eyed boy was horrifying. To try to humor him, as Margaret Fell was doing, was repugnant and painful. There he stood, a filthy human beast about to be slaughtered, locked up at the bottom of a well, dragging chains that had chafed the skin off his ankles and caused running sores; and there sat a lady presuming to have become part of his world by taking off her jewelry. To importune the boy, who must be going through torments of terror and apprehension, with melodious notions about his wondrous heart alternately freezing and frying seemed an obscenity. In a few weeks' time, at sunrise, his body would drop, his neck would snap, his heart would freeze forever after an agonizing struggle with death at the end of a rope. Each time Ann looked at him she saw the dropping body, the desperate struggle, the swinging rope slowly coming to a halt, like a stopped pendulum. It made her feel that she was an intruder, a fraud. The least offensive thing she could do was to make herself as inconspicuous as possible while waiting for her mistress to accept defeat.

As she sat there leaning against the bars throughout that interminable day, she had plenty of time to think. The truth, she concluded, was simple. Life, as revealed all around her, was a hideous nightmare. The only escape was to grab each fleeting chance for happiness, any opportunity for joy that might present itself, knowing all the time that this pit of the damned was the true reality. Whatever might happen to her in the future, she would never be able to forget this prison. It would be with her always, like the stench that she could not close out as she sat there dreaming dreams of canopied beds, marble floors inlaid black and white, gilded leather covering the walls, hundreds of candles in crystal chandeliers, velvet gowns, servants, greyhounds, cockatoos in jeweled cages. What she should really do the moment she was free was to find herself a rich old merchant who would adore her, indulge her slightest whim, give her riches, luxury, freedom to meet anyone she liked: young noblemen, officers . . .

Never before had she thought of the future in those terms. All her life she had pursued virtue, chastity, charity. By entering Lancaster Castle, she had thought, she was following Christ's example. Not in her wildest dreams had it occurred to her that within days, robbed of all her pious fancies and girlish ideals, she would cynically consider hunting down a rich old man. What had happened to the holy enthusiasm she had felt when Margaret Fell first mentioned the sufferings of prisoners? She yearned to go home to the inn; only by writing it all down could she hope to answer that question.

When at last Margaret Fell said, "Well, Ann, I think it's time to leave," she leaped eagerly to her feet; her heart sank when she heard her mistress add, "Be good now, children; I'll be back."

She was coming too! She had had second thoughts, the pretentious queen! Ann fumed with helpless rage as they stood waiting for the jailer to appear in response to the whistle. He seemed to take a long time; when finally the light of his lantern came swinging down the passage and the madwomen next door began their mindless crowing and shrieking at his approach, tears of disappointment welled in Ann's eyes. Why had she changed her mind? Why, why?

There could only be one explanation: she was afraid. At the last moment, the idea of having to spend the night in the dungeon was too much for her delicate sensibilities. Then why had she raised the children's hopes so cruelly? Why had she made such a song and dance of "her duty to share their world"? It had all been a rich woman's fancy, the last semblance of selflessness was ripped off her example of Christian charity. Ann forgot about the earlier hopes that her mistress might accept defeat; all she could think of at that moment was the cruel disappointment of seeing her dream of freedom come to naught. Oh, how she hated her! How she despised her imperious fickleness!

It seemed to her, in her state of angry rebellion, that even the turnkey was derogatory. Margaret Fell had dramatically announced her decision to stay overnight that morning; to turn tail now did not improve her standing with the prison staff, who thus far had been surly but respectful. When, as they appeared on the landing, an uncouth voice bellowed from one of the passages, "Hey! How's thy frying heart, Fogo?!" the turnkey shouted, "Shut yer trap or I'll Fogo thee, bull-sucker!" This time he offered no apology for his language.

Outside, the ramparts of the castle were orange with the sunset; in the alleys of the city twilight had already settled. They did not speak as they walked, swiftly and some distance apart, to the Three Swans; when they entered the taproom, the sound of buzzing voices ceased abruptly. Margaret Fell went to fetch the key and order their supper in an oppressive silence.

Normally, they chatted as they went about their dark, empty rooms, lighting the candles; this time not a word was spoken. Margaret Fell seemed preoccupied. It must be a novel experience to her to give up, she obviously did not like it. Supper was served; the maid left with the tray, they joined hands for grace.

The moment she held her mistress' hands in hers, Ann felt a twinge of contrition. She did not know whether it was the mere touch of Margaret's hands or the fact that they trembled slightly, but suddenly she was sorry for the woman. Even though she had given up, she *had* done a courageous and unprecedented thing by going down into those dungeons on an errand of mercy. Rather than blame her for fickleness, she should try to revive the admiration she had once felt for her. She opened her eyes; the face opposite her was a mask of such sorrow that she was about to ask, "Margaret Fell? What is the matter?" Then her mistress opened her eyes and smiled. "Well," she said, "I must be too tired to eat. I think I had better go before it gets too late." She rose. "I'll just pack a bag; it was foolish of me not to have thought of it this morning."

It came as such a surprise that Ann found herself tongue-tied with remorse and confusion. She helped her pack, trying all the while to think of something to say; when she faced her at the door, she blurted out, "Please, let me come with thee! Please! Thou canst not go there alone, it's too late to be on the streets . . ."

Margaret Fell, pale in the candlelight, shook her head. "No, my dear; this is my battle, not thine. Have a good rest. And bring me some food for the children in the morning. Good night, God bless; I'll have the landlord call a chair."

"God bless . . ."

She should have run after her, but she stood in the doorway, listening to her rapid steps going down the passage and the stairs. The din of voices from the taproom became louder when the downstairs door was opened, then it fell silent. She heard the door close; the voices started up again, excitedly.

She turned back into the room. The sudden emptiness made her feel forlorn and ill at ease. To eat alone, which she had dreamed of all day as a feast of languorous delight, turned out to be bleak and mournful. When finally she sat down with her diary she felt constrained, as if the presence of her mistress were more oppressive in her absence. Why had Margaret changed her mind? Or had she truly forgotten to pack a valise? The valise seemed incongruous: did she expect to lie down in that filthy straw in her nightgown? She should have taken a blanket!

For a moment Ann considered going after her with one, if only as far as the warden's office; but by the time she arrived, Margaret Fell would already have descended into the dungeons.

She could not get her out of her mind. She was haunted by the image of her trying to sleep in that foul-smelling cell, among those filthy, vermin-ridden children.

In the end, all she managed to write was, *"Tonight M.F. moved in with the children in Lancaster Castle."* After some brooding, she added, *"after all."*

She sat staring at the page. Would there be rats down there that came out at night? 'Oh, my God,' she thought, 'help her! Have mercy on her! Have mercy on *me!*'

* * *

Margaret Fell had returned to the Three Swans in momentary faint-heartedness. The day had been an exhausting one; it was proving so difficult to make contact with the children; she had the feeling that she made no impression on them whatsoever. But when she had taken Ann's hands in hers for grace, she had found that they trembled. The girl was troubled by her change of heart; it must be a deep disappointment to her. So, with wooden bravery, she had suddenly decided to return.

She managed to hold firm to her determination all the way to the castle; when she entered the office, however, she found a stranger sitting behind the warden's desk. It might have been the darkness that made him look unprepossessing; the light of the candles on the desk sharpened his hawklike features and seemed to give an unusual brilliance to his oddly wide-set eyes. Only when he rose did she realize he was a hunchback.

"Good evening, Madam. Henry Hathaway, assistant warden." He made a crooked little bow. For some reason he frightened her.

"Good evening," she said, as pleasantly as she could. "I am the wife of Chief Justice Fell. As you must have heard, I have permission from Warden Farragut to spend the night with the children."

"Yes, I know all about it." The hunchback seemed to think it amusing. "Dr. Withers has also been informed. You will be meeting him later tonight."

"Is he a surgeon?"

"No, he is the spiritual adviser of the inmates of this prison. He will be concerned with the boy in your cell who is due for execution. He told me before we went down tonight that he plans to pay you a visit if time permits."

"I see . . ." She became aware that someone was rummaging through her valise and saw it was a man she had not seen before, obviously a turnkey of the night shift. "Warden Farragut ceased inspecting my basket some days ago," she said sharply.

The man, sallow-faced and cavernous, did not seem to have heard. She watched, shaken and embarrassed, as his hands went on searching the contents of her valise, fumbling among the intimacies of her night apparel and toiletries.

"It is regrettable, Madam," Hathaway said, still with that irrepressible smile of amusement, "but at nighttime we have to be especially careful. Someone might grab your valise and use its contents for his own purposes. Anything in there?" His voice when he addressed the turnkey was not amused.

"No sir. Only candles. Do we allow candles?"

The hunchback looked at her, and there was that unpleasant smile again. She did not know what made him so loathsome; surely it was not his deformity. The thought made her submit more meekly to the search than she would otherwise have done.

"In your case, Madam," the hunchback said, "we'll let you keep the candles; normally, we would confiscate them. Danger of fire, you know. But as you are going to spend the night down there, let's allow you the comfort of some light. You will need it."

Something in the way he said it made it sound like a threat. "Why?" she asked, frowning.

"Rats, for one thing." His smile grew; his wet lips glistened in the candlelight.

"I—I should like to go down now." She tried to sound unconcerned, but the mention of rats was unnerving. He had probably said it only to frighten her; his ill will seemed obvious now.

"Certainly. Good night, Madam. Happy dreams."

"Is—is your man going to accompany me?"

The hunchback's face was a caricature of regret. "Alas, Madam, we do not have sufficient staff at night to provide you with an escort. But surely you know the way by now?"

"In that case, could I have a lantern?"

He threw up his hands in commiseration. "Ah, I wish I could oblige, Madam, but I'm afraid the one available lantern was taken by Dr. Withers. You have candles, haven't you? Parsons! Light one for M'Lady."

The cavernous man took one of the candles from her valise, without asking, and lit it from the one on the desk. He handed it to her without a word.

She felt a momentary confusion. She had to hold the candle, shield the flame against the draft and carry the valise; it would be awkward and difficult, once she started on her way down.

"Parsons, open the door for M'Lady! Good night, Madam, see you tomorrow morning. Or are you planning to stay with us permanently?"

She did not deign to answer that. "Good night, Mr. Hathaway," she said coldly. She nodded at the turnkey, who held the door open for her, and stepped out into the dark cave of the gateway. Instantly the draft blew out her candle; luckily, the entrance to the dungeons was marked by a lantern. As she approached, she saw there was a guard on duty; during the daytime the jailers had their own key. The guard lifted the lantern and shone the light on her face.

"Good evening," she said.

Without replying, he inserted the key in the lock of the grille with a rattle that echoed in the well beyond. The gate swung open, and she stepped inside.

The stench that met her as she approached the black pit of the stairs seemed even more repugnant than it was in the daytime; the very idea of having to spend the night at the bottom of that black, stinking shaft made her shudder. She tarried for a moment at the top of the steps, stricken with apprehension. Then she lit the candle with the tinderbox she had, wisely, put in the pocket of her cloak as she left the inn. The feeble, flickering light barely reached her feet, she would have to go carefully once she started her descent.

Never before had she felt such abject fear; she could not put the rats out of her mind. In the past, the mere mention of a mouse had been enough to give her the irrepressible urge to jump onto a chair and scream for help. She had never thought about rats in the prison, she had never seen one there. Now the idea that she would have to lie down in the straw to sleep while there might be rats burrowing all around her was petrifying. "Oh, God, God," she prayed, in a whisper, "help me, please help me . . ." But the instant response to her fervent plea was the thought: 'Which God? Where?' Standing there, gazing into the well below, she suddenly felt overcome by an angry scorn for George Fox and his fancies. If only God had been allowed to remain firmly established in the heavens, gazing down upon her with the fatherly concern of One who counted hairs and watched over each sparrow, she would have descended into that black pit like Daniel into the lion's den, whereas now . . . What comfort could she derive from the small, powerless voice within her, urging, *'Go, please, Maggie, go . . .'?* The voice of her fear was much stronger; anything was stronger than the pitiful whisper that pleaded with her to go to those children. Why should she? What were they to her? She had tried her best, hadn't she? Was there any hope she would ever get through to them? They were beyond human reach. And that horrible boy, spewing obscenities . . .

All He has is thee.

There was the boy about to be hanged, younger than her own son George. If he were her son, would she go down? Of course she would.

Well, he was God's child, and the only way his Father could reach him was through her. 'All right, God,' she thought, setting her jaw. 'Here we go, sink or swim together.' But it seemed that God, if He were indeed within her, was as apprehensive as she. Once she returned to the world, she would have a word with George Fox and tell him that she had tried out his fancy concept and found it worthless. "Come on, Maggie," she murmured. "Stop shilly-shallying."

She swallowed and groped for the first step with her foot.

That first step turned out to be the most difficult; once she had discovered the candle flame would survive as long as she went slowly, she took heart. She found that if she concentrated on going down those steps to the exclusion of everything else, the whole thing became possible. Gradually, as she went down, step by step, she gained confidence. But when she reached the first landing she was greeted by a storm of catcalls, whistles, boos and shrieked obscenities from the passages. It had happened before, but always in the presence of a jailer with a lantern; this time she froze with fright. Whether it was a jerky movement of her own or the draft from the passages, suddenly the candle went out. The laughter it caused was terrifying; it seemed as if the whole prison shook with roars of malevolent glee. A voice yelled as from the bottom of a pit, "Hey! Honey bear! How's thy frying Fogo?!"

The laughter doubled in volume; she stood in the darkness shaking like a leaf, about to burst into tears and flee back upstairs. A thought flashed through her mind, 'That of God. Appeal to that of God in them.' She did not stop to consider how grotesque the notion was; pinned against the wall, she cried, her voice shrill and puny in the roar of their laughter, "Friends! Friends, for the love of God, I am here to help the children! Please, *please* help me!"

She hardly knew what she cried, but it seemed to catch the interest of those invisible people. The sudden silence gave her the courage to cry, "Down there is a boy who is going to be hanged! He's only eleven! We cannot leave him to face that alone, *somebody* has to go there, somebody has to be with him! Please, please help me! I am so afraid!" Oh, she should not have said that! She should not have told those people how frightened she was.

A voice yelled from one of the passages, "He's a murderer!"

Without thinking, she cried back, "I don't care what he has done! What any of you have done! God is love! And His love can only reach that boy through me, through—through all of you!" She stood there, trembling, steeling herself for the roar of derision that would follow. But there was no response.

She managed to light the candle despite the shaking of her hands. When the flame had grown bright enough to reveal the first step, she continued on her way, bracing herself for the onslaught of the next landing. But they seemed to have howled their fill; she was allowed to pass without being harried. Shakily she pressed on toward the bottom of the pit, preparing herself for the shrieks of the lunatic women.

But whether it was the darkness or whether most of them were asleep at this hour, only one of the tragic creatures stood at the bars and stretched out a claw toward her as she passed with her candle. "Dearie," a voice whispered. "Dearie, love me! Love me too . . ." She hurried past, her arms covered with goose pimples.

At last she reached the end of the passage, the dungeon of the children, home. As she fumbled with the key in the lock, she wondered how a place that had at one time filled her with such revulsion could suddenly feel like home; then, as she opened the door with the screeching hinges, she saw the light of her candle glisten in the eyes of a child. It was the little girl, who came crawling toward her in the straw; the others lay curled up like animals in the center of the cell, huddled together for warmth. She heard the rattle of a chain, lifted the candle and saw the one-eyed boy pressing himself against the wall again, in the spot where he always stood. "Well, children," she said cheerfully, "here I am. I told you I'd be back." She put down the valise, stuck her hand through the bars of the door and locked it from the outside. She put the key in her bodice, bent down to pick up her valise and jumped back with a squeal when she saw a small black thing jump and scurry away into the straw. "Oh, God . . ." she whispered, her hand on her heart, eyes closed, leaning against the bars. "Oh God, dear God—I can't. I can't . . ." She heard a high, snickering sound, opened her eyes and saw the boy grin at her malevolently. For a moment she stiffened, then she said quietly, "Well, I am happy to see that thou canst laugh." It was a foolish thing to say, certainly not the way to endear herself to him, but she needed all her self-control at that moment not to flee. How silly, how stupid that her entire concern should come to naught because of her terror of mice! For it must have been a mouse. Rats were *much* bigger, and certainly not shy like that. It had been a harmless, curious little mouse at least as frightened as she was. She went to the center of the cell and, after wrapping her skirt tightly around her ankles, sat down with the children despite the certainty that the moment she did so rats would scurry toward her and scrabble inside her petticoats. She opened her valise, produced an empty bottle she had brought, stuck it in the straw and put the candle in it. "Well, children," she said briskly, "here we are. Now let's see. What shall we do first?"

Judged by their responsiveness, the huddled forms in the straw were fast asleep. Only the little girl, dull-eyed, her grimy face covered with sores and snot, gaped at her, breathing through her mouth with a snoring sound. Poor little thing; how long had she spent locked up in this cellar, away from light and air, from life? "Let's play a game," she said. "Knowest thou the game 'I spy with my little eye'?" The child said nothing, just stared at her vacuously.

"I'll show thee how it goes." She looked at the bottle, then she said gaily, "I spy with my little eye something beginning with 'B'—"

"Ballocks."

The boy. Oh dear, her choice of game had been unfortunate, considering he had only one eye. But this kind of delicate feeling was ridiculous under the circumstances. "Bottle," she said to the little girl in front of her. "B—bottle. Wouldst thou like to try? 'I spy with my little eye something beginning with—' what?"

"She's a mute," the boy said.

"Oh—I see . . ."

Suddenly there was a movement among the huddled shapes in the straw. One of the little boys lifted his head, listening. He scrambled to his feet, the others followed suit and the lot of them rushed toward the bars, trying to peer outside. Even the little girl scrambled toward the gate on hands and knees, to try and peer down the dark passage. There was a sound of voices and a loud clattering, as if a cart were being wheeled down the passage. There came a light, then the angular silhouette of a baker's cart pushed by a man in rags, accompanied by a small, disheveled woman of indeterminate age carrying a lantern. The children pressed themselves against the bars, stretched out their hands toward the cart; the woman suspended the lantern from a crook above the cart, opened the lid and started to spoon something from a barrel inside into a bowl. She turned around to hand it to one of the children, who all squealed and waved their hands and tried to grab it; she lashed at them with her ladle and gave it to the farthest boy. She turned to fill the next bowl, but the children could not wait that long. They set upon the boy, who spat and screamed and kicked, trying to defend his bowl, spilling some of its contents in the straw. The woman cried, "Here, you, varmint!" holding out another bowl; the pack of voracious urchins rushed back to the bars. Open-mouthed, aghast, Margaret watched their ferocious fight that came to an end only when each of them had a bowl, having lost most of the contents through their sense-less, hideous violence. The spectacle was so pitiful that she barely had eyes for the woman, who peered at her through the bars and said, "If you want food, you'll have to pay garnish, M'Lady."

"Garnish?"

"You don't expect to get fed for nothing, do you, now?"

"Oh, I'll—I'm not hungry, thank you."

The woman shrugged her shoulders and turned away. "Geddup!" she cried; the man in rags turned around between the shafts and started to pull the cart back along the passage. The lunatic women welcomed him with bangings and raucous cries; they sounded like famished beasts of prey. Margaret closed her eyes, overcome by hopelessness. She had never quite realized before how horrendous this place was, how futile her effort to relieve some of its horror. It was not fear that would defeat her, it was hopelessness, the conviction that she would never be able to change this place, that nothing could, that the one thing likely to happen was that it would change her. She belonged in her own house, with her own children, her own husband . . . She felt a sudden, desperate yearning for Thomas, for the baby, the delicate fragrance of fresh bedsheets, the—

Something made her look up. Behind the bars, peering down at her, stood a white-haired man in black.

"I am Dr. Withers," he said dourly. "You have the key, I believe?"

"Yes . . ."

"Pray let me in. I am here to see the boy Henry Jones."

She opened the gate for him with alacrity, for he was a harbinger of her own world. But when he stepped inside, his antagonism became obvious. He was a tall, stoop-shouldered man who would have looked forbidding under any circumstances; in the ghostly light of his lantern he looked the image of wrath. His cold, fanatical eyes gazed down on her with such hostility that she almost backed away. "What business is this of yours, Madam?" he asked harshly.

"I beg your pardon?"

He closed his eyes in exasperation. Then he opened them again and said in a voice taut with self-control, "I heard what you said on the stairs, and you heard my answer: this boy is a murderer. Do you know the punishment for blasphemy, Madam?"

"Blasphemy?"

"What you said was blasphemy. Only faith in Jesus' atonement saves, nothing else. He is the one to transmit God's love to the world; no one else can usurp His place."

"But I do not intend to. All I wanted to say—"

"Don't try and defend yourself, woman!" he cried. "I will be lenient this time! I will forget! But do not endeavor to convince me that you did not intend to say what I heard you say! Or that you did not know that the entire prison can hear every word spoken on those stairs!"

"I didn't know! My candle blew out and—"

"Sinner, do not defend yourself!" he cried. There was something majestic about his anger; she gave up trying to convince him. "As I have said: this time I will be lenient. But do not spout blasphemy again within these walls or I will be forced to report you." He gave her a peculiar look and added, "I will be lenient, that is, on condition that you shall now repent. Do you repent?"

She looked at him in bewilderment. Her first impulse was: go for that of God in him. But something about his eyes told her that for once this was hopeless. "What would you have me repent, Friend?" she asked, trying to convey to him a sense of good will.

"Repent claiming that you should have been singled out to convey God's love to these children!"

"I would repent had I said that, Friend."

"That is what I heard you say, woman!"

"I did not say that I had been singled out. I singled myself out."

"I would not go on trying to defend myself with sophistry," he said, suddenly without passion. "There is no argument here. Either repent, or I will report you as a blasphemer."

"I repent for anything I may have said that offended thee."

"Not me! God!"

She knew she was taking a risk, but she could not help herself. "Friend," she pleaded, "God is love! How could His love become a reality to these children if it weren't through thee or me?"

He stared at her for a moment in silence, then he said in a tone of finality, "I will speak to the boy now." She stepped aside; he waded through the straw toward the boy, who stood with his back to the wall, waiting for him defiantly.

"Henry Jones," he intoned, "thou art condemned to be hanged by the neck on the first Saturday of next month, at sunrise. I am here to prepare thee. Thou knowest that without faith in Christ Jesus and His atonement of all thy sins, there is no hope for thy soul."

"Ballocks," the boy said.

The old man did not seem to have heard. "Unless thou throwest thyself upon the mercy of our Savior, thou wilt burn in hell forevermore. Dost thou know that? Dost thou believe?"

"Shit," the boy said.

This time it dawned on the minister that he was faced by a rebel. "Dost thou *want* to go to hell, boy?"

"Any place where I won't meet thee!" The boy's voice was high and childish, heartbreaking in its lonely defiance.

The minister was taken aback, momentarily. *"What* didst thou say?"

"I don't want to go to heaven and meet thee there!" the boy cried; then the minister struck him in the face with his fist. The child squawked and crumpled into the straw. When Margaret saw the man lift his foot to kick him, she cried, "No, no!" She rushed toward the child and threw herself between the two of them, shielding him with her body. It was spontaneous and utterly sincere, yet she felt detached, as if in a charade. It did not seem real, none of it did.

The old man looked at her with cold, impersonal hostility. She waited for him to pronounce her doom, but he said nothing. He turned around and waded through the straw to the gate. He pulled it open, let himself out, shut it again, threw the key inside and was gone. She looked down on the huddled form in the straw. He did not move; she thought the priest had knocked him unconscious until she realized he had fallen asleep where he fell.

Suddenly she felt completely disoriented. For a moment the whole dungeon swirled around her; she closed her eyes and rested her head against the wall. 'Oh, God, dear God . . .' she thought, but she did not finish the prayer. She was crushed by the heartlessness, the cruelty, the suffering. She had never known that this could happen to human beings, not even after reading those hundreds of letters from imprisoned Friends. She felt as if all hope, all faith in goodness, beauty, all the gentle graces by which she had been sheltered all her life had been nothing but a dream. It became clear to her that it was not this dungeon, this brutality that was the dream, but Swarthmoor Hall.

She looked at the sleeping boy. She wanted to touch him, in a gesture of tenderness, but could not bring herself to do it. Here she was, pretending to embody God's love, and the idea of touching him, or any of them, filled her with such repugnance that she could not bring herself to do it. They had been symbols to her, not real human beings. She herself had been a symbol of mercy, descending among symbols of suffering with a symbolic message of love. She was nothing but a rich lady doing good.

She went to find the key in the straw and waded toward the

other children. As she sat down beside them, she remembered the rats, but her fear of them had dimmed. Weariness overwhelmed her; she closed her eyes, her hands in her lap, and the association with meeting for worship brought back, with almost unbearable poignancy, the memory of other times she had sat like this, under the illusion that she was experiencing the presence of God. It had all been a figment of her own imagination. She could not have sensed any presence of God, for there was no God. There could not be, for the God of righteousness personified by the priest and the God of love she had imagined were irreconcilable. It was impossible that the Spirit which had urged the Israelites to massacre women and children had anything in common with the loving Father Christ talked about. She had achieved her goal at last. She was free. Free of convention, tradition, inherited beliefs, free to face the truth. Well, here it was: tenderness, compassion, love, honor, hope—everything that had once made life worthwhile was a luxury, a dream. Reality was this. All she need do was look about her. But what was the point of an existence like this? Where was the sense of it? She covered her face with her hands. There was only one word to sum up the human experience as it had finally been revealed to her: absurd. The truth about life was that it was absurd.

Suddenly she jumped with fright as something touched her hand. She opened her eyes and saw it was the little mute girl, gazing at her, open-mouthed, with dull, mindless eyes.

She managed to smile. She wanted to speak to her, but remembered the child could not hear. It was all fake anyhow, for in her heart she shrank away from the horrible creature with disgust, hoping she would not touch her again. The child stank horribly; even in the feeble light of the candle she could see lice in her hair. If ever their bodies were to come in contact . . . Then the child snuggled up against her.

All that was fastidious in her cried out in repugnance, urging her to push the child away. But after a moment she relaxed and let her be. If she could give this poor, idiot baby a brief illusion of a motherly presence sheltering her from harm, why not? What was there left to defend? Even if this were no more than a mindless little animal's search for warmth, why not give it? With a sense of farewell, she put her arms around the child and pressed the filthy little head against her chest. She sat watching the lice until the candle flame twitched, sputtered and died, and darkness engulfed the dungeon.

She did not know how long she sat there in the dark, her arms around the little girl, waiting to feel the first crawling of lice on her scalp; they must be climbing all over her by now, seeking her hair. Suddenly one of the madwomen in the next cell started to clamor; as she looked up, she saw a light flicker on the bars. It grew brighter, throwing slowly drifting shadows on the wall opposite; it stopped just short of where she could see it and a man appeared at the door.

"Good evening, Mistress Fell. I hope I didn't disturb your sleep?"

It was John Sawrey. She was relieved it was he, not the clergyman or the woman with the cart. He stood there, small and elegant with his plumed hat and red cloak; the lamplight flashed on the buckles on his shoes as he moved closer to peer through the bars. "Is there anything I can do for you? Can I have them bring a blanket? Some fresh water?"

"No, thank you, Mr. Sawrey. It's very kind of you."

He looked at her, his face noncommittal, but his eyes seemed to show a concern that surprised her. "I'm ashamed that you should live in such filthy conditions. I'll tell Mistress Fraley to change the straw tomorrow."

"Oh—thank you." It seemed uncharacteristic of him, this sudden solicitousness. He must be up to something; her relief turned into wariness.

As if he had read her thoughts, he gave her a faint smile and said, "You must wonder at my concern."

"Indeed." There seemed to be no point in dissimulation.

"During Hilary this prison is my responsibility, and in a sense I am your husband's representative. I am as concerned about you as I would want him to be about my own good wife during his tour of duty."

"You're very kind."

"Are there any messages I can give him? Please consider me at your disposal."

"Thank you, for the moment I have all I need."

"Very well, then." He pulled on his gloves. "I'll make it a point to visit you every day about this hour, if that would be convenient."

"Oh—oh, yes."

"Should there be any problems at any time, please do not hesitate to have me called. I am residing in the castle during Hilary. Both wardens know where to find me."

"Thank you." She did not know what else to say.

"Good night, Madam. Your obedient servant." He swept his hat and made a leg; his shadow on the wall looked huge. She heard him mutter, "All right"; someone lifted the lantern. The next moment he was gone; the poor souls in the cell next door jabbered briefly at his passing; the light drew away, and all was dark again. The child she was cradling had not stirred, nor had any of the others.

He left her in a pensive mood. His courtesy and concern, however calculating, had somehow alleviated her desperation; there now seemed to be a ray of hope. She sat pondering on it for a while and realized that her suddenly taking heart was brought about by his promise to have the straw changed. That such a simple thing could make such a difference! She wondered why she herself had not thought of it; for some reason she had considered everything in the dungeon to be as permanent and unchangeable as the rock out of which it was hewn. It had never occurred to her that the straw could be changed; of course it was the first thing she should have arranged for! She might have to pay Mistress Fraley garnish for it, but that she would gladly do. How was it possible that she had not thought of it herself?

As she sat there in the darkness, with the child on her lap, she felt moved to go into meeting quite alone. She relaxed her body, emptied her head of thoughts, even the small, babbling ones, until she sat there blank and passive, waiting for that of God to rise within her.

What rose was a thought. A cold thought, almost angry: *'What is so godly about sharing their filth?'*

It startled her; she had expected something noble, soothing. Looked at coolly and without religious rapture, there was indeed nothing godly about her sitting there waiting to feel the first lice on her scalp. Rather than sharing their filth, she should make them share her cleanliness.

That of God within her manifested itself in the decision to clean out this pigsty first thing in the morning. She suddenly was sure that Christ, had He been a woman, would have done the same.

CHAPTER THREE

THAT night John Sawrey had himself and the constable taken by Warden Hathaway to the provost's quarters, for that was where he intended to lodge from now on, be it in acute discomfort.

The provost's quarters, two triangular rooms with narrow windows in the southeast tower, were notorious among judges. In winter they were impossible to heat, in summer they acted as a receptacle for all the odors that rose from the bowels of the castle. None of the judges during his three-month stint as provost ever availed himself of the quarters; everybody preferred to stay at an inn. But now John Sawrey had told the Fell woman, on the spur of the moment, that he would be available at all hours; as a consequence he found himself facing the dismal prospect of having to lodge for the remaining months in the dank, musty, pie-shaped little rooms in the tower. Even Hathaway, not a man to be easily surprised, was baffled by this sudden desire on his part to avail himself of the lumpy canopied bed, the rickety chairs and the threadbare, rat-shredded rugs of the provost's quarters.

That the constable would accept this sudden deterioration in his lodgings without comment was a foregone conclusion, he never protested. But someone would have to be found to do the cleaning and look after their meals. Mistress Fraley had her hands full, but perhaps Mistress Farragut, the day warden's wife, who lived three floors down, would be prepared to do so. Even if she were not, nothing could shake Sawrey's determination to make his headquarters here until the boy's execution; that long, at least, Fell's wife was certain to remain in prison.

She was really a quite remarkable woman, and would be the very devil to ensnare. Never before had he been challenged by a quarry of such intelligence and elusiveness. It would be a contest of wits; these austere rooms with their atmosphere of grim seclusion were better suited to the occasion than the noisy inn, where it was difficult to concentrate. And as a base of operations he could not wish for anything better; he would be on the spot, instantly available, yet enjoy total privacy.

That night it occurred to him that he was about to engage in what might well be the most crucial and dangerous hunt of his career. He had not expected the Fell woman to put herself so completely in his hands. He had tried to keep her away from those children, piqued by Fell's high-handed decision to allow his wife access to the dungeons without first consulting him, the acting provost. Now it seemed as if, by an extraordinary stroke of luck, he had made exactly the right moves to put the woman at his mercy. Voluntarily incarcerated for at least the next month, she had put herself in a position where, with a minimum of inventiveness on his part, she would soon consider him her benefactor rather than her adversary. It was a situation not unlike that of John McHair.

That night, as he paced his dark, triangular room, the poacher was very much in his thoughts. Trying to map out his strategy for the coming month, he found himself referring back time and again to things the rogue had told him. At the time he had not paid much heed to the substance of the endless monologues about hares and does and rabbits, runways and territory and routine; now he tried to recall the exact words with which the man had tried to convey to him the secrets of his trade.

What he did remember clearly was the first condition for the capture of game: the hunter should begin by identifying with his quarry. He should observe it, familiarize himself with its habits, absorb its character before making a move. It had come as a surprise to him to hear how conventional animals were, how settled in their daily routine. There was a remarkable similarity between the world of the woods as depicted by John McHair and prison. Both had the same routine, the same narrow range of interest: bodily comfort, food, sleep, power over others. Prison was like his own park; he himself, like John McHair, king of the woods.

Toward morning, as the sun rose over the hills and he stood looking at the distant bay, he formulated concisely the objective of the manhunt: to prove, with documented evidence, that the Fell woman was a subversive Quaker. Yet he knew, without being able to put his finger on it, that there was more in his determination to ensnare her. A cold passion seemed to have taken hold of him. Had it to do with his faith? As a devout Independent, he regarded Quakers as abominations. What was more, now that they had been officially classified as dangerous by the proclamation, it was his duty to hunt them down and bring them to justice. But this did not explain his excitement, the nervous alertness of all his faculties tonight. Watching the sun rise over the city, he concluded that what drove him was the passion of the hunt itself. That presented a danger. If he wanted to trap his exotic prey, he must keep a cool head, a sharp eye, be aware of his own shortcomings and plan his campaign accordingly. What he needed, before making the next move, was a cold-blooded look at John Sawrey and his foibles, especially his sense of inferiority. But he should also try to identify with her, beginning with Quaker thought, principles, aspirations. He would visit the few at present in prison; he would pick their brains, absorb their souls. She should not know of this, but that was easy. Quakers were now kept in solitary confinement, in chains, without visitors. Finally, he should make her incriminate herself. To encourage her to talk was not enough; even if she were to admit to the most heinous of crimes, it would be worthless without a written confession or a verbatim report duly validated by sworn witnesses. He should have a court recorder write down every word, once she started to tell all. The man must, of course, remain out of sight. But where to find someone able to perform such a delicate and confidential task, and with accuracy? Offhand, he could think of only one man: old Holofernes Stowe, scribe of the Assizes. Most intelligent and accurate; he used an abbreviated script that only he could read. But he lived in Kendal; it would either need a handsome reward or some kind of blackmail. The latter was the most dependable, but what dark secrets could an academic old bachelor like Holly Stowe be hiding? Well, if there were any skeletons in his closet, the constable would find them.

He watched the feathery night clouds catch fire in the sunrise. What patience he would need! What insight into the mind of that extraordinary woman! Would he be able to identify with her? How would she feel, for example, when, this very morning, fresh, crisp, fragrant straw was spread in her cell, bringing a scent of summer, of freedom, of home?

*   *   *

Ann Traylor returned to the prison in a mood of contrition, wondering how she would find Margaret Fell after what must have been a gruesome night. She herself had slept only fitfully, haunted by dreams of rats, screaming madwomen, pitch darkness, prowling men in cloaks and black hats. Several times she had found herself sitting bolt upright, heart pounding, overcome by a terrible sense of guilt. At one moment she had even considered dressing and going to join her, but one look through the window at the black mass of Lancaster Castle among the stars had sent her, shivering, back to bed.

She hesitated in the gateway, afraid to go in; then, disgusted with herself, she marched into the warden's office. Mr. Farragut welcomed her with the usual mocking smile. "Well, well, young lady! We're in a hurry this morning, aren't we?"

She scarcely heard him; she imagined Margaret Fell crouching in that filthy straw, terrified, her eyes demented from the horrors of the night. As she descended with the jailer carrying the lantern, the stench of the dungeons seemed worse than ever. But there were no yells or whistles from the black mouths of the passages; she ran past the cage of the lunatics, ducking away from the claws reaching between the bars; at the door to the children's dungeon she cried, even before the man with the lantern had caught up with her, "Margaret Fell? Margaret Fell! Canst thou hear me?"

"Good morning, Ann." The voice was cheerful. When the lantern lit up the inside of the cage, there she was, tall and dignified, wading toward the door to unlock it. "Hast thou brought some candles? I'm afraid we used them all."

"Oh—candles—yes, yes, certainly . . ." She rummaged nervously in her basket and produced one of the candles she had packed that morning.

"Splendid. May I light it from your lantern, my good man?"

"Yes, ma'am." The jailer opened the little glass door to enable her to light the wick from the flame.

"Thank you very much. Good day to you."

"Anything else, ma'am?"

"No, thank you. I'll arrange it with Miss Traylor, here."

"Very good, ma'am. 'Bye, miss." The lantern drew away.

There she stood, holding the candle, smiling. "Come in, my dear."

Ann watched her put the candle in the bottle. "Don't you want to lock up again?"

"No, for thou wilt be going out again in a minute. There are a few things I want thee to get for me. Then I would like thee to go to the warden to arrange for this straw to be removed and fresh brought in. Tell him Justice Sawrey approved it, and that I'll pay for it, if necessary. Perhaps thou hadst better ask Mistress Fraley and offer her garnish for it."

"Mistress Fraley?"

"Oh, of course, thou hast not met her yet. She is the housekeeper, or whatever it is called. She brings around the food, and grants privileges for money. Have a message taken to her by one of the turnkeys. I want the straw out of here this morning. Then I want the following things—here, a slate, write them down. It's quite a list." She looked as though she were facing her kitchen staff at home, as imperious as ever. Not a hair out of place, completely at ease, with a peremptory disregard for her surroundings and, for that matter, the delicate mood of her companion.

As Ann dutifully wrote down the list, she was so full of resentment that she had to bite back the tears. She could not wait to get back into the fresh air, away from this impossible woman, free to think.

"Or whatever else the apothecary recommends for the mange. Hast thou got that?"

"Yes."

"I also want some medication for Henry's eye."

"Henry?"

"The boy."

"Oh—oh, yes."

"A salve or an ointment for the empty socket, and an eye patch."

The night seemed to have widened the gulf that separated them. It gave Ann a feeling of loneliness; she had trouble not snapping back at all those ridiculous orders. Blankets, clothes, broom, bucket, bread, sausage, cheese, apples, combs, brushes, hunting water, cough lozenges, lavender—she would need a pushcart! But she did not protest; an argument would only keep her down here longer. At a given moment, waiting for Margaret Fell to think of one more item to add to the cartload, she glanced at the one-eyed boy leaning against the wall and saw him sneer at her. Suddenly she found herself thinking, 'He deserves to be hanged, the little ghoul!'

The thought pursued her when at last she found herself outside in the sunlit square. What had become of the noble feelings, the sense of godliness, the yearning to serve the helpless? All that was left was

anger and envy. Yes, envy: Margaret Fell had had an experience
that she had not shared. But this was ridiculous! She could not go on
being tied to Margaret Fell's apron strings! She was a woman herself
now. She must begin to lead her own life. Then she realized what
she was staring at, unseeingly: a hat in a milliner's shopwindow, an
extravagant hat, wide-brimmed, green velvet, decorated with an
audacious plume of pheasant feathers. Something about the hat, something daring, devil-may-care, seemed to personify the Ann of her
daydreams, the ravishing beauty, woman of the world, pampered,
contemptuous. Before she knew it, she found herself inside the shop,
trying it on in front of the looking glass.

The buxom woman who served her, wreathed in smiles, observed
her with shrewd little eyes. "It's the very latest London fashion,
miss. We just this morning finished making it up. You are the first to
try it."

Seen in the mirror, the ridiculous thing looked even more gaudy and
extravagant than it had in the window. Yet something about it,
something brazen, taunting . . . "How much is it?"

"Five shillings, miss. Very, very reasonable, considering the amount
of work. Do you realize how many delicate little feathers . . ." She
looked in the mirror over her client's shoulder. "Absolutely delicious! It
looks *adorable* on you, miss. It sets off your beautiful complexion."

Ann was about to say, "It's not for me, it's for my mistress." Then
the thought, 'There thou goest: hurrying back into servitude.' She set
her jaw and said briskly, "All right, I'll take it."

"Very good, miss. You will not regret it. It's most becoming. I'll get
a box for it."

"No, thank you. I'll wear it."

"Ah?" The woman was obviously dying to find out more about her.
She asked, with pursed-lipped unctuousness, "Where shall I send the
bill, miss?"

"No need for a bill. I'll pay for it now." She rummaged in her
basket for her purse.

It was ridiculous! She was out of her mind! One whole month's
wages! She counted out the coins on the counter, all the while feeling
that the next moment she would wake up. This could not be true,
squandering her hard-earned money on this ridiculous . . . She
dropped a coin. As she bent down to pick it up, the hat toppled and
fell to the ground. It seemed an omen.

"Oh, miss, you *do* need pins with this hat!" The woman was leaning
over the counter to look; as Ann straightened up, she caught a whiff of
orange blossom from her ample cleavage.

"No, I thank you. It'll do nicely." She wanted to get out, away
from those beady little eyes fascinated by her servant's dress. A moment
later she was back in the street.

The topheavy feeling of the wobbly thing on her head almost made
her turn around to tell the woman she had changed her mind. But as
she stood in hesitation, a young gentleman passed her, looked at her
and doffed his hat. She had no idea who it was, he was a total stranger;

then she caught sight of her reflection in the shopwindow. It was vague, but she saw in the little panel a fascinating vision of fashion and femininity, of sunlight glinting on golden pheasant feathers. Should she go back and get hatpins? But she had the feeling that the fat woman was watching, beady-eyed. The apothecary was just a few houses down; she would go there first.

She opened the door with a brisk tinkling of a little bell. The dusk inside was heavy with the scent of smelling salts and Peruvian balsam. She entered and stood nervously drumming her fingers on the counter, waiting for the apothecary with a new qualm of doubt and remorse. The walls were lined with jars; in a glass basin on the counter, slow, sluggish leeches were squirming. "Anybody home?" she called.

There was a rustle and a clatter in the back of the shop; a mousy little man in a white smock emerged with the double glint of a pair of spectacles on the tip of his nose. "Good morning, good morning, forgive me, ma'am, I did not hear you. What may we do for you today, ma'am?" He sang with servility; she had never been addressed so humbly in her life. She regained her composure.

"Let me see . . ." She produced the slate from her basket and studied it. "To start with, I need some hunting water."

"I beg your pardon?"

She gave him a withering look. "Hunting water, for lice. Surely you have that, haven't you?"

"Oh. Oh—yes, certainly, ma'am." He scurried away to rummage among bottles in a cupboard. "Here you are, ma'am. Will two pints be sufficient?"

"Ridiculous. That bottle doesn't contain two pints! I need at least— I don't know. You tell me. Six lice-infested children; how much would one need?"

"Six?" The little man's mouth fell open.

"Indeed, six."

"Very good, ma'am." He scurried again; a moment later he put a larger bottle on the counter. "That should be sufficient, ma'am."

"Very well."

"Anything else?"

"Certainly. I need something for the mange."

"Mange?"

She looked down on him haughtily. "I also need some ointment for the inflamed socket of a child's missing eye."

"Missing eye . . ."

"I suppose I'll also need an eye patch. Won't I?"

The little man now gazed at her with bafflement. "How—how did that happen, ma'am?

"Did what happen?"

"The eye . . . an accident?"   -

"No, no," she said, aloof. "Someone gouged it out. Let me see . . . I also need lavender, cough lozenges . . ."

"Gouged it out?! For mercy's sake, why?!"

She would have loved to reply, "Because he brained his papa with a poker," but thought better of it. "Oh, just one of those family tiffs," she said. "Is there a special ointment you would recommend?"

The apothecary, numbed, went through the motions with staring eyes. It was a long list and it took a long time; what it achieved was that when she left the shop, after telling him to send the bill to Mistress Fell at the Three Swans, she no longer felt as if she were masquerading. The hat, for better or for worse, had become hers.

The feeling of independence it gave her was such that she decided to take the medicine straight to the prison and to arrange for someone from the inn to accompany her to carry the rest. Decked out as she was now, she could not march through town carrying a broom and a bucket. Of course, her simple gown suddenly looked drab, the hat was like a flag on a peat barge. But she was so self-confident now that reality caught up with her only as she approached the prison. In the gateway, the wobbly thing on her head became ludicrous again. Impossible to descend into the dungeons like this! She must have been insane! Again she considered going back to the milliner's and telling the woman she had reconsidered. Maybe she could say that her husband . . . No! She would not knuckle under to Margaret Fell again! The hat was *hers,* and she was going to keep it. All right, she could not wear it going down; but what would she do with it? Hang it on the prison gate? She and her crazy, impulsive actions! What in the world was she going to do with it? She would have to leave it in the warden's office. The warden had a bit of a leer, but at least he would not gossip about it. Or would he?

When she opened the door to the office, her heart stopped. There, in front of the warden's desk, stood Judge Thomas Fell.

Her impulse was to flee; but it was too late. Blushing, she made a deep curtsy, mumbled, "Good mo—" There went the hat, crashing to the floor.

She was so mortified that she could not pick it up. She rose, eyes closed, wanting to be dead.

"Allow me."

She opened her eyes. There was the judge, his face noncommittal, proffering the hat.

"Thank you, sir . . ."

"Are you going down to see Mistress Fell?"

"Yes, sir."

"Pray ask her if there is anything she would wish me to do. Tell her I am at her disposal."

"Very well, sir."

"Come back to let me know, will you, please?"

She turned around and made a dash for the door. She dropped the hat on the chair by the door and slipped out.

The turnkey escorted her down. For the second time that morning she descended the endless steps. She was furious with herself and mortified beyond words. It was all Margaret Fell's fault; it was she who had driven her to buy that hat! She knew she was being unreasonable, but she had spent a horrible night agonizing about

that woman and about the way she would find her after a night in
a place like this, and then she had not even had a hair out of place.

When she arrived in front of the cell, there was Margaret Fell,
barefoot, her skirts hitched up, scrubbing the cobbles with a broom.
The straw was gone, the children were hopping and leaping around
her in obscure high spirits; the one-eyed boy squatted moodily in a
corner.

"Ah, there thou art!" Margaret Fell put the broom against the bars
and brushed her hair out of her eyes with the back of her hand.
"Hast thou bought the broom and the bucket yet?"

"No, I thought I would first bring the medicine."

"Excellent! Don't buy them, I have borrowed a broom from Mistress
Fraley; she lent me a bucket too. But I will need the chamber pot.
Come in."

She opened the gate, which was not locked; the children squealed
with glee, playing scotchhoppers. But not even children at play could
dispel the evil gloom of the dungeons. "Let me see what thou hast
got there. Is this the hunting water?"

"Yes. But I must tell you that your husband is upstairs."

"Thomas? What brought him here?" Her alarm was, for some reason,
gratifying.

"I don't know. He just asked me to tell you that he is at your
disposal. He wants me to go back and tell him whether there is
anything you might wish him to do. Would you like to see him?"
It was a gratuitous remark; the judge had not suggested anything
of the kind. She watched Margaret Fell's discomfiture with satisfaction.

"Oh? No . . . I—tell him I'll send him a letter. He should not
come down here—not now, not until I have sorted this out."

"So what shall I say? That there is nothing he can do for you?"

"Not for the moment. But maybe he will help thee carry the rest
of the things. I forgot, of course, that all this has to be paid for.
Ask him to take care of it."

"I had the bill sent to the inn."

"I see. Very good. Well, work it out with him. Careful, Jody!
Don't upset the bucket!" She went to the little girl spinning madly
on the hard, bare floor, took her by the arm, pointed at the bucket
and made an admonishing gesture with her finger. Then she came
back to the bars to pick up the broom again. "All right, Ann, come
back as soon as thou hast the rest. I need thee here."

"Very well." There was nothing else to say. She could not stand
and watch Margaret Fell scrubbing like a scullery maid. "Let's go,"
she said to the jailer, who stared into the cell, open-mouthed, and
followed him down the corridor. The lunatic women seemed to have
finally given up reaching for her through the bars. Their vague shapes
sat huddled in a corner of the dark cell, nobody shrieked or banged
chains.

On her way up, she braced herself to face the judge once more.
Devil take that hat! What in the world had got into her? She would
have liked to slip out into the square, leaving both the hat and the

judge behind; but after a brief hesitation in front of the door to the warden's office, she entered, her head held high.

Judge Fell was sitting in front of the warden's desk. He rose courteously; Mr. Farragut, somewhat surprised, followed suit. The judge turned to the warden. "I'll be back to discuss this further. For the time being, I would be grateful if you would give Mistress Fraley my respects and thank her for her kindness. Tell her I'll want to see her personally later today."

"Very good, Your Lordship."

The judge came toward Ann. This time she did not curtsy. He went to the door, opened it for her, then picked up her hat from the chair. "Here you are."

"Thank you." She decided she would just carry it; but when they walked out of the dark gateway into the sunlit square, she put it on. "Sir, your wife said—"

He put his hand on her arm. "Not here!" His voice was hushed. "There are a host of things I wish to know. Would you give me the pleasure of having luncheon with you?"

She stopped still with amazement. "Lu-luncheon?" she stammered foolishly.

"Forgive me, I sent Will Hartford and the coach back to the inn. Would you mind? It's only a short walk."

"I—I'll be happy to . . ."

"Very well, then. This way—"

They set out across the sunlit square; as they passed through the shade of the statue of St. George, a swarm of starlings that had alighted on it took off again and swept like a cloud around the square, shifting from black to silver as they banked. There was about their sweep a wild, restless urgency; it was that time of year.

*   *   *

"I must confess something to you . . ." The girl looked young and charming in her nervous solemnity.

Until that moment Thomas Fell had sat in the crowded taproom steeped in gloom, carrying on little more than a desultory conversation. The fact that all Margaret had been able to think of for him to do was to help carry a maid's purchases rankled; now he became aware of this charming young person with her impossible hat, about to make a solemn confession after only one glass of claret.

"Ah? What mischief have you been up to?"

Her eyes, green and grave, looked up at him, twinkling with the reflection of the candle flame. "Mischief? I don't understand," she said, taking herself seriously indeed. "What I meant was—I don't really understand your wife."

He smiled. "Well," he said lightly, "you are not the only one, my dear. There are times when I don't understand her myself. More wine?"

While he filled her glass, she stared at him with astonishment from underneath her hat.

"Don't look so surprised," he said. "Believe me, you are not the only one to be mystified by Mistress Fell on occasion. You should have seen the face of that old harridan Fraley when she was told to take a bucket and broom to the wife of the Lord Chief Justice in the children's cell. She looked as if she had seen a ghost, until I crossed her palm with silver. After that, of course, everything fell into place: a rich lady's whim indulged good-naturedly by her husband." He spoke more bitterly than he intended.

"Well . . . isn't that so?" The girl must have realized that she had gone too far, for she blushed. It was a ravishing blush; she actually was quite a ravishing little creature. He had never noticed it before; at home she had just been one of the nondescript young females with whom his wife surrounded herself, coming and going like pigeons, continually different, always the same. "The concept is somewhat simplistic," he said, smiling to put her at her ease. "I would have thought you to be one of the first to recognize this. Aren't you a Quaker yourself?"

She stared at her glass, frowning. "I was. Or, at least, I thought I was. But then . . ."

"Then what?"

She glanced at him, clearly of two minds whether to confide in him or mind her place. For a young woman who was, in effect, a servant, it must be difficult to seem poised and at the same time show deference to her master. Who was she, anyway? He remembered something about an alcoholic father, distant relation of the Rutledges. Yes, that was it: the women had arranged for her employment at the Hall through the intricate network of ladies-of-the-manor that reached from Land's End to John O'Groats. It must be one of the largest and most effective grapevines in the world.

She sipped her wine. "I was skeptical in the beginning, when George Fox first arrived." She had obviously decided to unburden herself. "I thought he was, frankly, a mountebank, and the way he proceeded to make your wife suffer made me more and more—" She stopped, and there was that blush again. She averted her eyes and looked accusingly at her glass.

"Pray proceed. I'm fascinated."

"But—I don't think I . . ." Her eyes were shy and wary like a doe's.

He suddenly felt himself relax; the hurt, the apprehension that had haunted him ever since his wife returned from Windermere suddenly seemed to lift. Maybe it was the wine; they served a deuced good claret in this place. "Look, dear child," he said genially, "don't go on blaming yourself for every honest word you say. I have been married to my good wife for over twenty years, and happily so; I must know her better by now than anyone else. The better one gets to know her, the more one loves her; and implicit in love is trust. So, trust her motives, trust her intuition, admire her courage and reserve judgment on her actions, even though occasionally they may appear—well—Dantesque." He was startled by his sudden ebullience, it was unlike him. For some reason, he had felt compelled to sing his wife's praises. All resentment seemed dispelled; he was overwhelmed by a humorous tenderness for dear, impulsive Maggie. "So, anything you can tell me about her present activity will give me a clearer notion of how to intervene, should the need arise. Which, between you and me, may be anytime."

"Oh?" She looked worried.

"Never mind; pray continue. How did you feel about George Fox when you realized that he made my wife suffer?"

She stared at her glass again, touching its stem with a slender hand. "He made all of us suffer, by first getting us all stirred up and then abandoning us, just like that."

"At that time, I gather, you still felt you understood my wife?"

She looked up, startled, but her aplomb was admirable. Apart from being good-looking, she had her wits about her. "Rather. It was she who pulled us together by saying that there must be many others like us who had been abandoned by him, and that instead of feeling despondent we should come to their aid, especially those in prison . . . but you know all that."

"Go on."

"Well, I became her—her assistant. I admired her very much. I still do. Very much." She looked at him earnestly.

"Then what happened?"

"Well, then you took us on that visit to Lancaster Castle and showed us . . . Why did you do that?"

"What?"

"Show us those hanged children."

"To impress upon my wife and yourself what you were risking by your involvement with the Quakers. You know, I presume, that to be a Quaker is now a punishable offense." He took a sip of wine. "Well—it seems that my treatment has been effective in your case but not in hers."

She smiled uncertainly; then she said, with a sudden rush of emotion, "But it's different for me. I *did* believe in our mission, until I was assaulted."

"You were *what?*"

"Assaulted . . ." She said it bashfully, her eyes downcast.

"For God's sake! When did that happen? Where?"

"In the dungeons, the first day, on our way up. A man burst out of a passage and—" She stopped.

"What happened? Surely somebody came to your aid?"

"Your wife did. She beat on him with her basket until he gave up."

"My God! Did you tell the warden?"

"Of course. The warden had warned us that this might happen."

"But nothing did happen, did it? I mean—nothing serious?"

"No, nothing serious." She reddened and looked away.

He suddenly felt embarrassed. He spotted a servingwench in the dusk of candlelight and tobacco smoke, and called for more duck. When he had been given a generous helping, he raised his glass and said, "Well, here's to your continued good fortune."

"Thank you."

She herself did not drink. She had more sense than he had thought.

"So, after that incident you felt a cooling of your missionary zeal?"

"Yes, I suppose you could say that. More precisely, a resentment against your wife. I hope you don't mind my saying this," she added hastily. "I must assure you that I love her very much. I have an intense admiration for her; I am sure it's all a matter of my own feelings—"

"Don't apologize. She defended you, didn't she?"

"Yes, she did. But—well, you see, that night I was very distressed, and she was very kind to me, kinder than she had ever been; I suddenly had a feeling, well . . . My mother died very young, I never really had a mother. That night I had."

"I see."

"When the next morning she told me we were going back down there, I—I felt hurt. Stupidly, I'm sure, but terribly hurt. Oh, well . . ."

How like Margaret! No wonder the poor child had doubted the sincerity of her motherly tenderness! "You see, my dear, once my wife and, I suppose, most determined people have a goal in mind, they pursue it with a single-mindedness that often hurts others. They mean no harm—as a matter of fact, we should admire their incorruptibility. For that's what it is. She has a very clear concept of values. Once she has decided to help unfortunate children in a dungeon, that is her supreme concern. She cannot be frightened away, or dissuaded, or sidetracked, not even by the distress of someone she loves. She is a remarkable woman, you know. You have much to learn from her, perhaps we all have."

She looked at him with an odd expression; then she said, "I think she is lucky to have a husband like you."

He stared at her for a moment. Was she more experienced than he thought? But her eyes were guileless, their innocence enhanced by that improbable hat. No experienced woman would have decked herself out with such a monument of *courtisanerie*. He had asked this harmless little wench to luncheon out of sheer, miserable loneliness, so as not to have to suffer through yet another meal all by himself in a corner of this raucous, reverberating den of jollity; now it turned out to have been an excellent idea. What if he invited her to supper too, after they had done their shopping for the empress in the dungeon? It might give rise to gossip; the place was full of people who knew him. A private room? He had to think of the child's reputation. But if he wanted to watch over his wife, he should know what was going on down there. He needed a spy.

"Well, we had better go and get the things she needs," he said, putting down his napkin. "Oh, forgive me, you have not finished your wine."

She smiled. "I have already had more than I should. This has been wonderful."

"Well, it's mutual, I assure you. By the way, we have only scratched the surface of all this. Would it be imposing on you to ask you to join me for supper tonight?"

*   *   *

Ann felt a momentary misgiving. Was this right? Should she? But his eyes were so sincere, his aristocratic gentility so evident that she brushed aside her timorous qualms. "I'll be happy to."

"Good. But there is one thing I must mention—I hope it will not offend you."

She felt a return of her apprehension. "Why?"

"People have the unfortunate disposition to suspect the worst in their fellow men. The only way to prevent tongues from wagging would be for us to sup in a private room. Normally, this would be a fairly intimate thing to do—I hope I need not assure you that my intentions are entirely honorable."

"Of course."

"I must remain fully informed about what goes on in the prison. If it would be agreeable to you, I would say: for the next few days at least, let us meet for supper. Would that be all right?"

She nodded.

"Well then, shall we go?" He rose, holding out his hand to her. Without the wobbly hat she could have accepted his assistance with smiling grace; now it was a rather hazardous operation, as if she were balancing a pitcher on her head. He did not seem to be aware of it; she felt grateful to him. From the moment he had helped her in the warden's office, he had guided her with the discreet expertness of a dancing partner.

Considering the circumstances, their shopping expedition was surprisingly lighthearted. By the time they arrived at the chamber pot on her list, they felt sufficiently at ease with one another to indulge in a rather juvenile private joke at the tinker's as they chose the largest copper vessel available. The man's obvious bewilderment while wrapping up the resonant thing sent her into almost irrepressible laughter. The judge had no trouble keeping his face straight until they emerged from the dark little shop; then he took her arm in a boyish eruption of pent-up hilarity. As they crossed the square on their way back to the castle, they again startled the starlings befouling St. George's headless shoulders; the swarm took off with a mighty rush of wind and swept around and around the keep, shifting color. In the warden's office, Mr. Farragut was about to hand over the keys to the hunchback Hathaway, the guardian of the night. The judge announced that some purchases would be delivered during the course of the evening, all of them intended for Mistress Fell, and he requested Mr. Hathaway to see that they were delivered to her. Then, without further ado, he invited Ann to leave with him.

It troubled her; she felt she should have gone down, to tell Margaret Fell that the things she wanted were on their way. He must have sensed her discomfort, for when they were out in the square again he said, "You must have wondered why I prevented you from going down."

"Indeed."

"I intend to go myself, tonight."

"I see."

"I expect you would like to change before supper. May I escort you back to your inn?"

"Yes, please."

"If you wish, I'll wait for you there. You won't be long?"

"Oh, no—not more than a few minutes."

What ridiculous pretense! She had nothing to change into. But after they arrived at the inn she went upstairs, let herself into her rooms and burst into giggles, leaning against the door. Well, she had better change into her traveling smock, the only other garment she possessed. She spent some time freshening up and ended by posturing in front of the mirror, trying on her hat at various angles, with various facial expressions. It was her first chance that day to study it properly; perhaps it was rather gaudy and pretentious, but, whatever else it might be, it was obviously effective. Fancy, Judge Fell taking her to supper!

She found him waiting by the side of a sedan chair; obviously, he had not cared to let Will Hartford in on their tryst. It added more spice to the already exciting occasion; it was amazing how safe and at ease she felt in his presence.

It was the first time in her life that she had been carried in a chair. He assisted her as she climbed into the small, dark cubicle; she sat down on the cushioned seat and he closed the door from the outside. She nearly cried out when the men lifted the thing, but when they started to walk, with practiced, steady gait, and Thomas Fell smiled at her through the little open window as he walked alongside, she reclined in the cushions and relished the faint, luxurious smell of stale perfume and musty velvet. Well, here she went: Ann Traylor in a chair! Ever since she was a child it had seemed the height of luxury to her, unattainable, another world. She had run alongside chaises with other urchins, jeering, to the fury of the linkmen who walked ahead; never had she expected to be carried like this herself one day: softly swaying, reclining in the cushions, with a Lord Chief Justice walking alongside.

It was a delightful evening. Never before had she talked so openly on such intimate matters to anyone, not even Margaret Fell. After the second glass of wine she told him about her childhood, her sad father, the harshness of poverty, the degradation of servitude; she even told him of her sudden awareness the other day of the bitterness of life and her determination to grasp every chance to enjoy beauty and comfort and joy. Their surroundings enhanced the intimacy of the evening—dark red hangings, a crystal candelabrum with seven candles, their flames reflected by silver cutlery, gleaming pewter, goblets of wine. It seemed as if during those few hours she blossomed into that different person, the woman of her daydreams. When at last he rose to take her back to the inn, she was tempted to take a memento of the evening, but for a lady of the world to walk off with a piece of cutlery would be incongruous.

He took his leave in the gateway at the inn. He kissed her hand, thanked her for a delightful evening and suggested he return the next day at the same hour, to take her out to supper. She graciously accepted, swept up the stairs to her room as if trailing the train of a costly gown, and was met in the mirror by a dowdy female in a drab traveling smock, with on her head a hat that looked like a pheasant on a dish, carried in for a banquet. She took it off and felt like tossing it into a corner, but she stroked it, murmured, "Good beastie" and laid it carefully on the dresser. She put the candle on the table and went to fetch the exercise book.

"Tonight, after a day of many unexpected happenings, I supped with Justice Fell in a private room . . ."

There was much to write, yet she suddenly felt prompted to put down the quill, go to the window, open the curtain and gaze at the sky.

'Ah! Life, life!' she thought, as the sweep of the Milky Way greeted her with all its glorious promise above the dark, brooding mass of Lancaster Castle. For the first time that night she thought of her mistress, incarcerated with those horrible children underneath that mountain of stone. A hundred feet deep.

For some reason, it spoiled the moment. She closed the window again, drew the curtain, picked up her quill and wrote, *"We have agreed to do so every day, for the time being, so I may keep him fully informed of what goes on in the prison. He is really most concerned about his wife. I told him she is lucky to have such a sensitive, loyal and loving husband to watch over her. And with such discretion! He is the most tactful man I ever met. There I sat, talking my head off virtually during the entire meal, but his attention never flagged, or if it did, he never showed it. The food . . ."*

The quill scratched on, page after page, as she recaptured the evening minutely, remembering every detail, every word, every thought.

* * *

Thomas Fell looked forward to seeing his wife again. When he arrived at the castle, he was filled with good will and understanding. He greeted Hathaway jocularly, told him of his intention and said he would be back anon. The guard at the gate, who lifted his lantern and saluted respectfully when he saw who it was, opened the door to let him in. He stepped inside and was assailed by the pestilential stench that rose from the well of the stairs; he hesitated and after a few seconds turned around. He mumbled something to the guard, went to hand in his lantern at the warden's office and left on the pretext that he had forgotten something.

In the dark square, looking up at the sky ablaze with stars, he asked himself why, for God's sake, he had not gone down. Out of sheer revulsion from the obscene place? Not very noble, considering his wife was at the bottom of that pit. No, there was more to it; he tried to fathom it as he walked the dark streets to the inn. Had it been the incompatibility of the two worlds: the private dining room and the dungeons? Had he been ashamed to confront his wife? Did he, despite the admiration he had expressed so volubly that day, hold her motives in contempt, and had he been afraid this would show when he confronted her?

When he arrived at the inn, he was too restless to go to bed. He turned around and walked back to the castle. In the warden's office he countered the hunchback's smirk with haughty authority. "I'll be working in chambers all night, Hathaway," he said, turning his back on the unsavory creature. "I would appreciate it if, toward dawn, one of your men could bring me a mug of ale."

Legs scissoring in the lantern light, he strode down the long, empty corridor, up the flight of stairs to the judges' chambers. The room was cold and desolate; its solitary window looked onto a blank wall, bleak and forbidding in the moonlight.

He sat down at his desk, solitary figure in the candlelight, and began to tackle the pile of petitions that had accumulated during his absence.

Only after he had sat scribbling patiently for several hours, the shadow of his quill reaching out into the night, did the true reason for his retreat from the dungeons occur to him. By then the sense of well-being of the aging *bon vivant* had been replaced by the unemotional realism of the judge. He knew now that, had he confronted his wife, he would have been aghast at the conditions under which she lived and would have been tempted to secure preferential treatment for her. That would have been wrong. She was playing with her life; Cromwell's proclamation was only the beginning of a systematic persecution of the Quakers. She must be prevailed upon to give up and return to Swarthmoor or she would end as a prisoner herself. He should see to it that she was discouraged, that things were made as harsh as possible for her, that she felt deserted, even though he would be watching over her day and night, unseen.

He sat there writing until the dawn paled the light of the candle and the wall opposite the window turned blue with the daybreak. A clatter of wheels echoed in the courtyard as Mistress Fraley pushed her cart to the well of the stairs; he heard the squealing of pulleys as the cart was lowered to the first level, where the debtors and their families rotted. He pushed back his chair and walked to the window to see the ramparts touched by the sunrise. As the first sunlight flashed on the weathervane on the northeast tower, he thought of the young girl now awakening in a small room in the city. She would stretch and yawn, swing her legs out of bed; then she would pull her nightgown over her head.

He turned away, gathered up his papers, locked them in the armoire and pocketed the key. He had better break his fast before he met Ann Traylor at the gate so she could tell his wife—what? There was nothing to tell, now that he had decided to make things as harsh as possible for her. Well, he might go to meet her all the same.

Outside in the square, untouched as yet by the sun, the starlings sat huddled close together on the shoulders of St. George, beheaded by the Ironsides. If that had been all they had done! In their fury against all popery and pagan contamination they had smashed the statues in every church, even the organs, thus not only smashing the face of idolatry but cutting out its tongue as well.

Ah, the folly of men! For some reason, the thought of the smashed organs caused a feeling of resentment toward Margaret and her suicidal folly. Unless he managed to save her, she might never again be able to teach her daughters a madrigal like "The Andalusian Merchant." Humming it somberly, he walked to his tryst.

* * *

On her second night in the children's dungeon, after a day of Herculean labor, Margaret Fell surveyed with satisfaction the sparkling-clean cell filled with fragrant straw. The children still looked scruffy, but she had doused their heads with hunting water. She gathered them around her and inspected their scalps; she could find no more lice. All of them were very affectionate now except Henry, who persisted in his morbid hostility and even refused the ointment and the eye patch. But she did not let him trouble her; she felt triumphant. She stretched out on the fragrant straw and, exhausted by the unaccustomed labor, dropped off to sleep.

Half an hour later she awoke with a start, to find the children scratching in their sleep. She lit the candle and discovered to her horror that they were crawling with sinister-looking bugs of a reddish-brown color, larger than the ticks that plagued the hounds in the fall. The sight filled her with revulsion.

Cleaning out the dungeon had not been enough; the children obviously carried the bugs in their clothes and on their bodies. On the morrow she would bathe them, cut their hair, put them all in clean clothes; it would mean another day of hard work, but she must not be lax now or all her labors would come to naught. Even if she had to dip them over and over until they screamed, she should not allow the bugs to infest her straw, so fresh and inviting, spiced with lavender, which gave it a hint of the fells in summer.

She settled down to sleep again, but found she could not come to rest. She felt itchy all over and began to scratch herself as fiercely as the children, even though she was sure her itching was just imagination. A tearful panic was getting hold of her when suddenly a light came down the passage. It had to be Thomas, it just had to be; she was at the bars in a flash, peering out, breathless with anticipation.

It turned out to be John Sawrey. Her disappointment was so acute that she could barely muster the courtesy to return his greeting as he appeared, cloaked and plumed, at the gate, carrying, of all things, a seat-stick. She detested the sight of him, which was unreasonable, considering she owed the fresh straw to him, if nothing else. When he said with a bow and a sweep, "Good evening, Mistress Fell, how have you been today?" she managed to hitch up a smile and answer, "Thank you, Mr. Sawrey, very well indeed, owing to your kind assistance."

"I am happy to hear that. Is there anything else you wish me to do for you?"

"No, I thank you. Not for the moment." The bugs seemed too intimate a subject to mention; she had trouble not to scratch herself while he was watching.

"In that case: your obedient servant, Madam." He made another bow and sweep. "Constable . . ." She realized he was not alone; obviously, he was too grand to carry his own lantern.

After he was gone, she sat watching the candle flame, with the children pressed around her like chicks in spite of the bugs. She realized she had been unfair; whatever Sawrey's ulterior motives might be, he was the only one who betrayed any interest in what she was doing. True, Thomas had sent word that he was "standing by," or whatever his virile term had been for dallying in indecision; Ann was a useful little thing, she certainly could not do without her, but the girl's reluctance was so obvious that her presence had become a burden rather than a comfort. John Sawrey alone seemed to have some notion of the reality of the prison, the small day-to-day things that were so important: fresh straw, fresh water, cleanliness, light. Should she have invited him in, to show him the clean straw? Well, tomorrow she would really have something to show him when he came.

The moment Ann arrived in the morning, Margaret organized a thorough cleaning of all the children, with the exception of Henry, who snarled like a chained dog the moment he was approached. Mistress Fraley brought hot water, soap and a brush, surlily but promptly. While Ann put ready the fresh clothes she had bought the day before, Margaret herself, sleeves rolled up above her elbows, her skirt hitched around her waist, stood up one squalling, naked child after another in the wooden bucket and scrubbed them with the brush until their pallid, sickly skin glowed. They hated it, but did not struggle; only the little girl Jody began to fight when soap got in her eyes, poor thing. The scene seemed to touch Mistress Fraley, for at a given moment, of her own accord, she brought a bucket of milk, which she proceeded to share out with a ladle among the naked children shivering in the straw, waiting to have their hair cut. Only when they were allowed to put on their new clothes did they become sprightly, especially little Jody, decked out in a gingham smock that was much too large for her but looked crisp and clean. The child was beside herself with delight and demonstrated it by standing on her head, emitting monotonous hoots of pure joy. The boys, bald, scrubbed little mannikins now their hair had been shorn, started to play leap-frog again; soon there was such infectious joy in the cavernous cage full of romping children that the three women were briefly united by a sense of tenderness and satisfaction. Ann said, "Oh, I wish the judge could see them now!"

"Who? Sawrey?"

"No, your husband. He'd see quite a difference from yesterday."

"Yesterday? He didn't see them yesterday."

The girl looked at her, puzzled. "I thought he came to visit you last night."

"Why? Did he say he intended to do so?"

"Yes . . ." The girl suddenly seemed embarrassed, as if she were sorry she had mentioned it.

Supper came, and with it the strenuous efforts to prevail upon the famished children to wait their turn. They were so happy and good-humored now, with the exception of Henry, that afterward they sang "The Andalusian Merchant" right through for the first time, without a single true note and each descant a discord, but with such zest that the mad biddies in the adjoining cell joined in, slamming their chains against the bars to beat the time. It was a cacophony that would have set a dog howling, yet Margaret sat beaming in the center of her little choir, filled with gratitude.

Finally, she fell asleep in a happy glow, her adoptive young tightly pressed around her. Half an hour later she woke up at a fierce sting in the side of her neck. She slapped it, but the sting burned viciously and did not diminish; she felt the spot with her finger and discovered a hard, alien body that she plucked out of her skin with a cry of revulsion. She inspected it by the light of the candle; it was one of those horrible bugs. She gazed aghast at the squirming insect she was holding between her fingertips, not knowing what to do with it; suddenly she heard a child's voice say, "Burn it."

She looked up and discovered that Henry had joined her. He squatted beside her, staring with his solitary eye at the squirming bug. "Stick it in the flame," he said. "Look . . ." He put his hand inside his clothes, produced another of the ghastly creatures, which, to her horror, he proceeded to hold in the candle flame. There was a brief, repulsive hiss; he shot the charred little corpse into the darkness with finger and thumb and turned to her, a smug expression on his face. "That's the way to do it," he said. "Try it. Come on, stick it in the flame."

Squeamishly, she obeyed. At the horrible hiss, she burned the tips of her fingers, and her hand darted back.

"Now shoot it," he said. "Go on, shoot it."

She did so with relief; only then did it penetrate to her that this was the first time he had ventured out of his corner. The difference between the snarling animal in the corner and this self-important little boy was deeply moving.

"Catch another," he said. "There are plenty of 'em. They are bedbugs. They hide in the wall and come out at night. So, better get used to them. Come, catch another."

So wonderful was the sudden intimacy between them, so miraculous, that she found herself hoping she might find another of those bugs on her. She had no trouble doing so; feeling something move, she looked at her ankles and saw to her horror that her legs were swarming with the filthy creatures. She could go on burning them all night without making any difference; she looked about her and it seemed she saw them everywhere in the trembling candlelight. Her beautiful, clean, lavender-scented straw was alive with the vermin; so were her clean, freshly furbished children. But the fact that the bugs had caused Henry to come out of his corner made them seem a mere nuisance, not the plague they really were.

She did not engage him in conversation. Intuition told her to let him take the lead and venture as far out of his shell as he wished. They put a few more bugs to their fiery death; then suddenly he turned around and crawled back to his corner. But, brief though their conversation had been, the chasm had been bridged; he would come back in his own time.

After he was gone she sat gazing at the candle flame, watching it grow tall and voracious toward the end of the wick until it twitched, sputtered and died. In the darkness she went into meeting for worship. 'God,' she thought, 'dear God, thank Thee. Now what do I do? Tell me what to do.' Her prayer was no longer directed at an all-powerful Father in an office in the sky, as George had put it. She knew now that there was a real, positive power within her, an inward Light that would rise to the surface and direct her thoughts, if she gave it the opportunity to do so. It was mysterious and yet, once the mystery had been accepted, utterly simple and real. This time again there rose within her a sense of direction. She had expected to be told how she could identify with the little boy in the corner. But the Light guided her to think, 'Thou canst not identify with a boy of eleven, mutilated by an unimaginable, horrendous act of violence and about to be hanged. Think for thyself.' She proceeded to think for herself. 'If I were asked: What is thy dearest wish, what would my answer be?' Well, that was easy: to liberate the children, all children, from the nightmarish dungeons of England's prisons. 'No, no— think of thyself as a prisoner, plagued by bugs, pining for fresh air, wind, sunlight . . .' A walk in the sun, that was what she would really enjoy. Would he too? Of course he would! She should ask permission to take him out for a walk in the sun! She would ask Sawrey. Where was he, by the way? Wasn't he coming tonight? And where was Thomas?

It was obvious now that Thomas was not coming, in spite of what Ann had said about his intention to visit her. What had made the girl so self-conscious? Suddenly she found herself yearning for him so passionately that she realized he had been wise to stay away. He should not come, not yet; if she were to see him now, she would be tempted to surrender and leave with him. For underneath her sense of triumph and achievement were weakness and terror. She dare not think of next month. If she as much as touched on the knowledge that Henry . . . She could not stand it. It made her want to flee into Thomas' arms, hide her face, cover her ears.

No, she must go one step, one day, at a time. Walk in the sun. Take Henry out for a walk in the sun. Ask Sawrey.

She sat listening in the darkness, her head turned toward the gate, waiting for the light of his lantern.

* * *

When Mistress Fell sprang her request on him at dead of night, John Sawrey was impressed. There she stood, already half a jailbird despite her comely gown and her hair, which still had a well-groomed sheen in the lantern light but was beginning to lose its shape. She must know herself that before long she would look like the rest of them: haggard, disheveled, vermin-ridden, disfigured by scabs, a creature of the lightless depths; yet her eyes were radiant and she sounded excited as she said, "Mr. Sawrey, there is something you can do for me! I should like to take Henry outside for a walk on the ramparts every day. Would this be possible, do you think?"

He tried not to show his confusion. What bothered him about the request was that it was unforeseen. In the contest in which they were engaged, victory would go to the one who managed to stay one move ahead of the other. He obviously needed to identify with her to a deeper level still. Where were those pamphlets about the Quakers he had ordered? Nobody in this town could be prevailed upon to move briskly, spring had turned even the heads of old billy-goats like Fell. He wondered whether she had an inkling that at this very moment her husband and her maid were supping together in a private room at the Red Lion. He hoped not; it might induce her to drop this mad venture and return to the world to reclaim her rights.

"I will certainly put it to the regents, Madam," he said. "Your concern for the boy is impressive, misguided though it may be."

She peered at him intently through the bars; again he sensed that never before had he faced such intelligence and awareness. His own smiling dumpling of a wife was enough to make him burst into sardonic laughter, compared to this bright-eyed, quick-witted female lynx. "Why the regents?" she asked. "Can you not grant the permission yourself?"

"In this particular instance, I'm afraid not, Madam. The boy's late father was a man of influence." That was true enough, but he suspected that she, with her experience of judicial affairs, would smell a rat. He must be careful, give himself time to think. "Well," he said, taking off his hat for the bow and sweep, "I must bestir myself, Mistress Fell. I have to make the rounds before retiring."

"I still do not understand why it is necessary for you to consult the regents," she persisted. "If you yourself feel that the boy should not be pampered by letting him smell the fresh air for five minutes a day, why not say so?"

He had to meet this challenge or she would brood about it during the lonely hours of the night. Uncharacteristically, he said at an impulse, "To tell you the truth, Madam, I want to consider this thoughtfully. On the one hand I am eager to oblige you as the wife of a distinguished colleague, on the other I have the duty to be consistent in my application of the law."

"Come, come, Mr. Sawrey," she said with a hint of her husband's mannerism, "surely, to permit a child an innocent walk on the walls cannot be interpreted as a judicial inconsistency!"

"I beg to differ, Madam. There is no more embarrassing sight than that of a judge who first sentences a criminal to death and then proceeds to coddle him to assuage his own uneasy conscience."

"You have an uneasy conscience?" She asked it in apparent innocence, but could not hide the dagger in her question.

"Indeed not." He smiled. "I will be happy to explain to you why not, tomorrow. Now you must forgive me." He made his bow and sweep. "Good night, Madam. Remember, I am at your disposal at all times. Constable." It was not necessary, she had registered the man's presence last night, but he must make certain she knew he was not alone, rather than have her discover this at an inappropriate moment later in the game.

"Good night, Mr. Sawrey. I thank you!" she called after him as he walked away; it expressed a radiant self-confidence.

Instead of going to the Quakers in the other corridor as he had planned, he climbed the interminable steps, to be waylaid in the gateway by little Hathaway, who called from the door of his office, "Your Honor! Someone has arrived for you!"

It was old Holly Stowe, bundled up to the ears, his beak-nosed face pale with fatigue, a worn valise by his side. Someone had moved briskly after all; but at that moment Sawrey failed to appreciate the man's eagerness. After Holly had been guided to the pie-shaped room next to his own, the old chatterbox struck up a snattering conversation with the constable, who had been steeped in gloom, exiled on the top floor of the tower, forced to sleep during the day with no one to relieve his boredom except sparrows and spiders. They went on blabbing and blathering; the walls of the tower might be three feet thick, those that separated the rooms were made of paper. It boded ill for the future, but to tell them to hold their tongues would be unwise; no point antagonizing them when he had to rely on their loyalty and discretion in the near future. He opened the door. "I'll be in chambers in the other wing, if I'm wanted," he said, interrupting their gabble. Holly Stowe, sitting on the edge of the bed in his bare feet, his broken boots beside him, was showing a huge big toe, inflamed by gout, to the constable squatting in front of him; the candle stood between them on the floor.

Sawrey went to fetch the key to the chambers. "No sign of Justice Fell?" he asked the warden as he took it from him.

"Not tonight, Your Honor," the hunchback replied. "At least, not yet. If he comes, shall I tell him you are expecting him?"

These infernal busybodies! "No, thank you, Hathaway," he replied coolly. "Just tell him I have the key."

"Very well, Your Honor. I expect he'll be back. There's a letter for him arrived tonight from London. I put it on his desk."

He found the letter on the desk, as Hathaway had said; it had been sent by magistrate's coach, first priority, and bore the seal of the Palace of St. James's. He balanced it on his hand, looking at it thoughtfully. Fell was safely ensconced with his little doxy; he had at least an hour.

He prised the seal open expertly and unrolled the parchment; another letter fell out, in a different handwriting. He read the parchment first; it was signed "Margaret Fell." *"Dear Heart! As the father of thy people, I come to plead with thee for one of thy youngest children . . ."* Dear Heart? As he read on, he discovered that it was a petition to Oliver Cromwell, asking for a pardon for the boy Henry Jones. She was raving mad! Calling Cromwell "Dear Heart," addressing him as "thou"? What had got into the woman? He read the accompanying note. It was signed "S." *"Amice. I received the accompanying screed this morning and thought it judicious to refer it back to you prior to presenting it, as it appears to be written by your good wife. Under the circumstances, her appeal might have an adverse effect on C as its salutation, mode of address and valediction smack of Quakerism, presently one of C's bugbears. Should you so desire, however, I will be happy to present it on return. I trust your good family is well; here matters have changed considerably since you left, and I often think of your remote eyrie with envy; yours has been the better choice. When the fires of passion are raging, the wise eagle soars out of reach of the flames, content to ride the thermals. Be well. S."* There was a postscript: *"The boy's victim had powerful friends in these parts, who would react adversely to a pardon, justified as it might appear considering the child's age and, no doubt, the nature of the provocation. The late lamented was notorious for his addiction to the sin of Tiberius."*

Who was "S"? What was the sin of Tiberius? Whatever it was, the letter put a new aspect to the case. It meant the woman was more reckless than he had thought, and at the same time had friends in London powerful enough to intercept a letter to Cromwell. He could be bolder in his approach than he had been thus far, but he must be more thorough in documenting his case. His proof that she was a Quaker must be irrefutable. More than that, he must prove that her concern for the condemned boy was a direct result of her blasphemous persuasion, and that she intended to disrupt the due process of law. In order to present incriminating evidence that would stand up in court, he must provide an exact definition of Quakerism, based on expert testimony, by someone versed in legal terminology. The obvious answer was Dr. Marshall, spokesman for the ministers at the trial of George Fox.

After carefully restoring the seal to the letter, he wrote a note to the good doctor, asking him for a succinct, unequivocal summary of the heresies subscribed to by the people calling themselves "Children of the Light" and also, as an afterthought, for the dossier on George Fox compiled for the Lancaster trial.

*   *   *

"So I said to him, quite frankly, "No, Oliver, this is as far as I can follow thee. Imprison him, although even that would seem excessive punishment for a man who, after all, is a monarch. But have him beheaded? No. That, to me, would turn thee into a tyrant.' "

"What did he say to that?"

Thomas Fell looked at the girl's eager face, and realized that he had never told the story of his break with Cromwell more compellingly. For some reason, the thought distracted him. He took a sip of burgundy, gazed at the glass, dark red, candlelit, a summer rose. Ah! If only he were still the dashing young barrister, favorite of both the King and his executioner! But the young barrister would not have known how to savor this moment. Ripeness is all. "I wonder whether Charles ever realized that by the manner in which he met his death he probably saved the monarchy, in the end. Despite his glaring faults, he was a wise, occasionally even a poetic man."

"Ah?"

He realized that he had been talking too much. "Sorry. Where was I?"

"You told him that the King's execution would turn him into a tyrant. How did he take that?"

"Oh, he turned around and walked away." He had not; it had been a harrowing outburst of profane fury, Oliver at his worst. "That was the last I saw of him. You must be tired, my dear," he added unfairly.

"Oh, no, no! Quite the reverse!" She looked aghast, and no wonder: he had never seen anyone look less tired than she.

"More wine?" he asked.

She seemed about to refuse, but had second thoughts and nodded, struck, no doubt, by the thought that another glass of wine would prolong the evening.

Perversely, her acquiescence prompted him to say, "Ah—but I should have more sense than to ply you with wine at this hour! Tomorrow is a busy day, for both of us." He rose; obediently, she followed suit and took his proffered arm. When he guided her down the dark stairs to the courtyard, there was about her a feminine fragrance of innocence and youth.

He did not call a chaise, but walked her back to her lodgings through the dark furrows of the streets under the starlit sky. He encouraged her to talk; she had not had a chance to say a word during supper. She chatted happily, aglow with the evening, which to her must be like a dream. She talked about Margaret, what a wonderful woman she was, what immense courage she showed in staying on with the children despite all opposition; it was the first time he had heard about opposition, but it came as no surprise. To the minor powers Margaret's interference must seem like a threat.

When they arrived at the dark door of Ann's inn, he held her hand and said, "I should like to invite you to supper again tomorrow, but I really wonder whether that would be wise. For your sake, I mean."

"Why not?" He could not see her face in the darkness, but her voice sounded anxious. "I would love to—unless I bore you?"

"No, no," he said, smiling. "Quite the reverse. But the walls have ears, the doors eyes. If we return tomorrow, there are certain to be whispers."

She was silent for a while, then she pulled her hand out of his and said, "I see. Well, in that case . . ."

"I do not believe you understand, my dear," he said hastily. "The only person who might be hurt by gossip would be you. People have a tendency to be lenient toward the frailties of aging Chief Justices. You are young, innocent . . ."

She tossed her head proudly, a rather risky gesture with that hat; then she said, "For Margaret Fell I would sacrifice anything, anything at all."

It was perhaps a mite theatrical, but he took it she wished to continue to sup with him. "I see. Well, in that case . . . I'll be here at the usual time tomorrow. Good night."

"Good night, sir." She vanished quickly in the shadows of the doorway, the bell inside tinkled as she opened it. He smiled and started toward the castle. It had been quite a feat, to call the acceptance of a standing invitation to supper from a Lord Chief Justice a sacrifice for the sake of the man's wife. But she had the prerogative of youth to have her chain of logic tested by its strongest link. She was a companionable creature who made him feel mellow and pleasantly disposed, as would a really superlative wine. What a boon, to have come across her! Imagine being condemned to have his meals alone, to go to bed at sunset full of morose broodings about his health! He arrived at the warden's office in high spirits.

"Good evening, Hathaway. How are we tonight?"

"Good evening, Your Lordship." The hunchback rose respectfully behind his desk. It did not make much difference, poor man. What a curse, to have to walk through life with that crooked back! Many women must have gone out of their way to touch his hump for luck.

"A lantern, please. I have some work to do."

"I'm sorry, Your Lordship, all lanterns are gone. Justice Sawrey is up there."

"What the devil do you mean? Up where?"

"He came in an hour ago, Your Lordship, and went to chambers. May I give you a candle? Shall I call the guard to accompany you?"

"A candle will do, thank you." That Sawrey should use the chambers at this ungodly hour seemed an intolerable intrusion. It was not, of course; as provost, he had a perfect right to be here. But why the devil would a man want to work in chambers at this hour unless

—unless he were carrying on a dalliance with a girl young enough to be his daughter, which filled him with such nervous zest that he could not sleep?

Sobered, he made his way down the dark corridor and up the flight of stairs toward chambers, shielding his candle flame as he went. As he approached the door, he saw a crack of light underneath it; when he opened it, he found Sawrey, hat on the back of his head, sprawled in the chair where he himself had sat the night before. He felt inordinately irritated at the sight. "Good evening," he said tersely. "What gives me the pleasure of your company at this hour?"

The little man stared at him noncommittally. "I was expecting you," he said. "I thought it was time you and I had a word."

"About what?"

"About your good wife."

It was perfectly legitimate and in order. As judiciary head of the prison this term, Sawrey had the duty to concern himself with what was going on. Yet the man's tone and the way he sat there rubbed him the wrong way. "Is this necessary?" he asked coldly.

"I'm afraid it is. I've just come back from a visit with Mistress Fell. She requested permission to take the Jones boy out for a daily airing on the ramparts. I need not point out to you that there are aspects to this request that need to be discussed."

"What the devil do you mean, visiting her at this hour? Wasn't she asleep?" It was a peevish question, but the idea of this creature going to see Margaret in her cell at dead of night revolted him.

"It is my custom to make the rounds of the prison at unpredictable hours. Ever since your good wife's arrival I have made a point of going to see her to find out if she might be in need of assistance. In my place, I trust you would do the same. I do not pretend I approve of what she is doing, but I am a married man myself. Women have their fancies. In my own case also, to indulge them has proven itself to be the best policy."

"What's wrong with taking the boy out for an airing?"

"For one thing, there is the possibility of an escape."

"From the ramparts?"

"Unlikely, but possible. I do not want the warden to grant permission unless we are covered against that eventuality."

"How, pray?"

"What I had in mind was bail."

His face stiffened. "Like the bail you suggested Herbert Marshall demand of William Best?"

Sawrey looked at him balefully. "I'll leave it to you to determine the size and the nature of the bail. The boy, as you know, has committed a murder of a particularly vicious kind."

"Five pounds?"

Sawrey spread his hands. "Anything you say. Then there is the fact that to take the boy for a walk every day might create a precedent."

"How so?"

"Other prisoners in the same straits might justifiably ask for the same privilege. Unless, of course, there should be the possibility of a pardon. But that I would know about, wouldn't I?"

"Of course."

"Well, let me talk it over with Hathaway and Dr. Withers and see what can be done to accommodate your wife."

"Do whatever you see fit. Now could I have the desk? I have a stack of petitions to deal with."

"Surely. Shall I leave the lantern?"

"Take it. I won't be leaving before dawn."

"In that case, good night." Sawrey picked up the lantern. "By the way, a letter arrived for you. It's on the desk."

"Oh?"

"Good night."

"Good night."

He picked up the letter thoughtfully. There was something in the way Sawrey had mentioned it . . . Magistrates' mail, the seal of the Palace of St. James's. He inspected the seal closely; it did not look as if it had been tampered with. He broke it.

As he unrolled the parchment, another letter fell out and he recognized, with a shock of alarm, his wife's handwriting. *"Dear Heart! As the father of thy people . . ."*

He read hers first, then old Shorwell's, then her letter again. This time he was struck not only by her incredible ingenuousness but by her undeniable sincerity. There could be no doubt as to her total involvement with the boy; her disregard of her own safety in the face of what she felt to be an urgent need for mercy was impressive. Chances were that Cromwell would have granted her request but at the same time, with typical puritanical righteousness, ordered her clapped in prison as a Quaker. Shorwell had rendered them a great service by returning the letter; Thomas wondered why the old fox had done it. By keeping it from Cromwell and writing that note to boot, he had taken a great risk, which was uncharacteristic of him. For the confidant of the late King to have continued as Cromwell's confidant was a feat of extraordinary political dexterity; to bring that off, a man had to be unemotional as a vulture, ruthless as a badger. Obviously, something in her letter had moved him to shield her from the consequences of her folly, despite the risk involved; it would seem she had been saved in the nick of time. But then there was Sawrey. He might have tampered with the seal, after all.

What was he to do? Go down there and tell her about the fate of her petition? He wandered over to the window and gazed out at the blank wall, the starry sky. No, if Sawrey had seen it, he had seen it; nothing he could do or say would change that fact. What could Sawrey do with the knowledge? He was crafty enough to realize that he would destroy himself if he were to engineer her prosecution as a Quaker under the limitations of the present proclamation, unless she committed an overtly subversive act. He need not warn her to watch her step with Sawrey, she was intelligent enough to do so of her own accord.

With a sigh, he returned to his desk to deal with the rest of the petitions, each one representing a human tragedy. A man could bear only so much; sufficient to each life the suffering thereof.

*   *   *

"So I replied: '*For Margaret Fell I would sacrifice anything, any-thing at all' and meant it wholeheartedly. I cannot understand now what made me feel so hostile toward her in the past; it is almost as if I had been another person then, a stranger. How could I fail to see the selflessness, courage, greatness of her gallant, self-effacing . . .*" Suddenly she felt moved by a devil inside to write "*ballocks*"—a word that had stayed in her mind ever since the boy had spat it at Margaret Fell and her high-tailed charity. She reared away from the book, aghast.

What did this mean? Well, it was quite clear: it meant that she had been trying to fool herself, even in her diary. For this was not the sweet, self-effacing Ann Traylor she had tried to foist upon herself. Sweet? A wolverine, a Salome . . . Oh, stop it! This was ridiculous.

"*. . . courageous, self-effacing . . .*" What had she been about to write? Oh yes, "*acts. The sheer moral purity of her . . .*" This time she found herself writing, "*savage determination to press-gang those miserable urchins into a choir, to scrub them as if they were gar-den statuettes, the insufferable high-handedness with which she sent her husband trotting all over town for children's clothes, a slop barrel, a piss pot . . .*" No! She could not write this! She was spoiling her whole diary! But something forced her to go on, as if she were rolling down the side of a hill. Her quill raced across the pages, describing herself crudely, mercilessly. She could no longer swallow the nauseating pre-tense of the sweet, ingenuous maiden who had no idea she was engaged in a deliberate effort to seduce a man who found himself temporarily disoriented because of his wife's refusal to have anything to do with him. Then the question that had been haunting her surfaced once more.

"*Who says that what Margaret Fell is doing is beautiful and godly? Who says that I must do the same as she, for the sake of my soul? If George Fox, that sanctimonious creeper, is right, if I am indeed unique, irreplaceable, never seen on earth before, never to be seen again, do I not have the right to be myself? The duty, even? What it boils down to is the question: Who am I? The pious churchmouse, mumbling about sacrifice? The weakling, infatuated with her mistress, who melted in the woman's embrace that night in her bed? Or the brazen hussy who bought the hat, caught the judge under it and, now she has captured him, does not know what to do with him? Or has the true Ann Traylor still not emerged? Is there still someone else within me, trying to get out? Is the fact that I*

*suddenly find myself writing all this poisonous nonsense part of the
effort of that true person to emerge? These pages of my diary are
spoiled anyhow, so I might as well continue. Well then: so far I
have been asking myself, 'What are T.F.'s intentions?' It is time
to ask myself what my intentions are, and to answer honestly."*

She frowned at her own frankness. Written down, it seemed terribly
calculating and cold-blooded. Yet she must find out the truth of all
this, soon. Time was short; in a few weeks the boy would be hanged
and that would be the end. She felt in her bones that Margaret
Fell would return home the moment the boy had been executed
—if only because of the shock, for, despite her scrubbing and house-
cleaning, she still seemed to live in a world of fantasy. The boy
would be hanged, the children would be left exactly as they had been
in the first place, once the moment came for her to return to her husband, her household. And what would happen to Ann Traylor in that
event? Was she prepared to take up life as a governess again, be
demure and subservient, wrap parcels for those dumbledores in prison,
write sanctimonious letters full of pious cant about *that of God within,*
as if it were the stuffing inside a turkey? And her hat? In a box, with
mothballs, stored away forever? And the judge turned blind again to
her presence? Whatever happened, she would not go back to that! Not
to the life of tight-lipped, tight-braided governess, primly trotting down
the road to heaven. The very idea stifled her.

She rose, went to the window, opened it, breathed the cool night
air and gazed at the stars. She remembered her premonition of a
few days ago, when she had stood here like this. What then had
seemed wishful thinking, a preposterous daydream, had become a
reality: a rich man was hers for the taking. Yes, the taking; no point in
deceiving herself. It was only a matter of days before she would have
him in the palm of her hand. She had no experience worth speaking of
in that respect, but feminine instinct told her: The trap is not yet
sprung, but he is sniffing the bait.

What should she do now? Continue listening with dove's eyes,
hanging on his lips, allowing herself to be plied with wine, pretending
to become reckless? Instinct told her not to fret; he would take the
lead at a given moment, the way he fancied he had from the beginning. What then? What was the future of the woman of the world
with the jaunty hat? A rich old man who would give her material
security and plenty of opportunity to entertain dashing young officers? Not a very edifying dream for someone who had at one time
aspired to saintliness. What was the next stage? Have herself set
up in rooms in an inn by Thomas Fell? Here in Lancaster, or in
Belfast, farthest on his circuit? It seemed a miserable existence:
endless, boring days of waiting, a feeling of uncleanliness, corruption,
dissipation . . . But what else? Stop this dangerous game, back away
from Thomas Fell while there was still time? That gave her an
unexpected feeling of emptiness, a sudden nausea, as if she were
about to be sick. She went back to the table, frightened by the
violence of her reaction. She took up the quill and wrote: *"What is*

this? Am I in love with him? Is that why I feel so terrible all of a
sudden, so torn up at the thought that the wisest thing would be to
send him away?"

Anguished, but determined to discover the truth about herself, she
went on writing, spoiling six pages of her diary, to arrive, in the
end, at: *"Oh! How I love thee! How I love thee, damned old*
judge! I count the hours, the minutes until tomorrow evening when
I will see thy shy, sad face break into a smile again, hear thee
say, 'Ah, good evening, Miss Traylor, good evening.' Damn thee!
Damn thee, Thomas Fell! I thought I was the spider and thou the
fly! What am I going to do? What in the name of God am I going to
do? Thomas! Thomas! God, I suffer! HOW I SUFFER!"

She stared at the scrawled words, underlined three times, a shriek
of anguish that seemed to leap off the page. Then, with grim determination, she began to tear the pages out, one by one, and to
burn them in the candle flame.

Each curling, blackening sheet devoured by fire was self-torture.
She *was* desperate, she *was* in love with an unattainable man, she
was doomed either to lead a life of sin and squalor or to waste
her youth in servitude and chastity—dull, gray chastity. Her despair
was real, her misery profound; when she went to bed at last, she
expected to lie awake, hot-eyed, for hours. But she fell asleep instantly, to dream about a kite in the sky, the wind in the trees, the
surf, sounding like laughter.

CHAPTER FOUR

CAREFULLY and with a finicky attention to detail, John Sawrey set the stage for Margaret Fell's self-incrimination. He accustomed her to his nightly visits, until, he was certain, she looked forward to them as the poacher had done. He managed to make her stand in a spot where Holly Stowe could hear her without being seen; this he contrived by putting himself on his seat-stick against the wall opposite her cell. He consistently discouraged any chit-chat and confined himself to reminding her that he was at her disposal. She had now, he knew, begun to deplore the brevity of his appearances; in this respect her husband had cooperated considerably by leaving her to her own devices. She had no one else to whom she could unburden herself; the maid was there only in the daytime and then they were both busy with the children. Everything was ready, there was no reason for him to tarry longer. But then Dr. Marshall's documents arrived, and they turned out to be disappointing.

John Sawrey scanned the doctor's letter gloomily in his room in the tower of Lancaster Castle. Next door the constable and Holly Stowe were starting what must be their fifteenth game of backgammon of the night; like himself, they had become adjusted to sleeping in the daytime and rising when the bats began to circle the tower. But whereas the bats had plenty to do, the two men were forced to while away the hours doing nothing except quarreling like an aged couple and playing backgammon. It was time Holly Stowe were given something to do, and that was another reason why John Sawrey had been eager to receive the information he had requested from Marshall.

Now the whole plan began to look like a private chimera.

"In answer to your request for a summary of the heresies of the so-called 'Children of the Light,' I enclose the malediction invoked on the people called Quakers by the Presbyterian ministers of Scotland when George Fox first visited that country. It gives an admirable definition, readily understandable by the layman, of the grotesqueries and aberrations of the infidel Fox cum suibus." The accompanying paper contained a dreary series of pompous anathemae: *"One—Let all those who say Grace is free be cursed, and let the people say Amen. Two —Cursed be all they who say the Scriptures are not the word of God, and let the people say Amen. Three—Cursed be all they that say faith is without sin, and let the people say Amen."* So it went on, one dreary curse after another, to end with, *"Seven—Cursed are all they that proclaim that every man has a light within him sufficient to lead him to Christ, and let the people say Amen."*

It might be very effective when intoned in church with the appropriate voice of wrath, but in a court of law it would produce nothing but amused smiles on the faces of the counsel for the defense. Trying to make Margaret Fell's utterances fit these vague and emotional maledictions would be an exercise in futility.

The dossier on George Fox turned out to be just as unpromising. It was extensive enough; it described and quoted all the young man had done and said over the past two years; but, at first glance anyway, it seemed extremely biased, obviously compiled by vindictive ministers whose church services he had disrupted. Undeniably, the whole affair was a wild goose chase.

The object of his campaign had been to induce her eventually to commit a subversive act, impede the course of justice, not in private but in front of sufficient witnesses to ensure that Fell and Best would be unable to intimidate them. Her letter to Cromwell had given him hope, but she had done nothing since that could in any way be called emotional or impulsive.

What she had actually done, as any astute counsel would instantly point out, was to heed Christ's exhortation, "Suffer little children to come to Me and forbid them not." She had, in the space of one week, transformed the cell into a nursery. She had, through her maid and her husband, arranged for cots to be brought down, a table, little stools, crockery, spoons; she and her maid had sewn curtains which could be drawn in front of the bunks in the wall, now used as cupboards. She herself slept on a field bed in a corner of the cell and had managed to establish a degree of privacy by surrounding it with a screen, also provided by her husband, whom she used as an errand boy. She not only read the Bible to the children before going to sleep, she prevailed upon them to kneel by the side of their cots and intone a prayer like a bunch of jackdaws. When described by witnesses, all this could not fail to present a heart-rending picture of child conversions.

The more he considered it, the less point there seemed to be in continuing. He thought of calling it all off and sending Holly home; instead he decided to start recording Mistress Fell's precious words that very night. The cause of his decision was a violent dispute between the two bored men in the room next door, the like of which he had not heard before. There were screams, curses, a rumbling of furniture; when he appeared in the doorway he saw Holly Stowe standing at the window, a picture of querulous indignation; the constable, ham-fisted, seemed about to throw himself upon him.

"What on earth is going on here?" he cried, like a mother bursting into her children's room. "What are you fighting about *this* time?"

"Guess what he did!" Holly Stowe squealed, pointing at the open window. "Guess what he did with the dice!"

"Which dice?"

"He couldn't stand losing any more, so he stuffed them in his mouth and spewed them out the *window!*"

Normally Sawrey would have been mollified by the spectacle this evoked; under the circumstances he came close to screaming at them and their childish antics. "Well," he said coldly, "it seems the time has come for you to do some work. Stowe, get thy papers ready. Constable, light the lantern. We are going down."

On the way, he repeated once more the instructions which, by now, they should know by heart. "Holly, thou wilt stand in front of the cell with the madwomen. Stay as close to the bars as thou canst without giving them a chance to grab thy writing tablet or any part of thy person, but make sure under all circumstances to remain out of sight of Mistress Fell. Constable, thou wilt hold the lantern for him, facing the lunatics, ready to warn Holly should they be up to tricks. Do so without a sound; we don't want Mistress Fell to realize that there are two of you. Holly, write only what she says; I will insert my own questions in thy transcript. Try and get her down *verbatim* . . ."

They crossed the courtyard and descended the interminable steps, the constable lighting the way. When they arrived on the lowest level and entered the corridor leading to her cell, Sawrey was overcome by an excitement, a sudden tension that made his scalp prickle, yet was quite pleasurable. He did not know what to compare it with, he had never felt a sensation like it. The poacher had mentioned it, in one of his monologues. *"You stalk a doe for the kill, a little closer each time, and when the kill comes, there's nothing like it, in the whole world."* At the time, he had judged it another of the man's sentimental absurdities; now he discovered the truth of it. There was in the gradual encirclement of Margaret Fell an excitement that was almost sensual. He should, really, give it some careful consideration later that night and decide if an extraneous emotion were building up inside him that might trip him up at the decisive moment. It certainly should be watched.

Her cell, as they approached, was dark, as it had been every night. He had made a point of arriving when the children were sure to be asleep, except for the boy, who seemed to be awake at all hours, peering at him from a corner with his solitary, unblinking eye. He took off his gloves and tapped on the iron bars with his signet ring, calling courteously, "Mistress Fell?"

Since erecting that screen around her field bed, she was usually asleep by the time he appeared; before, she had just dozed sitting there, the children gathered around her like a litter.

"Just a moment, Mr. Sawrey."

"Take your time, Mistress Fell, please. I did not intend to waken you."

It was by now the traditional gambit with which their encounters opened. He heard rustling and creaking behind the screen; the children were fast asleep in their cots, the infernal boy was crouching in his corner wide awake, his eye glinting in the lantern light. Holly Stowe, who despite his elderly fussiness was astute and decisive when it came to the point, took up his position without unnecessary dithering; the constable, less endowed with gray matter, had to be maneuvered into place like a mule. Holly Stowe had just signaled that he was ready, pencil poised on his slate, when she appeared from behind her screen looking, if anything, somewhat less tainted by prison life than last time.

"Madam, your obedient servant." He honored her with the customary bow and sweep. "I trust you are well?"

"Very well, thank you, Mr. Sawrey."

He smiled. "It is, Madam, a pleasure to inform you that permission for a daily walk on the ramparts has finally been granted by the regents. You will be allotted fifteen minutes, counting from the moment you arrive on the upper level. It has been arranged that a guard will accompany you, for obvious reasons."

He had delayed granting the permission until he was ready to start the interrogation, in the expectancy that it might put her in a mood to talk. He had not expected the emotional effusiveness with which she reacted. "Oh, Mr. Sawrey! How wonderful!" she cried. "Thank you, sir, thank you, thank you!" and she reached for him through the bars like the madwomen.

He took her hand and said, "But, Madam, it is nothing. It was a privilege to arrange it for you."

"Henry!" she cried, turning to the boy in the corner. "Didst thou hear that, Henry? Isn't that wonderful? Oh, Mr. Sawrey, I cannot tell you what a joy this is, how—oh, this is wonderful! Truly wonderful!"

He opened his seat-stick and took up his position against the wall. Her enthusiasm was not only surprising, it filled him with a hunter's excitement. This was better than he had dared hope; but he should proceed with great delicacy. "Well, Madam, I am glad indeed that I have been able to please you. I wish there were more I could do."

"Oh, Mr. Sawrey, you have done so much already! Truly, I can't tell you how—how grateful I am!" He had the impression that she had wanted to say "how surprised I am."

"I'm flattered, Madam, but I must confess that I have no idea what you mean. I have asked every day if you had any wishes; thus far you have made only one request. Now, is there anything else I can do for you? Don't hesitate, I am entirely at your disposal."

"I—I really don't know what else you could do, honestly. Just to know that I can count on your interest and support is sufficient. It truly is. I don't think you realize what a difference it makes, to know that someone—" She stopped; but it was obvious what she had intended to say.

"I think what you are doing is very charitable indeed," he said. "I have been wondering, though, how you expect to continue this sort of care, all by yourself."

She took the bait, without a moment's hesitation. "Of course I have been thinking about that all the time! You see, there is nothing special in what I have done, I just happen to be the first. I am convinced that there are many Christian matrons like myself who will be prepared to spend some time with these children."

"I am afraid I must disagree with you, Mistress Fell. I do not think you will find any ladies in this town prepared to do what you are doing. I'm afraid this needs a special kind of person."

Holly Stowe was writing furiously, the fool! He had told him not to take down his questions, but, obviously, there were limits to the old man's intelligence. Now was the moment she was going to commit herself, if he was lucky.

But, despite her ebullience, she had all her wits about her. "I think you'll be pleasantly surprised, Mr. Sawrey," she said, smiling. "You underestimate the Christian virtue of the ladies of this town." It was charmingly put, but the old wariness was back in her eyes. She was not going to show her hand. She was a match for him, that was sure.

Even so, he felt hopeful again. He wondered why. It had to do with something intangible, instinctive; nothing she had said or done justified this sudden reversal. Was it her emotional relationship with that boy? He was the central figure. She obviously had not quite realized yet what lay ahead for him. Could he risk hinting at that? What condition was she in? Was she beginning to show any nervousness, the gradual loss of self-control that was typical of prisoners?

He rose, folded his seat-stick, put it under his arm and approached the bars, pulling on his gloves. Close to the bars he said quietly, with concern, "Madam, there is something I must mention to you, if you will forgive me."

"Yes?" Her wariness was, somehow, extremely exciting.

"I do not wish to dampen your high spirits, but I wonder whether you are aware that to take the boy out for walks on the wall may make things more difficult?"

"For whom?"

"For him. I have experience in these situations. Do not be misled by the way he behaves now. It is the aggressive ones, the rebellious ones that, when the noose—well. Don't make it more difficult for him than is necessary."

"I fail to see your point, sir." She said it coldly, almost haughtily, but, close to her as he was at that moment, he sensed her nervous tension, as if it were a quiver transmitted to him through the bars.

"Forgive me, Madam." He smiled and pulled on his gloves. "I am sure you will find the strength to cope with that situation, just as you have found it to do this admirable work."

"It is not my strength, Mr. Sawrey," she said firmly. "It is my faith in God."

"Quite. Quite." He turned to go.

"I am convinced that when the time comes God will show the way."

He stopped. "The way to what, Madam?" It was bold, but something in her voice had made him prick up his ears.

"The Lord will provide."

He was certain that was not what she had intended to say. What had she meant? The way to what?

But he had gone as far as he could safely go. He doffed his hat, swept it, bowed and made a leg. "Madam, your servant. Forgive me for disturbing you."

"Not at all, Mr. Sawrey. Not at all. Good night to you."

"Good night, Madam. Constable!"

He walked down the corridor toward the stairs without acknowledging Holly Stowe's presence. Only when they arrived on the landing did he ask, "Didst thou manage to get anything down?"

"I think I got all of it, or most of it," the old man said eagerly.

"Well, work it out as soon as we are back in our quarters. I'd like to look over what she said, especially that business about God at the end."

"I got all of that. I'll work on it straightaway. It should not take long, an hour or so."

"Very good."

But as they mounted the stairs his newfound certainty dwindled; when they arrived in the tower it seemed as if his brief moment of self-confidence had been an illusion. As he sat in his chair again, his feet propped up on the bed, morosely gazing at the perpendicular sliver of starry sky caught in the embrasure, he reconsidered his optimism of a moment ago with bitterness. Even if her relationship with the boy were emotional, even if the hanging were to shatter her as it undoubtedly would, what good would it do? Downstairs, he had thought for a moment she might do something impulsive during the hanging, lose control, interfere, try to stop the hangman. But even if she did, could it be made to look like impediment of justice? She would simply be a pathetic, emotional woman pleading for mercy at the last moment, a subject for sympathy rather than the reverse.

Next door, behind the paper wall, the constable started to hum the infernal madrigal she made the children squeal each day, and Sawrey was about to silence him when he heard Holly Stowe's voice, "Oh, stop that! Canst thou not see I'm working?" The constable growled, "Excuse *me,* I'm sure."

Well, there was no point in going to bed yet; he had to wait around until Holly Stowe had something to show for his efforts. What was more, he was wide awake. He picked up the dossier that Dr. Marshall had sent him, marked *"The Case Against George Fox, Blasphemer, Lancaster Assizes, Trinity 1652."* It was, for the clergy, methodically done, complete with index of subjects and names. He looked up "hangings," not expecting to find the word at all, but there it was—*"hanging, interrupted by G.F., Derby jail, July 1650."*

Interrupted? He leafed to the page indicated. *"On the second of July, a woman named Hazel Hawthorne, sentenced to be hanged for stealing, was brought to the scaffold in the courtyard of Derby jail. George Fox was imprisoned there at the time and had written to various judges and magistrates in an attempt to have her sentence commuted, basing his appeal on the Scriptures, more particularly the commandment 'Thou shalt not kill.' When the moment came for the springing of the trapdoor, the executioners found themselves im-*

*mobilized by a shout from the window of the cell in which the
blasphemer was incarcerated. He shouted at them a word variously
interpreted as 'Stop!', 'God!' or 'No!' As a result, a spell was thrown
over the men, who were paralyzed to the extent that they could
not proceed with the execution. The woman was taken back to
her cell and the matter was brought in front of Sir Gervase Bennett,
acting provost. Fox was sentenced to serve a supplementary three
months after completion of his term, the charge being 'impeding
the course of justice.' The woman in question has not been executed
as of this writing; the warden of Derby jail moved into the prisoner's
cell and was subsequently dismissed, as he joined the people called
Quakers."*

He lowered the book. If something like this were to happen here
in Lancaster, in front of the crowd to be expected at this hanging,
the perpetrator would receive a much harsher sentence than three
months. Could she be prevailed upon to do the same? What exactly
had happened, anyhow? Was it indeed a spell the man had thrown
over the executioners, or what?

Whatever it was, it smacked of a miracle. That was, obviously,
why everyone concerned had been intimidated, hence their pussyfooting reaction to the extraordinary incident. Carter Barton, the
local hangman, would be less readily impressed by someone shouting
"Stop!" at the crucial moment during an execution.

Think, he told himself. Think it through from the beginning. Try
to put thyself in her place. There is the boy, about to be hanged.
It has not become reality to her yet; she will have to be made to
face it. Forcibly, if possible. An emotional shock of some sort . . .

He rose, went to the window and stared at the night. The stars
were hazy with thin, swift clouds from the sea. There was a new
moon, its back to the wind, blurred by the clouds scudding past. He
knew he was on the right track. Shock. An emotional shock. When?
Obviously, the first time she took the boy out for his walk. How?
What?

It took a while before he hit upon the answer; despite the hour,
he went downstairs to arrange it.

*   *   *

In spite of Sawrey's ominous last words, Margaret Fell was so
elated with his permission to take Henry outside that she could
hardly sleep. She had given up hope that her request would ever
be granted; now she realized how desperately she had been yearning
for a breath of fresh air, not only for Henry but for herself. She had
spent a mere three weeks in the dungeon, but already she felt as if
she had not seen the sun for years. She was happy now that she had
not given in to the temptation to sneak out for an hour or so, leaving
Ann with the children. She had always known that the only way to get
through to Henry was to share his world.

The moment Sawrey was gone, she could not contain herself; she went to the boy crouched in his corner, put her arms around him and said, "Henry, Henry, isn't it wonderful? Tomorrow! Tomorrow we can go outside!"

But he did not share her excitement. There was still a wall of suspicion between them. But it no longer disturbed her; least of all, that night. In her elation she knelt by her cot and thanked God from the bottom of her heart for this blessing, this wonderful surprise. It strengthened her conviction, unspoken but deep-rooted, that Oliver Cromwell would respond to her plea and grant the boy his pardon. It was the only condition on which she could face the fact that Henry was sentenced to be killed, brutally, ten days from now.

Her night was restless and she was up earlier than usual. Never had she looked forward so intensely to anything since she was a child. She expected the guard to come for them from the moment she awoke; only when she went to call the children did she realize it was a ridiculous hour even in the world of the prison, where life began before daybreak while it was still dark outside. To expect to be taken for a walk on the ramparts at four in the morning was ridiculous. She really had to get a hold on herself, this was foolish. But as the morning progressed, she became more restless, more impatient. Ann arrived with the laundry; they spent some time changing the children's clothes before starting the lesson of the morning; but not for a second could Margaret forget the treat that lay in store; she found herself running to the bars to try and peer down the passage at the slightest sound out there.

But the morning passed, agonizingly, without anyone coming for them. The hour of noon passed. Ann prepared to leave, as she had to hand in their washing at the inn; still the guard had not come. When Ann left, Margaret asked her to inquire upstairs; perhaps they had forgotten about them; perhaps Sawrey had forgotten to instruct the warden. Ann promised to do so; for the first time the girl's eagerness to leave did not disturb her.

Two o'clock. Three o'clock. Four o'clock; still the guard had not come. She was about to blow her whistle, something she had not done for a long time, when, all of a sudden, there he was.

"Mistress Fell? I've come to take you and the boy out for a spell. Are you ready?"

"Oh, we surely are! Yes, yes, of course! Henry, quick! Henry!"

The boy, sullenly, stayed in his corner.

"Come on, Henry, come on! We're going for a walk outside! Come, child, come!" She put her arm around his shoulders and tried to guide him to the door. To her astonishment, he balked.

"What's the matter? Dost thou not wish to come?"

The boy did not reply. He looked at her fiercely with his solitary eye, his face set in a scowl.

She knelt by his side, put her hands on his thin arms and pleaded, "Oh, Henry, please don't do that to me, please! I have so looked forward to taking thee out, now please don't be stubborn! Come! Come, if it were only to do me the pleasure. Yes?"

He peered at her, and the expression on his face changed. He seemed to look much older than his age, with a bitter, resigned wisdom. He did not say a word, but his shoulders slumped; it felt like a surrender.

"Come, Henry, come! It's not going to be terrible, it's going to be wonderful! Thou wilt see; once we are out there, thou wilt enjoy it immensely, I know it!" Chattering nervously, she led him to the open door, and they followed the guard as he went down the corridor. She had her arms around the shoulders of the little boy; he let himself be guided, but his steps were hesitant, not only because he had to drag his chains; it seemed as if he was prepared at any moment to turn around and shuffle back into the security of their cell. It was very odd, but she had the same sensation. The moment she set foot outside that cage where she had stayed only so short a while, she felt insecure. She was trembling with apprehension; the prospect of a walk in the sun suddenly no longer seemed at all attractive. What in the world had possessed her to ask for it? She was overcome by the compulsion to turn around and hurry back to the children. She should not have left them alone; she should have asked Ann to stay with them while she was gone. But she knew it was not because of the children that she felt this way; it was that strange sense of insecurity.

As they climbed the stairs, she discovered that she tired much more quickly. In the beginning she had climbed the many flights without pausing for breath; now she had to call "Please!" on each landing, to make the guard stop and give her a chance to catch her breath. She stood leaning against the wall, eyes closed, heart pounding; poor Henry had the same trouble; toward the end of their climb he could barely lift his feet with those chains. Her own feet seemed to weigh like lead; as they approached the top level she had to pause halfway up the flight of steps. At last, there was the door to the castle gateway, the first light of day in almost three weeks.

But they did not go out into the gateway; there was a small door in the wall that she had never noticed before. The guard opened it and, to her horror, she saw another flight of steps. "Must we?" she gasped.

The guard, surprised, turned around. "Beg pardon, ma'am?"

"Must we climb more steps?"

"Well, ma'am, I'm supposed to take you to the ramparts."

"How many more?"

"Huh?"

"How many more flights are there?"

"I don't rightly know, ma'am. From here on, though, there are no more landings."

"Oh. I see. Very well, let's go. So long as you don't mind stopping frequently. We really aren't used to this any more."

"Very well, ma'am." The guard seemed puzzled. "We will take it slowly, ma'am."

"Thank you, bless you."

It became the longest climb she had ever made. Poor Henry, when they got to the third turn of the spiral, sat down on the steps, whimpering with exhaustion. But there was light just above them, bright and inviting. "Look, Henry, look," she said, "there's the sunlight, right ahead of us! Dost thou see it? That's where we are going. We are nearly there! Come, love; come, let me help thee."

They stumbled on, like two convalescents after a long illness, until at last they reached the source of the beckoning light. It turned out to be an embrasure through which a narrow beam of sunlight slanted down into the well of the stairs. She was dying to inhale the fresh air, but so concerned about Henry not being able to make it that, with her last ounce of strength, she lifted him to look through the narrow opening. He was heavy because of the chains and her strength had been sapped by the long climb; she could lift him only for a few seconds. With a moan, she put him down again with a rattle of iron and leaned against the wall. "Didst thou see the sun?" she asked, eyes closed.

He did not answer. He sat at her feet, his head in his hands. Poor boy, because of those chains he must be more exhausted than she was, she had had no idea how heavy they were. They rested for a long time, while the guard waited patiently a few steps above them. It was quiet on the steps; once her heart had stopped banging, she began to discern sounds from the outside world that were as precious as the breath of fresh air she had caught: voices, hammering, the sounds of freedom and activity.

She opened her eyes, looked up at the guard and asked, "Is it far?"

"No, ma'am, three more turns and we are there. Do you think you can make it?"

"Yes, yes . . . we're almost ready." She put her hand to her breast; even to talk was exhausting. "He's very weak."

"Take your time, ma'am. I am in no hurry." He seemed a kind man; she should really pay a little more attention to him, instead of treating him as a means to an end. She wondered how George was, where he was, why she had not heard from him. Did he know what she was doing? Silly question. "Come, Henry," she said, "we are nearly there." She pulled him up by his arms; he lifted his feet wearily up the high steps. She picked up his chains and carried them for him the rest of the way.

When finally she staggered into the open of a bright, wind-swept afternoon, she was overcome by giddiness. The mere breath of clean sea air swirling around her made her lightheaded, almost drunk. She stood clutching Henry for support; during the first moments she felt as if she were about to dissolve in the boundless space of sunlight and wind. Then she heard the guard say, "Ma'am? If you want to go and walk, you should do so. We have not much time left."

"Yes . . . yes, thank you . . . Come, Henry."

With an effort, she started along the ramparts. When they reached the parapet, she stood still, eyes closed, blinded by the daylight. Merely to breathe that delicious air was pure heaven. She raised her face toward the sun, feeling its warmth, pressing the shivering little body of the child against her. The hammering was louder now, and she heard the rumble of planks; they brought memories of carpenters and masons, the bustle and the excitement of a house being built. She opened her eyes and looked down into the courtyard of the castle; sunlight glinted on the roofs, the towers; down there in the shadows were the carpenters, hammering. Then she saw what they were building. A scaffold, with a gibbet.

"Oh, no!" She cried out in horror, grasped Henry's head and pressed it against her so he would not see it. For a moment her mind was a blank; then her first thought was: 'On purpose! They did it on purpose! They kept us waiting so long on purpose!'

She turned around and, dragging Henry with her, stumbled to the parapet on the other side; there she stood, tears running down her face, swamped with horror. It was for Henry they were building it— no! She could not face it, she could not! In desperation she tried to look at the sky, the sea, but all she could see through her tears were three little buttercups growing in a crack between the granite blocks of the parapet. The sight of those fragile flowers trembling in the wind broke down her last defense. She slumped forward, her head on her arms, and cried her heart out, knowing that it was wrong, she should not be doing this to Henry, she was being weak, stupid; but she could not help herself, it seemed as if all her strength, her faith, her hope had suddenly collapsed. It was so cruel, so heinous, like an idiot pulling the wings off a fly to watch its mutilated body stagger, the way she and the boy had staggered up those stairs. "Oh, God, oh, God!" she moaned. "Save him, save him . . ." But even as she spoke the words, she realized their futility. There was no one to pray to, no fount of mercy in the universe, no God of love. Somebody touched her arm. She looked up, ready to follow the guard back down.

But it was Henry. He was holding something out to her; a little yellow flower, one of the buttercups. She stared at it, confused; then he said, "Here," and proffered it once more.

"For—for me . . . ?"

He nodded.

"Oh . . . Henry . . ." She could barely speak. She took the little flower and pressed his frail body against hers. "Oh, my dear, my very dear—oh, God . . ." She hugged him, kissed his hair, in a senseless, helpless outpouring of love. Finally she managed to get hold of herself, wipe her tears and say, smiling, "Well, who would have thought that I would be offered a posy on the walls of Lancaster Castle?"

As she said it, she saw that he knew. He looked at her with a terrible understanding. "Oh, God," she whispered, taking him in her arms again. "What can I do, what can I do?!"

It was a cry, not a question. Then he said, his voice stifled by her embrace, "Stay with me."

She knew at once what he meant. Despite her desperate concern for him, she froze. She had managed not to think about the execution at all; the certainty of Cromwell's personal intervention had blotted it out. Now it had suddenly become reality; to envisage that she would have to be present was unbearable. But, seeing the little flower, she realized that, despite his bravado and his lonely rebellion, he was a frightened child. She must not fail him. "Yes, Henry," she said. "Of course I will."

"Where I can see thee when they put it over my head," he said matter-of-factly.

"I will." She kissed his hair. "Come, let's go back." Together they turned around and walked toward the guard in the doorway.

"We are ready to go back," she said.

The man's face was impassive, but suddenly he said, "You take the lantern, ma'am. I'll carry him," and he picked up Henry, chains dangling.

She went ahead of them, down into the dungeons, wondering what had made him do that. He must have seen the boy give her the flower; it must have touched him. If a man like him could be touched, why not Cromwell? It gave her a brief resurgence of hope. Something would happen, something would prevent this monstrous crime, be it in the nick of time. The Lord would provide.

At the entrance to their corridor, the guard said, "Well, ma'am, you know the rest of the way. Can I leave you here?"

"Yes, of course. Thank you, thank you very much."

"Don't mention it, ma'am."

He lowered the boy gently to the ground, picked up his lantern and hurried back up the stairs.

"Come, Henry." Her arm around the child's shoulder, she set out toward their dungeon. As they passed the cell of the madwomen, a voice whispered, "Miss!"

At the bars stood a woman, looking terrible and pitiful, but with a face that, despite the scabs, was surprisingly sensitive and cultured. "Please," the voice whispered, "help us! Not just the children, us too! Please, M'Lady, help us, in the name of God . . ."

"But . . . but how?" she asked, gazing at the cage full of witches.

"Just come and talk to us!" the voice whispered. "Just come and talk, perhaps sing, read the Bible . . . We are not mad all the time, you know, only some of the time. It is when we realize it that it's—it's the worst." Suddenly the voice breathed, "Be careful! Be careful of that man who comes every night! There's someone writing down every word you say!"

"What's that?"

Suddenly, hair-raisingly, the woman burst into shrieking laughter and started to slam her chains against the bars, arousing all the other wretches in the cage, who instantly joined in making that terrifying noise. She hurried Henry to their cell, deeply distressed; there were the children, waiting for her. The delight with which they leaped on her, all wanting to be hugged at the same time, made her forget for a while.

After they had been fed and bathed, had said their prayers and been put to bed, and she had whispered a little private story to each one of them as her own children loved her to do, she finally sat down on her cot behind the screen to think.

So that was why Sawrey had come to see her every night, why he had been at such pains to offer his services. She did not doubt that what the woman had told her was true. Some mad compulsion drove him to weave this intricate web of subterfuge; he must have postponed his permission for them to walk on the walls until the building of the scaffold was started. But why? A mentality like his was totally alien to her. It was obvious now that every move he made, every word he spoke served some nefarious purpose, was part of some scheme in his sick mind. Had not George Fox named him as an example of those whose souls were beyond redemption, whose ultimate punishment he recorded in his Book of Rewards?

There was only one thing she could do: confront him. He was sure to turn up that night to find out how the outing had affected her. Well, she would tell him. She would tell him point blank that he was . . . She could not find the words to describe him. If ever she had despised a human being, it was he.

It seemed hours before she finally heard the sound of footsteps and saw the light of a lantern coming down the passage. She waited until he tapped on the bars with his signet ring; then, instead of replying as usual, "Just a moment, Mr. Sawrey, I'll be right there," she stepped from behind the screen and faced him.

"Good evening, Mistress Fell. How are we tonight? Did you enjoy your little outing?"

She took a breath to say, "You devil—" but could not bring herself to do so. His face with the dead, slitted eyes was masklike in its remoteness from reality, from life itself; suddenly his scheme, the whole elaborate nonsense of bringing a scribe to take down every word she said, seemed so insane that her resolve to challenge him dissolved.

"I'm a little tired tonight, Mr. Sawrey," she said. "It was kind of you to arrange for that walk, but it turned out to be more tiring than I had expected."

"Ah?" He observed her with that odd, insane intensity.

"It was not very kind of you, though, to arrange for the scaffold to be built just at this time."

His eyes did not blink. He went on gazing at her with that unnerving intensity. "That was regrettable," he said. "But it was time you started to face the inevitable. I am sorry to inform you that there is no hope for a pardon. I trust you are going to be sensible about it. I would not want you to try what George Fox did to the hangmen in Derby jail."

She managed to control herself. "You are very knowledgeable, Mr. Sawrey," she said with a smile.

"Should you be tempted to consider the possibility, then I must warn you that Carter Barton is different from those men. There are other differences, of which no doubt you are aware."

"Who is Carter Barton?"

"The executioner, Madam."

"Good night, Mr. Sawrey," she said, letting go of the bars.

"Good night, Madam, your humble servant." He made his bow and sweep.

Back behind the screen, she slumped down on her bed, exhausted. Yet, she told herself, something good had come of it all: Sawrey had given her the answer. She would do what George had done: appeal to that of God in the executioners. He had done it, so she could do it, despite what she thought about his miracles. He had said so himself, many times: it was not he who had the power; he had been in the power of the Lord. Wearily she rose and fetched the candle to have a look at the children before retiring for the night. She went silently from cot to cot, tucking them in, and ended by putting little Jody on the pot, fast asleep, leaning against her. There were only a few bedbugs on the child, and she plucked them off routinely; then she put Jody back in her cot and went to look at Henry, who still lay, every night, rolled up like a dog at the foot of the wall, although there was a cot for him. She stood looking down on him, his sad, old face, and decided to do what she had wanted to do for some time. She put down the bottle with the candle, picked him up without waking him and carried him to her bed. There she tucked him in, chains and all. She went back to fetch the candle and settled down to sleep the way she had slept the first nights, sitting in the straw, leaning against the wall. She was so tired she could sleep anywhere; he would probably be ready to use his own cot on the morrow. She might put it behind the screen with hers.

Suddenly she was struck by doubt, a quaver of panic. But she checked herself. She must have faith. Now, of all times, she must have faith. There was no turning away from it; she must face it now, prepare herself to let that of God in her fly with that one word, "Stop!" It would flash across the courtyard like an arrow, fuse with that of God in the hangmen as it had in Derby jail and they would not have the power to hang him. She folded her hands and bent her head and centered down, into the silence.

*   *   *

"Are these the normal effects of imprisonment?" Henrietta Best read. *"This sense of insecurity, of not daring to venture outside the cell? I know thou hast experience in this respect and I am sorely in need of some reassurance. Hast thou during thy incarceration known strange extremes of mood? From high spirits and over-confidence down to the depths of doubt and lack of faith in oneself, even, at times, in the power of God?"*

Henrietta Best lowered the letter and looked out of the window at the darkening summer garden. A nightingale sang in one of the ilex trees; the scent of roses was wafted toward her by the warm air, rising in the chill of the night. The dungeons of Lancaster Castle seemed far away from this world of beauty and gentleness. She closed her eyes and listened to the nightingale. How was it possible that men could do such atrocious things in the darkness under the ground, where they dragged their screaming victims by their hair to—no, no, not that.

What did the poor woman expect her to answer? 'Yes, *ma chère,* that is all quite normal; and there is more: there are whips, and iron stakes driven into the ground to which to tie spread-eagled, naked females. Thou wishest for my advice? Don't wait until the turnkeys have raped thee, become the warden's mistress while thou still hast the chance.'

She dropped the letter and covered her face with her hands. She did not hear the door, or the soft footsteps of the little girl who crept into the room. She nearly jumped when her wrist was touched by a small, cold hand. It was Mary, in her nightgown.

"What is it, *ma chouchou?* Canst thou not sleep?"

The child solemnly shook her head. It was these infernal long evenings; darkness fell so much later in Lancashire in summer than it did in France. But Tonton had always had trouble falling asleep too, summer nights. "Come," she said, "let me take thee back to bed. If thou art good, I'll tell thee a story." She bent down to pick up the child.

"When is Mother coming back?"

"She won't be long now. Another week or two and she'll be home again."

"I want Mother to come back."

"Of course thou dost. We all do. But she is doing something truly wonderful, something that one day will make you all very proud."

A harsh, hostile voice asked, "Will it?" She looked up and there stood Meg, the oldest girl, in the doorway, her young, unformed face, normally so bland and pretty, twisted in an unpleasant scowl.

"Hast thou come to fetch her?" Henrietta asked.

"I have. Come, Mary." Meg came into the room briskly, without tenderness.

"No!" Henrietta cried, despite herself. She could not stand unkindness at that moment. "Let me take her, I was about to."

"Why should you, now I'm here?"

"Because I want a word with thee. Wait here a moment, I'll be right back."

Hastily Henrietta gathered the child in her arms and carried her out into the passage and to her room. "I know I promised to tell thee a story, Mary," she whispered as they went, "but I have to talk to Meg. Wilt thou forgive me? I'll tell thee a long story tomorrow."

"Very well." It sounded resigned. How sad that one had to learn so early that life was full of disappointments and long stretches of loneliness. She put the child to bed, bent over her to kiss her and went to close the curtains more tightly; but the day lingered on the ceiling.

Meg was waiting for her by the window. She looked defiant, but it was a good sign to find her there at all. Margaret Fell had written on her long mother's list, *"Meg: At the age when she is trying to find her own feet and can do so only by being angry with her elders."*

"Tell me, Meg," she asked, "why art thou so angry with thy mother?"

The girl gazed at her somberly, or tried to; it was difficult with those exquisite features.

"Art thou not proud of what she is doing?"

Meg shrugged her shoulders and turned away to the window. "As far as I can see, all she has done is desert her own family. For the sake of what? Some criminal children in prison. What does she expect to achieve? Cancel their punishment? I can't see anything admirable in that."

"What she is doing is to fight inhumanity where she met it. We all meet inhumanity in our lives; the world, alas, is full of it. Few of us have the courage to do something about it; she had. And, believe me, it takes courage."

"I can't see anything courageous about it," the girl said surlily. "What courage does it need to go and mope around some moppets in prison if your husband is its highest authority? She even took a chaperone."

"Who was promptly raped the very first day."

"What?" The child swung around and faced her, her face blank with astonishment.

"Forgive me, I should not have said that. She was attacked by a man in the dungeons the first day. Luckily the worst was avoided. But keep this to thyself, I pray thee."

"But that—that is terrible! That's—what did Father do?"

What had the judge done? What could he do? "I don't know, dear. It is part of the reality of prison: women walking the corridors unescorted are likely to be attacked. He cannot change that."

"But the entire prison system is under his rule! Surely he can do something!"

How much the child had to learn! "My dear, even a man in the highest position of authority can do nothing about what happens in dungeons a hundred feet below the ground unless he goes there himself. That is exactly what thy mother is trying to show us: there is no point condemning evil and expecting others to fight it. Unless we are prepared to fight it ourselves, we had better turn away and hold our tongues. Which is what most people do."

"Why did Mother have to take Ann?" the girl cried suddenly. "Why could she not have taken *me?* We're the same age!"

It took Henrietta a moment to recover; then she said laconically, "And have thee raped instead of her?"

"I wish to be a Quaker too! Why should I be protected from something that Ann is supposed to be strong enough to face?"

Henrietta sighed, and picked up the letter. "Let me read this to thee." The girl sat down with her back to the lingering day. The nightingale sang exultantly behind her. Henrietta flipped open her lorgnette. "There are things in here that I am sure she did not intend for her children's ears, but then, thou art Meg Fell now, nobody's child but God's. Or dost thou object to God's parenthood too?"

"I do not object to anyone's parenthood," the girl replied. "Pray read the letter."

"Dearly beloved Friend. I am sitting here in the straw of the children's dungeon, by the cot of an eleven-year-old boy, his ankles chained together, due to be hanged nine days from now. I am writing to thee because I promised him I would be with him in his last moments, and I am afraid that, when the time comes, my strength will fail."

The nightingale sang in the darkening garden while she read. She did not look at the girl until she had finished the last line, *"So, although thou and I once doubted the validity of miracles, here I am with nothing left to hope for except that, at the last moment, God in His love and mercy may save this child's life, for the sake of His own martyred Son, Whose presence is about us tonight."*

There was silence; then the girl asked, "Will He?"

"What?"

"Save the little boy's life?"

"I doubt it." She folded the letter.

"Then, what will she have achieved? What good will she have done those children? When she leaves, all they will know, those who aren't dead by then, is that a woman came, spoiled them for a month and left. I doubt whether I would, in their place, be thankful for her visit."

Henrietta Best smiled wearily. Maybe this was why mankind had made so little progress, despite the shining examples of prophets and saints and Christ Himself. Each generation had to fight the same battle all over again, the battle for its own soul. She suddenly felt tired.

"And Ann Traylor? Is she going to be at the execution too?" It sounded peevish; perhaps because of the nightingale.

"I have no idea," Henrietta replied. "For all I know, Ann Traylor may have her own battle to fight."

"Exactly," the girl said with unsentimental briskness. "As I see it, Mother is fighting her own battle."

"If she is, dear, she is doing it for all of us."

"That," the girl said pertly, "I will have to see. Good night."

"Good night, Meg. Do look in on Mary if thou wilt. If she is still awake, I promised her I'd tell her a story."

"Don't worry," the girl said. "I'll tell her one myself." She opened the door and hesitated as if to say more. Henrietta braced herself, but, mercifully, she thought better of it, closed the door and was gone.

The nightingale sang exultantly in the garden, enamored of the night. Or of its own sound? What substance was there to the sermon she had given the child, other than the need to vent her own emotions, just as the nightingale was doing?

She rose and leaned against the window post, gazing at the darkening garden. The letter had been sent eight days ago. That meant the little boy in chains was to be hanged tomorrow. She wondered whether they had the same barbaric custom here as in France of serving those they were about to kill a three-course meal, with wine and liqueur; whether they would use the trap or push him off a tripod. How could a man live with himself after hanging a child? How could he face his own children afterward? For all she knew, the men who had killed her own children had gone back to their families without feeling shame or guilt, for they had done it not as men, but as soldiers. God, she should stop this.

She took a deep breath of the evening air. Come, think of something else. Think of the girl. She had sounded brutal and insensitive; other daughters would have admired their mother and her noble efforts, all she could think about, the silly goose, was what her rival Ann Traylor was doing.

As a matter of fact, what *was* Ann doing? There was little mention of her in the letter. *"Ann and my husband are faithfully trying to cope with the constant stream of requests that emanates from this dungeon."*

Suddenly some duenna's instinct smelled a rat. A lonely, middle-aged man, a restless, passionate girl . . .

'Voyons! Tout de même!' She closed the window, shutting out the nightingale. She would never be a Quaker.

CHAPTER FIVE

S ING," the boy whispered in the darkness.
"But that will wake up the others."
"Sing softly."

She sang softly, the way she now did every night. They had been lying like this, side by side in the darkness on her narrow cot with his head on her shoulder, every night for weeks. As she sang the slow melody of "The Andalusian Merchant," she hoped he would fall asleep; he usually did. But as she reached the end she braced herself for the questions: 'Will it hurt?' 'Will I go to heaven?'

She had expected those questions a long time ago; it was unnatural that he had not referred with a word to what was to happen on the morrow, as if he were not even aware of it. He must be thinking about it; he was an intelligent boy, aware of everything that went on around him. It was unbelievable that he could simply ignore it, behaving as if he had a whole life ahead of him which they would spend in each other's company. That was what bothered her most: the passionate, desperate way in which, since that walk on the walls, he now clung to her.

She waited for the first question, dreading it and at the same time yearning to broach the subject at last. They could not live through these last hours without referring to it at all. She had decided she would not talk about Jesus waiting for him, but someone he had known, someone he had loved. Surely there must be someone. Then she would ask him to prepare a place for her, to wait for her to join him, so as to take away some of his terror of the dark, of oblivion. But he was sound asleep again, relaxed and at peace. Did he not realize that in a few hours' time . . . ?

Even now she could not bring herself to confront the gruesome thing about to be done to him. The moment she felt that horror encroaching upon her she thought of the miracle God would perform through her, the power He would grant her to stop this evil. She forced herself to think: 'Have faith, believe, believe in Him, *believe!*' What she should do, she told herself, was sleep, gather strength for the ordeal ahead, were it only to bridge the hours that separated her from the moment when . . . Oh, my God!

Suddenly she was overcome by a sorrow so deep, so overwhelming that she knew it would paralyze her if she gave in to it. It seemed as though a mound of grief had been building up behind her and was about to crush her. She must not give in to it! She must not fail him!

She should not stay like this, staring in the darkness, his head on her shoulder, his small body pressed against hers; she should get up and move about, kneel, pray, for God's sake, pray! She tried to disengage herself without waking him up, but he gripped her tightly; a few minutes later she tried again, and this time he let her go. Cautiously she slid out of his small embrace and rose. The darkness was so deep that she could not see the outline of the cot; but she knew the small world in which she lived by now. She found by touch the edge of the screen, crossed the emptiness beyond with her hands outstretched until she felt the bars and pulled herself against them. "God," she prayed, "God, have mercy, God, give me strength, God, God, have mercy, for Jesus' sake, have mercy on him, have mercy, mercy . . ." She was startled by a sudden whisper. "Ma'am?"

It came from the passage, close by; whoever it was must have found his way in the dark.

"Who is it?"

"Hush! It's me, the jailer who carried him down from the wall, remember?"

"Oh—oh, yes . . . What is it you want?"

"Hush," the voice urged, closer. "I've come to give you this."

"What?"

"Where's your hand? Put it through the bars."

She obeyed; something cold touched her fingers.

"Have you got it? Take it, it's a bottle."

She took it. "What is it for?" she breathed.

"Give that to him in the morning, ma'am, after they bring his breakfast. When Mistress Fraley asks what he wants to drink, say lemonade, and when no one is looking pour this into it."

"Why? What is it?"

"Hush! It will make him drowsy, ma'am, so he won't really know what's going on."

"Oh . . . Are you sure that—"

The voice did not let her finish. "Yes, ma'am, yes!" it whispered urgently. "You give it to him! It's a great help, especially for children. But don't let anyone see it, don't tell anyone I gave it to you. It would go badly for me if they knew."

"Thank you," she said, trying to keep her voice calm and controlled. "Thank you very much. How very kind of you."

"There's one more thing, ma'am," the voice continued after a pause, as if he had been looking to see if someone were coming. "When Carter Barton comes to weigh the boy, take him aside and ask him to make it the long drop . . . Did you hear that, ma'am? The long drop."

"Y-yes," she whispered.

"It's important, ma'am, very important. Make sure you do."

"What is it?" She could not help herself, she had to ask.

"Never mind, ma'am, Carter will know what you mean. Just ask him to give the boy the long drop, he'll do it."

"But—but what *is* it?"

"Hush, ma'am, hush!" There was another silence; then the voice whispered, "Good luck."

"Thank . . . thank you."

She stood, the little bottle in her hand, her head against the bars. She tried to pray, to revive her certainty that she would save him through the power of the Lord, the way George had saved the girl in Derby. But she could not think coherently, she could only feel an inexpressible sorrow, not just for Henry, for all of them. God, she prayed, God, mercy, mercy . . .

But it was as if the only love in the universe she could call upon was her own, a faltering candle flame among the stars.

*   *   *

Justice John Sawrey did not sleep all night. He stayed up till the small hours preparing a document for Margaret Fell to sign; by the time he went to bed it was too late. He just lay there waiting for the dawn.

At first light he went to the window to see what sort of day it was going to be. The night before, Holly Stowe, whose gout forecast the weather, had announced there would be rain in the morning; to his relief, he saw the stars bright in the sky. He expected a large crowd; the crime had been notorious and the hanging of a child always attracted more people than other executions.

He lit the candle and dressed for the occasion. The prescribed garb for the sentencing judge was black hat with black plume, black cloak, black gloves, no ruffs or cuffs, black satin collar and turnovers. It was an uncomfortable costume and he would have preferred to put it on at the last moment, but he could not count on finding the opportunity to do so. Many magistrates and dignitaries were expected with their families; he should be on hand to welcome them and make sure they were given seats on the tribune according to their prominence. The common people would stand in the courtyard, early arrivals getting the best places.

When he looked out he heard the murmur of the waiting crowd; the first spectators had already gathered outside the gateway the night before. By the time the boy appeared on the scaffold, people would be packed in that courtyard as tightly as herrings in a cask, even in the gateway.

When the constable came to call him, he was fully dressed. "I suggest thou and Holly go down and ask the warden whether he can use your help. The gates will be opened any moment now."

"Holly is sick," the constable said. "His foot hurts something terrible. He has been moaning all night."

"In that case, leave him here. But do offer thyself to the warden. I want thee to keep an eye open for anyone from Ulverston. I want to know who they are, understood?"

The constable grunted.

With the aid of a candle, John Sawrey descended the narrow stairway to the corridor leading to the warden's office. When he opened the door he found the prison officials already present, despite the early hour. Both Farragut and the hunchback were there with their turnkeys, all of them dressed in black, Farragut wearing the red seal of his rank. Dr. Withers was lowering his surplice over his head when Sawrey came in; he went on talking inside the garment while the others bowed respectfully, the hunchback sweeping his hat.

"Mumble mumble mumble," Dr. Withers muttered, "I feel we should, for this hour is inconducive to . . ." His head appeared, white-haired and noble; alerted by the respectful silence, he saw who had joined them. "Ah, good morning!" he croaked, shrugging down the surplice with a feminine wriggle of his hips. "As I was saying, why must we have these executions at such an inconvenient hour? Is there any particular reason why they must be at sunup?"

"I always thought it had something to do with religion," Sawrey remarked coolly.

"Oh? I'm only a simple priest, but if the reason for this ungodly hour were divinely inspired, I would know about it, wouldn't I? Personally, I find—"

"When are the gates to be opened?" Sawrey asked, ignoring him.

"At the usual time, one hour before," the warden replied.

"As we are expecting a large crowd, would it not be wise to make it earlier?"

"As you wish, Your Honor. But we should wait until Carter Barton is through with his preparations."

"Has he arrived yet?"

"He is checking the gallows now. He has been here for some time."

"As have most of us, if I may say so!" Dr. Withers interjected. "For these infernal hangings a man has to be up at midnight! At least I have, if I want to prepare the soul of my prisoner properly."

"I'll have a word with him," Sawrey said, going to the door.

"Wait a minute! Are you going down? I'm coming with you!" Dr. Withers hitched up his skirts.

"I'd rather you did not," Sawrey answered. "I wish to have a word with Mistress Fell before you all start milling around down there. Pray, give me at least a quarter hour."

"But what about my preparing the boy's soul?" Withers cried. "Should we not be concerned with that, rather than fritter—"

"You have had a month in which to prepare his soul, sir; if you haven't done so by now, one quarter hour is not going to make much difference."

Sawrey opened the door and entered the dark gateway. The crowd beyond the gates fell silent at his appearance; he ignored them and went to the courtyard, his steps echoing in the vault. The platform of the scaffold and the gibbet were outlined in the sky, where dawn had begun: a blue, translucent brightening of the darkness. As he looked up at the black rectangle of the scaffold, a square suddenly sprang open in it and with a rumble and a creaking jerk something heavy plummeted through and dangled, swinging, from a rope reaching into the sky. He climbed the ladder irritably. "Next time, give warning before dropping that sandbag!" he cried to the silhouette at the foot of the gallows. "I was nearly knocked over!"

"Beg pardon, Your Honor," the mournful voice of the executioner answered. "It's the short drop; the bag is nearly ten feet off the ground."

"How was I to know?" Sawrey asked peevishly, crawling onto the platform. Of course the man was right. "And don't add any weights!" When there was a large crowd it was always best to give them their money's worth. For the execution to be over in a flash would be bad policy, people would feel deprived of something, especially Mistress Jones. But there were others who would disguise their ghoulish disappointment as righteous indignation if the boy failed to struggle for at least five minutes before giving up the ghost.

"Don't worry, Your Honor, I'll see it's done right," the shadow replied mournfully.

"I know thou wilt, I'm counting on thee." Carter Barton was, despite his bovine bulk, an executioner of subtlety; he could calculate the death struggle of his victim down to a few seconds. "Hast thou weighed the boy yet?"

"Not yet, Your Honor. I was just about to go down. The carpenter is waiting."

"Ah? I haven't seen him."

"He's somewhere under here. You must have missed him in the dark."

"Listen, Carter: I must have a word with Mistress Fell before anyone else turns up, I want to make sure she understands what's happening so there shall be no hitches. Give me a few minutes before turning up; I am going down now."

"Very good, Your Honor."

"And remember, I count on thee. An example, that's what we need."

"Don't fret, Your Honor. I'll see to it."

"Very good, Carter. Thou art a good man; thy work will be properly rewarded. The widow of the boy's victim is going to be there. I am sure she will not fail to express her appreciation."

The giant must have arrived at the same conclusion himself, or he would not have been here this early. It was customary for the next of kin of the victim to reward the executioner for the emotional satisfaction he was able to give them. A good hangman could achieve different effects by the type of noose, the length of rope, the weights attached to the legs. Some executioners were sentimental when it came to children; they made the rope so long and weighted the little body so heavily that the head was severed by the drop. In Carter Barton's case there was no need for worry; the man had the insensitivity of an ox.

When Sawrey's silhouette appeared in the gateway again, the crowd at the other end fell silent once more and watched him as he made his way to the door of the dungeons. They knew there was nothing happening yet, but after a long night of inactivity his mere appearance represented the beginning of the excitement. The guard at the doorway saluted him; he too was garbed for the occasion, in his case a black hood with two slits for eyes and a black capulet that reached halfway down his chest. Traditionally, the guard at the door followed immediately behind the prisoner, to prod him with a halberd should he stumble on his way up.

"Is Mistress Fraley down there yet?"

"I haven't seen her, Your Honor, I've just come on."

"If she happens by, tell her to wait until I'm through down there. I will call her."

"Very good, Your Honor." Respectfully, the man opened the door for him and handed him a lantern. "You'll need that on your way down, sir."

"Oh, yes, of course."

The stench, when he stepped inside, was stifling, and he felt the tension even as he entered; on the day of a hanging the excitement of the unseen felons in their cages was always tangible. It sent a prickly feeling down his spine; he started down, wondering what would be his fate if someone, in a moment like this, were to open all doors and let them out. He was sure that they would tear him apart, rip out his heart and eat it, as had been reported on one occasion in Brixton prison in London. Suddenly, with an ear-splitting squeal, a black thing carrying a human figure came plummeting down from above and streaked past, nearly knocking him off his feet with the turbulence it caused in the stagnant air. It was Mistress Fraley's cart; she must already have been inside when the guard came on duty. He hurried down to catch her before she started pushing the cart down the corridor where the lunatics were screaming and banging.

"Oh, Your Honor! You gave me quite a fright!" she cried when he tapped her shoulder.

"I'll thank thee to make thy descent more dignified next time," he said tersely. "On an occasion like this, it does not show the proper respect to come plummeting out of the sky like a witch on a broomstick."

"Oh—very good, Your Honor."

"Pray do not intrude for the next ten minutes." Without waiting for her reply, he turned away and entered the corridor. The crazy women went berserk at the sight of him; they shrieked and spat, slamming their chains against the bars in demented fury. He did not deign to look at them, but stayed well out of reach of their grasping claws as he passed. Their frenzied rage expressed the mood of the prison; as he approached the children's cell, he could almost feel the hatred swirl around him.

The moment he appeared at the gate, Margaret Fell came wading toward him through the straw to open the door. The gate swung inward, the screeching of its hinges inaudible because of the deafening din of the madwomen next door. "Oh, Mr. Sawrey, good morning! How kind of you to be so early!" She shouted it, almost gaily.

It would have been a bewildering welcome, had he not spent all this time on the study of the Quaker mentality. Her mind no longer had any secrets from him; after identifying with her through endless pages of clerical prose, he knew the exact meaning of every gesture, every word. His plan had worked to perfection; she would not be so calm and serene unless she were absolutely convinced that there would be no execution because God would prevent the hanging of the small, stoop-shouldered boy who sat crouched on the edge of the field bed, watching him anxiously with his one, unblinking eye.

After a glance at the boy, she asked in a whisper, "Mr. Sawrey, would it be possible for me to come with him?"

"Of course. That can be arranged."

"You're so kind."

"Don't mention it, Madam; it's the smallest of favors. I am not sure I can allow you to mount the scaffold itself, though. That, I'm afraid, is the prerogative of his spiritual adviser."

"Oh—but surely Dr. Withers is not his spiritual adviser. He has barely seen the child."

"I know, Madam. But, alas . . ."

"Can I not be his spiritual adviser?"

He did not betray that this was what he had intended her to ask. "I'm afraid that only a priest can be considered as such, Madam."

She hesitated, then she said, with a nervous smile, "Well, Mr. Sawrey, I know this has been a point of interest to you for some time; the moment has come to tell you that I am a priest, according to my religious beliefs."

"I beg your pardon?"

"Come, Mr. Sawrey, we do not have time for niceties! You know I am a Quaker, and I suspect that you know enough about Quakers by now to realize that to us every member is a minister. On that basis I now request that I stay with Henry to the end."

"You realize, Madam, that this will have to be acknowledged officially?" he asked quietly.

"How do you mean?"

"I cannot grant permission as a personal favor; the occasion is a public one. I cannot do so unless I am presented with a document stating that you, Margaret Fell, spouse of Chief Justice Fell of Swarthmoor Hall in the Parish of Ulverston, solemnly declare in the presence of sworn witnesses that you are a member of the religious sect known as the Children of the Light, commonly called Quakers, and consider yourself to be a minister of said religious movement, duly accredited. It must also state that the prisoner Henry Jones is a member in good standing of said religious movement, and that he has expressed the desire that a minister of his faith shall assist him in his last moments for the sake of his soul."

Her eyes searched his. "Do you by any chance have the document with you?"

He felt a quiver of excitement that he suppressed at once. He reached inside his sleeve and produced the small roll of parchment he had prepared overnight. "It will need your signature in the place I have indicated. Read it at your ease and hand it to Dr. Withers when he comes; I'll take care of the witnesses' signatures."

She took the parchment; he noticed that her hand shook, she must realize fully the consequences of signing this document. It was a moment toward which he had worked with total dedication for a long time; perhaps that was why it came as an anti-climax.

"Let me give you a quick summary of this morning's procedure as from now," he said.

She put her hand on his arm. It was an oddly gentle gesture at that particular moment. "Don't, Mr. Sawrey. I know it all."

"You know that Master Barton and the carpenter will be turning up in a moment or so? That a special meal will be served by Mistress Fraley?"

"Yes, I—I do know it all." For the first time she betrayed a strain. Her face looked haggard and deeply lined. No wonder: she was about to put an end to herself by trying to obstruct the execution. It was essential that she should do so in plain view of everyone in the courtyard. "I need not warn you, Madam," he said, "that any interference with the proceedings on your part would constitute an obstruction of justice, which is a felony."

She had been about to turn away; his words stopped her. "I know," she said, with a smile. She was, despite her delusion, an admirable woman.

With a clatter of wheels, accompanied by the shrieks of the lunatics, Mistress Fraley and her cart drew near too soon.

"Madam, I wish you Godspeed," he said, bowing. He gave Mistress Fraley a mortifying look; as he walked away, he overheard, despite the screaming of the wretches in the adjoining cell, the old harridan's question. "What'll he drink? Beer? Porter? Cider?" and Margaret Fell's answer, "No, thank you, Mistress Fraley. He'll have lemonade." She said it as if she were placing an order in a tavern; he could not help marveling at her fortitude.

*   *   *

The meal Mistress Fraley brought for Henry was unlike any meal Margaret had ever been served in prison. There were scrambled eggs and sausages and kippers and oat cakes, tartlets and scones and strawberry preserves and a dish full of butter. There was far too much for one person, let alone a small boy; but she received it with gratitude and complimented the housekeeper on her care. When Mistress Fraley had left, Margaret asked Henry, "Well, love, which of this wouldst thou like first?"

He swallowed, looked at the array of dishes, the delicacies spread out for him, and shook his head.

She felt herself weaken, but closed her eyes for a moment and thought, 'Hold on, hold on!' She smiled and asked, "Art thou sure?

Look at these sausages. Don't they look tasty? Jody! Take thy hand away!" The other children crowded around the glorious treats and could, of course, hardly resist helping themselves, but she had to make sure first that Henry wanted none of it. "Thou art sure, love?" she insisted.

He gave her a look that made her flinch inwardly. She patted his shoulder and said, "Very well. Shall we give it to the others?"

He nodded quickly.

"All right, children. Let's start with the cakes . . . Robert . . . Harry . . . No, Jody! Don't touch before I give it to thee!" She always forgot the child could not hear; she pushed the grabbing little hand away.

The sharing out of the meal among the others gave her a brief respite from the decision, over which she had agonized all night, whether to give Henry the potion from the jailer. She was still trying to make up her mind when, unexpectedly because of the noise of the children, she discovered two men standing at the gate. One was huge and sinister, dressed in a black tight-fitting suit and a hood that covered his shoulders, the other was small and elderly, in ordinary laborer's clothes. "Yes?" she asked shakily; she thought for a moment that they had already come to fetch him.

"We have come to have a look at the boy, ma'am," the huge man said. His voice was slow and mournful.

"Oh—I see . . . Are you Mr. Barton?"

"Yes, ma'am. And this is Saul MacDougal, the carpenter. Would you let us in, pray?"

"Oh—oh, certainly." She fumbled for her key, tearing a button off her dress in her haste to take it out. She tried to insert the key into the lock through the bars, but her hand shook so that she could not find the keyhole. The carpenter took it from her and opened the lock. The hinges screeched; the huge man stooped as he entered. "We won't take a moment ma'am," he said. "Is this the boy?"

All she could do was nod. She watched, hands tightly folded, as the big man went to Henry, touched his shoulder and said, "Just stand up for a moment, laddie. I'm not going to do anything, just stand up for a moment."

Henry obeyed fearfully; suddenly the man stooped, picked him up in his arms and lifted him off the ground. She cried, "No!" and dashed forward, but the man put him down again.

"It's all right, ma'am," he said. "I just wanted to find out how much he weighed."

"Oh, God . . . !" She knew she should be brave and calm and not show any emotion, but it was impossible. She put her arms around Henry and pressed him against her; he hid his face against her chest. As they stood there, stricken with horror, the carpenter approached, took a length of twine out of his pocket and measured Henry with it, behind his back, and tied a knot in the twine. "That's all, ma'am," he said. "You go and eat, there's plenty of time yet."

The men turned to go; she cried, "Mr. Barton!"

He stood still and turned around. "Yes, ma'am?"

"Could I . . . could I have a word with you? In private . . ."

The man frowned, his dull eyes looked at her uncomprehendingly.

"Come, Henry, come, my dear; just sit here for a moment, I'll be right back." She took the child to the bed and sat him down; then she turned to the carpenter. "Mr. MacDougal—would you mind? Just one moment, while I speak with Mr. Barton?"

"Yes, ma'am," the carpenter said. "I'll be right outside, Carter."

When he had gone, she took the big man's arm to guide him as far away from Henry as possible. His arm felt huge and alien, like part of some large animal. When they stood by the wall, close together, she looked up at him and whispered, "Mr. Barton, in the name of God, I pray you . . ." She could not help it, tears were running down her face.

"Yes, ma'am?"

Go for that of God in him, she thought, go for that of God. "Mr. Carter, Friend," she whispered, "I have a great service to ask thee, not for myself but for—for Christ's sake. Give Henry the—the long drop, please." Although she could only guess at the meaning of the words, she had barely been able to bring them out. She was overcome with despair; like her acceptance of the potion, it seemed a surrender.

He took a long time to answer. She realized that he was of two minds; she pleaded, whispering, "Friend Carter, I pray thee, he is so little, so afraid . . ." Suddenly she could not hold up any longer. She slumped forward, her head against the chest of the stranger, and wept as she felt all her firmness and certainty dissolve within her. Then a hand touched her shoulder and the mournful voice grumbled, "Very well, ma'am. I'll see to it. Bear up now, ma'am. It's best to be jolly. It helps them, you know."

"Yes—yes, Mr. Carter, Friend, yes . . ."

She managed to detach herself from him and groped for her kerchief in her apron. She wiped her eyes, saying, "Well, that's very nice. That's very nice of you, Mr. Carter, sir. We are obliged. See you anon . . ." It was idiotic babble, a frantic effort to undo the harm she had done in letting Henry see her weep.

"That's all right, ma'am," the mournful voice grumbled. "Take it easy now, there's plenty of time. Goodbye, laddie."

"'Bye, sir . . ." Henry's voice was high and tight. He sat, shoulders hunched, knees together, on the edge of the bed.

The carpenter locked the gate and handed her the key. She said with forced gaiety, "Goodbye, gentlemen! Goodbye, and thank you!" She watched them until they were out of sight, then she turned around, knowing she must be calm now, and jolly. But she could not help herself, she rushed to fetch the pitcher of lemonade. To her horror, she found it empty. "Who has taken this? Who of you has taken this?" she cried, her voice shrill.

The children froze, she had never spoken to them like this before. They gaped at her, mouths full, tartlets and sausages in their hands.

Robert, the oldest, murmured, "She got it," nodding at Jody. The little deaf-mute sat, oblivious of what had happened, happily drinking from the beaker. Margaret dashed for it, crying, "Give here!" but managed to control herself and not to tear the beaker from the child's grasp. Poor mite, she could not know. "Jody, this is Henry's," she said slowly and clearly, kissed the child's forehead and gently took the half-empty beaker away. She went to the shelf where she had hidden the bottle and poured its contents into the rest of the lemonade. She had nothing to stir it with, so she used her finger as she took it to Henry, who was watching her anxiously. "Here, sweeting, here, this is for thee."

He shook his head.

"Henry, please! Please drink it! Believe me, thou *must* drink it, thou *must,* please!"

He watched her tensely, his eye was full of fear and understanding.

"Do it for me," she whispered. He looked at the beaker, and took it. Holding her breath, her hand on her chest, she watched him as he drank; when he had finished, she closed her eyes and felt herself sway on her feet. Be jolly, be jolly! She smiled at him through her tears and asked, "Well? How did that taste?" It was a foolish question; her voice sounded shrill and unnatural.

He looked at her calmly, with an expression on his face that chilled her. 'God,' she thought, 'God, mercy.' Then, suddenly calm and firm, she said, "Come, let's thou and I have meeting, shall we? We need a moment with God." She knelt by the side of the cot, her back to the others, folded her hands, closed her eyes and bent her head. After a moment she felt him get up and kneel beside her. 'God,' she thought, at the end of her strength, 'help us, help us, we are failing.'

She waited for that of God to rise within her and bless her with that indescribable feeling of peace and light. But it was as if God, if He indeed dwelt within her, was as failing in strength as she. She sat there, slowly sinking in the awareness that she had no power. She had nothing; all she could muster within herself was powerless love, the candle flame among the stars. But that too flickered and died. She sat for a few moments in total darkness, total despair. Then something touched her hand.

It was Henry's, resting on hers. 'God,' she thought, 'mercy, mercy, for Thy Son's sake, Thy Son who died on the cross, Thy Child who cried for His Father.' And suddenly there it was, rising within her: stillness, peace, light.

But it was not from within her that the stillness rose. It was communicated to her by the small, cold hand resting on hers. Was that possible? Could it be that God had granted Henry peace? She glanced at him. He sat as she did, head bent, eyes closed; a lock of his blond hair that she had washed the night before hung down, silky and shining, on his forehead.

She wondered whether he knew, the way he had known when he had given her the flower, and she asked herself who, in the shadow of death, was sustaining the other.

*   *   *

When Ann Traylor came out of the inn, she found, to her relief, Thomas Fell waiting for her. The sight of his familiar figure in the pale light of dawn moved her so much that she needed all her self-control not to rush toward him and embrace him in gratitude. For she had been haunted all night by visions of the boy doomed to die at sunrise. It was not for him that she agonized but for Margaret Fell, who had spent the night with the child and who must now be suffering untold torments. She would have to go to her, stay with her and the other children while the execution took place in the courtyard; but the prospect was so harrowing that she might well have taken flight but for this dear, dear man. Her relief and gratitude were such that she greeted him with a cry, "Thomas!" that rang through the courtyard.

He took her arm and said, "I thought I'd come and escort thee. There's likely to be a crowd outside the gate. Thou wouldst have difficulty fighting thy way through."

"A crowd? At this hour?"

"Oh, yes. The ghouls who come to witness this kind of thing turn up early. Come, let's go."

They walked in silence, arm in arm, down the deserted streets toward the castle.

"I think we had better take the side entrance," he said as they approached the somber building. "I have the key."

"Can I get to the dungeons from there?"

"Art thou sure thou shouldst go down?"

"It's the least I can do. It must be terrible for her, right now. I can hardly face it myself."

"I wonder whether thou wouldst be of much help to her at this point."

"Why not?"

"It may be easier for her to be alone with the other children. Thy presence might make it more difficult for her to master her feelings while the execution is taking place upstairs."

"But she won't know when it happens, will she? Surely she can't hear what goes on in the courtyard that far down?"

"Oh, yes, she'll know exactly. I don't know how they do it, but all prisoners know. Maybe it is whispered from cell to cell; maybe they hear the crowd. The well of the stairs acts as an ear to the prison. It's uncanny, but they always know exactly. Quite often they shout, curses and the like; at the moment of execution itself, they usually go berserk."

She dared not confide to him the horror that filled her at his description. They crossed the square; there, at the foot of the walls of the castle, was a huge mass of people, indistinct in the semi-darkness, gathered at the gate.

"There are so many of them already . . ."

"This way, if we want to avoid them."

They made their way, almost furtively, around the square.

"I wish thou wouldst think it over, dear Ann," he said as they entered a dark portico in the wall. "Believe me, it would be best to leave her be."

"Oh, I pray thee! Don't make me feel more uncertain!"

"Forgive me." He pressed her arm. There was a click, a door creaked. "This way."

She entered the twilight of a long corridor, vaguely lit by a row of windows blue with the dawn. At the far end was a crescent of yellow light; as they approached it, she realized it was a door standing ajar. It led to the warden's office, bright with the light of candles and lanterns, full of people: Warden Farragut, the hunchback Hathaway, Dr. Withers. A slight man stood with his back to the door; when he turned around, she saw Justice Sawrey.

As they entered, silence fell. Outside, the waiting crowd murmured and laughed. There was a tension in the air that gave Ann the shivers.

"Good morning," Justice Sawrey said, smiling. "You are just in time, we are about to admit the crowd. May I invite you to join me on the tribune?"

Thomas replied, "No, thank you, Sawrey. Miss Traylor would like to be with my wife during the next hour. Could she be escorted there before you open the gates?"

Sawrey exchanged a look with the warden, who said, "Sorry, Miss Traylor, but that is not advisable under the circumstances. Why not wait until later? In an hour's time it will all be over."

"Oh, but I must!" she exclaimed, forcefully because of the lamentable relief she felt at his refusal.

Justice Sawrey said, "Young lady, it is the warden's decision, and I concur. The procession will be on its way in a few moments. You would not care to run into that, would you, now?"

Thomas took her arm and said, "If Justice Sawrey feels he cannot grant permission, that is all there is to it. He is provost during Hilary, this is his responsibility. Come, let me take you to chambers."

"You won't be able to see anything from there," Sawrey said.

"It is not our intention to be spectators," Thomas replied dryly. Without waiting for Sawrey's comment, he took her arm and guided her back into the corridor.

When they were out of earshot, she whispered, "I feel awful! Please! Is there no other way . . . ?"

"Hush." He pressed her arm. "Believe me, this is for the best. Thou hast no idea of the mood the prison is in right now. We'll go upstairs and wait until it is over; thou canst go to her the moment the crowd has left."

She protested no longer. Quickly they walked down the echoing corridor.

* * *

Margaret knew they were coming because of an angry noise of many voices that started far away and steadily increased. Finally the women next door began to scream and curse and slam their chains against the bars; outside the gate a small procession of men in black appeared, led by Dr. Withers in a white surplice, carrying a prayerbook. She saw the wardens, Farragut and Hathaway, and two jailers, each carrying a halberd. The children, who until that moment had been playing in the straw oblivious of the impending horror, backed away into the corner. There they sat huddled close together, watching the men.

"Pray open up," Dr. Withers said.

She looked at Henry; he lay asleep on the cot. She waded toward the gate, took out the key and handed it to the priest. While he was opening the gate, she went to Henry's side and put her arm protectively around his head without touching him, for she did not want to wake him up. A tremor took hold of her; she tried to fight it by praying silently, 'God, please help, God, help, please help, please help . . .' She opened her eyes and saw the priest and the wardens standing at the foot of the cot.

"Is—is this . . . ?" she asked softly, so as not to frighten Henry.

"I'm afraid so, ma'am." Warden Farragut's voice was kind, but he looked ominous in his black clothes. "I'm afraid you will have to wake him up, ma'am."

She closed her eyes for a moment, trying to draw strength from within herself, from God. Then she gently shook the boy's shoulder and called, "Henry? Henry, wake up . . . Henry, it's—it's time . . ." He stirred, but he did not open his eye.

"Henry? Henry, it's—it's time . . ." He could not be roused; the potion must have been stronger than she thought. Should she not have given him the whole bottle? In her anguish she looked at the two jailers with the halberds, seeking reassurance from the one who had brought it to her; but in their black hoods she could not recognize who it had been.

"Has this child been drugged?" Dr. Withers asked angrily.

Suddenly she was overcome by panic; all she could do was nod.

"Mistress Fell!" the old man cried. "Don't you know that is a punishable offense, ma'am? An obstruction of justice?"

"Oh, please, please, for the sake of God!" she cried, falling on her knees in front of him. In her panic, she threw her arms around his legs. She knelt there for a moment, not knowing what to do. But she must not give in! She must not give in to this weakness! She must stay with Henry, help him, be there. "Oh, God," she whispered. "Help me, help me . . ."

"He must be conscious for the sake of his soul!" the voice above her cried. "If we want him to be ready for the grace of Christ's atonement, he must repent before he dies! He cannot repent if he is unconscious!"

"Oh, please, please!" she pleaded, looking up at the angry face, the inhuman eyes. "He *has* repented, I know he has, he told me himself, he told me only last night, he *has* repented, he is very, very sorry, can't we now just let him be?"

"I cannot administer Holy Communion if he is unable to give the proper responses!"

"It will not be necessary," she said, "he—I—let me show you . . ." She rose, fetched the roll of parchment from the shelf in the wall and handed it to him. "I have asked Mr. Sawrey to allow me to be his spiritual adviser," she said. "It's all here in this document."

Dr. Withers gazed into her eyes for a moment, puzzled; then he unrolled the parchment and read it. As he did so, he shook his head. Her heart sank. He rolled it up again and asked, "Are you aware of the consequences of this document to you, personally?"

She nodded.

"May I ask what possessed you to do this?"

She had been ready to plead with him; to find herself attacked was more than she could bear. "For God's sake!" she cried in desperation. *"Look* at him!"

The old man looked at the child asleep on the cot. For a few moments no one moved. In the distance, far away, was a murmur, as of many people.

"I cannot allow you to take my place," he said. "All I am prepared to do is let you share my ministry. I will do my duty by him; after the final Lord's Prayer you can do your part, whatever that may be. You will have to give the signal."

"Signal?"

"To the hangman. When you are through, just nod at him so he knows he can go about his business."

She stared at him, aghast. "I cannot! I . . ." Then she remembered that it would not be necessary. By then she would have cried out, that of God in her would have fused with—with that of God in—in . . . She was overcome by giddiness. She closed her eyes and thought, 'God, please! Please, God, keep me going, please, please . . .'

"Well, let's get him on his feet and on his way," she heard Dr. Withers say. A hand touched her shoulder; it was Warden Farragut. "Would you waken him, ma'am?" he asked; there was kindness in his eyes. Dr. Withers had turned away, she saw him stoop through the gate.

"Must I?" she whispered.

"Pardon?"

"Must we wake him up? I'll carry him! He is very light . . ."

Warden Farragut looked at her, then he asked, "Why don't you stay down here with the children, ma'am? It would be much better for everyone."

"Oh, please, please!" Panic overwhelmed her again. "Please don't make me do that! I'll—I'll wake him."

She bent over the boy, but the warden held her back. "Let me do that, ma'am." He bent over Henry; she stood by, eyes closed, not wanting to see; then the warden's voice said, "Here he is, ma'am."

She opened her eyes. There was Henry, asleep in the warden's arms; he was holding him for her to take over. "Oh, thank you! Thank you, Mr. Farragut!" she whispered. She took the slight, sleeping body in her arms, put its head on her shoulder and whispered, "All's well, all's well, it's me . . ." Then she looked at the warden and nodded.

He touched his hat and went out the gate. She followed him; the chain, dangling from the ankles of the sleeping child, clanked against her as she walked.

In the gate she turned around and said to the children huddled in the corner, as cheerfully as she could, "Now be good, children! I won't be long, I—" Their faces were so knowing that she turned away.

Outside, the procession had formed again, led by Dr. Withers. Between Warden Farragut and Warden Hathaway was a space; she understood it was meant for her. She joined them; they started to move. The moment they did so, Dr. Withers began to read from his Bible, *"The Lord is my shepherd, I shall not want . . ."*

The sound of his voice was drowned by the cries of the lunatic women as they passed. "Goodbye!" they shouted. "Goodbye, Henry! Goodbye!"

Their cries were so loud that she was certain he would wake up, but he did not stir. He was getting heavier; she wondered whether her strength would reach all the way up those steps. Again she prayed for help; but she had done it so often that morning that her plea began to lose conviction. She must concentrate on the power of the Lord now, so she would be able to muster it when the moment came. She knew she would; George had done it, she would be able to do it too.

The cries of the lunatics receded as they continued down the passage toward the landing. When they arrived there, Dr. Withers' chanting voice was drowned again, this time by a sudden, huge sound of many voices crying, "Goodbye! Goodbye!" It came from the passages; never had they sounded so near.

She stumbled on the first step; behind her, Warden Farragut asked in a whisper, "Ma'am, shall I carry him?"

"No, no, Mr. Farragut," she replied, "I can manage."

As she hoisted herself onto the next step, Henry suddenly seemed to become lighter. It took her a moment to realize that Warden Hathaway, in front of her, had picked up the chain.

Slowly the procession mounted the stairs. When they reached the second landing, a new chorus of voices joined the unseen prisoners' cries of farewell. "Goodbye, Henry! Goodbye! Goodbye!"

Concentrating on carrying the child, she continued to climb the steps to the courtyard.

* * *

"What is that?" Ann Traylor asked. She was standing at the window of the judges' chambers. The hubbub of the crowd in the courtyard had suddenly ceased and a subterranean murmur become audible, that seemed to be drawing closer.

"Those are the other prisoners, saying farewell," Thomas Fell beside her replied. "They always do. It means the boy is on his way."

From where they stood they could not see the scaffold, but he knew from experience that the sounds would be explicit enough. As the farewell of the voices from the dungeons, projected by the well of the stairs, grew in volume, he was overcome by the emotion that always beset him during the last minutes before an execution, a mixture of melancholy and carnal excitement. It was not obscene; it was caused by a sudden awareness of his own evanescence; touched by the shadow of death, his flesh responded with a feverish lust for life. Had he remembered this, he would not have suggested that they wait here, for now the lust for life concentrated on the girl by his side.

"Oh, my God," she whispered, as the sound grew louder until it seemed to reverberate in the courtyard. "I don't know if I can stand this . . ."

He put his arm around her shoulders protectively. "If thou wilt, we'll close the window. But I believe it best if we do not." He tried to mask with solicitousness his urge to feel her soft, young body against him.

The sacrificial lamb was about to emerge into the open; the crowd began to growl in anticipation. He felt her shiver when suddenly there came from below a terrifying roar.

"Here they come," he said.

* * *

When Margaret Fell stepped out into the courtyard, she was, for a moment, confused. The procession was greeted by hundreds of jeering, catcalling voices that seemed to come from all directions; the gateway was packed with people. The wall of shouting faces, distorted with hatred, unnerved her; the determination that had sustained her until that moment dropped away; suddenly she knew: I cannot do it, I cannot live through this. As if he sensed her faltering, Warden Farragut sustained her. His face seemed to be the only human face in this nightmare of distorted, screaming masks. When the crowd in the courtyard saw them, the shouts and screams increased. She arrived at the bottom of a ladder, looked up and saw a platform where a ghastly gibbet waited.

Mr. Barton climbed the ladder, then Dr. Withers; when her turn came, she knew she could never do it alone, so she let Mr. Farragut take Henry. She climbed the ladder first, awkwardly because of her skirts; when she was halfway, Mr. Barton's head and shoulders appeared in the sky, and he stretched out a hand toward her. He pulled her onto the scaffold; she looked over the edge and saw Mr. Farragut climbing toward her, Henry on his shoulder. She knelt to receive him and was helped back onto her feet by Mr. Barton, who guided her to a spot underneath the gibbet.

The screams, curses, howls of hatred from the crowd filled her with terror. They were incomprehensible to her; it was as if she were surrounded by another species. Under the onslaught of their rage the men on the scaffold seemed like friends: Mr. Barton, Dr. Withers, the two wardens, the halberdiers. She looked from one to the other pleadingly as the shrieks and the howls increased; one raucous hoarse voice nearby went on bawling monotonously, "Let him dance, Barton! Let him dance, Barton! Let him dance, Barton!"

"He will have to kneel now, ma'am," a voice said in her ear. It was Mr. Barton.

"He can't!" she cried. "For God's sake, Mr. Barton, he can't!" Then the boy in her arms stirred. He lifted his head and looked around him, his arm around her neck. She knelt down to put him on his feet; a black-gloved hand came to her aid, lifting the chain so he would not step on it and stumble; it was Warden Hathaway.

The moment the child stood on his feet, the crowd shrieked and booed with redoubled fury. Dr. Withers' voice intoned solemnly, "Henry Jones, I am here to serve thee Holy Communion, so thou mayest partake in the blood and the body of Christ, who died for thee on the cross to grant thee now, in thy last moments, peace and the certainty of life eternal."

She whispered, "All's well, Henry, all's well, love; kneel, love, kneel, all's well, Christ is with thee."

She said it without thinking, but when Henry knelt and she put her arm around his shoulders, it was as if indeed they had been joined by a mysterious Presence. It seemed to fill her with an inexpressible tenderness, even toward the howling animals in the courtyard. She was filled with hope, until she realized that the tenderness totally disarmed her; she could not possibly rise in the power of the Lord and cry "Stop!"

"God," she prayed, as Henry sipped the wine that was Christ's blood, "God, save him, save him . . ."

The voice of Dr. Withers intoned, "Let us pray! *Our Father, which art in heaven . . .*"

The crowd fell silent.

*   *   *

"What is happening?" Ann asked, startled by the silence. It seemed more ominous than the howling of the crowd had been.

"The priest has started the Lord's Prayer," Thomas replied. "Look, some people down there are praying with him. Grotesque, isn't it? One moment they scream, 'Let him dance,' the next they mumble, 'even as we forgive those that trespass against us.'"

"And after this . . . ?"

"The boy's chains will be removed, to make him lighter. He will be asked if he has a last wish before meeting the eternal God. Then the game begins."

"Game?"

"I'm afraid it's going to be a long-drawn-out business."

"I thought it was all over very quickly!"

"I'm afraid not. There are many variations possible, and in this instance . . ."

Some unspeakable evil seemed to reach out to her from the mass of people below, waiting to see a child tortured to death. It seemed to give a sudden humanity to her sinful love for the man beside her. Suddenly she felt an overwhelming need for his sheltering arms. "Thomas," she whispered, "I . . . I think I'm going to faint . . ." It was the only way; he would never have taken the lead.

She swayed on her feet, and it was not all make-believe. She heard him say, "Ann . . . Ann!"

There were his arms. Outside the window, the crowd resumed its howling.

* * *

When the hangman put the noose over Henry's head, Margaret Fell's strength gave out. This should have been the moment for her to unleash the power of the Lord, but though she opened her mouth, her voice failed her. Her last strength dissolved when she saw Mr. Barton, after arranging the rope around Henry's neck, pat him on the shoulder.

Until that moment all her actions had been based on the assumption that she would stop the execution by submitting herself to God's power. Once again, she tried to do so in desperation, as Henry stood tethered by the neck to the gibbet above him. 'God!' she thought, with all her might, all her soul, 'God! Use me! Use me!'

What arose from the deepest resources of her soul was that indiscriminate tenderness, which squandered itself by reaching out to everybody: the wardens, the halberdiers, Dr. Withers, Mr. Barton, the howling crowd. Once more she tried to cry, '*Stop! In the name of God!*' but again her voice failed her. She thought despairingly, 'Take *me,* God, take *me,* take *me,* take *me* instead, take *me,* please, please take *me* . . .' The indiscriminate tenderness went flowing out from her to the people in the courtyard, rendering her powerless.

"Henry Jones," Dr. Withers intoned over the roar of the crowd. "Before thou goest to meet the Eternal God, hast thou a last wish to impart to me, thy shepherd?"

The tumult died down for a moment; voices cried: "Last wish! Let's hear his last wish!"

'God!' she thought, collapsing on her knees beside the child, her face in her hands, 'Christ, Jesus, mercy! Mercy . . . !'

The voice of Dr. Withers asked, "What was that thee said, Henry?"

Henry's small voice replied softly, "Sing it."

Her heart stopped. No, not this . . .

"Sing what, Henry?" Dr. Withers asked.

She found the strength to say, "I know what he means. He wants me to sing for him."

The courtyard became silent; everyone was straining to hear what was being said on the scaffold, but she did not notice it; she was conscious only of the priest. She asked, "May I?"

Dr. Withers nodded.

She had failed as an instrument of God; she must not fail this dying child. She took a deep breath and sang, *"The Andalusian Merchant that returns . . ."* Her voice, high and tremulous, caused the hush in the courtyard to deepen. *"Laden with cochineal and chi-china— dish . . ."* Her throat contracted; she was unable to utter another sound; her hands were folded in speechless supplication.

Suddenly a voice sang far away, *"Reports in Spain how fiercely Fogo burns."* It was a voice from the dungeons. Other voices joined in from the depths, *"In an ocean full of flying fishes. These things are wondrous . . ."*

As the sound of the singing voices grew, she seemed to be filled with light. Something immense, inexpressible revealed itself to her with overwhelming reality.

"Yet more wondrous I," the voices sang from the deep, *"whose heart with fear doth freeze, with love doth fry . . ."*

Someone in the courtyard cried, "Barton! Now!"

There was a crash as of a door slamming, a rush of wind. She opened her eyes and saw she was kneeling beside a hole in the floor, in which swung a perpendicular rope. Her heart cried out in unbearable sorrow, but the Light raised her to her feet. She stretched out her arms toward the sky. 'Henry . . .' It was as if she were reaching him up to God.

So real was the Presence as she stood there, arms stretched out toward the sky, that everyone in the courtyard stood motionless. Even in the gateway and on the square no one stirred, except the starlings.

* * *

On the tribune, Justice John Sawrey sat thunderstruck. It was incredible; somehow the woman had managed to change the bloodthirsty crowd around the gallows into a Quaker meeting. He himself was unable to shake the spell until she lowered her arms, turned to the hangman, shook him by the hand, then did the same to Dr. Withers. He knew the meaning of that handshake: she had broken meeting.

As the crowd, with a murmur of voices, awoke from her witchery, Sawrey made his way to the scaffold. It had all gone so quickly that he had not realized exactly what was happening; one moment the boy had been kneeling on the hatch, the next he was gone, as if swallowed up by the shadows under the scaffold.

He knew what had happened when he saw the remains. The boy had been deliberately, expertly, beheaded. Dr. Withers came down the ladder and joined him, to his astonishment, to give him back the roll of parchment. "I have no use for this, Sawrey. I'll leave it to you to dispose of it."

"No—no use?" Sawrey stammered. "What do you mean? It is her confession!"

"It would be if she had signed it," Dr. Withers retorted. "Carpenter! Close that coffin before Mistress Fell comes down! We are not savages!"

This was outrageous! There could be no doubt: Withers had deliberately refused to make the woman sign her declaration.

Hathaway, the hunchback, came down the ladder; Sawrey confronted him the moment he stepped down. "What the devil does this mean? Why did Barton not take the chains off? Why did he give him the long drop?"

"I don't know, Your Honor," Hathaway said. "Ask him."

When Barton finally came down, Sawrey was beside himself. "That was a pitiful job!" he cried, the moment the man appeared on the ladder. "What the devil dost thou mean, acting against my instructions?"

The giant stopped and looked down on him mournfully.

"Dost thou realize that this will cost thee thy job?"

Barton shrugged his shoulders and climbed down.

"God's fish!" Sawrey cried, losing control. "I'll see to it that thou payest for this! I'll report thee to the regents! I'll . . ." He might as well have shouted at the back of a receding bull.

The next one to come down was the warden himself.

"Mr. Farragut! I demand an explanation! What went on up there? Who told Barton to act against my instructions? Why was I forced to give the command myself, from the tribune?!"

The warden, normally a shrewd man who never lost sight of his own interest, looked at him with distaste and said, "You saw it for yourself, Your Honor."

"What I saw was a mercy hanging!" he cried. "I demand an explanation! What got into you people?"

The warden looked as if he were contemplating an answer; then he said, "Your Honor, if you do not understand after seeing it with your own eyes, nobody can explain it to you." He turned away.

"I want that boy's skull!" Sawrey shrieked, incoherent with rage. "I want it on my desk tonight!" He turned to the carpenter and saw that the coffin had already been closed. "What dost thou mean, closing that coffin before having had my instructions?"

The old man looked up with badly acted innocence. "Beg pardon, Your Honor?"

"I want that coffin opened and the head sent down to the kitchen! Is that understood?" He became conscious of people watching, realized that he was making a spectacle of himself and turned away, in time to see somebody climbing up the ladder instead of down: the red-haired maid.

Where was Thomas Fell? Why should only the maid appear, not the husband with whom she had been closeted in chambers?

He set out to fight his way through the crowd.

*   *   *

The moment the woman's voice had started to sing in the courtyard, Thomas Fell had recognized it. He had broken free from Ann's embrace and rushed to a window in the adjoining room, from there he had watched, thunderstruck, the happenings on the scaffold. Ann had joined him; he became aware of her presence only as she ran off when Margaret shook hands with the hangman and the priest.

He knew that he should have gone to the aid of his wife himself, but, stricken by an odd, weary awe, he had returned to the judges' chambers to slump down in the chair behind the desk. There he was sitting, head in hands, when the door opened.

He looked up; it was Sawrey. For a moment he thought something had happened to Margaret, for Sawrey's face was as white as a sheet; but his voice was as pedantic as ever when he said, "Well, I trust that now you will be good enough to take Madam home?"

It was not a question to put to one's superior, not in that tone. "Have a care, Sawrey," he said. "Control yourself."

His authority had effect. Sawrey asked in a more reasonable manner, "Surely you could hear up here what was happening?"

"I saw it from the window next door. Where is she now?"

"On the scaffold!" Sawrey cried, with a return of outrage. "She *must* come down! I cannot allow this!"

Thomas eyed the irate man calmly. His outrage gave him a feeling of kinship. Whatever the gratification was that the man must derive from witnessing executions, this time Margaret had robbed him of it. Both of them had been robbed of the consummation of a private passion by her indomitable willfulness. "Well," he said, rising, "let's go and have a look at what is going on down there."

"Can you give me the assurance that Mistress Fell will now leave this prison?" Sawrey asked.

For a moment Thomas considered a sharp retort; then he relaxed. "I am sure she will," he said. "She must be shattered. All her life she has been used only to gentleness. Come."

*   *   *

When Ann Traylor climbed onto the scaffold, Margaret Fell was sitting at the foot of the gallows, her hands in her lap, eyes closed. Her face looked worse in the sunlight than it had in the twilight of the dungeon; its waxy pallor made the sores and scabs that transfigured it look hideous. Her hair, matted and discolored by the medication against lice, was like that of any woman prisoner after a long incarceration; there was nothing left of the willful rich lady who had refused to accept defeat. She was defeated; she needed help.

Ann sat down beside her and put an arm around her shoulders. Margaret Fell opened her eyes and said, "Ann! I failed! He is dead!"

"Hush," Ann said, as to a child. "Thou art exhausted, Margaret. Thou hast done the impossible. Now thou must go home and rest."

"But I can't! I cannot leave the children! They will think they have been abandoned . . ."

"Hush. Don't fret about them; I'll go to them and stay until thou canst arrange for someone else to relieve me."

It looked as if the exhausted woman wanted to protest; then she closed her eyes and slumped against her. So they sat when Thomas Fell joined them.

"Come, dear heart," he said, touching Margaret's shoulder. "It is time for us to go."

"I must wait," Margaret whispered. "I want to be there when they take him down."

"He has been taken down," Thomas said. "The coffin has been taken away. It is finished."

He helped her down the ladder. Ann watched from above as they walked to the gateway. He had his arm around her, half carrying her.

Well—there he went. She wondered why she felt no pain, no grief at the thought that probably she would never set eyes on Thomas Fell again. She tried to feel the sadness she should be feeling, but she could feel nothing; all she remembered at that moment was Thomas sitting opposite her at table, saying, "At that time you still felt you understood my wife?" Suddenly she thought of her diary. God! If anyone found that! She must get back to the inn for her things as soon as possible!

"Miss Traylor? Are you still up there?"

It was Warden Farragut, at the bottom of the ladder. He had changed from his mourning clothes into his usual suit; his white-plumed hat looked rakish, seen from above.

"Yes, Mr. Farragut?"

"Anything wrong? Can you come down by yourself?"

"Certainly." She turned around to descend, then she stepped back and called, "Would you, pray, look away, sir?"

"Oh! Of course, forgive me." He turned around.

She climbed down; it was scarier than going up had been. There came a moment when she hesitated, about to call for his help; then she felt his hands around her waist. His voice said, surprisingly close, "That's it, Miss Traylor. You are there."

She let herself be lifted down and turned to face him with a smile. "Thank you, sir."

"Your servant. May I call a chaise for you?"

"I am concerned about the children. I should go down first, before I return to the inn to fetch my things."

"Your—things?" They had entered the gateway; he stood still.

She gave him her most ravishing smile. "I am taking Mistress Fell's place."

"But, my dear young lady—!"

It was the beginning of a fatherly speech. She had had enough of fatherly speeches. "What do you take us for?" she asked. "Sentimental flibbertigibbets?"

"But, my dear Miss Traylor—"

"What would you have us do? Occupy ourselves with those poor mites for one month, and then leave them to sink back into the amorph—morph—well, whatever? Once we started, we knew we would have to see it through to the end."

"What end, for mercy's sake?! These children are in here for years, some of them for life!"

"Nonsense," she said with growing self-confidence. "You can't lock up children for life."

"But, my dear young woman! They were sentenced in a court of law!"

"Well? Sentences can be remitted, can't they? We'll continue to treat them as children until you men have come to recognize them as such. Have you any children yourself?"

"Yes, but—"

"If they are naughty, do you lock them up in a dark cupboard?"

"I certainly do! But that is beside—"

"For life?"

He looked at her; his exasperation became resignation. "Very well. Do I call a guard to escort you down?"

"Your children have a father to forgive them after they have cried their hearts out in a cupboard for an hour. All the poor mites downstairs had was Mistress Fraley and Dr. Withers; now they have us. We treat them the way you treat your own when they have been up to pranks."

"Like murder? Armed robbery? Assault?"

She looked at him with a new authority. "Shame on us all for letting them sink that deep," she said.

"All right, Miss Traylor." He smiled. "Let's continue this discussion some other time. Like tonight? Would it be agreeable to you if I came to see you before going off duty, in case you need any assistance?"

She remembered the warden of Derby jail who had moved into George Fox's cell. She did not think he had done so on the same considerations she read in Mr. Farragut's eyes. But what could he get up to in a cell with six children? Five, now. She felt a pang of sadness. "Very well, Mr. Farragut, that would be kind of you." She picked up her skirt, to enter the door to the dungeons. "If you would be so kind, you might ask the maid at the Three Swans to pack my affairs in my valise and bring it to me." The maid could be trusted with the diary; she could not read. Would he open it before bringing it down? She had to take the risk.

"It will be a privilege," he said roguishly. "How long do you expect to be with us, Miss Traylor?"

"Until some other lady turns up to relieve me."

"Some *other* lady?" She left him standing with his mouth open.

At the top of the well of the stairs a first doubt hit her. The stench and the darkness suddenly gave her the same sense of foreboding as when she had gone down the first time. Again she felt with certainty that a grim fate awaited her down there, that if she did this she would set foot on a road to suffering from which there would be no return. As she stood staring down into the pit, a voice said behind her, "Don't you want a lantern, miss?" It was the guard.

"Thank you," she said, took the lantern and started down.

Her trepidation was gone. She felt calm and confident as she descended the stone steps. There was a difference from last time: this time she went down by choice.

On the third landing a voice hailed her from one of the dark passages. "Miss? Quaker miss?"

She swallowed, then answered calmly, "Yes?"

"Are you going back to the children, miss?"

"Yes."

"Would you be willing to teach some others?"

"Which others?"

"Ours," the voice said. "Here they come."

There was a shuffling sound in the darkness; alarmed, she tried to shine her lantern into the dark cavity of the passage. In the feeble light three, four, six children appeared, dressed in rags, their eyes glistening the way the others' had the first time she had seen them by the light of her lantern. How had they got out? They must be debtors' children, who were allowed to roam.

"Hello," she said shakily.

The children, close together, eyed her without expression. Something seemed to open up inside her, a feeling of tenderness she had never experienced before. She went toward the dismal little figures in the lantern light and said, "Well, isn't that a surprise! Come, let's go down. You'll see how happy the others will be! We are going to learn how to write, and how to read, and how to do sums, and we are going to sing songs for the whole of Lancaster Castle. What do you think of that?"

None of them answered; they just stared at her, the way the others had stared, like cornered rats. She remembered how long it had taken them to accept her. "I am called Ann," she said. "You'll have to tell me your names downstairs in the schoolroom. Shall we go? Come, let me carry thee." She picked up the smallest girl, despite the child's filthy appearance, and was shocked to feel how light she was for her size. "Here," she said, holding out the lantern to the tallest boy. "We're going all the way down."

The boy, after a moment's hesitation, took the lantern and started down the steps gingerly.

"God bless you, miss!" the voice called from the darkness. Before she had been able to answer, other voices joined from all directions, calling, "God bless you! God bless, Quaker miss! God bless!"

She did not know which were voices and which echoes.

CHAPTER SIX

THAT evening, John Sawrey did something he had not done for a long time. He told the constable to get him a bottle of sack, and when it was delivered to him he locked himself in his pie-shaped little room, determined to get drunk.

The sense of defeat had settled into a dull rage that, he knew from experience, could only be laid to rest if he either vented it on somebody else or knocked himself out with sack. He sat down in his chair, put his feet on the bed, and glowered at the slit-eyed window, bottle in one hand, glass in the other.

Margaret Fell had been too nimble for him. There he was, despite all solemn studies of the faith and the practice of Quakers, despite the beautiful document in which she had been supposed to incriminate herself—if he had not cried out to Carter Barton, there would not have been any hanging at all that day and the disaster would have been complete. Now, although some of the notables had complained, their wives had obviously received another kind of thrill which left them with enough gossip to last them through the summer. Even Mistress Jones, the widow of the boy's victim, had scurried out of the courtyard in an uncharacteristically subdued manner, avoiding him.

The point that rankled most was: How had Margaret Fell done it? How had she managed to throw a spell over hardened men like Dr. Withers and Barton? Had Barton expected to have his palm crossed with gold by Chief Justice Fell? No, incredible as it might seem, the dim-witted ox had done himself irreparable harm just to please her. And Dr. Withers? Only a week or so before, he had stood in the office downstairs foaming with rage about Quakers, swearing that if ever he could lay his hands on the Fell woman and prove she was a Quakeress, he would have her in chains; now he had conspired with her to suppress incriminating evidence. She was a witch, all right, a Quaker witch. And she had slipped through his fingers.

He was slouched in his chair, grimly nursing his rage, when there was a knock. "Yes?"

Somebody tried the door; he remembered he had locked it. He went to open it; Warden Farragut came in, hat in hand.

"Yes, Farragut, what is it?"

"Your Honor, I have news for you. Mistress Fell's maid has moved in."

"Moved in?"

"With the children, instead of her mistress."

"And you permitted it?"

"Your Honor, I do not have the authority to stop her. That's why I came to see you. What do I do?"

He was about to shout, "Throw her out, of course!" when the thought hit him: Hold it; Margaret Fell is putting her plan into operation. "Did the girl say how long she intends to stay?"

"Yes, Your Honor. Until someone turns up to relieve her."

"Thank you. I'll think about it."

"Very well, Your Honor."

His mood changed. Gone were the rage, the thoughts of defeat and failure. The woman was going to mobilize others. That meant she would be back. Only by her example could she persuade other women.

The bottle was three quarters empty and his spirits were high when there was another knock at the door.

"Come in!"

It was Carter Barton, huge and melancholy. "Your Honor, here it is." He held out a package wrapped in burlap.

"What is that?"

"The skull, sir."

"Oh—all right. Put it there, on the bed."

"Yes, Your Honor." The man put the package on the bed and shambled out of the room.

He rose unsteadily, went to the bed, opened the burlap and let the contents roll out. There were two parts; they had not attached the lower jaw. He glowered at the small white skull. Henry Jones. When the boy had appeared in court, his fate had already been sealed; General Evans, Mistress Jones' brother, had gone out of his way to suggest to him that there was no point in going too deeply into the whole affair; his late brother-in-law's reputation should not come under discussion during the trial. The trial had not taken more than twenty minutes: murder most foul, breach of trust, monstrous ingratitude, black cap, by the neck until dead, God have mercy on thy soul.

The ghoulish little skull precipitated the maudlin phase of drunkenness. Gone were the high spirits, the broad grin at the darkening window; he slouched back to his chair and slumped in it. He was weak, he was vile. Vile, vile; John Sawrey, thou art vile. For all thou knowest, it might have been Christ. Judas, that's who thou art. Judas Iscariot.

He pondered over the thought. Judas must have been a man like himself: brooding, turned inward; pity so little was known about him. Pity everybody had done nothing for thousands of years but spit at the mere mention of his name. Thirty pieces of silver, betrayed his Master, vile, vile, Judas Iscariot, thou art vile. But had Judas done his dark deed only for a paltry sum of money? Ah! The darkness of the human soul! What had driven Judas? What drove John Sawrey, who would not rest until Margaret Fell lay in front of him as Henry Jones lay now: a skull freshly boiled in the basement? Why, for God's sake, why? Ambition? Thirty pieces of silver? Judas had hanged himself after having done his foul deed; yet by that deed he had saved mankind.

Without him there would have been no atonement. Without Judas there would have been no crucifixion, no supreme sacrifice, no hope for mankind until the end of time. Judas was more important than any of the other Disciples; they had fallen asleep at the gate, and blundered about cutting off people's ears, and when it came to their Master's tortured death they had been nowhere to be seen. God, who in His unfathomable wisdom had ordained His Son to be murdered on the cross, had needed Judas. If Judas at the last moment had said, "No! I can't do it!" then God would have been forced to find Himself another.

He sat upright in his chair, with the drunken feeling of having touched upon a great secret. Judas had acted upon God's instructions. *That* was the dark power which drove him: God. God's plan for the world demanded that he, John Sawrey, do this foul deed: hunt down Margaret Fell and then stand, tears streaming down his face, among the crowd as she was nailed to the cross and raised screaming in the sky, where she would die in torment.

Suddenly, drunkenly, he burst into tears, his head in his hands. "Oh, Margaret, Margaret! Why must I destroy thee?"

But, though his grief was real, he knew that he would get her in the end.

* * *

In their bedchamber at the inn, Thomas Fell was helping his wife bathe by sponging her back for her. It moved him deeply seeing her there in the hip bath the maids had brought in, so fragile, so white, so utterly exhausted by the mad demands her indomitable will had imposed upon her.

He gently sponged her back with the insect bites and the mysterious weals. What a supreme effort it must have been for her, with her gentle upbringing and delicate constitution! He was full of admiration and affection; never had he felt more tenderly disposed toward her, never before had she seemed so hungry for his protection. It was as if she had emerged from a frightening dream.

He had arranged for supper to be served in their rooms. Candles, wine, he had even chosen the flowers. The maids knocked and asked if they could set the table; while behind the closed door the dishes and the tumblers were set out with a discreet tinkling of silver and crystal, he rubbed her down and produced the white, downy robe he had bought for her at the same time he bought Ann Traylor's riding cloak. It had been an infantile gesture of contrition; now he was happy he had done so. She was delighted with the robe; her eyes, large in the pallid face sharpened by deprivation, seemed to light up. He helped her put it on.

When he heard the outer door in the other room close, he led her in to see the table. The way she gazed at the candles, the silver, the crystal, the wine broke his heart. She gazed at the flowers, a bouquet of bright crimson tulips with sprigs of fern.

"Aren't they lovely?" he asked.

"Those are the colors the women should wear."

"Pardon?"

"It would prevent their being assaulted."

"Which women?"

"The ones that will work in the prison. I wonder how Ann is faring."

She rattled him for a moment; then he realized that she could not be expected to make the transition from one world to the other in a few hours. He had to be prepared for her harking back to those days and nights for a while yet.

The maids came in to serve supper. He had chosen light and tempting food and selected an innocent little claret to smooth out her tension. She did not touch the food or sip the wine, but she appeared to relax as he kept up an inconsequential chatter. She looked so tranquil as she sat there gazing at the candle flames that she jolted him again when she said suddenly, "I killed him."

"Excuse me?"

"My love pervaded the prison and tenderized all concerned; but they hanged him. Lovingly."

"Dear heart, I have no idea what thou art talking about."

"When George Fox saved the girl in Derby, he was not loving or tender. He cried, 'Stop!' and they stopped. I made everybody, including the hangman, lovable, but George Fox saved her life."

He sighed. "Dear heart, thou wilt have to enlighten me first. What is this business about George Fox in Derby?"

"He prevented a woman from being hanged by shouting 'Stop!' at the moment they were about to spring the trap door." She closed her eyes.

He observed her with a beginning of coldness. What was this tall story? He had never heard such nonsense in his life. Damn George Fox! But he should humor her. "Tell me a little more. Were there any witnesses? Was it a public execution?"

Her eyes, as she gazed at the candle flames, were filling with tears. Poor dear, she was shattered. Should he allow her to go on with this, or take her in his arms?

"The girl in Derby struggled and screamed and fought to the last. But I drugged Henry and took all the fight out of him, until he let them do with him what they wanted. I took away his will to live." The tears were running down her face now. She looked anguished at that moment, piteous.

Averting his eyes, he picked up his glass. "I can understand thou art distressed about this, dear heart, but suppose thou hadst stopped the execution this morning; what would have happened? Another execution would have been ordered and measures would have been taken that this time there would be no interference. Even if the death sentence had been commuted to life imprisonment, what would have been his future? He would have spent the rest of his days in prison, half blind. No wonder the child lacked the will to live." He put his hand on hers. "Frankly, dearest, I consider what thou didst a greater miracle than whatever Mr. Fox may have done in Derby. Thou didst prevail upon vicious and vindictive men to help a child they had planned to torture to death. The boy was executed in as swift and humane a manner as possible. That is what *I* would call a miracle. Admittedly, I may lack faith in not accepting the other one."

Her face seemed to soften. "George and I had an argument about this. I said that I considered miracles to be harmful, because only certain people could perform them. I could not accept that God would manifest Himself only to His chosen."

"I think the secret simply is, dear heart," he said kindly, "that thou art a woman. Mr. Fox's yelled command and thy tenderness are worlds apart."

"But the boy is dead."

"Indeed. The boy is dead because he had no will to live. Our Savior's determination to have Himself crucified must have bewildered rational people too."

"It's no good," she said. "Whatever thou sayest, whatever anybody says, I know I have the blood of that child on my hands."

He looked at her with concern. Would she go on blaming herself for the rest of her life for not having performed a miracle? "Just as a matter of interest," he asked, "did Mr. Fox happen to know the young lady he saved? Was she a friend of his? Had he ever had conversation with her?"

"I don't know. Does it matter?"

"What bothers me about Mr. Fox's love for humanity is its impersonal nature. He loves love itself."

"That's what Henrietta used to say. I have never understood what troubled her so. I don't think it's true."

Suddenly he had had enough of honoring Mr. Fox on this particular night in their lives. "My dear, I am sure thou wilt go on blaming thyself for a long time. But do not expect me to agree with thee. I was there. I saw a courtyard full of people who until that moment had been no better than rabid animals turn into a crowd in prayer. I saw their faces when they left. I seriously believe that what thou didst will have a greater influence on their lives and their values than any magic trick Mr. Fox might have performed." She looked at him intently; it encouraged him to add, "I think it philosophically possible that there is such a thing as elemental goodness in the universe. If so, thou wert, during those moments on the scaffold, its incarnation. As such, thou hast given a lot of people hope. At least, that's what thou hast given me."

Suddenly she rose to her feet and came to him. She threw her arms around his neck, cried, "Oh, Tom . . . !" and broke down in his embrace.

As he sat there, gently stroking her hair, he was struck by the thought: Perhaps she is a saint. It gave him a sense of unfairness. What had he done to deserve this? For whether one lost one's wife to a lover or to saintliness, the result was the same.

"Oh, Tom, Tom," she sobbed, "I love thee so."

He kissed her hair and continued to stroke it soothingly as he felt the return of the old, familiar melancholy.

* * *

"No!" Thomas Fell cried angrily the next morning. "I will *not!* I have arrived at an age where I am no longer prepared to put up with sudden changes of plan and fickle decisions!"

"I am sorry," Margaret said coldly. "I have not arrived at that age yet." She poured herself another cup of tea, careful to keep up a front of determination, but she was ashamed of herself. How was it possible? Twenty-four hours after Henry's death she was having a row with her husband at the breakfast table, he in his nightshirt, she in the beautiful robe he had chosen with such care and tenderness. How odious, how degrading!

"Very well!" he said with black determination. "Give me one good reason. Just one!"

"I could give thee two if only thou wouldst give me the chance."

"Oh!" he cried, and there he went, stamping up and down again in his nightshirt, looking ridiculous and very angry.

"For one thing, I promised the children."

He turned on her. "Thou didst promise the children! And what about thy own children, whom we promised that thou wouldst return today? Who will be waiting anxiously, peering out of the window?"

"They will have to go on peering awhile longer," she said calmly. "The children in prison have been abandoned all their lives. I cannot walk away from them saying 'I'll be straight back' and never be seen again."

"Oh, great merciful Turk!" he cried. "And thy second reason?"

"Dear heart, in thy present mood . . ."

"The second reason! That's all I ask!"

"All right: Ann Traylor. Do we leave her there? All by herself in that dungeon, without a soul who cares about her except that leering warden?"

"Which warden?"

"Farragut. His name is Hyman. And, it seems to me, that is what he is after."

He burst into laughter, somewhat forced, she thought. "Oh, all right! I give up. Is thy family ever to see thee again?"

"Don't be foolish. But I must arrange for someone to take Ann's place."

"Who?"

"There must be plenty of women like myself who—"

"Heaven forbid! One per generation is enough!"

"Don't start shouting all over again," she said. "I plan to ask Henrietta Best."

"I forbid thee to do that! I happen to like the woman. I don't want her to end up in the cell with the lunatics!"

"Would it not rather be up to her to decide?"

He leaned his fists on the table and bent over to her, looking elderly and frail without his wig. She should really not subject him to these strains.

"Beloved Margaret," he said, "thou canst not go on arranging people's lives for them. Thou must at a given moment make up thy mind to arrange thy own."

"Well, that's what I am doing. I am trying to arrange it so that I can go home as soon as possible."

He looked at her with determination. "Thou art going home today."

"But, dear heart . . ."

"Thou art going home today! If somebody has to remain behind to watch over Ann Traylor, I will. I'll stay here until thou hast caught some unsuspecting female and trussed her and carried her into those dungeons like a pig. For that is the way it will have to be done; thou wilt not find any woman ready to go down there voluntarily, not one!"

"I know one."

"Henrietta Best! I told thee, thou art not—"

"Meg."

"Which Meg?"

"Our Meg. Mistress Best wrote she is distressed that I took Ann Traylor instead of her." She knew that this was going to bring the roof down. But he had to know sometime, it might as well be now.

"Meg?!" he cried, the beginning of the cave-in. "That *child?!*"

"She is the same age as Ann, dear heart, and a good deal stronger."

"Never! Never in a thousand years! I—"

A knock upon the door cut him short. "Yes! No!" He gathered up his nightshirt. "Who is it?"

"The maid, sir," a voice replied from the passage. "There's a lady here to see Mistress Fell."

"Which lady?"

"A Mistress Jones, sir."

"Jones?" He turned to her. "Do we know any Mistress Jones?"

"Not in Lancaster." Then, suddenly, it struck her. "Wait a minute!"

"Huh?"

"Out!" she said, rising. "Quick! Into the bedchamber! Out, out!" She went to the door.

"What the devil—"

"It's *she!*" She pushed him toward the bedroom door. "Henry's mother!"

"What—?"

"Quick!" She closed the door behind him, crossed the room and opened the one to the passage. The maid stepped aside as a dark woman in widow's weeds emerged from the shadows.

"Mistress Jones? Come in, please. Forgive me, I am not properly dressed to receive visitors."

"I fear I have come at an inappropriate hour," the woman said. "But I had to see you."

"Please come in." The woman entered; Maragaret closed the door and gestured to a chair. "Please sit down."

The woman had not heard her. She stood there, forbidding in her black mourning clothes, her gloved hands clasped in front of her.

"Will you not sit down?"

Again it seemed as if she had not heard. She was handsome in a dark, fiery way, but her face, stark white, seemed distorted by an inner tension that must be almost unbearable.

"Mistress Jones? Would you not sit down?"

Tears welled up in those black, burning eyes; the woman said in a strangled whisper, "I have not slept all night. I—I had to see you . . ." She opened her purse and rummaged in it, searching for a kerchief, with which she dabbed her eyes. Then she took a breath, tried to smile and continued, "You loved him, didn't you?"

The question startled Margaret, but she took care not to show it. "Yes," she said.

"So did I. Believe it or not, so did I." The haunted eyes searched hers with chilling intensity. "But yesterday I came to see him tortured. I had promised the hangman three louis if he protracted it as long as possible." She had to dab her eyes again with her kerchief; her hands were shaking.

"Come," Margaret said, putting an arm around the woman's shoulders to guide her to a chair. "Sit down."

But the other would not be budged; her body was rigid. "I . . . You know, I presume, what happened? Why—why Henry was hanged?"

"You mean, what he had done?"

The woman nodded stiffly in a supreme effort to hold back her tears.

"I never wanted to know."

"You—you did not *want* to?"

"No."

"Why not?"

"Because it did not matter to me."

"You did not know that he murdered his father?"

Margaret wondered how she could coax the poor woman out of whatever it was that held her in its grip. "I heard something of the sort," she said, "but I did not know the details. And I don't want to know them now."

"But that's why I came!" the woman cried, her voice taut and harsh. "I came to tell the truth!"

Margaret had no idea what the woman was about to say, but beyond the bedroom door her husband stood listening. She could not allow this desperate soul to incriminate herself before an eavesdropping judge. "Mistress Jones," she said firmly, "please pull yourself together. You must not do this. I beg you!"

"I must!" the other cried. "I must tell *somebody!* I cannot live with it any longer!" She seemed about to break down.

Margaret put her arm around the shoulders of the woman again

and said urgently, "What is done is done, Mistress Jones. Henry
is dead. Now you must find a way to give a sense to his death, not
bring about more pain, more suffering."

"A sense?" She sighed. "You are right. They are both dead. There
has been enough suffering. . . . May I help myself to some tea?"

"Oh—of course, certainly. Let me, please . . ." Margaret wondered
whether Thomas indeed had his ear to the door.

"You know," the woman said, when she sat stirring her tea, "I have
the strangest feeling. To me, he is not dead." She smiled nervously.
"Is it because I don't want to believe it? To me, he is everywhere I
go. Do you believe in such a thing?"

"I don't know," Margaret replied.

"I see." She took a sip of tea. Putting the cup down, she said, "You
talked about giving some sense to—to it all. What did you mean?"

Margaret was confused; she had said it on the spur of the moment.
Suddenly she was moved to say, "Why don't we find out by going into
meeting?"

"Meeting?"

"Let's sit for a moment in silence and ask God for guidance."

Without waiting for the other to agree, she closed her eyes, folded her
hands in her lap and sank at once, with practiced ease, into the stillness from which that of God would rise within her. This time, what
rose was an image: the cell, the children, Ann Traylor. How was
she? Who was going to replace her? She opened her eyes and gazed
at the woman opposite as she was struck by a preposterous thought.
It was impossible! No, this was nonsense . . .

As if she had felt Margaret's regard, the other looked up. "Well?"
she asked in a whisper.

"Would you be prepared to do what I did?"

"I beg your pardon?"

"Go into that prison to help the children who are locked up in
there? There is a girl with them now, from my household. She is young
and inexperienced. She cannot stay there for any length of time."

"I don't quite understand . . ."

"You know what we are doing, don't you, for those children? Henry
was one of them."

The woman stared at her in disbelief. "You . . . you can't be . . .
You mean *me?*"

"Why not? Don't you want to?"

"But, my dear! You have no idea what you are asking! I mean, you
don't know . . . you don't know me at all!"

"What is thy name?"

"Bronwen . . ."

"Let's go back into the silence, Bronwen. If He whispers in thy
thoughts that thou must go, go. Do not judge thyself, just open thyself
for His will to rise within thee. Thou wilt know, the moment thy head
is empty of all thoughts, judgments, wishes, except for the desire to
love Henry, wherever he may be."

She closed her eyes again to escape from the other's haunted stare, folded her hands, bent her head and prayed, 'God, Love, whatever Thou art—help us.'

* * *

They sat motionless and in silence for so long that Thomas Fell wondered what the devil was going on in there. Convinced that they must have left, he opened the door and peered in, to be met by his wife's solemn face.

"Pardon," he mumbled, and hastily retired. The devil, he thought, the devil!

He dressed briskly; as he put on his wig in front of the mirror, he muttered, "What next?"

Suddenly the connecting door opened and Margaret stuck her head in. "Tom?" she asked, in her visitor's voice. "Come and meet Mistress Jones. She is going to take Ann Traylor's place."

He blurted out in spite of himself, "She is *what!?*"

Margaret gave him a stern look and said loudly, "Maybe thou wouldst be kind enough to keep Mistress Jones company for a moment while I dress quickly? Then perhaps thou wouldst escort us to the castle, so I can show Mistress Jones the way? We do have the coach-and-pair here, don't we?"

"Yes, er—yes!" he replied loudly, beckoning her into the bed-chamber. She came in and closed the door behind her. "Go along," she whispered, "be a dear, keep her company. I won't be a moment."

"Thou art stark, raving mad!" he said in an outraged whisper. "Not *that* woman! I forbid it!"

"Why not?" Her expression told him that she had dug her heels in.

"I have only heard part," he whispered, "but enough to suspect that it was not the boy who brained her husband with a poker, but she!"

"Hush!"

"Hush?! That boy was sexually abused by the man, she must have come upon them, and—"

"Hush!" She faced him, eyes blazing. "Thou hast heard nothing! Chief Justices do not listen at doors."

"Well! Of all the—"

"Unless thou art prepared to disprove that, under oath, in court!"

He looked at her incredulously. "My God," he said, more baffled than outraged, "and there was I, thinking thou hadst become a saint!"

"Well, perhaps I am."

"That woman belongs in prison!" he cried, in a last effort to bring her to her senses.

"Well—that is where she is going." She swept past him and began to unbutton her robe. "Don't keep the poor woman sitting there all by herself! Go and tell her about our roses. Her husband and she grew roses. Tell her about ours."

He straightened his coat and opened the door.

Mistress Jones turned out to be a surprisingly handsome woman; his composure was not aided by the discovery that she and her husband had never dreamed of growing roses. Damn Margaret and her tricks! A saint indeed! Suddenly he decided this was ridiculous. He could not, as Chief Justice, allow a murderess to get away so she might help his wife in her imperious concern. "Tell me, Mistress Jones," he said casually. "It was you who killed your husband, was it not?"

She showed an enormous amount of pluck. She faced him calmly, with only a slight hardening of the look in her fierce black eyes; then she replied levelly, "As it happens, I did not. I tried to tell your wife this, but she did not think it important."

"Just as a matter of interest, what *did* happen?"

She rose. "Justice Fell," she said in a tone that reminded him of Margaret, "I agree with your wife. I think it no longer matters. I did not kill him. As to the rest, let us grant the dead their peace."

He rose too. "Mistress Jones, I am afraid that this is not quite satisfactory. I may have to ask you for a more explicit explanation, at your convenience."

"To what end? To drag my husband's private life through the courts? What purpose would that serve, other than an abstract notion of justice? He was a good man. A kind man, a loving man. None of us are perfect, are we?"

He bowed. If the damn woman did not want to make a confession, there was no way of forcing her. "Indeed, Madam. Some of us lie, some of us steal, others hang an innocent child."

She did not flinch. "How true." She picked up her gloves; then she added, "Have you ever been the victim of a rage, sir? A rage so black, so satanic, that you no longer knew what you were doing?"

How Welsh she was! "Can't say I have," he replied.

She started to pull on her gloves. "Your wife is a noble woman, sir. She gives one back one's belief that God is a God of mercy. Which, I gather, is not your concept of Him. An eye for an eye, a tooth for a tooth, is it not? I thought so too, until I saw her on the scaffold, helping my child face—" Suddenly, alarmingly, she collapsed on a chair and burst into tears.

"Mistress Jones! I beg you . . ." He heard the door open behind him and there was Margaret, gown open, hair loose. She rushed toward the sobbing woman, put her arms around her as if she were a child and gave him a look that made him back into the bedchamber and close the door softly.

*   *   *

When Margaret told Warden Farragut that Mistress Jones was to take Ann Traylor's place, the poor man looked so flabbergasted that, despite the solemnity of the occasion, she had trouble keeping her face straight. Obviously, he thought it an elaborate joke, but Bronwen Jones' authority was such that when she asked peremptorily for a lantern to take with her down into the dungeons, he instantly obliged.

He even offered to take the good ladies himself, but the fiery Bronwen said, "No, thank you, that won't be necessary."

As they descended into the dungeons, Bronwen Jones' reaction was interesting. Margaret wondered whether she herself had looked like that when she went down for the first time: tense, her eyes filled with horror. Her feeling of empathy with the woman grew. At the inn, the idea of her taking over had seemed grotesque; it became less so during their long, winding way to the lowest level. Whatever Bronwen Jones might be, she was obviously a strong and fearless woman who would be able to cope with any situation that might arise. Whether she would have the love that the children needed above all else was not so evident.

Finally they entered the dark passage and heard the madwomen squeal and slam their chains against the bars at their approach. In the lantern light, Bronwen Jones' face seemed hard and impassive as they passed the cage with the sad creatures who stretched out their claws toward them; on an impulse, Margaret shook a few of them by the hand, saying, "Good morning, good morning. How nice to see you again!" To her surprise, a few voices answered, "Welcome back! Nice to see thee, Maggie!" Others, alas, beyond the reach of humanity went berserk and made such a racket with their chains that a fight broke out. It was deeply distressing to see the demented creatures go for each other, pulling each other's hair, throwing each other down, lashing out at one another with their chains. She took Bronwen Jones' arm and pulled her past the piteous scene. When at last they reached the gate of the children's cell, she called, "Ann!" Then her mouth fell open.

In the light of four candles sat a large group of children, in pairs, each pair with a hornbook in front of them. Ann, looking prim and stern, was in the process of teaching them the alphabet. When she saw Margaret, she rose to open the door for her; five of the children leaped to their feet and came running toward her. For a few minutes they swarmed all over Margaret, tugging at her gown, throwing their arms around her neck, her legs, kissing her; she knelt in the straw and little Jody, hooting joyously, climbed onto her lap. The child was so tenacious that when she finally had freed herself of the others and was able to rise to her feet again, the little girl clung to her. So, with Jody in her arms, Margaret asked, "Who are these new ones?"

"Children from other floors," Ann explained calmly; she did not appear disturbed or distressed by her first night in prison. "Their parents are debtors; I was asked to include them in the class."

"How wonderful!" Margaret said. She went to the children, shook them by the hand, asked them for their names, looking with pity and concern at their sad, dirty faces, the vermin in their hair, their filthy rags. Then she realized that she had not introduced her new companion. "Ann, this is Mistress Jones, Henry's—"

Bronwen Jones was in no condition to be introduced. She stood with her hands in front of her face, shoulders heaving. Margaret had forgotten the impact the sight of the children had on someone who saw them for the first time; to her, the dungeon looked so clean and neat and the straw so fresh that, foolishly, she had expected to be complimented on it. But her sense of relief was profound. Bronwen Jones would come to love the children just as she did, and that, she now knew, was the key that unlocked their humanity.

After her first moments of shock and pity, Bronwen was very practical in her discussions with Ann, who was obviously relieved that she was not going to be left to her own devices. There were things she needed: more hornbooks, slates and clothing for the new children. Bronwen promised she would see to it and return later in the day to help her bathe and change the newcomers.

Back in the warden's office, they were told that Justice Fell presented his compliments and asked his good wife if she would be so kind as to tarry awhile; he was in chambers with Justice Sawrey and would be out soon. "Come," Margaret said. "Why don't we go for a stroll in the sun while we are waiting? Mr. Farragut, when my husband arrives, would you tell him that he can find us by the statue in the square?"

"Very good, Madam . . . Madam . . ." The warden bowed to both of them.

Outside in the sunlit square they sat down on a bench near St. George. Pigeons were out in force, strutting and cooing; the starlings had gone. The square looked as if summer had finally arrived.

"Ah," Margaret said, lifting her face to the sun. "How good it is to be in the open! It makes one giddy to breathe this sweet, clean air after the dungeons."

The woman beside her studied her. "Thou art very pale," she said matter-of-factly. "And thou must do something about those pustules. Is it the food? I ask because I must know what to expect."

"No, it's the vermin."

"What kind?"

"Bedbugs. Rather like ticks, large, reddish; they live in cracks in the walls and come out at night; there's nothing you can do about them. I scrubbed the cell from top to bottom, had the straw changed, doused the children with hunting water, but the bugs won."

"I wonder if there is a salve that would stop them biting."

Margaret looked at her with admiration. Such equanimity! It was a miracle, as when George Fox had first brought in John McHair. How long ago that seemed, how little she had known then of the true nature of God, as well as her own.

Suddenly Bronwen took her arm. "We must talk about the children," she said. "We must get them out of there."

"How? I know how fiercely men cling to punishment and revenge."

"Not just men," the other said soberly. "I did so myself."

"But what could we do? With the children, I mean, once we had taken them out of there?"

"Put them somewhere where they can see the sun and breathe clean air; a house in the country. The men may surround it with bars if they like, but the inside should be like any other house: warm, safe, secure—a house for children."

"Ah! And no jailers! But motherly women . . ."

"Why not include men? Those children should have fathers as well as mothers. What we should try to find are married couples prepared to take a number of them under their wing and treat them as their own." She glanced at Margaret. "I know how this sounds, considering I started only this morning, but my husband and I have been thinking along these lines for a long time, about abandoned children, orphans. My husband—" She fell silent.

"It sounds wonderful," Margaret said lightly. "But let's discuss our next step first. We must begin with the wives of men in power. They should see the children; the rest will take care of itself."

"I hope so."

"Why not?"

"I do not think thou wilt find many women prepared to do what thou hast done."

"For someone who has just joined me . . ."

"Do not count me. My reasons are, pray God, unique." There was a moment of uneasy silence between them. Then the other said abruptly, "I want thee to know that I am not doing this as an act of expiation."

Suddenly the memory of Henry was so real that Margaret's eyes filled with tears. She saw his grimy hand holding the buttercup, heard him say, "For thee." She must not think about him; if she allowed herself to think . . . He was dead and gone forever. What had happened could not be changed.

"Well," she said, rising, "thou hadst better start getting those things together."

"I will." Bronwen Jones held out her hand. "Farewell, Margaret. Have a good rest. Come back soon. But not too soon; stay with thy family awhile. It is a great blessing to have a family. It is from them that a mother's strength derives." Abruptly, she rose and walked away, tall and elegant in her widow's weeds.

Margaret watched her until she was gone.

* * *

"Why do you want to know?" Sawrey asked.

Go easy now, Thomas Fell thought. "Oh, just as a matter of interest. I should like to know a little more about her, as she is going to take my good wife's place with the children here."

Sawrey's eyes acquired an odd remoteness, like those of a predator: without malice, without involvement. "That certainly comes as a surprise," he said dispassionately.

"I thought I would let you know. As provost, you may find cause to restrict their activities somewhat, or before you know it you'll have women swarming all over the prison, poking their noses into affairs that are none of their business."

"I would not worry about that," Sawrey said. "Mistress Jones is an exceptional case."

"Ah?"

"Was that not what you wished to find out?"

"What would her reasons be?"

Sawrey sized him up with that cold, impersonal look. "Are you familiar with Mayor Jones' reputation?"

"In what respect?"

"The sin of Tiberius."

So he *had* opened that letter! "Oh, that. Why?"

"I don't know whether you ever saw the boy; he had an eye struck out during the struggle."

"I only saw him once, briefly, when I showed my wife around the prison."

"But you have seen Mistress Jones. She would be capable of eruptions of rage, don't you think?"

"I wouldn't know. Handsome woman, if one is partial to the type."

"The type that commits violence in a paroxysm of Welsh fury?"

"Good heavens!" Thomas feigned shocked surprise. "Are you suggesting that not the boy, but the woman . . . ?"

"Her testimony was that she heard the sound of an altercation; when she entered the room she found her husband lying with his head in the fireplace, the back of his skull crushed; the boy standing over him with a poker. But I would not put it beyond Mistress Jones to have come upon her husband and the boy *in flagrante,* and to have expressed her emotions. Forcibly."

Very astute, Thomas thought, but this was where it had to stop. "Sawrey," he said, "if these are your findings, I expect a report, after which I will order an inquiry into the manner in which the trial was conducted."

"I was simply guessing." Sawrey appeared unruffled, but he had taken the hint.

"I could not remain amiably indulgent of the possibility that an innocent boy may have been condemned to death because of—what? Insufficient investigation? Pressure from outside? Those would be the questions that would have to be answered."

"Don't worry," Sawrey said with a faint smile. "I know that Mistress Jones has powerful friends. And that we have no case," he added judiciously.

Thomas picked up his gloves. "Indeed we have not." He rose. "By the way—I would appreciate it if you were to keep an eye on the member of my household who is still here. Miss Traylor."

"It will be a privilege."

"Thank you. Good day." He bowed perfunctorily and went to the door.

"Your servant," he heard Sawrey say behind him.

As he walked down the corridor, he decided that if the tide were favorable and they arrived in time, he would ask his neighbor the squire of Holker Hall to lend him a couple of horses so Margaret and he might cross the sands tonight, rather than be driven all the way around and have to spend the night in Kendal. He was eager to be home.

* * *

"No, dear heart, I don't think it's quite safe yet," Thomas Fell said. "We should wait another ten minutes. Let's rest for a moment."

He helped Margaret dismount; it was a strange sensation to her to slide out of a saddle again after such a long time. And yet it had only been a month.

"Let's sit down here," he said, leading her to the edge of the bluffs. "We can see what the tide is doing, and enjoy the sunset."

They sat down in the bracken. Behind them, the borrowed horses began to browse in the succulent heather. In another week or so it would be too tough, fit only for sheep. Strange, to come back to all this. It still was unreal to her, like a dream.

"Pity we can't see the house," he said.

She gazed out over the water, flashing and sparkling in the setting sun which obliterated the details of the bluffs across the estuary, the roofs of Swarthmoor. "How nice we can be home tonight," she said. "It was kind of Squire Holker."

"Yes." He tossed his hat aside and stretched out in the heather. "Ah, this feels good after the town!"

She smiled.

"I know," he said, eyes closed. "The contrast must be even more striking to thee."

She reached out and put her hand on his arm.

Without opening his eyes, he took it, brought it to his lips, kissed it and put it back on his arm. "Ah . . . This is bliss!" Then, after a while, "I wonder how Henrietta Best has been getting on. I gather you corresponded."

"She seems to have managed very well. The children appear to like her."

"I do too." He yawned and rubbed his nose. It was a long time since she had seen him so relaxed. They should do this more often, just sit in the bracken somewhere and watch the sun go down.

"I think I know what happened," he said.

"H'm?"

"To brain a man with a poker takes some doing, for an eleven-year-old boy. And the man was lying with his head in the fireplace, the back of his skull crushed. He must have stumbled, fallen backward and brained himself on one of the andirons. I think she went for the boy with the poker."

Her tranquil joy darkened. "Why canst thou not leave the dead to bury the dead?"

"Dear heart," he said, "it is my professional deformity. I happen to be obsessed by a passion for truth."

"Art thou sure it is for truth?"

He opened his eyes. "What else would it be?"

"Just for sport. The boyish desire to put salt on Mistress Jones' tail."

"That I would not mind at all."

She bent over and kissed his nose. There were lines around his mouth that had not been there before. Yet it seemed only yesterday they had sat like this on the other side of the water, in their courting days. He had toyed with his stick in the bracken and said, in the urbane tone that had impressed her so deeply at the time, "As old Aaron Cartwright once remarked, 'Life and the universe are not only much more complicated than thou thinkest, they are more complicated than thou canst think.'" She hadn't remembered that for years.

"How is the tide doing?" he asked, yawning. "Canst thou see Chapel Island shoal yet?"

She looked. The silver stretch of water still lay unbroken around the low silhouette of the island, the ruins of the monastery. "Not yet. Try and sleep awhile. I'll waken thee."

"H'm."

She looked at his delicate hands, folded on his chest; his face in repose. "Let me take thy wig," she said.

"H'm." He lifted his head, eyes closed.

She took the wig off, careful not to snarl the curls in the bracken, and put it on her lap.

"That feels good. Thank thee, love."

She smiled down on him, and was suddenly chilled. The way he lay there, his head with its shorn gray hair, his hands folded on his chest, he looked as if he had just died. What a horrible thought! She turned away and looked at the sunset, but the thought of death remained with her. How brief life was! Briefest of all, Henry's. She heard Bronwen Jones, "I have the strangest feeling he is not dead."

It seemed unacceptable that a person should vanish into nothing. It could not be; it made no sense. Yet here she sat, gazing at the setting sun, with a feeling of acceptance that she had never known before. Now that she had experienced the reality of God, she could accept His mystery.

Thomas sat up and looked at the receding tide. "We had better start moving," he said, "or it will be dark by the time we reach the quicksands. And we are not Mr. Fox and his friend."

As he fetched the horses, she sat watching the sun, thinking about George. She had not thought about him for a long time. Where was he? What was he doing? *All He has is thee.* She wondered if he really knew how right he had been.

"Dear heart, here's thy beast. Could I have my wig, please?"

They went down the bluff cautiously, the horses' hoofs slithering in the bracken. Once they reached the hard, firm sand, they set out at a gallop for the row of brogs that marked the path between the sink-holes. The setting sun touched the distant shore; they cantered into the immensity of the sands, trailing, for a brief moment, long shadows behind them.

HISTORICAL NOTE

OF ALL Protestant sects in seventeenth-century England, the Quakers were the most savagely persecuted, by both the civil authorities and the church. They were hounded, beaten, robbed, imprisoned; some Meetings were so brutally uprooted that only the children were left to gather for worship. At the time of the Restoration there were over forty thousand Quakers in England, all of them fair game for any minor magistrate or irate mob.

Margaret Fell and her household held out against the rising tide of persecution until, in 1660, Judge Thomas Fell died. Almost that very day Justice Sawrey moved in upon them. They were expelled from the Hall; Margaret Fell's property was confiscated; she and her daughters moved from house to house in the twilight of the Quaker underground until, in 1664, she was arrested and sentenced to six years' imprisonment in Lancaster Castle. It was the longest prison term ever imposed on any Quaker "for truth's sake." Friends did their utmost to help by bringing her food, books and especially paper and ink, as from her cell she blithely carried on her staggering correspondence. One of the recipients of her pleas for religious freedom was King Charles II, whom she addressed consistently as "Dear Heart."

Imprisonment was not the only punishment for being a Child of the Light. In the sixties many Friends were sentenced to exile in Massachusetts as "indentured servants." The New England Puritans had started a persecution of the Quakers which surpassed that of the motherland in savagery. All Quakers were arrested on arrival in Boston; the captains of the vessels that carried them were fined for putting them ashore; four were hanged on Boston Common, one of them a woman; many languished and died in prison, others were sent on to the penal colony of "Rhoad Island."

After Margaret Fell's release from prison, she and George Fox were married. It was, in the eyes of the world at least, a marriage of convenience; they were now joint leaders of the burgeoning Quaker movement. After her years in the dungeons Margaret was a white-haired, gaunt woman; George a benign, saintly man described by William Penn as "a bulky person." Margaret's courage never flagged. During a brief lull in the persecution of the Quakers she organized a women's brigade to help the prisoners in Brixton prison in London, at that time the worst of all. She dressed them in red and green, so they might stand out in the perpetual dusk and thereby escape assault.

In 1681 a hundred Quakers, headed by William Penn, set sail for America on the ship Welcome. Their plan was to start an ideal community in the wilderness, governed according to the precepts of the Sermon on the Mount. They lived for over a year in caves and huts on the banks of the river while building their first settlement, which they christened Philadelphia, City of Brotherly Love. Owing to their fairness in business, their paying the Indians promptly for each piece of land they bought and their silent meetings for worship, in which the Indians frequently participated, "the Holy Experiment" was successful. The colony prospered; before the turn of the century Philadelphia had grown to be the largest port in North America.

In 1691 George Fox died in London, aged sixty-seven; Margaret Fell eleven years later, at the age of eighty-eight. One of the last things she did was to oversee the publication of George's journal, a book that was to become a major influence in Quakerism. But as published, it did not contain all he had written; the manuscript had been heavily edited and in some instances changed by a committee of London Friends; there can be no doubt, however, that the final responsibility was his widow's. All miracles and supernatural occurrences were deleted, all references to "The Book of Rewards"; the hangmen in Derby Jail no longer obeyed George's passionate cry, but some vague impulse within themselves that was not explained. From its pages emerged not the man George Fox had been, but the one Margaret Fell decided he should have been. During his lifetime she and he had battled for supremacy in the Society of Friends, each trying to impose a different concept of love on the movement as its guiding star. Only after his death did sly old Maggie, mischievous saint, finally have her way; henceforth the accent in the spiritual life of Quakers would be on service rather than salvation, tenderness rather than righteousness, and on infinite patience with the foibles of others as well as one's own.

It was a concept that would lead to great things: the first prison reform, the first humane treatment of the insane, the first school among the Indians, the first abolition of slavery, but—

But this is where the second part of the saga begins.

PART TWO

THE HOLY
EXPERIMENT

Pennsylvania, 1754-1755

During the second half of the 18th century a transition took place in the plain language used among Friends. "Thou" was replaced by 'thee" as the first person singular and declined as "he." "Thou hast" became "thee has," "thou art" became "thee is," et cetera.

Although in 1754 the transition was not yet completed, I have used the new form throughout for the sake of clarity. It remains in use in some Quaker families until this day, and is presently being revived among younger Friends.

BOOK ONE

CHAPTER ONE

THE Delaware River lay glinting in the sunrise, in the immensity of the primeval forest. It was a clear morning, but, as usual at this time of day, the glitter of sunlit water was obscured by mist in one bend, fifteen miles below the city of Philadelphia. The mist was caused by a ring of warm springs in the riverbed, surrounding a narrow island called "Eden." The name was apt, for the warm springs gave the island a much milder climate than the surrounding countryside; even in winter, it teemed with almost subtropical lush vegetation. The Indians, after whom the river had been named by the first white settlers, had revered the fog-shrouded little jungle in the middle of the river, especially a huge, jagged boulder halfway between it and the Pennsylvania shore. The rock was mentioned as an Indian sanctuary in the first contract made between William Penn and the Unami tribe of the Delawares, with the assurance that it would be kept inviolate for all time. But that had been seventy-two years ago; the Delawares had long since retreated to the north under the ever-growing pressure of white colonization; now all that was left of the boulder as a religious shrine was its name on the charts of the river, "Altar Rock."

To the captains of the merchantmen plying the river to and from Philadelphia, Altar Rock was anything but a shrine. Combined with the perpetual morning and evening fog which obscured the narrows most of the year, it presented the greatest navigational hazard between Cape May and the city. The narrows had been the scene of many shipwrecks and collisions in the past; the worst tragedy had been the sinking of the ferry to the island by the brigantine *Margaret Fell* in 1703. In that catastrophe young Moses and Melanie Baker had perished, leaving their little son Boniface, aged two, to the care of his paternal grandmother, Ann Traylor Baker. During the ten years that followed, the old lady and the growing child remained the only white inhabitants of the island she owned, living, attended by seventeen slaves, in the big mansion that had just been completed when tragedy struck. Then a tutor was imported from the mainland, and eventually a bride for young Boniface, Beulah Best, granddaughter of William Best the shipwright. There were three children in rapid succession, and it was they who, with their high shrill voices and their wild games in the reeds on the water's edge, finally chased the last remnant of the Indian sanctuary: the hush of reverence that had covered the little island for as long as Boniface could remember and that had made his childhood one of silence, secrecy and loneliness.

On this particular morning, in the spring of 1754, it was as if he were enveloped once again by that peculiar, secretive hush as, sprawled boyishly, he drifted along in the old workboat down the New Jersey side of the island in the fog, watching it turn blue and golden as the sun rose above the forest. Ever since he was allowed to do so at the age of six, he had loved to set out from the jetty at the northern tip of the island early in the morning and let himself drift down the length of the island, all alone in a cloud like a planing bird, listening to the soft gurgling and lapping of the water in the reeds, the clanking of a bucket, loud in the mist, the sound of laughter and voices and the yapping of dogs as he drifted, unseen, past the slave quarters, until, with always surprising suddenness, he heard the mighty gushing of the river boiling around Altar Rock, which became audible only as his boat drifted past the shelter of the wilderness on the southern tip of the island. Unless the river was swollen with rain or with melted snow from the hills, the current took twenty minutes to carry him down the length of the island.

This morning, as soon as he lay down in the boat after rowing out into the fog, he felt as if he were being carried back into the world of his boyhood. The spell fell over him the moment the shadow of the island vanished in the mist. All at once he was no longer a portly, balding man of fifty who had felt like taking out the workboat after a restless night of tossing and turning in the first airless heat of spring, but the silent, secretive young boy who had sneaked out of the house before Grandmother was awake, to flit down the slope of the lawn in the blue of the daybreak, climb into the still, black boat waiting for him on the edge of the void, and push himself, careful not to waken anyone in the sleeping house with the rumble of oars or the splash of water, into the secret world of the fog that surrounded the island like a cloud resting on a mountaintop. And there he soared—eagle, condor—miles above scurrying earthbound creatures like Grandmother and Peregrin Moremen, the tutor, and fat Mammy, the house slave, and all the sky and the clouds were his, all the future, life . . .

Boniface tried, consciously, to evoke that boy: thin, wiry, quick as a squirrel; but, looking at his fat thighs cased in discreetly expensive broadcloth, his bulbous calves in their white stockings, it was difficult to imagine himself as that barefoot drifter again, lolling, hands behind his head, Quaker hat on his nose, in what at the time had been the vast expanse of the boat and now turned out to be a tight little tub indeed. But once he lay on his back and had kicked off his silver-buckled shoes to wriggle his toes as the barefoot boy had done, the spell fell. Suddenly he tasted youth again: the infinity of the future, the giddying rush of inarticulate promise—promise of adventure, godliness, love—a plethora of half-imagined yearnings for everything life could offer except, mysteriously he now realized, riches. At no time in his youthful dreams had he imagined himself in that far distant future as he had turned out to be: a rich, fat planter living in subdued Quakerly splendor in the selfsame house into which, forty-eight years before, he had been carried as a squalling little orphan, to be gathered in by Grandmother's arms and pressed to her breast.

Suddenly he felt an intense homesickness for his grandmother. For a moment he was beset by the unmanly longing to be touched by a magic wand and to return, just once more, to the sleeping house in the golden haze of the sunrise and knock on the door of her room and at her call to walk again across the coarse, doglike coat of the carpet to the fourposter in which she sat, propped up against pillows, having breakfast from a tray, talking to Mammy about the business of the day. "Well, well!" she would say sternly. "Since when do we enter our grandmother's room with bare feet? And look at those grubby toes! Don't tell me thee has been messing with that old boat again!" But despite the stern voice and the unsmiling scrutiny of those green eyes, he would know that she was not really angry with him; she never was—whatever he might have done there always was a secret tenderness in the depths of those un-compromising eyes. It was that secret, amused forgiveness, he now realized, that had been at the heart of the great sense of security which had been the governing element of his childhood. Had it been love? Or merely a sense of proportion, the secret amusement of one who had known prison and torture and exile at the innocence of his childish sins?

Well, whatever it had been, she would be proud of him now. The net profit was now double what it had been in her best days; the number of slaves had grown to two hundred; his daughters were ap-proaching maturity in an atmosphere of gentleness and quiet affluence; his son was being groomed to take over the plantation when he came of age; maybe that would be the time for his father to return to those dreams of his boyhood: a life of adventurous saintliness like that of Gulielma Woodhouse, ministering to the Indians in the wilderness beyond the mountains, or heading a hospital for the insane, or—

The peace in which he drifted was shattered by strident voices, star-tlingly close. They must come from the Hall, for he recognized the voices of his daughters; everything sounded close in the fog. Even though he could not make out any words, it was obvious they were having one of their quarrels; their altercation, jarring and ugly, destroyed the quietly jubilant feeling of youth and resurrection in which he had been drifting, hands behind his head, hat on his nose. What on earth could be the matter this time? Which infantile streak made an eighteen-year-old girl go, tooth and claw, for her little sister at the slightest provocation, as if she were still ten years old herself? Well, he had better go and find out.

He rowed back in the mist to the dock at the foot of the lawn with the unerring sureness of forty years' practice, tied up, put his shoes back on, and walked toward the white-pillared house looming huge and brood-ing in the fog, wreathed in slowly writhing shrouds that seemed to twist and reach in agony as they were dispelled by the heat of the morning sun. He climbed the flight of steps to the veranda, opened the glass doors to the hall, and entered the warm darkness of the house still smelling of sleep. The sound of the quarrel came from Becky's room above; he swiftly and silently climbed the carpeted stairs, opened the door, and silenced the suddenly loud voices by crying, "Children! What on earth is going on here?!"

The girls, still in their long white nightgowns, their hair in paper

curlers, stood facing each other beside a walnut secretary Becky
had inherited from Grandmother. One side of it seemed to have dropped
onto the floor; Abby was holding a stack of notebooks.

The moment she saw him, Becky cried, "Look what she did! Look
what she has done to my desk!"

"It is not thy desk!" Abby shrilled. "Thee gave it to me, it's mine
now!"

"That does not mean thee can tear it apart! Here, look, Papa,
look what she did! The whole side has come off! She ruined it!"

"I did not ruin it! That side was *meant* to come off! Otherwise, how
did these books get in there?"

"Abigail?" he asked quietly, in an effort to reduce the volume of
their voices, "why has thee taken it apart?"

"Why does she take everything apart?!" Becky cried. "She is not
a child, she is a monkey! Anything thee gives her, anything at all, she
instantly pulls apart to see what's inside!"

"Well, this time there *was* something inside!" Abby triumphantly
held up a pile of old exercise books, dog-eared and yellow.

"Whose are they?" he asked.

"Mine!" Abby cried.

"They're not!" Becky tried to grab them from her; they began to
fight like cats.

"Children! Please!" He put his hands on their shoulders to separate
them. It had been a long time since he had last touched them; the
delicate bones of their shoulders did not seem very different from
when they were little. To feel them again was extraordinarily moving;
how vulnerable the girls were, despite their flaring tempers, how fragile
and feminine! "What books are they?" he asked.

"They're diaries!" Abby cried.

"If they are Becky's diaries, then thee must give them back to her.
She may have given thee the desk, but anything a person writes remains his or her property."

"But they *aren't* hers! They have nothing to do with her! They're
at least thirty years old!"

"Then whose are they?"

"I don't know, I hadn't had a chance to look at them before she
came storming in."

"Storming in!" Becky cried, outraged. "This is *my* room! This is
my desk!"

"It is *not* thy desk! Thee gave it to me because thee was going to
get married!"

"Shut up!" Becky shrieked, beside herself. "Shut up! Shut up!" and,
picking up her skirts, she ran out of the room.

"Well, now," he said, feeling anger for the first time that morning.
"That is not a Quakerly way to behave, Abigail."

"I can't help it if Joe Woodhouse broke his troth! Once she gave
it away, it became mine. I can't give back what she gives me each
time a beau weasels out on her!"

"What nonsense! The boy is downstairs right now!"

She shrugged her shoulders. "Ask her thyself."

He sighed. They might be vulnerable and in need of protection, but there were moments when he simply did not know how to handle them. He held out his hand and said, "I think thee had better give those books to me, Abigail."

She faced him defiantly. "If it is to give them to *her*—"

Before he could reply, Becky's voice cried in tearful fury from the adjoining room, "Oh, *keep* them! Keep them, silly goose! I don't want them, they are boring anyhow!"

"Boring? Thee thinks it boring to find out that Grandfather Best was not the son of the judge who saved George Fox from prison?"

Becky appeared in the doorway, despite herself. "He was not?"

"Indeed not!" Abby exclaimed proudly. "He was a foundling."

"Nonsense," Boniface said. "Whoever gave thee that notion?"

"Read it! It's all in here! And *lots* more."

Becky had recovered. "I don't believe it!" She turned away.

"I'll tell thee more: he was a dwarf!" The statement was so outrageous that the child herself seemed taken aback by it. "I promise thee it's true, Papa. There's lots more, all about Grandfather Best, and Great-grandmother, and lots of other people."

"I'd better take those books," he said sternly. "Thank thee." Abby handed them over without protest, although he could see from the way she followed them with her eyes that she would try to get her hands on them again at the earliest opportunity.

"Now let's all get dressed for breakfast and meeting," he concluded, turning to go. "I hope you girls will appear in the Lord's presence in a more suitable mood." With that, he closed the door behind him.

He found his wife, Beulah, in the kitchen, preparing breakfast on the huge cast-iron stove. Despite the early hour, she was already disheveled and perspiring; wisps of hair stuck to her forehead, her cheeks were flushed. He had given up trying to convince her that there was no earthly reason for her to do the cooking, considering that Medea, the old Negro maid, was sitting idly by, watching her work. "Did thee hear the girls just now?" he asked, realizing too late how unkind that question was; she had been much troubled by her hearing lately and hated to be reminded of it.

"No, I didn't." She broke a new lot of eggs into the skillet with a hissing sputter.

"Has there been trouble between Becky and Joseph?" he asked.

She looked up. "Why? Did she confide in thee?"

He was tempted to say she had. Instead he told her what had happened and showed her the diaries.

She gave them no more than a cursory glance. "Those girls . . ." She sighed. "What is it that makes them complicate their lives so? I never was like this at their age . . ."

"Thy eggs," he warned.

* * *

At the news that her old tormentor's diaries had been found, Beulah
Baker's first thought was 'No, not again!' A foolish thought for a
sensible, practical person; the old woman had been dead and buried
twenty years; yet the news made her want to slump in the nearest
chair, eyes closed, head back, legs outstretched, arms dangling, thinking, 'All right, I give up! Take it, take all of it—and good luck to
thee, Ann Traylor, and good riddance!'

It lasted no longer than a few seconds; she instantly rallied, put
out with herself for indulging in such fancies. She must be more tired
than she had realized, and no wonder. It seemed as if the work in
the house and on the plantation had become more of late, instead of less
as she had hoped when her daughters were still small. Supervising the
slaves, cooking, washing, spinning thread, weaving the yarn into cloth
for garments for the whole family, knitting socks, stockings, comfort-
ers, woolens, bed socks, mittens, earmuffs until she felt drunk with
giddiness and, cross-eyed with exhaustion, fell asleep during meeting
for worship or, worse, while her husband was reading aloud in the
evening from William Penn's *No Cross, No Crown* or Besse's *Sufferings of the Friends During the Great Persecution.* She had been known
to keel over, as if struck on the temple by a snowball, waking up only
in the nick of time to keep her poor, worn-out body from hitting
the ground. Occasionally she asked herself what had happened to the
gay, sensitive, trusting young girl whom everybody had loved so much
and of whom her friends had said with envy: "Beulah? That one is
going to make off with the pick of the lot." Young, roly-poly Boniface
Baker with his apple cheeks, self-satisfied smile, jackets with sleeves
that were too short and a hat that was too small had not been the
pick of the lot, but even so her friends had regarded her with envy.
It had been just after the depression of the twenties, few new ships
were being built; under those circumstances the proposal of the future
owner of Eden Island, with its profitable plantation and its impressive
Hall overlooking the river, had seemed a stroke of good fortune. What
she found herself totally unable to cope with was the presence in
that Hall of the indomitable, queenly old woman who had regarded
her from the moment of her arrival as a silly, scatterbrained toy
poodle for her grandson. Under the icy, contemptuous stare of those
green eyes she had felt herself turn into exactly what she was considered to be, a jabbering idiot, all thumbs, who could not keep a
pot on the fire without its jumping malevolently to its death on the
tiles in front of the stove, or iron a shirt without burning it, who
starched the bed sheets, filled the lamps with vinegar and locked the
cat in the oven. It had been the cat incident that had broken her
resistance. She had left the oven open to heat the kitchen, the fire
had gone down, the cat had sought the warmth of the small, dark
cave; before going to bed she had closed the oven door and banked

the fire so as to arrive the next morning in a kitchen where, at least, the crocks would not be frozen to the floor. Of course it had been Grandmother who heard the faint meowing behind the oven door and who was, on opening it, knocked off her feet by the screeching cannonball exploding from the interior. The cat had lived to limp through the house for nine more years, turning every encounter into a mute reminder, and ever after that day Grandmother had gazed at her coldly, saying nothing, but with the word "cat" written almost visibly on her forehead, even when she lay on her deathbed.

Now, after twenty years, by God, here she was again: bursting out of a secret compartment in her desk like a poltergeist. Beulah could see it all: interminable evenings during which her husband would, in the reverent voice he reserved for religious occasions, read to his family, loud enough for her to hear, from the sacred writ of the insufferable old woman, who could be counted on to dispose of every living soul that had ever crossed her path with the damnation of faint praise, excepting, of course, poor martyred Bonny Baker the First, holy, holy, holy, dastardly done to death in the dungeons of Lancaster Castle, whose last gasp in the arms of his sobbing young bride had been a prayer for the souls of those who had persecuted him. Beulah knew she was poisoned by bitterness, but she could not stand the story of that unctuous couple martyred in the straw of England's darkest prison, clasping each other in the sight of God with such pristine purity that the only solution to the enigma of the child born to the young widow after her husband's saintly death was a repetition of the Immaculate Conception.

The thought of having to listen to the sanctimonious words of her resurrected tormentor for month after month filled her with such flaring fury that she took it out on the eggs while her husband and fat old Mammy, the kitchen slave, watched her with fascination.

*   *   *

Breakfast was tense and awkward; there could no longer be any doubt that Becky and Joe Woodhouse had had a falling out. Becky studiously refused to acknowledge his presence; his clumsy efforts at genteel conversation were embarrassing. Abby watched them with un-Christian glee; it was a relief when all of them finally entered the blessed silence of morning worship.

Boniface found that he could not center down. He went on thinking about the diaries. After meeting he went to his study with the books under his arm, looking forward to an undisturbed half hour before leaving to see about the business of the day. But Beulah intercepted him on the stairs, to urge him in the unhushable voice of the deaf to have a word with Joe Woodhouse and find out his intentions. He found the young man waiting awkwardly by the door of the study, a roll of paper under his arm. "Uncle Bonny—could I see thee for a moment?"

"By all means." He opened the door. "Sit down, Joe. Make thyself

comfortable." It was a rhetorical suggestion; obviously, the last thing
the nervous young man could do at that moment was make himself
comfortable. "How is thy father?"

"Very well, thank thee, Uncle." Then, as if he were waking up,
"Oh, wait a minute! I have a letter for thee." He dug it out of the
inside pocket of his morning coat, which was dutifully plain in cut
and color but made of very expensive cloth indeed. "This will explain
the purpose of my, er, mission, Uncle." He handed him the letter,
unsealed as a ritual sign of trust between father and son.

*"Dear Friend Boniface: I wonder whether by any chance thee has
among thy slaves a mature wench, preferably widowed but without
dependent children, suitable as a house servant. If so, perhaps young
Joseph can have a look at her, or, should there be more than one
available, view the various possibilities and report to me.*

*"As to the second reason for his visit, it seems best to leave the
explanation to him. He has with him all the pertinent documents and
maps, and he is sufficiently informed on the subject to provide thee
with a lucid explanation.*

*"With tender regards for all, and in the hope that we will soon
meet again, thine, Isaac Woodhouse."*

It all seemed straightforward; Boniface wondered why he sensed
subterfuge. "Certainly," he said, folding the paper. "I don't believe
we have any unattached females available, but I may be mistaken.
Thee will have to ask Caleb Martin."

There was an awkward silence.

"Well, Joe, what else has thee got to tell me?"

The boy looked up from a scrutiny of his fingernails. "Uncle, it
concerns Altar Rock."

"What about it?"

"Well, as thee knows, it is becoming more and more of an impediment to the growth of our trade, of the whole city. Because of it, the
size of the ships that can sail all the way up to Philadelphia is limited
to what they are now. In the meantime, the new trend is for larger and
larger ships, and—"

"Yes, yes," Boniface said impatiently. "I know all that. Are they by
any chance reviving that idea of a canal again? I thought it was decided—"

"No, no, Uncle!" the boy exclaimed eagerly, showing a youthful
excitement he had been hiding so far. "We have now come up with an
entirely new idea! We—Abe—Ben Franklin, really, was the one who
suggested it: we think we have found a way of blowing it up!"

"Blowing it *up?*"

"Look!" Joe leaped to his feet with such alacrity that he nearly overturned his chair. "Let me show thee the plans . . ." He unrolled the
papers that he had been carrying under his arm and spread them across
the desk. The first was a detailed map of the bend of the river, with
a cross-section. "This is the narrows, with Altar Rock," he said super-
fluously.

"What does it signify?"

"I'll show thee, Uncle." Joe pulled another sheet from underneath the chart. It was a plan of the rock itself, seen from various angles, complete with measurements.

"Who made this drawing?" Boniface asked, with a beginning of irritation; these plans were based on an extensive survey. "When was all this done?"

"I couldn't say, Uncle . . . But look!" He groped underneath the chart and produced a third sheet of paper, which he spread out on top. This time the base of the rock was surrounded by a series of bell-shaped objects, connected with the surface of the river by chimneys. The whole thing had a fantastic quality, like the drawings of sea monsters by imaginative explorers.

"What are these?" Boniface asked, pointing at the objects.

"They are meant for the gunpowder. I don't quite understand the workings of it, but it seems that with those chimneys the fuses will go on burning until they reach the charge. If the explosions take place simultaneously, the rock will be shattered."

"I see." Boniface leaned back in his chair. "That is an interesting theory."

"Yes, isn't it?" Joe, oblivious to his displeasure, continued with some pride, "Father authorized me to ask thee what thy price would be for Altar Rock." When Boniface did not reply, he added, less confidently, "Although the rock itself is worthless and its removal would benefit all ships, Father would be prepared to part with a substantial sum of money for thy permission to remove it." When his uncle still said nothing, he said in a strained voice, "I am sure thee would like to consider this at thy ease, Uncle. I'll leave these plans with thee," and started toward the door.

"I don't think that will be necessary, Joe," Boniface said. "I could not possibly consider this proposition."

"Oh?" It stopped him in his tracks.

"To start with, I am not at all sure that I am the one to give permission, because in the original treaty Will Penn made with the Delawares it was agreed that the rock would be considered an Indian sanctuary for all time. I suggest that thy father take his proposition to the Delawares."

"But, Uncle! The Delawares moved out of here ages ago!"

"I know. But before I consider the proposition, I must be sure that they have no objection."

"And if the Delawares were to release thee, Uncle?"

"Let's cross that bridge when we get to it."

There was a silence, then the boy said, with a hint of Woodhouse steel in his voice, "I think Father would like to be reassured that thee and he see eye to eye on this matter, Uncle, before—well, before we decide on other matters."

The boy could not touch old Isaac in the subtle art of diplomacy. "Is that why thee is hedging in thy relationship with Rebekah?" Boniface asked.

"No, no, Uncle! Not at all, not at all!" He rolled up his plans and put them under his arm. "Well, Uncle, if it's all right with thee, I'd like to take a look at those slaves . . ."

"Very well. Ask the stableboy to bring out the chaise for thee."

"Thank thee, Uncle." He hesitated, as if to say something more; then, thinking better of it, he made for the door.

After the boy had left, Boniface was overcome by anger. The pipsqueak! How dare he use his betrothed as a pawn in a business transaction? Poor Becky! Suddenly the whole affair seemed vile and hideous. How callous to use a human being like this, with total disregard for her uniqueness, her innocence, her young, vulnerable love for this oaf! His anger became so unsettling that he picked up one of the dog-eared exercise books to escape from un-Quakerly thoughts.

The first entry was dated October 1652. The writer had obviously been Grandmother; not only did he recognize her handwriting but the methodical way in which these jottings of a lifetime had been indexed and cross-indexed was typical of her. The index listed the names of all the leading Quaker families of Pennsylvania and Rhode Island. She had, first as a member of the Fell household and later as one of the first settlers in Pennsylvania, witnessed the making of Quaker history at first hand. There must be some personal information on a number of weighty Friends, or the diarist would not have taken such pains to keep them away from prying eyes.

"I hope she is asleep at last, poor woman. How is it possible that one person can make another suffer such agonies without noticing it? And all that while he is holding forth about 'love' and 'tenderness' and 'answering that of God in everyone' . . ."

He stopped. He had the strange feeling that Grandmother had not intended him to read this. Odd that she had not left any instructions as to what should be done with these books; it was unlike her.

He looked up in the index *"Baker, Boniface."* The first entry referred to the first page.

"Considering the way he has treated Bonny and Margaret Fell, all I can say is—well, let me be charitable. The one who really stood up to him today was Mistress Best, bless her . . ."

He remembered what Abby had said about Grandfather Best. If indeed this legendary figure had been a foundling and a dwarf, then that information could only embarrass his descendants. The only person to read these books should be a historian who could be counted upon to treat them with objectivity. But after seventy-two years of intermarriage there was no objective person left in Philadelphia. The one who came closest to it might be Jeremiah, Beulah's brother, who was toying with the idea of a Friends' Historical Library and who, as clerk of Philadelphia Monthly Meeting, could be counted upon to handle any explosive disclosures with diplomatic discretion.

He turned his chair to face the window and gazed at the wide, tranquil view of the river and the Pennsylvania forest, cleared of mist now the sun had risen. A brigantine, her sails gold and starkly shadowed in the sun's low light, was working her way upriver through the narrows, helped along by three longboats manned with slaves. As always at this hour, Altar Rock, wet with spume, glistened like black marble.

The sight of the rock turned his thoughts back to Becky and that miserable boy. She would be best off without him; but it was obvious she was completely moon-sick where Joe was concerned. What if he gave his permission for the rock to be removed? Why not sell it at a reasonable price and grant Becky her dream? Old Isaac would not have sent those plans if he had not ascertained first that the person to grant permission was he.

He gazed at the colossal boulder, black and alien in its bed of foam in the heart of the green and blue landscape. As a boy he had listened to countless stories about the spirits that lived in it, told by old Hadrian, the house slave, long since buried beneath the chestnut trees in the graveyard on the other side of the island. Stories about nymphs, winged serpents, a big toad with eyes the size of saucers that lived in a cave underneath the rock; the stories had filled him with awe of that black, spume-slick monster gurgling and hissing in the silence of the night, a musical sound of chortling water that now summed up all his childhood. Was that why he felt so reluctant to have it destroyed? Or was it indeed to keep faith with the Indians? In one thing Joe had been right: the Unami tribe of the Delawares with whom William Penn had made his treaty had long since left the area. They now lived on the high reaches of the river, hundreds of miles away.

The brigantine had labored her way past the rock and was now about to start her first tack toward the Jersey shore. The longboats had cast off and were moving toward the stern of the vessel, to have themselves towed back to Philadelphia. Again his thoughts returned to Becky. What a pity that she should have fallen in love with such a spineless boy, entirely dependent on his father and his brother Abe. For Becky's sake, he should give the boy some responsibility that had nothing to do with his father or his brother.

What if he asked him to deliver the diaries to Jeremiah? He had no taste for reading any further. He wondered why.

With a vague feeling of guilt, he wrapped the books securely. Then he sat down in his chair again to gaze at the river.

*　　*　　*

Joe Woodhouse viewed with dismay the rickety chaise and the knock-kneed, sagging old horse the stable slave was rigging up for him to visit Caleb Martin about those Negro wenches. He was planning to drive by way of the fields so that he could have a good look at the indigo crop; just as he was about to climb into the contraption, a girl's voice called, "Wait!" It was Becky, running across the lawn.

His first reaction was one of exasperation. After their painful talk the last thing he wanted was a confrontation; but when she joined him, breathlessly asking if he could give her a ride to the slave hospital, where she had some work to do that morning, he said politely,

"Certainly, Becky. It will be a pleasure. Allow me," and he held out his hand to help her into the chaise.

Had it been Abby, she would have scornfully refused it and swung herself into the unstable little carriage; Becky went through a great show of feminine helplessness as he handed her up into the carriage. She sat down, opened her little parasol to protect her hair and restored a few stray curls disarranged as she came running. Flushed, breast heaving, she looked strikingly beautiful; he could, he reflected as he swung up beside her, quite easily fall in love with her again, despite her treacherous temper.

As the little chaise bounced out of the yard and onto the rutted road, he suddenly found himself filled with anger toward Uncle Boniface. It was ludicrous that Philadelphia's future as the largest port on the continent of North America should be put in jeopardy because of one man's stubborn determination to honor the superstitious claim of some tribe of savages who had long since moved away. Well, he had done what he could, now on to the next thing: the appraisal of the state of the indigo harvest, without betraying to the girl by his side what he was up to.

"I'm happy to have this chance to apologize to thee, Becky. I'd like a chance to explain myself."

"Oh, there is no reason for that," she said. "Thee explained thyself very well indeed."

She sounded as if she was spoiling for another fight; his eagerness to impress his father faltered. "Even so," he ventured, "I would appreciate it if thee would give me a chance to talk. Could we not make a little detour?"

"Detour?" She gazed at him from the roseate shade of her parasol as if she had never heard the word before. "What an extraordinary suggestion for someone who told me only last night that we must return to being just good friends."

He was sorry now. "Forgive me," he said, "it was a foolish suggestion."

"Foolish? I must say, thy choice of words is surprising!"

He was overwhelmed by the desire to kick her shins, as he had in the past when he was sent here for a month each summer. At that time there had been no indigo culture yet; he had chased her down the long, straight alleys between the rows of peas and runner beans, up a tree in the graveyard, and they had ended up, perilously, on one of the heavy branches overhanging the water, hearts pounding, heads close together; her eyes had been huge and blue, full of unfathomable thoughts.

He looked sulkily away to inspect the first untidy field of indigo. It looked healthy but unkempt; the roots were choked with weeds, yet the plants were more than man-high; in the blessed climate of this island anything would flourish, despite the sloth and incompetence with which Uncle Boniface and that drunkard Caleb Martin ran this plantation. Abe was right: white Indians, that's what they were.

His father had asked him to note especially which type of plant

Uncle Boniface was growing: *Indigofera tinctoria* or *Indigofera anil.* The first was less hardy but produced more leaves, the second smaller but easier to cultivate. If it were *tinctoria,* then the island was a potential gold mine, for it would give as many as four cuttings of herbage each year. The difference could only be seen in the pods; as it was too early in the season for pods, he should take a sample of both bloom and foliage, for analysis.

The field they were crossing in the creaking chaise was in full bloom. The silvery branches of the shrubs shimmered in the sunlight; each was heavy with torches of mauve flowers, which gave the field the same hue her face had in the luminous shade of the parasol. He wondered how to get hold of a sample; he could not stop the carriage and pick a branch without explanation. Becky was not interested in business matters or anything else that did not concern her directly; but even so, she would be bound to ask questions. Luck helped him out. The bouncing little cart reached a part of the tracks where the ruts were so bad he had to pull the horse over to the right. It caused a plunging movement so violent that Becky threw her arm around his waist, afraid of being thrown out; the branches of the shrubs streaked along the side of the carriage and he managed to break off a small one with two torches of flowers. Turning toward her, he held out the flowers and said, "I'm sorry if I hurt thee. Forgive me."

She sat for a moment dumfounded, her arm around his waist, her parasol awry; her eyes searched his. This was how she had looked last year when they had sat down on her great-grandmother's grave and suddenly, without warning, kissed each other for the first time. Just before his lips had touched hers, she had looked at him with that same expression. She straightened up, pulled her arm away and accepted the untidy little bouquet as if it were made up of roses. "Dear Joe," she said, as if they weren't surrounded by acres of the flowers.

Whether it was the way she had looked at him or the tenderness of her words, he suddenly felt ashamed. He seemed to wake up, disoriented, from a dream of meaningless schemes and abstractions; for a moment the only reality seemed to be her lips, her face, her eyes, the whole lonely, vulnerable person next to him. Why couldn't they forget about Altar Rock and be themselves, stroll hand in hand through the long grass along the river, to the cluster of shrubs near the graveyard, where they had so often lain in the past to watch the clouds sailing through the branches? He felt like taking the flowers from her, throwing them away and telling her that he had been put up to this deception by his father.

But self-preservation made him remember the past, when, time and time again, as she had been about to lose one of their wild games, she had suddenly turned on him to taunt him with some confession he had been foolish enough to make earlier. They might share an hour of tenderness and comradeship, but she would be sure to turn around later, blue eyes flashing, and say "Kiss me? Did thee ask thy father?"

All he could do was put his hand on hers, but she had no hand available. One held her parasol, the other the flowers; she was still sniffing their scent. It irritated him; he had expected her to put them aside with bored familiarity and forget about them, so he could pick them up unobtrusively at the end of their ride. Her behavior did not seem true; those flowers smelled, in the mass, unmistakably like cats' urine. Abe had once remarked with that poker face of his: "Those indigo flowers make the whole of Eden smell as if the Lord had, in a moment of absent-mindedness, created more tomcats than He had planned." It was the kind of joke his father disapproved of.

He suddenly wished the drive were over. Although she was sitting there lost in her own thoughts, Becky aroused a disturbing hunger in him. Last night he had renounced all notion of marriage as being premature; what was it that made him sit there daydreaming about kissing her, pressing her body against his, feeling once more her warm, soft lips? He glanced at her; oblivious of his presence, she was gazing at the fields, holding the meaningless posy, her face aglow with the parasol's shade. How easy it had been to mislead her! When they finally reached the slave quarters, he was grim with self-reproach.

They stopped in front of the hospital, the first of a row of identical cottages, all paintless and almost derelict. She turned to face him; her radiant face made his heart sink.

"Joe, dear heart, I'll be waiting for thee here; come as soon as thee has attended to thy business."

"I will," he said in a hoarse whisper that made her laugh. He helped her down with a recurrence of the desire to kick her shins.

"All right, whenever thee is ready, dear heart." She turned away toward the little building where two Negresses crouched on the porch, one holding a naked pickaninny by a rope around its belly, like a puppy. He clicked his tongue at the horse and whisked the reins; the chaise, creaking and swaying, rattled off.

Caleb Martin, the overseer of the plantation, was not in his cottage at the far end of the row. He was not at the factory either; Joe finally found him in the field on the southernmost tip of the island, where a band of slaves was harvesting the first task of indigo shrubs. Young Joshua Baker, apprentice overseer, hovered in the background. It was late to do any cutting; Joe knew from his father that the plants should be harvested very early in the morning, before the sun could wilt the leaves. It was another sign of the carelessness with which this plantation was run; the crop itself, however, looked succulent and abundant. The slaves bore the mark of the same duality: their clothes were coarse and shabby, their bodies exuded strength and animal well-being. Most of them were men; the few women were stacking sheaves onto a flat-bed cart. Their smocks were ragged and torn; one buxom young wench showed the cleft between her breasts, glistening with sweat. He caught her eye; the bold look with which she responded made him look away in embarrassment.

"Well, young fellow, what brings thee here this morning?" an unfriendly voice asked behind him.

It was Caleb Martin, hostile and swarthy, on a mean-looking gray gelding. Joe had always disliked the man, whose twisted scowl made him feel uncomfortable. Caleb was the black sheep of the Martin family, an incurable drunk; Boniface Baker was considered godly for having given him this job.

"My father sends his compliments, Caleb Martin," Joe said with formality. "He desires to buy a good, trustworthy wench as a house servant; Boniface Baker directed me here to discuss this with thee. He requests thee to show me what thee has available in the way of unattached young females."

The suspicious eyes narrowed; the man was obviously displeased by the request. "Thee comes at an inopportune moment, Joe. We are at the beginning of the harvest, I need every field hand I have."

"It is a wench we want. A house wench."

"There are no house wenches in this plantation. There is one lazy old crone at the Hall who staggers about whisking feather dusters, but I wouldn't wish her on my worst enemy." His face broke into a smirk. "Let alone on thy father."

"Be that as it may, Caleb Martin," Joe said with dignity, "the message Boniface Baker gave me for thee was to show me some wenches so I may make a choice. He does not want to separate any couples, and asks thee to show me only loose women—I mean, unattached ones." He felt himself blushing at his slip of the tongue.

Caleb Martin reveled in it. "Loose women, Joseph? Come, I will show thee some loose women. We have two right here at the cart. That is Phoebe"—he pointed with his whip—"the fat one in the calico smock. She is past breeding, but a good worker and unlikely to cause any mischief. Then we have this sassy one here, young Cleo—a lusty wench, eager to be bred, likely to be a pack of trouble in town."

It was the girl who had given him the bold look. She pretended to be unaware of their attention, and swung the sheaves onto the cart with lithe, sinuous movements. She had the spindly legs common to black women, but conspicuous breasts beneath her skimpy cotton frock. "She lost her buck a month or so ago," Caleb said behind him, "and she has made nothing but trouble since, so I wouldn't be sorry to see her go. She isn't worth a farthing. All she is good for is to be bred for litter. Well—that's all I have, those two. Make up thy mind."

Joe felt his cheeks redden again, this time with anger. Like his father, he did not agree with the sentimental arguments against slavery from Friends who did not keep any slaves themselves, but he did agree, as did all Quakers, that the Negro should be treated with kindness and humanity. To discuss these women in their presence as if they were cattle insulted his ingrained respect for that of God in every man. "It would seem that our interests converge here, Caleb Martin," he said coldly. "Thou wouldst be happy to see Miss Cleo go, it is my opinion that she offers the best prospect for my mother's purpose."

"I see," Caleb said. "Is thee sure it is thy mother's purpose, Friend Joe?"

Joe felt his stomach muscles contract and he answered tautly, "I fail to get thy point, Caleb Martin."

"Come, come," the other said, patting the neck of his horse. "Don't think that young bitch is not aware of it; she asks nothing better than to be bred by a young blood like thee, to her it would be a way of getting ahead in the world."

It was not only the man's words that angered him but also the sweet, sickly smell of rum they carried. He was about to make a sharp rejoinder when Caleb suddenly looked up. Joe looked around; there was nothing to be seen. Then he heard voices in the distance, wailing, shrieking. Caleb swung his horse around, spurred it and galloped off toward the noise. The Negroes had downed their sickles; all of them were gazing in the direction of the sound, all except the girl, who turned toward him, smiling. It was her look, rather than his curiosity about the disturbance, that made him lash the horse. The chaise bounced off across the stubble field in pursuit of Caleb Martin.

Joe caught up with him in the courtyard of the factory. Caleb was standing in the midst of a group of slaves, all dressed in ragged smocks streaked with blue. As Joe climbed out of the chaise, they respectfully moved aside for him. He wished they hadn't.

On the ground lay the body of a Negro. The head was crushed, the face covered with blood; pink and gray brain matter protruded sickeningly from a jagged hole in the black skull. "For the last time: who did this?" Caleb Martin asked, his voice vicious with menace. Then he noticed that Joe had joined him. "An accident," he said, "the poor brute was brained by the paddle wheel. Somebody put the thing in motion without first making sure that everybody had left the vat."

"Shouldn't—shouldn't he be taken to the hospital?" Joe asked, remembering too late that was where Becky was.

Caleb Martin shrugged his shoulders. "What's the use? He's as dead as a doornail." Then, perhaps realizing that this callousness might be reported to the Meeting, he said grudgingly, "All right, pick him up, take him to the hospital. Quick! Quick!"

The slaves lifted the body by arms and legs and started to carry it across the field, head dangling. The brain matter began to ooze from the skull, making a ghastly trail. Joe had had enough. "I'll go ahead," he said. "Becky is in the hospital. She should not see this."

Caleb Martin paused to look around, his foot in the stirrup. "No, of course not. Go ahead. I'll hold them back until she is gone."

"Thank thee, Caleb."

The reins whisked, the horse jerked ahead; the chaise, lurching on its worn springs, lumbered off across the field toward the quarters.

*   *   *

Much as Caleb Martin detested the young hypocrite and riled against doing his bidding, he held back the grisly procession until he saw the chaise leave the quarters and vanish among the fields, Rebekah's parasol swaying like a large pink flower in the sea of green and mauve. To see the youth make off with one of the girls he had adored and protected all their lives enraged Caleb; the slaves took the brunt of it.

He urged them on until they were lugging the corpse at a trot. He made them dump it unceremoniously in the hospital; then he handed his horse to Scipio, the head driver, and went to his cottage. As he tramped down the dusty road between the hovels, spurs clanking, clumsy and ungainly because of the back harness that hampered his movements, his rage mounted. Of course it had not been an accident! He knew what had caused it: jealousy over that bitch Cleo, flaunting her teats and swinging her rump until every buck in the compound was raving. There was only one way to stop this: if young Joe Woodhouse did not take her, he would have her bred, forcibly if need be. But it must be done by an outside stud, or there might be another murder.

What worried him was the revenge that was sure to follow this afternoon's slaying. Always after a deed like this some mysterious tribal justice was meted out to the murderer. He had never been able to get to the bottom of it, neither had any of the overseers of the neighboring plantations; but it was certain that in every compound there was a nigger court that took care of murderers by executing them: always by hanging, always on the spot where the murder had taken place, and always with the victim's rope belt for a noose. The only way to forestall the loss of another slave would be to find out who the murderer was and sell him as soon as possible. He did not for a moment consider reporting the murder to Boniface Baker; that would mean a trial, followed by the loss of a good slave by imprisonment; it would have to be another accident.

He stamped onto the veranda of his cottage. He never allowed his drivers to enter, all discussions took place out here. But this time, knowing they were surrounded by listening ears which could pick up a whisper from fifty feet away, he reluctantly left the door ajar for Scipio. The parlor, if it could be called that, was dark and barren, the room of a bachelor who rarely spent any time there during the summer. He left the moment he rose in the morning; at night he lolled in his rocker on the veranda until the mosquitoes drove him inside. The furniture consisted of a couple of cane chairs, a table and an oil lamp without a shade. The windows were shuttered; on one wall was a plan of the plantation, with lettered fields divided into numbered tasks; task one in Field A had been crossed out.

He took off his harness, tossed it on the floor, slumped in a chair and was trying to pull off one boot with the other when there was a knock on the doorpost.

"Come in, come in!" he called irritably.

Scipio hesitated, he needed angry urging before he obeyed and gingerly closed the door behind him. He was a magnificent animal in the prime of manhood who might have brought a lot of money in stud fees if his previous owner had not, in a moment of aberration, had this handsome beast castrated after his fourth attempt to escape.

"All right," Caleb said, "who did it?"

The Negro opened his eyes wide in incomprehension. "Cap'n?"

"Thee knows what I mean! Who killed Quash?"

"Killed Quash? Him killed by machine . . ."

"Don't humbug me! He was murdered by someone who was after that bitch Cleo, the way he was. Who was it?"

The huge Negro shrugged his shoulders and spread his hands. "Dunno, Cap'n. I seen nothin' an' nobody tell me nothin'."

The histrionics and the exaggerated nigger talk meant that he was not going to own up. There was one possibility left of getting at the truth: ask young Joshua to find out from Harry, the stable slave. It had worked in the past when they had shared one bed, but recently Harry had been sent back to the quarters and they had adjusted to their new roles of master and slave.

In the street outside, the wailing of women's voices increased as the hands came in from the fields. The day was lost; if he were to order them back into the fields, Boniface Baker was sure to countermand that order. A death among the slaves meant a holiday for them; they could be counted upon to make sure that the Hall heard their lamentations. He had better go and report the incident before Boniface came barreling down here to find out what was going on.

When he hoisted himself wearily out of his chair, his back hurt viciously. As always, his reaction to the pain was to reach for the bottle, but he was about to go to the Hall, better not have any rum on his breath. He would have to grin and bear it until he came back; if the niggers were having a holiday, he might as well have one too.

"Help me into that thing," he said through clenched teeth.

Scipio hurried to pick up the harness, relieved that he was not going to be questioned further. He helped his captain into the heavy contraption with fawning concern.

"Leave that," Caleb said curtly as the Negro tried to buckle the strap under his arm. "Go and tell them to pipe down out there."

"Yes, Cap'n." Scipio was eager to leave.

"And don't let them take the body home!" Caleb called after him. "I don't want any whooping and hollering around that corpse. Crate it in the hospital and keep it there until meeting for burial."

Scipio bowed in the doorway in an excess of servility and muttered, "Sure, Cap'n, I'll tell 'em!" The bluish black of his shoulders, wet with perspiration, glinted for a moment in the sunlight as he stepped off the porch; then he was gone. A few seconds later his voice began to bellow angrily above the caterwauling of the women outside; when Caleb appeared on the veranda, the demented shrieks had become a low wailing. Scipio brought his horse.

As Caleb trotted past the crowd outside the hospital, he noticed that the wench Cleo was not among the mourners; he spotted her as he passed the factory. She was trying to hide behind the vats; he thought for a moment of rounding her up and forcing the truth out of her, but decided against it. For an overseer the only way to handle slaves was never to chastise them personally, but to leave it to the drivers. Many an overseer had ended up murdered in his bunk after thrashing a slave, and no wonder; there was not a white man alive who could whip a slave without going berserk. Were he to lash out at a cringing black female, he too would lose all self-control and take out on her all the rage and frustration locked up within him waiting to be released, like an evil genie. Unrealistic Quaker notions notwithstanding, slavery could never be anything but brutal, violent and corrupting to all concerned. The best that could be hoped, for a weighty Friend who dreamed of respecting that of God in his slaves, was that he would find himself a discreet overseer who would do the dirty work for him, just as he hired a butcher to slaughter the lambs that inspired him to such soulful ministry during meeting for worship. Caleb had no quarrel with that; he carried with pride the burden of shielding the family in the Hall from grisly reality. Why confront fey and delicate creatures like Rebekah and Abigail with the foulness and obscenity of slavery? It was not their function in life to confront the violence, cruelty, suffering and death that surrounded their sunlit world of beauty and love. At times, in meeting with the family, he gazed fondly upon those children who only through his undying devotion and watchfulness were enabled to embody every mortal man's dream: to create a peaceable kingdom where the lion would lie down with the lamb and the tiger with the fatling, and where love, tenderness and compassion would reign forevermore. To a much greater degree than anyone would ever realize, Eden Island was enabled to remain a paradise garden by the swarthy, sinister, pain-racked man now cantering up the drive to the Hall.

Caleb dismounted, handed the reins of his horse to Harry the stableboy and slowly stumped and creaked his way to the house, spurs jangling, formulating in his mind a story that would be acceptable. As it turned out, his work had already been done for him by Joe Woodhouse, who obviously had given a lurid account of the scene. Boniface Baker, benign, portly and shrewd, came to meet him with outstretched hands, saying, "Friend Caleb! How tragic, how sad! And how awkward for thee, just on this first day of the harvest!" He put an arm around Caleb's shoulder and led him to the office. "I hope that the slaves, in their innocence, will not take this to be a bad omen?"

Caleb assured the worried owner that this would not be the case and took this chance to prepare him for another by saying, "The only superstition they may be prone to is that accidents come in pairs."

Boniface Baker shot him a searching glance, then replied, smiling, "Let us pray that, like all superstitions, this may be proven false," and ushered him into the office.

Meeting for burial was held that afternoon underneath the huge, softly foaming chestnut trees of the graveyard near the river. All the slaves were there, both field hands and house servants, all the members of the family, even young Joe Woodhouse, who had been eager to get away but felt unable to do so without appearing callous. The slaves had put up three garden seats underneath the largest tree; on these, facing the slaves, sat Boniface and Beulah Baker, Rebekah and Abigail, young Joshua, Joe Woodhouse and, on the corner, Caleb Martin. Between them and the silent mass of Negroes squatting in the grass the simple coffin lay on two trestles.

They sat in silence for more than half an hour; overhead, the leaves hissed like the surf in the breeze. Finally, Boniface Baker rose to minister. He spoke about George Fox and his lovely helpmeet, Margaret Fell, about his gallant grandmother Ann Traylor Baker, who had homesteaded the island, called it Eden, not as a hope but as a goal. On this sad day when they were all gathered together to say farewell to their friend and brother Quash, they could not honor him more, nor give more meaning to his life spent in honest toil and humble servitude, than by reformulating that goal called Freedom, realizing that real freedom was attained only by turning even the most menial task into a sacrament. For by that token all worldly differences between master and slave, parent and child, man and woman were abolished. This island blessed above others could, with divine assistance, become a shining beacon to all men.

The wind in the trees washed the slow, rolling phrases away; the slaves sat motionless, heads bent; only a few children, restless and bored, stirred in their midst. As Caleb listened to the unworldly admonitions that had nothing to do with reality, he felt reassured. There could be no doubt that Boniface Baker was sincere; he really believed that his slaves were as content as slaves could be, and that their small, blessed community of men and women of good will was inching closer to the Quakerly ideal of the Peaceable Kingdom every day.

Caleb surveyed the sea of sullen, closed faces and wondered who the murderer was, when the hoodoo court in the secret of the night would condemn him to be hanged by the neck on the spot where he had killed his brother. But the faces impassively turned toward the mellifluous speaker were inscrutable; he would never know the murderer until his body was found dangling from a tree, or a gibbet in the fields. He would remove all traces of the execution before anyone turned up from the house; it would be another accident, another clumsy jackass having himself brained by the paddle wheel of the thrashing vat, for by that time the body would be locked away in its coffin, hiding from the delicate eyes of the Baker family the black face twisted in terror, the protruding tongue, the elongated broken neck.

That night, as darkness fell, Caleb sat rocking on the veranda of his cottage later than usual, despite the mosquitoes. Nothing stirred; he went to bed and lay listening in the darkness, expecting the drums to start. But all remained still; it would not be tonight. He wondered why not. That was the trouble with slaves: nothing they did made any sense at all; they were secretive, treacherous, totally unpredictable, even to a man who had been working and breeding them for over a decade.

*   *   *

The moment Joe Woodhouse in his sulky saw the swinging lantern signaling him to stop, he knew he was in trouble. A spasm of fear twisted his stomach; he considered lashing his horse and driving the fragile vehicle straight into whoever it was that barred his way. But reason prevailed; the miscreants swinging that lantern and hollering, "Halt! Who goes there?" might have put a barricade across the road.

The shape of a man with a musket loomed ahead of him, holding the lantern high, then it was lowered and white-stockinged legs came toward him in the swinging light. The man stopped beside him, lifted his lantern once more and cried, "Faith! A Quaker! Boys!"

Other shapes came out of the darkness into the lantern light; grinning faces under tri-cornered hats; the barrels of muskets glinted dully. Joe Woodhouse sat staring straight ahead, trying to keep his jittery horse in check.

"Where art thou going, saintly Friend?" the man asked, his voice unctuous with mockery. "Thou art not by any chance hiding any slaves underneath thy coat, art thou, Friend?"

Joe knew now what they were: a slave patrol, ready to beat up any Negro who could not show a pass signed by his master and to collect the four pounds' bounty granted by law for each runaway slave they caught, dead or alive. These patrols were out mainly to make mischief; no slave in his senses would follow the road at night.

"Well, Friend?" the man with the lantern asked, still in that mocking tone. "Art thou carrying any stowaways? Let me see!" He stretched out his hand; Joe instinctively reached for the whip.

The hand stopped. "Faith! A Quaker going to be violent?"

Joe went on staring straight ahead at the shifting hindquarters of his horse, which began to get more and more nervous as it sensed the mounting tension.

"Well, then! Let's see if thou art hiding any darkies in thy Quaker britches."

Joe stiffened with shock as the impudent hand went for the front of his breeches. "I believe I can feel a little nigger right here!" the man cried. It was more than Joe could bear. Casting aside all caution, he shrieked, "Get!" and whipped his horse; with a scream and a tearing jerk at his trousers, the sulky leaped ahead. Blinded by the lantern, he was unable to see the road in the darkness.

He heard the shouts behind him recede as fast as if he were falling into a precipice. He fully expected to be thrown out of the sulky by a violent collision, but his horse had obviously not been blinded and, thank God, there had been no barricade.

The wind roared in his ears, his coat seemed to have taken on a life of its own, it flapped and tugged behind his back; never before had he hurtled through the night at such reckless speed. He let the horse race ahead until he saw the faint yellow glow of distant torches: the Rose and Crown at the corner of Chester Pike.

He reined his frenzied horse; it was not until he was abreast of the smoking torches that the mare finally slowed down. He thought of spending the night at the inn; but the sight of his breeches in the torchlight urged him on. The front of them was torn away; his white smallclothes were exposed; he could not show himself in public. He must pay for his folly with four more hours of driving through the night, his heart in his mouth, cursing his own stupidity.

Only after he had turned the corner and his horse had settled down to a steady trot did he become aware of the trembling of his body; he shivered uncontrollably from head to foot. His reaction was rage; he felt like shrieking as loud as he could to release his pent-up fury, but realized in time that this would scare his horse all over again. It was powerless rage, anyhow; had he been a man, he would have beaten that swine's brains out. Maybe, with luck, he had knocked him for a loop when he took off like a cannonball; maybe the wheel had broken the brute's leg, mashed his filthy face.

He spent the next half hour daydreaming of what he should have done and railing against the non-violence imposed on him by tradition and education. He tried to concentrate on something peaceable, but found only envy. The lout with the lantern had one thing he lacked: freedom. Philadelphia must be the most staid town in the world; the heavy hand of the Meeting lay on everything. Other towns had clubs, dancing schools, theatres; in Philadelphia the Meeting stamped them out the moment they reared their ugly heads. Temptation! Creaturely activity! All a young Friend was allowed in the way of entertainment was tea parties or discussion groups. And there was no escape, unless you defected, like Abe, risking disownment. Abe taunted the Meeting, the rascal! He had boldly joined the horse-racing, fox-hunting set of the wealthy young Anglicans and become a member of Bachelors' Hall, a meetingplace for youths who had been to Europe. The members of Bachelors' Hall had tried to open a theatre a year ago, but the first performance had been broken up with boos and hisses and shouting of psalms by weighty Friends who would not tolerate such salacious antics in the city they controlled. Oh! How Joe hated their mirthless repression of everything jolly and adventurous and daring!

As he drove on at a boring trot, to spare his horse, he grew more envious of the very yokels who had tried to subject him to their favorite humiliation of "Quaker ninnies." He had heard about it being done to others; it had never happened to him. What would those louts do if they ever caught a nigger? Beat him half to death, no doubt. And if it was a nigger wench? Suddenly all that was kept away from him by the staidness of the Meeting became embodied in the saucy slave girl with the bold eyes, her dirty smock half open, her cleavage glistening with sweat, her taunting breasts. What would *he* do to her, if he were one of those louts and captured her on a night like this, alone in the forest? What would happen if Mother took his advice and bought her as a house servant? Many sons of slave-owners did it, even after they had wives . . .

The thought of Becky sobered him. Whatever his daydreams, he would never dare break away from the security of the Meeting, lest he fall prey to that of the devil in him. He was not sure about that of God, but that of the devil was real and alive; he could feel it as he trotted through the night. He entered the security of the first sleeping street of Philadelphia with a feeling of relief and began to think of what he would tell his father. He hoped to be able to sneak up to his room without exposing his disgrace.

But as he entered the mews behind the house, he saw light in the window of his father's study. Blast it! The old man was working late again! The clatter of the hoofs and the rattling of the wheels could be heard in the house; he had better think of a good excuse for his torn breeches, or of a way to distract his father's attention.

As he unstrapped the valise and the roll of plans from the back of the sulky, he remembered the package that Uncle Boniface had asked him to deliver to Jeremiah Best. He would ask his father to do it for him; maybe that would work.

* * *

Isaac Woodhouse saw that something was wrong the moment his son entered the study. Joe looked haggard and disheveled, his clothes were torn, his eyes were wide with shock; Isaac's first thought was that he had been robbed by highwaymen. It turned out he had been manhandled by a bunch of rowdies; from the state of his clothing Isaac realized what humiliation the boy had been subjected to; of late it had become common practice among the growing numbers of those who felt like baiting Quakers.

"I trust thee comported thyself after the manner of Friends?" he asked.

"I did not lash out at them with my whip, if that is what thee means," Joe answered with a wry smile. "But I will not hide from thee that I was tempted to do so."

"I can well believe it." Isaac resisted the impulse to put his hand on his son's shoulder in a gesture of comfort. Instead he asked, "Well? How did thee fare with Boniface Baker?"

The boy shrugged his shoulders. "Not very well, I'm afraid," he replied, putting the roll of plans on the desk. "I don't think he'll ever agree to having that rock blown up."

"Money?"

"No. He said that it was not up to him to give permission, but to the Indians, as the rock was declared a sanctuary in their treaty with William Penn."

"When Ann Traylor Baker bought the island from the Proprietors, the rock was not mentioned as a sanctuary. Did thee mention the marriage?"

"It made no difference. And I can't say I felt proud of doing so."

Maybe it was the way Joe stood there, disheveled and shaken, but suddenly Isaac saw it from the boy's point of view. "Forgive me," he said. "I should have explained to thee at greater length that it is not as cold-blooded as it seems."

"Oh, I understand," Joe said with a wry smile. "Don't worry, should I love her sufficiently to pass Meeting with her, I intend to do so, apart from any other considerations."

"Of course." There was an uneasy silence. The boy seemed suddenly to have reached maturity. Was it the effect of the assault? There was a difference between the happy-go-lucky youth who had set out for Eden and this bitter young man.

"Anything else thee would like to know, Father? Or may I go to bed?"

"No, nothing else. Unless thee would like to discuss anything?"

The boy smiled that odd smile of bitter maturity. "No, Father. I've said all I want to say. Good night."

"Good night, Joseph." Again he felt the impulse to put his hand on his son's shoulder, but the boy turned away. Isaac saw him go with a sense of farewell; suddenly the boy turned around and said, "Wait a minute! I forgot these . . ." He came back to the desk, opened his valise and produced a parcel wrapped in brown paper. "Uncle Bonny gave these to me with the request that I hand them to Uncle Jeremiah for his historical library. I wonder whether thee would do so for me."

"I'll be glad to. What are they?"

"Diaries. They were discovered in a secret compartment in a secretary that belonged to Becky's great-grandmother. They seem to go back as far as a hundred years."

"Which great-grandmother?"

"Ann Baker."

"Fancy that . . . How very interesting."

"Good night, Father."

"Good night, Joe."

The moment Isaac was alone he unwrapped the parcel; the reason Boniface Baker had donated these diaries to the Historical Library must be that he wanted other Friends to read them.

The first of the dog-eared exercise books turned out to be an index, filled with names and numbers in spidery handwriting. "Woodhouse" was followed by a string of references to volumes and page numbers; he looked up the first one.

"Thomas Woodhouse became leery of 'raptures' when Mabby and Harry Martin pranced naked in the moonlight and ended up in each other's arms . . ." Harry Martin? That must have been old Peleg Martin's father.

He wondered whether the incident was described more fully earlier, and he looked under *"Martin, Harry."* But that sent him back to the same page. Maybe under *"Peleg"*? That took him to the third volume, 1712. *"After Peleg Martin's wife was killed by the sickness, his state was so pitiful that the Meeting decided to loan him sufficient money to buy a couple of slaves and make a fresh start. The wisdom and forbearance of the Committee on Ministry and Oversight were sorely tried when it became known that he had fornicated with one of his women slaves and that as a result she had given birth to a baby boy. It was the first time we found ourselves faced with a dilemma of this nature. We had firmly believed that, although these practices were prevalent among slaveholders of other faiths, no Quaker would ever sink so low as to exploit the condition of servitude of the Negroes entrusted to his care. The first reaction among the women members of the Committee was one of stern condemnation; some of them proposed that he be disowned. What seemed to enrage them most was that he had acquired the object of his sin with money loaned to him by the Meeting. I put up a plea for a loving response to Peleg's transgression. After all, so I pleaded, he had lost one wife and child and must still be in a sad and lonely state; rather than cast him out in self-righteous indignation, we should, as Quakers, give thought to the innocent victim of this tragic affair: the child the slave had borne as a result of Peleg's sin. Surely we could not allow to happen what happened in similar cases among the denizens of the world, namely that the child was sold in the open market. I am happy to say that I prevailed upon the Committee to take the child under its care and to place it with a foster mother until Peleg Martin found a virtuous, loving wife prepared to accept it as her own. I suspect the women acquiesced in this only because Ezra Atkins, who saw the child, reported him to be fair-skinned; only his eyes were black. Had the innocent little thing been like his mother in coloring, no doubt even my most fervent pleas would have gone unheeded—such are, despite our holy words, our pagan practices. The men on the Committee were more easily convinced than the women had been. Ezra Atkins and Uriah Moremen were appointed to collect the child; they returned, looking awkward and ill at ease, with the baby in a basket. I volunteered to take him in, as I had intended to do from the beginning. Now he is the most bonny little boy, much more lively but just as affectionate as my own dear Moses used to be at that age. It is strange to have an infant in my arms again; it seems that age does not extinguish our motherly instincts; I feel just as protective and tender toward little Caleb as I did toward my own when I nursed him."*

Caleb Martin part Negro! This was not the kind of trivia Isaac had expected. This was tragic, terrible; he was convinced that Caleb himself had no inkling of it, nor had anybody else in the Meeting. He had to hand it to Ezra Atkins, and the other old members of the Committee, they had never so much as hinted at this dark secret in old Peleg Martin's past. He wondered whether even Hannah Martin knew that the child she had reared and loved as her own was not a survivor of the epidemic of yellow fever as was Grizzle but a bastard sired by her husband out of a nigger wench in a moment of salacious brutality.

One thing was obvious: these diaries should not be given to any

historical library. They should not be seen by anyone, except, un-
avoidably, Jeremiah Best. He did not see clearly as yet what Jeremiah
should do with the books; probably the kindest thing to all concerned
would be to destroy them. But that was something only Boniface
Baker could do; after all, she was his grandmother.

Disturbed but fascinated, he read on.

Isaac stepped out into the cool of the morning looking forward to
the walk from his house to the shipyard. He set out with vigorous
steps, carrying the parcel of books, jauntily swinging his cane, a small,
wiry figure in Quaker garb striding down the street of shuttered houses,
their rooftops touched by the rising sun.

When he turned the corner of the street, the mere sight of the
waterfront filled him with pride. The scores of docks and jetties jutting
out into the stream seemed to mirror the forest across the river with
hundreds of masts soaring above the roofs of the warehouses as far
as the eye could reach. The river itself swarmed with shore boats
and barges; at the first pier of the four that belonged to him, the
brigantine *Gulielma Penn* had just been pulled in, direct from London.
She was loaded—as he knew, for he had received her bill of lading—
with crates of earthenware, casks of nails, barrels of ink powder,
plowshares, scythes, sickles, reams of paper, bolts of buckram, linen,
fustian, oznabrig, garlix, calico, Persian and Chinese taffeta. In the
warehouse, her return cargo had already been assembled: corn, lumber, fur, salted pork, barrel staves, hoops and shingles from inland
Pennsylvania, fish from New England, rice from the Carolinas, brought
to the city by coasters and destined for Barbados. There the vessel
would take on sugar, molasses, rum and wine for London.

Already her holds had been opened, the quayside was swarming
with stevedores, traders and townspeople eager to meet the mail. Her
bowsprit hung above the street, its dolphin striker made an eddy in
the crowd. He should go to the office to welcome her captain, but
this was a good opportunity to leave the formalities to Abe. Also, he
should see Jeremiah as soon as possible.

It was so long since he had last walked to the Best yard that the
distance turned out to be greater than he remembered. By the time
he reached the first of the three long, low sheds, he was hot and
tired. The Bests were doing well, like everybody else: they had three
ships on the stocks in various states of completion; the largest, a
three-master for Stephen Atkins, was almost ready for launching; the
other two were Henderson ships, a sloop for the coastal trade and
a brig for the West Indies. Despite the early hour, all three hulks
were beehives of activity; the racket of hammers and calking cudgels
was deafening.

One thing was obvious from all this activity: Abe would not find
an ally in Jeremiah Best in the matter of Altar Rock. The yard would
have to be retooled for the building of bigger ships; Jeremiah would
certainly not opt for such a costly change. Isaac had promised Abe
support on this issue; pity that, at the time, he had not realized that

he himself was against it. He had decided to let Abe go ahead because it had seemed a good opportunity to let the boy flex his muscles; now he was saddled with it.

He made his way to the office at the far end of the central shed; only as he was about to open the door did it occur to him that Jeremiah was retired now and might not be there.

Indeed, he was not. Young Obadiah was sitting at his father's desk, his tall frame perched on a stool, his long legs spread out in front of him. Obadiah, despite his thirty-four years still called "young Best," looked much the way Isaac's own son Abe must look at this very moment: *quasi* at ease, trying to hide his nervous insecurity. "No, Father is not here, Uncle Isaac. No, he's not in the yard either; he probably can be found in the library room of Fourth Street Meeting House, where nowadays he spends most of his time." Young Obadiah cleared his throat. "And how is Cousin Caroline? Keeping well, I trust?" The question was remarkably inept for a man of his age. Obviously, the fool was indeed smitten with eighteen-year-old Carrie, with lovesick disregard for the difference in their ages. How tiresome!

"Very well, thank thee, Friend Obadiah," he said, trying to keep his irritation from his voice. "I shall endeavor to join thy father at the Meeting House."

Obadiah sprang to his feet. "May I take thee there in the company carriage, Uncle Isaac? It's just standing idle . . ."

"All right," Isaac said, smiling wistfully at the defeat of old age. "I would be grateful. It is foolish for a man not to realize the limitations of his years."

As hints went, this one was rather pointed; but it was lost on the knuckle-headed young man, who guided him, as fawningly as Quaker practice permitted, to a phaeton with two overfed horses waiting in the shade beside the building. After helping him into the carriage with irritating solicitude, the young man climbed into the driver's seat and set off like the sun god, after whom the contraption was named and who had been notorious for his bad driving. He went in for much unnecessary whip-cracking, intended to frighten the pedestrians rather than to spur on the horses; before long an Irish voice yelled from the crowd, "Slow down, damn Quaker, or we'll make you walk!" Another spat a large, well-aimed blob of phlegm at the miserable driver; despite the revolting sight, Isaac could not take his eyes off its slow downward ooze on the back of Obadiah's coat.

Finally the carriage drove up Fourth Street, past the building site of the new Meeting House and the Friends' public school, and drew up outside the gates of the old red brick building opposite the courthouse. He thanked the young man with some restraint, and heaved a sigh of relief the moment he entered the quietude of the walled courtyard. He walked to the door and pushed it open.

The silence inside the building was deeper than the quietude outside. There was a musty smell of beeswax, old wood and motionless air that had been locked up for half a century. The clerk's office was underneath the stairs that led to the gallery; as he reached the glass-paneled door and peered inside, he was relieved to see Jeremiah perched at a table stacked high with books, scribbling, steel-rimmed spectacles far down his long nose. Seen through the fly-blown glass, he looked the same tall, gregarious wood-stork with whom Isaac had played as a boy among the old pulleys and steering wheels in the loft of the main shed on the shipyard. This idea of starting a Friends' Historical Library was no different from all the wild schemes Jeremiah had conjured up as a boy, new games with esoteric rules that only he himself could fully comprehend. For some reason, this had bothered girls much less; Jeremiah had always got on very well with girls. It seemed an irony of fate that he had ended up marrying Grizzle Martin, an overbearing gossip whose arrival in any gathering, large or small, instantly created a silence.

Isaac opened the door; Jeremiah peered greedily into the shadows. He must have looked exactly like this when his little nephew Isaac Woodhouse was sent crawling toward him on a blanket at their first confrontation.

"Good morning, Jeremiah."

"Ah, it's thee." Jeremiah's disappointment was obvious. "What can I do for thee?"

"I'm afraid there is a conflict between Boniface Baker and myself that may need thy arbitration," Isaac said dispassionately, sitting down in front of the desk.

"The price of indigo?"

"No. Altar Rock. Young Joe went to see Boniface Baker with the plans, to acquire his permission to blow up the rock, for a substantial sum of money, needless to say. Bonny turned him down flat."

"Ah?"

"He says he has no power of jurisdiction because of the treaty between Will Penn and the Delawares. Abe went through the records; there is no mention of the rock being a sanctuary in the contract between Ann Baker and the Proprietors. And no wonder: the Delawares had left the area already."

"I don't think Abe's going into the records is enough," Jeremiah said. "The whole Indian situation is very sensitive right now. I would submit it to the Meeting."

"Yes, I suppose that would be best."

"Anything else I can do for thee?" Jeremiah picked up his quill.

Isaac put the parcel of diaries on the desk. "I bring thee something on behalf of Boniface Baker that may be of interest to thee, in view of thy latest fancy."

"What is it?"

"Diaries of Great-aunt Ann Baker, from a secret compartment in her secretary. They were discovered yesterday; Bonny gives them to thee for thy collection."

"Good heavens!" Jeremiah dropped the quill and stretched out his hands toward the treasure. "This is just what I need! Are they personal?"

Isaac looked with disapproval at the bright, greedy eyes. He had forgotten how Jeremiah gushed over anything new or unexpected. "Before thee starts crowing with glee," he remarked dryly, "let me warn thee that in my considered opinion these books must be destroyed."

"Destroyed?" Jeremiah's jaw dropped with astonishment. "Thee must be mad! Historical documents? They do not belong to us, they belong to posterity!"

"For the time being, they belong to Boniface Baker," Isaac retorted, "and I am certain he has not read them. Maybe we had better send them back, for him to destroy."

Jeremiah recovered; his face resumed its impersonal expression. "Now, now, Isaac—of course I'll give them back to Bonny as soon as I have looked through them, should that be advisable."

Isaac eyed the unscrupulous cheater in forgotten children's games with suspicion. Collecting historical documents, Jeremiah's new fad, had obviously filled him with the usual all-consuming passion. Indian artifacts, double corn, a steam engine—in the pursuit of these fads he had always been totally unscrupulous for as long as they lasted; probably he would gladly sacrifice his wife in the throes of his passion— although that particular human sacrifice would have some beneficial aspects. At the thought of gossip-hungry Grizzle, Isaac became sure that the diaries should not be given to Jeremiah.

His wily cousin must have read his thoughts, for he leaned back in his chair, folded his hands on his stomach with a gesture of pious relaxation and said amiably, "Isaac, let us both try and shake off the spell of boyhood, alluring as it may be at our age. I am not planning to steal thy marbles or hide a counter up my sleeve. I am merely expressing interest in whatever thee is keeping so tightly under thy arm. Come, give them to me." He stretched out a hand once more, smiling reassuringly. When this did not produce results, he added, "If it would make thee feel better, I am prepared merely to leaf through them while thee is here. Just let me have a quick look, that's all."

As on previous occasions sprinkled over a lifetime, Isaac felt himself weakening despite bitter experience. "Jerry," he said, "thee is a liar, a cheat and an unmitigated scoundrel."

He saw a grin of triumph dawn on his cousin's face as he answered comfortingly, "I know, Isaac, I know," and waited for the marbles to be placed in his outstretched hand.

*   *   *

When it became obvious that wily Isaac was not going to let him have a look at the tantalizing books without the emotional gratification of haggling, Jeremiah was overcome by a feeling of sympathy.

It had always been Isaac's dilemma whether to go on hoarding or to invest; he had reacted in this same tight-lipped, stubborn way before ultimately putting some of his money in real estate outside the city limits, a move which had later been lauded as one of wisdom, courage and foresight. Isaac had never been wise, courageous or farsighted; his patient amassment of wealth had been the outcome not of some superhuman instinct. He was one of the most pedestrian of the Quaker grandees who ruled the Commonwealth, totally devoid of imagination, flights of fancy, any form of inspiration other than the Queries and the Advices of the Society of Friends. Without daring or originality, he had succeeded where others had failed, only by virtue of his unquestioning adherence to the Testimonies.

"What disturbs thee so in Aunt Ann's diaries?" he asked.

"Some highly personal indiscretions," Isaac replied. Lowering his voice and glancing at the door, he added, "She reveals, for instance, that thy grandfather was a dwarf."

Jeremiah was about to tell him that, as far as he was concerned, his grandfather could have sported a tail, when he realized that this might jeopardize his chances of being given the diaries, which became more promising by the minute. "My goodness," he said obligingly, "that comes as quite a shock."

Clearly, he had lacked conviction, for Isaac narrowed his eyes. "He was also *not* Judge Best's son, as we were led to believe, but a foundling given to Henrietta Best by her husband to keep her from becoming too deeply involved with the goings-on in Swarthmoor Hall."

"Those 'goings-on' were the beginning of the Quaker movement," Jeremiah remarked. "Is there more information of this nature?"

Isaac's look of suspicion remained. "A great deal," he said grimly. "What would thee say if I tell thee that thy brother-in-law Caleb is not old Hannah's son, but the outcome of a dalliance between Peleg Martin and a Negro slave?"

Jeremiah suddenly felt his enthusiasm doused. If ever Caleb were to discover . . . He realized that Isaac was right: it would be disastrous if those diaries were to fall into the wrong hands. "That's bad," he said.

"Aha! So thee is beginning to see my point. Well, there is information of this nature on every family in Philadelphia. The worst indiscretion concerns poor Bonny Baker himself."

"What is that?"

"Read for thyself." Isaac put the books on the desk. "Read them. I am certain thee will agree with me that these diaries must be taken back to Bonny Baker. He is the one to destroy them; we cannot usurp that authority."

"Quite."

"It would be best if thee were to take them back to Bonny thyself. I'll run along now." He rose. "Maybe thee should read as much as thee can before meeting for business tomorrow."

"Indeed. Well, see thee tomorrow."

"If God wills it," Isaac said didactically, went to the glass door and left.

Jeremiah opened the first of the diaries.

CHAPTER TWO

THE dispute over Altar Rock was presented the following afternoon to the men's meeting for business of Philadelphia Monthly Meeting. Jeremiah Best, in his function of clerk, read aloud a request by Isaac Woodhouse that two Friends be appointed to labor with Boniface Baker and himself in a spirit of love, so as to determine whether the treaty between William Penn and the Delaware Indians was still binding now that the Delawares had left the area. Where this concerned the delicate distinction between the letter and the spirit of the documents involved, Jeremiah suggested that the matter was a legitimate subject for a sense of the Meeting.

The two hundred-odd men gathered in the hall pondered upon this in somnolent silence. Sparrows chirruped loudly on the sills of the open windows; beams of sunlight full of dancing dust slanted into the room, checkering the tiers of benches. The partition had been lowered to enable the women to conduct their own meeting; behind it a female voice droned on monotonously. Jeremiah waited until it would be proper for him to suggest that he himself go and labor with Bonny Baker. The diaries had to be taken back, whatever happened, but to do so under the guise of this mission would not arouse Grizzle's curiosity. There had been a moment early that morning when he had dozed off in his chair in the study and wakened to find his wife standing by his side in her nightgown, leafing through one of the books. She had insisted on knowing what he had been reading all night; he had managed to fend her off by muttering something about "historical documents," but now he wondered how much she had seen. She was drawn to scandal with unerring instinct and indomitable perseverance, like a homing pigeon to its roost.

Finally he judged that the moment had come, and said, "If it is agreeable to the Meeting, I offer my services, as both parties are related to me."

"I unite." That was Isaac Woodhouse.

He looked around him for further signs of agreement.

"I approve," said Israel Henderson. "And I propose that Peleg Martin be invited to join thee on this mission."

It was an astute choice. Peleg was about the only one whose authority young Abe Woodhouse, who obviously was at the bottom of this, might grudgingly accept.

"Peleg Martin, would thee be agreeable to this?"

"Yes." The old man's dry voice created, as usual, a deepened silence.

"Philip Howgill, if thee would be so kind . . ."

The recording clerk began to write the minute. The Meeting waited in silence until he had finished. He read it aloud; it was approved without discussion.

The next item was an official communication from the Governor's office. Chief Running Bull of the Unamis had filed a request that a surveying party be sent to reassess the boundaries of a property sold by his grandfather to the Proprietors of the colony and asked that at least one Quaker be included besides Barzellai Tucker, the Indian agent. The Governor's office invited the Meeting to appoint one of their members; the expedition was due to leave in a week's time.

This was a tricky assignment. In 1686 the Delawares had sold to William Penn a parcel of land "extending in depth as far as a man can walk in a day and a half." Will Penn's shiftless son Thomas, who, on top of everything else, had seen fit to join the Anglican church, had these lands walked off anew in 1737, this time on a prepared trail and employing professional runners. The episode had been a bone of contention ever since; it was certainly in the interest of peace to have this injustice redressed. The mission would need a young, healthy Friend, in view of the hardships of the wilderness; after a lengthy discussion, young Joseph Woodhouse was appointed. He had been sitting in the back row with the other young bloods, betraying no particular interest in the proceedings. He was so surprised at being singled out for this important assignment that his voice was too high when he spoke to accept; he cleared his throat, continued in a startling bass and sat down, flushed with embarrassment.

While the recording clerk sat scribbling the minute, a note was passed to Jeremiah from the floor. He opened it and frowned in dismay. It came from Isaac Woodhouse and ran, *"A complaint has been lodged by Joe against Caleb M. for excessive drinking. I suggest thee take it upon thyself to go and labor with him in company with his father."* There was nothing Jeremiah could do; the moment a complaint was made against a Friend, it had to be submitted to the Meeting, although his identity could be kept secret.

"A complaint has been brought against a Friend for excessive drinking," he said. "May I ask the Meeting to appoint two Friends to labor with him?" He looked about him and added, "I realize that today's appointments have already put a heavy burden on this Meeting, so I suggest that Peleg Martin and I undertake this mission, as it will be on our way to Boniface Baker. Peleg Martin? Wouldst thou be prepared to join with me in this?" The old man's nod was barely discernible; he went on staring stolidly ahead of him. "May I have the sense of the Meeting on this?"

"I unite." Israel Henderson's voice sounded bored and formal. Others muttered their approval, Philip Howgill started to scribble. In the silence, Jeremiah heard a familiar voice raised behind the partition. He could not make out the words, but whatever it was his wife had felt moved to communicate to her sisters in the Lord, she was presenting it with her usual forcefulness.

* * *

The women's meeting for business had ground its dreary way for hours when Hannah Strumpf Martin was jerked awake by the cantankerous voice of her daughter Grizzle.

Until then the deliberations had hardly warranted anyone's staying awake, let alone an eighty-year-old woman who, like an eight-month-old infant, needed sixteen hours of sleep a day. After the soporific reading of the minutes of the previous meeting by the recording clerk, Millie Clutterbuck, the preparations for the coming yearly meeting had been thrashed out interminably: who was going to take care of the lodging of Friends' families from out of town, who was going to take care of the covered-dish supper on First Day, who was going to organize games for the children, *et cetera, et cetera*—Hannah had heard it all nearly forty times before. She had been drifting along on the somnolent river of verbiage when Grizzle's voice shrieked, "I don't care *how* this Meeting handles the matter, but I am sure I speak for everybody here when I say that I am *not* going to suffer that dirty old man's repulsive practical jokes again! I propose a messenger be sent to the men to say that we insist Benjamin Lay shall be told to stay away from yearly meeting!"

Oh dear! Hannah knew her daughter well enough to realize at once that poor old Benjamin Lay was not the true cause of her fury. Grizzle had applied this stratagem countless times: to have an outrageous request turned down and then, once the other party was off balance, to make the real demand she had had in mind all the time. Of course her point about Benjamin Lay was not outrageous, but he was a harmless old crank who, after his last prank at yearly meeting, would find it hard to rattle the women again. Last year he had hidden a pig's bladder filled with blood under his cloak, and when the minute on slavery was defeated once more because her dear husband, among others, refused to unite, he had leaped to his feet, crying, "Thus shall God shed the blood of those persons who enslave their fellow creatures!" He had thrust a dagger through his cloak, blood had come cascading down the front of his breeches, the women had screamed, several had fainted, the result had been pandemonium. All he could do to top that performance this year would be to arrive naked under his cloak and to expose himself when the minute on slavery was postponed again, as it was sure to be as long as her husband was alive.

Grizzle's request was tactfully laid to rest by the clerk, Mary Woodhouse, who was then judged ripe by knowledgeable Grizzle to receive the real harpoon in the corseted blubber of her massive hips.

"There is another point, Friends, that I feel it is my duty to bring to your attention," Grizzle continued, suddenly in a tone of sweet reasonableness. "It has come to my attention that young Rebekah Baker of Eden Island has made an important and very embarrassing discovery."

The silence was suddenly full of tension. "She discovered," Grizzle continued, "a stack of diaries in a secretary left to her by her great-grandmother Ann Traylor, whom we all remember with such loving fondness. By an unusual combination of circumstances I have been granted a glimpse of their contents, and let me tell you, Friends, in all sincerity"—she looked about her with a baleful expression in her bulging eyes, as if she were racked by gas—"one glimpse was sufficient to make me realize that our late Friend Ann has set down information about her contemporaries so intimate, so scandalous . . ." Again she paused to look around, stretching the motionless silence with the astuteness of a peddler. "It has come to my attention that the men are considering placing these diaries in my husband's historical library. I do not want to sound overanxious, but the few items I read, Friends, are of such a shocking, such a painful and damaging nature that I feel we women must make the voice of reason sound in this matter. I propose that we appoint a committee to examine the diaries before they are put on display." She sat down with dramatic suddenness.

To her mother, gazing at her noncommittally, her intention was clear: she had sniffed at those diaries and discovered they were a gold mine of information; her only means of getting her hands on them again was to elbow her way onto that committee. What could vindictive old Ann have written? That Isaac Woodhouse had had his portrait painted on the sly and hidden it in his attic? That Israel Henderson had a wine cellar stocked with Madeira? That her husband, Peleg, in his time . . . Suddenly she froze. Caleb. Ann Baker might have written about Caleb.

Her detachment evaporated and she sat there, heart pounding, praying to God that He might protect her baby, protect him, protect him; dear, dear God, protect him for Thy own little Son's sake . . .

Suddenly, Mary Woodhouse's New England voice sounded in the silence with the authority of her husband's princely status and her own majestic weightiness. There could be no doubt that the calm, rather prissy voice was the voice of the real power in Philadelphia. As it happened, Mary said, she knew about those diaries too, she had not had occasion to read them herself, but her husband had. She agreed with Friend Grizzle that the diaries contained some information on the personal lives of various people, mostly dead by now, that might be embarrassing to their descendants, so she was happy to assure Friend Grizzle that her admirable concern for the reputation of others was shared by the Men's Meeting, who had decided to return the diaries to Boniface Baker, advising him to keep them under lock and key until such date as the information contained in them could no longer embarrass anyone.

It was a dignified reprimand; but Grizzle was not one to give up easily. There she was, jumping to her feet, saying, "I do not think that the men should be the only ones to decide on this, not after the parts *I* have read! I maintain my proposal that a committee be appointed from this Meeting to join with the men in an examination of those diaries and to determine what should be done with them to protect the innocent."

Again Hannah Martin felt her heart beginning to race; she pressed her hand against her breast. Calm, she told herself, calm, calm, all is well. She won't get away with it, he is going to be all right . . .

Mary Woodhouse gazed upon Grizzle from the facing bench and said, "I am not sure I understand what exactly thee proposes, Friend Grizzle. Thy suggestion of a moment ago was that we endeavor to keep those diaries from public scrutiny. Well, that has been done. Now thee seems to propose that, whatever the men may have decided, thee would like us to ascertain exactly what embarrassing information they contain, before Boniface Baker locks them up for another ten years. I will be happy to ask for a sense of the Meeting on thy modified proposal, but maybe thee should first explain to us how, and in what measure, a further perusal of the diaries by thyself and other members of this Meeting would serve to protect the innocent." She waited for the reply with a charming smile.

Grizzle sat glowering at the woman with hatred in her bulging eyes. Then she answered, with complete composure, "Even so, Mary Woodhouse, I would like to hear the sense of the Meeting on this. Maybe this complete trust in thy husband's discretion is justified in thy case; in my experience, and I am sure in that of others present, tattling, though commonly considered a feminine activity, is a typically male one."

It was a nimble effort. Her opponent, sitting there with her velvet-swaddled bulk like an immovable mass, let the women have their titter before she answered, "I'll be happy to put thy proposal to the Meeting, Grizzle Best. Will the Meeting please express its sense on the proposal that Grizzle Best acquaint herself with personal information concerning its members from the private diaries of Ann Traylor Baker, for the protection of the innocent?"

Ruth Henderson asked, "Considering the intimate knowledge of the proceedings next door claimed by some members of this Meeting, does anyone know whom the men have appointed to take those diaries back to Boniface Baker?"

Nobody knew, at least nobody spoke up.

"In that case, I suggest that we send a messenger next door to inquire," Ruth Henderson continued, poker-faced. "For us to interfere with their decision would depend on whether this Meeting has confidence in the men concerned."

"Is it the sense of the Meeting," Mary Woodhouse asked sweetly, "that a messenger shall be sent next door to inquire which men have been appointed to deliver the diaries to Boniface Baker?"

It was the moment for Grizzle to strike her colors. "I don't think that is necessary," she confessed with some effort. "I am sure that they will be weighty Friends. I, for one, am content to abide by the decision of the men, at least as far as their choice of representatives is concerned."

"I'm a little confused," Mary Woodhouse said. "Do we want to embarrass the men as ruled, do we want Friend Grizzle Best to read those diaries for us, or what?"

Ruth Henderson's masculine voice boomed, "Friends, let's stop beating about the bush. We are all going to end up with mud on our faces unless we suppress our curiosity and let this treat go by, with regret. I suggest that we forget about the whole thing and do not include it in the minutes, let alone make it the subject of a solemn quest for a sense of the Meeting. I know we will all heave a sigh of relief once we are allowed to move on to the next point in the business; none of us, I am sure, is in a position to throw the first diary."

They all laughed, somewhat more abundantly than warranted; Mary Woodhouse, quick as a flash, seized the opportunity to move on to the next item: "The overseers understand that there has been a tendency of late amongst our younger people to increasing worldliness. It is proposed that this Meeting shall issue a minute warning against plays, parks, balls, treats, romances, music, love sonnets and the like, as being pernicious in the light of truth. The sponsor is Bathsheba Moremen."

While the women, with the zest of relief, attacked this issue, Hannah Martin sat worrying about her son Caleb. No one would ever understand how a woman could love a child carried under someone else's heart as if it were her own flesh and blood. Maybe it had to do with the kinship she had felt with the poor, terrified little baby when it came to her, for they had both been outsiders in a community as clannish and exclusive as any tribe of savages. Before marrying Peleg Martin, Hannah had been forced to forswear the church of her fathers, all loyalty to her family and her hometown; amidst the suspicious strangers her only ally had been little Caleb, the stone the builders had rejected. It had not bothered her for a moment whether he was indeed the son of Peleg's late wife as was Grizzle, or the outcome of a *Seitensprung* on his part with one of his Negro slaves, for where she came from there were no slaves and nobody condemned a child for its origins. Her childhood town had its own language, customs, music; it had been jolly and warm and earthy and kind; she had sung in the church choir at the top of her voice, everyone did everything at the top of their voices. Still, after all these years, what she missed most was to hear cantatas and oratorios performed by full orchestra and chorus, as she had in the church of her youth. She loved her husband, she had become convinced that the Quaker way was probably the most sensible and civilized way in which men and women could live together as a community, but there were things she would go on pining for until the day she died, and music was one of them. When writing down her last will, as Friends were exhorted to do while still in good health, she had wanted to add the request that during her meeting for burial some musicians from Nazareth, Bethlehem or Lititz might play, but wisdom and common sense had prevailed. Instead, she had written a note to Caleb, to be opened after her death. *"Thee is the only one who will understand*

*why I considered including this wish in my testament and why I de-
cided to omit it. I know that we will miss each other very much,
even though we have not seen each other often during the last years.
Whenever the memory of me might come to thee, from now on,
hum 'Schlafe, mein Prinzchen, schlaf' ein,' the lullaby I used to sing
for thee when thee was little, and my spirit will unite with thine
in love. Be well, beloved son, thank thee for the abundance of happiness, tenderness and joy thee has given me, and be blest in thy
ways forevermore, until we meet again. Have a happy life, Caleb,
my love, and mind thy back."*

After the meeting, she discovered that her husband had been appointed by the men's Meeting to travel to Eden Island the next day.
She had the boldness to suggest that she might go with him to visit
their son. It was only then that she found out that Peleg had been
appointed to go and elder Caleb, once again, for drunkenness.

It struck her with such sorrow that she did not sleep all night,
trying to think of a way in which she could protect him, not from
his father's wrath but from his own sensitive conscience, the sense of
inferiority of naturally gentle men.

All she could think of was to bake him some *Mandelkuchen* and a
Himbeertorte; she did so in the early hours of the morning. She
wrapped them carefully for the long trip, although she knew that
her husband would eat them on his way there, for he considered it
wrong to pamper a son who had sinned.

*   *   *

Jeremiah Best and Peleg Martin were gathered in earnest labor with
Boniface Baker in his study at New Swarthmoor Hall.

The doors to the balcony stood open; Jeremiah's words were almost drowned by the jubilant sound of the birds in the trees. The
bees were out in force; one of them came buzzing into the room
to alight briefly on the flowers that Becky Baker had put on her
father's desk early that morning. A huge, masterful June bug whirred
in, crashed into the looking glass over the mantelpiece and lay struggling on its back for a while, wings rustling, before whirring back into
the open. Jeremiah's peroration became louder and more irritable; the
birds, the bees, the June bug, all were part of life in the garden of
Eden, which reacted with total indifference to the momentous issue of
Altar Rock, key to the future of Philadelphia. Bonny Baker refused
to look at the plans for the removal of the rock, saying he had seen
them. When it was explained to him that, legally, Altar Rock could
no longer be accepted as Indian territory, he smiled with infuriating
smugness and replied, "The fact that Abe Woodhouse put the issue
in front of the Meeting indicates that he feels the way I do."

"Forgive me, but I don't understand," Jeremiah said curtly.

"Obviously, he is also of the opinion that the only people to make
this decision are the Delawares."

"But the Delawares moved away from this area nearly fifty years ago."

"Be that as it may, I will not proceed until I have their explicit, written authorization."

"Very well," Jeremiah said, "if that is thy attitude, I will present it to the Meeting. Is thee prepared to abide by the sense of the Meeting in this?"

Boniface Baker's pale, slightly bulging eyes contemplated him; it was an unnerving experience, like being scrutinized by a large frog. "Let's cross that bridge when we get to it," he said.

Jeremiah sighed. "Peleg Martin? Does thee have anything to add?"

The old man grunted. "I unite with his sentiment. It is one of our testimonies that we must use creation with moderation. To allow Ben Franklin to start blowing up rocks violates that testimony, whether they are Indian sanctuaries or not."

Jeremiah sighed. "In that case, let me suggest to the Committee on Indian Affairs that Joe Woodhouse ask Chief Running Bull what his feelings are in the matter. Would that be in accordance with your wishes?"

The old man grunted. Boniface Baker said, with a hint of satisfaction, "That seems the logical next step."

"All right," Jeremiah said, "this brings us to the second purpose of our mission . . ." He opened his valise and took out the parcel of Ann Traylor's diaries. "These journals were delivered to me for inclusion in the Friends' Historical Library. I am sorry to say that Isaac Woodhouse, myself and, I am sure, Peleg Martin consider this a dangerous idea."

Boniface Baker raised his eyebrows, which made him look even more like a frog. "May I ask why?"

"Because they contain highly personal information on members of the Meeting which we do not feel should be made public."

"For instance?"

For a moment Jeremiah considered jolting his brother-in-law's smugness by revealing what he knew about his antecedents from the diaries; but he conquered the un-Quakerly impulse. "Forgive me, Peleg, for mentioning this, but the diaries reveal, for instance, that Caleb Martin is part Negro."

At last that seemed to make some impression on Boniface. His bulging eyes seemed to harden, Jeremiah could not make out whether with anger or concern.

"I see. Thank thee, Jerry." He gave him a smile that had about it an odd finality. "I had better look through these diaries again. Now, if thee would like to visit with Caleb before supper, it would be better not to tarry. I will ask the stableboy to bring out the chaise for thee and Friend Peleg."

"Don't bother," Jeremiah said, rising, "I should like to see Beulah first."

While making his way through the semi-darkness of the landing and the stairs in search of his sister, Jeremiah felt overcome by a strange, irresistible melancholy. The atmosphere of the place, remembered from previous visits, got the better of him again. It seemed to exude from everything: the furniture, the walls, the house itself. The Bakers lived in what could be called baronial squalor. He had never forgotten his first visit to Beulah after her marriage, when he had been received in audience by the imperial grandmother, enthroned in a rocking chair in front of the stove in the kitchen, where she spent her days watching her granddaughter-in-law make a mess of things. Beulah had barely been able to talk to him, so busy had she been boiling water for tea, stirring a pot of soup large enough to feed an army, sweeping the floor of the kitchen; during their stilted conversation the old woman had helped herself to one hard-boiled egg after another, stuffing the shells into the hollow of her clawlike hand as she peeled them, only to throw the shells over her shoulder onto the floor behind her when she was through. It had seemed a sign of utter contempt; there could be no doubt that she despised her new granddaughter-in-law. Only later, after he had become familiar with the household, had he discovered that she threw whatever she wanted to discard over her shoulder, regardless of whether Beulah was there or not; so did everybody else. Babies crawled about the living-room floor followed by puppies, or cats, or tame crows, or geese, all of them completely uninhibited; even when there were visitors, nobody bothered to cover the children's buttocks or, for that matter, to run after them with a mop. To see gentle, innocent Beulah, who had been adored and protected all her life, trying to cope with this bedlam had been heartbreaking.

He found his sister in front of the kitchen stove, clanging and clattering the same pots and pans she had battled with during that first visit. The only thing that seemed to have changed was that now, instead of the grandmother, a fat, sleazy black woman sat lolling in the rocking chair, watching her work; all that was lacking was a bowl of boiled eggs by her side so she would have something to throw over her shoulder to keep her mistress busy. He had known the fat slave for years; every time he saw her she seemed to be a few pounds heavier and to sweat more profusely, with dark patches under the huge black arms, her face, built up of layers of fat, perpetually glistening with perspiration.

"Hello, Medea," he said grudgingly; his sister stood with her back to him and would not have heard him even if he had shouted. The Negress, as by some complicated mechanism inside her huge body, slowly wheeled the top half of it in his direction like a gun turret, spat out a sunflower seed and flashed a grin when she recognized him.

"How do, Massa Jerry?" Her voice was girlish and charming, like that of a fairy confined in a sow by a witch's spell. She stuck out a leg the size of a bowsprit and nudged her mistress' rear with her foot. "Look who's here, honey!"

Beulah dropped the lid of a pan, startling a cat asleep on the table; it jumped to the floor and stalked away. "Jerry!" she cried and was about to run toward him, but some ghostly apron string of her own creation drew her back to the stove to put the lid back on the pan and shuffle another one around before she finally greeted her brother.

As he held her in his arms and kissed her hair, he felt that she was even thinner than she had been the last time. "I'm so happy to see thee, Beulah," he said, "and looking so well."

She searched his eyes with a helpless, haunted look, as if she detected the insincerity in his words; then he realized that she simply had not understood.

"Thee looks well!" he shouted, nodding and grinning. "I love thee!"

"Oh, Jerry," she said with a sigh of relief and happiness, "I missed thee . . ."

He pressed her against him, suddenly overwhelmed by the brevity of their lives, the evanescence of love. Yesterday they had dressed up together, in front of the looking glass in their parents' bedroom in the old house on Front Street, giggling and full of excited whispers; tomorrow they would be gone forever, their bones crumbled to dust, their smiles forgotten, their love returned to God. "How is thee, love?" he yelled, aware that he could express very little of anything at the top of his voice.

But she saw in his eyes what she could not hear from his voice, and the happiness and sadness with which it filled her were unbearable to watch. "I'm well, Jerry, I'm really very well . . ." She said it with the harshness of the deaf and he knew that the words meant nothing; all she was telling him, with everything she had, was that she felt as he did. He had always been protective toward her, always known that she was not meant to be sent out into the wintry day of life alone; he had often thought that they would both have been better off had they never married, but gone on living together in their parents' house. But that would have meant no Obadiah, no Melanie, no Becky, Abby or Joshua; they would merely have hoarded life in front of that looking glass, giggling and whispering, frittering the years away in uncreative happiness. He discovered to his dismay that, however hard he tried, he could not make it sound like a bad idea.

"Wait! I have some soup for thee!" she cried. She turned to the stove, wiping her hands on her apron. He knew she was trying to express her emotions with the only means at her disposal; he hated the grinning presence of the fat Negress behind her back, watching her every move, hearing their every word. He turned around and said, "Come, Medea, leave us alone for a while."

"Oh, sure, sure," the young, melodious voice said, full of understanding, while the monstrous edifice in which it was held captive rose rustling from the chair with multiple motions and shuffled out, taking a purely ornamental broom along, like a monarch his scepter. He sat down on the chair she had vacated; when Beulah turned around to give him his soup, he relished her joy at the discovery that her black shadow had gone.

"Thank thee, Beulah," he said, stretching out his hands to receive the bowl.

"Careful, it's hot," her dead voice clacked.

"I will, Beulah!" he cried reassuringly. "Stop worrying about every-body else, come and sit with me!" He gestured toward his side.

She pulled up a stool and sat down beside him and watched him as he drank his soup. Suddenly he had a strange sensation, as if all that had happened during the intervening years had been but a dream and they were about to wake up in front of that looking glass. It lasted only a moment; it came and went like a flash of reflected sunlight.

He drank his soup, which was hot and tasteless; he lowered the bowl with a happy sigh and said, "Oh, that was good!" She was looking at him with an expression of love and knowing sadness, as if she had been touched by the same fleeting thought as he. He put his hand on hers; for a moment they sat gazing into each other's eyes; then, as by a common impulse, they lowered their heads and turned their reunion in front of the stove into a silent meeting for worship.

As Jeremiah Best and Peleg Martin drove to the quarters in the swaying chaise, there was no small talk between them. The reason for the awkward silence was the purpose of their expedition, to go and berate Caleb for trying to find solace in rum. What gave them the right to loom in front of this tortured soul, driven crazy by excru-ciating pain, and hold forth at him about the damage done to that of God within him by his drinking? Jeremiah did not know how Caleb had broken his back; it must have happened when he was still a child; he had never known him without that contraption of leather and iron that he had to wear. This much was certain: Caleb had spent most of his life on the rack.

It had been some time since Jeremiah had visited the slave quarters of the island; as they approached the compound, he became aware that something had changed. A taint had attached itself to paradise, an odor so penetrating and offensive that he wondered what on earth it could be; it smelled as if, somewhere in the fields of flowering shrubs, a corpse lay rotting. "What on earth is that stench?" he asked.

Peleg replied, without looking around, "Indigo."

"Thee means it's the blossoms that spread this horrible smell?"

The old man shook his head. "It's the fomenting leaves in the vats over there. They also bring the flies."

There were indeed a great many flies about, the horse was plagued by them. "I did not know that," Jeremiah said. "What a horrible thing to live with!"

Peleg grunted. "That's why only Negroes will work with indigo. Their sense of smell is different from ours."

They were passing what seemed to be a series of open cesspools at different levels, connected by a wooden aqueduct with a pump in the distance, worked by two slow-moving Negro slaves. A flatbed cart pulled by two oxen, loaded with sheaves of leafy branches, had just arrived; field hands were pitching the sheaves into the highest of the cisterns, others were working a creaking treadmill that kept a paddle wheel churning in the second. On the edge of the field stood a large, open shed with a series of lattice floors, like a drying shed for tobacco. "Is that where they dry the plants?" Jeremiah asked, to make conversation.

"No, that's where they dry the sediment. First they steep the leaves in the top one of those vats until they ferment; they beat the juice in the next one with that paddle wheel, drain it off and heat it in the third until crystals form. Finally they scoop out the sediment, pour it into molds and put them up on those shelves in the shed, out of the sun. That's how it's sold, in cones, like sugar."

The slaves looked well fed and reasonably contented despite the stench and the horrible flies that must be swarming around those vats by the millions. "It's a hard life," Jeremiah said.

"Nonsense," Peleg snorted. "A sailor has a worse life at sea. It's sentimental vapors, this modish jeremiad about slavery. If I had to choose between being rounded up by a press gang and shipped out around the Horn or being put to work as a slave on a Quaker plantation, thee would find me treading that mill with a song of praise." He grunted derisively. "That snake in the grass John Woolman with his sermons against slavery does not know what he's talking about. He has never had any slaves himself; he just tells other people what to do. Nowhere in the writings of George Fox or Will Penn will thee find one word against the keeping of slaves, as long as they are treated in a Quakerly fashion. My first slaves were paid for by the Meeting; would they have done that if they had not been clear about slavery? Let Woolman talk about coats and britches, not about slavery or how to run a plantation; he could not run a plantation without niggers and make it pay, neither can anybody else. And yet that man is given precious time each yearly meeting to hold forth at us about how sinful we are to keep slaves, how sensitive and tender is the soul of our black brother, how evil it is for a Quaker to keep him in bondage like a beast. Brother? They are no better than monkeys, and vicious ones at that."

Jeremiah did not know what to say. Now that he was aware of Peleg's past and the truth about Caleb, he could not understand how the old man could talk like that. If this was his concept of the Negro, his dalliance with the slave wench had been a foul deed: not a desperate man finding solace from his sense of loss and his loneliness in the arms of a woman of another race, but a randy farmer finding relief with one of his animals. That made Caleb the outcome not of an illicit dalliance, but of a visit to the outhouse.

Some of his disgust must have communicated itself to the old man, for he suddenly heard him say stiffly, "I'm sorry if I offended thee. The truth is often unpleasant."

Jeremiah turned to face him. The expressionless black eyes met his unflinchingly; the craggy old face, hewn out of bedrock, was set in the scowl of self-righteousness that had not changed as long as he could remember; it was as if all he had ever known was not the real Peleg Martin but his statue. What could he say? One did not argue with a monument. Yet who was it that had said if you dig deep enough, you will find that most men never grow up beyond the age of seven? Gulielma Woodhouse, of course; only a spinster could come up with a statement like that. For a moment her image came back to him as he had last seen her, in that impossible Indian outfit, a man's Quaker hat to shade her eyes, a rifle slung across her shoulders, trotting off on her pony, stringing along a mule that was virtually encased in a traveling apothecary with a hundred little drawers, all of them labeled in her mannish handwriting. He wondered where she was; probably somewhere beyond the mountains, where the only white people were outlaws and the only Indians wandering hunters. He envied her her strength and her untrammeled tolerance, and was grateful she was five hundred miles away, enabling him to admire her without being disturbed by her presence. Saints could be tolerated only *in absentia,* especially mischievous ones with pale gray eyes that instantly spotted the seven-year-old boy hiding inside the clerk of Philadelphia Monthly Meeting.

"Phew," he cried, "those flies are vicious!" He concentrated on chasing them and the smiling eyes of Gulielma Woodhouse.

* * *

During the ride Peleg Martin spotted the weakness of the management of the plantation, the vacillation, peculiar to Friends, between unctuous coddling of the slaves and hard business sense. He did not mind either attitude, as long as it was consistent. He respected any man who set his slaves free out of honest conviction, like Benjamin Lay, although he considered him a fool. He was the first to understand what prompted an owner to consider niggers sub-human; he should know, he had dealt in slaves long enough. A good thing he had retired from the trade before the present fashion started of condemning their importation as reprehensible, as if that were morally worse than to breed them from stock. It wasn't, for the only hope for the nigger ever to become human was improvement by selective breeding. Look at Caleb; he might be a weakling and a drunkard, at least he was better than the rest of his nigger mother's brood. 'Ah!' Peleg thought. 'If marriage and old age had not castrated me, how many generations of Calebs and super-Calebs could I not have bred in the years of my manhood! How many sub-human critters could I have improved by granting them the gift of my own seed! Scores of them!' But he knew that he too had been guilty of inconsistency; not out of virtue, out of sheer cowardice: fear of the consequences, fear of his wife, fear of hell. If, verily, whosoever looketh upon a woman to lust after her hath committed adultery with her in his heart, he was guilty of the sin of fornication a thousand times over, not only before he married Hannah but after, when the devil began to feed upon rejection, prissiness, frigidity. He had sown a thousand bastards in his mind and sold them in the open market, and why should that be sin? Look at the poor brutes! It would take many, many generations of selective breeding before they could take their place as full human beings; it might well be that the last trace of their blackness would have to be bred out of them to achieve it. Would that not be the only true, realistic way to lift them out of their bestial darkness? Would that not be the only honest, truly godly activity for Quaker males like Boniface Baker, caterwauling about "respecting that of God in our Negro brethren" while keeping them chained? What good did it do to sit with them in meeting for worship every First Day, to nurse their sick, teach their children to read and write, while keeping them beasts of burden? What hypocrisy, to sermonize at your niggers, telling them how all men were equal before God while working them like mules in the stench of rotting pulp under the torture of a million flies. It seemed a graver sin than to open the road to humanity for their future generations by mounting their wenches and breeding them. Look at those slaves there, right now: lazy, sullen, squalid. Look at the mess: fields unweeded, shrubs choked with vines, sheaves flung into the brine without cutting the twine! And that treadmill would turn twice as fast if it were worked by chimpanzees instead of by those lazy lollards, who must have acquired the knack of turning it just short of stopping. Where were the drivers? Was that hulking, one-eared moron squatting on the platform of the pump and picking his nose supposed to be one? He must be, for he carried a whip. There you went again: any slave, however dull-witted, knew by now that whips were shown but never used on a Quaker plantation. Another bit of mealy-mouthed hypocrisy! And where was Caleb? Why pretend to be the overseer of a plantation if you are nowhere to be seen? No wonder the slaves got out of hand; the hospital must be a roost of malingerers.

As the chaise, creaking and swaying along the pot-holed cart track, entered the quarters, Peleg began to notice something else. Nothing looked different from what he had already observed: sullen slaves, unruly bands of shrieking children, flea-ridden dogs scratching themselves on the dilapidated porches of hovels, but an instinct he had acquired during his many years in the ebony trade warned him. An atmosphere of secretiveness, a sense of brooding insurrection was in the air; he could not shake it off. When they finally drew up in front of the overseer's cottage and were welcomed by his son, who had obviously been warned of their visit and was waiting for them on the porch, he confronted him absent-mindedly and, once inside, eldered him about his drinking without conviction. Something was going on here, something was wrong. What could it be? Were they planning an insurrection? There could be no mistaking the smell of conspiracy, the surreptitious excitement that electrified nigger communities whenever there was trouble brewing. It always restored the tribal rapture; all sense of separateness and individuality was drowned in the ecstasy of planning an act of communal violence.

He stared at Caleb, listening to Jeremiah Best's assurance of the loving concern of the Meeting for Friend Caleb and his rumored failure to adhere to the testimony on alcoholic beverages. The somber, measured voice of his son replied, "I am sorry if I caused offense by having rum on my breath during the visit of young Joseph Woodhouse. That day I was plagued by pain in my back, for which there happens to be no other remedy." It seemed for a moment as if the dark eyes of the boy conveyed a wordless accusation as he shifted his gaze from Jeremiah to his father. It must have been a trick of the shuttered light, or maybe only his own bad conscience. The boy could not possibly remember how it had happened. Someday he might find out about his mother, God forbid; but nobody knew what had happened that morning, long ago, when the baby had come crawling into the house where his tormented, drunken father lived, who, taunted unbearably by his mere presence, had kicked the child with his heavy boot, with all his might, as if a cur had come crawling in from the quarters. Nobody knew, the child had been too little to remember; the only one who remembered was the man who had done it and who had tried in vain to expiate it by nursing him day and night, making a little harness to support his back that would not heal, swearing off alcohol forever after, restraining his violent temper with an unrelenting, self-punishing effort of will until he had turned into a man of stone who no longer betrayed by the flicker of an eyelid whether anything enraged or delighted him. As he sat there gazing upon the child that God, in His enigmatic omnipotence, had created when his seed sprang into the womb of that writhing, eye-rolling black temptress, he realized that the only redeeming element in his sinful life had been his love for his son. For deep inside him, the tenderness he had felt for the hurt child survived. What he missed most was picking him up, carefully so as not to hurt his back, pressing the incredible softness of his little cheek against his, no longer smelling the babyish scent of his hair, feeling the fragile, throbbing miracle of life contained in his little body. No wonder Hannah had never suspected that Caleb was not a survivor of the yellow fever, but a bastard. He had loved that child as Adam must have loved Abel; sometimes he wondered how that first father had felt as he squatted beside mankind's first grave. Maybe he too had felt this sense of mourning, tinged with the faint, fleeting hope that there was a land across the River Jordan where he would hold Abel in his arms again and whisper, "I love thee, mannikin; I love thee, little beastie . . ."

"If it is all right with thee, Friend Jeremiah," he said, "I would like a moment alone with my son."

It was obvious from the hesitancy with which he rose and walked away that Jeremiah assumed he intended to berate Caleb in private. How little people knew one another, how dark was the glass in which they discerned their own faces!

* * *

During Jeremiah Best's sanctimonious ministrations Caleb Martin had been shaking with rage; the moment he was alone with his father, his fury subsided. Once again, he was overcome by the nostalgia that always overwhelmed him in the old man's presence, a yearning for the goodness, rectitude, strength of character of the majestic old Quaker. If at times his work made him think of the human race as a sickness of the earth, he need only think of his father to halt the rush toward the black chasm of despair. Mankind could not be all bad if it produced noble men like Peleg Martin. If only he could live up to his father's standards! If only he could make him feel proud of his son! Listening to Jeremiah Best's Quakerly reprimand, he had felt like wringing young Joe Woodhouse's neck, not because of the boy's perfidy, but because he had demeaned him in front of his father. He had planned to tell the old man the whole thing had been an act of revenge by a despicable young pipsqueak, but the moment they were alone, his father's eyes made him feel like breaking down, sobbing on his shoulder, crying it all out: the pain, the loneliness, the despair. For although the expression on the granite face did not change, the eyes looked at him with love.

For a moment they sat opposite each other, motionless, while a desperate hope flickered in Caleb: maybe this time it would happen, maybe this time his father would open his arms for him and shelter him while he, at last, dropped all pretense, all the pathetic fakery that neither of them believed in, and became for a few minutes of truth the terrified, lonely boy he really was. During those moments of stillness full of promise he almost mustered the courage to fall on his knees and hide his head in his father's lap, but he left it too long. His father turned around and picked up a dish tied up in a kitchen towel, which he had brought with him. "Thy mother baked thee a pie," he said, his voice cracked and hoarse.

"Thank thee, Father." He took the dish and went to put it on the table.

As he did so, the old man spoke again. "What is the matter with thy slaves?"

"What does thee mean?"

The old man gazed at him. His eyes seemed all-seeing, all-forgiving. "Thee knows what I mean. I felt the tension in the air as we drove in. What is it?"

Caleb hesitated. The chance of unburdening himself had passed; now, suddenly, here it was again. Should he tell him about the murder, the impending execution? His father must know as well as he did that the entire so-called reality in which the plantation lived was a fiction, artfully nurtured by the slaves; that they had a secret life of their own which was the source of their defiance. His father must know that, to the niggers, the names they had been given by their masters were a mockery, that once they were out of earshot of the white man, they called one another something different. At times, listening in the darkness of the night, he had speculated as to what their true names might be: Scipio, Big Barlow or King; Cleo, Silent Panther; Cuffee, Flashing Snake; but even as he dreamed them up he knew that these were the imaginings of a frightened white man trying to identify, to understand, so he might dominate them at last. Sometimes he had the nightmarish suspicion that the real masters were they, that the real sanity was theirs, that the secret of salvation had slipped from the hands of their masters, himself included. But these were nighttime thoughts, the musings of an overseer who lay listening in the darkness to the rustlings, the squeaks, the whispers, the distant laughter that turned out to be nothing but the wind in the trees, the wavelets lisping in the reeds. "Maybe thee is right, Father," he said. "We had some trouble after one of them was killed in an accident a few days ago."

"What kind of accident?"

He dared not look at his father's eyes, for they would see the lie. "We just started processing the first crop, they had to get used to the machinery again; one of them was brained by the paddle wheel."

"The paddle wheel? At the speed thy slaves are turning it, it could not brain a fly."

The eyes could not be fooled; he turned to face his father. "Someone crushed his skull with a rock. I don't know who. But I know why: a young wench. A widow. Any man who sets eyes on her dreams of nothing but grabbing her for himself. I'm sorry I lied. I did not want the house to know."

As always, there was no reproach in his father's eyes; only love. "Was her husband killed too?"

"No, he died of snakebite."

"Never trust snakebites when it comes to slaves."

"I am inclined to believe it in this case, for there was no revenge."

"Ah?" The old man frowned. "Is there a nigger court in this plantation?"

"Yes," he said uneasily. "Isn't there everywhere?"

"I should say not." His father's disapproval was disturbing. "What form does their revenge take?"

Caleb began to get nervous. "Well, it begins with a night of working themselves up into some sort of trance . . ."

"How? By singing?"

"No. With drums. The next morning, the man they have sentenced is found hanging from a tree or from a gibbet in the fields, always in the same spot where the murder took place. He always has the rope belt of his victim for a noose."

"How many times has this happened?"

He looked away again. "A few times. Four, five . . . I never know when it will happen; sometimes the victim is found the morning after the murder, other times it takes days, even weeks. That's what makes it so difficult to do something about it."

"Well, that is easy: They only carry out their executions when there is a full moon."

He gazed at his father with awe. Of course, that was the answer! Each time he had lain on his bunk listening to those drums until his temples felt as if they would burst, there had been shafts of moonlight across the room; when he rose at intervals to peer out of the window at the deserted road between the cottages, it had been as light as day. "Of course," he said. "I should have known."

"There is one way of stopping this kind of thing. Take their drums away the day before full moon and tell them that if anything happens before morning all males will be sold."

"I am sure that would be the solution," he said with a wry smile, "but Boniface Baker would never allow it. I have tried to take away their drums before, but was told that on a Quaker plantation slaves must be free to make music and sing and bang their drums whenever they feel like it, except during working hours."

"In that case, remove the wench that causes the trouble."

"I thought Joe Woodhouse was taken with her, but I understand Jeremiah brought a note from Isaac Woodhouse saying his wife had changed her mind, and does not want a house slave after all. Boniface Baker will certainly not agree to selling her in the open market. The only thing to do is to breed her, maybe that will calm her down. Not by any of the bucks here, of course," he added quickly. "That would only compound the trouble."

The old man said nothing.

"The overseer of one of the plantations downriver offered me the services of a stud buck that he rents out. He would let me have him for a morning, in exchange for a service I rendered in the past."

"Boniface would agree to that?"

"I'll have the man brought in by rowboat early in the morning, at the southern end of the island, away from the house. Nobody need know."

His father was silent for a while; then suddenly he rose. "Let me have a look at thy harness before I go."

Caleb obediently took off his coat, his shirt, his vest, and showed the harness.

"Has it been comfortable?" the old man asked, behind his back, while his cold, dry hands tested the strap around his son's waist.

"It's all right."

"Let me see." The strap was snapped tighter; it bit into his flesh, he could not help wincing. "That too tight?"

"No, no . . . It gives me better support."

"That's what I thought. Thee has been wearing it too slack. If this doesn't give thee solace, I'll measure thee and make another one."

"I don't think that will be necessary for a while, Father. This feels good."

"Watch out for the temptation to leave the strap too slack. This may hurt thee for a moment, but it will give thee much more comfort all day. I should know, after all the harnesses I built for thee."

"Yes, Father," he said, too moved by the ritual to feel the discomfort. "Thank thee."

"All right." There was a moment of stillness and waiting. Then he felt the cold hands alight on his bare shoulders. The voice said behind him, "God bless thee, son, and keep thee."

He closed his eyes. He had never found the words to express what he felt at that moment of blessing; it was a moment of pure light.

"Well, I'd better be going. Jeremiah Best will be wondering what is keeping me."

He turned around, the light still about him. "Yes, Father."

The old man held out his hand; he shook it gently. It never failed to amaze him how fragile it felt, such was the strength of those eyes.

"I'll thank thy mother in thy behalf for the pie." Then he was gone.

Caleb, unwilling to expose his twisted back and harness to public view, did not go out to the chaise with him. He would tell Scipio to buckle the strap tighter for a few mornings, as a tenuous tie with the old man, until the agony of the tortured muscles would force him to loosen it up again.

He heard the old voice say, outside, "All right, Friend Jeremiah, let's go." There was a silence, then, with a creaking and a muffled sound of hoofs, the chaise rolled off.

He went to the table, untied the knot in the kitchen towel and took out the pie. Blackberry pie and tea seemed a good idea for supper. He put the kettle on, lit the kindling in the stove; then he sat down and wrote a note to his colleague in Septiva Plantation. *"Dear Friend, further to thy offer to avail myself of the services of thy buck Cudjo . . ."*

As the quill scratched, the water in the kettle on the stove began to sing.

*   *   *

That night, just as he was about to go to bed, young Joshua Baker heard the call of a chuck-will's-widow in the tree outside his window. It had been so long since he last heard it that for a moment he was sure it was indeed a bird; then the call was repeated, slowly and urgently. There could be no doubt; it was Harry.

As he had done many times in the past, Joshua took off his shoes, crept out onto the dark balcony, climbed the balustrade, grabbed a branch of the chestnut tree and swung himself on top of it. When he straddled it, he was frightened, so long it had been since he had last done this. What the devil could Harry want? It had better be serious; the time of childhood games was over; the secret call of friendship had turned into an impertinence on the part of an uppity nigger. But when, after sliding down the branch in the darkness, he discerned Harry's silhouette in the heart of the tree, it seemed as if he were returning to the land of boyhood.

Harry and he had been inseparable after his father had given him the little nigger boy for a playmate at the age of three. They had slept in one bed, giggled at the same jokes, trembled in the darkness at giants and ghosts and explored together their fascinating bodies. Exploration had turned into sin; one morning, while making their bed, Mammy had called them back to their room in an angry voice, shrieked at them that they were sinful little buggers, that they ought to be ashamed of themselves and that she would tell Massa and Missus what they had done. That same night Harry had gone back to the quarters, where he belonged anyway.

Never before had Joshua gone through such bleak loneliness as during the week that followed; then, on the seventh night, the chuck-will's-widow had called in the chestnut tree outside his window and he had flitted across the balcony, beside himself with longing. The house and the lawn had been bathed in the stark light of a full moon, but inside the old chestnut tree it had been pitch dark; only at the last moment did he discern Harry as he came leap-frogging down the branch. He had stretched out his hands toward him, Harry had grasped them in the darkness, and so overwhelming had been the relief of feeling that hard, sinuous body against his again that the only way he could release the fullness inside him had been in a kiss. Harry must have felt the same; the moment their mouths found each other in the darkness, he had slumped against him, grabbing his head as if it were a gourd from which he could not drink enough to slake his thirst. They had made elaborate plans to escape together on a raft downriver and to ship out on a whaler; but they had been unable to shake off the growing awareness that Harry was a slave now and always would be, that no other relationship was possible for them in the future than that between master and slave.

They had met a few more times in the tree at dead of night; but by the time Josh became Caleb's apprentice, the transition had been complete. That was over a year ago; so it filled Josh with an eerie sense of reliving the past to hear Harry whisper in the darkness of the tree again. Harry told him why, after more than a year, he had called him out with the call of the chuck-will's-widow. "Scipio has been orded by Cap'n Caleb to take a note to Septiva Plantation," he whispered. "Scipio cannot read, so he gave me that note to tell him what it said, for on his last plantation the overseer once gave him a pass and when the paddy-rollers caught him it turned out it said, 'Give this nigger hell,' and they did. But this note," Harry whispered, "asks Cap'n Harris, the overseer of Septiva, to come by in a boat day after tomorrow with a big nigger called Cudjo, a stud buck he rents out to breed wenches who refuse to remarry after their husbands are sold. I know why he wants Cudjo, Josh—he wants him for Cleo. Now, thee doesn't want that to happen, Josh! Thee doesn't want Cleo to be raped in the fields by that man who has never even seen her before, only because she won't marry again! For God's sake, don't let this happen, Josh! If she has to make little niggers for Cap'n Caleb, don't let it be this way! Surely thy father would not allow this? Tell him, Josh—tell him! Let him stop Cap'n Caleb before it is too late!"

The voice in the darkness was urgent, desperate. For a moment they sat there again the way they had in the past. "I'll tell my father," Joshua said, with a proud sense of power. "I'll talk to him tonight. I'll tell him thee wants to marry her."

"No, no!" Harry cried, alarmed. "I don't want to marry her! I just want to protect her!"

"Why not? She is not thy sister, is she?"

"No, no! They would do me in for it, like they did Quash! No, Josh, please, don't say that to thy father!"

It was the first Joshua had heard about Quash's death being other than an accident. Maybe Pompey's had too. "What happened to Quash?" he asked.

But Harry was not telling. "Take her into the house, Josh!" he whispered. "As a favor to me, after all the years we have been friends: make thy father take her in as a house slave! Thee won't regret it, I promise thee. She'll be good to thee, I know, I know!"

The words shocked Josh, for Harry obviously loved the girl. "All right," he said, "I'll see what I can do. Has the letter gone?"

"Yes, oh, yes! Scipio had to do it, Cap'n Caleb would have found out if he hadn't!"

"All right, I'll go and see my father now." He turned around on the branch cautiously. He was about to crawl away when something moved him to turn his head and whisper, "Goodbye, Harry." It was not all he wanted to say, but he did not know how to put the rest into words.

Back on the balcony, he stood still for a moment, listening. Not a sound came from the garden; Harry had flitted down the tree and across the lawn with the noiseless agility Josh had always admired. He went to the doors of the study. His father was sitting in his easy chair, with his back to him, reading in the candlelight, so absorbed that he did not notice the still presence on the balcony.

He intended to tell his father about the note; but as he stood there, his hand on the latch, he was not sure it was the right thing to do. He needed time to think. Tomorrow morning would be early enough to stop Caleb's scheme.

As silently as he had come, he tiptoed back to his room, opened the glass doors and stepped inside. He started to undress, as he had been about to do when the chuck-will's-widow had called him. As he pulled his shirt out from his breeches, he caught sight of himself in the mirror. Why had he not told his father? The words had been ready in his mind. Why?

He pulled his shirt over his head, tossed it aside. He took off his shoes, started to unbutton his breeches, avoiding his reflection. Why had he not told his father? Did he want her in the house for himself? Years ago, as children, when they were playing Indians and Squaws in the wilderness at the southern tip of the island, Harry and he had done it to Cleo, as a game. He had wanted to cry off, but ended up doing it out of pride, as she had taunted him when Harry had done it first. It had not meant a thing to him at the time; he had just lain on top of her for a while, noticed that she had golden flecks in her eyes the same way Harry had; then he had got back to his feet and left her to play alone while he and Harry went for a swim in the river. He hadn't thought about the episode for years. Now, he thought of it again.

He undressed further until he stood naked in front of the mirror. "Cuckoo!" he said. "Hello, there!" He was prancing up and down, pulling faces at his reflection, when he heard a noise on the balcony. His sister! He ripped his shirt off the chair, held it in front of him and backed, heart pounding, toward his bed. He blew out the candle on the night stand, slipped underneath the covers and lay listening the way he had done as a child after doing something no one was supposed to see, such as staggering about his room drooling like a vampire and pouncing upon the pillow to sink his fangs into it.

How innocent he had been! He was suddenly overcome by a sense of damnation. It made him turn over, bunch up his knees underneath him, fold his hands and whisper his prayers.

* * *

It came as a disappointment to Abby Baker when her brother blew out his candle, plunging the room into darkness; she had been fascinated by his antics. Standing in the shadows on the balcony, she had watched him dance in front of the mirror, talk to himself, giggle, make little horns with his fingers at his reflection, swing his buttocks and wriggle his shoulders, oblivious of her presence. What fascinated her most was his ability to play games all by himself, something she was totally unable to do. The moment she was alone she became bored, unless she found something to do with her hands, but even that soon failed to interest her because she wasn't allowed to do what she really liked: take things apart, like clocks or the rusty old pistol she had found in the attic. The pistol had got her into trouble when she had rushed into her parents' bedroom one morning to show it to them. Her father had been sitting up in bed, his nightcap still on his head, a glass of milk in his hand; the moment he saw the gun, he had, with a cry of alarm, slammed the glass onto the bedside table, spilling its contents, and pulled the bedclothes up to his nose, crying with a stifled voice through the blanket, "Take it away! Take it away! Would thee shoot us all?" She had answered, "But, Dad! It's all rusty and old, it can't go off!" and he had replied, "If God wills it, even an umbrella can go off!" Her mother had taken the pistol away from her and, later that morning, had dropped it in the river, as if it were a dead snake; that night at evening worship her father had ministered on the peace testimony. After that, she had not dared take anything apart for a while, until Becky gave her the desk; and look what had happened.

The unfair thing was that she had taken the desk apart not just out of curiosity, but because she wanted to find a hiding place for her own diary. For the time being, there was only the title: *"These are the Secret Diaries of Abigail Baker of Eden Island, a Wanton of 10½ Years Old."* She had written "10½" very thinly, so she could change it into "11" after her birthday. The word "wanton" would

certainly pin Becky's ears back, should she come across it; she did
not quite know what it meant, but one thing was certain, it was much
more interesting than "bride." And if Becky sneered at it and said,
"What in the world makes thee think thee is a wanton?" she would
answer, "And what makes thee think thee is a bride?" Of course
Becky would marry Joe Woodhouse in the end, anybody could see
that, but there were sure to be many more fights between them before that happened, and Abby loved fights. She also loved to observe
people talking to themselves, pulling faces in front of their mirrors
or pushing up their breasts, the way Becky did. She had watched and
eavesdropped on them all for years; whenever she got bored doing
her samplers, she would sneak out onto the balcony and peer through
the curtains of people's rooms.

She knew a great deal more about the members of her family than
they knew about one another; she also knew things that, strangely
enough, had not happened yet. Not big events, small things: Harry
raking the lawn in the sunlight, Mammy huffing and puffing past him
with a basket on her way to the vegetable garden and pulling his
ear as she passed. All those things, she realized as they happened,
she had seen before. Once she had seen a silver tankard standing on
the little table in the hall, stretched out her hand to pick it up and
found it was not there; a week later her father had brought it with
him from Philadelphia and he and Mother had had a long argument
as to where to put it; sure enough, it was finally put on the little
table in the hall. One morning when she was on her way with Harry
in the chaise to the hospital with a basket of goodies for Messalina,
who just had had a child, they passed the old tree by the graveyard
and she asked Harry who was in that coffin on trestles underneath
it; Harry, astonished, said there was no coffin and she angrily told
him to turn the buggy around and see for himself; but by the
time they came back to the tree the coffin was gone. Four days ago,
there it had been again, underneath the tree exactly as she had seen
it before: standing on trestles, with Quash's body inside, and all the
slaves squatting in the grass, and the birds singing and the leaves
rustling and her father's voice wailing about Man whose days were as
grass.

When she was sidetracked by Joshua's antics in front of his mirror,
she had been on her way to Father. She wanted to ask him if she
could have a look at those diaries again because she was interested
in Great-granny Baker. She was interested in something she had
glimpsed just as the books were taken away from her: *"I think
that Willie Best may have come from a traveling circus, or be a
gypsy's child, for he can foretell the future."* Willie had been the
dwarf, her mother's grandfather, so she might have inherited her
second sight from him. She desperately wanted to find out about it.

But just as she was about to knock on her father's door, Becky
came banging out of her room with the sound of a mule train, making
Abby dart back into the shadows. Of course Becky did not notice
her; she never noticed anything that did not concern her directly.

She went into Father's room, in her nightgown; if only she wasn't going to ask him for those diaries!

The moment Becky had stepped inside, the wanton of ten and a half years, secret shadow of the night, tiptoed to the door to eavesdrop and find out what it was all about.

* * *

Boniface Baker had been lost to the world for hours. He had fallen under the spell of his grandmother's voice whispering in his thoughts and identified so intensely with the young girl who had written these lines a century ago that it was as if she were in the room with him. Alerted by a small movement out of the corner of his eye, he looked up from his reading and saw her standing in the doorway, like a hallucination; then he realized it was Becky.

To see her there at that moment moved him deeply. The Ann Traylor of the early diaries must have looked exactly like her: eighteen years old, determined, with that same transparent, vulnerable beauty. He had never thought of his grandmother as beautiful or vivacious or young; to him she had always been a stern old woman. Now he had discovered a ravishing creature who had sacrificed herself to join her husband in prison. He had just arrived at that moment in the story, and was still surrounded by people who had become real to him—Margaret Fell, Henderson, the housekeeper, Thomas Woodhouse, the steward, Mistress Best, little Bonny Baker with his lame leg, John McHair the poacher, the evil Justice Sawrey. It was as if he were talking to his daughter in the middle of a crowd when he said, "It is hot, isn't it, love? Thee cannot sleep?"

Becky smiled, the delightful smile that never failed to deflate him in moments of anger. "May I come in?"

"Of course. Sit down . . ." He pulled up a chair for her.

"Thee is sure I am not interrupting thy reading?"

"No, no, I'd love to talk with thee."

She sat down with grace. Whatever had made him think of her as merely an overgrown child? For the first time she seemed to have acquired womanhood in his eyes. Who was she? What was she really like? Maybe it was the crowd of ghosts that made him think: 'I now know the young girl who was her great-grandmother more intimately than I know my own child.'

"These diaries are absolutely fascinating," he began. "I'd love to tell thee about them."

She looked at him and smiled that smile again.

"All right," he said good-naturedly. "What does *thee* want to talk about?"

She took a breath as if to answer, then hesitated and looked down at her hands.

"Come, come, I'm thy father. There's no reason to be reticent with me."

She looked up; her eyes were like moonstones: limpid, pure, full of mystery. "I received a letter from Joe. Uncle Jeremiah brought it along. There is a line in it that baffles me. Maybe thee can help me understand."

"What does it say?"

"'I hope thy father will come to the right decision in the matter of Altar Rock. If he does, I will be delighted to pass Meeting with thee.'"

The miserable little twerp! The first time young Joe had brought this up it had seemed he was merely under the spell of his father. Now no other conclusion was possible: he was deliberately using his so-called fiancée as a pawn in a political game. The cad! She would be better off without him.

She was watching him intently. "I don't want to pry into thy affairs, Father. All I want to ask thee is: before deciding, think of me."

His first impulse was to put her mind at ease and say, "All right, dear heart, I will," as he had so many times in the past after requests that were a great deal more outrageous; then Ann Traylor intervened. She had been the same age when she made her decision to throw in her lot with the Children of the Light; she had married out of compassion, in the power of God. To give in to the girl's request merely to make life easy for her was to abdicate as her father. She was about to make a decision that would alter the course of her destiny; he should treat her not as a willful child, but as he would Ann Traylor.

"I'll be glad to tell thee what all this is about," he said. "First, let me ask thee a question. Is it thy intention to marry him?"

She met his searching gaze with composure. "Yes, Father."

"I need not tell thee that marriage is not something a woman enters into because she is charmed by the notion, as by a toy or a gown. It is not a credential of being grown up, it is a bond for life, a manifestation of the love of God in human flesh, as thy great-grand-mother put it in her diary the day she married thy great-grandfather so she might accompany him into prison." He looked at her gravely. "Knowing this, can thee truly say that thee loves Joe Woodhouse?"

That, obviously, was a question she was dying to answer. "Yes, oh, yes!" she exclaimed passionately. "I do promise thee, I do! Truly, truly!"

"What makes thee think so?"

She frowned. "Well, I—just *know*. I have all the symptoms: hot and cold flushes, I cannot think about anyone or anything else, I yearn to be close to him when he is not there and I act cool and distant when he is, I have written at least fifty letters to him and torn them up and . . ." She caught his eye. "Is—isn't that love?"

His heart sank. He had decided to treat her as a woman because of Ann Traylor, but these were not the words of a woman. Then he remembered that Ann Traylor had been twenty-eight when she married. "And why does thee love him?" he asked.

Her face lit up. "Well, for a thousand reasons. He is handsome, he is jolly, he is healthy, he is fun to be with, he—he loves *me*.

I cannot give any reasons, really. I just love him. I know I do. I know."

"What about his character?"

The question seemed to reassure her. "Oh, he is a dear. He is kind, he has a heart of gold, he . . . Why?"

He did not know quite how to proceed. "Before we go on, let me tell thee what the decision is that he refers to. Abe Woodhouse and the young Quaker merchants of Philadelphia want Altar Rock removed to allow the passage of bigger ships. I feel we should honor Will Penn's treaty with the Delawares, which mentions the rock as a Indian sanctuary to be respected in perpetuity. Apart from that, to destroy it would be wrong. As Peleg Martin says, it violates the testimony that we must use creation with moderation."

She looked at him suspiciously. "Does thee honestly believe that the Delawares still want it as a sanctuary?"

"No."

"If the entire city wants that rock removed, why not give in?"

She looked at him with the confident expectancy she had shown so often in the past when waiting for him to decide to do her bidding. He said carefully, "Before we go into that, I would like thee to answer a question, not to me but to thyself. What is the character of a man who holds his betrothed to ransom to achieve material gain for his father? I ask thee as an adult, not as a child."

She looked at him musingly for a moment, then she smiled that ravishing smile again and said: "Let me ask thee a question, as an adult. What is the character of a father who goes on procrastinating after he has made up his mind, knowing that his daughter may lose her fiancé as a result?"

He gazed at her, stunned.

"I have wanted to ask thee this before: Why does thee always tarry when someone asks thee for a straight answer? What purpose does it serve? I do not want to harass thee, I want to understand thee."

It was as if she had dropped a mask. She must be as tired of the father-child relationship as he was. "It usually is a wise thing not to decide on anything, however clear-cut it may seem, before having achieved clearness on it in meeting for worship."

"Is this common Quaker practice?"

"No, a personal peculiarity."

"I suppose the same can be said about Joe's dependence on his father: a personal peculiarity. He is not grown up in every respect yet, but I am sure that once we are married he will."

"But that dependence on his father makes him treat thee with utter callousness! As if thee were not a real person whom he loves, but—but an abstraction!"

She smiled. "That's just because he's a man. He wants to prove he is not a little boy on a leash any more by making it appear that he and his father made this decision jointly. Also, I suspect he likes the idea of having *me* on a leash for a while, panting for his proposal. He may not have admitted it to himself yet, but to break free from his father and to pass Meeting with me merely means exchanging one leash for another."

This was not his sweet, spoiled little daughter, this was a woman ready to take a man in hand the way Margaret Fell had taken George Fox, and Ann Traylor Bonny Baker. What was it that gave Quaker women such strength? "How can thee love him, knowing all this?" he asked. "The way thee describes him, he is a weakling!"

"Maybe this is what all sensitive men are like when they are young."

"What if he does not grow out of it? What if he turns out to be truly a weakling?"

She shrugged her shoulders. "In that case, I'll have to accept it. I cannot go on waiting for him to grow up before making up my mind. It would mean remaining a spinster for the rest of my days, like Aunt Gulielma."

"Thy Aunt Gulielma did more good than most married women."

"Perhaps so," she said, with a first trace of irritation, "but we can't all put on leather pants and gallop off with a medicine chest to look for sick Indians. Some of us will have to bear children, or there won't be any Quakers left, worthy or unworthy of the name."

"I did not intend to anger thee," he said. "I wanted to be the devil's advocate . . ."

She rose and kissed the bald spot on his head. "I know," she said, her breath a brief warmth on his skull. "It is just that my patience is running out. I love him, I hate him, I want him, I am furious with him, furious, furious, for not being strong and independent and coming galloping across the lawn on a white charger to elope with me, and a pox on both our parents."

He took her hand. "I marvel at thy wisdom," he said, suddenly feeling lonely.

Her eyes seemed to search his from a distance, despite their proximity. "Don't weaken, devil's advocate," she said. "I have not been proposed to yet."

He kissed her hand and let her go. She went to the door, turned around, blew him a kiss and was gone.

He took up the diary he had been reading. *"When I rose to ask to be married to the prisoner before he entered jail, Justice Sawrey looked at me with benevolence. 'Faith! The Quaker lad seems to have been sowing some oats!' he exclaimed. 'Certainly, young woman, thou canst give the fruit of thy womb a legal father before he starts his sentence.' When I told him that I was not with child but that I merely wanted to accompany him to prison, he looked at me as no man had ever looked at me before. It was as if I had done something unforgivable to him, personally. Then he said, in that icy voice I can still hear sometimes, 'I will not legalize fornication. I will sentence thee to two years in prison for blasphemy, wantonness and re-*

fusal to pay tithes. Then if thou wishest to make a mockery out of holy matrimony, marry yourselves, as I am told is the Quakers' wont.'

"So it came to pass that, on our first evening in Lancaster Castle, Boniface Baker and I rose amidst the small, unhappy group of Friends who had been rounded up and incarcerated that day, and he spoke, 'In the presence of God and this assembly I take my Friend Ann Traylor to be my lawful wedded wife, and I promise, with divine assistance, to be a loving and faithful husband unto her for as long as we both shall live.' I clasped his hand tightly and said, 'In the presence of God and this assembly I take my Friend Boniface to be my lawful wedded husband, and I promise, with divine assistance, to be unto him a loving and faithful wife for as long as we both shall live.' Then we sat down again in the straw, and it was as if there were a light about us and a great stillness, and so we were married.

"But alas, it soon became obvious that he was wasting away. The cell was a dank dungeon like the one in which the children were incarcerated. Its walls dripped with water; cavities the size of coffins, hewn out of the rock, served as bunks. Normally, prisoners remained there only until they had paid garnish to Mistress Fraley for better quarters, but in our case the Judge had given orders not to grant us any privileges, even if we paid the garnish. Not even lighter shackles were granted us, which was the first thing even the meanest felon bought for garnish. We crawled or crouched, unable to stand because we were chained by wrists and ankles, sickened by the stench of our own excrement and of the heads of the hanged being boiled in the kitchen below us.

"Although he was by far the most cheerful and loving among us, Bonny became rapidly weaker, and on Christmas Eve of the year of our Lord 1663 he died. He was lucid and at peace until the end, whispering to us he had no fear or pain, because of his knowledge that it was so ordained by the Lord in His infinite love and mercy. I, from my mortality, cried out, 'Why? What could be the purpose of God in letting thee die so young?' He looked at me as if he were already drawing away; I thought it was the light of the candle shining in his eyes and I begged Thomas Woodhouse to remove it. I heard him whisper, 'It is the seed of the future.'

"I did not want to disturb his last moments, yet I could not help but cry, 'What seed? Bonny, what dost thou mean?'

"He was silent for so long that I thought he had passed. But then his voice came, quietly, and with a strange joy which at that moment seemed, to me, demented. 'Remember me, and do not rest until . . .'

" 'Until what, Bonny? What?'

" 'Until, by thy labor, the seed has grown a harvest of light and love.'

"It seemed meaningless to me. I asked, 'How? When will there be a harvest?'

"Again he took a long time before he replied; I realized that he had to gather strength to speak. Then he said, 'As soon as thou canst say: if Bonny had not died in prison . . .'

" 'Yes?' I urged. 'If Bonny had not died in prison . . . then what?'
"This time there came no answer. He had gone home to God."

* * *

"In the presence of God, and of this assembly . . ." Becky Baker thought as she sat daydreaming at her great-grandmother's desk, an empty sheet of paper in front of her; then she shook off those girlish musings with determination. She wrote the first line of her letter. *"I love thee, Joseph Woodhouse, thee alone—not thee and thy father."*

It had seemed witty when she had thought of it on the way back to her room from her father's study. Now, after that daydream about their wedding ceremony, she was suddenly afraid that it might infuriate him sufficiently to make him cut off his nose to spite his face, by deciding he had to go on his European tour first or finding some other excuse for indefinite postponement. In truth, she had been surprised by her own brazenness when she had described his character and pretended mature detachment to her father. What nonsense! That was how she *wanted* to be! If only it were true! If only she could really feel like that, think like that, not for just a few minutes, showing off to her father, but when Joe and she were together, or when she woke up yearning for him in the middle of the night, or now, sitting here, about to write him in a lighthearted manner that it was time to let go of his daddy's hand and to come toward her on his own feet, not like a puppet on a string. And why not? Why should she not write it down exactly as she had planned? Heaven knew it would not be the first letter she had torn up.

"Dear Joe, I love thee dearly, thee alone, not thee and thy father."

Her uneasiness deepened to dismay. To think these things was one thing, but to write them down . . . She tore the sheet to pieces, small pieces, the smallest pieces she could manage. If ever, by accident, he were to set eyes on those words . . .

She pulled out a fresh sheet, put it in front of her and suddenly felt ashamed of her cowardice. Ridiculous! How could he ever have got hold of that piece of paper? And even if he had, wasn't it the truth? He was big enough to take it. Let's try again.

"Dearest Joe. I love thee dearly, thee alone . . ." But instead of maintaining her independence, she slid into the same old nauseating treacle again: *"and that is why I am overjoyed, nay, beside myself with happiness to be able to tell thee, in the strictest confidence, that my father has agreed to the removal of Altar Rock, according to thy father's sensible and selfless wishes . . ."* Ugh! To grovel for him was one thing, to grovel before his father . . . She tore the sheet up again, this time without going to the length of disintegrating it. Obviously, this was not the time to write any letter. She would have to sleep on it, write to him in the cool, objective light of the morning instead of at dead of night. She took her night bonnet from under the pillow, went to the mirror to tuck in her curls and was struck by the harrowed face that scowled at her as if it were stuck through

the board on the stocks. What made her think she was irresistible? He must be seeing hundreds of girls every day in Philadelphia, going to parties with them, drinking tea with them from the same cup, seeing them get tipsy on the rum and sugar that nowadays could be found in every Quaker parlor in town. What about Minnie Martin, or Anna Henderson, with her haughty airs and buck teeth? She wasn't ready for competition at all; sometimes, for a few moments, it might seem as if she were, but she was not really. Look at her! Look at that peaked, petulant face, those hurt calf's eyes, that minny little mouth! He might as well kiss the crease of his own thumb. What made her think she could afford tantrums and airs and impatience with such a buttonhole for a mouth? She had better grab him while the grabbing was good. She had better write that note, quickly, and never mind about groveling in front of his father; better grovel some more. What on earth had possessed her to feel so sure of herself? Look at her! Just look!

She looked at her weak little chin, her long, thin neck, her sloping shoulders; then she opened her nightdress, let it drop off her shoulders and bared her chest. Now, that was different! The rest of her might be mediocre, but her breasts were better than most. Let Anna Henderson try to compete with these, she thought as she pushed them up to make them stand out more conspicuously. Why, not even Minnie Martin . . . A small movement caught her eye in the doorway to the balcony. She said wearily, "Go away, Abby. Go to bed." She did not wait for a reply; she just closed her nightdress, got into bed and snuffed the candle.

She would decide tomorrow what to write.

*   *   *

Abby, filled with hatred for mean, sneaky Becky, slouched back to her room and heard, as she was about to light the candle, a soft yowling outside the door to the landing, followed by the wheezing of Bilbo sniffing at the crack. She did not really care for the huge, slavering animal and his whacking tail that always knocked things over, but tonight she opened the door and allowed the boisterous beast to burst into her room. She did so because of a strange sense of oppression, as if something eerie was afoot in the night.

She managed to make Bilbo lie down on the mat beside the bed, but it was obvious he did so only because he thought it was the beginning of a game. He lay restlessly, his great tail thumping; she had never known any creature able to express such frenzied activity while lying down. She lit the candle; the dog's huge, moist eyes gazed up at her, unblinking, with two bright reflections of the flame. She picked up her sampler and, sighing, continued to needlepoint the O of "thou" in the sampler's motto, *"But what dost* THOU *say?"* The "thou" was in red, the rest in black, and the motto was surrounded by pansies.

It was too dark to see the tiny stitches; she held it at arm's length and muttered, "I say: Poops to thee" and was about to throw it onto her bedside table when suddenly Bilbo lifted his head and looked at the doors to the balcony, his ears pricked up.

She froze, her hand with the sampler stretched toward her bedside table; then Bilbo began to growl. She knew as she saw him rise on his forelegs that the next moment he would go bouncing to the doors and start barking fit to raise the dead. She hushed him angrily with a whisper and blew out the candle; he lay down, a deeper shadow in the darkness, but went on growling, staring at the doors.

At first she did not dare; then she could no longer restrain her curiosity, swung her legs out of bed, hushed Bilbo once again, opened the doors and tiptoed out onto the balcony.

The moon was almost full. The world lay steeped in its eerie light. The trees on the lawn were shrouded with shadows, the outbuildings of office and laundry with their whitewashed walls seemed phosphorescent in the night. It was so still that she could hear the hiss and gurgle of the water foaming around Altar Rock clearly, as if it were close by. She was about to conclude that it must have been a coon or a bird in the chestnut tree when suddenly she saw a horseman cross the lawn in the light of the moon.

No one ever did that; only a total stranger—but he could not be a stranger, the ferry did not run after dark. A ghost . . . ?

She wanted to break away and run back into her room, but she could not, petrified as she was by the feeling that she had seen this before in a dream, a nightmare: a horseman slowly coming toward her with, dangling from the knob of his saddle, two ghoulish round things trailing long black hair, two death heads smeared with blood, Indians; he was carrying the heads of two Indians.

As she stood there, helpless under the spell of that power afoot in the night, she knew that none of this was true and yet it was unavoidable; he came slowly, inexorably, riding toward her until he reached the house, right below the spot on the balcony where she stood. The horse snorted softly and tossed its head with the tinkling of a bridle chain. She saw that the horseman was dripping wet; his clothes were sticking to his body, his hair was slick with water. A drowned man; the ghost of a drowned man on a horse . . .

Then a booming voice bellowed, "Ahoy there, Cousin Abby! Top o' the morning to thee!"

Phooey! It was George McHair!

Bilbo started to bark furiously; his roar, reverberating under the eaves, broke the spell. She heard her father come out onto the balcony and call, "Who's there? Is that thee, Caleb?"

She ran back into her room and climbed into bed, furious with stupid George McHair for riding across the lawn at dead of night. The clodhopper! Those mountain Quakers had no manners and no sense of time either; at home they were up and about at all hours, tending their traps, clubbing those poor little animals to death. If he had brought her another raccoon skin, complete with tail and legs, expecting her to put it on her head, she would scream.

She lit her candle again, picked up her dreary sampler; then she heard voices coming from her father's study. As she silently drifted back onto the balcony, headed for her father's room, she reflected glumly on the mystery of why she should want to eavesdrop on Cousin George's dreary stories about Indians and Calvinists that bored her to tears in the daytime. Why did a person have to be such a riddle to herself? Would she find somthing better to do nights, once she was a grown-up? She certainly hoped so.

She peeked from the shadow of the moonlit tree and saw them come in; George's leather pants squeaked as he walked. She heard her father's astonished voice, "Why, thou art soaking wet! What happened?"

George's bass voice answered, "Oh, I swam across the river with Betsy."

"Betsy?" her father asked, nonplussed.

"Me horse. I said to myself, why spend money on a bed in the inn when there may be a bit of straw waitin' for me in me uncle's house? So we just swam the river and here we are. I left Betsy to graze in thy pasture, Uncle, is that all right with thee?"

Pasture! And that about the lawn, where nobody was allowed to walk!

But her father replied, "Certainly, George, this is thy home. I'm glad to see thee, lad. But doesn't thee want to change into dry clothes first?"

She hoped that one day she might be as good a person as her father, but it did not seem an exciting prospect.

*   *   *

Boniface Baker concluded that young George McHair must be in some sort of trouble, or he would not have come swimming across the river at dead of night. Of course it was possible that he did not have the money for an inn; one tended to forget that there were poor Quakers in Pennsylvania; George McHair was one of them. He called Boniface uncle because their mothers had both been Martins, although only distantly related to each other; almost every Quaker in Philadelphia had a Martin among his ancestors. Tiny, frightened Saraetta Martin McHair had been ill equipped for frontier life; she had died young, leaving her widower to run wild on the prairie. Thomas McHair, otherwise known as "Buffalo," had gone over the hill years ago; now his son probably needed help. What with a senile old grandfather and an Indian half-sister, George must have plenty of problems; the village of Loudwater where he lived, homesteaded by his great-grandfather, was now overrun by hostile Scotch-Irish Calvinists.

"Well, lad, what can I do for thee?" Boniface asked.

George promptly lowered his huge, soaked buttocks onto the embroidered seat of the largest chair. His leather suit stank more than usual now that it was wet; even so, his body odor managed to get through; the swim across the river must have been the first bath he had taken for a considerable time. On previous occasions Boniface had felt irritated by the boy's uncouth manners, his propensity to knock over anything that the dog's swinging tail left standing; that night he was moved by the youth because he had just been reading about his great-grandfather the poacher, who must have been much the same. George obviously had inherited his love for the wilds and the big sky, as indeed had all of them; not a single male McHair had ever gravitated back to the town, and there did not seem to have been any female McHairs—other than the boy's half-caste sister, whom Buffalo had tried to pass off as a foundling. Of course nobody had believed him, so he had left, heaping abuse on the heads of the "sniveling, chicken-lipped Philadelphia Quakers."

"Uncle, there's going to be trouble with the Indians," George began. "Something has to be done, or there's going to be a massacre."

"Of whom?"

"Of everybody," the young giant answered solemnly, "Indians and settlers alike. It's those Paisley boys."

"The who?"

"Paisley, Uncle. Twins they be; their father is the preacher in the kirk. He is bad enough himself, the way he carries on in his sermons about God telling him to rout the savages from the promised land; but his boys are wicked, really wicked. A foreigner would not be able to tell them apart, but I have known them all my life, I'd recognize either of them in the dark. The both of them are no good, but Petesey is the worst. Petesey stands for Peter, Uncle, the other's called Polly, for Paul; but don't be fooled by the names, they are rattlesnakes, the both of them. They're always looking out for trouble, wanting to string up Indians from trees just for the hell of it. Sorry, Uncle, I did not mean to curse, but now Petesey is after Himsha. He hangs around the house all day, watching. He's not courting; he doesn't want an Indian for a wife; all he wants is to have his way with her and then pull up his britches and . . . Sorry, Uncle. Just because she's Indian." He paused, then he added casually, "She *is* Indian, isn't she?"

"Oh, yes," Bonny said blithely, although he did not really know. "Thee knows thy father brought her home as a foundling."

The innocent eyes gazed at him. "Is that really true, Uncle? Some people say that she is my sister."

"I know they do."

"Well, is she?"

He looked at the worried blue eyes that seemed to have brought into his house a bit of the mountain sky. Could this be why the boy had ridden all those miles on horseback, swum across the river and burst in upon his sleeping house? "Does it really matter, lad? I mean: she is thy sister, whether she is thy father's natural daughter or not, isn't she? But tell me more about this business of a massacre. If it is serious, it should be presented to the Meeting. As it happens, Jeremiah Best and Peleg Martin are here, both of them are on the Indian Affairs' Committee. So thy coming tonight may prove timely. The Lord has guided thee."

"Yes, to be sure," his nephew mumbled halfheartedly. "Thee knows that the French have been stirring up the Indians against the British?"

"Yes, I've heard about that. But haven't the Quakers the Indians' confidence?"

"No, Uncle, no longer. The Delawares may still be friendly, but these wild Indians from across the mountains, to them a white man is a white man, an intruder who wants to get rid of all Indians. Uncle, it's a powder keg."

"What makes thee think so?"

"My own ears and eyes. I trade with the Indians, I meet them all the time. And, well—there is another reason."

"Ah?"

"I have talked to my father."

So Buffalo McHair was back! It was an un-Quakerly thought, but this was not an unmitigated blessing. A drunken, rowdying, whore-mongering Quaker outlaw was an embarrassment not only to his relatives but to all of Philadelphia Yearly Meeting. "Did he come to see thee?"

"No, we just happened to meet on the trail. He had some Black-feet with him, told them I was an honest trader, and told me to pay them a fair price for their pelts. Well, the pelts were not very good, they had left paws and heads on to build up the weight, but they had on their war paint, so I did his bidding and bought the pelts at top price." He shifted uneasily in his seat; his pants squelched and oozed some more river water into the embroidery. "Then Father took me aside and said, 'George—thy name is George, isn't it?' And I said, 'Yes, Father,' thinking it was a joke, but he said, 'Thee knows, me boy, at my age a man loses count, if he is a man.' I have not often had the temptation to strike a person in the face, but this time I had, Uncle, God forgive me, for I was thinking of Himsha, and the hard life she has ahead of her as a half-breed—if she really is his daughter, that is. Is she?"

Again Boniface said, "Honestly, George, I do not know. Nobody knows except thy father. The thing to do would be to ask him straight out. If he still is the way he used to be when I knew him, he'll tell thee bluntly. Evasiveness was never one of his vices."

"I know," the boy said unhappily. "But I don't think I'll see much of him. He's a wild man, Uncle, truly a wild man. More akin now to the lion than to the lamb."

Boniface felt a stirring of envy at that unselfconsciously poetic description of the black sheep of the Pennsylvania Quakers. Maybe it was an echo of his admiration for the boy's distant ancestor John McHair the poacher, who had become something of a black sheep too, after migrating to America. "Well, tell me. What bad news did he bring?"

"He warned me that the Frogs were stirring up the Feet, and that any day now—"

"Who was doing what?"

"Sorry, Uncle: The French were stirring up the Blackfeet Indians.

That's what we call them in the mountains: the Feet, as a manner of speaking, and the Frogs . . ."

"The French. I understand. Now tell me what he said."

"Well, he said that there was going to be trouble with the Feet, that they were ready to raid the villages on the frontier, and he told me to go and see thee so thee might tell thy fancy Friends—sorry, Uncle, that's what he said—that they had better make peace with the Delawares in a hurry, or—well . . ."

"Well?"

"What he said, Uncle, was a little coarse."

"Never mind that. Tell me what he said."

"He said that otherwise the Quaker women would have their bowels around their knees and their babies would roast on a spit. He also described what would be done to the Quaker men, but I think thee has the drift of it."

"Did he suggest anything?"

"No, that was all he said about the Indians. But he said a lot of other things . . ." The boy's face took on an almost rapturous expression; he seemed caught up in the moment he had met his wild father, of whom he was obviously proud, in spite of himself. "I asked him where he lived and he said 'with the birds and the buffalo'; I asked him if there was anything he wanted and he said, 'Yes, what we want out there is a Quaker preacher. We need a good sermon now and then, underneath a tree, by a man who can make his voice heard above the roar of the boulders in the torrents. Don't let them send us one of those traveling ministers who just squat there saying nothing, as if they were about to—to relieve themselves.'"

"Quite, quite."

"'Send us a man who raises his voice,' he said, 'who brings the Quaker message as it used to be and kicks us in the ballocks with it.' Sorry, Uncle. 'For we are powerful men out there, and powerful sinners,' he said. And when he left, 'Go with God, Jim.' That time he called me Jim. 'Get lively, boy. No McHair should sit on his arse picking his nose waiting for the Indians to bring in their pelts. Come with thy father! Get drunk, get shot, get thee an armful of wild, randy woman and become a man instead of a pack rat! Is thee coming?' Then he said without waiting for the answer, 'No, thee had better not come now, thee had better go and tell those tight-buttocked Quakers in the countinghouse in Philadelphia that they must get back into the wilds with their message of that of God in every man, or they'll find themselves buggered by a Blackfoot, right in Fourth Street Meeting House, among all them fancy cushions.' Sorry, Uncle."

He could not help asking, "Does he still consider himself a Quaker?" It was a question not so much to the boy as to himself.

"Oh, yes, Uncle, yes!" young George replied. "He wears a Quaker hat, only he has stuck some red feathers in it. And inside it is where he keeps his tobacco pouch; I saw that when he took it off, to take a quid. He offered me one, but I did not take it, of course. Then he said, 'Boy, come where the free life is! Have the guts to face God on thy own, as the old Quakers did; stop hiding thyself among the rest of the crows thinking He will not spot thee. He will, Joshua, He will!' This time he called me Joshua. 'He will single thee out with His slingshot and make thee jump with a squawk, even if thee hides thy head under one of those cushions. Cushions!' I thought that was the last he was going to say, but he put his hat back on with the tobacco pouch inside, and said, 'Go and tell thy Uncle Bonny.' Then he raised his hand and said, 'Come, Friend Timawah,' that means Ax of War in the language of the Feet; and he rode back into the forest, with the Indians. He had a beautiful little horse, a salmon-colored mustang stallion. I would have given my right arm for that horse."

"Has what he said been confirmed by others? If I want to convince the Meeting, his word is not likely to be taken as final." That was putting it delicately.

"Well, no," the youth answered. "But I heard later from Uncle Ellis—that's Lone Seeing Eagle, an Indian trapper we know—that Timawah is a chief. Lone Seeing Eagle said that Father is a powerful man between the mountains and the river, and those pelts had just been an excuse, he said. I thought they were poor pelts, very poor. I didn't think my father could have really meant it when he asked me to start trading with the Feet at those prices. It would ruin me in a month. He is a strange man, isn't he, Uncle?"

"Yes." He felt moved to add, "But maybe less strange if we could only rid ourselves of some of our prejudices."

"What does thee mean, Uncle?"

"Thy father, the way thee describes him, is in many respects like his grandfather John McHair; I have learned a lot about John McHair in this journal of my grandmother Ann Traylor." He pointed at the book with the spidery handwriting that he had put aside when the barking of the dog had alarmed him. "Thee knows, I assume, that he was one of the earliest Friends?"

"What does she say about him?"

"He was a woodsman, like thy father and thyself; he ended up in prison for poaching on a judge's land, and because he was a friend of Margaret Fell, they lopped off his hand. That's why he later wore an iron hook."

"Ah? I wonder if that is his hook, the one with the straps, in our stable. I used to play with it; now I hang the horses' gear on it. Could that be?"

"It certainly could. As thee knows, he homesteaded Loudwater. He left Philadelphia because of some trouble with the Meeting and moved into the wilderness as a trapper. He became a friend of the Indians, and married a girl they had kidnaped during a raid in one of the other colonies. A white girl who was mute."

"Deaf mute?"

"No, she could hear all right, but whatever had happened to her seemed to have robbed her of the power of speech. She never spoke a word for the rest of her life."

"That must have been hard on him."

"I don't think he minded. He was a kind man, a real Quaker. My grandmother says that he built a house beside a little waterfall; that was why he called the place Loudwater. The house was struck by lightning before it was finished; the second house collapsed; the third was crushed by a tree—then he understood God's purpose and built a Meeting House first, for him and his wife and the Indians. His next house was spared. Thy grandfather was born in it. He was their only child."

"Does she say who Himsha is, Uncle?"

"I don't know, George," he answered patiently. "I haven't got that far yet. But my grandmother died twenty years ago. How old is Himsha?"

The boy's face fell. "Eighteen, nineteen . . ."

For a few moments they sat in awkward silence. Then Boniface asked, "Is there anything I can do to help thee, George? Thee knows that, to me, thee is a member of my family."

The innocent blue eyes battened onto his with disturbing intensity. "As a matter of fact, Uncle, the real reason why I came to see thee is that I want to ask thee for thy daughter Becky's hand."

It came as such a shock, and was spoken in such a colloquial tone, that Boniface gaped at him with incredulous astonishment. "I beg thy pardon?"

George gave him a peculiarly smug grin that might have been intended as a coy smile. "I know it's sort of sudden," he admitted. "But I haven't had much chance to come a-courting, as it is a good ride away. I promise thee I will be a good husband. I have a solid house, I earn money—oh, yes, Uncle, I earn a lot of money. After the wedding I would build a new wing to the house, to make room for the wee ones. And my old grandfather would be very happy to have somebody to play with. He's now gotten so daft, poor man, that he runs out to play with children whenever he can."

"Did thee discuss this with Becky herself?" Boniface asked, unable to believe that such brazen self-confidence could be entirely self-generated.

"No, not yet, but I'll talk to her now, if thee will grant us thy blessing. I brought her some coonskins for a hat."

The coonskins restored Boniface's sense of proportion. The whole thing was harmless, despite its alarming pretensions. "I'm sorry, George," he said kindly. "But I'm afraid thee is too late. Becky has been spoken for. As I understand it, she is about to pass Meeting with Joe Woodhouse."

"Oh? I didn't know that." He did not seem crushed by the information. Then he asked blandly, "And what about Abby?"

This was ridiculous. Maybe mountain Quakers arranged their marriages in this manner, but there were limits to the charm of rustic customs. "My daughter Abby is ten years old," he replied, more sternly than he had intended. "I would suggest that thee scout about for a future bride among more suitable prospects. Aren't there any girls where thee lives?"

"Oh, yes, Uncle, plenty of them, but they are all Presbyterians."

"I'm sure the Meeting would make an exception, in view of thy isolation, and agree to thy marrying out of Meeting."

"It's not the Meeting, Uncle, it's them. To those girls I am a fool, the butt of all village jokes; children follow me in the street jeering, *'Quaker, Quaker, no buttons on his coat'*—the rest thee knows. When Parson Paisley gets tired of preaching against the Indians, he preaches against the Quakers—which is me. I would never find a Loudwater girl, or any other girl on the frontier, ready to marry me; they'd sooner marry the village idiot."

"Well, I am honored that thee should think first of my daughters," Boniface said evenly. "But what about yearly meeting? Thee might meet some girls there."

George shrugged his shoulders. "I suppose so. I'll just have to wait until then. In the meantime, if thee should think of a suitable person, will thee let me know?

"I certainly will, George." It had been a narrow escape; the mere thought of fragile Becky, after her gentle upbringing, being jeered at in the village streets of Loudwater . . . "What is the rest of that song the children chant?" he asked.

"Thee doesn't know it?" There was that ghoulish, coy smirk again. *"'Quaker, Quaker, no buttons on his coat, but his britches are buckled, for he's as randy as a stoat.'* Has nobody ever sung that at thee, Uncle?"

"I can't say they have." The occasion seemed to ask for more, so he added, "But then, of course, I have never lived among hostile Puritans. I must say, I admire thee. I don't think I could have adhered to the peace testimony under that provocation."

"Oh, it does not bother me." The young giant shrugged his shoulders. "They don't actually do anything, not since I embraced Petesey Paisley some years ago."

"Embraced?"

There was that grin again. "As a Friend, I could not strike him; he went on shoving me and tripping me up, so one day, after thinking it over in meeting for worship, I put my arms around him and said, 'Friend Petesey, I love that of God in thee, now let me squeeze the rest,' and I squeezed him in the power of the Lord. Since then, nobody in Loudwater has actually done anything. They just jeer."

"Meeting for worship? I thought the three of you were the only Friends for miles around."

"We meet regularly, Himsha and the old man and I. The old man chortles sometimes, like a baby, but that does not bother us, as it does not seem to bother God. For He's there; we are three, so He's there, in the midst of us. And when I am by myself in the forest, I sit by a tree, or in the shade of a rock, and there He is all about me, and I drink His peace like water from a spring."

It made Boniface embarrassed about his feeling of superiority. "I wish we could send out some doughty Friends to face the world with thee," he said. "But I'm afraid not many Philadelphia Quakers are likely to get the leading to move to the frontier."

"Oh, it doesn't worry me, Uncle; as long as they do not harm my family, it doesn't worry me at all." He rose; his soaked leather pants came away from the cushion with an ominous sucking sound. "Well, I'll be going to rub down Betsy now, Uncle. Is there room in the stable for her and me?"

"Don't be ridiculous. I cannot allow thee to sleep in the stable, thee is a member of my family. Go along the balcony, second door on thy right, that's Josh's room. I'm sure he'll be delighted to share his bed with thee. But I'm afraid there might not be room in his bed for thy horse as well."

"Oh, no, ha ha ha!" Young George threw his head back; his laughter was so colossal that the dog started to bark nearby.

"Hush! Thee will wake the girls!"

"Sorry, Uncle, but that was very funny. Imagine! The horse!" There must be a singular lack of humor in the wilderness for him to react so extravagantly to what had been, frankly, a very poor joke.

"All right, my boy, off with thee," Boniface said, trying to guide him to the doors. He might as well have tried to guide a boulder; the mere touch of those biceps gave him an idea of what his loving Friendly embrace must have been like; he was lucky not to have killed that boy. The thought of Becky in those arms . . .

"Good night, Uncle," the boulder said. "Thank thee, thee has been very good to me."

"I wish I had been able to help thee."

"Oh, thee has. See thee in the morning, God willing."

"Sleep well."

The giant moved away; Boniface called after his receding back, "Second door on the right, remember!" as the possibility of this land-slide entering Abby's room occurred to him; with his inexperience, George might not discover he had climbed into bed with a girl until her first terrified scream.

"Good night, Uncle. I'll be going to look after Betsy first."

"Good night." He sighed; then he settled down in his chair and picked up the book again.

"On Christmas Eve of the year of our Lord 1663 he died . . ." He had read that, and about the prison in Newcastle, the docks at Liverpool . . . Here: the holds of the slaver that had taken Ann Traylor, Mistress Best and her little son to the New World. *"Then came the night when, driven up to the deck by the feeling that I was suffocating in those holds without a breath of air, I was suddenly grabbed in the dark, my scream was stifled by a cruel hand, I was thrown down onto some ropes and, despite my desperate struggle, raped by someone whose face I never saw. Until this day I have no idea who the man was who became the father of my son; I am sure that God forgave me for never divulging that it had not been Bonny Baker."*

Boniface could not believe his eyes. He read the sentence again, slowly, carefully; he put the book down as the truth dawned on him. It had always been terribly important, to know he was the grandson of a saint, member of an exclusive family; it was the ground on which the whole edifice of his self-esteem had been built. The revelation struck him with such bewilderment that he picked up the book again and read on.

"I must confess that in the years that followed I was sorely put to find an answer to the question uppermost in my mind: If everything that happens is the will of God, why had He willed me to be impregnated by a faceless brute, cursing my womb with the sins of unknown generations? Was my child to be punished for the sins of his unknown fathers? It seemed cruel, vicious, utterly ungodly. I harked back to my husband's last words with an awful, deadly doubt, growing into despair: What in the name of the merciful Christ could the 'harvest of light and love' be that would grow from the seed so cruelly implanted in my womb? And this was truly a virgin birth; the faceless monster in the darkness was the first man I had ever known."

Boniface had barely registered what he was reading. He was so shocked, so shaken, that he sank to his knees and asked God, "Why? Why has this truth been revealed to me? Why now? Is there a reason? What is it?"

But there was no answer; only the soft, secretive chirp of a cricket in the night, and the distant hiss of Altar Rock.

CHAPTER THREE

I T was only at breakfast the next morning that Becky Baker learned, shocked, that Joe Woodhouse had been appointed by Philadelphia Meeting to join an expedition into Indian territory as their representative in a new survey of the Walking Purchase. She could not believe her ears, Joe had not mentioned it in his letter; then Abby said evilly: "Ah, that must be the massacre I dreamed of last night." Although everybody ridiculed her, it set Becky worrying and prompted her to take George McHair aside after the meal to beg him to go with Joe, to protect him—well, not quite protect him, for he did not need protection, but he did not know the Indian language and it would be a great help to him to have someone with him who did.

Poor George, who, despite his lumbering hulk and a voice like a bullhorn, was about the weakest and most vacillating person she knew, hummed and hawed and finally said that it was not up to him to decide, but to the Meeting. So she got hold of Uncle Jeremiah on their way into meeting for worship in the living room and boldly proposed that he suggest to the Meeting that George McHair be appointed to accompany Joe Woodhouse. Uncle Jeremiah did not seem enthusiastic, neither did Peleg Martin, whom he called in on this, but George spoke Delaware, because he had often been left in the care of the Indians as a child when his parents went to yearly meeting, so he was a natural choice. At their probing, George admitted that he had never met Running Bull, the chief of the Unamis, but that his father knew him. As she had hoped, Uncle Jeremiah ended by asking him to go; he was authorized to do so as both he and Peleg Martin were members of the Committee on Indian Affairs and this was an emergency. George mumbled that he had urgent business in Loudwater, so maybe they had better appoint someone else; but Uncle Jeremiah, who had come to like the idea, replied that the expedition would not leave for another week so he had plenty of time.

During meeting, thinking about Joe, Becky decided to give George a letter for him. Then she conceived the plan to write not one but ten letters, one for each day the expedition was expected to take; she would number them with stern instructions to Joe to open not more than one each day.

After meeting, everybody prepared to leave: her father for his office, Josh for the fields and the guests for the ferry. She went to George as he was saddling his horse in the stableyard. "Cousin George! Would thee mind tarrying awhile, to give me the chance to write Joe a letter?"

The youth gazed at her with a hunted look in his eyes; Uncle

Jeremiah called from the carriage that was about to take them to the ferry, "Oh, let him be, Becky! Give the boy a chance to get home!"

She was about to say something biting when, luckily, George himself decided it. "Oh, well," he grumbled weakly, "I don't mind. It's going to be full moon tonight, so I can ride after dark . . ."

"Full moon?" Peleg Martin asked in his croaking voice. "Thee says it's going to be full moon tonight?"

"That's right, Uncle," George replied. "I don't mind waiting, not at all—"

"Joshua!" Peleg Martin shrieked at Josh, who was about to ride off. "Tell Caleb it is full moon tonight. He had better watch out for trouble!"

"What kind of trouble?" Josh called.

"Never thee mind, boy! Just make sure thee tells him."

Josh dismounted and handed the reins of his horse to Harry. "Hitch her for me." He walked away.

Ten letters, all of them tender, loving, witty, entertaining, fascinating—Becky had her day's work cut out for her. As she was about to go, she saw the hangdog expression on George's face and tripped toward him, rose on tiptoe and kissed him on the cheek. "Thee is a treasure, George," she whispered. "I would not know what to do without thee . . ."

She left him staring after her, rubbing his cheek, and ran back to the house, filled with a radiant self-assurance.

"Dear, dear Joe: Here thou art, thy first night in the wilderness, and here am I, on an island far away, thinking of thee. If love has wings, our lonesome souls should meet somewhere halfway, above the clouds, over Philadelphia . . ."

She would teach him to think that he could sneak away!

* * *

In the unsentimental light of the morning, it all seemed less dramatic to Boniface Baker than it had the night before. By the time he sat down to breakfast with his family, he could not understand why he had felt such panic at the discovery that his grandfather had been not a saint but a rapist. After all, what difference did it make? He himself was no different, only an illusion had been shattered, and maybe it had been time it was. He was going to give it all some solid, unemotional thought; he would take the boat and, alone on the river, bring his doubts and his fears before God. But first there was work to attend to.

He sat down in his office and began the day's task by studying the spring request for yard goods. Caleb's estimate for the two hundred slaves was five hundred yards of men's blue cloth, six hundred yards bleached shirting, six hundred yards stuff for women's underwear, six hundred yards calico for frocks, one hundred handkerchief pieces and one hundred straw hats. He had added a footnote, *"I request no socks, on the assumption that knitting hose will remain one of the indoor tasks of women slaves."* The request represented a hefty sum, to which must be added Caleb's own salary of a hundred pounds a year and a two-shilling bonus for every cone of indigo over one hundred and fifty. The way the harvest looked now, they should do well this season; two hundred cones was a reasonable estimate. But the extra profit had to be plowed back into repairs and improvements such as a new paddle wheel, before they had more accidents like the one that had killed Quash. It also was time the whole lot of hutches was shifted again. To teach slaves cleanliness was a futile undertaking; the only way to cope with the accumulation of filth and vermin was by shifting the shacks every summer to burn the repulsive mess found under the floors. He could, of course, pare down the request without hurting anybody much; but Caleb, dour and unforthcoming as he might be, was a good overseer.

He was adding it all up when Josh knocked on the doorpost. "Father? Could I have a word with thee?"

He looked up, irked by the interruption. "What is it, Joshua?"

Josh came into the room. "Father, there's something I should tell thee. It—it's about one of the wenches. Caleb is planning to have Cleo forcibly bred by an outside buck, and I'm afraid there may be trouble."

"Caleb *what?*"

The boy repeated warily, "He intends to have Cleo bred tomorrow morning by a stud buck from Septiva, brought in by rowboat."

"What in the world possessed him to do this?"

The boy shrugged his shoulders. "I don't know. Thee had better ask him thyself."

"I will, I will! Right now!" He rose. "By the way, I'm grateful to thee for telling me this. This is not the way we want to handle our slaves, is it?"

The boy shrugged his shoulders again.

"The chaise is at the ferry. All right if I take thy horse?"

"Of course, Father."

He patted the youth's shoulder and strode to the stable, where he found Josh's mare saddled, hitched to the post.

The moment he mounted the spirited young animal, he knew he would have his hands full. It was exactly the kind of horse that would delight a callow youth; like its owner, it had little sense as yet and was alarmed by a whisk of wind in the indigo leaves, the swoop of a bird, even a sudden whiff from the pulp trench at the factory.

Boniface found Caleb at the factory, supervising the unloading of a cart of sheaves. "Caleb! What is this ridiculous idea of having a wench impregnated by a brute she has never set eyes on? What in the world got into thee?!"

Caleb, astounded, asked levelly, "What would be wrong with that, Boniface? All I'm proposing is to breed a slave who has become a bone of contention among the bucks. Since young Pompey died she has refused to pair up with anyone because she enjoys having all those males fight over her; this is the only way to put a stop to it. Who told thee about this, by the way?"

But Boniface was not in a mood to answer questions. "I don't care what thy arguments are! No wench on my plantation is going to be subjected to that kind of barnyard treatment! It's—it's an abomination!"

Caleb remained unruffled, an admirable quality in an overseer. "Look, Boniface, I appreciate thy interest in thy slaves. But as it is I who am supposed to run thy niggers for thee—"

"I don't care! I cannot allow this to be done! It shall *not* be done! Not while I am around!"

"Thee need not be around," Caleb said, still with admirable composure. "I intend to have it done at the far end of the island where there will be no witnesses whose sensibilities might be offended."

"But I *am* around!" he cried.

"I wish thou wert around more often," Caleb said quietly. "There is no better manure for the fields than the master's footsteps."

"Caleb, I want a clear answer to a clear question: is it understood that this—this abomination shall not take place?"

Caleb looked at him through narrowed eyes. "Why suddenly make an issue out of something we have done before?"

He was right; they had. They also had taken children away from their mothers and wives from their husbands, to sell them in the open market, always because the arguments were reasonable. Suddenly it struck him that what Caleb proposed to have done to the girl was exactly what had happened to Ann Traylor. "Where is that girl? Let's ask her what *she* wants."

Caleb's composure faltered. "Ask *her?*" he repeated.

"I do not object to the principle of selective breeding; what I object to is arranging for the violation of any woman, even if she is a slave."

"But she will never accept it willingly!" Caleb cried, provoked at last. "That's what I've been telling thee! At the moment she is the uncrowned queen of all thy slaves because she drives every single male rabid!"

"She won't do so forever. One of these days she'll choose a mate, and—"

"She will!" Caleb exclaimed angrily. "But *why* does thee think she's holding out like this? She wants a white man! She wants thy son!"

For a moment Boniface stood thunderstruck. Then he said, shaking, "I want her in front of my desk in my office one hour from now. And thee too." He got onto his horse.

The colt leaped forward as if triggered from a catapult; Boniface needed all his wits to prevent himself from being thrown as she streaked across the littered yard and down the straight furrow of the road through the fields.

By the time Caleb brought the girl into his office, Boniface had worked himself up into such a furor that her appearance came as

an anti-climax. Her face expressed nothing, her behavior was sullen.
But she was a statuesque, handsome specimen. No wonder all the
bucks were after her.

He asked her if there were anyone she wanted to marry; it needed
a prodding from Caleb to make her reply, "Nassuh."

It became an inconclusive, embarrassing interview. He tried to
arouse a spark of response in her, to no avail. It was a clear victory
for Caleb; even so, Boniface refused to let him go through with his
odious plan; little else was settled when Caleb left with the girl, yet
Boniface felt a sense of relief. It was inconceivable that Joshua, with
his upbringing, could be tempted by this creature; for one thing,
there was her funk; not just the reek of an unwashed body but a
musky animal scent, like that of a reptile. To a boy brought up as he
had been, accustomed to the perfume sachets and scented powder of
his sisters, this could be nothing but revolting. So on that score at
least, he could breathe easier. He sighed and rubbed his eyes; then
he got up, walked to the dock, untied the old workboat and rowed
out onto the river.

The birds were singing in the reeds and in the trees of the graveyard. Barely a week ago he had drifted past the island like this
and thought how fortunate he was, how it lived up to its name.
Now Paradise seemed suddenly lost because innocence was lost. The
decision to save the girl from his grandmother's fate had not brought
back his lost sense of virtue. He felt soiled, unclean, tainted. How
much was there to heredity? His father had been a gentle, sensitive
man, but Jahleel Yarnall, a Friend who bred cattle, had told him
once that individual characteristics usually jump one generation before showing themselves in a bull's progeny. He had always blithely
trusted his own impulses and motivations as being inspired by inherited saintliness, now he had to consider them suspect. He could
no longer trust the small, still voice that prompted him in prayer or
in meetings; for all he knew, it might be that of his grandfather
whispering to him in the silence.

There was only one solution: adhere to the letter of the Sermon
on the Mount. He could no longer decide for himself what was good
or evil.

*   *   *

"Who peached?" The question obsessed Caleb. He must find the
informer; there was nothing so damaging to an overseer's authority as
gossip between the quarters and the house.

In this instance, some nigger must have told young Joshua. The
logical thing to do would be to put pressure on the boy to make
him reveal his source of information. But although Joshua was
officially his apprentice, one day he would be master. So Caleb had
Harry brought in.

The moment the scowling, surly young slave stood in front of him,
Caleb knew that it must have been he. He was the living example of

the sentimental folly of making a pickaninny the pet of the master's children. Harry had been treated as an equal by everybody in the Hall for the better part of his life; no wonder he could not accept being suddenly thrown back into the quarters and treated like the rest. Caleb looked at him narrowly as he stood there, arms dangling, thick lips parted in a slack-jawed expression of stupidity, in his bulging eyes the expression of all animals in captivity: 'I will be slyer than he, I will break out one day.' Yes, here was one slave who would try to escape at the earliest opportunity.

"Did thee tell the Hall about my asking Mr. Harris to bring Cudjo?"

The boy grunted stupidly. A little too stupidly for him.

"Answer me! Did thee tell the Hall about Cudjo?"

This time the boy shook his head.

"If thee does not answer, I will have thee hung by thy thumbs until thee does!"

A flash of rebellion flickered in the sullen eyes. "If you touch me," the boy said menacingly, "I will tell Miss Becky."

Before Caleb realized what he was doing, his fist had crashed into that black mug, hard. It had been years since he had used violence on a slave; but what the boy had let slip had been unbearable: ruined by years of pampering and the pretense of equality, he now lusted after the daughter of the house. Caleb needed all his self-control not to batter the black ape with his fists until he was exhausted. What alarmed him was the gratification that would bring him; the blow had given him a foul, sensual pleasure, a physical satisfaction. Suddenly the door to the cottage was kicked open and a frenzied creature threw itself at his feet. "Cap'n, Cap'n, I didn't do it! Please stop 'em! Please, Cap'n, stop 'em, stop 'em!"

It was the little runt Cuffee. His behavior was so unprecedented that Caleb stood for a moment nonplussed; then the groveling man held up a rope and, folding his hands in supplication, begged, "Please, please, Cap'n! Save me, save my life, Cap'n! They're going to kill me!"

Caleb understood at once what had happened. There should be no witnesses to this, especially not young Harry. "All right!" he said sternly. "I'll see to thee in a minute. Shut up!" To Harry he said, "Go to thy hutch and stay there until Scipio comes to fetch thee. I have not decided yet what I'll do with thee, but this much I can tell thee here and now: thee will be taken off house duty and sent to the fields."

That wiped the insolent sneer off the creature's face; he obeyed in an abject hurry, suddenly reduced from a rebel to a scurrying cur. Well he might; to be thrown back into the fields foreclosed any chance of social betterment. He turned to Cuffee. "Get up!" he said. "What the devil is going on?"

Cuffee scrambled to his feet, jabbering with fear. "They'll kill me, Cap'n, they'll kill me! They threw this at me through the window!" He showed him the rope.

"Why? What is it?"

"It's Quash's! It's Quash's! I didn't do it, I swear I didn't do it!

I didn't kill him, it was an accident, but this means they are going to hang me for it!"

"Nonsense! If they wanted to hang thee, they would have done so before now. Give me that rope and go back."

"No, Cap'n, no, Cap'n, please, please! It will be tonight, it's full moon!"

He had to do something; to ignore this dramatic revelation would be a sign of weakness. "All right," he said. "Go out and wait for me on the veranda. Thee can stay here until tomorrow. Nobody is going to hang thee while I'm around."

The slave grabbed his hand and covered it with kisses. "Oh, Cap'n, Cap'n!" he stammered. "God bless you, Cap'n, God bless you! You are the best Quaker in the whole wide world! You are—"

"That's enough!" He now regretted having made that suggestion, the mere idea of having this nigger in his house— "Get out!" he cried. Cuffee did.

He spotted Scipio on the veranda and called him in. When the driver had closed the door behind him, Caleb asked, "Is this true? Are they planning to hang him?"

Scipio was ill at ease. "No, Cap'n," he replied in a throaty murmur. "It is the evil in the guilty man himself that hangs him. No one else can do it to him."

"I don't know what thee is talking about."

Scipio glanced at the door. "If he has killed Quash," he whispered almost inaudibly, "Cuffee will hang himself. If he hasn't, he won't. No one will lay a finger on him. He will do it himself if he is guilty."

Through the grimy window Caleb saw young Joshua dismount in front of his cottage. "All right, I'll see thee later. For the time being, make sure that Harry does not talk to anyone from the Hall any more."

"Yes, Cap'n, yes!" Scipio replied, relieved, and he made off with such alacrity that he almost collided with Joshua in the doorway. He stood back to let the boy enter, then, with an agility that was astonishing for a man his size, he vanished from sight.

"Good morning, Joshua," Caleb said. "I want to talk to thee."

The boy looked ill at ease.

"It has come to my knowledge that Cleo has been making sheep's eyes at thee."

"Nonsense!" the boy protested unconvincingly.

"I know the thought would never enter thy head, but let me tell thee, just in case, that to fool around with a nigger wench means playing with fire for a boy thy age and in thy position."

"I must say—"

"Thee must say nothing until I've finished!" This was not the way one should talk to one's future employer, but he had had enough of sweet reasonableness. "I can give thee fifty examples to prove that when a white boy fornicates with a nigger wench, it becomes an addiction. Once he starts, he is unable to stop even if he marries a decent white girl. He is unable to help himself; for the rest of his days, whenever he has the chance, he will sneak back to the quarters to have his way with some filthy wench or other. He will be sick with disgust at himself, but he will be unable to free himself from that stinking cesspool. All it takes is one roll in the hay with a slave, and thee'll be sucked into that pit forever."

The boy stood there sullenly.

"All right," Caleb said. "Go and see how they're doing at the factory; they should be unloading the second cart by now. Make sure they don't bruise the leaves."

Joshua hesitated as if to say something, then he shuffled off, rebellious in his obedience. There went another problem; suddenly there seemed to be so many problems that Caleb went to find the bottle in the back of the cupboard, underneath the pile of underwear.

He was too experienced a drinker to fool himself with the thought, 'Just the one.' He knew that once he started there would be no stopping until he dropped; and after a short hesitation he decided that was not a bad idea. It would not solve any of the problems, but it would cut them down to size.

After the first swigs of the sweet, burning liquid he stopped caring about what happened to young Joshua, or to Cuffee cowering outside in fear for his life, waiting to be let in. It did not touch him any longer, not the real Caleb Martin, future owner of a small plantation on the mainland, with just a few slaves, just a few, to make it profitable. Presently he hit upon a brilliant idea for the future: Why put all his money on one card? Why limit himself to raising first-class vegetables for the refined palates of the Quaker princes of Philadelphia? Better get himself a brace of good hunting dogs and do some custom-hunting of escaped slaves on the side. He knew their secret runs, their wayside stations, their secret calls like that of the whippoorwill. There was another proof that they were sub-human; everyone knew that once a whippoorwill started, it knew no stopping; yet the slaves stuck to one or two calls. They were unable to grasp that they might as well light a torch and wave it about. It would be a snap.

He finished the bottle to seal his pact with the future. Why not open a second one? For him to stay sober would achieve nothing; if the poor devil on the veranda wanted to hang himself, nobody could stop him. The thing to do was to turn your face to the wall and pretend to be asleep.

He proceeded to drink himself into a stupor so deep that he was barely roused by the sound of drums in the distance. He muttered drunkenly, "I can't do a thing about it. Not a thing. Nobody can."

He turned over and fell asleep again.

*   *   *

Joshua Baker was awakened by the sound of distant drums and went out onto the balcony to have a look. It was full moon; if Peleg Martin had not given him that cryptic warning for Caleb, he would not have given the drums a second thought. On mild, moonlit nights it was customary for the slaves to hold a frolic with fiddle and banjo that went on until the small hours. On other plantations drums were forbidden, as it was assumed that they were used for signaling; most Quaker slave-owners discouraged them too in order not to provoke their neighbors. But on this remote island, his father had decided, the Negroes could pound their drums without upsetting anybody.

This time there seemed to be a great many of them thudding heavily in the night. What did they mean? What had old Peleg Martin meant? Josh decided to go and find out for himself. He had been warned many times never to go near the quarters after dark, nobody did, not even his father. But the call of the drums was so compelling that he felt himself irresistibly drawn toward them. He could easily creep up unnoticed, the slaves would be too busy watching the dancers or dancing themselves. He would leave his colt at the factory.

As he crossed the patches of moonlight and shadow in the courtyard, he heard, even before he reached the stable, that his horse was restless, almost in a frenzy. He would be insane to try and ride her tonight with all those shadows criss-crossing the road and night owls likely to be flushed by their passing. It was a good distance away, but he would have to go on foot.

When he reached the fields, he left the open track and continued along one of the straight, narrow alleys between the shrubs. The night was full of strange, lisping sounds; the shadows of the shrubs sometimes looked like crouching figures, he frequently stopped and waited before he dared go closer, only to find it had been a trick of the moonlight, part of the spell the drums were throwing over him with their incessant thudding. "Come, come, *come* boy—*come* boy—come, come . . ." He began to make out whole sentences as he ghosted down the narrow alley. He approached the angular black-and-white cubes of the factory buildings standing gauntly in the moonlight like a dream landscape, and suddenly the drums were louder. Peering from between two bushes, he saw a spectacle that filled him with awe.

Weaving in and out of the cones of moonlight between the buildings were two naked dancers, a huge black female covered with weird daubings in white paint, and a small, frenzied man. As the strange pair came slowly spinning and prancing toward him, he recognized Mammy; the other one was Cuffee. They seemed to be performing a kind of snake dance; Mammy was swaying back and forth, her arms above her head, holding a white rope that she let slither down one arm, around her neck and up the other arm. She appeared to be the leader: Cuffee was moving with nervous leaps and twirls that at first looked erratic, but later seemed to follow some pattern imposed upon him by the slow, elephantine woman who, despite her size, moved with a lithe, catlike grace. They disappeared behind the wagon shed, followed by a crowd the size of which was difficult to judge in the moonlight, but it looked as if all the slaves were there. Four men were beating the drums; the rest were working themselves into a frenzy, clapping time. They all disappeared from sight behind the shed.

When the last stragglers had vanished, Joshua ventured recklessly into the open. He ran as fast as he could across the yard, aware that he must be starkly visible in the moonlight; when he reached the shadow of the stable, he stood still, his back to the wall, panting, listening, glancing nervously about him.

Nothing stirred. The mules banged and grunted on the other side of the wall; the drums thundered rhythmically beyond the dark building. It was foolhardy, but he had to see what was going on. Carefully he crept along the stable wall toward the corner from where he would be able to see the moonlit yard. His heart was in his mouth; although he had no idea what they would do to him, the mere idea of being discovered was terrifying. Obviously, the Negroes, whom he had always considered docile and friendly, were not like that at all. This was not a childlike revelry of subservient darkies; he had stumbled into some pagan rite of an independent, primitive tribe. As he approached the corner, he sensed a frightening power. The drums seemed to be reaching a crescendo of controlled rage strong enough to break any chain, breach any wall.

At the corner, he stopped. He was terrified now, yet irresistibly drawn to go on. He had to see, he had to. He lifted his foot; as he did so, he kicked something soft that suddenly exploded with a huge, buzzing sound and a sickening odor. For a split second he was about to sprint back to safety, then the odor made him realize that he had kicked a mound of indigo pulp and disturbed the flies that had settled on it for the night. There must be thousands of them; the angry buzzing whizzed around him in monotonous fury; finally it subsided.

The mishap had for a few moments absorbed all his attention; when he caught his breath again, he realized that something had changed. It took a moment of sheer animal fear, cowering against the wall, before he realized what it was: the drums had stopped, it seemed as if they were holding their breath.

Come on, he said to himself, it's only a bunch of niggers! Don't be intimidated by their antics, they wouldn't dare touch thee! They would be committing suicide if they assaulted the son of the house! But this was empty babble, for it was not the niggers he was afraid of. By venturing out among them he seemed to have become part of something much larger, the animal world, the wilderness, nature itself. He peered around the corner.

He saw Cuffee standing on the edge of the middle vat with the paddle wheel, writhing in bizarre contortions, now holding the white snake of the rope; he saw Mammy's huge black bulk, arms stretched out toward the squirming, writhing figure in the moonlight above her. He heard a rhythmic, guttural noise and realized it was she, growling with the same beat with which the drums had pounded until they fell silent. It was a scene of such fascination that for one moment he was off his guard; in that moment someone pounced and threw him to the ground.

The next few seconds were a frenzy of sheer, stark fear of death; overwhelmed, he collapsed and felt his strength ooze out of him. The first thing of which he became conscious was the buzzing of flies. Then it penetrated to him that the body pinning him down was very light. It was not Scipio or some other Negro buck, it was a child or a woman. He had been unable to register anything in that panic-stricken struggle; now he realized that he was touching a woman, a naked woman, slippery with sweat. She was straddling him, his legs were caught in the grip of her thighs. Then she slowly bent over him, silhouetted among the stars; a soft, hot, hungry mouth found his, and he realized it was Cleo.

The recognition gave him back his strength. He struggled violently while the hot mouth choked him and a darting, probing tongue searched for his; then a weakness from within overwhelmed him.

She sensed the moment with uncanny awareness, leaped to her feet and pulled him up by his wrists with surprising strength. He wanted to resist, but his body did not. She hissed, "Hush!" and pulled him with her into the moonlight.

They flitted across the open space toward the bushes; when the shadows enveloped them, he collapsed, with a rustle of leaves and a brief crackle of snapping twigs. He looked up and saw her standing above him, her shoulders and her breasts, wet with sweat, glinting in the moonlight.

*　　*　　*

Beulah Baker awakened in the airless night from a dream about war. Soldiers were falling, screaming with pain; women, wailing in agony, rocked to and fro over the bodies of their dead children; a baby was born in the ruins of a house, a group of slack-jawed soldiers stood watching. Finally she woke up, overwhelmed by a sense of doom and disaster. She could not stay in bed, she had to get up. Then she realized that her husband was not with her. Because of that dream, her sense of despondency turned into foreboding: something had happened; he had had an accident.

She hurriedly put on her morning gown, went out onto the balcony and saw light coming from the open doors of his study. With immense relief she found him reading in his chair. "Dearest? Thee is not coming to bed?"

He looked up, like a man awakening, smiled and said, "Oh—yes, I'll be there in a minute. What's the time?"

"I don't know. It must be past midnight. Has thee been reading all this time?" She recognized the diaries and for some reason that brought back her feeling of foreboding.

"Yes," he said, "I must confess, they are fascinating. I know now, for instance, why John McHair—"

"Hush!" She lifted her hand and listened intently.

"What's the matter?"

"Ssh!" Despite her deafness, she had heard a sound, a heavy sound in the tree, like a big animal. "There's something out there . . ." Suddenly afraid for her children asleep with their doors wide open, she rushed out onto the balcony, in time to see something leap off the balustrade and vanish into Joshua's room. "Bonny! Quick! I saw someone slip into Josh's room!"

He joined her on the balcony. "What did thee see?"

"A man! He's in there now . . ."

With admirable courage he walked down the balcony toward the doors through which she had seen the intruder vanish; out of concern for his safety, she ran to join him. Together they reached the doorway to find Joshua himself, undressing by the light of a freshly lit candle.

Relieved, she asked angrily, "What on earth does this mean, sneaking out at dead of night? Where has thee been?"

Her husband shushed her. "Was it thee who came climbing across the balustrade just now, Joshua?"

"I suppose so." The boy sounded surly and hostile. He looked guilty; he always looked like that after some mischief. She became aware of a strange, musklike smell. Where had he been?

"Explain thyself, Joshua," her husband said sternly.

The boy shrugged his shoulders. "I heard drums and I thought, as apprentice overseer, I should go and find out what was going on."

"And what did thee find, may I ask?"

"Nothing. Just the niggers carrying on by the light of the moon. Harmless horseplay, that's all it was."

Her husband's anger was deflated. "Well, don't do it again. Thee should know better than to go down there after dark." He put his hand on her arm and turned to go. "Good night, Josh, sleep well."

"Sleep well, Mother, Father."

"Good night, child," she said. There could be no doubt: Joshua had been up to no good. He could not fool her, not his own mother. What was that odor? It seemed familiar, but she could not place it. Maybe Bonny knew. When they reached the door of their bedroom, she tried to steer him inside, but he balked.

"Let me put away those books in my study," he said.

"What has he been up to, Bonny? He looks very shifty to me."

He put his mouth to her ear. "Hush! I am sure all is well! Come, go back to bed!"

She could not see his face clearly in the moonlight, but something told her he knew more about this than he would have her believe. What was going on? She was overcome by that sense of foreboding again, the dying soldiers shrieking with pain, the burning house, the child born like a dog in front of those gaping men covered with mud and blood. "I think," she said, "that he should be sent to Abe Woodhouse as an apprentice, or Obadiah Best. He is too young to be a slave-driver."

"Hush, dear heart!" he cried in her ear. "This is not the time to discuss it! Go to bed! I'll join thee in a few moments!"

"Yes . . ." She realized that she must have been shouting, and suddenly felt tired and defeated.

He went back to his study, she to her room. She wondered if she should take some Daffy's Elixir to calm her nerves, but could not be bothered. She would be unable to sleep, but the night was half over.

She lay for a while on her back, open-eyed, in the dead light of the moon. Eventually she fell into an uneasy slumber, to be awakened by cries outside, from the lawn. She went to look and saw Mammy, ghostlike in a white nightdress, standing in the red mist of sunrise. "Massa! Massa, come! Massa! It's Cuffee! Cuffee has hanged himself!"

Terrible as the message was, it gave her a sense of relief. That must have been the foreboding that had oppressed her all night: a slave hanging himself. She turned back to the bedroom. "Bonny, come! Cuffee has committed suicide!"

"Oh, my God . . ." He sat upright, his nightcap awry, his normally ageless face old and haggard.

*　*　*

The body was a grisly doll with elongated neck and huge, protruding tongue, suspended from the beam over the paddle wheel. When Joshua Baker set eyes on it, the truth struck him: he had been living in a fool's paradise with his boyish dreams of marriage and love and tenderness and buying a covered wagon and moving with Cleo into the wilderness beyond the mountains. He had lain awake until dawn, hot-eyed, daydreaming, still drunk with the delirium of the violent rites of manhood in which he had been possessed by a creature, half animal, half woman, who, in a struggle full of fury and tenderness, had unleashed in him the power of his virility. He had a mistress, he was a man! But he was more: a pathfinder, a breaker of new ground. He would show that Negroes were human, that Cleo had that of God within her, that she was as unique and irreplaceable in her individuality as he.

But one look at the grisly doll with its monstrous purple tongue and he knew. She had thrown herself on him not because she loved him, but to prevent his witnessing a murder.

After the first shock he was overwhelmed by the wish to revenge himself, to treat her as what she was: a filthy, conniving whore, a sub-human animal with the evil power of arousing him to frenzy, nothing but a soulless female body for him to ravish and possess whenever the mood took him, and to kick aside the moment he was through. He would not rest until he had made her cringe at his feet, until he had shown her who was the master, brought home to her what happened to bitches who dared to hoodwink their owner.

He went to see Caleb and found him on his bunk, an empty bottle on the floor beside him. It was the first time he had seen the man drunk; yesterday he would have been terrified, now he could look down on the pitiful weakling with indifference.

When he told the half-conscious, drunken Caleb that he wanted Cleo assigned to the house, the man rose to his elbows in sudden sobriety. "Never!" he croaked. "I'll never agree to that! Not in the house! Does thee hear? I won't have thee fornicating in the house! Not in the presence of thy sisters, thy mother! Good God!" He slapped his forehead and fell back as if felled by his own hand. There he lay, moaning drunkenly, "No, no, not that, not that."

"Dear friend," Joshua said with an icy calm that surprised himself, "either thee assigns Cleo to the house or I will tell my father that Cuffee's death was murder, that Quash's death was murder, and Hannibal's, and that Pompey's death from snakebite probably was murder too."

Caleb covered his eyes with his hands and shook his head in drunken misery. "Tell him! But I will never let thee! Never!"

"Just a minute," Josh said coldly. He seemed a different person, formed from his own rib during that wild night of initiation. "I will also tell him that thee has been torturing the slaves."

That worked. "What's that? Who told thee that?"

It had been a shot in the dark; but this morning on his way to the quarters he had seen Harry, who had looked like a kicked cur. So it was true. Of course there was secret torture, Quaker overseers had to control their rebellious slaves like anyone else, only they agonized over it, let it turn them into human wrecks like this pathetic drunkard. What a prospect! Not for him. "Come," he said, "pull thyself together. Listen: thee sends Cleo to the house, I keep my mouth shut. Let's settle this now."

"But why?" Caleb asked, weaker and more desperate than Josh would have thought possible. "What has gotten into thee? What does thee want?"

"I want her," he replied coldly, "whenever I please."

"Oh, God, oh, God," Caleb moaned, covering his face with his hands again. "God, what have I done?"

It turned Joshua's contempt into rage. "Sniveling coward!" he cried. "Get off thy bunk! There's a dead man out there, a burial to be arranged! Get up and do thy work, instead of eldering me! It has nothing to do with thee! It is my life, my wench! Get up!" He kicked the bunk. "Get up, I say!"

Despite his new self-assurance, he was surprised to see Caleb Martin obey meekly and swing his legs out of bed. "Please, Joshua," he moaned. "Please give me my harness . . ."

Josh was shocked to hear himself answer, "Get it thyself. Don't expect me to pamper thee from now on! Find thyself another apprentice!"

He strode manfully out the door, yet he felt a profound alarm. Without realizing it, he had counted on Caleb not letting him get away with it.

But that was nonsense. With Caleb out for the count, he must take control. It was up to him to create order in the chaos of milling slaves, the shrieks, the wails, the lamentations, the pandemonium of two hundred wily animals who saw their chance to malinger for a day. Well, he would teach them! He would show them who was the master!

To his satisfaction, he saw that he took them completely by surprise. With a new authority that brooked no refusal, he ordered them back to the fields. He called Scipio, told him to get the hands back to work on the double, and to see to it that the lost hours were made up before they were allowed to return that night. He picked two old slaves, who usually sat dozing in front of their hutches all day chewing sunflower seeds and spitting the husks at the dogs, to cut down the corpse from the paddle wheel, put it on a cart and take it to the hospital. "Quick, quick!" They obeyed arthritically; as he saw them scurry to the factory on their pale, flat feet, it occurred to him that they might no longer be able to handle the mules. It gave him an evil satisfaction to order Harry to drive the cart. Harry obeyed meekly, as Caleb had, without a glance of reproach.

When the compound was cleared, Joshua started back to the overseer's cottage along the empty street. The old women and the children had fled indoors; he knew they were peering at him through the cracks, terrified, conquered. His was the only way the primitive tribe he had observed last night could be subjugated. Love, respect, humane Quaker treatment could never conquer them, for they were a different species that could never be domesticated. All they understood was violence. "Do as I say or I will kill thee." That was the secret: the knowledge that, when the chips were down, he only had the power to kill *first*. So, never go unarmed, always be wary, never trust them. Last night, Cleo had pounced on him, catching him utterly by surprise; she must have watched him from the moment he started out. There was no other explanation: they must watch every movement of the people from the Hall, waiting for a chance to pounce. She had taught him a lesson he would never forget.

Caleb was still in the cottage. He sat at the table, his head in his hands; when he looked up, his eyes were bloodshot and bleary.

"Well?" Josh asked.

Caleb cleared his throat and looked away. "I cannot do it, Joshua, I cannot do it! Not to thy sisters, not to thy parents, not to thee!"

"All right," he said, with again the flickering hope that Caleb might stop him. "I am going home now and shall report thee to my father for torture and intimidation. Good day."

Caleb did not even hold out until he had reached the door. "No, no!" he cried. "Don't! I've been thinking! I—I will let thee have my house, my bed, tonight, any night, while I am at meeting for worship. I'll tell thy parents that thee has agreed to guard the compound in my absence. But, for the love of God, do not take that girl into the house! Please!"

With deep disgust, because Caleb had failed him once again, Joshua answered, "All right. That'll do, for the time being. And don't bother to explain anything to my parents. It is no concern of thine." As he opened the door, he saw Caleb trying, awkwardly, to struggle into his harness. Remorse urged him to give him a hand—after all, the man was virtually helpless without assistance. But his power was too new, too tenuous; he did not dare test it by an act of kindness. He

said, "Take thy time. Everything is taken care of. As far as I'm concerned, thee can go back to bed and sleep it off." He slammed the
door behind him.

He nurtured the secret hope that his father might put him down, but
when he stated that during meeting for worship that night he would
remain in the compound, there was no protest. His father seemed to
think it laudable that he would forgo his spiritual nourishment in order
to devote himself to his duties. His mother seemed relieved, in some
mysterious way; Becky returned to her own preoccupations; Abby, who
normally would have been burning with curiosity for all the ghoulish
details, seemed indifferent to the fact that a slave had hanged himself
in the paddle vat.

When Josh appeared on horseback at the far end of the road between the hutches an hour later, everybody scurried inside. As before, he rode to the overseer's cottage down a deserted street. Caleb
was gone; Josh found him in the fields. All hands were at work;
it seemed to him that the moment he showed himself there was a
marked increase in activity. He spotted Cleo at the far edge of the
fourth field, squatting by her water buckets. She looked up at him
impassively as he drew up on his horse. "I want thee in the overseer's cottage after the bell," he said. "Make sure thee is there or
I'll kick thee in the guts."

He thought he saw a flicker of alarm in her eyes, but, to his surprise, her face broke into a grin. "Sure, sure," she said, as to a child.
"I'll be there, Joshua."

Never before had she called him by his name. No nigger had ever
dared, except Harry. He knew he should strike her now, ride in
on her, kick over those buckets and make her scurry, but, confused, he
jerked his horse around and galloped off.

That night he was prepared for her wiles. He sat waiting for her
in the cottage, well in advance of the bell. He could hear the slaves
outside, scurrying about furtively, aware of his presence behind the
closed door. The bell sounded; at the second stroke the door opened.
There she was.

He had worked it out carefully in his mind: he would begin by
taking that silly grin off her face. She closed the door behind her
and leaned against it; then, with a sensuous shrug of her shoulders,
she dropped her skimpy dress to the floor.

"Come here, bitch," he said.

She came, lithely, with all the self-confidence of the magnificent
animal she knew herself to be. Her scent made his desire stir within
him. "Thee tricked me," he said, with a tremor of rage in his voice.
"Thee tricked me out of seeing Cuffee hanged last night."

She made a guttural sound that he did not understand. There was
no point in trying to comprehend it; it was the sound of a different
species. And he was not interested in her thoughts or her feelings;
all he wanted was her body. But first she had to be tamed.

"I will show thee what happens to wenches like thee," he said.
With all the force he could muster, he struck her face.

She squawked and crashed to the floor. There she lay cringing for a moment in lugubrious agony. He stood, shaken beyond expectation, looking down at her; he had hit her harder than he had intended. But what shook him was the carnal excitement the blow had unleashed in him.

She stopped moaning, lay still, turned her head and leered up at him with that twisted grin. "Joshua," she whispered, "strong Joshua. Oh, what a strong man! Come, strong man...Come.."

All that was sensitive in him urged him to run, as fast as he could, back to the house. But the desire was stronger.

*   *   *

Caleb Martin sat in the circle of the family in the drawing room of the Hall in meeting for worship.

Normally, he derived some peace, some comfort from meeting, but not tonight. He was crushed by the tragedy he had been too weak, too witless to prevent. At that very moment, as they sat in holy silence, the son of the house was fornicating with a nigger wench, a calamity that might well tear asunder the fragile fabric of love and kindness they had woven between them over the years. He was to blame, he should have been strong, masterful, but, like all of them, he was limited in his power by his nature and by the destiny God had set for him. All, as they sat there, were feeble, weak, vacillating; yet, through some peculiar grace, a divine blessing that had been vouchsafed them, they had managed to build out of their individual imperfections a communal strength, a corporate power that was the secret of every Meeting, whether made up of the people in a community or the members of one family, as long as they returned daily to the source.

In the silence of the darkening room, Caleb prayed, with all his heart and all his soul, that God might use this power generated among them to save the boy. Only God could save him now, for the girl would not rest until she became pregnant. He had never dreamed that in New Swarthmoor, as in so many other plantations, the day would come when a master would have to sell his own offspring as slaves. But no, it would not get to that point; the Quaker way of life would force the family to accept the child. Dear God, what then?

The first of the innocent had fallen. He wondered grimly who would be next. Abby? Rebekah?

The fury that rose within him at the thought was so overpowering that his knuckles went white with the strain of prayer. Save me, God! Save me, save me, dear, dear God! Save us all . . .

With a feeling of relief he heard Bonny Baker's voice. The little man had risen and taken off his hat, which meant that he was addressing God.

"Heavenly Father," he chanted in the sing-song of prayer, "a man, a Negro man, took his own life on our island last night. As no sparrow falls lest it be ordained by Thee, as Thou countest the hairs on the heads of all Thy children, there must be in this sad and obscure death a hidden meaning for us to perceive. Is it, dear Father, that we in this house have erred in our ways? Is it that we should pursue more vigorously the preaching of Thy gospel among those steeped in darkness and ignorance? Is it that each one of us should turn within ourselves, search our consciences, to discover in what way and to what degree we are responsible for Cuffee's desperate deed?"

The voice, solemn and pontifical, droned on; the words began to lose their meaning. What was the use of those rhetorical questions? Of course all of them were responsible, for what had killed Cuffee, as it had killed all the others before him, was slavery. There were no two ways about it: either they kept their slaves and held their peace, or they freed them, as the rural Friends in Philadelphia Yearly Meeting had been urging Quakers to do since 1688. But to set the slaves free would not solve the problem either; for what means of support did they have? Negroes without means of support could be snapped up by the first landowner they met; it would be the ultimate cruelty to grant them freedom only to let them be snared by a more ruthless master. The problem of slavery was insoluble, like war. Every Quaker mouthed the peace testimony; but what if their own homes were attacked, their wives raped, their children slaughtered? Would they just stand idly by? During the Indian war the Rhode Island Quakers had been faced with the choice either to kill or be killed, and they had, despite their best intentions, become involved in war. And weren't some wars necessary? Had not Jesus himself said, "Think not that I am come to send peace on earth: I came not to send peace but a sword"?

The problem was insoluble because it lay beyond the boundaries of reason. There was no reasonable solution; certainly not the one the mellifluous voice enamored of itself was now chanting; "Love, kindness, that of God in every man . . ." Words, words! Their only hope was an act of redemption, by one of them or all of them; pious evocations of the presence of God no longer worked. Through Joshua's fall they had all been reduced to mummers making ritual gestures, speaking ritual words without substance. The Presence in their midst had drawn away. The circle was empty.

CHAPTER FOUR

TOWARD sunrise, as he reached the foothills, George McHair began to feel tired. And no wonder, he had ridden virtually without stopping since the ferry had put him ashore the night before. Man is a strange animal: a week ago, on his way to the island, he had been drawn so strongly by the lure of civilization that he had not stopped to sleep then either; now he was eager to get away from it all. There really was no better life than in the forest; he began to live again after he had left the last of the small German farms behind him and entered the woods. The virgin forest, his home, was still an undisturbed paradise. In the open glades the deer fed by the hundreds, even in winter, their cast antlers whitened the thickets. Bears, elk and panthers roamed the woods, beavers dammed the brooks, partridges drummed on hollow logs. He could eat the choicest venison, salmon steaks, fat trout whenever the fancy took him.

The moment he entered the forest all tiredness left him. After resting his horse under a huge old chestnut tree, and breaking his fast with wild berries from the stony briar patches on the southern slopes, he mounted again and rode on steadily for some hours, until he heard the first haunting call of a lynx. He had better stop now, he was getting groggy and hot-eyed; Betsy was beginning to falter. He knew a little glen nearby where a row of beaver dams had turned a mile of stream bottom into a swampy meadow; he would bivouac there. If he left at dawn, he would be home before dark. He dismounted to pick some spearmint and sheepsower; by the spring in the glen he would find some cress and wild horseradish to spice his supper.

But when he reached the clearing he discovered he was not hungry; worry took away his appetite. He had failed to come home with a bride or a betrothed, so now he would have to go through the same torment again that had made him flee a week before. What had come over him was no mystery; all animals on reaching maturity began to look for a mate. If only Himsha were not his sister! He couldn't think of a better, more loving, more patient, more even-tempered, more exciting wife. That had been the shock: not the deep, instinctive urge to find a mate, but that it should be Himsha.

A slight drizzle started, more like evening dew than rain. He roamed on foot through the falling night in a state of agitation, trying to shake the vision of Himsha, whom, to his undying shame, he had started to spy on of late; he had even taken to the incomprehensible aberration of surreptitiously opening the cupboard where she kept her clothes to inhale the clean, girlish scent of her undergarments. Never in his life had he been so deeply troubled; could she really be his sister if he felt like this about her? Had his father indeed found her as a wandering orphan? His misery deepened as his excitement mounted. It was as if the urge for procreation had taken over his life, contemptuously oblivious of his will, his sense of decency, his earnest desire to be a good Quaker, a good brother, a clean, decent man.

As he no longer felt hungry he did not make a fire. The ground fog had risen to his hips, Betsy's body seemed to float, legless, on a gray cloud. He unsaddled her and rubbed her down; then he slapped her rump to tell her she could roam. There was no need to tether her, she always made her way back to him at daybreak, however far she might wander during the night; if she caught the scent of a big cat, she would trot back to him for protection, like a dog. The spring gurgled in the silence, muffled by the mist that narrowed the world. He took his two leather water bags and filled them at the spring, the fog all around him.

Of course, it had been sheer panic that prompted him to ask for Becky's hand, and Abby's. He should have known better than even to think of proposing to the daughter of a rich Friend. The whole notion was nonsensical: he needed freedom, the unbridled life of the huntsman, the forest, where a man prepared to live a natural life like the animals could make a good living as long as he kept the peace with the Indians and never slept soundly enough at night for a big cat to stalk him. It was the only life he knew; and the only girl who would fit into that life, because she was accustomed to it, was Himsha.

He lay down under his blanket, shivering as the chill of fog-soaked earth penetrated his fancy outfit. He had put it on only to go courting; in the wilderness deerskin was useless, the surest way of catching a chill. And a hunter with a chill was like a wild goose in the molting season: a caricature of a bird, floundering helplessly with enough noise to advertise its presence for miles around.

He lay on his back, eyes closed, feeling the light woodsman's sleep creep over him as it always did the moment he lay down in the open. He heard, with the heightened awareness that came just before sleep, every sound. If a cougar were about, he would hear its soft, tensely controlled breathing, the only sound it could not suppress. But he heard nothing; Betsy was grazing rhythmically a short distance away, like footsteps on gravel. From the forest came the distant, mournful wail of a wolf, calling in the moonlit night.

He dreamed about Himsha all night. At sunrise the mist on the meadow came alive with birdsong and the excited chittering of squirrels. In the distance sounded the first sustained drumming of a woodpecker beginning its working day. He rose reluctantly, loath to exchange this peaceful, primitive world without problems or temptations for the troubled, confusing one of the cabin and the village.

As only Betsy's head was above the flat cloud of the morning mist, he let her find her own way back toward the trail. When he reached it, his thoughts began their dreary round again, around and around;

he knew they would go on doing so until finally he was faced with the challenge of Himsha's presence.

Later that morning he cursed his deerskin suit again when he rode into a steady rain. It turned his shirt and trousers into wet, ice-cold chamois leather. For the first time that day the idea of getting home became attractive. Shivering, he began to yearn for the first glimpse of the village, the smoke from its chimneys floating in thin layers between the trees, the measured fluting of the whippoorwills. It became a vision of such comfort that he cantered up the last steep slope that overlooked the valley; the sound of musket fire took him by surprise. He reined Betsy, his heart in his mouth. Indians! Then he recognized the agonized squeals echoing off the walls of the forest as the shrieks of squeakers, not of Indians on the warpath, and he remembered what day it was. Of course! How could he have forgotten? Instead of returning hime to the quiet village of his daydreams, he was riding smack into the rowdy celebrations of Muster Day, when the village militia, composed of all able-bodied male citizens over the age of fourteen, was called together for drills. It was the Scotch-Irish who had started it, to prepare for attacks from Indians that so far had not materialized. Like most Calvinist festivities, it seemed to consist mainly of competitions: who could leap highest or run fastest, shoot straightest, all of which entailed prizes; the main competition, however, for which there was no prize, was who could drink the most. He was bound by the Friends' testimony against bearing arms, so he always made a point of staying away on Muster Day to avoid being harassed by drunken revelers, thrown on his back on the common and having his breeches wrenched off, as had happened once before.

When he began the descent toward the village, the sharp crackle of rifle fire echoed by the forest frightened Betsy. As usual, his mood communicated itself to her; she was nervous and fretful. He talked to her and patted her neck, wet with sweat after the exertion of cantering up the slope. The racket was tremendous; they must be prize-shooting down there. He left the road and ghosted along the edge of the forest; through gaps in the trees on the common he caught glimpses of the crowd, the marksmen and the posts with the torches and the targets: live turkeys, flapping their wings in panic. It always enraged him to see them degrade a bird by using it for target practice. They were not hunters, these people, they were peasants turned trappers, still obsessed by the peasants' hostility toward any animal that might harm their crops.

On the outskirts of the village near the old Meeting House, a band of rowdies caroused, so he led Betsy into the graveyard. Despite their strutting violence, the Scotch-Irish were superstitious, they would never hazard into a burying ground after sunset. The ghosts of the harmless people slumbering underneath the small, identical Quaker headstones were not likely to bother anyone: McHairs, Martins, Tuckers, Yarnalls—there was not an angry spirit among them. All of them had labored patiently on the small fields they had wrested from the wilderness; their lives had been spent peaceably, without hatred or hostility toward anyone; they had been plain people, raised to a kind of grandeur by the lifelong practice of their faith. He remembered some of them from his childhood: his mother, always tired; eighty-year-old Aunt Mary, stern and forbidding, who when she was finally laid out was found to have beautiful, long, auburn hair, scarcely touched with gray. How would they have stood up to the taunts, the hatred of those newcomers now yelling and screaming in the streets, setting the dusk aflame with bonfires on the common? They must be roasting hogs, maybe a moose or an elk; their muskets and rifles went on crackling in the silence, the helpless birds on the target posts fluttered in agony. He stood in the little graveyard listening to the unholy racket in the distance, the raucous bellowing of the revelers nearby. Betsy was restless; it was best to leave her here behind the old Meeting House, out of sight from the street. "Hush, Betsy," he whispered, patting her. "Still, love, be still, all's well, I'll be back for thee." He tethered her to the tree behind John McHair's grave that his grandfather had planted as a sapling; to distract her, he gave her some oats from his saddle bag and left her munching.

He forded the little brook and crept along the forest's edge. The neighbors' houses were all dark; he aroused a few roosters, but luckily there were no dogs, they must all be on the common, roaming around the bonfires and the roasts. Then he forded the brook again and approached the cabin stealthily through the truck garden. It too looked deserted; for a moment he thought that Himsha had overcome her shyness and wandered into the village to watch from a distance; but as their own rooster started to trumpet imperiously at his approach, setting the ducks snattering, he saw the feeble light of a candle behind one of the windows. She must have stayed home, of course, to keep an eye on Grandfather, who always became restless when the villagers started firing their rifles. He found the latch in the darkness of the back porch, and frowned when the door opened readily. How often had he told her to keep it locked when he was away? Not only because of Petesey Paisley; on a night like this the roaming bands of revelers were just as dangerous.

He went inside and did not see her at first. The long, narrow room was dark except for the small pool of candlelight at the far end. "Himsha?" he called.

She rose between the table and the chimney; she must have been kneeling on the floor. She was wearing her quilted doeskin robe; the candlelight gleamed on the two braids of black hair hanging over her shoulders. His mouth went dry, and he felt the cowardly impulse to turn around and flee back into the night. "I'm home," he said, unnecessarily. It came out as a croak.

"Come here," she whispered. "What does thee think is the matter with him?"

"Who?"

She did not answer, but knelt down again behind the table. He joined her and saw she was bending over a basket. Beside it were a bowl of water, some rags and a saucer of milk with a spoon; in it lay

her cat, Casey, a nondescript black-and-white animal that she adored
with what seemed to him excessive tenderness. "What's the matter?"
he asked. "Is he sick?"

"I don't know. Something must have happened to him . . ." Her
voice, like her eyes, seemed placid.

"When?"

"I found him a few hours ago, under the shrub outside. I'd been
calling him for a long time, but he didn't come; then I heard a little
sound under the shrub and there he was, covered with dirt. When I
picked him up, he cried horribly. Look—see how pale his tongue
is, and the inside of his mouth? I think he's been hurt, terribly hurt."

"Let me see." He knelt beside her and looked at the cat. Its head
rested on the edge of the basket, its eyes were closed, it seemed to
be asleep. But its mouth was open, and it breathed in short, labored
gasps. "Maybe it was a bobcat."

"No," she said, "I think I know . . ." She gave him the sideways
glance without moving her head that was typical of her; he had never
seen anyone else do it just like that. "I think he was kicked by a horse."

He had seen the look and did not believe her. What was she hiding
from him? He stretched out his hand toward the cat, but she held it
back. Her touch made him swallow.

"Don't!" she whispered urgently. "If thee touches him, he'll scream."

As if the cat had been listening, it gave a plaintive cry. A shiver
ran through its body, it retched and heaved, and a slimy, colorless
liquid dribbled from its mouth. She dipped a rag in the water, wiped
its lips, cleaned up the small mess on the floor, dipped her fingers in
the milk and let the cat lick a few drops. It did so with alacrity,
but without opening its eyes or moving its head. *"Gnusha, gnusha,"*
she whispered. *"Gnusha kashnee, gnusha, gnusha . . ."* She pretended
she did not remember Algonquin, but when Lone Seeing Eagle said
something to her in that tongue, she always obeyed him. The only
living beings to whom she spoke in her native language were the
cat and Grandfather, if they needed comforting. Where was Grandfather, anyway? Usually he welcomed him with cooings and chortlings.
George peered at the bunk in the darkness, but could not make out
whether it was occupied.

"Where's Grandfather?" he asked. "Outside?"

Again she gave him that sideways look. "He's been gone for some
time."

"Some time?" he asked incredulously. It was just like her, she would
get completely carried away over a sick cat and shrug off the disappearance of her own grandfather as if it did not matter. "Was he here
last night?"

"I don't think so."

"Thee does not *think* so! But, Himsha! He's childish! He doesn't
know where he's going! With all this shooting going on, he may have
wandered off into the forest!" He put his hands on her shoulders.
"Look at me! When did he leave? Look at me!"

She faced him with a swift, snakelike movement, her black eyes flashing. "I don't know!" she said defiantly. "And don't worry about him! Uncle Ellis will look after him; he'll bring him back when all is quiet again."

He dropped his hands. She was right, the old Indian would indeed be watching over him.

She turned back to the cat; the sight of her soft, slender body made him leap to his feet. "Well, I'm going to look for him!" He went to the door, expecting her to call after him, but she did not. He turned round in the doorway and cried dramatically, "We have to start looking for him at once! I'll go and see the sheriff and ask him to make up a posse!" It was nonsense; he would be insane to show himself to that drunken crowd on the common; even when sober, nobody would start searching the wilderness after nightfall. But she said nothing; he could not see her behind that table. "Well, I must say! Thee is a loving granddaughter!" he cried angrily, and slammed out into the night.

As he stood there to let his eyes get used to the dark, he realized how frighteningly her closeness had excited him. What could he do? God, dear God, what could he do? If he went back to the cabin that night, he would be unable to keep away from her. And he was certain, absolutely certain that she was his sister. His father was not a man to pick up stray children; he would never have taken her in if she were not his own. She was his sister, and here he was, lusting after her every moment of day and night. "Oh, God, what can I do, where can I go?" he prayed, eyes closed, but there was no answer; all there was afoot in the night was a rat or a coon rustling under the cabin, the sleepy stirring of a hen in the chicken coop. He had to find an excuse for staying out, something that would prove stronger than the pull of his desire. To go to the sheriff about organizing a posse was pointless; but where else could he go? Everybody was out on the common, gorging on ale and hard cider from the vats rolled out by the innkeeper for the occasion—everyone except Parson Paisley, that was.

Parson Paisley! Before George realized that to appeal to his arch-enemy was lunacy, he found himself on his way to the parsonage, as if his body had taken over control from his mind. It was madness; Parson Paisley, with his sermons against Quakers, was obviously determined to hound the last of them out of town. But surely no man of God, not even a firebrand like the old parson, could refuse to arrange a search for a senile old man who had wandered off into the wilderness.

The parsonage was the largest house in the village, and the only one built of stone. It had been the first thing the newcomers had done: built a parsonage and a church, in that order. First their priest had to be housed, then God. There was a light in a downstairs window; somebody must be about. It could only be the parson; his sons were certain to be on the common. George hesitated at the gate; then he went boldly up the path that led to the porch. He knocked on the door; a harsh voice called, "Come in!" A dog started to bark furiously.

"Shut up!" the voice called, and the dog fell silent. George opened the door and found himself in a dark hallway.

"Where are you, Parson?" he called; he realized he had fallen into the servile "you."

"Here! First door to the left!"

He opened it; a huge black shadow came for him, growling. The voice yelled, "Caesar, down! Down, I say!"

It was the parson; white-haired, myopic, behind a desk in a dimly lit room lined with books, peering at his visitor through a pair of spectacles on the tip of his nose. "Who are you? What do you want?"

"It is I, Parson Paisley," George said, intimidated by the alien surroundings and the dog. "George McHair."

"McHair?" The old man sounded as if he couldn't believe his ears. He tried looking over his spectacles, but they did not seem to make any difference. "Come here," he said, "let me see you."

George obeyed, hat in hand, with a sense of betrayal; it proved too .much for his Quaker conscience, so he put it back on.

As if that finally convinced his host, he said, "Ah, yes. And what brings you here, young man, at this hour?"

"I've come for help," George said nervously. "I've just come back from Eden—near Philadelphia—and my grandfather has disappeared. My sister said he wandered off, maybe as long ago as yesterday, which means that this is his second night in the forest . . ." His voice trailed away; both the dog and the old man watched him with hostility.

"I'm sorry to hear it," the parson said in a tone that belied the words. "But what has that to do with me?"

The hostility was tinged with satisfaction; George now hated himself for coming. "I—I thought that maybe you could help organize a search party," he mumbled. He felt trapped in a situation he no longer controlled; the sense of ensnarement deepened when he saw a sudden look of cunning in the old man's eyes.

"I'm glad that you consider yourself a member of my flock, at least when the water reaches the lips," the old man said. "Of course I'll be happy to help find your grandfather. As your shepherd, I am bound to watch over my black sheep too."

George realized that somehow his request must be serving the old man's ends. "Thank thee," he said, returning to the Quaker vernacular. "Would it be possible to set out now, Friend?" This must antagonize the parson, he hoped it would, maybe it would undo the harm he had done.

But Parson Paisley did not seem to notice. He sat smiling in the candlelight like an old tomcat that had just caught a fat, juicy mouse. "You know that is not possible," he said with fatherly patience. "I can understand your anxiety, and it honors you; but there is no point in starting a search before daybreak. Have you any idea where your grandfather might have gone? Does he have a favorite spot in the woods? Surely he has done this before?"

He had; but to tell this cunning old buzzard about his Indian protector would be worse than folly, it would be inviting disaster.

George was certain none of the villagers had ever seen Lone Seeing Eagle; should they come to know about his nightly visits, they were sure to lie in wait for him. "No," he said. "He just wanders off without any notion of where he's going. Maybe it would be better to forget about it. I'll just go out there and take a look around."

The old man brushed it aside with contempt. "Don't talk rubbish," he said. "Come back at dawn. Now leave me alone, I've got work to do. Good night." He picked up his quill and resumed writing, as if his guest had already left. Even the dog stopped gazing at George; it heaved a sigh, put its head on its front paws and went to sleep.

George hesitated, then he turned away and left the room. There was nothing else he could do; everything was settled. He would come back at daybreak to find a posse waiting and they would set out to find his grandfather, and Parson Paisley would have achieved some mysterious purpose that George failed to fathom. Whatever it was, it could only bode ill for Himsha and himself, even for Grandfather.

Back outside, hearing the drunken singing of the revelers on the common, he did not know what to do. What else could he dream up to keep himself away from the cabin? Betsy, of course; he should not leave her tethered in that graveyard any longer; even this close to the village she was not safe from bears or panthers, and the scent of roasting carcasses always attracted them. He set out toward the old Meeting House, this time going directly to it, down the dark street with its heavy black trees standing in pools of shadow in the moonlight. There was not a soul to be seen, not even the urchins of the village who normally would lie in wait for a lonely man at night and pounce on him in a pack, out of sheer mischief. When he reached the graveyard, it occurred to him to spend the night in the old Meeting House. It was empty but for some stacks of old benches and piles of hoops; it had been rented to the cooper for a warehouse by the town council, who had calmly appropriated it once they discovered all that was left in the way of Quakers was senile old Jim McHair, his little grandson and a half-breed baby. When he stepped onto the creaking porch of the gloomy old building, an owl swooped screeching from under the eaves, startling him. He heard Betsy snorting and pawing in the darkness underneath the trees, walked toward the sound, and stopped dead in his tracks when in front of him a ghostly figure rose, barring his way.

"Good evening, Uncle," he said reverently. It was the attitude he affected the moment he set eyes on the old Indian, of whom he had stood in awe ever since he was a child.

Lone Seeing Eagle stepped into the moonlight. The black eyes peered unblinkingly from the spider web of crags and folds on the incredibly ancient face; the short Delaware crest stood out from his skull like a cock's comb. A quiver of arrows was slung across his back; he did not have his bow with him; he must have left that with his horse, nearby in the forest. George had never seen his horse; it was as secretive and elusive as he; like all Indian ponies, it must have been trained not to neigh or whinny when left alone.

"Thy grandfather is well," the old Indian said in the toneless voice he seemed to affect only when he spoke English; whenever George heard him speak Algonquin to Himsha, it sounded quite different: animated and surprisingly jocular.

"Thank thee, Uncle. We were terribly worried about him."

"Do not be concerned," the wooden voice said. "Let him be, or thou wilt cause great harm."

It was a strange thing to say. "What does thee mean, Uncle?" he asked. "I have already called for a search party tomorrow morning . . . But of course, if I can call it off . . ."

Something strange happened. The old man looked at him for a moment with intense alarm; then, without another word, he vanished like a ghost.

He left George bewildered and worried. It was the first time in his life he had seen Uncle Ellis alarmed. What had he done? Could he indeed call off the search party?

He went to fetch Betsy, forded the brook with her and walked her down the bridle path to the cabin. What on earth could be wrong? He should call off the search party, but what could he tell Parson Paisley? That his grandfather was all right? How was he supposed to know that? He could not say that he had received the news from an old Indian; then the fat would be in the fire. No, now he had done this stupid thing, there seemed to be no other solution than to see it through.

He put Betsy with the chickens in the lean-to; the racket her entrance provoked among the silly birds was enough to raise the dead. In the house, he found Himsha still on the floor beside the basket, nursing her cat. It looked exactly as it had looked when he left: motionless, eyes closed, head resting on the edge of the basket, stirring only to retch and vomit and to lick some drops of milk off Himsha's finger with a bloodless, pale tongue. He told her to go to bed; the cat would be all right, at least there was nothing she could do to help it. But she told him to go to bed himself, she was going to stay up.

Glumly he lay down in the corner of the room on the stack of pelts that served him as a bed. The faint, musty smell of dust and rain, which the old buffalo must have collected over the years while roaming the prairie before being felled by a shot from a hunter's rifle, made him think of his father. Huge, coarse, thundering across the prairie with his bunch of rowdies in pursuit of a stampeding herd of buffalo that set the earth aquiver for miles around . . . He fell into a fitful slumber.

At first light he awoke and found everything as it had been the night before: Himsha crouching on the floor, the cat in its basket, its head resting on the edge. He felt he had not slept at all; yet there was the blue of daybreak coloring the windowpanes. He pulled on his leggings and left for the village.

It seemed unlikely that the parson could have roused anyone after the riotous night; but when George rode up, he found, to his dismay, a dozen men and their horses gathered outside the gate of the parsonage, dressed for a raiding party. Blankets, leggings, breechclouts, powder horns and bullet bags, their rifles in greased leather covers lashed athwart their saddles. When he arrived, they were passing around the bear grease and rubbing their faces with it; obviously, they counted on staying out for more than just a day. Polly Paisley was the first to spot him. "Here he comes!" he called, and his cronies turned their greasy, grinning mugs toward him. "No need for you to come, Quaker boy!" one of them called, the sheriff's son, a prime bully. "We'll find your grandpappy! Why don't you stay home with your squaw?" There was a cackle of laughter, then the parson's harsh voice cried out, "Enough of that! We are on an errand of mercy!" His authority, the only real authority in the village, had the usual effect; there were a few grumbles, but they obeyed. They turned their backs on the new arrival, as if they had decided to forget about him. "Everybody ready? Mount!" They mounted. "Follow me!" The old man, with his black parson's clothes and the two tufts of white hair on his head, looked like a creature from a fairy tale, a booted cat astride a horse, as they rode off, their mounts skittish with early morning jitters. The rumble of their hoofs rattled windows, roused roosters and unleashed dogs, which followed them, yapping excitedly at the horses, until they crossed the bridge and started to climb the steep, winding trail into the forest.

George, bringing up the rear, was worried about Himsha. She had been left alone before, but always with Grandfather. The Paisley twins rode right in front of him, so there was no real reason to worry. And Grandfather? Maybe he was dead, maybe he had been abducted by the Indians. If he had been abducted, he would come to no harm at all; not only was he a Quaker, but senile old men were revered by the Indians as people of wisdom. His father had said, months ago, "Why keep the old manchild cooped up in that smelly cabin? Take him across the mountains and let him loose; the Shawnees will pick him up and he'll be treated as an oracle for the rest of his days. After the way he used to minister in meeting, that's just what he would like, if he had the choice—to minister himself to death, with everybody flat on their faces in admiration. And now look at him: locked up, dribbling and drooling like a mangy old fox dreaming of ducks. Shame on thee, sanctimonious little fart." Then he had thundered off into the bracken, leaving, as usual, a sense of outrage and loneliness.

They were riding into Paisley territory now, where George had never ventured, just as the Paisleys never set foot in the territory that belonged traditionally to the McHairs. They might despise one another in the village, but, like the panthers, mountain lions and the elusive lynx, they respected one another's hunting grounds. Nobody except the Quakers bothered about the territorial rights of the Indians.

George began to watch carefully. This was unknown country to him; if for any reason he should find it necessary to leave without the others, he must be able to find his own way. They roamed through the woods all day, searching every hollow, every cave, every thicket, without finding a trace of the old man. They called his name, time and time again, their voices echoing eerily in the caverns of the forest:

"Jim McHai-ai-r . . . ! Old Jim . . . ! Where are you?!" But not a sound, not a trace; he must either have fallen into some crevice or been abducted by Indians. At nightfall the posse was far from the village; they camped in a small clearing on the southern slope of a hill. They shot a deer and a couple of turkeys and dismembered them, sharing out each man's portion in raw meat, for him to roast the way he fancied around the big log fire. They told stories, swapped jokes, passed the gourd; crouching around the lonely light of the campfire in the dark ocean of the forest, they felt kindly disposed toward one another, even toward George, stony-faced under his Quaker hat, gazing morosely at the fire. When the meal was over, they rolled themselves in their blankets and lay down with their feet toward the dying embers of the fire, like the spokes of a wagon wheel. They had drawn straws; Polly Paisley was the first to stand guard.

The night was peaceful. The moon was out; the stars shivered with brightness overhead. There simply was nobody left in the village who could hurt Himsha except maybe the urchins, and she could cope with those. So why should he feel so restless? Damn old Uncle Ellis! Why hadn't he spoken up? And his grandfather—dying old man wandering about the forest . . . Quite suddenly he knew Grandfather was dead. He knew it with the eerie certainty with which, at times, he knew which direction to take in the fog even though he could see no farther than his horse's ears. For some reason, the notion gave his concern about Himsha new life; he rose on his elbow to look at Petesey Paisley and saw to his relief that he was lying fast asleep, his hat on his face.

George fell into the hunter's half sleep, waking and listening many times that night. Sometime toward morning he saw Charley McAdoo get up and Jake Devlin lie down in his place. Polly was fast asleep, rolled in his blanket; Petesey's hat had fallen off his face and now lay beside the dark blotch of his head. There was something strange about his head; it gleamed oddly in the faint glow of the embers. George strained to look; with a sickening cramp of his stomach muscles, he saw it was not a head but a gourd.

Petesey Paisley was gone.

*   *   *

Of course Himsha McHair knew what had happened to her cat, but she had kept it to herself. George had become so irritable of late, quick to anger, like his father; if she had let it slip that Casey had been kicked to death by Petesey Paisley, who had roamed around the cabin the night before, George might have gone for him. She had never cared for the Paisley twins, but never before had she felt such loathing for them as these last months. They roamed around the cabin at all hours, like male dogs hanging around a house where there was a bitch in heat. They made her feel as if she were not a person but a thing, to get hold of and ravage. Their fevered male lust was vicious and hostile; to rape a squaw was a deed that

God would countenance as part of His great retribution against the heathen that their father roared about in the kirk on Sundays. They had no mother to counter their father's violence; their worst impulses were stimulated every Sunday by that raving man in the pulpit, bent on the massacre of all Indians. Yet a raid would inevitably result in the Indians descending on the village in their thousands, shrieking over the thunder of their horses' hoofs as they raced in narrowing circles around the cluster of houses in the valley; what would happen once they swamped the village and took their revenge, no white man could imagine. She had seen it once, and although it had happened long ago, the images of violence and murder, the screams of women, the insane roar of frenzied men hacking and stabbing, dancing around with dripping scalps they had ripped off the horrible pink skulls of their victims, had been branded upon her memory. Her life seemed to be drenched in blood and violence; she had never trusted the peaceable interlude with Grandfather and George in the cabin; she had never given in to affection, always stayed uninvolved, in order to remain inviolate from the horror and the pain of the massacre that was inevitable. Instinct had told her that it would utterly destroy her if, when the massacre happened, she were tied to another human being by love.

But that did not apply to animals—and now little Casey was dying. There were no outward signs of violence on the little cat; only his fur was dusty and dirty, something a cat would never permit unless it was sick unto death. His tongue and gums were so pale as to be almost white, and there was a heartbreaking wail every time he moved.

For the second night she sat with Casey, helplessly watching him suffer until finally, in the small hours, the animal opened his golden eyes wide and tried to lift his head as if looking for her. Then something changed; the light in the dark pupils of the eyes flickered and went out. There was no change; the eyes went on staring fixedly, but they were different, the light was gone. Casey, her playful companion, was dead.

She felt no sorrow, no shock; like the glass eyes, now staring unseeingly, she seemed devoid of all feeling. As she sat there, hands in her lap, gazing at the dead cat, a memory from long ago came to her. She had sat like this before, with the same feeling of remoteness, even from her own body, but still a captive of it, held by a tenuous thread that seemed to tug and sway, like the string of a kite. Everybody was dead, even her little dog, and all the wigwams were burning; the crackling of the fire was the only sound. She sat motionless, her hands in her lap, staring calmly in front of her, for a long time; then boots came walking across the embers, stepping over the bodies around her. They stopped in front of her, and she was picked up. The memory frightened her; it seemed again as if everything that had happened since had been an illusion and that the truth was this: to sit, her hands in her lap, staring in front of her, waiting for the thread to snap, without thought, without hope, without dread, just waiting. Then she heard a sound. Someone was trying the latch.

She did not look at the door; she felt no fear, not even curiosity. Where she floated, held only by a thread, nothing mattered any more. She did not wait for the door to open, but for the thread to snap. It tugged and swayed, as it had when she was little. The door remained closed; she was aware of being watched through the window, but it did not concern her.

She sat there for the rest of the night, motionless, her hands in her lap. Only at daybreak, when the room became light and the square of the window was reflected in Casey's eyes, did she move. Gently she picked up the basket with Casey's stiff little body and carried it to the door. She opened the latch with her elbow and found the door bolted. George must have done it before he left and gone out through the hatch to the chicken coop. She opened the door and carried the basket to the spot she had in mind: in front of the sunflowers, which were already quite high and would soon burst into bloom; seen from below, they would look like a sky full of gay, swaying suns drawn by a child, just the kind of thing kittens and babies could look at for hours in innocent fascination. She gently put down the basket in the grass, fetched the spade and began to dig Casey's grave. As she put her foot on the spade for the second time, she was grabbed from behind.

That was the moment the thread snapped. Suddenly it was as if the whole sky caved in on her; she was cut loose and swirled, spiraling, in an emptiness filled with terror. She fought, screamed, bit, clawed, but the arms that held her were stronger than she. She was thrown onto her back, her arms pinned underneath her, a hand ripped open her robe, a heavy weight fell on top of her. She frantically tried to throw it off; when a knee forced her thighs apart, she opened her eyes wide and recognized Petesey Paisley.

"No, Petesey, please, no . . ." she pleaded desperately; but he laughed and muttered, "Nice, you'll see it's nice, nice . . ." She felt naked, defenseless; her strength was failing, she was about to give up the struggle and surrender when suddenly he gave a startled cry. His eyes opened wide, he gaped at her in utter astonishment, tried to speak, but instead of words, blood spurted from his mouth as if he had been drinking it and choked. His eyes stared at her incredulously; then she saw it happen for the second time that day: something went out of them, a light, a secret in the depth of the pupils. He slumped forward, on top of her.

She lay for a moment paralyzed. Then, in a frenzy, she struggled from under the lifeless body; it thudded, sluglike, on its side in the grass. She scrambled to her feet; as she stood looking down at it with unspeakable horror, it slowly rolled over on its face. From between its shoulderblades stuck the shaft of an arrow with three colored feathers.

She ran into the cabin and vomited in a corner.

*   *   *

The moment George McHair saw that Petesey Paisley was gone, he knew something had happened to Himsha. He threw himself onto his horse and raced back through the forest, following the trail he had memorized on the way out. He reached the village, thundered through the empty streets and slid out of the saddle before Betsy had come to a stop in front of the cabin. He ran inside, calling, "Himsha! Himsha!" Then he saw her.

She was sitting in a corner, on the floor, her hands in her lap, her eyes wide with shock, her shirt torn and covered with blood. "Himsha!" He knelt in front of her and touched her cheek; she did not move, she just sat staring at him with those huge black eyes. He took her in his arms, cradled her, whispered, "Hush, hush, all right, it's all right." Gradually she became less rigid; finally she began to talk, in a wild, disconnected way, about a body in the garden. He hushed her, soothed her, carried her to the bed and covered her with the quilt. Then he went outside. He could find nothing, only a spade and the beginning of a little grave; the basket with the dead kitten stood beside it. There were signs of a struggle; he knelt down, searched in the grass and found traces of blood.

He stood up, at a loss. What should he do? Childishly, he felt the urge to throw himself into the saddle again, gallop back to the campsite, pretend nothing had happened and continue the search for his grandfather. Could it have been Grandfather? He heard a crackling noise behind him, swung around and saw Betsy greedily ripping beans off the row. He tethered her to the post of the porch.

Inside, he found Himsha exactly as he had left her. She looked as if she were asleep, but when he came in her huge, dark eyes seemed to reach out to him in a mute plea. He felt a sickness, almost a pain, under his midriff; he waited until it had abated, then sat down on the edge of the bed and put his hand gently on hers. It felt cold. "What happened?" he asked softly. "Can thee tell me what happened?"

She shook her head and closed her eyes.

"It's all right," he whispered, caressing her hand clumsily but with great tenderness. "Tell me, Himsha, tell me . . ."

She shook her head; tears welled from under her eyelids.

What should he do? He went on caressing her cold hand, unable to shake off a sense of unreality, waiting to wake up from this nightmare.

Then she whispered, "Is he . . . Is he still out there?"

"No, there's no one there. I've searched everywhere. What happened, Himsha?"

He saw in her eyes a flicker of hope, as if she thought for a moment that she had imagined it all. Then she lifted the quilt and looked at the blood on her clothes and dropped it again.

"Yes," he said, "there was blood out there. It was Petesey, wasn't it?"

She nodded, eyes closed.

"Was it his body?"

She nodded again.

"Who did it?"

She did not react.

"Was he shot?"

She nodded.

"How? By an arrow?"

She nodded.

There could be no doubt now; it had been Uncle Ellis, their guardian angel, who had watched over them ever since they were children. He must have taken Petesey away to bury him somewhere in the wilderness, or put him in a tree near the run of a cat, so that when he was finally found, people would think that was how he had been killed.

He got up and went back to the garden. He buried Casey in his little basket, effacing the traces of blood as he did so. The impersonal activity of digging the hole cleared his mind; he must get back to the search party as soon as he could and have a good excuse for his absence. It meant leaving Himsha alone again, but there was no other way. He put the shovel back in the lean-to and hurried inside.

"Himsha, thee must get rid of those clothes at once, bury them in the garden, burn them; whatever thee does, get rid of them. Come, pull thyself together, get up, show thyself in the village; but whatever happens, *whatever happens,* tell no one, not one living soul, about this morning! Promise!" He put his hand on her arm and shook her, trying to be gentle but at the same time to get through to her, which was difficult. "Promise me, Himsha, promise me thee will not tell anyone!" She merely nodded; to his despair and misery, he saw tears running down her face again. To leave her like this was inhuman, but he had no choice. He turned away and ran out of the house without looking back, threw himself into the saddle and sprinted off at a thundering gallop. He felt the wind on his face and hoped it would keep him from bursting into tears. He forced Betsy up the slope to the trail at breakneck speed; as he rounded the bend, he suddenly pulled back on the reins and shrieked, "Whoa!" avoiding by a hair's breadth a horseman coming down the trail with a pack mule strung behind him. Betsy reared, whinnying, on her hind legs; as she stood there, bolt upright, pawing the air with her forefeet, the horseman said in a high-pitched voice, "Good grief! Little George! What's the hurry?"

Only then did he recognize who it was. "Aunt Gulie! Please! Please go and see Himsha! She's in trouble!"

The leathery face underneath the weatherbeaten Quaker hat lost its grin. "What trouble? Where is she?"

"She's at home, Aunt Gulie, at home! In the cabin, the door is open! She's sick, terribly sick, she's . . . she's upset . . ." He did not know what he was saying. He must not give it away, he must not. Even Aunt Gulie must not know what had happened.

"Upset by what?"

"I don't know." He soothed Betsy, who had finally come down from the sky and was going into one of her theatrical panics. "Her cat died . . ."

"Her cat?" The sky-blue eyes, almost white in the weatherbeaten face, narrowed.

"Yes, Aunt Gulie, yes—I must go now! I must join the posse,

Grandfather is lost, but do go and see her, she really needs thee, Aunt Gulie . . ."

"All right, I'll be there when thee comes back. Don't worry."

"Thank thee, Aunt Gulie," he said, biting back the tears. "God bless thee!" Spurring Betsy once more, he galloped off into the forest.

* * *

Gulielma Woodhouse, still a little shaky, slowly worked her way down the hillside toward the village, pacifying her poor old mare, Annie. Luckily, the mule had no nerves, you could fire a blunderbuss underneath that jackass and he would merely start moving.

Young George had really scared Annie, bless her spinstery soul, and herself too, bless her *idem idem;* now she had an acute attack of hyperacidity. Interesting; she had noticed those symptoms of late only after strenuous physical effort, never after a silly emotional shock like this. Well, she was getting older; it was a miracle that she had not been plagued by hyperacidity before, considering the atrocious diet she had lived on for the better part of forty years. Man could abuse his inner organs only so far: pemmican, parboiled jackrabbit and, in the desert, rattler steak or breast of buzzard, yum, yum. At least she would not die of overweight and its complications, as would most of her affluent Quaker relatives. After piously forswearing all carnal vices like dancing, fornication and booze, the saintly Philadelphia Friends had proceeded to dig their graves with their teeth. Seen from a purely medical standpoint, the first two vices would have been preferable, as they involved at least some physical exercise. Well, she had better try to control her stomach juices, if such a thing were possible, for she seemed to be heading for another emergency. Little Himsha in terrible trouble because her cat had died. What on earth could be the matter with the child?

As she rode into the village at a plodding trot, the first urchins started to jeer at her outlandish appearance. During the four months since her last visit many newcomers must have arrived; to any child who had spent a modicum of time on the frontier the sight of a buffalo hunter in his bizarre outfit and his nut-brown face burnished with bear grease was commonplace; even the fact that she was a woman was of no particular interest. She was surrounded not only by children but by a milling crowd of gaping, yoo-hooing idiots to whom she seemed to represent the joke of the century. The throng she attracted slowed her progress; at first they expressed little more than good-natured curiosity, but when those damnable urchins began to chant the ditty about *"Quakers and Indians, traitors both,"* a few of them became unpleasant. Someone started to fumble with her leggings in an uncharming effort to ascertain whether she was a goose or a gander; finally she unstrapped the prehistoric musket given her by her beloved Hunis from the pommel of her saddle and pulled it out of its leather casing. It was worse than useless; to fire a shot from the thing at its age would constitute a baroque form of suicide. But it looked formidable, especially when she snapped back the hammer-lock the size of a door handle, opened the breech, directed the trumpet of the barrel at the nearest rowdy and peered at him. It was pure bluff, but it worked, as she had known it would. Maybe it was the certainty on her part that made the cure effective; in any case, the crowd inched back and gave her a chance to proceed. It was a good thing they did, for her poor old Annie, whose nerves had already been jolted by young George, was beginning to show signs of an approaching crisis of menopausal jitters. The crowd accompanied her to the cabin, watched her dismount with slack-jawed fascination and showed no signs of dispersing when she walked toward the door; they obviously were going to wait until she came out again. God knew why; maybe they expected her to fetch a broom on which to continue her journey.

She knocked on the door; there was no response. She had not expected any; it had been a diagnostic knock. Had there been a response, that would have meant the end of the emergency. She opened the door and found the girl in bed, barely conscious and in a state of shock, but alive. She drew back the quilt and saw blood. Nosebleed? No traces of blood in the nostrils, no temporary anemia of the mucous membranes; somebody else's blood. Her clothes were torn, her hair was disheveled and had some grass in it; it looked like rape. A cursory inspection showed that, if so, it had been only an attempt. A pretty Indian girl living among frontiersmen could not go long without some rabid male trying to rape her, not nowadays. Why this overwhelming need for suppression of the event? Had it been her brother? These two creatures, lonely Quakers in a lawless town full of antagonists, must have been thrown together for mutual support like two quail among a pack of foxes. But where had the blood come from? She tried to recall George's image as he had towered above her on his rearing horse and stormed off into the forest like a stag with hounds on its traces. There had been no scratches on his face, no sign of a fight. There was only one explanation: whoever had attacked her had been clouted by George for his pains. Considering the boy's size and the elephantine strength he had inherited from his father, chances were that he had brained the man and splattered her with his blood.

If so, where was the corpse? Buried, most likely. But to go out now and start rummaging in the garden for a body under the eyes of that crowd would be ill timed. So she had better try to restore the child to consciousness; as a rapee, she would be considered innocent by any court, if not by the drumhead court of the frontier.

Well, back to the old routine. Gulielma pulled the arrow from her Quaker hat, which she tossed on a chair together with her leather jerkin, and set about heating water for tea. With a shot of rum and a dash of pepper, the brew would raise anything except the dead. Meanwhile, she could get those blood-soaked clothes off the child and clean her up. While being undressed, the girl seemed to protest, in her half consciousness; when at last the poor thing lay naked on the grimy sheet, Gulielma, despite her clinical detachment, could not help looking at the child with admiration. She had the figure of a Greek statue; no wonder she had caused havoc in this rabbit warren full of randy males. Ah, if only she herself had looked like that as a young girl! What a swath she would have cut among the Quaker swains! She might even have renounced her medical career and started a family, probably with some outside beau, one of those gorgeous Huguenot boys, for instance. It would have meant slightly more misery for a few thousand Indians, which, spread over a period of forty years, was not exactly world-shaking. She sighed, covered the girl with the quilt and went to look at the water, which seemed to be taking a long time. Perhaps she had better give the child some mild medication instead of the explosive dish of tea, which was more appropriate for comatose buffalo hunters than for this fragile Indian Venus. The crowd was still outside, however; she could hear murmuring beyond the gate. Well, there was nothing for it. She opened the door and strode briskly to her pack mule. In the sudden, expectant silence she unstrapped the angular edifice of the pharmacy the beast carried and heaved it onto the ground. She unsaddled her old horse while she was at it and sent them both into the vegetable garden with a slap on their bony haunches. The two old nags instantly went for the string beans and started to rip them off sideways with alacrity; young George would be aghast when he came home; it would have to be the fee for her professional services.

She was about to take out some laudanum when, with thundering hoofs and raucous war yells, a posse of horsemen came tearing down the street, scattering the crowd like sparrows. They cannonballed past, clods flying, and drew up their whinnying, rearing horses in front of the parsonage. George was among them; it must be the search party coming home, empty-handed by the look of it.

The attraction of the homecoming posse was irresistible; like a herd, the crowd started to stampede in the direction of the parsonage. Gulielma was on her way back to the cabin when young George turned up, looking pale and drawn despite his ruddy complexion. He slid off his horse and allowed it to join the other two that were vandalizing his garden; obviously, he was a badly shaken young man.

"Did you find Grandfather?" she asked with therapeutic casualness.

"Petesey Paisley is missing," he replied nervously.

"Who is Petesey Paisley?"

"The parson's son."

"Was he a member of your party?"

"Yes . . . He—he disappeared overnight; there hasn't been a trace of him since."

His lack of talent for dissimulation was such that she found herself pushing him into the house, as if his bad conscience could be spotted from the parsonage, three hundred yards down the road. He obeyed; when he stooped through the doorway and saw Himsha, he asked worriedly, "How is she? Will she be all right?"

"Of course she will," she replied. "But I think it's time thee told me exactly what happened, if thee wants me to help you two."

"Happened?"

"Come on, don't try and fool thy old aunt. Was it this Petesey who attacked thy sister?"

It had been a blind guess, but obviously she had hit a bull's eye. He gaped at her with round, innocent eyes, then he stammered, "How—what—I don't know what thee is talking about . . ."

"Come, boy," she said, "stop acting like a two-year-old and tell me the truth. Thee had better tell me in a hurry, because if I'm not mistaken, thee and she are in bad trouble. I may be able to help you or I may not, but I certainly cannot help you unless thee tells me exactly what went on, how she ended up in this condition and why thee is now looking at me as if I were a ghost." He seemed to need one more little push, so she added, "Come on! Out with it!"

"Yes, Aunt Gulie, yes—it was Petesey Paisley. Petesey must have attacked her this morning while she was burying her cat, and somebody, I don't know who, killed him . . ." Out came the whole story in a rush, incoherent because of his nervous exhaustion. She was trying to find out whether his absence from the posse had aroused suspicion, when a church bell started to peal clamorously. It was an urgent, alarming sound that seemed to have little to do with religion; it sounded like the warning of an approaching raid. "What does that signify?" she asked.

He was so wrapped up in himself that it took a moment before he said, "I—I don't know, but I'm sure the parson is up to no good. I don't know what possesses him, Aunt Gulie; I think he's mad . . ."

"Why?"

"All he does is rile up everybody against Indians and Quakers . . . I don't know what he's up to now, but I'm sure he'll make things worse, whatever he does."

She went to fetch her hat and her jerkin. "I'll go and find out." She stuck the arrow through the hat, but on second thought decided against it; the less conspicuous she looked, the better.

"Oh, but thee shouldn't go out there now!" George exclaimed, still in the state where everything looked like a threat. "They'll turn on thee; if they are angry or worked up, the first they turn on is Quakers!"

"Don't worry," she said, and patted his shoulder, about a foot above hers. He was like a frightened horse to the touch. "I can take care of myself. In the meantime, make thy sister a dish of tea, put some pepper in it and a shot of rum. The water is boiling." She went to the door, lacing her jerkin. She turned around and added, "As a matter of fact, it might not be a bad idea if thee thyself had a dish of it. In thy case, make it two shots of rum." He looked at her with big, startled eyes; he obviously adhered to the testimony on temperance with religious zeal; the rum she had found must be a legacy of his renegade pappy.

Outside, people were running toward the church from all directions. Her presence did not seem to bother them, although they were aware of her; they were too preoccupied to pay her much attention. The entrance to the church was crowded; she had some trouble getting in; when she finally did, as one of a group of rough and highly pungent yokels, she found the inside packed with people jammed together like herrings in a cask. The atmosphere was one of excited anticipation, more like that of a crowd waiting for a bear-baiting than for a religious service.

A white-haired old man, two tufts standing out from his skull above his temples like furry ears, climbed into the pulpit and bellowed, "Let us pray!" In the silence that followed he proceeded to exhort the Lord of Hosts to smash, exterminate, dismember, draw and quarter all enemies, Hittites, Philistines, idolators and pagan varmints, and to vouchsafe courage, determination and holy fire to His chosen. Whatever else the old buzzard might be, he was an accomplished animal trainer; after his first words he had his audience in the palm of his hand.

George had been right. There was not a spark of godliness in anything he said; with flailing fists and a voice that could win any hog-calling contest, he went on to announce that both his beloved son Peter and old James McHair the Quaker had been abducted by marauding Indians and that the moment had come to go and do the Lord's work; the Lord's work being the extermination of any Indian man, woman or child they could round up between now and nightfall. He even appointed from the pulpit those who were to join the raiding party and those who were to stay at home to defend the women and children; he told the raiders what to take, and the women how to prepare themselves for all eventualities; the sermon turned into a briefing, couched in Biblical terms. "Hittites," "Philistines," "godless heathens" and "fire-worshiping varmints"—all these seemed to be synonyms for "Indians"; at each new epithet the congregation whooped and hollered like a crowd watching a wrestling match, an occasional "Amen" being their only sign of deference to their surroundings.

It was such a distressing performance that Gulielma was tempted to emulate George Fox and interrupt the blasphemous harangue, but alas, she was bound to the approach to conflict after the manner of Friends not only by principle but by experience. The aggressive George Fox approach only increased the havoc that was being wrought, whereas the meek, cheek-turning patience that was the contemporary form of the Friendly persuasion at least tended to defuse a tense situation. She suffered through the old demagogue's hour-long ranting with a deepening sense of disaster; when finally he let his congregation go in a state of frenzied excitement and climbed down from his pulpit, obviously drained emotionally, she made her way against the current of bodies toward the back door through which she saw him disappear. She assumed it led to the vestry; when she opened it, she found a covered walk leading to the parsonage. She made her way to the house and knocked on a glass door. There was no reply except for the threatening bark of a dog, so she went in. The dog came bounding toward her from the shadows; she spoke to him, softly, in Algonquin, telling him that if he did not keep his mouth shut she would tear off his tail and stuff it down his gullet; it was not exactly the approach to conflict after the manner of Friends, but in the case of dogs it worked like magic. The huge, hairy windbag instantly slunk off; not so, however, his master, who appeared in a doorway in the dark passage crying angrily, "Who's there? Don't you know that I do not receive any member of the congregation without an appointment?"

"Good morning, Friend," she said with the sanctimoniousness that, alas, had turned out to be the most effective when pacifying raving lunatics and fiery prophets, the difference between whom seemed to diminish as she grew older. "I would like to have a word with thee about thy sermon, if I may."

He sputtered, "Who are you? What do you mean, barging into my house?" But his lion's roar had been replaced by his watchdog's wariness.

She stepped into the light, gave him a radiant smile and said pleasantly, "I am Doctor Gulielma Woodhouse, physician. I've just come in from the prairie, and I am on my way to Philadelphia. I happened to be present at thy sermon, and I would like to offer my services."

Had anyone approached her with this kind of unctuous blabber, she would have suspected it at once; but, obviously, the old man's sensibilities had been blunted by all that raw emotion. He tried to focus his eyes on her, both with and without the benefit of a pair of glasses that hovered on the tip of his nose; he needed new ones, for neither effort seemed successful. Finally, he let her into his study, be it with reluctance.

It was a small room with books, a desk, a dilapidated horsehair chair and other sticks of furniture, most conspicuous among them a huge white cuspidor into which he squirted a jet of tobacco juice the moment he sat down. He must have had years of practice, for, in spite of his failing eyesight, his aim was perfect. "What do you mean, Madam, er, Doctor," he grumbled ungraciously. "How do you think you could be of service in this matter?"

"Oh, I don't know," she replied airily, sitting down in the horsehair chair that seemed to snarl as she did so; it must be the dog, who now lay by the side of his master's chair, slavering. She whispered to him in Algonquin, with a mendacious smile.

"Pardon?"

"I was talking to thy dog, Friend Parson. I assured him that I am a friend, and I hope that I will be able to assure thee likewise."

But he was not that easily hoodwinked; after all, she was now dabbling in his profession. "Let's cut that, Madam," he said, without an effort at graciousness. "If it is your intention to stop the people of this village revenging their dead, then let me tell you here and now that you can save yourself the trouble."

"Dead?" she echoed, with badly acted astonishment. "I didn't know that any bodies had been found."

"As you very well know, Madam, there is no need to find any bodies to know what has happened to my poor son. If you are who I think you are, then you should know that Indians do not kidnap people for ransom, but for torture and execution."

"I did not intend it as a criticism, I just would like to be fully informed."

"Why?"

It was a good question. A good question deserved a good answer. Step number one: "Never use a man as a means, only as an end." In other words: Identify with thy adversary. She took a deep breath and said, with the feeling of sudden authority that the old Friends had optimistically defined as "being in the power of the Lord": "Friend, I think that, of all the people in church this morning, I may have been the one to understand thee best. Thee is the shepherd of a town that is being swamped, not by thy Scotch-Irish flock, but by freed indentured servants, pimps, prostitutes, robbers, murderers, the most vicious dregs of humanity. It is a crushing burden; no man of God can be asked to shepherd a more unrewarding herd." As had happened countless times before, in spite of her cynicism, she felt the beginning of that mysterious process of identification which was a *conditio sine qua non* for the emergence of the spirit of love, the only spirit in which any conflict could be solved.

The old man must have felt something other than the quivering spirals of hatred with which the room was filled; he leaned back in his chair and watched with grudging fascination the vague blot she must represent to his myopic eyes. "Thank you kindly for your concern, Madam, but may we please get to the point? As you must know, we are now organizing several search parties—"

"If they are search parties, Friend," she interrupted, "then I will be happy to join, in whatever function thee might set aside for me. But when I left the church I had the feeling that, whatever the spirit of thy words might have been, they were interpreted by thy congregation as a call to a raiding party, with unlimited license for murder." This was stage two of the Friendly approach to conflict: after having identified with it, speak truth to power. The fact that she knew what had happened to his son gave her a sense of guilt—for a moment she was tempted to tell him. But she discarded the notion; at this point the revelation would only make things worse. "I am deeply sorry that thy son—"

"Whether it concerns my son or someone else's son is of no consequence," he snapped. "Will you please come to the point, or leave me alone?"

She smiled, reassured that she could take him at his word. "Friend," she said, "I would be a fatuous jackass if I were to come here to tell thee what to do, or to bore thee with my private opinion. However, maybe the voice of an outsider who has just come from beyond the mountains deserves to be heard, to ponder upon as thee sees fit. May I, on that basis, take a few minutes of thy time?"

The old man sighed and slumped wearily in his chair. The dog beside him, as if it were his double in the animal world, also sighed and put its weary head on its forepaws. The parson took his useless glasses off his nose, rubbed his eyes and finally said, his voice hoarse with fatigue, "Doctor, or Madam, whatever you want me to call you, you are the most accomplished liar that ever sat in that chair."

"Liar, Friend?" she inquired charmingly. "How so?"

"Because," he replied, putting his glasses on again, "all this holy folderol only serves to cover up your tracks with your tail, like a vixen. Why not be honest and confess, 'Even if I have to grovel and fawn for it, I'll try to stop that old man from harming my Indians, whatever they may have done'?"

She smiled. It was a miracle; it never failed. There he went, after all these years, actually identifying with someone else in a spirit of, at least, equality. She wondered how long ago this had last happened to him. "Friend, of course that was my first thought when I came in here. But there is such a thing as falling, inadvertently, under the sway of the power of God. Thee would not still be listening to me if thee did not feel that what I am saying is no longer premeditated. To make absolutely sure of this, I would suggest that we sit together for a few minutes in silence, considering that where two or three are gathered together in His name, there He is in the midst of them." She did not wait for his reaction, but closed her eyes, folded her hands in her lap and bent her head; "Step three: Prevail upon thy adversary to join thee in meeting for worship." At once she sensed, with almost physical awareness, the silence between them dive to a deeper level. It was no longer mere silence, the negative absence of sound; there was a sudden presence between them, a spiritual energy in quivering suspension. She wanted to formulate words, a prayer, but the reality of the Presence was so overwhelming that the need for articulation left her. All she wanted to do as she sat there, surrounded by the infinite ocean of light and love, was to be aware of it, submit herself, like a vessel becalmed in infinity, to the urging of its current.

They sat like this for minutes on end; then, as at the close of every meeting, she held out her hand to him. He shook it gingerly, to flee in a self-conscious display of breathing on his spectacles, rubbing them with the edge of his frock coat and putting them on again. By then he had at least partially recovered his aplomb.

"Apart from all this, what is it you have to say to me, Doctor?" he asked. It still sounded masterful, but it was no longer. Through the mysterious process all violence and self-righteousness had been purged from the atmosphere; they now confronted each other, however briefly, in a weary spirit of tolerance.

"I have just come back from the wilderness," she said. "The Indians are spoiling for a fight. The French are behind it, but that's beside the point. All they are waiting for is a spark to hit the tinder. Only the Delawares are hesitating; they are the ones with whom William Penn made his original treaty, and after seventy-two years, they still are reluctant to break it. In my considered opinion, there is a chance, a small chance, that war can be avoided if everyone on our side behaves with the utmost restraint and responsibility.

"That's all very well—" the old man began, but she cut him short.

"Pray let me finish, Friend, so I may have done with it and go. I am not here to persuade thee, nor even to labor with thee, I am here to speak my piece and leave thee to act in whichever way the Light may guide thee. It may be God's will that there shall be war; I am in no position to determine what is His will and what is not. This is a moment when the only responsible stance a Christian can take is that of total submission to the Light. What would be the consequences of thy sending out raiding parties into Indian territory? A response from the side of the Indians so massive that only the word 'massacre' can describe what would happen to this village as a result. Seventeen tribes, war paint on their bodies, arrows in their quivers, their horses pawing the ground, are poised to swarm across the mountains in their thousands, to kill and scalp every single paleface in sight, man, woman and child. Whatever violence the males of thy village can unleash, there is no hope that this town can withstand the tidal wave of destruction that will wash over it within hours after the first Indian village has been raided. As a Friend, I can swear no oaths, but thee must believe me when I avow to thee that thy sermon of this morning, if its intent is carried out, will be the direct cause of the death by torture of every living soul that sat listening to it in thy church this morning. What thou hast read to those people, Friend, may be the will of God, but it can only be interpreted as God's determination that Loudwater shall share in the fate of Sodom and Gomorrah. If it is thy conviction that thy sinful flock deserves total extermination, so be it. If not . . ." She rose. "I will not pronounce judgment on that, Friend," she said with sincerity. "For it is a matter between thee and God. Good day." She turned to the door, prepared to leave without any further discussion.

But he called her back. "What do you want me to do?" he exclaimed angrily, as if he now held her responsible for his predicament. "Two people of this village are gone, vanished into thin air! Of course the Indians abducted them! Am I to acquiesce in their disappearance and call off the search altogether?"

Again she felt a pang of guilt. Should she tell him what she knew? The temptation to do so was strong, but intuition, or the Light, told her not to. "Friend," she said, "it is obvious what thee must do. Call the men together and simply organize search parties to look for the two that are missing until they are found, dead or alive. And warn them not to lift a finger against any Indian. At least look first, before inciting thy people to a massacre." Then she added, "I'll tell thee what. I'll organize a posse to look for old James, I think I may have an idea where he is; thee organize the posse to look for thy son. Let's give ourselves twenty-four hours; if after that time neither of them has been found, let's have another sermon. How's that?"

He eyed her balefully, as did his dog. "And how am I supposed to justify all this to my congregation?" he asked belligerently, but unable to disguise the humility of his question.

"Friend," she said with a smile, "surely that is a rhetorical question. I have not come here to flatter thee, but thee is a past master at handling crowds." Without waiting for his reply, she opened the door and left him alone with his dog and God.

When she came outside and saw the angry crowd milling around the men and the horses of the raiding party, she realized that the old minister might well have unleashed an evil genie that even he might prove incapable of coaxing back into its bottle. There could be no doubt that the excited, vicious crowd wanted blood; man's elemental tribal insanity was unleashed once more, the tragic affliction of the only animal in existence that devoured its own kind. But even if Parson Paisley was able to restrain them, how could she collect a posse to look for a senile old Quaker, with the people in their present mood? She, a Quaker herself and a woman to boot? The only chance she had of collecting a few people would be to tell them where to look for old Jim; maybe his grandchildren had an idea.

She made her way back to the cabin, where she found Himsha sitting up in bed, sipping tea. Young George was so surprisingly nonchalant that she concluded he had followed her prescription to the letter. "Hello, Aunt Gulie!" he cried, as if it were the first time they had met that day and the sight of her filled him with well-being. "Come on in! Would thee like a drop of tea?"

"No, thank thee," she replied wryly. "How's our patient?"

"Himsha? As thee can see, she's as frisky as a filly."

Well, that was an overstatement; she was very pale and, clearly, still shaken. Gulielma went over to her and patted her hand. "Glad to see thee perking up, Himsha," she said kindly.

"Perking up?" the young drunk roared behind her, with an echo of his father's ear-blasting boom. "She's ready to burst into the meadow and test the fence!"

"Hush," she admonished him and guided his massive body to the only chair in the room. "Why doesn't thee sit down and talk to me?"

"Talk to thee, Aunt Gulie? I'd rather do a little jig with thee!" He giggled alarmingly. His tipsiness would have been touching in its innocence if he hadn't been so large; once that bovine bulk started lurching about, it could become a menace. "Keep quiet," she said, managing to make him sit down. "There is something I have to ask thee. It is important."

"Important," he repeated earnestly.

"I am trying to make up another posse to go and look for thy grandfather, but no one will come unless I know where to look for him."

"Look for him." He nodded, his blue eyes grave but unfocused.

The thought crossed her mind that he also might be suffering from delayed shock; his youth had been very peaceable, owing to the *Pax Amicorum* in which he grew up; his nerves were obviously not of the same tough fiber as his father's.

"Now stop playing the fool and listen carefully, George!" She needed that information, whatever ailed him. "Senile people have a tendency to return to their early childhood in their fantasies; there is a good chance that thy grandfather has wandered back into the forest to where he used to play as a little boy. Is there anyone alive in these parts who knew him at that age? I need that information before I can go and look for him. Does thee understand me?"

"Yes, Aunt Gulie, yes, yes . . ." He nodded solemnly; she suspected that he was not listening but captivated by what happened to her image when he moved his head.

She shook him by the shoulder. "George! Listen or I'll slap thy silly face! Who is there that played with thy grandfather when he was a little boy? Is there such a person? Think!"

He seemed at pains to express thought. He was eager to please, but incapable of concentration. "I—I dunno . . ."

"Think, thou brittle guzzler!" She hoped the Quakerly reproach would have a greater effect on him than "damn drunkard."

But, alas, he had slipped out of reach. "Think . . ." he said thickly, closing his eyes and leaning back in his chair. "Think . . ." and that was that. His alcoholic babyhood had lasted but a flicker, now he was back in the womb. He would lie there, sprawled in his chair in peaceable gestation like a huge, blissful fetus, until the stupor wore off and he woke up in the frightening world again.

She sighed, straightened up and stood looking down at him, scratching her head. Well, she might as well renounce the idea of the search party; on to the next move. Trouble was now unavoidable; she had better get both of them out of here, quickly. But how was she going to move the ton of senseless beef snoring in the chair? She turned to the girl. "Dear heart, we had better start packing our things, the moment has come for us to move out of here."

"And Grandfather?" the girl asked.

"I'm afraid that we'll have to forget about him."

"No . . ."

"Thee heard me tell thy brother: there is no point in my trying to get another search party going unless I know where to look for him. And I haven't the faintest idea."

"Oh . . ."

"What's more, just between thee and me, he's probably dead. If he hasn't succumbed to exposure, chances are a mountain lion got him. I can do no more. I must look after the living and see to it that they remain that way."

"Uncle Ellis would know," the girl said quietly.

Uncle Ellis? Of course: Lone Seeing Eagle. "Know what?"

"Where he is."

"Why should he?"

"He always looks after Grandfather when he runs away. And they knew one another as children."

"Where do I find him?"

"He is never found. He finds thee."

"Where?"

The girl looked at her before she replied, an enigmatic look from large black eyes. It now seemed clear that she was not a white man's child; only Indians looked like that. The way she sat there, her delicate, aquiline face framed by those heavy braids, she was a beautiful creature from another world. Then she said calmly, "Go to the old Meeting House."

"What does thee mean? Just go there and wait for him?"

"Yes."

"How will he know I am there?"

"He will know."

Ah, those Indians! "I see," she said. "It is thee who will tell him."

The girl shook her head and, surprisingly, tears began to roll down her face.

"All right, child, all right," she said, and she stroked her hair. "I'll go to the Meeting House." She went toward the door. "Thee had better tie down the latch after I'm gone. When I come back, I'll show myself at the window there." She did not wait for an answer; she suddenly had had enough of both of them.

Outside, the street lay empty in the sunlight. It was a stroke of luck that everyone in the village had been drawn to the excitement on the common; this was the wrong moment for an Indian to be around, however adept he might be at making himself invisible. It was a relief to walk the streets without being followed by a jeering crowd; it seemed like old times, when the entire population had consisted of Friends. What blissful days they had been! The Quaker families of Loudwater had lived unarmed among the Indians for generations; the Indians had helped them with food in the harsh winters and taught the white boys the art of hunting, the Indian children had gone to the village school, and when the Friends went to yearly meeting they left their babies with the Indians. The result had been people like Buffalo McHair, who were treated by the Indians as their own, to the extent that one of them still watched over this family as a guardian angel.

The old Meeting House lay in the small clearing of the burial ground, swathed in the shadows of chestnut trees that whispered secretively in the breeze. It was so quiet there, on the edge of the forest, that she could clearly hear the gentle, musical tinkling of the little waterfall that had given the village its name. The last time she had been inside the old building was as a young woman on her first journey out, with her life still before her. She had gone in to worship; she remembered sitting in the small, still crowd of elderly Quakers, seeing in her mind's eye the legendary John McHair building this crude edifice for a meetingplace with God. He must have built it together with his mute, mysterious young wife, gone out into the forest all alone and lugged the heavy timbers back himself, back-breaking labor that must have taken forever. But the result had stood for almost a century and it did not look as if it were about to fall down yet. It was now overgrown with honeysuckle; Virginia creeper had wound itself up the posts of the porch, where she remembered gathering with the women after meeting. She climbed the rickety steps and looked at the posts that the old patriarch must have carved himself from the peeled trunks of saplings. She had never really looked at them before, having been too preoccupied with herself at the time. They were slightly fluted, surprisingly graceful for a primitive crafts-man with only one hand.

Despite its air of disuse and dilapidation, there was a serene at-mosphere about the little building: it was still obvious that it had been built as a house of God. The door on its cracked leather hinges stood ajar; when she pulled it open, it creaked eerily in the silence.

The inside was dark. Grime and vegetation had covered the windows, creating a green twilight like an underwater world. The floor was covered with refuse, old bottles, rags, the droppings of generations of bats; all she could discern in the darkness was the penumbral shadows of a stack of barrels that partially obscured the windows and, against the walls, benches piled together. Two of them still stood upright, opposite each other; she sat down on one of them and closed her eyes. The God of her girlhood seemed to be all about her as she sat there, at the sunset of her life, in the same spot as she had at its sunrise. Ah, the dreams, the hopes, the illusions! All centering on the great, mysterious lover who had seemed to beckon at the end of the trail that led into the wilderness. Now, forty years later, there she sat: a leathery old woman feeling the first surreptitious gnawings of death in her stomach, still following that trail. What would he turn out to be? God, or merely death itself? It did not matter. *Sub specie aeternitatis,* nothing mattered that happened on the planet called Earth, with its ephemeral creatures, in the unimaginable vastness of the interstellar void. But as the terror of death crept upon her from those shadows filled with ghosts of the past, she told herself this was the delusion she had been combating all her adult life: measuring the values of the universe by human standards. The only mind that could conceive its meaning was the mind of God. Why this abject terror of the unknown, without ever stopping to wonder with the same terror where she had come from? Wasn't she heading for the same darkness, or light, she had emerged from sixty-four years ago? The same "infinite ocean of light and love" that had once miraculously spawned the squalling spark of life called Gulielma Woodhouse was about to re-ceive her back, that was all. Why should she be filled with terror? She sighed and opened her eyes; opposite her, on the wreck of the facing bench, sat an Indian.

After forty years among them, she should be accustomed to their magician's trick of appearing and disappearing at will, but once again, as she had done many times before, she gave a frightened start. This time with reason: the Delawares must have made their decision at last, for the old man opposite her was covered with war paint. Naked except for loincloth and moccasins, he was decorated with yellow stripes that ran up his belly and over his chest. The upper half of his face was a yellow mask, with red blotches on his cheekbones and over his eyes. His crest was reddened also, and from it dangled two eagle's feathers. Crooked red and black streaks went down his thighs, and around each arm a band of orange and green. But his eyes were closed; despite his alarming exterior, he exuded an extraordinary serenity. He might be an aged Quaker immersed in the Presence. He seemed to have joined her in her solitary meeting for worship.

They sat facing each other in silence. His tranquillity, in bizarre contrast with his menacing appearance, pervaded her with a sense of peace, an extraordinary awareness of the Presence. She became confident that, to a higher consciousness, the enigma of the past made sense, and that the menace of the future was merely a projection of her own anxious mortality. When she finally heard a movement opposite her and opened her eyes, it was with a sense of loss. The old Indian was holding out his hand, as would any Quaker at the break of meeting; she shook it and said, "Friend Lone Seeing Eagle, peace be with thee. I have come to ask whether thee knows where I can find James McHair."

"I know where he is, Friend Man-Woman," the old man replied in Algonquin; his voice was soft and measured. "I shadowed him for two days. Like an animal that knows it is about to die, he was looking for a lair. I helped him climb into a tree where he and I once played as children. I did not stay to wait; I knew he was at peace."

Despite the fact that he spoke in his own dialect, he obviously adapted his words and phrases carefully for his white listener. It was extremely courteous, and rather touching. She felt a little less overawed by the weightiness of his presence. "Whereabouts would that be?" she asked.

He looked at her without expression. "It does not matter," he replied. "Whatever is left in that tree is of no importance to Friend James or anyone else."

She realized that this was all he intended to tell her. "And the young boy Petesey Paisley?" she asked.

He replied calmly, "His body is outside, on my horse. I killed him; I am on my way to deliver myself to his father."

The statement took her completely by surprise. She stared at the old man for several moments; then, doing away with all decorum, she said urgently, "Lone Seeing Eagle, thee cannot do this! Those people out there are not reasonable men, they are violent fanatics who treat the laws of the land with contempt! Even if the boy's father were to agree to it, they will never let thee stand trial; they will hang thee from the nearest tree! Thee cannot do this. Thee must not. I understand that thee wants to assuage thy conscience, but this is suicide." She spoke forcefully, with the authority of the physician.

But it was to no avail. He gazed at her with those dark, expressionless eyes, then he answered, "I know, Friend Man-Woman. But this is what I must do to prevent a great killing. They are about to raid the villages, the way they raided mine sixteen winters ago. Then only one girl child was left alive; this time there would be none."

Despite her abhorrence of what seemed a senseless act of self-destruction, she felt a first doubt. However persuasive Parson Paisley might be, the males of the village had been roused to such a state of bloodthirstiness that even the most convincing argument might fail to deter them. For this Indian to offer himself as a sacrificial lamb did indeed present a small hope that their violence might be diverted.

As if he read her thoughts, the old man produced a leather thong which he held out to her. "I ask thee, Friend Man-Woman, to bind my hands behind my back."

But even though her reason understood, she could not let him do this; forty years of determination to save life proved insurmountable. "I'm sorry, Friend Lone Seeing Eagle," she said, "I cannot help thee. I will not stop thee, but I cannot help thee."

He gazed at her with expressionless objectivity, as if he were already looking at her from a world of larger consciousness, greater understanding. "Friend Man-Woman, I ask thee again: tie my hands behind my back, take me to my horse on the edge of the forest, guide me to the father of the boy I killed, and tell him thou found me and decided to take me to him." His eyes, despite their detachment, seemed to show cunning. "I know that thy form of worship will not allow thee to speak a lie. Think, though, Friend Man-Woman: thou *didst* find me, and thou *wilt* decide to take me to him. Say no more and thou wilt not have lied." He held out the thong to her once more. "Do as I ask thee, as a last service to Friend Lone Seeing Eagle."

His typically Indian bargaining suddenly gave him a heartbreaking humanity. He obviously was determined to go through with this; no argument would hold him back.

"But if they ask thee why thee did kill the boy, what is going to be thy answer? The truth?"

There was that look of cunning again. "Friend Man-Woman, that will be for me to decide. Thy God will not allow thee to help me speak a lie, so do not concern thyself with this. Help me, as a friend of my people, to save our women and children. Do not take away from me the responsibility for my own fate."

It had been an extraordinary speech, one she might expect from a learned colleague asking for her assistance in an act of self-destruction to end his own pointless suffering. Here was a man planning to do more than that, to forestall the pointless suffering of countless others. All she could do was to submit herself to his destiny, now about to find its catharsis in this awesome act of atonement.

She took the thong from him with the curious feeling that she was handing something over; then she looked at him critically and said, "Friend Lone Seeing Eagle, I would advise thee to remove the war paint from thy body." At his sudden look of distress, she added, "I know what that means to thee, but by appearing like this thee will suggest that thy people are now at war."

It was an irrefutable argument, but she agonized for him. It was asking for a sacrifice almost as great as that of giving his life: to a Delaware, to enter eternity without those credentials of virility meant that his ghost might be captured by his enemy and used as a slave. She was so keenly aware of the agony her suggestion caused him that she tried once more to dissuade him.

"Dear, dear friend," she said, "thee knows and I know that the avalanche of war, once unleashed, cannot be stopped by any man, however brave and self-effacing. Why not accept thy act of killing that boy? I know what he did, I know the girl, I can tell thee that if thy arrow had not struck him down, he would have destroyed her as surely as if he had plunged a dagger into her heart. Why give thy own life as an act of purification?"

But he was not for one moment deterred by her subtle effort to weaken his resolve. He stretched out his hand and said calmly "Thank thee, Friend Man-Woman. I have no cloth, hast thou anything I might use to clean myself at the brook?"

She gave him her neckerchief. Then she went to the door, looked up and down the deserted street and beckoned him.

Surreptitiously they scurried toward the brook, beyond the tombstones that marked the era of Friendly peace now drawing to a close.

*   *   *

George was shaken awake from his alcoholic stupor by Himsha so agitatedly that he reacted with a sense of alarm. "Wha—what's the matter?"

"Wake up, wake up!" she urged, her voice hushed as if she were afraid of being overheard. "Uncle Ellis has been captured! He's being taken to the parsonage now, by Aunt Gulie!"

"Aunt Gulie?" he repeated stupidly.

"She found Petesey, put him across Uncle Ellis' horse, she tied Uncle Ellis' hands behind his back and she's—she's . . ." She burst into tears, her face in her hands.

He sat, mouth open, staring at her. Aunt Gulie capturing Uncle Ellis? It made no sense. "It cannot be," he said firmly. "Aunt Gulie would never do such a thing."

"I saw them! I saw them!" she sobbed. "She is taking him to the parsonage; they'll—they'll . . . Listen!"

In the distance sounded a deep-throated roar. He knew it was the crowd, but he had never heard a sound like that before. He rose unsteadily to his feet and shook his head to clear it; then he went to the door and peered, eyes aching, into the sunlit day. People were coming out of their houses and running toward the church; a woman's voice shouted, "They found the parson's son! He's dead! They caught the Indian who did it!"

It sobered him. Uncle Ellis was indeed in danger. Despite the lightheadedness that made him unsteady on his feet, he ran toward the parsonage.

The crowd in front of the parsonage was so dense that he did not even try to fight his way through. The roar, huge and sickening now, had nothing human about it; it was as if the whole population had turned into a single monstrous beast, roaring with rage, shaking fists, shrieking; nearby, an idiot voice bawled monotonously, "Show's thy jig, child-eater! Show's thy jig, child-eater!" A blowsy wench, flushed with excitement, was sitting on a man's shoulders to look over the heads of the crowd; she shouted, "Ouch! Sweet Jesus, if they did that to me . . . But he doesn't feel anything, I tell thee they're like fish, they . . . Ouch, Ouch! Oh, Jesus . . . Oh, no!" She had her skirts hitched up, her stark white thighs squeezed the head of the man beneath her, she held on to his hair with her fists.

George felt like turning away and running home; but he must do something, defend Uncle Ellis, get him out of their hands . . .

The woman above him gave a shriek, then she cried, bucking back and forth on the man's shoulders as if she were riding a galloping horse, "They've cut it off! They've cut it off! Ahhh . . . ! He felt *that,* all right!" Indeed, an awful wail of agony rose above the roar of the crowd; it was drowned by a massive bellow of approval that made George sick to his stomach. The woman screamed, "They're stuffing it in his mouth! They're stuffing it in—" Her voice too was drowned by the bestial roar of the crowd and a deafening sound of applause. Then the female shrieked, "There he goes! There he goes! They're hanging him, now, *now!"*

Something in her voice made him stare at her. Whatever was happening over there, she no longer looked at it; she lay slumped forward over the head of the man beneath her and for a moment he thought she had fainted, but she was covering the man's hair with kisses.

Beyond her he saw, to his horror, a twitching body, blood running down its thighs, being hoisted into the tree that shaded the parsonage.

"Now show's thy jig, child-eater!" the idiot voice bellowed. *"Now* show's thy jig!"

George turned away and ran.

*   *   *

Gulielma would never have believed that she could stand calmly by while a frail old man was tortured, obscenely mutilated and finally garroted to death by a herd of human beings in the throes of communal insanity. The serenity the old Indian had brought with him surrounded her, active, alive, almost as if she alone, among the lunatics shrieking in damnation, realized the spiritual portent of this ghastly ritual slaughter. A mystical feeling sustained her, as if her presence were desperately needed, as if through her awareness she held up a mirror to the poor, tormented victim. Her fortitude seemed essential to the spiraling Presence sweeping around that tortured man like a whirlwind of pure, breathtaking energy. She knew as she stood there, petrified, that she was watching not an orgy of destruction but an awesome moment of creation, that in this apparently senseless sacrifice there was a sense beyond the reach of her reason.

What the obsessed, mad-eyed ghouls were doing to that old male body was, in a realistic sense, unspeakably obscene; had she witnessed it from the everyday immediacy in which she spent her life, she could not have borne it. It seemed an act of mercy when, finally, they put the noose around their victim's neck and hauled his jerking, struggling body up into the tree; but they lowered him again when his motions slackened, to go on desecrating the dying body in a paroxysm of cruelty and utter damnation. She thought, as in meeting, slowly and unhurriedly, 'Strength, my friend, strength, strength, He is here, thee and I are gathered together in His name, and He is in the midst of us.' She knew, beyond all possible doubt, that Lone Seeing Eagle was aware of it, even as his tormented body was hoisted, squirming, into that tree for the fourth time. Suddenly there was a flash of light and an explosion; a red star spat open on the chest of the tortured man, and with a shudder the body went limp. She turned around and saw, on the porch of the parsonage, old Parson Paisley, a smoking rifle in his hands. Beside him, ears cocked, stood his dog, waiting for the dove to hit the ground.

After a second of stillness, the crowd started to murmur and stir; old Paisley, with the fire of the prophet in his eyes, roared at them, "Woe, woe, ye evil sinners of Loudwater! What have you done? Is this the way to behave in front of the house of the Lord?" While he went on berating them, shouting about foulness, blasphemy and retribution, she left. The crowd, hypnotized by the wrathful voice roaring its awesome exhortations, let her pass unnoticed. She left not as a protest against the cold-blooded belatedness of the old man's intervention, for she understood why he had waited so long. He had granted them a small symbolic massacre; it was the only way he could undo the harm he had done by inciting them to a holy war. She left because, should she have to face these villagers on some future occasion, it would be better if she were not identified with the shameful thing they had done.

It seemed an anti-climax, after the cosmic awe in which she had witnessed the old Indian's death and transfiguration on this shabby rural Golgotha. But Lone Seeing Eagle, wherever he was now, no longer needed her to hold up a mirror. He had crossed the surf of pain and set sail on the infinite ocean of light and love.

She returned to the cabin. When she came in, George and Himsha stared at her with such horror that she realized they did not understand why she had been the one to lead the old man to his certain death. She explained how it had come about, briefly, for they should get out of Loudwater as fast as they could. In the backwash of this brutal murder, the Indians might descend upon the village.

She managed to get the two bewildered infants moving. Half an hour later, before the populace of Loudwater had come to its senses, they were ready to leave.

*   *   *

George prepared to abandon his home in a daze. He worried about the livestock; who would look after them? But he still had a feeling of unreality and his legs felt so weak that all he could do was to follow Aunt Gulie's lead. She told them to pack as little as possible; he would take the luggage, Himsha would ride with her, although it would be quite a strain on the poor old mare.

They were about to go when they heard Betsy and Annie whinny excitedly in the garden; George hurried to the door and caught a glimpse of a furtive gray ghost in the forest across the brook. It was Uncle Ellis' horse; he went back inside to tell Aunt Gulie. It must have broken loose during the execution and fled into the forest, but it was an Indian horse, no white man could hope to capture it, let alone ride it. It would have to fend for itself until it found a herd it could join or until a panther or rattlesnake got it. Then Himsha said she would try to coax the horse to come to her, she had fed it in the past. She took some bread with her and a rope and, mysteriously, the quilt off the bed. They watched her go down the narrow path to the brook and wade across it. At the edge of the forest she put the quilt around her shoulders with her back to them; a moment later she dropped it and slipped into the wilderness, stark naked.

"What on earth is she doing?" George asked, alarmed.

"It's an old Indian trick," Aunt Gulie replied.

"But what is she *doing?*"

"If a horse is frightened or a stray has wandered into their territory, Indians take off their clothes before attempting to approach it. I don't know why; I think it has something to do with assuring the horse that they mean no harm."

It troubled George to know that Himsha was out there so close to the village without any clothes on; he should go after her to protect her from those rowdies. But Aunt Gulie was not concerned. "After their outburst of insanity this morning," she said, "they are going to lie low for some time to come."

"Insanity?"

"Of course. Jesus said it, 'Forgive them, Father, for they know not what they do.' It's not our wickedness that makes us the biggest menace on earth, it's our sudden paroxysms of lunacy."

"Thee is prepared to forgive those men for what they did to Uncle Ellis?" he asked incredulously.

"I'm prepared to," she replied dryly. "But I cannot say that I have reached that degree of loving-kindness yet. I should, for the very reason Christ gave: They knew not what they did. They were insane."

It was a bewildering statement and he wanted to talk about it, but suddenly she cried, "Look!"

There was Himsha, astride a pale blue roan with gray mane and tail; she was leaning forward, her arms around its neck, as if she were whispering in its ear. It was a beautiful and deeply disturbing sight, for she had not had time to put on her clothes. Then, slowly, gracefully, she slid off the horse's back; George saw that she had managed to put the rope around its neck. When she stooped to pick up the quilt, the horse shied, jerking her upright; she held on to the rope with both hands and spoke to the animal calmly; George could not hear what she was saying, but the horse acquiesced. She bent down again; this time it allowed her to pick up the quilt, which she put around her shoulders. She walked it to where her clothes were, tied the rope to a sapling on the bank of the brook; the horse, though its nostrils flared and its mouth worked, did not try to break away while she dressed. She folded the quilt; then, with a sinuous bound, she leaped onto the horse's back. Amazingly, it did not protest; guided by the rope around its neck, it forded the brook and came down the narrow path to the cabin, nervous and apprehensive, with small mincing steps, past the other horses, which neighed and stretched out their muzzles to sniff with curiosity. The pale, wild horse had no eyes for them, it did not even glance their way. When Himsha slid off its back at the door, it made as if to follow her inside. It stuck its head in, sniffing, the rope dangling from its neck.

"Is thee not going to tether it?" George asked.

"No," she replied. "He won't run away. But we should go now, before anyone sees him." She went to get her blanket roll and looked once more about the cabin, slowly. He knew she was saying farewell; until then it had not occurred to him that probably they would never return.

They slipped out of the village unnoticed. Even the dogs seemed to be off somewhere, brooding about what had happened.

Uncle Ellis' roan turned out to be totally unlike any of the horses George had ever owned. Its relationship with its rider was different; rather than being handled by Himsha, it seemed to treat her with an odd, protective care. They made camp in the little glen where he had spent the night on his way home; the horse stayed with her, like a dog. It refused to wander off to graze with the others even when she said, in Algonquin, "Go get thyself something to eat. I'll be all right." It snorted as if it had understood, but stayed where it was, and she let it be.

"Shouldn't thee make it feed at least a little?" he asked. "Tomorrow's going to be a long day."

"No," she replied. "Why should I tell him what to do? He's old enough to know what he wants."

"Well, obviously, he wants to be with thee," Aunt Gulielma said briskly. "Come, George, let's get a fire started and boil some jerky. At my age, I can't chew it unless it's cooked."

As George went to collect dead wood, his thoughts returned to the happenings of that morning. He wanted desperately to talk about it with Aunt Gulie, because for the first time in his life he was unsure of the rightness of the peace testimony. If those men had been insane, should those who were not, like himself, have tried to stop them? Did non-violence mean that a lunatic should be allowed to butcher people unhindered? For the first time his Quaker tolerance, ingrained in him since his earliest childhood and second-nature to him now, found itself faced with the intolerable. He could not accept Aunt Gulie's acquiescence; something should have been done, somebody should have stopped them, it could not have been God's will for him to hover nervously on the periphery while their guardian angel was being tortured, mutilated, lynched. It could not have been His will that Aunt Gulie should stand there, calmly watching the proceedings, thinking, 'Forgive them, Father, for they know not what they do.'

That night, at the campfire, he tried to broach the subject, but she was uncommunicative; after they had eaten and rolled themselves in their blankets around the fire, she reached out and nudged him. "In the morning thee should not continue with us to Eden Island, George," she said. "Leave early and get thyself to Philadelphia as fast as thee can, to tell the Meeting what has happened and give them an urgent message in my behalf: They murdered an old chief, this may be the excuse the Indians have been looking for. Something will have to be done by the authorities, or this colony will see a massacre the like of which it has never seen before. Tell the Friends that in my considered opinion they must make up their minds, now, whether to meet violence with violence or to abdicate all political power. They can no longer have it both ways. Is that clear?"

"I think so, Aunt Gulie."

"Shall I write it down for thee?"

"No, I'll remember. It's quite clear."

"I should hope so," she snapped and, sitting up, started poking the fire, sending up a shower of sparks that briefly revealed Himsha already asleep and the blue ghost of the Indian horse watching over her.

"Well," Aunt Gulie said, throwing the stick into the fire, "we had better get some sleep; we must be on our way at first light. Good night."

"Good night, Aunt Gulie."

They did not need to keep watch; the horses would tell them if anything approached under cover of darkness. George felt the drowsiness of sleep come over him. It seemed unbelievable that only the night before he had lain like this with the posse, Petesey already gone, leaving his hat and his bedroll in his place. Little had he known that he was sneaking off to his death.

He was drifting into the smoky, glowing darkness of sleep when it occurred to him that he had not lusted after Himsha since Petesey died.

* * *

The next day, as Himsha and she rode through the gradually more civilized world, Gulielma Woodhouse was haunted by the notion that at some time during the last few days she had done or omitted to do something seemingly small and innocuous that was bound to have disastrous consequences. What? Was it something she should have done intead of standing there, petrified, while the lunatics tore a human body apart? She could not find the answer and ended by putting the whole notion out of her mind.

Toward nightfall they approached the village of Media. Friends would be gathering for evening worship at this hour in their somber, red brick Meeting House, but for some reason she could not stand the idea of meeting, not right now. They camped out in the open, away from the village, like fugitives.

The next day they arrived too late for the ferry to Eden Island and had to stay at the inn. They shared a bed; the moment they lay down, Himsha nestled close to her with such passion that Gulielma realized the child was ravenous for tenderness. For some reason, the notion of having committed a crucial mistake caught up with her again; could it have something to do with Himsha? Poor little thing, she must be terribly lonely now, with both old men gone. When the girl pressed herself hungrily against her, she told her, on the spur of the moment, the story all children loved: how she had come by her antique musket. A remote Indian tribe at the very edge of her territory had, centuries ago, stolen it from a Spanish conquistador. They had also kept the conquistador himself, as a mummy, and put him, wearing helmet and breastplate, in a stone chair in the entrance to their sacred cave of the bats. She had been made prisoner by them when she blundered into their territory, but after curing the chief's gout she had become the man's blood-brother in a ceremony in front of that mummy, by torchlight; hundreds of naked Hunis prancing around them while her blood and that of the chief were being mixed in a bowl from which they finally drank, like a loving cup, their elbows entwined. She had been given the musket, which was one of a pair, as a safe-conduct in the tribe's territory for herself and her descendants, but there was one condition: in order to ensure safe passage for her descendants, she must return to the tribe the moment she felt death drawing near.

Only when she had reached the end of the story did she realize that Himsha had fallen asleep. As she tried to disentangle herself from the embrace of the sleeping girl, it suddenly occurred to her what her mistake had been: she should have gone back into the forest to find the body of old Jim, for to leave him in that tree for the

Loudwater rednecks to find had been reckless. They were bound to find him sooner or later, and would undoubtedly use him as a pretext for raiding the Indian villages after all. How could she have been so stupid? She should not have rested until she had found old Jim's body and buried it; now his remains might undo all the good Lone Seeing Eagle had achieved by his heroic sacrifice.

It was too late to go back; the best she could hope for was that a mountain lion or a catamount would find the body before the Paisleys did. It would be days before they recovered and took up their forays into the forest again. 'Calm down, dear,' she told herself, 'it's pure hysteria.'

But she fell asleep with a feeling of impending disaster.

CHAPTER FIVE

GEORGE McHair arrived in Philadelphia at nightfall and went straight to the house of his Uncle Peleg, the only one among his relatives in the City of Brotherly Love on whose doorstep he felt he could arrive unannounced.

Peleg arranged for an emergency session of the Committee on Indian Affairs the next morning; once the august body was in session, after twenty minutes of ponderous silence, George made his report and was appalled by the lack of response. The weighty Friends on the committee reacted to Aunt Gulielma's desperate plea for action with prayers, rhetorical exhortations, interspersed with periods of silent meditation; even Joe Woodhouse turned out to have no idea of the seriousness of the threat on the frontier. The sense of the Meeting amounted to the recommendation that George McHair join Joseph Woodhouse and Barzellai Tucker in the surveying party due to leave the next morning. After meeting broke, each member of the committee gave the two young delegates his fatherly blessing, telling them "to mind the Light"; Uncle Jeremiah assured George on their way home that "The Quaker mill may grind slowly, but it grinds exceeding small." In his mind's eye George saw him scalped and mutilated, dancing the jig of death like Lone Seeing Eagle, and his dismay was edged with desperation.

The party with which Joe Woodhouse and he left the next morning did not promise anything better in the way of realism. It was an unlikely procession made up of young Anglican fops in full city regalia complete with ruffs, cuffs and periwigs, accompanied by a bevy of black servants, a portable laundry, a collapsible bathroom, a screened tent in which to play pinochle and to sip Madeira in the evenings and a special cubicle for the powdering of their wigs. It was more like the caravan of an Arabian potentate than an expedition into the wilderness of northern Pennsylvania. What distressed George most was the platoon of Hessian mercenaries on horseback that accompanied them to protect the expedition. Nobody was quite sure what they were supposed to be protected from, but one thing it was sure to do, George knew, and that was to irritate the Indians before even a word was spoken. The presence of the soldiers might wreck any chance of success.

George himself was treated with subtle condescension by the young city blades, as was the interpreter, Barzellai Tucker, with whom Cousin Joe and he were to share a tent. The tent turned out to be a great deal simpler than the fancy contraption in which the young blades slumbered through the hours of darkness and well into the day; the expedition was late leaving each morning, as they had played cards and quaffed Madeira until the small hours, waited upon by blackamoors proffering trays of tidbits prepared by a pastry cook in a special wagon. George assumed that his exclusion from the lordly goings-on in the gaming tent was due to his being a Quaker; but he soon found out that this was not the distinction made by the young Anglican gentlemen. On the very first day Joe Woodhouse was invited to join them and, to George's indignation, he accepted, despite the explicit minute of the Meeting condemning all fiddling, dancing and playing of cards, as well as wigs or indecent caps. Joe had not gone all the way yet; he still sat among the crowd of revelers in his sober Quaker garb, wigless, but it seemed only a matter of time before he would join the others in their worldly attire as well. The way he toadied to them made George so furious that the second night out he broached the subject to Barzellai Tucker, who, as a Friend, must be as distressed by the spectacle as he.

Barzellai, a gloomy little man with a scholarly mien, agreed but in a rather chilling fashion. He turned out to be a "peculiar" Quaker, convinced of the total corruption and damnation of the world, an attitude shared by many Friends. To him, Joe's defection was one more proof that the Society of Friends must either return to "the original concept of Quakerism" or perish. As evoked by him, the future Society looked depressingly like a small, self-righteous crowd of Barzellai Tuckers, their pursed-mouthed wives and their sanctimonious broods, scowling at the world behind a hedge intended to keep them "pure."

In his misery George gravitated toward the other center of communal activity in the darkness: a large bonfire where the lower-class members of the expedition gathered, with, in the background, the dimly discerned flashes of the gold braid and the buttons of the mercenaries, who were of a still lower class and hovered on the periphery. George sought out the hunter-guide, who turned out to be so impressed by the fact that he was Buffalo McHair's son that he introduced him to the other members of the party and launched into a lengthy discourse about his father, to their amusement and George's growing anger, for the picture evoked by the hunter was that of a carousing, coarse, roistering bully and insatiable womanizer. The men roared with laughter at this description of a Quaker, but when George mentioned his Aunt Gulielma in an effort to balance the picture, the hunter took over again and made things worse. According to him, the saintly woman who had spent her life serving the Indians was called "Pissing Gulie": a tobacco-chewing, boozing, man-eating Amazon, tribal blood-brother of scalp-hunting savages, drinking partner of the outlaws roaming the prairie between the mountains and the Mississippi River. How was it possible that a person could spend an entire lifetime as an example and an inspiration and be seen by people like this hoary lout as a monstrosity? When the man began to sound off about her amorous exploits, suggesting that she had lassoed, thrown and straddled the worst of the outlaws and left them gasping on their backs in the sawgrass, their britches around their ankles, he could no longer remain silent. He rose, a colossus in the firelight, and growled at the startled raconteur, "Friend, thee is a shameless, foul-mouthed liar. Thee disgusts me, so I bid thee a good night. Next time keep thy tongue bridled with the truth." His bulk, combined with the fact that he was Buffalo McHair's son and Pissing Gulie's nephew, kept the gathering around the campfire from voicing any protest or derision. Only after he had left did the hunter explain that the Quaker Amazon owed her nickname to the fact that, without any false shame, she would walk away from a campfire surrounded by men to relieve herself in full view on the edge of the forest; to somebody's question why she did not absent herself a little farther, she had once answered, "No, thank thee, Friend, I'd rather have my posterior seen by a bunch of louts like thee than bitten by a rattler." Her nephew was a true specimen of the family.

Oblivious of the impression he had made, George wandered off miserably in the direction of the tent. The horses in the corral at the edge of the camp sounded restless; he went to have a look at them and saw his own Betsy nervously trotting along the fence, stopping now and then to sniff the night with flaring nostrils, neighing apprehensively. One thing the Indians could do nothing about was the scent of their silent ponies. When George stooped into the tent, he found Barzellai Tucker, nightcap on his head, lying reading Barclay's *Apology of the People Called Quakers* by the light of the lantern.

"No sign of Joe Woodhouse yet?"

Barzellai Tucker pointedly put his finger on the place where he was interrupted and answered tersely, "Not that I know of. Look in the back." George lifted the trade blanket hung across a rope which divided the tent into halves. The two field beds in the back were empty. Behind him, Barzellai Tucker's grating voice remarked, "Do not fret that I put the two of you together in there; I am sure thee will have it all to thyself before long."

George retired morosely into the tiny cubicle. He lay down to sleep; when he stretched out at his full length, his feet protruded under the blanket into Barzellai Tucker's part of the tent. He lay, open-eyed and fully dressed, staring at the roof that slowly billowed in the wind as if it were breathing. He knew, as Betsy knew, that the Indians were close by in the forest, watching. They must view with disfavor the antics of the young men with their powdered wigs and their finery, their fashionable expletives like "Zounds!" and "Strike me vitals!," their code words like "buxom wench" and "Faith!" and "prithee," calling one another "sir" and "your humble servant" and playing pinochle for high stakes, in which Joe Woodhouse was taking an enthusiastic part. He sighed; Cousin Joe was rapidly turning into a replica of his brother Abe, a wet Quaker if ever there was one. These people were not Friends, they were a mockery; yet the Woodhouses and other Quaker princes like them represented the true power in the Society of Friends; if they foundered, Quakerism would founder

with them. There was, that night, no way that George could see
to prevent that happening.

* * *

Joe Woodhouse was bewitched by the debonair way of life, the
elaborate mannerisms, the hedonistic fashions and the witty conversation of his Anglican companions. For the first time he understood
why his brother had opted for this civilized way of life.

He had been prepared for an arduous journey during which he
would never get out of his clothes, eat pemmican and drink only
foul, brackish water; not in his wildest dreams had he expected
Madeira at sunset, five-course dinners with wine, roast fowl, broiled
boar, venison, followed by tobacco, mocha, brandy and, finally,
pinochle, in which the stakes were outrageous but immaterial. He
was especially impressed by the frankness of his companions; he
could not believe his ears when, the very first night, he heard the
most modish and aristocratic of them all remark calmly, during their
card game, "Of course I cheat, old fruit; my grandmother was an
Irish indentured servant, sold for a hogshead of tobacco on the banks
of the James River." Compared to his father's pretense that all
Quakers in America were the descendants of well-to-do English
citizens impoverished by persecution, this honesty was refreshing. Joe
had felt ill at ease at first because of his drab Quaker garb and the
boorish cut of his hair, but discovered that he need not renounce
those peculiarities in order to be accepted. He made himself acceptable to them by turning out to be pretty broad-minded for a Friend.
He drank and smoked, he even enjoyed the military procedure: the
buglers, the drummer boys, the harsh discipline, the precision with
which the soldiers moved during the ceremony of the daily muster
before the caravan set out in the morning. This must have been the
way Caesar, Claudius and Hadrian marched their legions through the
wilderness of Europe and the British Isles; the Gauls and the Celts
must have been as savage and backward as the Indians were now.

After the first night at cards, heady with generous helpings of port
and hot-eyed with tobacco smoke, the youth whose grandmother had
been sold on the banks of the James River and whose name was
Saul Urquhart offered him a bed in their communal dormitory. "You
don't want to crawl into that smelly little tent of yours at this hour."
Joe accepted, with a sense of belonging he had never known before.
He slept better and with a greater sense of security than in town;
the following morning, a little after dawn, when the first coffee had
been served in bed and everyone gotten shakily to his feet somewhat
the worse for wear, there followed an incongruous ceremony. A
recess to their portable bedroom turned out to be a wig closet; each
of the young gentlemen secreted himself in there in turn to have his
periwig powdered by two slaves. The night before, the wigs had been
collected after they went to bed; they must have been recurled since,

for when they were brought in, they looked immaculate. A cloth was wrapped about the gentleman's neck, his face was protected from the flying powder by a glass cone which he held himself, the Negro barber blew the powder on through a clear pipe, with long, heaving gasps, taking turns with his companion in what was, obviously, a heavy exertion. The entire wagon train of well over a hundred men was held up for this preposterous ceremony. When finally the young gentlemen were ranged around the table, spotlessly attired, their wigs resplendently white, their linen freshly starched, their velvet coats and breeches brushed, Saul Urquhart raised the first glass of the day, said, "Gentlemen, His Majesty," and they all repeated the toast. Joe felt no sense of betrayal when he removed his hat and raised his glass to drink the King's health too. It was an extraordinarily moving moment; again the ancient Romans came back to him—so must the generals and their centurions have raised their beakers in the wilderness to say, "Hail, Caesar!"

On the second night out, after they had played cards into the small hours, Joe, in bed in a pleasant, giddy daze of inebriation, opened the first of Becky's letters George had given him. He expected it to be filled with pious chit-chat; to his surprise, he found it to be witty, and rebelliously worldly. This was not a letter from a Quaker maiden demurely waiting to pass Meeting with her swain; this Becky would charm and captivate any of the young stags now snoring around him in various stages of alcoholic stupor. He was tempted to read all ten at once; but the prospect of reading one of the deliciously mischievous monologues every night seemed delightful.

After he had snuffed his candle, the last in the room, he turned over contentedly and fell asleep with a tipsy swoop. It never occurred to him that he had forgotten his prayer.

* * *

When the wagon train of the surveying party arrived at the outskirts of the village of Chief Running Bull of the Unamis, Barzellai Tucker came into his own. The train came to a halt at the edge of a surprisingly large stretch of cornfields, beyond which the wigwams of the village could be seen profiled against the shimmering expanse of a lake. The Indian agent rounded up his two companions to give them instructions for the coming parley; he had some difficulty corraling Joe Woodhouse, who now spent all his time with the young dandies; to George's surprise, Barzellai brooked no nonsense from him, nor from George himself, for that matter. "Neither of you has an inkling of what's really going on," he said. "The official purpose of this expedition is to reassess the boundaries of the territory bought from the Indians by the Walking Purchase. In actual fact, it is not just the Walking Purchase that is going to be surveyed, but a much larger territory, for the purpose of claiming it at next month's Albany Convention. You don't know about the convention? I thought as much.

Well, next month there is going to be a meeting in Albany where all claims to Delaware territory by whites as well as Indians are going to be settled. Pennsylvania, represented probably by young Mr. Urquhart, is going to claim not only the original Walking Purchase but much more. At the convention he is going to try to confuse the Delawares with highly technical documents, which is why we have all these experts with us. He is going to produce maps with compass courses, degrees of longitude and latitude, obscure measurements; I would not be surprised if they were to include Russian *wersts* or French *kilomètres*. The Delawares own the land north of here, as far west as the Ohio River. As I trust you know, the Iroquois, supposedly the protectors of the Delawares, are in reality their sworn enemies and always have been. Now they are about to sell them out at the Albany Convention."

Joe made as if to speak, but Barzellai snapped, "Don't interrupt me! I'll answer any questions you may have later. So: the Iroquois are about to sell out the Delawares by trading their territory for certain privileges promised them by the British. They have no love for the French, as the French treated them abominably, especially General Champlain. They have other rewards coming to them for staying on the British side, but their main concern is revenge. The Delawares find themselves between hammer and anvil, between the young gentlemen we have with us and the Iroquois. They are not in a position to bargain, for they have no other power than the threat that they will join the French. In fact, they have no chance of doing so; the Iroquois are poised to slaughter them, on any pretext, and so are large numbers of our own settlers, virtually everyone except the Friends and the Germans. However, the Delawares have now been humiliated to a point where they are about to declare war, regardless of their chance for victory. The only hope they have left"— Barzellai looked solemnly from one to the other—"is ourselves. They have trusted the Friends ever since Will Penn made his treaty with them. Before we go in, let me read you the words of his first letter to them, written in the year of our Lord 1682." He pulled a piece of paper from his coat pocket, and after an intimidating glance at them he intoned: *"The Great God, Who is the power and the wisdom that made you and me, guides our hearts to righteousness, love and peace. These words I send to assure you of my love, and of my desire for your love, my friends . . ."*

After reading the letter to end, Barzellai folded the paper, put it back in his pocket, folded his hands in his lap and bent his head. Without another word, they united in meeting for worship. Outside the covered wagon, soldiers laughed, armor clanked; the call of a bugle echoed from the wall of the forest. They sat in meeting for at least a half hour before Barzellai shook hands with each of them and said, "Take this spirit with you, Friends." He was about to leave when as an afterthought, he added, "By the way, Running Bull will not be alone. He will have with him two men. One, wearing a necklace of beads and two feathers hanging down from his scalp lock, will be the shaman, the chief's most powerful adviser. The other will probably be an older man without any sign of rank or office, wearing his hair in two braids instead of the Delaware crest. He will be an Iroquois sachem, he represents the occupying power." He crawled toward the back of the wagon, lifted the canvas flap and the sunlight streamed in, dazzling them. They climbed out.

When the column entered the village, the Indians stared with hostile indifference at the procession of wagons, carts, pack mules and staggering Negro slaves carrying casks and luggage. What alarmed George was that most of the men were in war paint.

Fortunately, common sense had prevailed upon the arrogant young peacocks in the party and they had left behind the company of soldiers, who camped outside the town to await developments. The wagon train came to a cumbersome halt near the center of the town and it soon became apparent that Chief Running Bull would receive the delegation only when he was good and ready. They were going to have to await his pleasure.

George whiled away the hours by strolling about the town. It was his first visit to a permanent Indian settlement; all he had known thus far were temporary camps of the small nomadic clans that roamed the mountains. This was a large, obviously prosperous town of hundreds of wigwams, constructed of bark and skins, ranged in rows with thoroughfares between them, like any white settlement. When he reached the banks of the lake he had seen shimmering in the distance, he found a fleet of canoes bobbing at anchor in clusters of four behind a breakwater made of logs. That was why there were so many men about: they must have arrived from other settlements across the lake.

They were finally summoned to their audience with Chief Running Bull by a haughty delegation of warriors painted in lurid colors. Even the gentlemen from Philadelphia noticed by then that there was something amiss; they were decked out in their most gorgeous finery, their stark white wigs resplendent in the sun, but their bearing had lost some of its arrogance and a number of them were nervously taking snuff on their way to the chief's lodge. George followed, with Joe Woodhouse and Barzellai Tucker, in the invisible wake of perfume the twelve young men trailed behind them. No one spoke. Finally George asked Barzellai in a hushed voice, "Has thee met Chief Running Bull before?"

"Yes."

"What's he like?"

"Shrewd and amenable, when sober."

"Let's hope he's sober now."

"Quite."

They arrived at a high, imposing edifice in the center of the town. Outside, another delegation of Indians received them, also decked out in lurid war paint; their behavior was so contemptuous that George stooped through the low doorway of the lodge with the feeling he was about to go on trial for an unspecified crime.

Inside, all he could see at first was the smoky glow of torches and a round, dazzling hole in the roof. The place smelled as if he were in the presence of scores of Lone Seeing Eagles; the stench of body odor and bear grease was made more pungent still by the sooty reek of the torches lashed to posts supporting the concave roof. As his eyes grew accustomed to the dim light, he found himself in a long, oval room, surrounded by an amphitheatre full of Indians, with at the far end a platform on which three men were seated. In the center, on a stool covered with animal skins, sat a huge Indian of indeterminate age, so large and bulging with fat that he had a woman's breasts and looked eight months pregnant. Naked but for a loincloth, he wore no bracelet or beads; his skull with the Delaware crest was without feather or roach of deerskin. The two other men, seated on either side of him, were those described by Barzellai Tucker. The one to the left, of skeletal build and surprisingly dark-skinned, was dressed in a cloak adorned with wampum embroidery, wore a necklace of teeth and shells, two feathers were attached to his scalp lock, and from the lobes of his ears, which had been pierced and opened until they formed loops of living flesh, dangled the dried-out heads of two skunks or young badgers. In his right hand he held a gourd that rattled when he moved. The Indian to the right, dressed in leather shirt, kilt and leggings, his hair in two plaits, looked stolidly ahead.

The young men from Philadelphia lined up in front of the dais and executed a beautifully coordinated bow, scrape and sweep. Saul Urquhart said, in a strained but assured drawl, "Your Excellency, we are honored to present to you the compliments of the Provincial Council of the Commonwealth of Pennsylvania, and of His Excellency the Governor, representing the Lord Proprietor, all of us subjects of His Majesty King George the Second. Greetings." They executed another bow, scrape and sweep, and relaxed with apparent relief, as if they had taken care of the main part of their mission.

The three Indians on the platform remained motionless. The two men flanking the chief went on staring straight ahead without betraying that they had been aware of the mission's arrival, let alone its elaborate courtesies; the chief himself, softly snoring, sat gazing at them with eyes so dull and listless that his deep-socketed navel, which appeared to follow the proceedings with fascination, seemed to be the most interested part of his person. George wondered if he was drunk, but there seemed to be more to his groggy indifference than inebriation. In the end the twelve obtuse and self-confident young men lined up in front of him found themselves reduced by his unfocused, heavy-lidded indifference from a delegation to a row of prisoners in the dock. George's feeling of standing trial deepened.

"Let me present to Your Excellency the members of our delegation," young Urquhart said, with less assurance. "On my far left: Philip

Thurmond, Esquire . . ." The young man made a bow. "Jerobiam McAllister, Esquire . . ." The second young man bowed, but neither the chief nor his two companions so much as glanced at him. They kept their eyes fixed on a point some two feet above the head of Saul Urquhart while the twelve, with growing discomfort, presented their compliments. Then a calm voice beside him said, "Friend Running Bull, greetings. I present thee my two young companions, Joseph Woodhouse and George McHair. Peace, o mighty bull."

For a moment it seemed as if the chief would ignore that greeting too, then the huge body slowly leaned sideways, lifting one colossal thigh; to George's shocked amazement, he broke wind with such force that, apart from demonstrating that he was sitting on a drum, he expressed the most profound contempt possible.

The twelve young dandies froze in incredulous bafflement; Barzellai Tucker seemed unperturbed. "As always, great one," he said with composure, "thou hast the power to express great wisdom."

The chief peered at him; it was unclear whether with amusement or anger. Then he lowered his majestic posterior and said in a high-pitched, feminine voice that came as a surprise, "Step forward, mouse. Show thy little snout where I can see thee." For the first time the crowd on the amphitheatre reacted; a weird cackle ran through their ranks. The men on the platform stared stolidly ahead of them.

Barzellai Tucker walked toward the platform, followed by George and Joe. The fat chief looked down upon them with his unfocused eyes, alien and enigmatic, like a whale. His navel still seemed to be the most human part of him, watching them with deep-socketed fascination; Barzellai addressed himself to it. "The bull and the mouse have always lived in harmony, as they in no way intrude upon one another's territory. I am happy the bull is still chiding the mouse for its size, and I return the friendly greeting. I cannot tell thee how happy I am to hear that mighty roar again."

The silence in the lodge was profound. It seemed to George that their fate hung in the balance; then the high-pitched voice piped, "Little mice who do not know their places get trampled upon by the mighty bull." For some reason, the words sounded harmless; maybe it was the voice. It was so high and effeminate that George wondered if the breasts were real; perhaps the chief was a woman.

Barzellai Tucker was unperturbed. He walked to the platform. "Stop trying to frighten me, o mighty bull, and let me greet thee warmly, dear friend." He stretched out his hand toward the chief, who, without a moment's hesitation, slapped it away. But he seemed to do so playfully, like a woman being wooed. "Thou knowest we never touch each other, mouse," the voice squeaked. "Next thing, thou might want to mount one of my heifers; think of the monstrosity the outcome would be."

"A bull-mouse?" Barzellai asked. "It would be an interesting animal. At least it would live in peace with both its father's and its mother's totem."

"A mouse with horns?" the chief asked. "Or hast thou horns already?"

After a short silence, the crowd on the amphitheatre roared with laughter. George realized someone was translating the chief's jokes for them. He had never suspected that Indians had a sense of humor; they had always been solemn, even pompous. The intriguing part was that, by the laughter of the crowd, the chief had reduced the twelve young men to sheepish spectators. He seemed to decide that the moment was ripe to finish them off. "Thank you, gentlemen, for your compliments," he said, addressing them at last with insulting casualness. "I will be happy to receive your spokesman sometime today, tomorrow or the day after, as soon as I can find a moment. Good day." Dismissing them with a wave of his hand, the chief turned to Barzellai again. "Tell me about the two whelps thou hast brought with thee."

"This is Joseph Woodhouse, son of Isaac Woodhouse of Philadelphia, nephew of thy friend the man-woman."

"Pissing Gulie," the chief said.

The crowd, after a brief silence, tittered.

"That name, brave bull, is for campfire use only," Barzellai replied calmly. "On my other side: George McHair of Loudwater, son of Buffalo McHair, grandson of James McHair the bird man, great-grandson of Iron Hand, thy grandfather's blood-brother."

The chief seemed to contemplate them with distaste, then he pointed at Joe and said, "All right, I will talk to that one, but I want to talk to him alone."

For the first time he seemed to have got the better of Barzellai Tucker. "But—but the idea was that I should be present . . ."

"Whose idea, little mouse? Thine?"

"Well, this is a very complex situation, so it was the sense of the Committee on Indian Affairs—"

"Pah!" The chief seemed to slap the words away as he had slapped away Barzellai's proffered hand.

The little man recovered quickly. He smiled and said in the same pleasant tone as before, "When the bull roars, the mouse scurries. Let me know, o mighty one, when thou art through snorting and pawing the dust, so thou and I may hold a true parley." He turned to leave, drawing George with him.

Joe cried, "But *why?*" It was a cry from the heart; he stood there clearly terrified out of his wits.

George saw Barzellai frown, but the chief seemed to accept it at face value. "I will tell thee, young man," the high, effeminate voice said. "Because thou art a blood relation of Pissing Gulie. He—" he pointed at George—"is a son of Buffalo, whose temper is violent. What we need now is a clear head, a wise voice."

"But you cannot judge a man by his father!" Joe exclaimed passionately. "Friend George is a man in his own right, unique, irreplaceable, never seen on earth before . . ." The old, impressive words burst out of him, then faded into silence, the speaker reddening with embarrassment. "I mean—it's not fair," he added.

The chief smiled. "Dost thou see now why I chose him, little mouse?" he asked.

Barzellai nodded and turned to leave.

Joe, thoroughly rattled, grabbed his coat and asked in a whisper, "What must I do?"

Barzellai answered, "Mind the Light." Holding George by the arm, he walked to the door. As they emerged into the dazzling sunlight, they were set upon by the young gentlemen, who had gathered outside the entrance and were conversing in querulent voices. "What the dickens does this mean?" one of them asked shrilly. "I've never been so insulted in my life! What game are you playing, you—you Indian expert?"

To George's surprise, Barzellai brushed him aside, muttering, "Excuse me."

"But we cannot let ourselves be treated like this without protest!" the youth called after him. "After all, we represent the Provincial Council! The Governor! The Proprietor! His Majesty the King!"

Barzellai Tucker did not reply, but urged George on toward the wagon, pulling him as if he were a child; George asked irritably, "Why the hurry, friend?"

The little agent stopped in his tracks and looked at the huge youth with exasperation. "Because we must join in meeting for worship as soon as we can!" he snapped.

"Why, what's the matter?"

"Why dost thou think Chief Running Bull isolated that boy the way he did? Even thee must have realized that he is no ordinary man!"

"Yes, I asked myself—"

"He has been to London, he has been received among nobility, ten years ago he was the most important and sought-after young chieftain among the Delawares. But it all turned bad. Why? I don't know; it just did. Now he is a glutton, a torturer—"

"Torturer?"

"I know I should be appealing to that of God in him, but after today . . ." He gritted his teeth and pulled his young companion along with him briskly. "That's why I want to go into meeting: to cleanse myself of hatred and contempt!"

George began to realize that the apparent jesting between the chief and the Indian agent had been serious. "But why would he keep Joe behind?"

"Thou hast seen it with thy own eyes; heard it! That fart! Never before . . . Even the voice was a mockery! He has never talked before with that silly woman's voice. And that business of choosing him because he is a nephew of Gulielma Woodhouse—pure wickedness! He detests her; it is the first time I heard him mention her name without spitting!"

George did not know what to say. It was disturbing to see so disciplined a man reduced to furious vituperation.

They reached the wagon. Barzellai lifted the flap and gestured him inside. George obeyed, the other followed him, lowering the flap behind them. "All right," he said, "let's go into meeting and pray for Joseph Woodhouse in his hour of need."

Dutifully, George sat down and obliged.

*   *   *

'Mind the Light!' Joe thought. That was fine in meeting for worship, but here? What light was there for him to follow? His wits?

If he had any sense, he would run for it before that fat man-eater, who now had him all to himself, made a feast of him. While he stood there agonizing, the chief rid himself of the presence of everyone else in the hall, including the two men on the platform. The crowd shuffled out, leaving the two of them alone among the fluttering torches.

Mind the Light . . . Which light, dear God? He had been picked because of his Aunt Gulielma, so what would she have done in this situation? He did not have the foggiest notion. He tried to visualize her reaction to the malevolent stare of the small whale's eyes now fixed on him; but he did not know her well enough, he really did not know her at all, only her mannerisms and the mannish way she conversed during dinner parties, which had made them giggle when they were children.

"Well, Quaker boy," the chief asked. "What news hast thou for me?" It sounded pleasant enough, yet there was something wrong. It took Joe a moment before he realized what: the fat man no longer spoke in a falsetto, but in a normal male voice.

It did not diminish his apprehension, but it made him face the danger, no longer wanting to flee. Never mind Aunt Gulie; the only thing he could do was to meet this menacing man according to the approach to conflict after the manner of Friends, as he had been taught during endless, fly-buzzed hours in First Day school. *'Facing an adversary, try to go into meeting with him.'* So he said, in a voice that made him clear his throat, "Before we labor together, Friend Running Bull, I suggest we center down for a moment of silence." He did not wait for an answer; he boldly sat down on the floor where he was, folded his hands in his lap and closed his eyes.

He expected the silence to be broken by the chief's laughter. But nothing happened; the silence seemed to sink to a deeper level and become stillness. There, waiting for him as it were, was the second step: *'Identify with thy adversary.'*

How? How could he identify with an Indian? They had not a single point of common reference. But the Friendly approach to conflict provided for this eventuality. *'Center down on the only value common to all creation, truth.'* At the time, it had sounded sanctimonious; now he had no choice but to try it. The truth. He opened his eyes, saw the fat man above him peer at him and said, "Friend Running Bull, I must tell thee that the real objective of this expedition is not to redress the injustice of the Walking Purchase, but to survey a larger tract of thy land that will be claimed as the original purchase during the Albany Convention next month."

The inhuman eyes went on staring at him without expression.

"That, I assure thee, is the truth."

Then the fat chief made a sound. It seemed to gurgle upward from deep inside his huge body. It was an unpleasant sound, a malevolent chuckle. "I know the Quaker approach to conflict. *'Speak truth to power.'* Very good, Quaker boy. What comes next?"

The fact that he had been sized up threw Joe for a moment into confusion; then he thought: 'That does not mean it will not work.' "I am glad thou hast recognized my approach to thee, Friend Running Bull. There is no secret about it; on the contrary, truth and openness are essential for mutual understanding."

The chief's masklike face seemed to change, but it was difficult to make out what it signified. Had he smiled? Was it a scowl of derision? Joe did not know; but he had no choice except to continue. Step four: *'Muster all love, tenderness and concern for the other within thee.'* Not easy; but somewhere in the mountain of fat poised above him there was an Inner Light, a human identity crying out for recognition. The only way to edge closer to it was by the truth. The truth. The word echoed down the corridors of his memory, so often had he been admonished with it during those First Day school lessons. "As thou must have realized at once," he said, "I was sent to accompany this expedition in total ignorance. I had no idea what it was all about, and I have told all I know of its intent. But I wish to do whatever I can to help prevent the outbreak of war." It had been a muddled little speech; the "approach to conflict" had led him nowhere. Now what?

The little whale's eyes stared at him fixedly. Suddenly the voice said, "All right, little Will Penn. Thy beloved Delawares are about to be robbed and massacred. Some young braves feel they must go down fighting, not pleading for their lives like squaws. We have a treaty of mutual assistance. What are the Quakers going to do about it?"

This new sign of the man's perspicacity seemed to convey some reassurance. Even though he himself was unable to identify with the chief, the chief obviously could identify with him. Running Bull must be shrewder than most men he knew, including Barzellai Tucker.

"Look, Quaker boy," the chief said, "why dost thou think I singled thee out?"

"Because of my Aunt Gulielma."

"Because thou art the son of one of the richest and most powerful merchants in Philadelphia. What I want from thee is the answer to one question: What are the Philadelphia Quakers going to do? Are they going to stand by my people, or is all they have to offer us summed up in thy person?"

Of course! How could he have been so stupid! That was why he had been chosen: as the son of his father. In the chief's place, he would have made the same choice. Instead of depressing him, it gave him something to hold on to. He was in no position to know how Aunt Guliclma would have confronted the man, but he had a fair notion how his father would. "I cannot answer that question," he said calmly. "If they have a plan, they did not tell me about it. I doubt they have."

"Why? Aren't they aware of what is happening? Do they not realize that the Delawares will be wiped out unless we receive help?"

"I honestly do not believe they know that. If thou wilt forgive my bluntness, I don't believe it matters to them." He saw a flicker in the little eyes, and added, "There are among us people to whom it would matter, who feel that to break faith with the Indians, especially yourself, means breaking faith with the principles on which the Holy Experiment was founded. But these people do not hold the power in Philadelphia Yearly Meeting, nor in the Provincial Assembly."

"Art thou telling me, boy," the voice from inside the whale said ominously, "that as a representative of the other party of the treaty, thou now givest me the advice to die fighting or move out altogether?"

Joe sensed that a critical point had been reached. All he could do was to continue speaking the truth as he knew it. "I am not a true representative of the Quakers in power," he said. "I was given no instructions other than to mind the Light. The only light for me to mind, as far as I can see, is to tell the truth as I see it."

"Well," the chief said, "for want of anything better, let's have it."

"Very well. If I were in thy position, I would move out." It was a preposterous thing to say; he knew nothing about the politics involved. But that was not the point; the chief had chosen to ask for his opinion, there it was.

"And where would I move to, o wise one?" the fat man asked mockingly. But something told Joe that he was taking him seriously. If nothing else, it was a measure of his despair.

"Surely there is plenty of room to run to in the west."

"There we would run into the French."

It brought to Joe the memory of something Aunt Gulie had said, about the wide, open spaces behind the backs of the French. "According to my Aunt Gulielma, the lands beyond the French lines are free for the taking."

"Thy Aunt Gulielma is an ignorant woman. Beyond the French there are the Wyandots, then the Miamis, then the Potawatomis. There is no land between the sea and the great prairie that does not belong to some tribe."

"But are they more powerful than the Delawares?" Joe asked. It was a strange question for a Quaker, not exactly an expression of the peace testimony. But he added, for good measure, "It would give thy young braves something to look forward to other than shame."

He had gone too far in his newfound self-assurance. The chief snapped, "Thy snatter is as empty as that of gooses!" It was the first error he had made so far in his excellent English.

"It may be," Joe replied, "but thee insisted that I give thee my opinion, Friend Running Bull. I have tried to answer thy questions truthfully; if thou hast come to the conclusion that what I say is foolishness, I trust thou wilt allow me to retire." For the first time in his life he felt he was someone in his own right; the amazing part of it was that he had begun to feel that way the moment he was treated as merely his father's son.

The chief scowled. "And what assistance may the Delawares expect from their Friends the Quakers, should we decide to leave the lands of our ancestors and vanish into the sunset?"

Joe closed his eyes to think. Suppose the Delawares decided to remove themselves from the disputed land. What would his father's reaction be? As a Quaker, he would be impressed by their adherence to the peace testimony, but he also would look for an opportunity of maintaining some influence within the tribe. "I would say, Friend Running Bull," he replied thoughtfully, "that if the Delawares were to decide upon this course of action, they could count on support from Philadelphia Yearly Meeting."

"And what would the substance of that support be? Beautiful words?"

"I think there might be more."

"Weapons?"

"Thou knowest better than to ask that. But there might be a contribution in money and goods."

The chief stared at him fixedly. It was impossible to know what he was thinking, but there was in his huge, flabby bulk the tension of a coiled spring. Something in those hard little eyes suddenly reminded Joe of Abe. How delighted Abe would be, should the Delawares decide to remove themselves, thereby relinquishing Altar Rock forever! The thought unnerved him. Was this what he had been doing in the power of the Lord: serving the interests of the house of Woodhouse? It could not be! This *was* the right solution for the beleaguered tribe. He was sure that the Meeting would see it that way too in the end, and would do all in their power to help. But how? What would their first reaction be? "I think, Friend Running Bull, that the Meeting would begin by contributing a school for your children."

"A school!" the chief scoffed. "I need weapons and I am offered a school!" He rose ponderously to his feet. "When you return to Philadelphia, Mr. Woodhouse," he said with sudden formality, "pray pay my respects to your aunt, the man-woman."

"I will," Joe replied uncertainly.

"Pray say to her, 'Running Bull, the fat one, sends his greetings to Pissing Gulie.' Then, pray spit in her eye."

Joe's heart sank. "Friend Running Bull, thou knowest full well I'll say no such thing. That is not the sense of our meeting."

The inhuman little eyes contemplated him without interest. "And what would the sense of our meeting be?" It was asked in the mocking, high-pitched voice.

"That—that the Quakers and the Delawares are still friends."

The chief said, "Show me." Then he waddled off into the shadows. Deep in thought, Joe walked toward the doors. There must be a way of showing the Indians that the Quakers were still their friends; he should not rest until he had found it. He felt confident that he would, for during a few fleeting minutes he had reached the man in side the whale, the real Chief Running Bull. He had also, in some mysterious way, reached the man inside himself.

When he stepped out into the bright sunlight, there was no one to be seen; the village lay deserted in the afternoon torpor. He strolled down the street between the wigwams to the lake, sat down on a log at the water's edge and looked at the nets drying, the canoes, the water, thinking about the young braves, ready to fight until death rather than surrender like squaws. Since his talk with the chief, the humanity of those luridly painted young men, who had seemed so unreal and romantic, emerged as something akin to his own. Suppose one of those young braves were to turn up in Philadelphia, go into a huddle with, say, Jeremiah Best, after which the Quakers would be told they had to leave and move out into the Northwest Territory, taking only the things they could carry? No more Water Street, no more strolls along the banks of the Delaware, no more looking at the ships and dreaming of distant places; farewell forever to all the things that spelled home. He looked at the canoes, the nets, the lake; they must mean the same to those young braves as the banks of the Delaware did to him. Or did they? He was, after all, a city dweller. Was this village, despite its aspects of permanence, as important to them as Philadelphia was to him? Or would they be eager to strike out for the unknown prairie beyond the mountains? Maybe they had dreamed about it as children just as he had dreamed about the sea and the foreign lands beyond the horizon.

"Oh, there thee is!" a voice said, angry with relief.

He looked up and saw Barzellai Tucker, harassed and cross, standing beside him. "Where has thee been? Why did thee not come straight back? What happened?" For an experienced Indian agent, the little man seemed oddly flustered.

"Oh, we just talked."

"What does thee mean, just talked? Tell me! What did he want to know, what did he ask, what did he do?"

Suddenly Joe felt sorry for the man. It must have been hard for him to be ejected from a parley with Indians. Yet all that nonsense about roaring lions and little mice had been a caricature, as if Running Bull had pandered to the man's concept of Indians, showing up its absurdity. "I was asked how Quakers can be expected to help the Delawares."

"Well? What did thee say?"

"I said: Nothing."

"What does thee mean, thee said nothing? Surely thee must have given some answer?"

"That was my answer: Nothing."

Barzellai Tucker stared at him, perplexed. "Thee means thee told Chief Running Bull that the Quakers would do *nothing?*"

"Isn't that the truth?"

Barzellai Tucker slapped his thigh in exasperation and turned around as if he were about to walk into the water. Then he cried, theatrically for so stolid a Friend, "My God! What have I done to be cursed with two such—such incompetents!"

"Come, Friend Barzellai," Joe said, with more authority than he realized. "Does thee expect the Quakers to support the Delawares?"

"Of course!"

"How?"

"By bringing it to Yearly Meeting, for one thing!"

"And what is Yearly Meeting likely to decide?"

"To honor our treaty!"

"To what extent?"

"To the extent of instructing our Quaker representatives in the Assembly to undo this—this outrage!"

"We do not have the necessary majority for that. Only if the Germans join us."

"Of course the Germans will join us!"

"I don't agree. It's exactly on the subject of the Indians that we differ."

"Well, all that is secondary! Thee should have told the chief that the Quakers could be counted on! Thee had no business speaking of things thee knows nothing about!"

Suddenly Joe had had enough. "Friend Barzellai," he said calmly, "thee told me that I should mind the Light. I followed thy advice, and the Light urged me to tell the chief the truth. This I have done; however, it was the truth as *I* see it. If thee sees it differently, thee should tell him so. But, in my opinion, thee would increase the chances of war by raising the hopes of the Indians for a Quaker intervention. Thee would strengthen the hand of the young braves, who want to stand and fight even if it means the destruction of the Delawares. I think it is our duty, as Quakers, to tell these people the truth. The whole truth, not just part of it."

The little man stared at him for a moment blankly. Then he asked, "And what is the whole truth, in thy opinion, Joseph Woodhouse?"

"Unless we provide the Delawares with arms to defend themselves, they will be massacred. Philadelphia Yearly Meeting will not consider arming anybody. I told Chief Running Bull that if he cut his losses, pulled up his stakes and moved through the French lines into the prairie beyond, he could count, to start with, on a school for his children."

Barzellai Tucker stared at him in silence for a moment, then he asked, "Is that what the Quaker princes have instructed thee to say? Why didn't thee inform me of this beforehand?"

"Nobody instructed me," Joe replied. "This is my opinion, no more."

"Ah! I see! Thy opinion." Barzellai Tucker shrugged his shoulders. "In that case . . ."

"I'm sorry, Barzellai Tucker," Joe said. "But this is my truthful assessment of the future. I may be proven wrong."

The Indian agent gave him a thin smile. "I'm sure thee will be proven right, Joseph Woodhouse," he said acidly. "Thee reads the mind of the Quaker establishment better than I do."

Joe wanted to leave it at this; on the other hand, it was important that they should end up with some semblance of unity in their advice to the Indians. "I don't think it has to do with the Quaker establishment, as thee calls it. This way we will have kept the peace and prevented the massacre of innocent people. Does thee remember what George Fox told Friends in England who were dispossessed by the persecution? Do not take a stand, move away across the ocean and carry the Seed to a new land."

"But the Indians are not Quakers! What thee has told them is to give up their tribal territory, the graves of their ancestors, the spirits living in every rock, every tree!"

There was Altar Rock again and the bewildering circumstance that Abe might well be prepared to help the Delawares with money if that would ensure their voluntary removal. But the thought no longer distressed Joe; it now seemed proof that he was on the right track. He asked, with increased self-confidence, "And what would the alternative be, Barzellai Tucker?"

"Stand firm! Exert political pressure to stop this exploitation of the Delawares here and now!"

"And if the political pressure fails?"

"That is not certain! Not at all certain!"

"All right, let's assume the Germans vote with us in the Assembly on this. Then what? Would that stop the Albany Convention from taking place? Would it stop the Proprietors making a deal with the Iroquois regarding the Delaware lands? Come, Friend Barzellai, let us sit down together and share a few minutes of silence. I think we need it, both of us."

It looked for a moment as if the other were about to turn away; then he gave in. He sat down on the log beside him; together, side by side, they joined in the silence of the lake, the sky, the town.

That night Joe Woodhouse returned to the Quaker tent to sleep.

CHAPTER SIX

I T was two German Friends from a village called Gnadenhütten who, on the eve of yearly meeting, sounded the alarm: a band of Scotch-Irish from the mountains were on a rampage, massacring Indians in revenge for the death of some old man from their village murdered by an Algonquin. The whole countryside was in an uproar, the Friends reported in their highly excited Pennsylvania Dutch: Indian refugees were clogging the roads to Philadelphia—they themselves had hardly been able to get through with their wagon and regretted they were so late.

Jeremiah Best, who received the news in the Meeting House, did not take it seriously. For one thing, the German Friends were not late, they were almost a day early, the first of the rural Friends to arrive asking for a place to sleep. But the hour certainly was late, if that was what they meant; it was past ten in the evening, they were lucky to have found him still there. During the past hour or so he had been about to leave for home several times; each time he had been held up by some petty detail. Had the water jugs arrived yet? Who was supposed to take care of inkwells and quills for the clerks of participating Monthly Meetings? What about that support of the east gallery, was it eaten by termites, in which case the whole of the gallery must be condemned as unsafe? After ten minutes of assiduous peering through his spectacles by the light of a candle, he had decided that it looked like woodworms, but a carpenter had better inspect it in the daylight, first thing tomorrow.

All these preoccupations were the curse of the clerk of Yearly Meeting; they always came to a head just before the convention was about to start. Tomorrow thousands of Friends from the outlying Meetings, of all social classes, languages, temperaments and ages, would descend upon the city like locusts; to see, just as he was about to leave, a bunch of over-excited country folk turn up in a state of fluster, jabbering about a massacre which they pronounced "mah-sucker," was one complication too many. He dismissed their story as the result of too many steins of beer, put the alarmists up with a local family of Pennsylvania Dutch who had asked for "Friends of their own ilk" and finally left for home.

Walking the dark, quiet streets, he found that the Germans' story did not leave him in peace. Gulielma Woodhouse, who had arrived with the Bakers, had given a disturbing picture of the preparations for war by the Indian tribes of the plains; he wondered whether he should alert her. But when he entered their sleeping street, he could not discern any lights in the Woodhouse mansion and decided it would keep until morning.

Around three o'clock that night he was startled from a fitful sleep by a banging on his front door. He went down in his nightgown to see who it was, stubbing his toe as he went; when he opened the door, he found Philip Howgill, the recording clerk, who had agreed to stay in the Meeting House overnight to receive any new arrivals. "Friend Jeremiah!" the man cried breathlessly. "Come, come quickly! A whole crowd of Indians has arrived! Women, children, old people, all asking for asylum! They say they are about to be killed by an army of Ulstermen and ask the Quakers to protect them! Please come, come quickly!"

Jeremiah felt a quiver in the pit of his stomach; but, despite his inward turmoil, his mind worked with cool precision. "Do we have any confirmation of this?" he asked. "Or is it just the Indians' story?"

"Oh, no, no!" Philip Howgill cried, with the unfortunate dramatization that seemed to afflict everyone prior to yearly meeting, "more German Friends have come in and they all tell the same story: a posse of horsemen, yelling and screaming and firing their muskets in the air, are looking for Indians to avenge an old man killed in a tree. They even fired at the weathercock of the Lutheran church in Gnadenhütten! It's true, all of it! What are we going to do, Jeremiah Best? We cannot possibly protect these people! How do we put them up, where? God only knows how many there may be at daybreak! What's to be done with them all?"

"Philip Howgill," he said sternly, "control thyself. Nobody will be helped by thy losing thy head."

"But—but they're all in the courtyard, right in front of the Meeting House! What am I to say to them? What—"

"Listen to me!" Jeremiah's voice was so authoritative that Philip Howgill, not normally given to hanging on other people's lips unless he was supposed to record what they were saying, swallowed the rest. "Go back to the Meeting House, tell their leader that someone will take care of their affairs in a few minutes, give them water, invite them to join thee in meeting for worship, anything to keep them from getting into the same state of agitation thee is in at the moment. I'll join thee as soon as I have dressed and alerted Gulielma Woodhouse next door. Quick!" His firmness seemed to have fortified the flustered man, who, zigzagging like a winged bat, ran back to the crisis.

Upstairs, Grizzle's voice shrieked from the landing, "Jeremiah! What's going on down there?"

"Nothing, dear," he replied appeasingly, groping his way up the stairs. "Just a tribe of Indians who turned up at the Meeting House, asking for asylum."

"Asylum?! What asylum? I never heard such nonsense in my life! And who was that banging and screaming? One of thy night-owl friends?!"

As usual, she held him responsible for the disturbance. She was a highly strung woman who could not be held responsible for everything she said when excited; the best defense was to divert her with interesting tidbits of information. So, as he climbed toward the light of her candle, he told her about the old man shot in a tree and the weathercock of the Lutheran church in Gnadenhütten. To his surprise, she took the whole thing seriously, which in her case meant emotionally. "Who is there to help them?" she asked, alarmed. "Is there anybody who speaks their language at the Meeting House? They must be in a terrible state!"

"If not, what does thee suggest I do about it? I'm going to have my hands full as it is."

"Oh, *thee!*" she cried, managing to express in the word all she thought of his efficiency, compassion and common sense. "I'm coming with thee! It's high time somebody was there to receive those people and look after them. What's it like outside?"

For a second he recoiled from the prospect of adding Grizzle, shrieking like a banshee, to the confusion in the courtyard of the Meeting House; then he said, "That seems an excellent idea, my dear. I'm sure thy presence would be a help. I think I'll also call Gulielma Woodhouse and Himsha McHair, as they both speak Algonquin or whatever the language is."

"Is it cold outside? Is it raining?"

"I don't recall," he muttered. He was putting on his clothes when he was brought up short by another banging on the door, reverberating in the empty hall.

"Now, who on earth can that be?" He stumbled down the dark stairs in his stockinged feet.

"Take a light! Don't break a leg on top of everything else!" she shrieked after him, but he was already at the door. When he opened it, he found the familiar figure of his father-in-law, Peleg Martin; an invisible horse snorted and jangled behind him.

"Is thee ready to go, Jeremiah?" the old man asked.

"I—yes, yes . . . But how . . ."

"Philip Howgill alerted me, as chairman of the Committee on Indian Affairs. Why is thee not dressed yet?"

Jeremiah mastered an unfilial impulse; then Grizzle was upon them, fully dressed. "Thee has the buggy out there, Dad?" she asked in the tone of wary jollity she always affected in the face of her dour father.

"Yes, I knew thy husband could not be counted upon to purvey thee with a conveyance at this hour of the night."

It was so patently unjust that Jeremiah felt like slamming the door in the old man's face, but he managed to thank him for his foresight while struggling into his coat, which Grizzle had brought down with her.

He was about to climb into the buggy after her when he remembered Gulielma. So he left them, with a sense of liberation, and hurried toward the dark Woodhouse mansion. It was his turn to bang on the door; he heard what Philip Howgill must have heard: a shuffle of slippers approaching, a voice muttering, "Yes, yes, yes . . ."

Then the door was opened. "Who is this?" It was Isaac Woodhouse, with a candle.

"It's I, Jeremiah. And a good morning to thee!" In his eagerness to exude calm, he sound flippant; Isaac reacted accordingly. But once he heard the news, he instantly grasped the potential danger. "Whatever happens, we must not let this thing get out of hand," he said, with surprising briskness. "Whatever thee does, don't let those Indians spread all over town, keep them confined to the Meeting House grounds, at least until we have seen the Governor."

"The Governor?"

Before Isaac could elaborate, the women arrived, in various degrees of nightly attire; the only one fully dressed was Gulielma, but then she had no skirt or bodice to contend with. "What's going on?" she asked.

Jeremiah told her about the Indians and the Irish roughnecks from the mountains.

"Who are these people?"

"Which?"

"The Ulstermen? Who are they?"

"Something with 'boys.' Peace—Pars—Parsley boys."

Gulielma reacted with uncharacteristic alarm. "Those are the men I told thee about! The dead man in the tree must have been old Jim McHair! We had better get going." With those words she strode out the door, down the stoop, and down the dark street in the direction of the Meeting House.

There was nothing Jeremiah could do but follow. He wished he had taken the buggy; he was too old for this. As he ran breathlessly after the vanishing shadow of that impossible woman loping like a stag, he wondered what had possessed him two years ago to aspire with such tenacity to the post of clerk of Philadelphia Yearly Meeting.

Campfires among the tombstones, whinnying horses running loose inside the gates—the grounds of the Meeting House had been transformed in a matter of hours from a hallowed garden of remembrance into the campground of a tribe of nomads. The Meeting House itself had fared no better; when they arrived in its dimly lit hall after making their way through groups of stony-faced Indian squaws cooking food for their children, they found Philip Howgill in a state of utter frenzy, surrounded by rural Friends and their families, old Indian women, over-excited Quaker children playing tag and even a pack of roaming dogs that must have followed the Indians. Philip was trying to get everybody to camp on the Commons; all the poor man could think of under the pressure of this onslaught was to get them to leave.

Gulielma, with great authority, took control of the Indians in the grounds; Jeremiah helped handle the new arrivals inside; by daybreak they had managed to impose some semblance of order on the chaos. The scattered campfires had been concentrated into a large one in a corner of the yard; there Gulielma, helped by Himsha, Becky Baker, her little sister Abby and a number of other women was now running a communal kitchen. The horses had been rounded up and tethered; Jeremiah had managed to direct most of the new arrivals from the countryside to Quaker families in town; everything gradually came under control, but there could be no doubt that this yearly meeting was going to be an impromptu one, he might as well tear up the agenda. If the armed men were to pursue the Indians right into Philadelphia, then the Meeting would have to decide what to do with the Indians who had come running to them with touching but disturbing confidence in the old treaty with William Penn.

Jeremiah did not have much time to think about it; during the odd minutes he could give it some thought it became clear that, whether they liked it or not, the moment of truth had arrived for the Quakers. What were they going to do? Defend the Indians with force? Impossible. Then what? Load them on ships and spirit them off downriver before the rowdies arrived? There would not be time for that, and it would not solve the basic problem. The Quakers would have to decide whether to adhere to the peace testimony in the face of the approaching calamity; despite his preoccupation with the immediate emergency, Jeremiah realized that he was living through historic hours which would affect the lives of generations of Quakers to come.

For the moment, he tried to salvage the structure of the meeting by pretending that the agenda could be adhered to; but he told John Woolman, who was to give the major address the first day, that urgent business might take precedence over his presentation. The kind little man took it philosophically, murmuring with a smile that way would open. All Jeremiah could do was to smile back. There were a thousand things clamoring for his attention when he was dragged away to join Isaac Woodhouse, Peleg Martin and Israel Henderson for an emergency audience with the Governor; as clerk of Philadelphia Yearly Meeting, his presence was mandatory. It was an awkward assignment; what they were reduced to doing was to ask for the militia to protect the Indians. It was a moot point whether violence furnished by someone else on request was a breach of the peace testimony or not. But what was the alternative? Go for that of God in the ruffians threatening the Indians? How? When? They drove to the audience in gloomy silence.

It seemed that the rumor of the emergency had not yet reached the Governor's palace. When their carriage entered the courtyard after traversing the echoing cavern of the gateway, they found the cloistered garden with its geometrical landscape of hedges and fountains as remote from all strife as the sunken gardens of Hampton Court, after which the courtyard had been modeled. The carriage drew up at a flight of marble steps leading to the front doors. Flunkeys observed their arrival through panes of tinted glass. As they descended from the carriage, Jeremiah heard a strident shriek from one of the peacocks which strutted on the lawn like huge, walking flowers. One of the horses neighed; a covey of white pigeons swooped down from the roof of the main building with a loud flutter of wings to alight, a sprinkling of white blossoms, among the flowers of the peacocks' tails. The contrast with the hurly-burly in the grounds of the Meeting House seemed to sum up the political reality: the Proprietors and the Crown serene with self-confidence, the Quakers in a state of total confusion.

Inside the palace, the tranquillity seemed deeper still. They stood waiting in the hall for an uncomfortably long time; finally a door to the hall opened, the Governor's aide-de-camp, Colonel Urquhart, emerged to suggest they make themselves comfortable while His Excellency finished some urgent business that had, regrettably, come up at the last moment. There was nothing else to do but to follow the Colonel's advice and sit down.

Seated on two carved settees in the hall, they found themselves centering down into silence. For the next twenty minutes, while the Governor kept them waiting, they sat united in meeting for worship; the flunkeys, gazing at the lawn through the purple-hued glass of the doors, yawned in somnolent boredom.

When at last they were admitted, they felt stilled and strengthened; had they been ushered into the regal quiet of the Governor's chambers without this restorative interval after the frenzy of the Meeting House, they would have been at a distinct disadvantage.

Governor Morris was exquisitely mannered and charming. His massive wig, cut after the latest fashion, befitted an occasion of state more than an early morning audience, as did his carmine velvet coat and the modish lace ruffs that protruded from its sleeves like roses. When Isaac Woodhouse as their spokesman presented the reason for their visit, he appeared highly sympathetic. Of course, he would not have hesitated to send a company of militia to protect the Indian refugees at the Quaker Meeting House, had any troops been available to him. As ill luck would have it, the troops guarding the city of Philadelphia had been seriously depleted: two platoons were accompanying a wagon train on its way to the frontier, another was on escort duty with the surveying expedition to the Delawares, the rest had been deployed in strategic locations along the western border, since, as the gentlemen undoubtedly knew, the tensions between England and France had increased dramatically of late. Colonel Urquhart hovered in the background, making discreet appreciative noises; Jeremiah saw, with distressing clarity, that this was the chance the Proprietors and the Crown had waited for to demonstrate to the obstreperous Quakers that their fanatical pacifism was an unworldly pipe dream.

He took no active part in the discussion, but he registered every word, planning to write it all down at the earliest opportunity, for future generations. Isaac Woodhouse's composure was admirable; Jeremiah had never thought the moment would come when he would admire his cantankerous little cousin, but Isaac countered the Governor's insincere and almost gloating commiseration with restrained dignity.

Governor Morris' exquisite manners could not hide his obvious hope that those ruffians would actually invade the grounds of the Quaker Meeting House, even if it meant the death of a few squaws and papooses.

They took courteous leave of the Governor; he bowed and scraped, humbling himself before them as had become the fashion among magistrates when dealing with Quakers ever since King Charles had said to young William Penn, who refused to take off his hat, "In that case, Master Penn, I'll take off mine; it is the custom that in the presence of the King of England only one person shall wear a hat."

They climbed back into the carriage in silence. No one spoke even after they had left the echoing gateway behind and were making their way back through the crowded streets. There was excitement in the air; the news had spread quickly; to the worldly inhabitants of the city the impending confrontation between the sanctimonious Quakers and a bunch of yahoos from the mountains promised great entertainment. When they finally reached the Meeting House, an even larger number of covered wagons had drawn up outside, hundreds more Friends from the outlying areas must be clamoring for board and lodging. Jeremiah could restrain himself no longer. "Well?" he asked. "What *are* we going to do?"

The silence that followed became awkward; then Isaac replied, "Way will open."

It was a worthy sentiment, but Jeremiah instantly translated it as "Maybe I will think of something." Despite his cousin's canniness, he doubted that anyone could. As he entered the grounds of the Meeting House, he saw among the throng in the lobby the burly figure and lion's mane of Stephen Atkins of Rhode Island. The sight of the famous fighting Quaker, symbol of what was euphemistically called "Holy Violence," filled him with despondency. Stephen Atkins was only forty-eight years old and already his exploits were legendary, the most famous being the occasion when his ship was attacked by pirates; when the first one clambered on board, he had grabbed him by the scruff of his neck, saying, "Sorry, Friend, thee has no business here" and dropped him into the sea. In the past Jeremiah had secretly relished that story, thinking that no pirates could conceivably threaten the City of Brotherly Love.

Stephen's booming voice hailed him over the heads of the crowd. "Greetings, Friend Jeremiah! Back from thy audience with the Governor? What did he say?"

How did the man know? The whole thing had been arranged in utter secrecy; he himself had told no one except—of course. It was a moment in which he found it difficult to love his wife.

Silence fell in the lobby. Everyone was waiting; he must say something, anything. "We will discuss the matter in our first meeting for business, which I suggest we enter into now."

Stephen Atkins took a deep breath as if to make a retort; but a dry, uncompromising woman's voice cut him short. "I unite!" It was

Gulielma Woodhouse, bless her heart. Others voiced agreement; and with a sigh of relief Jeremiah made his way into the meeting hall.

* * *

As the surveying party made its ponderous return to civilization, Joe Woodhouse and George McHair broke away and reached Philadelphia hours ahead of the wagon train. In the outskirts they were struck by a commotion that increased as they approached the center of the city; the crowds thickened as they neared the Meeting House, until in the end they had to force their way through a tightly packed mass of humanity. The atmosphere of excitement suggested an impending spectacle such as the arrival of a circus.

They were in sight of the Meeting House when a hunter friend of George's shouted to him that the Paisley boys from Loudwater were on the rampage, killing Indians, and on their way to the city, where hundreds of Indians had taken refuge with the Quakers. It seemed incredible, but when they arrived at the gate they saw it was true.

Hundreds of squaws, children and old people were camping in the courtyard in teepees and pup tents that must have been provided by the Meeting. Rows of horses were tethered to the iron fence; in a far corner, a field kitchen had been erected, surrounded by trestle tables and benches; a number of Quaker women were busy preparing a meal in huge pots over an open fire; girls were setting out plates and mugs. There must be at least three to four hundred Indians there, but no Friends were in sight, other than the women preparing the meal; there must be a meeting in progress.

Joe and George entered the hall and found the partition lowered; Joe was sorry, for he would have liked to catch Becky's eye to show her that he had returned safely. Somebody was speaking from the rostrum: Joe's uncle Stephen Atkins. He cut a fine figure with his powerful shoulders, his rebellious eyes; what he was saying turned out to be pretty provocative. He was berating the overseers for appealing to the Governor for troops to protect the refugees. He found it intolerable that Friends should appeal to others to do violence for them. Didn't Friends realize that this destroyed the basis on which the spiritual power of Quakerism was founded? Didn't they recognize the hypocrisy of it? He had had occasion before to say this to Philadelphia Yearly Meeting: "The course of events will force upon you the consequences of the violent reality surrounding you, as it did upon us in Rhode Island. Now the challenge has arrived. Are you going to defend the Indians or are you not? Are you going to tell them that the old treaties are no longer valid because the realities of today are different from the realities of seventy-five years ago? You cannot sit here and deliberate erdlessly on what to do. Wake up, Friends! The time has come to face the truth!" He looked about him with hypnotic eyes; the silence in the hall was such that no one dared move. Then he said, "There is no other way: you *must* take up arms and defend the helpless, or the power of the Lord will be drawn away from the Quakers of Pennsylvania, from you in this hall, each one of you! *Inasmuch as ye have done it unto one of the least of these My brethren, ye have done it unto Me.* What is going to be your answer when, in the after life, He challenges us and asks, 'What have ye done when I took refuge in your temple from the fury of those bent on killing Me?' Will He be satisfied with the answer, 'Lord, we appealed in Thy behalf to Governor Morris'? Answer that question, Friends. Answer it any way you may feel moved, but *answer it!"*

He stepped down from the rostrum; at the foot of the steps he said, looking about him, "Those who want to discuss with me the practical means of protecting those women and children outside, please follow me." With that he strode down the aisle to the doors.

After he had left, it seemed for a moment that no one was going to follow him. Nobody stirred; the silence seemed to be turning into worship. Then Uncle Jeremiah cleared his throat and asked, "Would any Friend present care to comment on this statement?"

A voice came from the audience, "I want to say a few words in loving response to Friend Stephen's ministry." It was Israel Henderson; he made his way calmly toward the rostrum, but Uncle Jeremiah had broken the spell and prevented the meeting from turning inward. The moment Israel Henderson rose, others followed his example, but started toward the doors. They were, without exception, young Friends; Joe knew most of them.

It was a dramatic moment; a clear separation between the generations. When George beside him started to make his way to the doors, Joe followed suit. He had no taste for Uncle Stephen's fighting Quakerism; he was convinced that the worst thing that could happen at this juncture was for Friends to take up arms, but he could see no other solution. How else protect those poor Indian women and children if not by facing down the armed rabble with rifles and swords?

When he reached the courtyard, he saw that the gates had been opened and that riders were streaming out, led by Uncle Stephen on a huge bay mare. He already looked like a general leading his troops; all he needed was a train of cannon and he would be indistinguishable from any other commander of the militia. Joe saw Josh Baker skitter past and called to him, "Where are they going?"

"The new Meeting House!" Josh answered, then clattered out of the gates in pursuit of the others.

"Well, let's go and join them," Joe said wearily, "we might as well find out what they're up to."

"Whatever it is, I'm game!" George cried, and made for his horse at a run.

As Joe was about to follow him, he was hailed by one of the women preparing the meal. "What is going on? Where are they all going?" It was his mother.

"They're off to the new Meeting House," he replied. "Uncle Stephen wants us to arm ourselves and ride out to meet the raiders for a showdown."

"He would!" his mother exclaimed angrily. "See if thee can hold them up, Joe; I'll go and warn the women!" Without waiting for his answer, she hurried toward the doors, wiping her hands on her apron as she ran.

The rebellious young Friends gathered in the shell of the new Meeting House among stacks of lumber, drainage pipes and masons' tables. When Joe and George entered, Stephen Atkins was speaking. The solution was quite simple, he said, all they had to do was appeal to the Governor for arms. There might be no soldiers available in the city, but surely there were enough rifles.

Joe's despondency deepened. He was haunted by Chief Running Bull's last words: "Show me!" His uncle Stephen's proposal seemed the only answer to that request, and a few weeks ago he would have joined him enthusiastically; now he sensed this to be wrong. It made no sense that God should ordain that man must not kill without providing an alternative. There must be another way, there must be— but what alternative could he suggest? Flee with the Indians? Too late. Hide them? Where?

He looked about him at the empty hall, the stacks of building materials surrounding them; at that moment they looked inexpressibly sad, like a promise doomed to go unfulfilled. He gazed at the triangular stack of drainage pipes that seemed, in his present somber mood, to stare at him like the muzzles of so many cannon. In a far corner lay more cannon: stovepipes.

"But, Stephen Atkins, if we go to the armory and ask for guns and rifles, this would have the most serious consequences in the Assembly, wouldn't it?" It was Israel Henderson, Junior, a level-headed young man. "I do agree we must do something, but the fact remains that if we do as thee proposes, it is our fathers in the Assembly who will have to face the consequences. Can we do this?" But his was a voice crying in the wilderness. The others were irritated by his words, even though they could not answer the argument.

Stephen Atkins did it for them. "It will be your decision, not mine, because I'm only a visiting Friend," he said. "I am fully aware that political consequences for the Society of Friends in Pennsylvania are unavoidable if you act as I propose. But what alternative is there? Go back to the Meeting and leave the fate of the Indians to endless deliberations? What your elders are doing right now is what they have been doing for fifty years: they argue and argue until matters are decided for them by circumstances beyond their control. They do not want to face the dilemma, they want to mark time until a solution is forced upon them; then they can say, 'We have not violated the testimonies, we have been overtaken by events.' Friends, it is not our words that count, it is our *acts*. Nobody will remember in future generations what Philadelphia Yearly Meeting *said* in the year of our Lord 1754. They will remember how we *acted,* or how we failed to act, when the Indians came to us for protection."

His argument seemed irrefutable, yet Joe knew with instinctive certainty that it was wrong, it was a lie; if Uncle Stephen got away with this, something would be destroyed forever. He closed his eyes in despair, praying for guidance. But all he could do was wonder, idiotically, whether those drainage pipes would fit inside the stovepipes.

"What would be the most effective weapons to use?" somebody asked.

Uncle Stephen replied matter-of-factly, "The best way would be to confront them with a row of cannon across the road, outside the city. But the commander of the militia will not give us any cannon, even if he has them. All we can hope for is muskets, rifles, swords, lances—"

With a quiver, Joe rose to his feet. "Friends," he said, "we have the solution with us, right here in this room! To take up arms in defense of those Indians is the world's solution, not ours. But we can build from the materials we see around us four or five decoy cannon that from a distance will be indistinguishable from the real thing. There!" He pointed at the drainage pipes. "I am sure that those drainage pipes will fit into those stovepipes over there. Together they will look exactly like the barrel of a gun. Let's mount them on those bricklayers' buggies and I am sure that from a distance no one will see the difference. If we block the road with decoy guns that can fool the raiders, we shall have lived up to our promise to the Indians without breaking the peace testimony. We must not let go of our testimonies just because we cannot think of another solution in five minutes. If we cannot use violence, we must use something else: our wits. We will not come out of this as heroes or as saints, but if we succeed in stopping the raiders by training decoy guns on them, at least the world may say, 'With that canniness, who needs violence?'" He looked about him, sure of himself, yet shaking like a leaf.

Uncle Stephen's voice broke the tense silence. "Well, well," he said with dour admiration. "Thee is a true Woodhouse, Joe. All right—let's give it a try."

*   *   *

Gulielma Woodhouse had joined the Women's Meeting that morning with a sense of detachment induced by exhaustion. She had been up with the Indians all night, to miss a night's sleep was already a debilitating experience at her age, even if that night was not spent leaping about like a twenty-year-old. At this point each snap of a reticule sounded like a pistol shot to her and each cough like an explosion; as she sat there, listening to the fatuous arguments and unworldly proposals of one female orator after another, she blamed herself bitterly for not going to look for the body of old Jim McHair. Now here they were, helplessly arguing in circles while any moment the ruffians from Loudwater might be upon them. She had expected them to arrive before now; obviously, they had made camp somewhere in smug self-confidence, certain of their victory. Then Mary Woodhouse came in with the news that the young men of the Meeting had

ridden off under the leadership of Stephen Atkins, to arm themselves
for a showdown with the Paisley boys.

The Women's Meeting, which until that moment had been droning
on interminably, was suddenly jolted awake; above the clamor of
snattering women sounded a calm, quavering voice. It was Hannah
Martin; for as long as Gulielma could remember, the old woman had
never spoken in meeting; now there she stood, small and shriveled
and very German, saying in her heavy accent, "Friends, shouldn't we
do something now, as women, as mothers? Should we not think of
those Indian girls and their babies out there as our own children, our
grandchildren? What would we do if they were? Would we not take
them home and settle them safely in the cellar or in the attic? Would
we not stand in the doorway to wait for those boys with their guns?
And when they came, we would say, 'If you want to kill the Indians,
you'll have to kill us first.' Wouldn't we do this for our children? Of
course we would. So, let those of us who live here in Philadelphia
and who have room agree to take in some of the Indians, then let's
stand with our families in our doorways and confront those over-
excited boys in a spirit of love."

The effect of her calm, sweet little speech was profound. For a
minute it was so silent in the Women's Meeting that the voices of
the men on the other side of the partition could be heard clearly.
Gulielma felt her confidence in corporate witness restored; there could
be no doubt that Hannah Martin had spoken in the power of the
Lord. She rose to say, "I unite!" To her surprise, she sat down shaking.
Surely she should have said something more? But words had failed her.

A voice asked somewhere, "And if those boys say, 'All right, we'll
kill you'?"

There came Hannah's quiet voice again. "It is a possibility, and
if it comes to that, we'll have to face it. But I don't think it will.
They are just young men in a rage. We have all dealt with boys in a
rage, haven't we? And haven't we found that loving, motherly firmness
has always been the solution?"

There was a silence in which each of the women visualized the
consequences of the proposal. Then Ruth Henderson, the presiding
clerk, asked matter-of-factly, "Is this the sense of the Meeting? That
we propose to take into our homes a number of Indians and that we
shall stand in our doorways with our families to face the raiders
in a spirit of love?"

Somewhere a voice said, "It is."

There could be no doubt; miracle of miracles, the Women's Meeting
had minded the Light. Gulielma felt tears come to her eyes.

"In that case," the calm voice of Ruth Henderson said from the
rostrum, "we shall send a delegation to the Men's Meeting to inform
them of our proposition. Will Friends please indicate whom they want
to send as messengers?"

"I'll be happy to go," a voice said, after a few moments of silence.
It was Mary Woodhouse. "I do not want to impose myself on the
Meeting, but I must speak out, as I am under a concern to do this,

especially because the young Friends seem to be planning their organized violence under the leadership of my brother."

Before anyone else had commented from the floor, a young voice rang out from the back. "In that case, I would like to join Mary Woodhouse! I feel under a concern to represent the young Friends here. I am speaking, I am certain, not for myself alone when I say that I think it is a wonderful thing to do. I am sure, absolutely sure that we must do this, especially we young people. I beg the Meeting to allow me to accompany Mary Woodhouse, so that the men next door shall be confronted not only by their wives, but by their daughters!" Gulielma's mouth fell open in astonishment; it was Becky Baker. Of all the silly young things . . .

There was a moment of silence.

"May I conclude that the sense of the Meeting is that we send as messengers to the Men's Meeting Mary Woodhouse and Rebekah Baker?"

From the body of the Meeting a voice answered, "I unite. And praised be the Lord."

Despite herself, Gulielma answered with a Methodist "Amen."

*   *   *

Becky did not know what had made her do it. Something stronger than her shyness and her self-preoccupation had suddenly brought her to her feet. Now, with her heart in her mouth and shaky knees, she was walking down the aisle of the Men's Meeting toward the rostrum, where, like judges in a court, the overseers sat scowling down on them, obviously irked by the interruption of their deliberations. Uncle Jeremiah, normally an easy-going man, sat frowning behind his table with unmistakable irritation; thank God that Mary Woodhouse was with her. Becky felt suddenly sobered, almost paralyzed by the disapproving stares of all those men as she walked in an unnerving silence toward the rostrum.

Mary Woodhouse sounded calm and sure of herself when she spoke, yet Becky sensed in her the same insecurity. "On behalf of the Women's Meeting, Rebekah Baker and myself have come to inform you of the following decision. It is the sense of our Meeting that, in view of the temptation to violence to which young Friends are now exposed, our response to the present crisis is the following . . ." She outlined Hannah Martin's proposal in words that suddenly sounded emotional and utterly impractical. It was obvious that their proposition would be turned down without dissent; never before in her life had Becky felt herself exposed to such tacit censure.

After an uncomfortable silence Uncle Jeremiah asked, "Is it the wish of the delegates of the Women's Meeting that they return with this Meeting's response?"

"It is," Mary Woodhouse replied. Becky did not know why, but she was certain now that Mary had given up hope. It was an emotional and impractical proposal. But why had she felt such absolute certainty, such surging joy in response to Aunt Hannah's suggestion? What had made her speak so forcefully, with such conviction? It could not have been just a flight of fancy . . .

"May I invite Friends to comment on this proposal?" Uncle Jeremiah asked formally.

And then it happened. Without warning, something flared up within Becky, something bewildering but irresistible. Before anyone had been able to say a word, she was clambering boldly onto the rostrum, an indecorous act if ever there was one. But she did not care, she was propelled by the compulsion to confront them, not on her own behalf but on behalf of all those women whose sympathy and agreement she had sensed when she spoke. She faced the sea of male faces with love. "I know how you feel," she said, "I know that this is not the moment to do anything impulsive. But believe me, Friends: please, please believe me! What is at stake is not only the fate of the Indians who come to us for help, not only the fate of the political power you—we—have as Quakers. Believe me, Friends—fathers, uncles, brothers—what is at stake is the future of our Society itself. I have, as have all young Friends of my age, heard you talk in meetings, lectures, ministry about 'the future of Quakerism.' But the future of Quakerism is us, the coming generation; yes, us—I, Becky Baker, one of a thousand, but Becky Baker, unique, irreplaceable. I have been talked at for years: Quakerism is this, Quakerism is that . . . But now is the moment to show us a Quakerism that consists of practice, not of preaching. How often have I heard, have we all heard, the story of the Quaker who met a highway robber to whom he said, 'I would not have myself killed for any of my material possessions, Friend, but if it came to thy soul, I would lay down my life to save it.' What was that, Friends? The truth or a pious story? For years we have been beaten over the head with stories like that one: George Fox said this, Will Penn said something else . . . Now the moment has come for me to ask you: I know what George Fox said, I know what Will Penn said; but what dost *thou* say?"

As she said this, she trembled so violently that she was sure the men must notice it and realize that she was bluffing, that she did not have the strength or the conviction she pretended to have, that she was merely the pawn of something that had risen overwhelmingly within her.

In the silence that followed, someone rose from the body of the Meeting. When Becky saw who it was, her heart sank: dour old Uncle Peleg. All was lost.

"Friends," the dry old voice said, "I am sure that I speak the mind of this Meeting when I say that here indeed is a chance for us to show that we old Quakers are prepared to act upon our convictions. I inform this Meeting that my house will be open to as many Indians as my rooms can hold, and that I and my wife will stand in the doorway to confront those men, in a spirit of love." He sat down.

Suddenly unnerved, Becky groped behind her for the table for support. She heard Uncle Jeremiah say, "Is it the sense of the Meeting that we shall unite with the women? Will Friends who do not unite please make themselves heard?"

There was a silence in which Becky prayed; then came Uncle Jeremiah's voice again, formal as ever. "It is the sense of this Meeting that we shall each take into our home a number of Indian refugees, and confront the raiders in a spirit of love. May I now ask for a few moments of silence before we act upon this concern?"

They remained in motionless silence for what seemed to Becky an endless time. She felt drained, yet elated. She had no idea what the consequences would be, but she knew that whatever had happened to her in those moments was irrevocable.

Uncle Jeremiah said, "Friends, may God help us all." Her hand was touched, she turned around, and faced Uncle Jeremiah. His face was full of tenderness and understanding.

With a rumble of seats and a hubbub of voices, the Meeting rose. Mary Woodhouse took Becky back to the Women's Meeting, where all this lofty spirituality would now have to be translated into action. On her way out, Becky suddenly saw her father seated at the end of a row. He was staring at her with a look that made her realize, to her dismay, that he was terribly angry. She felt like rushing to him and begging his forgiveness, asking him to help her, but she could not. As she slowly walked past, she realized for the first time in her life that to go with God meant to go alone.

* * *

After Becky had passed him on her way to the doors, Boniface Baker remained seated. He did not trust himself to confront anyone; he was furious. There had been a few regrettable occasions in the past when he had lost his self-control; it was about to happen again unless he kept a tight rein on himself. The impudence of Becky standing there, announcing to the Meeting that all she had ever known of Quakerism was talk! He could not begin to enumerate the instances where he had shown her by his conduct the meaning of Quakerism; he sat there glowering with a sense of outrage. To denounce him as a mere lip servant of the Testimonies! It was despicable; he could not bring himself to leave for fear he might find himself face to face with her again.

Caleb Martin, who had sat beside him all through the meeting, hovered uncomfortably in the aisle, obviously waiting. Boniface forced his thoughts away from Becky and her accusations; everybody was now hurrying home, their carriages full of Indians, to make a spectacle of themselves in the doorways of their houses. He was merely a guest of Isaac Woodhouse; if he were to join in the demonstration, he would, truly this time, be nothing but a lip servant. With the countryside in an uproar, it would be unwise to leave the plantation under the care of Scipio. He would have liked to go there himself, but he could not leave his family to Isaac Woodhouse; he sent Caleb instead. Caleb, relieved by the assignment, left with alacrity.

Boniface could not help himself, his thoughts were constantly drawn back to the scandalous incident, like a tongue probing a sore tooth; he had to find a quiet corner where he could recover his senses. He ventured into the crowded lobby, stood for a moment in doubt, then decided to go to the gallery, which by now should be empty.

Upstairs, the noise and the commotion below sounded far away. There was a narrow passage between the wall and the last row of benches; he followed it into the far corner. When attending yearly meeting as a little boy, he had tiptoed down this same narrow passage with a few of his friends, their hearts in their mouths, while downstairs the voice of some speaker droned on, driving all children to distraction. When he reached the corner, he looked at the posts and crossbeams that supported the tier of benches; he remembered seeing rows of feet and hearing a continuous creaking as all those bodies shifted in the torture of boredom. How safe the world had looked then, how decent and reasonable! Would he have challenged his elders in public? Never! The thought would not have entered his head. It was outrageous! She . . .

Hush, Bonny, he said to himself, calm down, come to thy senses. Center down, take thy fury and thy outrage to God. He folded his hands, bent his head; it seemed indeed that the balm of the Presence descended on his troubled soul. The stillness of the ocean of light and love pervaded him with tranquillity; God, omnipresent and all-knowing, gathered him in, sheltering him with the wings of the morning. God, he prayed, God, God, Light of my soul, thank Thee, thank Thee. Then, as he stood there savoring the balm of the Presence, a voice intruded. It sounded far away, but was quite clear. "Heavenly Father," it said, "for some reason Thou hast brought me here to speak, although there is no one present except Thee and me. So, let me speak to Thee."

Boniface opened his eyes and looked about him; he saw no one.

"I am here to explain the color of my hat," the voice said. It seemed to be coming from the well of the hall.

He peered through the forest of crossbeams at the rostrum. At the speaker's lectern a small, slight man in gray clothes was standing, wearing a gray hat. The hat identified him as John Woolman, appointed to give the address of the day. Obviously, he had decided to deliver it anyhow to an empty hall. He really was a crazy little man.

"For those of you who may not know this," the gentle lunatic continued, "the fact that my hat is not dyed is a testimony. For all your hats, dear Friends, as well as your coats and your breeches, have been given their fashionable blue color by slave labor; indigo is grown only in plantations where there are slaves. Let me elaborate on this witness."

Boniface sat thunderstruck; the fact that the madman down below should unknowingly be addressing him personally seemed incredible. For even if the hall had been packed with Friends, he would have been the only one to whom those words applied; owing to the blessing of the warm springs, his was the only plantation in this Yearly Meeting where indigo was grown. The lunatic below began to tell the empty hall about the heinous sin of slavery, and the sense of outrage that had driven Boniface into this hiding place returned with a vengeance. This was unbearable! The crowning impudence! For a tailor, who did not even belong to this Meeting, to berate a member because he employed slave labor . . . He ran down the narrow passage, strode toward the front of the gallery and shouted at the little man below, "John Woolman, stop that nonsense! Stop!"

The man looked up, startled; then he asked, "Who is thee?"

"Never mind who I am," Boniface replied, trembling with fury, "let it suffice to say that I am a landowner growing indigo! I want to ask thee, Friend Woolman, by what right, what authority thee has the audacity to lecture me about my ungodliness, without thy ever having had a single slave thyself? I might listen to thee if thy conduct had ministered to me before thee raised thy voice!"

The little man below took off his hat and said, "Dear Friend, thank thee. I have not come here to berate thee. Bring thy burden of keeping slaves before God." He turned to go.

But Boniface could not let him get away with this. He cried, "Don't go away, Friend Woolman! Listen to what I have to say!"

The little figure stopped.

"Suppose I were to decide that slavery was wrong," Boniface cried, "what consequences would that have? I am responsible for a family, for the land, the house that has been left to me, for the very slaves that thee urges me to set free! If I were to say to them, 'You are free to go wherever you like,' what would happen to them, once they set foot on the river's bank? As they would have no visible means of support, they would be considered vagrants, a burden to the community, and any owner who happened to be there first would be entitled under the law to re-enslave them on the spot! So, before thee continues telling slave-owners what to do, thee should reflect upon the consequences of the decision thee urges upon us with such presumption! If I want to grant my slaves their freedom, I must provide them with means of support. How, Friend Woolman? There is only one way: by partitioning my land among them. I myself would have to move away with my family across the mountains, to homestead a piece of prairie large enough to feed me and those in my care. That, my holy Friend, is what thee is demanding of me! No man has the right to demand that of another man! Thee is not serving God, John Woolman, thee is blathering in ignorance. Go home to thy tailor shop and return to thy craft, which God has ordained thee to do, instead of telling me to ruin myself, my family, all those who depend on me, and start all over again in the wilderness, like Adam after the fall of Man!" He stood trembling with rage and indignation, glowering down upon the little man below.

Then the gentle voice said, "Forgive me, Friend; it was not I who spoke. It was the Eternal, speaking through me."

"Nonsense!" Boniface cried contemptuously. "What gives thee the

right, thee—thee brittle creature, to presume that God would speak
through thee and not through me?"

"Because," the little man replied, "something forced me to deliver
the ministry I had prepared to an empty hall. I did not see thee.
I did not know there was anyone around to hear my voice, yet I was
forced to speak. If thee is indeed the only one in this Yearly Meeting
to whom my words could apply, whom does thee think forced me to
speak, if it was not the Lord?"

Boniface Baker could not accept it. Maddened by the unfairness
of it all, he searched for words with which to crush the brittle creature
who had now committed the ultimate impudence of claiming to be
the voice of God. But all he could do was turn away, stride down
the passage toward the doors and down the stairs into the lobby.
When he emerged into the courtyard, he saw a carriage drawn up at
the steps, in the process of being filled with squaws and children.
He recognized it as belonging to Isaac Woodhouse; the girl who was
helping was Becky.

*   *   *

George McHair, peering down the straight, empty road beyond the
muzzles of the six cannon, was the first to see a surreptitious movement on the horizon, as if a swarm of beetles were jerkily crawling
toward them. His heart pounded, he prayed it would not be they,
but as the scurrying beetles drew closer, he saw a flash of sunlight
reflected by a rifle; it was the Paisley boys.

"Friends," he said hoarsely, "here they come."

For a moment the young Quakers behind the clumsy guns stood in
doubt; it seemed impossible that adult men, familiar with the tools
of violence, would fall for these toys; then Stephen Atkins restored
their confidence.

"Quick!" he cried. "Strike the tinder, ready the rods! The moment
you see the whites of their eyes, light your torches so they can see
them. Lively, now!"

His confidence was infectious; even George, who had never believed
in Joe's plan, was almost convinced, but it did not last. He knew the
viciousness of the Paisley boys, once they were maddened; they would
ride through the lot of them. But he was swept along by the activity
of lighting the wicks, readying the torches. Ah, if only these were real
cannon! They would hurl their deadly load with a roar, the bombs
would explode among the riders, shards of red-hot iron would tear into
the horses' bellies, the men's arms, legs, chests, faces . . . He felt a
sudden yearning for violence roil in his stomach; he had never suspected he was carrying it inside him. He glanced at the others and
saw their jaw muscles work, their eyes flash, their hands turn into
fists; then a cool voice above him said, "George McHair, thee knows
those men, doesn't thee?" It was Stephen Atkins, astride his horse,
a drawn saber in his hand.

"Yes, I know them."

"In that case, ride out and meet them the moment they stop. Tell them that they must either turn back or be blown to smithereens."

George thought he detected a tone of uncertainty in this martial bluster, but to all the world Stephen Atkins looked certain of their impending triumph.

He looked down the barrel of his cannon. He saw the posse of riders quite clearly now; it was hard to judge with one man riding behind another, but there could not be more than a dozen. It gave him some heart; even if they did not fall for the decoy guns, the fact that they were outnumbered might discourage them. But he knew he was whistling in the dark; Polly and Parson Paisley would not be deterred by numbers; if they were mad enough, they would take on an army.

"Ready now!" Stephen Atkins' voice cried in the tense silence; then, "Light the torches!"

The wicks atop the rods sprang to sputtering, smoking life.

"Present rods!"

Behind the six cannon the flaming torches were raised in view of the approaching horsemen. They were not deterred, but rode on with disdain for the guns trained upon them.

"Lower rods!"

The flames were poised a few inches above the wicks of the cannon; it caused the first hesitancy among the riders. One of them, it looked like Parson Paisley, seemed to be reining in his horse, but he did not stop.

"Halt!" the stentorian voice of Stephen Atkins bellowed. "Stop, or we'll fire!"

This time there was confusion among the horsemen; their phalanx halted raggedly and their horses began to skitter. "Lower your rifles! An emissary will be sent to you!" Stephen Atkins' voice had an unmistakable note of triumph. "All right, George McHair! Off with thee!"

Obediently, George rose to his feet and went toward Betsy, peaceably grazing among the horses by the side of the road. Only as he hoisted himself into the saddle did he realize how weak his knees were. He clenched his teeth and flicked the bridle; Betsy let go of the succulent grass with reluctance and trotted obediently toward the riders in the distance, munching as she went.

George reined her in a few yards away from the parson. The old man was the only one whose eyes seemed to have some sense of reality left; the others gazed at him with the glassy stare of men in the spell of violence.

"Greetings, Parson," he said.

The old man glowered at him. "Jim McHair's own grandson! What are you doing here, coward? You belong with us, to avenge your grandfather's murder!"

"Murder?" George echoed, more shrilly than he had intended. Betsy wiggled her ears, as if pained by that silly voice.

"Why else do you think we have come all this way? We found

him in a tree inside our territory, an arrow in his back, the same kind
of arrow that killed my son. So make room, chickenheart, let us
through!"

"I am sorry, Parson," George said in the voice of a woman servant
refusing to open the door to a stranger. "The Quakers have promised
the Indians protection. So I must ask thee, in behalf of Philadelphia Yearly Meeting of the Society of Friends, to turn around. All we
have in town are women, children and old men—very old men."

The parson, his eyes slits, peered at the cannon. Suddenly George
remembered that he was shortsighted. It was a ray of hope; maybe
this was where God showed His hand: Parson Paisley had forgotten
his spectacles, and he was the only one in that bunch intelligent
enough to spot them as fakes. The old man said, "Well, well! Don't
tell me the Quakers are going to behave like men at last?" He said it
gloatingly, but he seemed impressed.

"I—I'm sorry . . ." George said, with a giddy rush of relief. "We
don't want to do thee any harm, but this is as far as we'll let thee
go!"

"Well, I am glad we have forced you Quakers to behave like men at
last," the parson repeated with contempt; but he swung his horse
around. "Come on boys, let's go!"

Polly Paisley, drained of all reason by the excesses in which they
must have indulged, gaped at his father vacuously and cried, "Like
hell we will! Let's get them, boys!" But the parson grabbed his horse's
bridle; the horse reared and nearly threw its rider. "Come on! Turn
about!" The old man dug his spurs in, forcing his own horse and his
son's to swing around, hoofs skittering on the cobbles, striking sparks.
The others followed suit, and the lot of them rode off at a gallop,
yoo-hooing and yodeling as they must have done all along their bloody
trail from the mountains.

George, staring after them, heard behind him a wild cheering. It
was the young Friends, elated by their victory. He turned to join them,
wondering why he should have a feeling of defeat.

* * *

When the jubilant young Quakers rode into town, the crowds which
had jammed the streets as they rode out had vanished. There turned
out to be no one left at the Meeting House either, even the Indians
had gone; it looked as if everyone had gone into hiding, afraid of the
coming massacre. As they rode on, they heard a murmur of voices
that grew as they approached Water Street; they rounded the corner
and found it packed with spectators craning their necks, too en-
grossed to make room for them. Stephen Atkins commanded, "Gangway! Gangway!"

The crowd parted reluctantly; Joe Woodhouse wondered what was
going on. Then he saw, in the doorways of the Quaker mansions,
people standing woodenly, as in a vigil; his own doorway was filled
with motionless people; he saw Becky among them.

"We turned them back!" Stephen Atkins shouted triumphantly. "We blocked the road with cannon and they turned tail! The Indians are safe, and so are you!"

"Cannon?" someone asked incredulously.

"Yes!" Stephen Atkins shouted back proudly. "It was young Joseph's idea! We made up a set of dummy cannon and they fell for it!"

It was surprising that he could still sound so self-satisfied; it was becoming obvious to everyone that they were being greeted by their families with disapproval.

"Was it really thy idea, Joe?" a girl's voice called.

Joe turned his head and faced her. "Yes, Becky, it was," he replied, no longer the victorious young warrior of the Lord.

Stephen Atkins cried belligerently, "What's the matter with you people? We turned them back, didn't we? And not a shot fired! Where are the Indians?"

"In our cellars and our attics," Joe's father replied. "The raiders would have had to kill us first."

The street fell silent, eerily so. It was as if the old man's words had struck even the most dull-witted spectator. The Quaker guns, divinely inspired as the idea might have seemed, had been un-Quakerly compared to the witness of all these unarmed people in the doorways, united in a testimony of love. Suddenly a ripple ran through the crowd; a voice cried, "There they come!" To Joe's horror, the sound of hoofs came thundering down the waterfront, rounded the corner and a posse of horsemen rode down upon them, scattering the crowd like sparrows, shrieking and whooping in frightening elation.

"Jesus Christ, help us!" a voice cried out somewhere; Joe, after a moment of shameful paralysis slid out of the saddle and ran to join the people in the doorway of his father's house. He gripped Becky's hand, groped with the other until he had found that of his mother, then he closed his eyes and waited for the confrontation, this time the real one. Then he heard Stephen Atkins cry, "For mercy's sake! Buffalo McHair!"

Joe looked and his mouth fell open. The horsemen now slithering to a screaming, flint-sparking stop were not the men who had been halted by the stovepipes; they were a bunch of outlaws and rowdies on wiry little horses, led by a bearded giant with two bullet belts slung across his barrel chest, on his head a Quaker hat crowned with a bunch of red feathers. "What happened?" the man cried in a voice like a foghorn. "Where are the wounded?"

George hollered back, "Pa! There are no wounded! Didn't thee meet the Paisley boys on thy way into town?"

"That's why! The parson told me there had been a gun battle and that his boys had won!"

Before anyone had a chance to enlighten him, there was Becky's voice, high and strident. "He was right too!" she cried, for the whole street to hear. "We *were* defeated! By so-called Friends!"

Joe suddenly realized that she was a virago in the making. The guns had been an honest effort, earnestly made; it deserved better than censure by a self-righteous little battle-ax.

Obviously, Uncle Stephen felt the same. "Young woman! Keep thy nose out of this! Thee was not with us, thee has no notion of what happened!"

But Uncle Jeremiah, with the prestige of clerk of the Yearly Meeting, cried, "I unite with Rebekah Baker! To confront those men with guns, real or imaginary, was a brittle thing to do!"

Stephen Atkins turned on him. "I knew that would be the word thee would choose, Jeremiah. I am mortified."

For the second time that day, a gentle old voice quavered in the uneasy silence. It was Hannah Martin again. "May I invite thee and thy friends to supper in my kitchen, Stephen?"

Stephen Atkins raised his hat. "Aunt Hannah," he cried, "for thy food I would come riding a hundred miles!"

To Buffalo, Hannah Martin said with smiling innocence, *"Büffelchen,* I can't tell thee how happy I am to see thee! *Glücklich,* I am, real *glücklich!* Come, join us with thy friend."

"All right, men!" the giant bellowed. "The stables are at the back of the house! I promise you the feast of your lives!" His little salmon-colored mustang wheeled around and he clattered off in the direction of the mews, followed by the posse of yodeling rowdies, striking sparks.

*   *   *

Half an hour later they were gathered around the big kitchen table in the old house: Gulielma, Isaac, Joe and Mary, Stephen Atkins, Jeremiah and Grizzle, the Baker children, George, Himsha and Buffalo McHair, and the seven wild men from the prairie. Gulielma had seen to it that she sat beside Buffalo, for she had a few questions to ask him. Hannah, eyes closed, hands folded, her voice flutelike with its soft German lilt, said "Dear Lord, let there be peace and love and tenderness among us, even though we shout." Buffalo mumbled, "Amen."

When the hubbub of voices rose and the dishes were passed along, Gulielma tackled him. "Where was thy father found, Buffalo?"

He gave her a quick look. At close quarters, his eyes were shrewd and secretive. "In a tree."

"With an arrow in his back?"

He took a piece of bread and stuffed it into his mouth.

She waited until he had finished chewing. "Well?"

"I don't know what gave thee that notion. The story about the arrow was made up by the parson."

"I see," she said. "Thee'll have to get jug-bitten first, before I hear the truth."

He laughed. "I could drink thee under the table, Gulie, and walk away sober."

"Let's try."

He took another piece of bread and mumbled, "Not here. I might get amorous."

She looked at him with fondness. "Thee is an extraordinarily tactful man, Buffalo. I have often marveled at that."

There was that wary glance again. "What's that?"

"Never mind. Thank thee for the compliment. But there is something wrong about thy father's death. I intend to find out the truth."

He munched; then he asked, "To what purpose? Why not leave dead old men alone?"

"Because in this instance the dead old man might cause a war," she replied. "Also, I saw Lone Seeing Eagle being crucified. I owe him something."

"Thee owes him nothing but a prayer for his soul's rest." He took the plate handed to him by his neighbor; it was heaped high with beans and pork. "There is no gain in the truth, Gulie, for thee or anyone else."

"He was killed by Lone Seeing Eagle, wasn't he? Why? Was it a mercy killing?"

He turned his attention to his plate and began to shovel heaped spoonfuls of pork and beans into his mouth.

She was not given to perseverance against the voice of reason, so she decided to let it go and enjoy his company. She would get the truth out of him at some campfire, some starry, coyote-haunted night.

* * *

After the first glasses of his father-in-law's claret had smoothed out the anger and the exhaustion of the day, Jeremiah Best began to feel thankful for the miraculous way in which they had been saved. Old Isaac, who sat across the table from him, looking like the cat that had swallowed the cream, had been proven right: way had indeed opened. But at the same time Jeremiah began to suspect that canny old Isaac might not have supported the women's proposition so readily had he not known about the plan of the Quaker guns. Be that as it may, the combination of the two had worked wonders. Once again the Quakers had been saved from the ultimate choice, be it in the nick of time; but how much longer would they be able to hang on to their political power without having to violate the testimonies? The decision would lie with men and women like those now gathered around Hannah Martin's table: the members of his generation, but especially their children, Joe Woodhouse, Joshua Baker, Becky, Abby, George McHair, little Himsha.

The thought suddenly brought him to his feet in an irresistible urge to minister. He tapped his glass until silence fell around the table. He looked at the faces, turned toward him expectantly, took off his hat and said, "Heavenly Father, thank Thee for Thy blessings today. We know that often our efforts to hear Thy voice and do Thy will are faulty, tinged with creaturely desires and wishes. But today once more Thy voice has been heard and we have, each in our own fashion, tried to act upon it. Thank Thee, Lord, for revealing Thyself to us once again as pure love, pure light, the infinite ocean George Fox spoke about. Let us, as we sit here, remain aware of the essence of Thy nature and open to it, ready to let it work through us for the peace of all mankind."

He sat down with a feeling of incompleteness. As always, after he had ministered with true conviction, he ended feeling he had said too much, or not enough. The silence around him was deep, but he could not help whispering in his thoughts, 'God, forgive me for failing Thee.'

*   *   *

When the plates were passed once more, heaped full of *Himbeertorte,* Hannah Martin surveyed her table and thanked the Lord that Caleb had not been here today. Violence always excited him, in a bad way.

All at once she felt a pang of anxiety about him. She assumed it was a passing thought, but suddenly it seemed as if, behind the laughing faces of her guests, she saw his hands stretched out to her in supplication. Fear gripped her; she felt the need to be alone for a moment.

She took the bowl of butter and went to the larder. There, the bowl pressed against her and the cat rubbing against her leg, she prayed to God to protect her Caleb. She came back to the table feeling better; but as she sat down and looked at her plate, there was his desperate face calling, "Mother!"

She knew something terrible was happening on Eden Island.

CHAPTER SEVEN

CALEB Martin had been delighted when Boniface Baker sent him home. It was the same every yearly meeting: sheer torture to sit there during the interminable deliberations, knowing that the slaves had the run of the island and the Hall. They could roam freely about the house and poke their noses into the study, the bedrooms, the girls' wardrobes; he even saw them in his imagination defiling Rebekah's bed by sleeping in it. True, when he came home, there never was a trace of any of this; on the contrary, Mammy used those four days every year to spring-clean the house; yet every time he was convinced that something untoward had gone on during his absence. Now, for the first time, he had a chance to find out for himself.

By driving his horse to exhaustion he managed to arrive at the ferry landing before sunset. He was about to ring the bell for Charon when it occurred to him that it would warn them of his return. Young George McHair had swum the river, he could do the same. He forced his horse down the bank and proceeded to swim across, clinging to the pommel of his saddle. The tide was coming in, slowing down the current; even so he panicked when he felt the pull of the swirling water. Finally they emerged on the other side, halfway down the island, breathless and shaken. When he tried to mount his dripping horse, his strength failed him; the weight of the water in his clothes seemed crushing. But he managed to hoist himself into the saddle and the gelding set out for the house of its own accord, drawn to the stable like a homing pigeon to its nest.

The ice-cold immersion, the exhausting struggle had sobered him to the point where he began to think of those fears about the slaves as hallucinations; yet, without warning, he began to tremble with rage. It was an unreasoning anger, maybe he was just furious with himself. If he had had the strength, he would have dug his spurs into the poor horse's flank; but he let himself be carried slowly through the fields, the vegetable gardens, to the barnyard, where, whinnying gregariously, the other horses welcomed them from their stalls. His gelding trotted to the door of its own stall and stopped there, swaying on its legs, image of exhaustion. He himself staggered to the door, water squelching in his boots; his soaked harness was heavy and as tight as a vise. He yearned to go to his cottage in the compound, but he had to unsaddle the beast first and rub it down. While he was doing so, a sound penetrated to him: singing, somewhere in the distance; nigger voices. There was nothing wrong with that, they often sang when they thought themselves alone. What was wrong was that it came from the house. God damn their souls! They *were* in the house! They *were* making merry there while everyone was gone! He had been right, they were up to something!

As he stood listening, fury uncoiled inside him again. In the house, were they? He would teach them, God spare his soul! All of a sudden he seemed to acquire a light-footed nimbleness. He ghosted along the wall to the footpath across the lawn; before venturing into the open he pulled off his boots; the squelching might give him away. He wanted to surprise the slaves in their revelry before they had a chance to dissemble their carousing; so far, he was certain no one had seen him. Whatever they were up to in there, it absorbed them completely; it had never occurred to them that he might swim across the river and plummet down on them like a falcon from the sky. How could he surprise them? To reach the balcony unnoticed, he would have to climb the chestnut tree in front of Joshua's room, the way he had seen Harry clamber toward his tryst. It was not something he would have contemplated doing under normal circumstances; now he seemed to have the agility of a cat. He did not know what had taken possession of him; all he knew was that he must materialize in their midst before any man, woman or child could scurry away.

He climbed the tree as if it were a ladder, walked down the branch in his stockinged feet with the sureness of a bobcat; as he stood poised on the balustrade, a movement to the right caught his eye. He saw a furtive shadow slink through the open doors of Rebekah's room onto the balcony. There was something white in the creature's hands. It was Harry, whom he had once heard mention Rebekah in a way he would never forget; casting to the wind his decision to surprise them, he cried, "Halt! What has thee got there?!"

The boy recoiled as if he had been struck; he turned around, his eyes wide with shock; before he could run, Caleb bridged the distance in one bound and grabbed him by the throat.

"Help!" the boy shrieked. "Mother, Mother!"

"Show it to me! Give here! What has thee got there?"

The boy was too terrified to obey; Caleb wrenched the piece of clothing from his hand and saw that it was a girl's undergarment.

For a second he stood there, stupefied; then the violence that he had felt uncoil inside him broke from the grasp of his self-control. With a shriek of rage he started to batter the boy with both fists, to kick him, maul him, shrieking "Filthy nigger! Filthy black nigger!" It tore from his guts like the howl of an animal; when the boy started to lash out at him in sheer terror, the last vestige of sanity left him. He grabbed the squirming creature by belt and throat, lifted him above his head and hurled him over the balustrade onto the flagstones below.

He came to his senses only when someone standing beside him cried, "Your brother! You've killed your brother!" It was Mammy.

As the words penetrated to his consciousness, he turned slowly around with only one wish: to undo it, undo it all. But there stood Mammy, her shapeless bulk heaving with sobs, her eyes filled with horror, yelling, "Kill me! Yes, kill me! You just killed your own brother, you half-nigger! Now kill me! Now kill your mother as well!"

For a moment there seemed only one way out: to jump, to undo it all by undoing himself. But something held him back, some mindless will to live. He turned around and fled into the house, down the stairs, out the door, across the lawn, home, home to the quarters. On the flagstone path the boy Harry lay dead.

* * *

Scipio went to alert Boniface Baker—at the risk of his freedom, for there was no one left on Eden Island to sign a pass for him. When he arrived at the Meeting House, he asked for his master; when Bonny saw Scipio standing in the lobby, his first thought was: 'A fire, the house has burned down.'

He was told that Caleb Martin had killed Harry in a fit of rage and barricaded himself in his cottage, threatening to shoot anyone who came near. Scipio said, "Please, Massa, please come on home, please . . . He will kill more people, he won't listen to anyone, he won't even listen to his mother . . ."

His mother. With a sick feeling, Boniface realized: Caleb had learned the truth.

He had Peleg Martin called out of meeting. "Dear Friend," he said, "I have sad news."

"Ah?" The old man, who had been irritated at the interruption, froze.

"Caleb has killed one of my slaves, a stableboy called Harry, in a fit of rage. He learned the truth about his parentage."

"I see."

"I am going there at once. Would thee join me?"

"Yes."

"I will round up my family. We'll meet here in the lobby."

Boniface sent word into the Women's Meeting; Beulah and the girls came out and were told the ghastly news. Together with Joshua, Peleg Martin and Scipio, they all squeezed themselves into the coach and set out for Eden Island.

During the ride, as the hours crawled by, Boniface's mind was a turmoil of visions of complete chaos: the slaves out of hand, Caleb firing blindly into a mass of screaming Negroes, anything was possible, and it was all his fault. He should have done something the moment he learned of Caleb's parentage—told the man the truth, removed him from the plantation, instead of which he had reclined in the smug conviction that every problem, every conflict, every horror could be solved, as long as he remained calm and trusted in that of God in all concerned. His entire life he had behaved that way: skimmed over conflicts and problems with blithe confidence in the goodness and reasonableness inherent in all men, even in his slaves. Now, as he jogged and bounced along with the others in the swaying coach, he realized that he had lived his life on the surface only. What had dominated his life had been the conviction that the ultimate solution to every conflict was compromise.

At nightfall they were ferried across; after dropping the women at the Hall, Boniface made his way to the slave quarters with Peleg Martin. First of all he went to the hospital, where, so he had gathered, the boy's body had been taken. As he and Peleg descended in front of the ramshackle little building, a mass of silent slaves surrounded them in the gathering darkness. As they went in, Boniface was hit by a stench of dirt and neglect. He had not been inside the hospital for years; the smell seemed to gainsay the illusion that Quakers treated their Negroes as loving parents would treat their children; it was the reek of slavery.

Harry's body lay on a cot at the far end of the ward. By its side a woman crouched, praying or sobbing, Boniface knew not what; she was holding on to one of the corpse's hands. It was Mammy.

"What happened, Mammy?" he asked. The habit of a lifetime made him sound calm, master of the situation.

"He killed him! He killed him!" the woman sobbed. "He didn't do nothing! The poor boy done nothing! He was helping clear out Miss Becky's room, I sent him to take some clothes to the laundry that she had dropped behind the bed, and suddenly I hear a scream, and there he is, there is Caleb, beating him, kicking him. I cry, 'Caleb, Caleb! He's your brother! Stop!' But Caleb, he just went on kicking him, beating him, and when the poor boy tried to defend himself he grabbed him by his throat and . . ." Convulsive sobs shook her huge body; she could not go on.

The truth did not shock Boniface. He had suspected it was Mammy when he read about Caleb's mother being a Negress. She had always been treated by his grandmother as if she were not a slave or a servant. He knew he should be moved by her elephantine grief, but something about the huge, jellying bulk, the high-pitched wails left him unaffected.

"Maybe I had better go and see him first," Peleg Martin said beside him. He had forgotten about Peleg. He looked up and saw the old man standing there, relaxed, unconcerned, his face with the harsh, craggy furrows of age was without expression. Then it occurred to him that long ago the dour old man had embraced the huge body now sobbing at their feet. "Is she indeed his mother?" he asked.

"Yes," the old man replied without emotion. "Thy grandmother gave her shelter after the child was born."

"But when did she have Harry . . . ?"

"Harry? Who's Harry?"

He indicated the glassy-eyed corpse on the bed.

"That's not her son. Too young. She may have had any number of children later, but not that one. Too young."

"But she said—"

"Oh, she'll say anything that enters her head. That's what they like, to make mischief. As long as they can make mischief, they're happy."

The woman who had been sobbing inconsolably a moment before

was now listening intently, her heaving controlled, her breathing held in check. "Let's go," Boniface said as the evil of it all overwhelmed him.

* * *

Peleg Martin was relieved to leave Medea behind. He did not care about the dead boy on the bed; death had ceased to awe him. But love still did, or lust, or whatever it was that drove man and woman together to lie panting for a few moments in illusory unity, twin-backed animal racked by convulsions, writhing in the grip of the power that had hurled the seed of life into the womb of the void. It seemed inconceivable that once upon a time he had known ecstasy in the arms of the bulk of blubber now squealing wails of badly acted grief, clutching the hand of a dead boy with whom, he was convinced, she had no relationship whatever. She was no more than twenty years younger than he, and what could the boy be? Seventeen? Eighteen? She always had been an inveterate mischief-maker, even in the days when, moaning, she had arched beneath him in the spasms of passion. She had been a beautiful black beast full of wild, raw lust who had un-masked his embraces with his late wife as prim posturings of passion, copulating toads in the primeval sludge. How that black devil had tried to tear his manhood from him by the roots! How he had roared and reared! But for old Ann Baker, the black pudding now jellying at his feet would have robbed him of all reason, will and awareness forever, so obsessed had he been with the raptures of her glorious body.

He turned away in disgust. Her body, that was all it had been, that was all they had. For one brief summer, no woman had a better body or a more seductive one; then it bore fruit and wilted and turned into sagging, repulsive fat drooping toward the grave. Any man who attrib-uted a soul to a black body during the brief season of its bloom was insane. A soul? All they dreamed of was to have themselves bred by the demigods that dominated them, in the hope that their offspring would attain that ultimate goal: humanity, a soul.

As he slowly made his way to the overseer's cottage, Peleg Martin wondered about Caleb's soul. There had always been a doglike streak in him, a tendency to lick the hands of the master. Now the dog had turned upon his mother's kind. Murder? Who could call the outcome of a dogfight murder? If those busybodies in the Meeting who had never kept a slave were to impose their concept of slavery as a sin against humanity, the result would be disaster. For the moment the animal trainer freed the wild beast, something in the animal's half-conscious brain would snap, it would hurl itself upon its erstwhile master out of an irresistible compulsion to kill, as irresistible as the compulsion to copulate and create life. Between those two blind, ir-resistible compulsions the nigger's individual half-consciousness was tossed until eternal darkness engulfed him, the same darkness from whence he had sprung. Peleg was certain that poor Caleb had never fallen under the sway of the compulsion to create life; now he had fallen prey to the other compulsion and destroyed life, thereby condemning himself to death by his own hand, or by the hand of someone else, it made no difference. A man who had never created life was unable to stand the shock of destroying it; that was why whores were as essential to an army as cannon.

The dark mass of slaves outside in the falling night made room for him, silently, respectfully as he walked down the street to the overseer's cottage. Bats gamboled between the dark crowns of the chestnut trees; the façades of the hutches shimmered like tombstones. In front of the cottage there was no crowd. No horse was tethered nearby; it seemed deserted. As he climbed the steps to the rickety veranda and the floorboards creaked under his weight, Peleg wondered whether the slaves considered Caleb one of theirs and would claim him for their own hoodoo court of justice. Whatever happened, he must prevail on the boy to come with him and submit himself to the judgment of a proper court of law. He would be acquitted, of course; if he stayed here, he was bound to die a death unimaginable to a white man. He had to get the boy out of here, it was a matter of life and death. With a sudden sense of urgency he knocked on the door of the cottage.

There was no answer; he knocked three times before a slurring voice groaned, "Who's there?"

"It is I, thy father. Open up."

There was no answer. Peleg listened at the crack, holding his breath; he could not hear a sound. "Caleb! Open up, son! It's thy father, I must talk to thee!"

No reaction. He tried the door. It was locked. "Caleb? Open up, boy! I am here to help thee! Let me in, it is urgent!"

Silence. The boy was drunk, probably unable to stand on his feet. He should break down the door; he needed help. But Boniface Baker was nowhere to be seen. They were all worthless, with their fancy ministry and their flatulent prayers and their deadly ignorance of the dark crevasses of life, the depths of death as well as the pinnacles of love. "Come, son! Open up! This is an order!"

Suddenly there was Caleb's voice: clear, calm, chilling. "Is she my mother?"

Peleg hesitated. If he said no, the boy might believe him and allow himself to be coaxed out of this valley of death. But some awareness of the nature of the torment Caleb was going through warned him that to lie at this moment would be a mistake; only if the boy could stand the truth might he be saved. "Yes, Caleb," he said.

This was the moment in which the boy had to decide, alone, whether to live in the face of that knowledge or to give up and die. Even his father, to whom he had submitted so obediently all his life, could not help him now. Only God could—or a woman. A woman! Hannah? He considered sending for his wife, who really loved the child now hovering on the edge of the eternal darkness. But all she would be, poor woman, was a reminder of the lie in which the boy had lived since the day she had first held him in her arms and called him *Bubchen.*

If only there were a girl! Someone he had dreamed about, however chastely, someone young, feminine . . . "I'll be back, Caleb," he said to the door.

He went down the rickety steps to the road and walked away from the house, knowing that the boy was lying there, holding his breath, listening to his footsteps receding into the silence.

* * *

Becky Baker was in the drawing room, working by the light of the chandelier on an interminable cross-stitch of Job Five, verse seventeen, *"Happy is the man whom God correcteth."* Each time she stabbed the needle through the linen, it made a loud sound in the silence which lay like a fog over the small group of people in the room. She wondered, with mounting irritation, why on earth it had been necessary for George and Himsha McHair to come after them on their horses. Couldn't they have stayed with the Woodhouses? There they sat, stolid, motionless, each of them weighing a ton in the silence, which seemed more stifling as the seconds ticked by. Her mother and Abby did nothing to relieve the insufferable gloom; her mother, with the demonstrative somnolence that was supposed to hide the anxiousness of their waiting, sat by the empty fireplace with a book called *Awake, Ye Daughters of Jerusalem!* on her lap. Abbey was sitting on a stool beside her, messy little sampler on her lap, gazing into space while biting her nails. Becky was about to reprimand her when she heard a carriage rattle to a stop outside the front door. That must be Father and Uncle Peleg!

Suddenly she was overcome by excitement. They might have brought Caleb with them! Never in her life had she been face to face with a murderer. She was both relieved and disappointed when the two men entered the drawing room alone. They looked grim, adding to the gloom.

Nothing had prepared her for her father's request: "Rebekah, would thee come back with us to the quarters and persuade Caleb Martin to leave his cottage? We must get him out of there, tonight."

She gaped at him in blank astonishment; then she swallowed and asked, "Why I, for heaven's sake?"

Before they could answer, her mother barked in that toneless voice of hers, "What's going on? Where is Caleb?" Nobody paid any attention to her.

"He must be convinced by someone that he should stand trial, like a man," her father replied.

"What's going on?" her mother persisted. "What do you want of Becky?" Her voice might have been that of a parrot shouting from a cage in the corner of the room.

Becky looked at her father. He was pale, he looked frightened, hurt. "Have you seen him?" she asked.

"No, he would not let us in," Uncle Peleg replied.

"But why should he listen to me if he will not listen to his own father?"

"Will someone please tell me what is going on! Becky, what do they want of thee?"

"Hush, Mother!" she shouted irritably. "I'll tell thee in a minute!" She turned to her father. "But I hardly know him. I've known him all my life, but never—never *really.*"

They shuffled uneasily, like guilty little boys. What was the matter with them? She became suspicious. What gave them the idea that she could succeed where they had failed?

"Do they want something from the kitchen?" her mother cried. "Where is Caleb?" She was at a complete loss; her deafness seemed to get worse in the evening.

"I'll be honest with thee, Becky," her father said. "This is not my idea. I am not sure that Peleg is right, and that poor Caleb will listen to thee rather than to us . . ."

"But why?" she repeated impatiently. "Why not Joshua, who has been working with him all these months?"

"Thy Uncle Peleg is convinced that he will not listen to a man," her father replied unhappily.

"A man?" her mother queried. "What man? Where is he?"

Becky went to her, put an arm around her shoulders and spoke slowly into her ear. "Caleb Martin does not want to come out of his cottage. Father and Uncle Peleg want me to try and convince him."

"Thee?" Her mother looked up with an angry frown. "What gave them that idiotic idea?"

"I don't know, Mama," Becky answered loudly. "Ask them."

Before her mother had been able to do so, her father took Becky's place and began to repeat, at the top of his voice, what he had said earlier. Uncle Peleg led Becky aside. "I must explain to thee, child, that Caleb is not only confused because of what he did to that nigger boy. He has been hit by a—a revelation about his parentage."

She felt his hand tremble on her arm, though his voice remained calm and unaffected. "What does thee mean?" she asked.

The old man's discomfort was so obvious that she began to feel embarrassed; suddenly a hard child's voice behind her said, "He means that Caleb's mother was a Negro."

She turned angrily on Abby sitting there with a face of know-it-all. "How does thee know?!"

"I read it in Great-granny's diaries."

"Well . . ." She was overcome by an incongruous curiosity. A Negro? Had Uncle Peleg been married to a Negro? She looked at the wizened old man beside her; his hand was still trembling on her arm. He said grouchily, "Yes. His mother is Medea—Mammy."

Her father joined them and said, "Well, Becky, if thee thinks thee can face it, let us not waste any more time. Shall we go?"

She saw the dirty, spooky little cottage with its dilapidated porch, its shuttered windows, its sinister atmosphere of decay, herself approaching it in the dark, unaccompanied, knocking on that door, hearing slow, slouching steps approaching . . . "No, Father," she said. "I'm sorry, but I can't do it."

"Why not?" Uncle Peleg asked harshly. "Thee is not afraid of him, child?"

She faced him squarely, "Yes, Uncle, I am."

"Don't keep on at her if she doesn't want to!" her mother cried beside her, as if from a distance. "If she does not want to go, leave her be!"

But Uncle Peleg gripped her arm with that trembling old hand; his eyes looked haggard and distraught. "How now? Thee, who was not afraid to face a hundred men in Meeting, is afraid of one desperate, frightened boy?"

"When I did that, Uncle, I was in the power of the Lord."

"Then *go* in the power of the Lord, child! If thee could do that, thee might save him." Uncle Peleg gave her a meaningful look. "All He has is thee."

"What did he say?" her mother shouted. "Don't have thyself talked into something thee does not want to do!"

But a point had been passed beyond which there was no return. It was the same as when she had spoken in meeting: despite her determination not to become involved she was suddenly conscious that she could not go back. Although she had not said a word, Uncle Peleg squeezed her arm, his eyes filled with tears and he whispered, "Thank thee."

She wanted to cry, 'No, it's not true, I didn't say a word! I didn't say I would!' But it was too late. Her father put his hands on her shoulders, looked at her with tenderness and kissed her cheek; then he said, "Let's go." Her mother clung to her and cried, "Don't go if thee doesn't want to! Don't go, child! Don't go!" But Becky freed herself of her mother's grip as if she were casting off in a boat, all alone, headed for a whirlpool. As she passed George McHair, he suddenly rose to his feet and mumbled, "Shall I come with thee, Becky?"

She managed a smile. "No, thank thee, George. Two men will be enough, I think." She went into the hall to fetch her shawl.

She let herself be helped into the waiting buggy in the darkness by her father; the horse started to move invisibly in the night, and the buggy, creaking, drew away from the safety of the house. She lifted her face to the sky; perhaps if she prayed, she might draw some of the peace and the majesty of the starry night toward her. There was no moon, the stars flashed coldly, like diamonds; beyond them shimmered the luminescent swath of the Milky Way. Was God there? Oh, sweet Jesus, how far, how unimaginably far! Was Jesus up there, or here with her, right inside her, as she had been taught all her life? Oh, she wished He were, she fervently wished He were here within her right now; but she felt no stillness, no serenity beyond her turbulent thoughts. They were not really thoughts but flitting images, whiffs of terror that became stronger as the buggy creaked and swayed its way along the furrow of shadow between the embank-

ments of the fields of indigo toward the quarters, the cottage, the
murderer waiting for her. She was about to cry out, 'Please take me
back!' but as if he sensed her terror, her father put a hand on hers.
She glanced at him, he looked straight ahead; comfort and tranquillity
seemed to flow from his hand smoothing her trembling terror. After a
while a semblance of self-confidence rose within her as she reflected
that, although she could not perceive His presence, God must be with
her in this hour, for He was a God of love. Yet when finally they
entered the compound and the thudding of the horse's hoofs echoed
off the little houses that stood shimmering in the night, her body was
rigid with fright.

They drew to a halt in front of the cottage. It looked exactly as
she had imagined it: spooky, the darkness of its dilapidated porch
utterly terrifying. She wanted to hide her face on her father's shoulder,
cling to him; Uncle Peleg stretched out his hand to help her down
and she saw no way of extricating herself from the consequences of
her folly. When she had spoken to all those men in the Meeting House,
she had succeeded because she had felt as if she had the power to
move mountains; as she stepped down into the sand in front of Caleb
Martin's cottage, she had no power, not a shred. Beset by nervous
hiccoughs, she advanced toward the steps of the porch. She climbed
the steps like a sleepwalker, crossed the shadow line that separated
the translucent darkness of the night and the blackness of the veranda.
She tried to whisper a prayer, but her lips were so dry that they stuck
together. She closed her eyes, held her breath and knocked on the door.

The sound she made was louder than she had expected. It seemed
to reverberate as in a cavern. She was overcome by the urge to turn
and flee when she heard the buggy draw away between the houses,
into the night. She wanted to call out to them to wait for her, but could
not utter a sound. She stood petrified, sick with fear, listening for the
steps to come toward her, for the door to open.

But nothing happened. The sound of the buggy drew away, leaving
only the eerie, furtive lisping of the wind in the tree overhead. No
sound came from the cottage, no floorboard creaked; suddenly it
occurred to her that he might have left. Of course! He was not there;
she had worried for nothing. Emboldened, she knocked again, more
forcefully this time. The sound reverberated in the empty cottage.
She was about to turn away when a voice asked, "Who's there?"

She froze; but a remnant of courage enabled her to answer, "It is I,
Caleb. Becky Baker." She sounded surprisingly calm and controlled.

The voice behind the door asked, "Rebekah?"

"Yes, Caleb, it is I. May I come in?" Her own composure amazed
her; then she realized why she suddenly felt sure of herself: he had
sounded like a frightened boy.

He took a long time to answer; but she no longer felt as if the
world were holding its breath. The wind lisped in the leaves, somewhere an owl hooted; night sounds, normal night sounds. "Is thee
alone?" the voice asked.

"Yes, Caleb, I'm alone." Her fears had been unfounded. She was strong, she was calm, she knew how to handle him; the voice was that of someone who needed help. "Well? Is thee going to open up?" She asked it almost playfully.

Then the door slowly creaked open. Behind it was darkness. He must have been sitting there without a light. A recurrence of fear gripped her when the voice urged her in a whisper. "Come in! Quick! Quick!"

She stepped inside without thinking; it gave her a shiver when she felt him brush past her in the darkness and heard the bolt of the door shoot home. She thought idiotically, 'Locked up with a murderer.' What nonsense! He was not a real murderer, he needed help. But in the pitch darkness, with his invisible, stealthily moving presence seemingly all around her, she was becoming afraid again. "What about a candle, Caleb?" she asked, hoping he would not hear the tremor in her voice.

She felt him standing still. For a moment he seemed to be fixed somewhere in indecision. Then she heard a floorboard creak; a tinderbox was opened, a match scraped; surprisingly, the little flame sprang up behind her. She whirled around. He stood at the table, the flame in his cupped hands. He looked disheveled, swarthy, wearing only his breeches and the harness. She had never seen the harness before, only heard its surreptitious creaking during meeting. He lit the candle; when he looked at her, his eyes were wide with fear. His terror was so tangible that self-assurance returned to her, motherly firmness. "Good evening, Caleb," she said calmly.

"Good evening." His voice was hushed; he glanced at the door as if afraid of being overheard. Yet she had seen no one out there, heard no sound except the leaves, the cry of the owl. There was no one out there except the two old men in the buggy, waiting apprehensively in the darkness; the slaves must have barricaded themselves in their hutches, at least as frightened as he appeared to be.

"Caleb, I have come to ask thee to return with me to spend the night with us, thy friends and thy family, so we may decide together what to do?"

"Do?" She saw a wondering look in those haunted eyes. Maybe it was the candle flame, jerkily growing brighter.

"Yes, Caleb. Thee is our friend, our relative; we do not doubt that thee was provoked into violence. I am sure that the judge will accept that too. So, come with me; we will have meeting before going to bed and maybe a glass of toddy."

His eyes were odd. He looked as if he had not been listening to what she was saying at all. "Thank thee, Rebekah," he said. "But I'm afraid it is not as simple as that."

Without stopping to think, she blurted out, "Is it the fact that thee is"—she almost said 'half Negro,' but checked herself in the nick of time—"Mammy's son?"

The words seemed to strike him with a frightening impact. His face was contorted in a spasm of pain, his haunted eyes seemed to search hers, then something strange happened: he seemed to shed his fear.

He changed, in front of her very eyes, from a frightened boy into a self-assured man.

"Rebekah," he said quietly, "I am not sure I can face that."

"What, Caleb?"

"The truth."

She wanted to say something reassuring, understanding, but the eerie stare of those black, haunted eyes seemed to paralyze her, all she could do was shake her head.

"It is not that I suddenly feel different from you all, it is things I have done, thought. All my life I have thought of niggers as being not human, something between cattle and man. I could never have taken on this job if that had not been my conviction. Does thee understand? To me, nigger wenches were heifers that had to be bred when in season; I arranged for a buck to be brought to the island to breed one of them, without feeling shame."

His quiet, undramatic manner gave his words a strange intensity. She found she could not react with traditional Quaker phrases. "I understand, Caleb," she said. "But I assure thee that to us thee is no different today from what thee was yesterday."

He smiled, a curious smile of melancholy resignation. "I wish I could believe thee, Becky. But thee is young, innocent, pure. Life has not yet touched thee, and I am proud to think that I have helped make it so."

She did not understand what he was talking about, but something about him impressed her deeply. Thus far, he had been a vaguely depressing presence which intruded upon the gaiety of the family like a piece of darkness, a somber emissary from the world of the slaves. She had never thought of him detached from that brooding mass of Negroes whose dark-lidded looks seemed at times like those of caged animals. Now she became aware of him as a man, lonely, tormented, but undefeated. She did not know from what unearned insight, what unlived experience the knowledge came to her, but as she stood there she suddenly knew that she would never be able to induce him to follow her with words, not even if she were in the power of the Lord. The only way she could persuade him was by an act, a kiss.

The notion was so wild, so totally unexpected, that eighteen years of Quaker education recoiled within her. With an unnerving sense of revelation she realized that she was becoming aware of his masculinity, her own femininity. A bewildering temptation came over her; for a few moments all that was elemental and feminine within her reached out to him, with utter disregard for that of God in either of them. She felt the urge to throw her arms around his neck, draw his tormented face down toward her, drown his fears in a kiss, a kiss of life. But she was brought up short by the thought: 'The consequences!' If she surrendered to him, she would have to marry him, have children by him, nigger children . . .

As those last two words, despicable but utterly involuntary, flitted through her mind, he seemed to see them. His eyes that had searched hers with a growing hope darkened until she was faced once more by the gaunt, tragic mask that had stared at her before. She wanted to comfort him, shield him from the darkness into which he had stepped back, but it was no longer the sensuous woman inside her who had for a few breathless moments taken over her will, her destiny; what reached out to him now was all that was good and noble and kind and loving in her, that of God. With all the love of the Lord she could muster, she said, "Please, Caleb, please come with me! Please come and stay with us tonight!"

He smiled that melancholy smile again. "Thank thee, Rebekah, but I'm all right here. Don't worry about me."

"Then promise me that thou wilt go and see the judge and accept a trial!"

"I will," he said, but something in the way he said it filled her with foreboding.

"Promise?" she repeated feebly, despising her own coy, virginal ways. Oh! If only she had had the strength, the real, warm-blooded—no! It could not be. Anyhow, it was too late now. The moment had passed.

"I promise."

"Promise: 'I will stand trial and accept the verdict.' Promise."

"I will stand trial and accept the verdict."

She searched his eyes, knowing he was eluding her; she was about to press him further when she was overcome by a sense of shame. Who was she to demand of this tormented man that he promise her anything? She turned toward the door; he startled her by brushing past her to open it for her. He seemed no longer afraid of whatever he thought lay waiting for him out there in the night.

As she stood on the threshold, it seemed to her that everything remained unsaid. She thought of touching his cheek with her lips in a chaste little kiss, but whispered, "Good night, Caleb . . . God bless thee" and fled. She heard him close the door behind her.

She stood still for a moment to allow her eyes to become adjusted to the dark, her heart pounding; then she gathered her skirts around her and ran as fast as she could toward the buggy with the two old men waiting for her.

*   *   *

After Caleb Martin had closed the door behind her, he had a fleeting sense of achievement. There had been a moment during her visit when he had felt he could hold out no longer, but he had been able to keep the dream inviolate; she had come and gone, her kindness rewarded, her courage blessed, her innocence intact. She had faced him, during those dreamlike minutes of her visit, as purity incarnate; he had allowed her to leave despite his desperate yearning to take her in his arms, to seek shelter in her virginal innocence from the demons about to devour him. The moment she was gone, the powers of darkness rushed back into the void.

The horror was all around him. He felt he could touch it: something living, palpable. But there were only shadows in the room, dancing with the candle flame. Did that sense of approaching damnation come from within? He did not know and he did not care. Yet maybe his only hope to survive was to care; only: survive for what? What was he? White man or Negro? All his life he had lived a lie, a man without a real identity, without a soul. For if Negroes did not possess a soul, why should he? The notion "soul" was intertwined in his mind with masculinity. The ultimate despair he faced was that as a half-breed he carried no seed of life within him—that, like the mule, he was a sexless freak.

He broke his firm decision not to drink until he knew what to do, what to be. He found the bottle under the palliasse of his bunk and took a long, greedy draft, head back, his shadow, broken at the hips, twitching on the bed and the wall with the dancing of the candle flame. But when he came up for breath and wiped his mouth with the back of his hand, he knew that it would be to no avail. His body would end up groggy with the effects of the rum, not his awareness. If Negroes had souls, he had abused them beyond hope for salvation; if they had not, it made him a nobody. The whites would never consider him one of theirs again, he had seen that in the eyes of the innocent girl who had not even been aware of it herself. He would be an outcast from the family to whom he had belonged, were it only as an emissary from the world of the slaves. And the Negroes he had abased all his life would certainly not accept him, all they had for him was hatred. Suddenly he wished, fervently, that one of their wenches, a soulless nigger wench, would look at him with lust, desire him as a buck; she need not be young or comely, just a female, conscious of his maleness.

He flung the bottle from him; it hit the wall, thudded to the floor, rolled and fell still. He went to the table, pulled up a chair with his foot; the noise grated on his nerves. He slumped, his elbows on the table. Jesus, have mercy! Mercy on whom? If he was a neuter, there was nothing to receive the precious grace, no soul, nothing but a void. Caleb. Belac. Belac Nitram. What did it matter? His name no longer meant anything either way. He was getting drunk.

Spirals of giddiness began to cloud his brain. He cried aloud, "Nigger, white man, I don't care! But *something!* God, dear God, let me be *something!*" Then something thudded on the floor. He looked up; the door was closed. The windows were closed. There was nothing, nobody, there could not be. He was drunk. Then he saw it. On the floor, a few feet away, lay a gray snake. He shook his head; the fog of inebriation cleared for a moment. It was not a snake, it was a rope. As he sat staring at it, mouth open, a throbbing started outside in the night; the rhythmic throbbing of a drum. The drunkenness dissipated. Unemotionally, he thought: 'They are not going to wait until full moon.' Then the thought hit him: 'To them I am a nigger! Whatever I may think I am, *to them I am a nigger!*' He felt a crazy elation. He belonged to them. He belonged! He was somebody! His prayer had been answered. But his ecstasy was short-lived, for with desperate urgency his will to live brought home to him that his life was in danger; the rope was meant for him.

He pushed himself away from the table to get his rifle. As he stumbled to his feet, his legs seemed to be filled with wet sand; he could not lift them. He realized with alarm that he was giggling.

This would not do! He must get rid of the liquor. He tore himself free of the table, staggered to the door, ripped it open, stumbled groggily onto the veranda, grabbed hold of one of the posts for support; clutching it, he heaved; but nothing happened. He bent over and stuck his finger down his throat; his stomach responded at last and regurgitated some sour liquid that burned in his nose. He continued until the last drop of alcohol and bile had been wrung out of his heaving, wretched body; when at last he straightened up and took a deep breath of the cool night air, he felt weak and sick; but his body, though shivering uncontrollably, obeyed his will once more. He opened his eyes, about to head back for the door; then he saw her.

She stood in the middle of the road, quite still, arms dangling by her sides. Although he could not see her clearly, he knew she was a woman, he knew she was black. Her face was painted white, so were her arms and her legs, thin and fragile like a bird's. Was she meant to be a bird? Then she began to move. With slow, rhythmic movements she came toward him as in a dance, high-stepping, like a heron. She approached until he could see the outline of her black body in the starlight, and he realized that it was not a bird she represented, but a skeleton. Facing him in the night, swaying slowly to the rhythm of the drums, stood Death.

He broke away from the spell, stumbled back into his room, slammed the door and leaned against it, panting. The drums throbbed louder; it seemed they were conveying a message, a word. He listened, holding his breath, trying to comprehend what the drums were saying; then he felt a knock on the door behind him. In panic he stumbled toward the back of the room, the cupboard where the gun was, realizing too late that he should have bolted the door. He tore open the cupboard, groped among clothes, bottles; a shoe fell, candlelight sparkled on a buckle: his First Day shoes, the ones he wore to meeting. The thought of meeting broke his resolve to find the gun. With a sense of resignation, he turned to face as a Quaker that of God in the woman behind that ghoulish mask of death.

In front of him, smiling, her eyes full of impersonal tranquillity, stood Cleo. She was naked; the skeleton painted on her skin could not hide the beauty of her body. He had never dreamed the moment would come when he would see beauty or seductiveness in a Negro wench; now there stood before him the most beautiful, desirable woman he had ever seen. Her teeth as she smiled were dazzling, her breasts as she slowly lifted her arms rose to immaculate beauty; her hands, with infinite grace, held out the rope. He thought she wanted him to take it from her; then slowly she put her arms around his

neck; something soft stroked the back of it; the outstretched arms drew
away from him, dragging the rope across the back of his neck until
it fell and dangled, a living snake, in her hand once more.

He knew a moment of cold, chilling awareness; he realized that a
spell was being thrown over him, that she herself was in a trance. His
only hope was to shake her awake, to answer that of God in her,
appeal to the real, unique, irreplaceable Cleo who had never been on
earth before and would never be again. "Cleo!" he cried. "Wake up!
Cleo, it is I, Caleb! Look at me!" She smiled, unawakened, and
advanced on him again, slowly, hands outstretched. Again she put her
arms around his neck, but instead of drawing the rope across the back
of it, her nimble fingers fumbled with the clasp of his harness. She
stepped back, arms outstretched, rope dangling, receding slowly, as if to
guide him.

"Cleo, wake up!" he cried; but his body no longer belonged to him.
He shook off the harness; the drums pounded in jubilation. He took
off his stockings, his breeches, until he stood naked.

Smiling, sleepy-lidded, she began to rock to and fro with sensuous
movements, thrusting her pelvis toward him with the rhythm of the
drums. But when he stretched out his hands toward her, she stepped
back as in a dance, taunting him to follow her.

He was not aware of leaving the cottage, the veranda, the shadow
of the chestnut trees. Thrusting and withdrawing his pelvis in response
to the slow, sensuous undulations of her body, he danced slowly down
the road, toward the dark banks of indigo shimmering in the starlight.

On and on they danced, thrusting to the throbbing of the drums,
a naked man and a skeleton, with dangling between them a white
rope.

*   *   *

Stunned by Harry's death, Josh Baker had roamed around all day,
dreaming of revenge; even after going to bed, he could not sleep but
lay daydreaming about strangling Caleb, torturing him to avenge the
murder of his friend. George McHair, who shared his bed, lay snoring
happily when, between his wheezing and snarling, Josh caught the
sound of distant drums. He slipped out of bed and onto the balcony
to listen.

The rhythmic pounding of the drums seemed to draw slowly closer;
as his eyes became used to the darkness, he discerned figures in the
starlight, indistinct and unreal, a host of dancing shadows on the lawn.
Prancing, twirling, they made their way toward the house; among them,
dancing backward, luring a pale body toward the house, was a
phosphorescent skeleton. Not until they were right underneath the
balcony did Josh recognize Caleb; then the skeleton began to climb
the chestnut tree, a white rope in its hand.

Josh tore himself free of the spell and ran back into his room. For a
moment it seemed he had dreamed it all; George snored placidly
in the silence. Then there was an ominous rustling in the tree outside

the window; in childish terror Josh tore open the door to the wardrobe and hid inside. He worked his way frantically toward the back, through hanging clothes, lined-up boots, toys stored and forgotten, the smells of childhood. The far end of the wardrobe was silent, safe. It seemed as if even the news of Harry's death had not penetrated into this secret corner yet. Then he heard, even in this safest of all places, a high, blood-curdling scream.

He covered his ears with his hands and sank to his knees, praying.

* * *

Abby, awakened by a scream, ran outside and found Becky, in her nightgown, lying in a faint on the balcony; above her, gruesome and grotesquely alive, the naked body of a man hung swinging from a rope, legs kicking, hands clawing at his throat; at the sight of him, she screamed too. As she stood there, hands on her mouth, eyes wide with terror, watching speechlessly the dying contortions of the hanged man, someone came running toward her, put his arms around her shoulders, turned her away. She looked up and recognized George.

She tore herself free and fled back into her room. There she threw herself on the bed, screaming into her pillow, waiting for her mother to come, as always if she screamed loud enough. But no one came. She heard running steps outside, voices, shouts, a thud, the sound of something heavy being dragged across the floorboards. A glass door banged in the distance; it became still.

She lay there for a long time, listening; at last she dared lift her face and look at the doors to the balcony, which were open. She was more afraid than she had ever been, but something drew her toward those doors, a compulsion stronger than fear.

She was standing in the doorway to the balcony, staring at the empty tree, when someone touched her arm. She stifled a cry, a voice whispered, "Hush! It's me—Josh . . . What happened?"

To see him there unhinged her. "Oh, Josh!" she cried. "Caleb Martin has hanged himself!" Wild sobs began to shake her; she fell against him; he half carried her back into her room and helped her onto the bed. There she slumped against him, howling, hiding her face on his chest.

He stroked her hair, saying, "Don't cry, Abby, don't cry, it's nothing, it's all right, everything's all right, I'm here, I'm with thee."

His strength and his love were so comforting that her sobbing abated.

* * *

Toward morning Boniface Baker was overcome by weariness. Ever since it happened he had been calm, firm, lucid—the chaos into which his family was plunged after Caleb's suicide had left him no choice. With the aid of George he had cut the body down; after trying in vain to revive it, they had laid Caleb out in Grandmother's room,

which had never been used since her death. Peleg helped them clothe
the body; after that they sat down in silent meeting at the bedside,
joined by George, Becky, Beulah and eventually Joshua. Now only
Peleg was left to wake by the body of his son; he would leave for
Philadelphia at dawn to tell Hannah and bring her back for the funeral.
It was decided that the boy Harry would be buried next to him in the
graveyard by the river.

Exhausted, Boniface dragged himself to his study to catch a few hours
of sleep. He slumped in his chair, head back, eyes closed, feeling as
if he were being rocked by a ship at sea. He felt slightly sick; probably
exhaustion, or the delayed shock of finding that ghastly body with
its bulging eyes, poor unconscious Becky, Abby sobbing on George
McHair's shoulder.

He must put it out of his mind; he picked up his grandmother's
diaries and opened one of them.

*"So I said to the jailer, 'Please, Friend, look at her! She is sick, her
mind is wandering, we must do something to ease her suffering! Why
not give her a blanket? Why treat her worse than thou wouldst a
suffering dog?' But his heart was hardened by hatred provoked by the
Puritan minister who called us 'antichrists,' 'putrid seed of the devil,'
'whores of Babylon.' He spat at me through the bars, said viciously,
'I hope she rots in hell and thou too, blasphemous whore, and the
whelp of the devil in thy belly!' and went away. He took the lantern
with him.*

*"I could hear Mistress Best moaning in the darkness; the straw
rustled as she stirred. To my shame, I was beyond caring. I had en-
dured too much. I was sick and cold and losing blood; this I had done
ever since arriving in Boston. I crawled to a corner of our cell and
sat there, my hands over my ears, trying to shut out her whimpering,
trying to think only of how to survive this numbing cold. There came
a moment of utter despair when I contemplated taking off her clothes
the moment she died, if only she would, to cover myself with them
and burying myself in the straw, pressing her little boy against me,
not to protect him but to rob him of his warmth. I was an animal
fighting for its life, pregnant with the cursed fruit of rape, starved
into madness, dying with cold. I was steeped in the darkest, blackest
bestiality that had ever overwhelmed my soul. I hated her, I hated
her bloody foundling, I hated the ravenous little bastard stirring in
my womb, eating my sustenance away, but most of all I hated myself. As I sat there, my head on my knees, locked in hatred and bitterness, I knew that it was only a matter of time before I would die in this
freezing cage, just as the old woman in the darkness was dying:
hallucinating, whimpering gibberish, thrashing in the straw. I knew
at that moment that there was no real love, real faith within me. I had
been lured astray by a concept of myself that had taken my fancy:
the self-sacrificing, saintly maiden radiating a constant awareness of the
presence of God. It had been a delusion; I was nothing of the kind.
But it was too late now; I should have had the courage to face myself*

earlier, at the beginning, when I took it upon myself to replace Margaret Fell in the dungeons of Lancaster Castle.

"What a greedy, selfish bitch I had been, even then! Dazzled by her saintliness, I had wanted to be a saint too, attain that human greatness myself, get my hands on that blinding, awe-inspiring radiance as if it were some jewel, a trinket sparkling in the candlelight. I was attracted because of greed, not selflessness. Now here I was, with child by a brute whose face I had never seen, in a dungeon in Boston, Massachusetts, freezing to death, with a poor deluded wretch thrashing her last close by in the darkness. And all St. Ann could think about was how she would strip off the woman's clothes before she turned cold, how she would grab the child to kindle the dying ember of her life with his warmth. As I sat there facing the truth at last in the frozen darkness of hell itself, a hand tugged my skirt and a frightened little voice whispered, 'Ann? Ann? Please come, I think Mama is— I think she needs thee . . .'

"Even today, all these years later, I know what I thought at that moment. My first impulse was to push him away. Then I thought: 'If I do that, I'll frighten him and he may not want to come to me once the old woman is dead.' So I crawled toward the corner where I could hear her whimpering and talking gibberish in a high, crazy voice. She must have been pitiful, but there was no pity left in me. Henrietta Best was dying in terror and agony, as senselessly as a dog twitching on its back in its final throes, just before its consciousness is blotted out and it turns to nothing. That was, I knew, what she was muttering and whimpering about: the realization of her nothingness, her self-delusion of being unique, irreplaceable, an eternal soul in ephemeral flesh. Compared to Bonny's death in that other dungeon, hers seemed a mockery, a pointless cruelty, an utter waste. Yet, even as I groped in the straw reluctantly for her hands, I realized that it was better than the sweet, pretty passion play of Bonny dying, surrounded by adoring admirers imbuing him with their own dreams and delusions. At that time I still lived under the illusion that I was a self-sacrificing, saintly maiden who had joined her young lover in prison so as not to let him go alone; here, in the darkness, at the moment of extinction, I saw the truth that I had suspected before at odd, frightening moments. Our birth an accident, our life a brief succession of delusions and illusions, our death as meaningless as that of a rabbit or a star. I have never been able to shake that conviction.

"Maybe it is the secret of my ultimate ineffectualness that at the core of my being there is the knowledge, the immutable conviction, that we are nothing. But as I sat there, that terrified hand in mine, listening to that wandering voice gibbering in the terror of death, I realized that unless I could grab hold of some hope, some belief, true or false, I would quite literally lose my mind. I could face the ultimate truth only for a few seconds; even I, indestructible in my self-centeredness, could not survive in the vacuum of nothingness. I had to find something I could hold on to, some delusion that would give me the notion that there was some sense in my fighting to survive other

than the animal urge that made the little monster in my womb grow
and flex its muscles and buck its knees, driven toward its tormented
half minute of consciousness called life. Had I been a Muslim or a
Buddhist, I would have grabbed hold of some other notion. But as the
accident of my birth had placed me in England, where a delusion held
sway called Quakerism, all I could grab hold of in that slide toward
insanity were the words 'All He has is thee.'

Why these particular words? I do not know. I felt at that moment
no tenderness or compassion toward either the old woman or her
dwarf. But there I was, thinking: 'All God has to reach her with
His love is me.' So I stroked the old woman's hand and felt it relax
in mine. 'Well,' I thought, 'one on the books for God. Now let's be
kind to the little runt. And let's pretend to love even whatever it
may be that will eventually emerge from my womb, man or reptile.'

"Henrietta Best died that night. I covered her body with straw and
gathered the shivering child to my breast, not to rob him of his
warmth but to share my own. I was overwhelmed by the motherly
urge to whisper to him, in the darkness, soothing things, as to a baby,
until he burst into tears and clung to me desperately. Before I knew
what had happened, he had become my son, for he was a frightened
child who had no one else in the world except me. It was as if by
my acceptance of him I became the mother of my own child as well.
I no longer thought of the little creature in my womb as the evil
seed of the brute who had mounted me on that heaving deck like a
billy-goat, but as another helpless orphan who, once he emerged into
the world, would have no one but me.

"That was all there was to it. Stripped of unctuous phrases, all that
happened to me in the night Henrietta Best died was that I accepted
motherhood.

"Henrietta's body was dragged away the next morning by two
turnkeys as if she were a dead cow. I held the little boy and sheltered
his head against me as they grabbed her by the ankles; her skirts
came up over her head, and her stiff, wooden arms, spread out as
she was dragged along, became hung up in the doorway. They pulled
her through with a brute force that must have broken something;
I stroked the child's hair and murmured endearments to keep him
from remembering his mother being broken as she was dragged away
to the dungheap. If ever there seemed to be a pointless death, it was
Henrietta Best's. I am in no position to gainsay this. But one thing is
irrefutable: the death of her children and her rape by the soldiers of
the Cardinal were given some sense when I collapsed in her arms in
the hold of that ship and breathed to her in horror that I had been
raped. She could say to me, 'Hush, it happened to me too.' And those
words saved my life and my reason. What resurrected me were
her love and her understanding, which, clearly, were the fruit of her
own suffering; she could identify with me without pious pretense.
When she consoled me and took me in her arms, I experienced the
presence of God. So I found out that, indeed, God needs us as much
as we need Him. For it is only in our acts that He can fully express

Himself. In one thing Margaret Fell was incontestably right: miracles are immaterial. Man, in his ultimate despair, is not helped by an omnipotence who, like a magician in a cosmic circus, suspends the laws of nature. If God is anything at all, He is what St. John said He was, what George Fox said He was and what Margaret Fell, bless her soul, showed He was: love. All other definitions are efforts on our part to evade the demands of that final realization.

"I have not been able to live up to that realization. The moment I realized that slavery was evil, yet continued to keep slaves, I turned my back on the infinite ocean of light and love. How insidiously it crept upon me! First, I gave shelter to a poor black woman, abused by a white man, and her half-breed child; then I found how useful she was in the kitchen; then a black couple was offered to me who would otherwise have been sold at auction and found themselves at the mercy of a harsh master; before I knew it, I was keeping slaves with the notion that I was doing them a favor. The plantation prospered, I needed more and more money—not for myself, oh, no: always for others; and now I find myself with a stable full of black beasts of burden, whom I abuse, lovingly, and who—I am sure—consider themselves fortunate. Yet, whenever I face God in meeting, I know that this is an abomination in His eyes. I know, because He manifests himself in those rare moments through an emissary: Margaret Fell. When I think of her, see her eyes gaze upon me, I know: only after the last slave has been set free, and care has been taken that he will remain free, will I be able to take up life again at the point where I cut it off, for myself and mine, when I did that unforgivable deed. There are certain things that are totally evil, with which a compromise, however enlightened or reasonable or loving, is impossible. Slavery is one of them."

Boniface Baker closed the book, put it on his desk and went to his grandmother's room. He touched Peleg's arm and took his place beside the bed. Caleb's face was blue in the dawn, the eyes partially covered by the lids, the hands folded. If ever there had been two meaningless deaths, they were Caleb's and Harry's. He wanted to pray, 'Deliver them from absurdity,' but he was overcome by a sense of fatuousness. If anything had become clear from his grandmother's self-revelation, it was that to deliver a neighbor's life or death from absurdity was something you did yourself; it could not be left, unctuously, to God. Was he prepared to do so? No, he was not. But the least he could do was to be as honest about it as his grandmother had been.

He would not bury Harry among his family, after all. It was hypocrisy to bury a child among people with whom he had not been allowed to live.

* * *

Joshua entered the slave hospital stealthily, ready to sneak out again. There was no one in the dark ward except the body stretched out as if asleep on one of the cots, underneath a window.

A patch of sunlight lay across the bed, making the sheet whiter and the arms resting on it blacker. Joshua took off his hat and approached the bed on tiptoe. The illusion that Harry lay asleep or unconscious vanished when he stood by the bedside and looked down on the corpse. The black wooden doll, a faint smirk frozen on its face, had nothing to do with the eager, mischievous boy he had known. Harry was dead.

He stood staring at the body for a long time. A horsefly, flashing in the sunlight, bounced against a windowpane, buzzing. Memories of kisses, intimacies, words—he heard Harry's desperate voice again during their last meeting in the tree. He was overcome by the urge to kiss the black hand that had caressed him so often, throw himself across the body that had once been so warm and alive, trembling with passion, tender and comforting. He had known that body better than his own.

He should not weep now, for outside were the slaves whose overseer he had become. He hurried out, walked to the cottage as fast as he could, ignoring the slaves. He slammed the door shut behind him and stood panting in the twilight of the closed shutters, then he went to the cupboard where Caleb kept his rum. He felt around inside, found a buckled shoe; the feeling of Caleb being there became almost a reality when, as he walked back to the table, his foot kicked the harness, the shell of the crab. It was more evocative of Caleb's presence than his body had been on Great-grandmother's bed.

As Joshua stood there, at a loss, a shadow passed across the shutters. The door slowly opened. It was Cleo. Seeing her slip furtively inside seemed to unite them for a moment in a memory of the childhood they had shared; it was as if Harry had come in with her. Had he?

She came toward him; the sense of Harry's presence became stronger. She stood close to him and looked into his eyes. He searched hers, but saw only golden flecks. Then she raised her arms and pulled him toward her for a kiss.

For one eerie moment it seemed as if she were Harry, as if it were the dead boy's last, desperate farewell. Then he began to respond to her kiss. Fear and sorrow, shame and sadness, loneliness, childhood, all were swept away by an onrush of desire. They sank to the ground where they were standing, eyes closed, without breaking their embrace, until he lost his balance. They fell to the floor together; from that moment on, Cleo took the lead. She changed into the panther that had pounced on him from the night. Never before had they made love with such wild, insane abandon. As he cried out in the agony of fulfillment, she suddenly pushed herself away from him and stood above him, astride his body, staring at the door. "Cleo?" he asked.

She did not answer. He thought he saw the door close, but he was not sure. He scrambled to his feet, pulled on his breeches and stumbled out onto the porch to see who it had been. The road was empty. As he turned around to go back into the room, it penetrated to him: the road was empty, not a slave in sight. There could be only one explanation: Massa had been here. Cleo had seen his father.

He hurried back into the room, and found it empty too.

* * *

Boniface Baker raced back to the house in the bouncing buggy, lashing the horse to an ever faster pace. His mind was in a turmoil; all he could feel was outrage, fury. His first coherent thought was: 'Sell her. There is no other solution, sell the devious black whore! For God's sake, what can I do to protect him?' Only as he approached the house did he remember he had gone to the quarters in order to arrange for a meeting for burial. He would have to do it; but he could not face anyone yet.

He jerked the reins, swerved onto the track through the fields that led to the dock, tethered the horse and took the rowboat out onto the river. As he rowed away from the dock, a gray heron, flushed by the splashing of the oars, rose from the reeds and winged away, croaking angrily, into the mist that surrounded the island. He rowed slowly into the secret world of the fog; it smoothed out the turmoil within him. He let the boat drift. Water dripped from the oars onto the still surface. When the last drops had fallen, the turbulence within him had turned into stillness.

Joshua, little Joshua, his white, childish legs clutched in the vise of the black legs of a slave . . . Sell her! Sell her! But in the stillness he realized that it would not pull out the root of the evil. He might be able to convince himself for a while that by selling her he had saved Joshua from an addiction to Negro wenches, but he would merely have taken away one wench. After a while the boy would, inevitably, start looking for another. The only thing that would cure him was the insight that to abuse a black woman for his own bodily gratification was a sin against humanity, against goodness, compassion, tenderness, love, against God. Becky had said it with shocking bluntness in front of the Men's Meeting: the only thing that could convince was example, not words. If he wanted to save Joshua, not merely bring about a postponement of the boy's damnation, then he must show by his conduct that he held slavery to be totally evil. By granting his slaves their freedom he would also give meaning to the deaths of Harry and Caleb. It would give a sense to all the pointless deaths that had gone before, far into the past, as far as the dungeon in Lancaster Castle where Bonny Baker, stableboy of Swarthmoor Hall, had died. His grandmother's ravishment, the death of Henrietta Best and that of her children in that village in France—all those apparently senseless caprices of fate would achieve an ultimate purpose: the liberation of the slaves of Eden Island.

But what would be the practical consequences? He had shouted them at the man on the rostrum with his colorless hat. To set the slaves free without giving them land would mean to abandon them to the first rapacious owner who could lay his hands on them. But if he parceled out his land among them, he would have no choice but to homestead a new farm somewhere beyond the mountains, where there was land for the taking, for he would have no capital left with which to buy a farm or arable land near Philadelphia. He was a farmer, it was all he knew. But he was a farmer in a slaveholding world; how would he fare in the wilderness, without blackamoors to do the work for him? A spoiled, fat man who had never held a spade, with a deaf wife and two pampered daughters who had never touched a broom or baked a loaf, let alone attended the birth of a calf? It was all very well to decide that God had communicated His wishes to him; it would be pointless to set about obeying those wishes without the proper means to do so. He was a member of the Society of Friends, not of some emotional evangelical sect. He could not undertake this in the reckless assumption that the Lord would provide. It might be God's will, he was not going to move until God had provided him with the means to do so responsibly. He would wait until way opened.

He sat waiting in expectant silence for an answer, some intimation of a better solution. When no answer came, he rowed back to the island.

As he was tying up the boat, the solution came to him. He would send Josh on a tour of the world with one of the Woodhouse ships, and get himself another overseer.

He went to arrange meeting for burial.

CHAPTER EIGHT

DURING meeting for burial at the graveyard, Beulah Baker sat with her family and Caleb's relatives, facing the slaves. How recently, it seemed, she had sat there to bury Cuffee the slave! Now there were two coffins on trestles between them and the slaves, a large mass of squatting black figures in the sun. The family on the facing bench was protected from the heat of the summer noon by the shade of the chestnut tree.

As usual during meeting for worship, Beulah's mind was a babbling blank. She hoped there would not be ministry; she would be unable to hear a word. Her deafness was fast becoming worse; perhaps she should think about an ear-trumpet. A few more years and she would be as deaf as a post, and a virtual half-wit to boot, as she would have lost all touch with life around her. For the moment, to be freed of the constant clamor of her self-centered family, lazy servants and useless pets was a relief. She had no inner life worth speaking of; after a day's work in the household she was too tired to meditate on anything more ennobling than past birthdays or counting sheep while the intellectual fireworks of her family crackled around her; but there was about the semi-silence in which she now lived a certain harmony, peace. Ever since they uttered their first yells the children had conversed only at the tops of their voices, banged doors, kicked furniture in imperious exasperation. It had not bothered Bonny much, nothing seemed to be able to ruffle his complacency, but she had suffered over the years, were it only from the continuous headaches the aggressive racket of family life had given her. She wondered occasionally how she had managed to bear it all; probably because after the old woman's death everything had seemed benign in comparison . . .

Beulah's meandering thoughts were interrupted by a movement beside her. She opened her eyes to find Hannah Martin risen to her feet, clutching her black reticule, her eyes staring fixedly at the coffins, speaking. Or was she singing? Occasionally some Friend, in a moment of ill-advised abandon, would burst into a hymn during meeting for worship; it never failed to embarrass everybody. Yes, Hannah Martin was singing. In her case, it was rather touching.

Then Beulah saw, with a tightening of her stomach, that Bonny, sitting at the other end of the half circle of white mourners, was staring at the old woman with eyes wide with horror. It seemed as if her singing had conjured up for him some awful image. Suddenly Beulah was overcome by the same sense of impending calamity she had felt on the morning of the day when Cuffee the slave was killed. Here it was again, stronger than before: a darkness approaching, tragedy, disaster.

She saw her husband looking at the slaves as if he were trying to locate someone; then he closed his eyes with unutterable weariness, as if about to collapse in a faint. But he rose to his feet, lifted his face to the sky and began to speak. His face was so sad, so tragic, that her heart went out to him without her having an inkling of what he was saying. Then she became aware of a growing tension around her, not only among the white mourners but also among the slaves, who normally never listened to a word. All of a sudden they sat staring at her husband, mouths open, motionless, in a silence of which even she, despite her deafness, became aware. What was Bonny saying?

She tried desperately to read his lips, but could not make out a single word. She looked at other members of the family; they all sat blank-faced, stunned by his words. Then a hand clasped hers, hard. It was her brother; whatever Bonny was saying had upset him terribly. He saw her mute plea for understanding; undecorously, considering the occasion, he put an arm around her shoulders and pressed her against him in a gesture of protection. She was certain now, disaster had struck. But what? She went on scanning the faces of her children for some hint, but they just sat there, thunderstruck.

Finally, one of them stirred. Becky's face started to beam with joy, or delight, or pride, or . . . Dear God, which? What was Bonny saying?

Bonny sat down, his face pasty white. She could not contain herself and whispered to her brother, "What did he say?! Please, Jerry, what did he say?"

Jeremiah said in her ear, "He has given the slaves their freedom! He said he will share out the land among them!"

She stared at him, horrified; he pressed her against him and said, "Don't worry, I'll talk to him, don't worry . . ."

But he had misunderstood the look on her face. He could not know how many times the old woman had said to her, "If I were worthy of the name Quaker, I would give the slaves their freedom and share out the land among them." She could hear the cantankerous voice now, as clearly as if the old woman were actually there, in the midst of them. Then she saw her oldest child staring at her father with ecstatic admiration, tears rolling down her cheeks, and she was suddenly struck by an awful faintness, as if the old woman had come back to claim him.

*   *   *

All Jeremiah Best could feel, as he sat there sheltering the frail body of his sister, was shock and anger. Of all the irresponsible, harebrained, things to do! What about the man's family, his wife?

Rarely had he felt so protective toward Beulah; he would call the madman to task as soon as possible, but first he must look after his sister, assure her that she could under all circumstances count on him, more solidly than on her husband.

For once his wife Grizzle helped him. He had always known that she was a warm and generous woman at heart; after meeting broke, she urged him to leave Beulah to her. Beulah agreed, weakly, to go with her, and Grizzle led her, her arm around her shoulders, to the buggy waiting to take them back to the house, where a funeral banquet was to be served for the relatives. The Negroes still sat motionless in mute disbelief; although he had always felt a certain pity for them, this time the sight of those bovine black faces infuriated Jeremiah. But he told himself that he should not take out on those poor creatures the anger and indignation his crazy brother-in-law had aroused in him. Ignoring the family, several of whom tried to drag him into a conversation about the baffling development of that morning, he climbed onto the driver's seat of the first chaise at hand, had himself driven to the Hall and hurried to the office, where he found his brother-in-law.

Bonny was not alone. Becky was with him, and by the look of it she was as crazy as her father. Her face radiated adulation; obviously, she would not support the voice of reason. Bonny himself looked like a man who had just heard that he was about to be hanged; if ever he had seen despair, Jeremiah thought, here it was. He assailed his brother-in-law with the full brunt of his outrage. "May I ask, dear Friend, whither thee intends to go with thy wife and children after bestowing upon thy slaves the gift of all thy possessions?" He knew that he should be calm, but he could not help himself; he was shaking with anguish and fury.

Bonny's eyes were haggard; he looked ill. Maybe that was the answer: he was sick. A doctor should look at him, Gulielma. He could not be held responsible for his own acts.

"I intend to homestead a farm beyond the mountains," Bonny said wearily.

"Homesteading? In the wilderness? Thee must be mad! There is thy wife, deaf as a post, exhausted after all these years of back-breaking labor in thy household! How could such madness enter thy head?"

Becky rallied beside her father; she put her hand on his arm. "Don't heed him," she urged. "Uncle, why don't we discuss this later? Give Father time to recover . . ."

"Recover from what?!" Jeremiah cried. The martyred face of poor Beulah dominated his emotions; he would protect her if he had to arrange for this madman and his hysterical daughter to be locked up in strait-jackets.

"I understand thy anguish, Jerry," Bonny said, "but I must mind the Light."

"Which light? Thy private light? Only by submitting thy private guidance to the corporate guidance of the Meeting can thee determine whether thy light derived from God or the devil!"

Becky took over the defense. "Did George Fox submit his leadings to the judgment of a Meeting? Did Margaret Fell?"

"For heaven's sake, child!" he exclaimed. "He is not George Fox, he is Bonny Baker!"

"Precisely! And thee is Uncle Jeremiah! His brother-in-law, not his conscience!"

He had to fight the impulse to slap her silly face. "His brother-in-law, yes! Let's talk about that! What, in case thee should go through with this—this madness, is to happen to my sister?"

"Jerry, please," Bonny pleaded wearily. "Does thee think I came to my decision on the spur of the moment? Please, grant me that I considered before all else the well-being of my family!"

"Very well!" Jeremiah cried. "What *has* thee decided to be best for thy wife? Where is she supposed to live, once thy slaves are freed?"

"They have been freed."

"Where will she live? To take her with thee is out of the question, so: *where?* In the house? Impossible! What will she live on, once thee has given everything away? There can only be one answer to that: she will have to live on charity! With relatives, like myself!" In the midst of his tirade Jeremiah was struck by the possibility that Beulah and he might get back together. Such baffled surprise, such joy washed over him that he stammered in confusion, "What—what are her own feelings on—on this?"

"I have no idea," Bonny replied.

"Thee did not discuss this with thy wife?" Justified as his indignation was, it no longer carried conviction.

"No." Bonny rubbed his eyes. "I did not expect it. It just happened today, as these things will. Suddenly, when Hannah Martin sang that lullaby, way opened."

"No way has opened!" Jeremiah snapped. "This decision involves too many other people for thee to decide on thy own!" He left the office with a flourish of self-righteousness, but he was beset by uncertainty. Beulah would be delighted to move in with them, but Grizzle might think otherwise. The moment he considered it in cold blood, the plan seemed a pipe dream. Even so, he went to look for his wife.

He found her in the kitchen, in the company of Beulah and Hannah Martin, who, despite her grief, had rallied to help them prepare the feast. They did not notice him as he hovered in the doorway, intimidated. It seemed as if at least fifteen women were running back and forth carrying plates, chopping parsley, carving up parboiled beasts; the clatter of crockery, pots and pans was deafening. Yet Grizzle's voice dominated the ear-splitting din. "Let him simmer down, first!" she yelled, slapping a limp roll of dough. "Let him make the suggestion himself! Never put a man under pressure!" To his astonishment, Beulah flung her arms around his wife's neck and cried, "Oh, Grizzle dear! Thee cannot know how wonderful it is to have a friend like thee, whose every word I can *hear!*"

Grizzle's eyes filled with tears. "Beulah, I can't tell thee how lonely I've been since Melanie left the house!" she shrieked. "No one to talk to in the kitchen, nobody who cared whether I was alive or dead! Why don't we tell him thee has come to live with us only until thy husband has had a chance to settle down?"

He turned away and wandered into the garden.

*   *   *

Isaac Woodhouse spotted Jeremiah in the garden and heard that Bonny Baker was indeed determined to ruin himself and his family. For a moment he felt a nostalgic longing to partake of that radiant righteousness; then he realized that this very reaction summed up the threat Bonny's crazy action presented to the stability of the Commonwealth. This manumission of his slaves and sacrifice of all his possessions might well sway the Meeting's stand on slavery by their spiritual grandeur. Were the Meeting to condemn slavery, they would have to commit themselves to the cause of abolition and thereby upset the political balance that had kept them in power for three quarters of a century. He and the other merchants might eventually be able to reduce Bonny's act to a personal eccentricity in the eyes of the Meeting, but better if it never came to that; the man must be dissuaded from going through with this folly.

He found him in his office, with Becky, They were studying a map of the island, actually deciding how much to give to every slave. The key figure was Becky; Isaac knew that if he could dissuade her, Boniface would follow.

He drew her aside; the moment they were outside the office, standing in the draft between the buildings, he put it to her that, noble as it might seem, her father was actually giving away her mother's money and her own dowry, the key to her future happiness.

She reacted with adolescent outrage. "First it was Altar Rock, now it is my dowry! If that is all Joe Woodhouse is interested in, I expect to hear so from him personally, not his father!"

"Don't be a silly goose! Emotionally—"

"What on earth moved thee to support my stand in yearly meeting two days ago? Politics?"

"Of course not! I—"

But she did not let him finish. "Well, this is exactly what thee applauded two days ago: a man practicing what he has been preaching! If thee will forgive me, I'd like to help him to get on with it."

She turned her back on him and went inside. He knew that once her father was gone and she remained behind in the marriage market without a penny to her name, she would find out soon enough which side her bread was buttered on, but in order to make her realize this in time, he had better have a word with his son. Being of the same age as she, Joe might be able to make more of an impression.

He looked for Joe in the crowd and found him talking to young Joshua on a bench at the back of the house, overlooking the fields of indigo. Joshua looked pale and very young. Isaac wondered if he should approach the boy directly; better leave him to Joe too.

"Joe, excuse me—there's something I have to discuss with thee, urgently. Could thee give me a moment, please?"

His son rose, obediently; together they walked down the path between the flower beds, away from all the people milling around the house, waiting for the banquet. Alone underneath the surf of the wind in the trees, he said, "Joe, I just had a word with Becky. Thee would do her a service if thee could persuade her to give this matter some level-headed thought before urging her father to go on with his folly."

He felt his son's discomfort even as he spoke. Since the Indian expedition and the business with the Quaker guns, the boy had been restless and brooding.

"Father, I am not so sure it is folly. Slavery—"

He cut him short; the last thing he wanted at that moment was a lecture by a callow youth on the evils of slavery. In every yearly meeting during the past quarter century some blatherskate had risen from the ranks of the have-nots to hold forth on the subject. "I'll thank thee not to lecture me on manumission," he said. "I assure thee that there is not one consideration I have not turned over in my mind before thee was born. Let me tell thee instead about the consequences of Boniface Baker's act. To start with, the slaves themselves . . ."

They paced up and down in the shade of the trees; in the distance the guests and relatives chatted in the sun. The wind tousled the leaves, the fields billowed in the breeze, whorls of summer heat spun across the island.

The future of Eden Island, Isaac said, could only be seen in terms of melancholy and neglect. The slaves were not ready for it, they had no idea how to run things, how to grow a harvest without supervision, how to market their crop, how to organize a self-governing society that could stand up under the onslaught of the owners of the surrounding plantations, who would undoubtedly try to make life as hard as possible for them the moment their present masters had left. For Becky's father to hand over the island to them was a disaster for everybody: not only the slaves, for Uncle Bonny himself, his children, his wife, everything old Ann Traylor Baker had built up. And there was more: politically . . .

He continued to tell his son about the dire consequences of taking the Sermon on the Mount literally, and gradually he felt that his patient, sober words began to carry weight with the boy at his side.

* * *

Joe Woodhouse hesitated at the foot of the stairs in the dusk of the hall. "Luncheon will be soon!" some woman's voice called after him as he climbed the stairs. He went down the dark passage and knocked on the door of Becky's room. It was opened by Himsha McHair; behind her, Aunt Gulielma's voice asked irritably, "Who is there?"

"It's I, Aunt Gulie, Joe! I am looking for Becky."

"She is next door in Abby's room. Close the door, Himsha, there's a draft."

Himsha smiled at him; he realized that, with the exception of Aunt Gulie, he was the only member of the family who really understood Indians. He would like to talk with her, or, rather, let her talk. As she closed the door, the odd thought occurred to him that, rather than seek out Becky, he would like to go for a walk with Himsha, let her restore his sense of direction by talking to him, knowing that he understood her the way he had understood Chief Running Bull. He went to knock on the door of Abby's room.

"Yes?"

It was indeed Becky; he had never realized that her voice was like Aunt Grizzle's. It had a commanding ring about it, in contrast with the helpless, huge-eyed femininity of her appearance. "It's I, Joe. May I have a word with thee?"

"Surely." A skirt rustled, the door was opened and, blast it, there was Abby, the miserable brat. He had not counted on her being there; he would have to inveigle Becky into coming with him to the garden.

But Becky proved capable of dealing with her younger sister. "All right, Abby, leave us alone please."

"But it is my room!" the child protested. "I have as much right to it as thee!"

"Don't be silly," Becky said briskly. "Go for a walk or, better still, go and help Mother and Aunt Grizzle in the kitchen. Along with thee! Lively, now!"

"I hate thee," the little girl said calmly. She brushed past him into the corridor, stuck out her tongue at him and slammed the door.

"Well?" Becky asked, with a gimlet glint in her eyes. She obviously expected trouble and was ready to meet it.

"My father and I thought it would be a good idea if we had a word together." He realized too late that it had been a poor opening.

She bared her teeth in a crooked smile. "That would be the day, wouldn't it, when thee were to do something without thy father?"

He felt a rush of anger. "That's unfair," he said coldly. "Thee can hardly say I went to stop those roughnecks at the instigation of my father."

She gave a scathing little laugh. "And what a Quakerly demonstration *that* was!"

He was overcome by the unsettling desire to take her across his knee. "More so, I would say, than the demonstration thy father has seen fit to indulge in," he retorted.

She turned on him like a fury. Never before had he been confronted by her like this. "If that is all thee has to say to me, Joe Woodhouse, please leave! And ask thy father in my behalf to keep his bull calf roped, rather than send it blundering into people's rooms! Get out!"

His hands itched to slap her. "That's enough, Becky! I am thy fiancé, remember? I'm not going to stand thy nonsense!"

His masterfulness did not impress her in the least, she did not even notice it. "I asked thee to leave my room," she said with exaggerated formality, "I will ask thee once more, and if thee refuses—"

"Well?" He began to feel oddly joyous in the face of her flaring anger.

"I will call my father to throw thee out!"

"I see," he said. "Thee too still needs thy father."

She set her jaw and clenched her fists; warned by the memory of earlier days, he stepped aside, knowing she was about to kick his shins. He strolled toward the bed and sat down on it; it sagged with a twanging of springs that unsettled him. He should have taken the chair.

She pressed home her advantage. "If thee thinks, Joseph Woodhouse, that thee can walk into my room, loll on my bed and scandalize my father, thee is mistaken! My father at least had the courage to act upon his convictions, to set an example for his children! What has thine done? Made money, and hoarded it, and trained thee to guard his pile of gold like a watchdog, to wag thy tail the moment thee hears thy master's voice!"

"Damn thee, Becky!" he cried, jumping to his feet. "I forbid thee to speak so about my father!"

"Forbid! Hah!" She clapped her hands in mock astonishment. "Young Joe is becoming masterful!" Then she turned on him again, "Joseph Woodhouse," she said, her voice low, "thee embodies all I hate and detest in the Quaker louts who are to defend our testimonies for the next generation! Thy pompous, smug snottiness makes me *sick!*" She spat the word at him, her face close to his.

He was speechless with fury and indignation. Suddenly, against the frantic clamor of his reason, he flung his arms around her and smothered her shriek of shock and rage with a kiss.

*   *   *

Becky struggled violently in his arms; then her fury faltered, and with astonishment she submitted to the onslaught of his masculinity. She felt herself go weak and soft and giddy, and was about to surrender when an image imposed itself between them: a jerking white body; clawlike hands plucking at a throat, in the spasms of death; she gave a strangled cry, pushed him away, and stammered, "No, no . . . Don't, don't! Not now . . ."

Joe looked at her, startled. "Why—dear heart, I assure thee . . ."

"Don't, don't, *please!*" She stood swaying on her feet, her hands holding her head. She felt, with crazy detachment, that the left side of her hair had come loose; even though she was torn with horror and confusion, she rearranged it deftly, her face turned away from him. Betrayal, everything was betrayal . . . She had betrayed Caleb by refusing him what Joe had been about to take, she had betrayed her father by collapsing, helplessly, in his detractor's arms; and as to Joe himself . . .

She felt his arm around her shoulders.

"Becky, Becky, dear heart, what ails thee? Hush now . . . Hush, hush . . ."

He wanted to lead her to the bed, but she freed herself. Stupid ninny! Now, if he had taken her to the chair . . . How was it possible that she could break down and at the same time hear that cool voice in her mind? Was she two women? Was she mad? Was it the voice of the devil? She went to the window, away from him. He was sitting dispiritedly on the edge of the bed, a befuddled male. She felt the impulse to take him in her arms and comfort him, but it was unthinkable; she could never touch a man again, the image of dying, Caleb had rendered her incapable of surrender to a man for the rest of her life. It was that notion, that fear of a lifelong loneliness that made her rush toward Joe, throw her arms around his neck and sob, "Don't go away, don't! I love thee, I love thee, I'm—I'm . . ." Her brief, desperate effort to escape from the memory of that twitching, naked body died in despair. She collapsed on the bed, her head on her arms, and handed over to the convulsions of weeping what her mind could no longer bear. She had the hope that Joe, undeterred by her wailing sobs, would gather her in his arms or take her hand or stroke her hair, communicate to her that she was safe in the shelter of his masculinity. He was too stricken with confusion by her antics to budge. 'Oh, the oaf, the oaf!' she thought. 'Good thing I find this out now! That for a husband? Worthless! Oh, God, no, no, don't take him away!' She wailed and sobbed with abandon; the thought that he would never dare to approach her again made her desperate with loneliness and frustration. She lifted her tear-streaked face, conscious of the tresses of her disheveled hair that framed it tragically, and whispered, "Joe . . . Joe, dear heart . . . forgive me . . . forgive me . . ."

He gave her a tight little smile, as if he were afraid that the smallest movement on his part might unleash another avalanche of emotion. "There's nothing to forgive," he said in a voice so mouse-like that, unwittingly, she burst into giggles and dropped her head on her arms again, hoping he would take it for sobs.

He did, or else he would have seized his chance. He went on sitting there, petrified, clearly with only one thought: 'Let me out, dear God, let me out of here.'

At that moment she realized that of course Abby must be watching them.

* * *

With the intuition of the experienced peeper, Abby foresaw her sister's rush toward the balcony the moment Joe Woodhouse had left. The doors were flung open, Becky stood for a few moments on the threshold, looking around, then she stared at the tree into which Abby had fled, and retreated abruptly into the room, closing the doors behind her.

Abby heaved a sigh of relief. She knew why Becky had not approached her hiding place: the memory of Caleb, hanging from the very branch on which she was now crouching. For the next few weeks she need not worry about her sister pouncing on her, as long as she hid in this tree. But the memory had given her a shiver too, and she lost interest in spying on people, for a while.

It was not until late that night, when the banquet was over and the guests had retired, that she ventured onto the balcony again. Every room in the house was occupied. In the one next to hers she saw Aunt Gulie lying on the bed, a towel on her forehead; Himsha sat beside her, holding her hand. Like most of the mourners, Aunt Gulie had obviously eaten too much. In Josh's room George was pacing up and down, holding forth at Josh; Joe Woodhouse lay disconsolately on the bed, obviously still recovering from his bout with Becky. In the next room Uncle Isaac, writing at the table by candlelight, was telling Bilbo to leave, get out, go away! Bilbo just sat there, panting, ears cocked, expecting a lump of sugar; Uncle Isaac sighed and resumed his writing. In her parents' room Aunt Grizzle was yelling at Mother about living in Philadelphia after "he" had made off on his "wild goose chase." It was the first hint Abby had had about the future; it made her frown. Aunt Grizzle was a trial to stay with, always watching her sprinkle chocolate ants on her bread at breakfast and saying, "Well, now, Abigail, that is sufficient, I would say, for a person with a normal stomach and proper manners." Next door Uncle Peleg and Uncle Jeremiah were conversing about something that must have to do with her father, for she saw Uncle Jeremiah gesture at the wall of the next room, Father's study. She moved on to cast a look into the study and saw Father sitting in his chair, looking lost and forlorn. At the sight of him she was suddenly overcome by sadness; never in her life had she seen such loneliness. She felt impelled to go and sit on his knee, but as she was about to open the glass doors she saw him kneel by his chair.

He took such a long time praying that at last she could stand it no longer. She opened the doors a crack and said softly, "Papa?"

He looked up, his eyes unfocused. 'Abby? What is thee doing here?"

"Why did thee do it, Papa?"

He rose to his feet and said, "Come in and I'll tell thee."

She obeyed. He sat down in his chair and patted his thigh; she climbed onto his lap. "Well, now, what is it thee wants to know?"

"Why did thee tell the slaves they were free?"

"Because I could no longer keep them in bondage."

"Why not?"

"I came to the conviction that it was wrong."

"Does that mean we have to leave the island?"

"I'm afraid so."

She remembered what Aunt Grizzle had shouted to Mother. "Is thee coming with us to Aunt Grizzle and Uncle Jerry?"

He frowned; it must be news to him. "No, I'll be going away."

"Where?"

"To the wilderness beyond the mountains, to build a farm."

It sounded exciting. "Who's going with thee?"

"For the time being, nobody."

"Nobody? But thee can't build a farm by thyself! Thee'll get blisters, and who is going to wash thy clothes and cook thy supper and tuck thee in at night and bring thee a dish of tea in the morning?"

He smiled. "Nobody, I'm afraid."

She folded her hands in her lap with determination, the way she had seen her mother do, and said, "Whither thou goest, I'll go."

The blank look on his face was a disappointment. "That's very sweet of thee, but it's out of the question."

"Why?"

"Out of the question!" he repeated sternly. Then he added more gently, "But thank thee very much for the thought."

"But why not, Papa? Why can't I?"

"Thee is too young, that's all."

"Too young to wash thy clothes, to make tea?"

"To go into a wilderness without women," he replied, with a beginning of irritation.

She knew from experience that she should not press him further; raising her face demurely for a kiss, she said, "Good night, Papa." He gave her a peck; she slipped out of the room, back onto the balcony.

Her plan was made. It was very simple. All she needed was someone to come with her. Aunt Gulie would be the best, but she was always busy with sick people. Himsha? She hardly knew her. No, there was only one person: Becky. The prospect of having to live with Becky in the wilderness was depressing, but if it was the only condition, so be it. Her skirts rustled as she hurried to the doors of her room; she found Becky sitting in front of the mirror scrutinizing her eyebrows. "Becky! Becky! Father is going to build a farm in the wilderness!"

As she had expected, Becky whisked around. "What?"

"I was walking down the balcony and happened to look into Father's room and there he was, all alone, and so sad, so I went in and I asked him if he was going to live at Aunt Grizzle's too, he said no, he was going to build a farm beyond the mountains, and when I said I wanted to go with him, he . . ."

Becky rose and swept out onto the balcony.

After she was gone, Abby was overcome by doubt. How stupid of her to blurt it all out! Now, of course, Becky would talk Father into taking her instead! She hurried after her down the dark balcony, past the pale oblongs of the candlelit windows. When she arrived outside her father's study, her mouth fell open. For there was Father, sobbing, his face in his hands; Becky was stroking his hair. "Joshua?" she heard Becky ask incredulously.

"Yes, yes!" her father sobbed. "Suppose she is with child? What do we do? What do we do?"

"All right," Becky said, in a grown-up way, as if she were Mother. "All right, all right. Don't be upset. Way will open."

What was all this about?

*   *   *

Gulielma Woodhouse was just falling asleep when there was a knock on the door. She called uninvitingly, "Who's there?"

A timid voice replied, "It's Becky, Aunt Gulie. Please open up, there's something urgent I must ask thee."

She sighed and nodded to Himsha, who opened the door. Becky came in, carrying the urgency and secrecy of her mission like an eight-month pregnancy. The eyes, the prominent cheekbones, the chin looked remarkably like her great-grandmother's, that cudgel-swinging termagant. Gulielma decided that, unfairly, she disliked the child.

"Father wants to see thee, Aunt Gulie; there's something very urgent, very important . . ."

That infernal sense of drama! There was no decent way to turn down the dramatic plea, so she wearily put on again the dress she had borrowed from her sister-in-law, Mary Woodhouse, to look appropriately mournful. "I'll be back directly, Himsha," she said to the Indian girl, who watched her leave with a look of concern. Ah, what a boon to have her here! There really was no more sensitive or tactful human being on this earth than a civilized Indian.

Becky preceded her to Bonny's study; he rose at their entrance and grabbed her hand. For a moment she thought he was about to kiss it and was ready to snatch it free; then she remembered that she was a lady today, swathed in black, impersonating Mary Woodhouse. "Well, Cousin, what can I do for thee at this late hour?" she asked. The hour was not all that late; downstairs people were still clinking glasses and clattering dishes in honor of the dead.

"Forgive me, Gulie," Boniface said, his voice hushed and secretive. "But this is of the utmost importance."

"All right, out with it. Come on, man."

He took a deep breath, then he said with an effort, "Would thee be prepared to go to the slave quarters, I mean the ex-slave quarters, to find a girl called Cleo, and to take her to the hospital to . . . to . . ."

"To what?"

The man was suddenly overcome by embarrassment; she could have sworn he had reddened. "To find out whether she might be pregnant."

She looked from one to the other in astonishment. "Why?"

"Please! Please, dear Gulie, don't ask questions!"

That was not good enough. "I'm sorry, dear Friend," she said, not sounding sorry at all. "I'll be happy to give medical assistance, but thee cannot expect me to ride into thy compound, pick out some unsuspecting wench and wrestle with her until I have ascertained whether she is *virgo intacta*."

Father and daughter exchanged a pained look. They must have been confident that she would comply with their request without question. He hesitated, then he asked, "I can count on thy discretion, can't I, Gulielma?"

"I'm a doctor. Who's the father, thee?"

She could not have provoked a more startled reaction if she had slapped his face. "I?" he cried. "God forbid!"

"Come, come," she replied irritably, "it would not be the first time a Negro slave has been impregnated by her owner. Is it Josh? Is that why thee suddenly felt moved to abrogate slavery?"

Boniface faced her with dignity. "Indeed it is not," he replied. "But if she is pregnant, I'll adopt her as my daughter and take her with me to the Northwest Territory."

She felt sorry for having derided him. There was a sort of grandeur about his unworldliness. "Isn't that rather drastic?" she asked kindly. "Surely a solution could be found that is not quite so final?"

"If there is, it escapes me." He sounded like himself again, with a faint note of smugness. God knew, there was little left to be smug about.

"But is it necessary to take her with thee into the wilderness?"

"I do not want my son's chances ruined before he starts. No one must know of this, not even he."

So that was it. Josh, the little rat, was to be spared even the discomfort of knowing that he had put a slave girl with child. "I doubt whether thee does thy son a service," she said. "In my experience, a man grows to the measure he faces his responsibilities."

"That sounds very impressive," Bonny retorted with a flash of anger, "but look at Peleg Martin! The misery he caused! If at the time someone had taken mother and child away, all our lives would have been different. My grandmother would not have felt moved to give a home to the child's mother, thereby starting slavery on this island. Caleb's life would not have ended in murder and suicide. One such curse in our family is enough! I am determined that no one outside this room shall ever know about the child, including Joshua."

All this was news to her; she had no idea that Caleb had been the result of a dalliance between Peleg and a slave. There were more guilty secrets behind the staid Quaker façade than even she had suspected. "Dear Friend," she said, "an examination of the Negro girl against her will is out of the question. I'll be happy to go to the compound and bring her here so you'll be able to ask her yourselves."

The idea seemed to perturb them; they exchanged nervous glances. "What is her name?"

"Cleo," Becky said. "Shall I come with thee?"

She went to the door. "There is apt to be some revelry in the quarters; I had better go without any members of thy family." The prospect of twenty minutes in a buggy with this brainless chatterbox was appalling.

As she groped her way down the dark passage to tell Himsha where she was going, a huge bulk loomed in front of her and exclaimed,

"Hold on!" It was Buffalo McHair. "Where art thou going at this hour?"

"None of thy business," she replied, sweeping past him with swishing skirts. It was amazing how quickly one fell back into the role, wearing these clothes. She forgot about Himsha.

"A tryst, eh?" he bellowed after her.

She did not deign to reply, but floated down the stairs, hoping she would not trip and make a swan dive into the darkness below. Outside, the air was hot and muggy. She wondered if she should not go back and change; wet patches under the arms might ruin the dress. But she decided it would have to be Mary Woodhouse's contribution to the Baker family's testimony.

She groped her way to the dark stables and saddled up her faithful old mare by the light of a flickering lantern. As she tried to mount, she realized that she would have to pull the skirt of the dress up around her waist. Muttering un-Quakerly language, she unsaddled the horse again and went to look for the bay gelding that pulled the buggy. She wondered where the stable slave was and remembered that, of course, he was dead. Then the barn door squeaked open and a voice asked, "Can I help thee, Aunt Gulie?" It was young Joe.

"Yes, bless thee!" she exclaimed. "I have to take the buggy. Could thee rig it for me?"

"Why, yes," the boy answered obligingly. "May I have thy lantern, Aunt?"

They chatted while he rigged the buggy; in the distance she could hear the sound of drums.

"Shall I accompany thee, Aunt Gulie?"

"No, thank thee, I'll be all right." She climbed into the buggy, clutching her skirts.

"Will thee be gone long, Aunt Gulie?"

"No, all I have to do is find a girl and bring her back."

"They sound very noisy over there. Won't thee let me come with thee?"

"It is better if I go by myself, without a male escort."

"Oh, but they'd trust me!" the boy exclaimed. "I think I understand Negroes the way I understand Indians!"

Of course, he had been to see fat old Running Bull. She had intended to ask him about that.

"I think I may have thy knack for understanding Indians," he continued.

He was very young; yet the foolish remark moved her. Who knows, somebody among her nephews and nieces might indeed have inherited the idiosyncrasy that had ruled her life. "Let's talk about that in the morning," she said. "Now thee had better get out of the way; this beast is impatient." The horse seemed restless and irritable, chafing and pawing the ground.

Young Joe pushed open the stable doors; the moment the black square of the night opened in front of it, the gelding set out at a

canter before she had sorted out the reins. It gave her a pang of
apprehension, but it became obvious that the beast knew where it was
going. The flickering lanterns of the buggy served little purpose except to fill the night with dancing shadows. As she bounced and
swayed down the track toward the quarters, the sound of drums grew
louder until it drowned the creaking of the buggy and the thudding
of the horse's hoofs. There was a red glow in the sky ahead, as of a
huge fire. When she reached the compound, she saw it was a bonfire; Negroes were dancing around it. She reined the horse and slowly
approached them. She noticed that most of the dancers were naked;
what they were throwing into the fire was their slave smocks, symbols
of servitude. The drums pounded in wild excitement; most of the
dancers had covered their bodies with paint, they leaped and pranced
in the fire glow like bizarre animals, feathered serpents, deities of
an alien culture with which she had not the slightest contact. She
watched them, fascinated, with a growing sense of pity. What chance
would these poor creatures have to live their own life on this island,
once the Bakers had moved away? How long would they be allowed
to carry on like this, stark naked, savage, before the owners of the
surrounding plantations would subjugate them again? Boniface Baker's
testimony seemed cruel and thoughtless, as if he had opened a cage of
parakeets and set the poor creatures free, condemning them to death
in an environment they had never learned to master. Then one of the
revelers spied her.

A tall, thin Negro with a white mask and white stripes on his
arms and legs, he had been strutting around the fire like an ostrich.
The moment he saw her, he emitted a piercing cry and pointed at
her. The dancers stopped and turned to face her. Shrieking and squealing, the mass of birds, skeletons, feathered serpents and ghouls came
rushing toward her; the horse took fright and bolted into the night.

She thought she would be thrown out, but managed to hang on,
kneeling in the well of the careening buggy. It could only be seconds
before it overturned; never had she been so terrified. She knelt there,
clutching the seat, shrieking high-pitched screams that could only
frighten the horse even more. A shadow appeared alongside the buggy
as it plummeted driverless through the night; someone grabbed the
reins. After a struggle in the flickering light of the lanterns that looked
like a battle of gods, the vehicle was brought to a halt and she collapsed, sobbing, on the floor. A voice asked, "Gulie, is thee hurt?"
She was lifted bodily onto the seat; with a sob she collapsed against
Buffalo McHair's shoulder.

It was a novel experience; she had not indulged in the sheer delight of letting herself go since she was a child. The scientist in her
watched her antics with fascination as she wailed and heaved, rubbing
snot into poor Buffalo's beard, clawing the stiff cloth of his jerkin;
had it been daylight, even the most gullible spectator would have
raised his eyebrows in wonder. When finally she prevailed upon
herself to calm down, they were in motion again. The horse, probably

shamefaced after its tantrum, was plodding down the track on its way back to the house; Buffalo's Indian mustang was trotting nervously behind them, tied to the seat by its bridle. To whoop it up on Buffalo's shoulder was one thing, to confront those Philadelphia Quakers in her present state was something else. She straightened up and said, "Thank thee, old friend . . . That was a fortunate coincidence. How come thee happened to be around?"

"I asked Joe Woodhouse where thee had gone and he told me," he said blandly. "Here, have a swig, this will do thee good." He was proffering a flask in the darkness; if it was the one from his hip pocket, she would do well to abstain.

"Have a pull, it will perk thee up."

She hesitated a moment, then she grabbed the flask. The liquid gushed into her mouth in a larger quantity than she had intended; it seared her gullet and hit her stomach like boiling lead. For someone with her delicate digestive tract this was sheer murder, but, mercifully, the boiling lead numbed her stomach instead of burning it.

"Woof!" she breathed, casting the last remnant of delicate femininity to the wind.

"How is thee feeling?" he inquired.

"Buffalo McHair," she said, her old self again, "thee knows very well that the swig thee gave me just now is far more perilous than anything else that happened tonight."

He chuckled. "Well, thee scared the wits out of me. What the devil was thee doing down there in these impossible clothes?"

"I'll have thee know that this dress belongs to the richest woman in Philadelphia."

"That's what I mean," he said. "On the poorest woman in the prairie it looks preposterous."

"All right." She stretched out her hand in the darkness. "Where's thy flask?" This time it did not feel like boiling lead but like warm oil, setting her stomach aglow with well-being. "Where art thou taking me?"

He peered into the darkness. "To the graveyard, I reckon."

"Aha!" She lifted an admonishing finger. "That's what I thought." The scientific observer winced; this was worse than her feminine tantrum of a few minutes ago. Well, the devil take it. "Give me that bottle again," she said. "It steadies my nerves."

"Thy nerves are steady enough. I don't plan to carry thee into the house, not with all those beady-eyed Quakers watching."

"Buffalo McHair," she said, nestling against his shoulder, "thee is a bully."

Eyes closed, she basked in the glow from her stomach. It seemed to relax every muscle of her body. "Poor Bonny," she said, all mellow and compassionate.

"He is going through with it, is he?" the deep voice rumbled.

What a chest! The sound reverberated in the thorax; she realized with irritation that she was listening to his chest as a physician instead of as a damsel in distress. She should ask him for the recipe of that booze of his. Marvelous stuff. "Of course he is," she answered. "He's planning to move west and to take one of his girls with him."

"That's a pretty reckless thing to do."

"Of course. They'll be scalped, raped and buggered before they reach the river. He's a saint," she added, "a Quaker saint, and I'll thank thee to keep thy paws off his testimony."

There was a silence; then he said, "Gulie, thee is drunk."

She decided to ignore it. "I'll take him as far as the Ohio," she said. "Him and his harem. After that he'll have to fend for himself."

"Thee isn't going back to the prairie?"

"Of course I am. Why not?"

"Thee knows as well as I do there's going to be war! Thee has no business traipsing about the wilderness when the place is swarming with madmen bent on killing every living thing in sight."

"I'm not going to traipse around," she said with dignity. "I'm going home to my tribe."

"Thy what?"

"My Hunis. My blood-brothers."

There was a silence; then he said calmly, "Gulie, I am going to dunk thee in the river before I let thee loose in that house."

"That's right. First fill me full of liquor, then elder me for getting raddled. Men. That's what I should never trust: men."

"Gulie," he admonished sternly, "stop that. I've seen thee drunk before. Thee is as sober as I am."

She opened one wary eye. "Why would I pretend?" she asked.

"Is thee really going to surrender thyself to those savages?"

For a moment she felt like telling him why: because she was dying, because of the way the pink and orange towers soared in that deep blue sky, because of the peyote, the way it changed fear of death into yearning for the deep blue sky waiting overhead. But she checked herself; of all the men she knew, Buffalo was the most adult, wise, discreet, yet she could not bring herself to tell him, as if the telling would somehow make it inevitable. She sighed and said, at random, "Poor Himsha."

He did not press her. "I don't think she need be pitied," he said tactfully. "I have arranged for her to stay here in Philadelphia and go to the girls' school. Maybe she could stay with the Martins."

There it went: her glorious moment, the warmth, the happiness. She had refused to trust him, now he had withdrawn. "That's a good idea," she said, sitting up, her cheek cold after leaving his shoulder. "Where are we?"

"The graveyard."

She saw the silhouettes of tombstones vaguely outlined against the dark fog on the river, and heard the lisping of trees in the night breeze. In the flickering lantern light it looked as if dark figures lay prostrate on some of the graves.

"Tell her, if there's any problem, to see Joe Woodhouse," she said.

"Why Joe Woodhouse, for heaven's sake?"

"Because he understands Indians. Now let's go back."

He flicked the reins and they drove off. She remembered the girl
Cleo only as the lights of the house drew into sight. 'Well,' she thought,
'I'll tell Bonny I'll go and see her in the morning.'

* * *

Hannah Martin waited until the buggy had left before she stirred.
While it had been standing there with its unsuspecting occupants, something seemed to have been decided for her, beyond the power of her
will. Until they arrived, there had seemed to be only one way to help
Caleb, lonely, frightened child in hell: to join him there, do away with
herself and thereby commit a mortal sin that would send her wherever
his helpless, terrified soul was wandering, calling her name. But the
notion of mortal sin was a remnant of her Lutheran childhood; to
Quakers there was no mortal sin, no hell other than what man made out
of life for himself. In that sense Caleb had been in hell most of his life;
maybe he was free now. Maybe he had slaked not only his mortal flesh
but his pain, his fear, his loneliness, and set sail on the infinite ocean
of light and love from which he had come to her. Oh, Caleb, Caleb . . .
Her tears ran idly; she should not do this, this would upset him,
wherever he was. Oh, *Kindchen, Kindchen* . . . Her Quaker faith told
her that what she should do for him now was to make of his death
and his suffering an inspiration for others, but her heart, her poor
heart could not lift itself out of its selfish sorrow. She could not help
it, she missed him so.

But she had better join the others at the Hall before they started
to look for her. She rose to her feet with difficulty, for her old joints
were not so nimble as they had been; she straightened her bonnet,
took hold of her purse and turned to leave; then she discovered that
she was not alone.

On another grave, a short distance away, lay a dark figure. She
knew it was a woman even before she approached, cautiously, afraid to
disturb the mourner. It was in the slave section; she must be a
black woman. The grave must be that of the boy Caleb had killed.

She could not help herself. She stretched out her hands and touched
the shoulder of the figure in the darkness. It sprang up with a sudden,
lithe movement as if it were an animal caught in its lair. Something
glistened in the darkness, she thought it was the woman's eyes; then
a hiss made her freeze with alarm. She realized that whoever it was
sat crouched there, ready to leap at her throat.

"Don't be afraid," she whispered. "I'm Caleb's mother, I am sorry,
so very, very sorry . . ."

There was no answer; this was not the boy's mother. This was
someone younger, filled not with grief but with anger, despair, loneliness. Maybe she was the boy's fiancée, maybe they had been about
to marry. Then suddenly it came to her. "Is thee carrying his child?"
she asked.

The girl in the darkness moved; her huddled figure seemed to
become smaller; Hannah heard the sound of a sob.

The sound moved her beyond words. All that was motherly in her reached out toward the lonely soul in the darkness. She knelt, put her arm around the shoulders of the weeping girl and said, "Come, *Liebchen,* come . . . I know, I have been here myself, but we must not stay here. Come with me. Let's go home."

She had not expected it, but when she rose the girl rose with her. With gratitude and tenderness she guided her, shuffling in the darkness, to the road that led to the house.

* * *

Becky was downstairs in the hall when Hannah Martin came in, her arm around Cleo's shoulders; the moment she saw them, her heart sank. "Good evening, Cleo," she said bravely.

Before Aunt Gulie had come home, shaken after her horse had bolted, Becky had been certain that this nightmare would be taken away from them; now, even before old Hannah whispered, "We must do something for her, she's with child," she knew that God, whatever His mysterious purposes were, was driving Cleo west with them with implacable determination.

"Thank thee, Aunt Hannah," she said wearily. "Come, Cleo, I'll take thee upstairs. Thee can stay with me for the night, and Abby."

She did not wait for the girl's reaction; with an authority that seemed to convince everyone except herself, she took her by the hand and led her to the stairs. The hand was cold, clammy, alien; the touch of it gave her gooseflesh. She could not help it; the thought flashed through her mind, 'This is the hand of a different breed.'

She muttered some vague niceties as they climbed the stairs, but her mind was racing. Should she take the girl to her room at once, or first have her meet Father? As they were standing in front of her bedroom door she decided that he would have to see her first; she could not take Cleo in without his knowledge.

"Come, my dear," she said, kindly enough, but with the superiority she reserved for horses. "Let's go and see my father before we go to bed. This way." She took the cold hand again and led her down the passage toward the study. Father must be hoping that this cup would pass, as she herself had hoped until Hannah Martin came in out of the night. She knocked.

"Yes?"

She saw the smile on her father's face freeze as he recognized her companion.

"Come in, Cleo," he said; by the way he said it Becky knew that he realized it was no longer in their own hands.

"Aunt Hannah brought Cleo home with her to look after her. She seems to be with child." She saw the look that crossed her father's anguished face and turned to Cleo. "Isn't that so?"

The girl nodded. Something in the way she did so made Becky see her for the first time as a person, not merely as an instrument of fate. There was about the black face, the erectness of the body, the way she held her neck, an improbable dignity, considering the circumstances. She gazed at the enigmatic creature in bewilderment. This person had nothing to do with a slave or a servant. On the contrary, she lived in a world akin to the wilderness; if they were to take her with them, it might well be she who would protect them, rather than the other way around. It was unsettling.

"Is it true, Cleo, that thee is with child?" her father asked kindly.

The dark eyes of the girl slowly directed their gaze at him. The way she looked at him filled Becky with a sudden, instinctive fear that had nothing to do with reason, experience or even her incoherent fears of the future. Cleo was looking at her father as a female appraising a male. The way she must have looked at Josh . . . Oh, God, not that! She turned away, horrified at her train of thought. She was overwrought, the strain had distorted her common sense.

"In that case," her father said, in the slightly pompous tone that he could not shake even now, "I would like thee to come with us to our new home in the Northwest Territory. We would like thee to come with us not as a servant, but as a member of our family."

Suddenly Becky felt that he was terribly naïve. How could he assume so blithely that the girl would want to leave her own people, particularly now, after he had set them free? Was he, despite his noble deed, truly aware that there must be that of God in Cleo—an Inner Light, tenderness, forgiveness, love? To take her with them, she realized, could be a testimony only if they truly accepted her as their equal. By freeing the slaves Father had made a witness of their humanity; now they must go for that of God in Cleo, or they might as well stay home. It would be, she thought solemnly, another Holy Experiment.

"Come, Cleo," she said, putting her hand on the cold, alien one again. "We'll talk about all this tomorrow; we have had enough for one day. Let's go to bed."

Before she closed the door she smiled reassuringly at her father; her heart broke when she saw the desperate weariness on his face. It would, she knew, be his night in the Garden of Gethsemane, and there was nothing she or anyone else could do to help him. She had realized it herself as she went down the aisle after addressing the Men's Meeting: to go with God meant to go alone.

CHAPTER NINE

AH, those Woodhouses! When at meeting for business a week later Isaac suggested that Boniface Baker step into a side room, as a matter concerning him was about to be presented to the Meeting for its consideration, Jeremiah suspected that Isaac was up to no good. Now, after Isaac's first humble words, he was certain. He looked at the faces of the weighty members of the Meeting in whom, all pious principles of unity notwithstanding, the power of decision rested. Could it be that the whole thing was a premeditated effort on the part of the Quaker princes to neutralize the danger Bonny Baker so suddenly presented to them?

The institution of slavery was a keystone to their wealth. It had never really been challenged, despite the holding forth by rural abolitionists. Now one of their own had collapsed under the weight of his Quaker conscience. After being momentarily taken aback, they now were going to make short shrift of him. And Isaac would not be Isaac if he did not exploit the situation for his own benefit, at the same time loyally serving the common interest.

"Like all of us present," Isaac began, "I have been deeply impressed by Boniface Baker's witness. Very properly, Friend Boniface decided that merely to set his slaves free would deliver the helpless creatures to the rapaciousness of other slave-owners—not members of the Society, of course. To share out his lands among his erstwhile slaves was the logical consequence of their manumission. However"— Isaac gave the Meeting a compassionate smile—"there is another side to the matter. It concerns the offspring of Boniface and Beulah Baker: a boy, Joshua, two girls, Rebekah and Abigail, all three birthright members of this Meeting, none old enough to decide for themselves on such a grave and far-reaching issue. Let us make no mistake, Friends: what is in jeopardly is their heritage. It is very well to make a doubtless sincere gesture such as freeing one's slaves, but, as a Quaker, one has not only one's own conscience to consider in the matter. The Baker children have rights that would be violated. Their father's sacrifice amounts, in effect, to one made by *them* before they are of an age to decide for themselves. Is it not the duty of this Meeting to safeguard their interest? Let us consider, in a spirit of love, whether we might have cause to appoint a committee of trustees from our midst for that portion of the Baker property that would rightfully go to his heirs. Let us consider holding it in escrow until such day as the beneficiaries attain their majority. Should the Meeting decide to appoint such a committee, I will be happy to serve on it."

It was that last, seemingly selfless suggestion that gave Isaac's game away. Jeremiah understood now why Joshua Baker had been offered a partnership in the Woodhouse empire and was to be sent abroad for a European tour in preparation for it. Becky Baker, earmarked to marry Isaac's son Joe, would bring her share of the Baker property with her; as to Abby, poor child, no doubt the Meeting would entrust her interests to the selfless Isaac as well. It was distressing, yet somehow admirable; once again the Quaker genius for compromise asserted itself—a far cry from the original genius embodied by George Fox and Margaret Fell. As a spiritual force for the liberation of man from prejudice and violence, the Quaker movement seemed to have run its course; what was left was a political power which, no doubt, would continue to dominate the Assembly, thereby further shaping the future of the Commonwealth. It would be better than handing the future to the Scotch-Irish on the frontier and the slave-owners in the valley. For the slaves a Quaker domination was the better of two evils.

Israel Henderson rose, majestically, to unite with Isaac's proposal with some more pious verbiage on the necessity of protecting the young and an admonition to the Meeting to keep a firm grip on reality. After Israel Henderson, Peleg Martin rose to speak, most vociferous anti-abolitionist of them all; he could be counted on to agree with what was obviously a foregone conclusion. There he went, croaking away in his grating voice: "Friends, let us reconsider for a moment the core of the argument we are discussing: Are Negroes human? If so, then they obviously cannot be treated as cattle in matters of property. However! Are they? For the better part of a lifetime I have maintained: No. Whatever our attitude toward the Negro may be, he cannot be granted humanity in the sense of the word as we understand it." The old man paused, impervious to the heavy-lidded apathy that was settling over the Meeting, who had heard it all before. "I am sorry to say," he continued, "that I have been unable to revise that opinion, despite Boniface Baker. In the past, Boniface Baker has united with everything the slave-owners, including myself, have proposed to this Meeting. Now, here he goes and sets them free." He paused. "Friends, I am an old man. I have, during my lifetime, seen but few people who truly were in the power of the Lord. I am convinced that Boniface Baker, by freeing his slaves and sharing out his property among them, faces a future as blank as a stone wall. But I have no doubt whatsoever that, in doing so, he has answered that of God in himself, his children and, yes, his slaves."

The pen dropped from Jeremiah's hand. The stillness in the hall was so intense that the buzzing of flies against the windowpanes could clearly be heard. The old man looked about him. "Does this mean that I have changed my mind? No, it does not. I cannot change the conviction of a lifetime; I am old and fixed in my ways. To me, Negroes will never be human. But Boniface Baker has convinced me that God considers them to be so. And I have decided to take myself out of God's way." There was a commotion among the princes; Isaac whispered to Israel Henderson. Peleg continued stolidly, "Therefore, I cannot unite with Isaac Woodhouse's proposal. If we are so concerned about the Baker children, there is one way open to us: Ask *them.*

Never mind their ages, never mind our own notions of what is responsible, or sensible, or prudent. Let us ask *them* what they want, and
abide by what the Light leads them to decide." He sat down.

For several minutes no one moved. Jeremiah realized, with a feeling
of awe, that this was the watershed, the moment of truth in which
the Society of Friends would finally choose between the testimonies
and political power. What stunned them, himself included, was that
the decision had been forced upon them by the staunchiest of all
defenders of slavery.

Isaac Woodhouse rose to answer the challenge. He exuded self-
confidence. "Before we follow Friend Peleg's suggestion and consult
the Baker children in this matter, it is proper to reflect upon the
consequences of such action. I will not be so trite as to point out
that Friend Peleg no longer owns any slaves himself; neither do I,
so we may both be accepted by this Meeting as speaking from
principle, not self-interest." That was dirty, Jeremiah thought; Isaac's
self-interest was clearly involved. "Let us indulge for a moment in a
quality we have always claimed but rarely shown of late: old-fashioned
Quaker bluntness. What will be the consequences if this Meeting agrees
with Peleg Martin that the Negro is human, if not in our eyes, in
the eyes of God? As God-fearing people, we will have to submit our
imperfect wisdom to the supreme wisdom of the Inner Light. That
would mean we accept slavery as wrong, and we would be forced to
act upon this conviction, which is clearly in conflict with the spirit of
the times. We, who spend our lives in the business of this Commonwealth, know better than anyone else that without the institution of
slavery our prosperity will come to naught. I submit that if we do
Peleg Martin's bidding, if we invite the Baker family to speak for
themselves, we allow them to decide not only on their own fate, which
may be defensible, but on the role of the Society of Friends in the
political structure of Pennsylvania, on the future of the Quaker movement, of the Commonwealth itself. If we feel that this matter can be
left to three children, so be it. But it is my opinion that we should,
after having listened to the children, submit this concern to our corporate divine guidance. Only then will we attain a true sense of direction: the sense of the Meeting."

He sat down; again, silence fell for minutes on end. Unobtrusively,
meeting for business changed into meeting for worship. Then Israel
Henderson rose. "I wonder whether this weighty matter should not be
decided by the full Meeting rather than by half its membership. I
propose that the partition be raised and the women be invited to join
our search for truth."

Jeremiah could not remember a precedent for this. The partition
between the two Meetings was raised only for worship. In Rhode
Island, once, the partition had been raised before the full Meeting
arrived at a decision as to whether to adhere to the peace testimony
or to defend themselves against the aggression of the Indians in King
Philip's War. He became aware that all eyes were on him; he said,
"May I have the sense of the Meeting on Friend Israel's proposal that
the partition be raised?"

Several voices said, "I unite."

"In that case, may I solicit a messenger?"

"I'll go." It was Joe Woodhouse.

Jeremiah looked around him; when there was no demur, he said, "Joseph Woodhouse is appointed as a messenger to the Women's Meeting."

Philip Howgill's pen scratched in the silence as he wrote the minute.

* * *

Becky was so preoccupied with the presence of Cleo beside her at meeting for business that she lost track of the proceedings. It had been her decision to bring Cleo with them; once she and Abby had settled down with her in the back of the hall, she asked herself what had moved her to do so. Not that Cleo looked unpresentable; in one of Becky's own dresses which she had lent her, the girl made a figure of striking dignity. What troubled Becky was her own motivation. What good could it do Cleo to attend this endless discussion about libraries to be searched for worldly books and covered-dish suppers to be arranged if the weather held? She saw that Abby, sitting on the other side of the Negro girl, was picking her nose with dreamy concentration. She hissed at her sister angrily; suddenly the door opened. To her amazement, Joe came in, obviously bearing a message from the men next door. He went to his mother, who was presiding clerk, and whispered to her. She nodded and raised her hand, silencing Bathsheba Moremen, who had been carrying on about the virtues of brevity for the past ten minues.

"The Men's Meeting requests that the partition be raised," Mary Woodhouse said, "as they are laboring on a matter on which they desire the measure of light granted to us. Does the Meeting unite with this request?"

The Meeting united; Joe went back to transmit their reply; moments later the partition began to rise, ponderously, with shuddering creakings and rumblings. The women craned their necks to look at the men, who seemed at pains to pretend that they were unaware of anything unusual taking place. When finally the squealing of pulleys and the gnashing of chains ceased, Uncle Jeremiah, who presided over the Men's Meeting, graciously asked Mary Woodhouse's permission to take over the chairmanship. Mary nodded in agreement.

"Friends, at the request of the Men's Meeting, we are now united in our full membership," Uncle Jeremiah began. "We have made this request because we are about to pose a serious question to the children of Boniface and Beulah Baker."

Becky sat dumfounded. What on earth was all this about? She looked for her father, but could not find him; her mother was sitting only a few rows in front, but did not turn her head; she had probably not heard a word.

"The Men's Meeting has been deliberating on its responsibility to protect the interests of the Baker children," Uncle Jeremiah continued, "in view of their father's decision to liberate his slaves and to parcel out his lands among them. It was the sense of the Men's Meeting that we should invite the children to voice their leading on this matter before we join together in silence to seek divine guidance. Let me explain to them, and you, what the issues are ..."

He sallied forth into a rambling monologue on the grave consequences of her father's actions, not only to the future of his children but that of the Society of Friends and the Commonwealth of Pennsylvania. When the full meaning of the maneuver sank in, Becky began to tremble with outrage. How dare they! How dare they interfere with a decision that had been so personal, into which had gone such agonies of self-searching? To pretend it was for her sake and Joshua's and Abby's was ridiculous; a child could see it was their own well-being and comfort that were threatened, not by Father but by their own uneasy consciences. What they were in effect demanding of her was that she would take the burden from them, so they could stop Father at the request of his own children. It was such a scandalous effort at intimidation that she boiled with indignation. Was this what Quakerism had come to? Was that of God in Father, in herself, which had driven them to submit to its promptings regardless of the consequences, to be overpowered by the sense of the Meeting, the corporate leading by the Inner Light? It was not their Inner Light but their own miserable self-interest! They wailed and prated every First Day about submitting themselves to the Light, begging God to avail Himself of them, to test them; but they did not want to be tested, all they wanted to be was comfortable!

"Will the Baker children come forward and face the Meeting, please?" She became conscious that everyone seemed to be looking at her, at Abby, at—suddnly she knew what she must do. She said to Abby, "Take her hand!" and, standing up, pulled Cleo to her feet. Hand in hand, the three of them walked down the aisle toward the rostrum.

As she did so, shaking like a leaf, doubt and confusion began to beset Becky. How would Joshua feel about this? What gave her the right to decide this for Abby, for Cleo herself? After the three of them had climbed the rostrum and turned to face the mass of people in the hall, she was overwhelmed by a sense of helplessness. She tried to find her father's face, her mother's in the sea of white blotches, but she could find neither of them. Then she discovered Joe Woodhouse staring up at her from a seat on the aisle; she recognized the boy next to him, sitting with his head in his hands. It was Joshua.

The realization that the three of them were facing a sea of disapproval made her close her eyes in a silent plea for help, for mercy. At once she felt a stillness within that was beyond words. Then she heard a sound. It was that of a slow movement of a massive body, a huge, sleeping animal turning over. She opened her eyes and saw that both Meetings had risen to their feet.

As she stood there, bewildered, awe-struck, she felt what everyone in the silent hall felt at that moment: the indefinable, unmistakable presence of God.

BOOK TWO

CHAPTER ONE

THE good ship *Margaret Fell,* bound for Kingston, Barbados, Bermuda and London, came ghosting down the Delaware River through the summer haze. Standing apart from the bustle of the sailors on her deck, the forlorn figure of a young man in black clothes and Quaker hat was gazing disconsolately at the shore. The captain, who had received this extra passenger at the last moment somewhat ungraciously, saw his chance to make amends. He approached the young man, future partner of the firm, with an innkeeper's smile.

"Well, Mr. Baker, there we go!" he said with a heartiness that ill befitted his sullen mood. Departures always affected him that way; he hated every minute of them, sinking deeper and deeper into uncharitable gloom until he passed Cape May, to leave the ever increasing din of his household behind for another eight months and come home in time for yet another baby.

The young man looked at him with the elongated melancholy of a rain-soaked horse. "Quite," he said; rather tartly, the captain thought.

"We'll soon be passing your father's island. Devil of a hazard, you know, what with that rock and the confounded fog. Curse to the sailor, that's what it is."

"I'm sorry to hear it."

Damn it, those landlubbers took offense at even the most innocent remark. "I did not intend to cast aspersions on your property, Mr. Baker," the captain said with a smile, while behind his back his hands clasped and unclasped in secret strangulation. "It must be a blessed spot to live in."

"Indeed it was," the boy said stiffly.

Devil take it, of course, the boy's father had given the whole damn island away to his niggers! How could he have forgotten? Always the same with these departures, too much on a man's mind. "Yes, of course, I heard about your father's beautiful testimony. Beautiful, beautiful. The entire waterfront is full of it. He sets an example to us all, he does indeed. Terrible business, slavery. You should see the ships that bring the poor brutes. Made me vomit meself, when . . ." He checked himself in time. To start reminiscing about his days as mate of a slaver would be imprudent. They had been wild days, during which he had done things he cared to remember only once he had passed Cape May, outward bound. "Well, I'd better see to my business, Mr. Baker. Any time you care to join me for a glass of Madeira in my quarters, just give me the word. I'll be on the poopdeck." With that, the captain turned around and marched to the aft castle, spyglass under his arm, tri-cornered hat cocked to shade his eyes from the glare of the morning sun.

Joshua heaved a sigh of relief. He could not bear to talk to anyone right now. He stared fixedly at the bend of the river where, any moment now, the north end of the island would come into view. It had all gone too fast: the decision to go on the world tour, the buying of his outfit, the instructions by Uncle Isaac and Cousin Abe, the farewell from his family . . . It all had been part of a turbulent, chaotic torrent of events that now, suddenly, had come to a stop. There he stood, clutching the rail, biting back the tears, facing the future, to discover that it was a blank emptiness. He had cut off his roots and set himself adrift in a void. In a sense he had committed suicide as surely as if he had followed Cuffee's and Caleb's example. For the old Joshua Baker, the boy who had lived on Eden Island, was dead forever. Gone were the fields where he had played as a child, the little wilderness where he had made his first fumbling on-slaughts on Cleo as a boy. When he returned, if he ever returned, nothing would be left of the old Joshua, not a thing. No jolly family with its joys and quarrels, no cupboard with children's clothes and the old rocking-horse, no stable loft in which he had played with Harry, two toddlers shrieking with delight, throwing hay at each other. As he gazed at the bend of the river they were approaching, he found himself hoping that the island might be shrouded in fog and the ship might pass swiftly, coasting through a cloud.

But as they rounded the bend, heeling in the wind and carried by the current, there it was: green and luscious, the foliage of the chestnut trees shimmering in the sun, the red chimneys of the house soaring above them. The sight of the chimneys undid him, and when the house came into view with its pillared façade, the balcony, the lawn, he knew that the whole thing had been a monstrous mistake. They came abreast of Altar Rock; for a mad moment he thought of jumping overboard and swimming ashore; but it passed quickly. If he were to wade ashore on the beautiful, beckoning island, he would find the house in upheaval, all the furniture out of place, in the process of being stacked in the hall for the coming sale; he could not face that. He wanted to remember it as it had been, not witness its dissolution. When the southern tip of the island came into view, with its little wilderness, he saw a human being, the first he had seen on the island, the lonely figure of a black woman. He strolled to the captain standing wide-legged on the aft deck and asked, "Could I use thy spyglass for a moment?"

"Certainly, Mr. Baker."

He put the telescope to his eye and tried to focus it on the lonely little figure. The captain's voice said, "Let me help you, sir." He adjusted the telescope, and suddenly there she was, sharp and clear: a black woman standing on the beach of the little wilderness, gazing at the ship as it passed by. Was it Cleo? It was too far to see. He was overwhelmed by homesickness, not for her embraces but for those hours after his first experience of love, when he had dreamed about a different future: married, a farm in the wilderness, children, their life a Quaker testimony of love and human dignity in the presence of God. He felt like waving farewell to her, although he had no idea who it was, but the presence of the captain, watching him curiously, restrained him. He handed back the telescope and said, "Well, Captain, thee suggested we share a glass of Madeira; I think the moment has come for us to do so."

"By all means," the captain said, with a broad smile that somehow seemed inane. "Mr. Robotham, take over, if you please. Call me when we approach Newcastle."

"Aye, aye, sir."

"Come, Mr. Baker," the captain said, putting an arm around Joshua's shoulders. "Let's have our first, I hope, of many. Mind your head, please."

Joshua stooped through the low doorway to the captain's cabin and stepped, lips trembling, into the future.

* * *

After meeting with the Committee on Indian Affairs, Joe Woodhouse was deeply alarmed. He had made a report of his parley with Chief Running Bull, of the desperate situation in which the Delawares found themselves, beset by both the Iroquois and the colonists; he had told the committee about his promise that the Quakers would help with a school for the children if the Delawares would avoid warfare by removing themselves to uncontested territory. It was the promise that did it; he was severely snubbed, be it in Quakerly fashion. Nobody said outright that he had had no business committing the Meeting without specific instructions to do so, but the upshot was that the whole matter was tabled until some future date when, as Uncle Jeremiah said, a sense of the Meeting would be more readily available. Joe left in a high state of emotion, but found no one to commiserate with him, not even his father, who listened politely enough but who proved unresponsive to his suggestion that Running Bull be helped to make up his mind with a loan, considering that the removal of the tribe to the Northwest Territory would mean that Altar Rock could no longer be considered as an Indian sanctuary. Abe was more forthright in his response. "Look, Joe," he said, "why should we volunteer to lend the man money if he is planning to remove his tribe anyhow?"

It was callous and cold-blooded. Nobody seemed to realize how desperately important it was that Friends should give some visible sign of support now; the alternative was a war between the Delawares and the Iroquois. Could they not see that it was only a matter of time before the tribe would join the French? But nobody seemed concerned. It was as if standing in the doorways of their houses to shield the Indians had been a symbolic act which left everybody free to return to his own affairs. Joe had the distinct impression that nobody wanted to hear the word "Indians" for a long time to come.

It was therefore in a somber frame of mind that he accepted his father's invitation to accompany him to Eden Island for the auction of the contents of the Hall. When they arrived at the inn opposite the island, he was amazed at the number of carriages, coaches and sulkies lined up in a double row on the river's bank. The Hendersons' coachman, who was whiling away the time with some of his companions playing cards, advised them to leave their carriage here, as those who had taken their conveyances across were likely to have to wait for a long time to return to the mainland; the ferry could hold only one carriage at a time. They followed his advice and rang the bell for the ferry; presently the flat, cumbersome vessel detached itself from the wooded shore of the island and came crawling toward them with a long, ponderous loop downstream of Altar Rock; the little figure of the ferry slave walked to and fro, pulling the vessel along its chain with a worn wooden block. Joe stared at the rock; of course, it was the reason for the change in his father's attitude toward Uncle Bonny's sacrifice; the moment the slaves became the owners of Eden Island, Altar Rock would be bought from them by the house of Woodhouse and blown up; Abe had no sentimental regard for promises made to departed Indian tribes by the late William Penn.

The realization filled him with a sense of finality, as if part of his life were drawing to a close. Becky and he would probably not see each other again; her decision to go with her father into the wilderness seemed irrevocable. It was a wry thought: 'We have been continuously fighting because of my so-called dependence on my father, now it is she who cannot live without her father.'

The hall when they arrived was filled with members of the Meeting; the auctioneer, a garrulous Friend by the name of Hazeman, was chanting the bids in a rapid, melodious sing-song that rose in pitch as the bids went higher. On the block was a grandfather clock; Joe knew it well. Looking around at the crowd, he did not register at once the price at which the bidding had arrived; when he heard the figure "Nineteen," he gaped in amazement. Nineteen guineas for that broken-down thing? With its carillon that had at least five teeth missing and its inability to strike the proper hour? Yet, someone called from the crowd, "Twenty!"

"Twenty guineas twenty guineas twenty guineas!" Friend Hazeman chanted. "Anyone else anyone else? A beautiful timepiece manufactured in London, brought over from England at great expense, a true heirloom, anyone twenty-one anyone twenty-one?"

"Twenty-one!" someone called.

"Twenty-one I hear twenty-one when do I hear twenty-two twenty-two?" Hazeman, hand lifted, scanned the faces. "Anyone twenty-two anyone twenty-two?"

And there came Israel Henderson's weighty voice, "Twenty-two."

While Joe watched with baffled fascination, the old clock was finally sold for twenty-seven guineas, which was at least twenty guineas too many. When a scratched and wobbly dining-room table with five chairs was sold for twenty-three, Joe understood what was going on. Everyone knew that Boniface Baker needed money to pay his debts and buy the wagons, horses and tools necessary to homestead a farm in the wilderness; this was their way of helping him. It was very moving; even so, it was a sad occasion. Joe saw that Becky, who sat apart from the crowd with her mother and Abby, facing the jumble of their belongings, had difficulty holding back her tears. When a *secretaire* came up for auction, Becky covered her face with her hands. Joe realized it was the desk in which the diaries had been found that had started the chain of events which had led to the dissolution of the world of the Bakers, the voluntary exile of a man who had sacrificed all his possessions to make a witness. There he sat, rotund, benign, in a high-backed chair beside his family. Of all the people Joe knew, Boniface Baker was about the most unlikely hero. Yet, what courage it must have taken to come to this decision! Maybe Aunt Beulah deserved to be admired even more, watching stony-faced as all her furniture, china, silver, knickknacks, linen were sold piecemeal in front of her eyes. How must she feel, with not a single thing left to remind her of a lifetime of unrelenting labor?

As he watched her, Joe concluded that she was the true hero of the day; the day when the Hall was picked clean by the raven, which would leave but an empty shell of what had been a woman's life.

*   *   *

When Grandmother's bed came up for auction, Beulah Baker understood why, contrary to her expectations, she had been overcome by such indecent exhilaration as the auction progressed. She was witnessing not the end of her life, as the people who eyed her with such commiseration assumed, but merely of one period in it, an unhappy one at that. What was being dissolved was the identity of Beulah Baker—house, furniture, porcelain, linen, plate, knickknacks, children, husband—and what was left was Beulah Best, the eighteen-year-old girl who had come to the island with her trousseau and little red parasol, wearing a velvet gown. How charming that gown had been! She remembered the very feel of it, the luxury, the pride in being a married woman. And that little parasol, how she had agonized before she finally chose that particular one! She had gone out into the sunny street to try it out, watching her reflection in the shopwindow to see if the effect of the red sheen on her face was as flattering as she had been told it was. After her first confrontation with the old woman whose bedstead was now being sold for an exorbitant price, she had never worn the gown again, nor had she opened the little red parasol; many years later she had found it, trampled and broken, in the mud of the yard after the children had played with it, trying to ride a pig.

As she sat there impassively watching the dissolution of her world, the little red parasol became the symbol of the fate that had befallen her. None of the potentialities of the young Beulah Best had been given a chance to unfold in the shadow of that woman. She had become somebody else, unpleasant, harsh; only now that she was being dismantled, bit by bit, did she realize that she had never liked Beulah Baker, there had even been times when she hated her. But Beulah Best! That innocent, generous child, so full of hope and expectations, with such infinite capacity for love! . . . A hand was put on hers; she looked up, startled.

It was Jerry. He looked at her with such infinite concern, such sorrow that she was about to whisper to him, "Don't concern thyself, dear heart, I love it, I love every minute of it," but she checked herself in time; he must not know, he would not understand. Confiding in him would also increase the temptation to confess that, although she piously asserted she would of course join her husband and children in the wilderness as soon as they had started the farm, she did not really want to. She had assumed it was because she was frightened of the wilderness, but now, watching the auction with that growing sense of liberation, she realized it was not so. She did not want to go because she hated Beulah Baker; she wanted to go home to Philadelphia and become Beulah Best again. She still was Beulah Best, whatever anybody said, whatever she told herself; she still was the girl who had arrived on the island that summer morning long ago. The gown and the parasol were gone, but her capacity for love was still there, as strong as it had ever been.

There went the bed, knocked down at thirty-seven guineas, if you please. What would Israel Henderson use it for? A guest bed? That man must have more furniture in his house than he knew what to do with. It was all conscience money, an effort by the Meeting to buy peace of mind for letting Bonny do away with himself for a testimony none of them had the slightest intention of upholding. And that was a good thing, alas. Even in this short period of time the slaves had become quite unmanageable. They no longer did a stroke of work on the island, the house had not been cleaned for weeks, she and the children had had to drag the furniture into place themselves. And that silly little slut Cleo, lying about like a cat all day because of her "delicate condition"! Nobody had mentioned it to her, but it was obvious why they were taking her with them, why Joshua had been spirited away so precipitously. It left her unmoved; it was all part of the world of Beulah Baker, now drawing to a close. She had watched Joshua embark without shedding a tear, she had acquiesced without protest in Bonny's decision to take Becky and Abby with him; she had not even mentioned money, although part at least of what was being sold today had been bought with her dowry. All these people considered her to be a heroine because she faced the dismemberment of her life with equanimity; even dear Jerry had no idea. 'Farewell, Ann Traylor, farewell,' she thought; 'a few more hours and I will be free of thee forever.'

She bent her head, as she was afraid her true feelings must be visible on her face. Jerry put his arm around her shoulders and whispered, "Bear up, dear love, it's almost over. Tonight thee'll be in Philadelphia, and tomorrow I'll buy thee a present, something to put thy mind off all this. What would please thee? Tell me! What would give thee pleasure?"

She looked at his dear face, radiant with tenderness and love. "A little red parasol," she whispered.

She had said it jokingly, but he took her seriously. His eyes probed hers as if he were trying to see into her very soul. Then he nodded and said, "Thee shall have it, Beulah, dear."

Did he remember? She put her hand on his. So they sat, hand in hand, while the last of Beulah Baker's world fell under the hammer of the auctioneer.

* * *

Boniface Baker and his daughters left precipitously, not only because of the impending war but because of the shortness of the season during which travel by wagon train into unorganized territory was still possible. As it was, they were unlikely to arrive at their destination before fall; it would take a supreme effort to get a log cabin built before the snow came. Their winter, in any case, would be one of hibernation; their wagons were loaded with foodstuffs that would keep, to see them through till spring. There were two wagons, each drawn by a team of four mules, plus three riding horses and a flat cart drawn by Herbert, the old gelding, with on it a skiff and a plow.

To Gulielma Woodhouse, Herbert the gelding personified the enterprise: a fat, innocent animal that had lived on the island all his life. Out there in the mountains and the wilderness beyond, he would be worse than useless; nothing in his somnolent, uncomplicated life had prepared him for the ordeal. He would not know what to do when attacked by a mountain lion or a pack of timber wolves; he would not have the sense, while grazing untethered, not to wander away from the campfire. Her guess was that Herbert would be one of the first victims of Bonny Baker's folly, with Bonny himself a close second. There he went, looking ludicrous in his brand-new trapper's outfit of leather pants, Indian jerkin, rifle slung across his chest, blanket roll behind him, bull's horn filled with bear grease dangling from the pommel of his saddle. He might have looked convincing if he had not insisted on wearing a gray Quaker hat, in deference to John Woolman and his protest against slave labor; it made him look like a city Quaker in disguise, which was exactly what he was. The idea of this man homesteading a farm in the wilderness was preposterous; he must be so convinced of the godliness of his deed as to be certain that the Lord would provide where reason saw no hope for survival.

This was exactly what worried Gulielma as she rode ahead of the small wagon train. Her mind was too scientifically trained to accept this concept. Indeed, good deeds were rewarded, but only by the satisfaction they gave those who performed them. Her mind balked at the crude presumption of George Fox's infamous Book of Rewards, in which every enemy of the early Friends who was hit by a roof tile or vanished in quicksand was crossed off with the words "The Lord prevails!" Bonny Baker's present witness, so piously supported by the Meeting, was an act of stupidity that could not fail to bring about the wrath of a more cold-blooded and dangerous god than the one who had hurled George Fox's roof tiles. The man did not know how to dig a ditch and would probably have heart failure should he try; for him to live off the land with his two charming butterflies, a Negro girl and that innocent Sancho Panza George McHair, was a preposterous notion.

It was not only the blithe confidence with which Boniface Baker and his hapless crew set out toward their doom that troubled her, but the sanctimonious way the Meeting had encouraged him. Philadelphia Meeting had among its members some of the most intelligent men in the Commonwealth; surely Israel Henderson, Jeremiah Best, her own brother Isaac must be aware of the recklessness of this undertaking. If they had really wished to support Boniface Baker's testimony, they could have found a function better suited to his capabilities than this travesty. But merely because he was putting into practice the principles of the Society of Friends, everybody piously assumed that he would be safe under the wing of the Lord. She could not remember ever having seen her brother so sentimentally enraptured; it had been he who arranged for the exorbitant sums of money to be paid at the auction, he had provided the wagons and most of the stores from his own warehouse; to anyone who did not know him as well as she did, he must seem a man transported by a saint's example. What she suspected to be closer to the truth was that he and the others wanted to spirit poor Bonny away as fast and as far as possible, for fear his disease might prove contagious. It filled her with a distaste that grew into anger as the wagon train ponderously made its way deeper into the countryside, its arrival heralded by the Quaker grapevine. In every village they were met by representatives of the local Meeting, virtually with cries of "Hosanna!" She had the feeling that, had they lived farther south, the women would have spread palm fronds at their feet. These people were farmers, they knew from experience how hard it was to carve a living for a family out of the virgin wilderness; how could they stand there and applaud, the women with tears in their eyes? Many of them carried gifts of salted pork or weevil-proof biscuits or grain in mouse-proof barrels, like a sacrifice put at the feet of some tribal god.

Even George McHair did not seem to realize what lay in store for them. He had agreed to go with the Bakers for the winter without a second thought; he should have known better than to take on the responsibility for a useless man and his two useless daughters, one of them ten years old, for heaven's sake! The only one likely to come through unscathed was the Negro girl, who, despite her lithe femininity, seemed pretty well indestructible.

Gulielma knew nothing about Negroes, but she had worked with Indians long enough to know that the worst mistake a white man could make was to assume he could identify with those of a different race, and she was a slave to boot. Some things about the girl troubled her: the fact that she was not with child and never had been, the coldness of the black jewels of her eyes, unblinking, like those of a panther. The freedom she had received when Bonny gave his slaves their liberty amounted, in her case, to the freedom to do nothing. She lolled most of the day in the wagon she shared with the two other girls, stretched out languorously on her palliasse or on the tailboard. As the caravan reached the region where slavery was unknown, the adulation of the local Meetings was as much for the exotic creature as for Boniface Baker himself. To them, the whole thing was such a marvelous, dramatic example of the Quaker testimonies that Gulielma began to feel she was guiding a religious peepshow. Nobody seemed to consider the consequences of taking a black girl with such obvious powers of seduction into the lawless lands beyond the mountains, where she could not fail to set horny males like Buffalo's hunters whinnying like stallions in rut. Bonny, with his little hat and his prairie boots, might find himself obliged to lie in front of her cabin overnight like a watchdog, his rifle at the ready, to fend off inebriated swains. As it was, she had herself paraded past the popping eyes of the farmers, draped on the tailboard of her wagon, dangling a slender black leg, languidly spitting the husks of seeds at them. What was the creature up to? What were her motivations? Revenge? Conquest? Boniface Baker, preoccupied with being a saint, had not as yet become aware of her as a woman; but Gulielma, observing the girl from the corner of her eye, occasionally caught her contemplating her erstwhile master as a lazy cat contemplates a plump white mouse. Boniface Baker was nobody's concept of a satyr, but he had fathered three children and thus must have received his share of the explosive force that drove all living things to procreation. During the long months of winter, cooped up in a cabin with this singleminded Delilah, with nothing else to do but whittle or read the Good Book, he would find himself faced by a challenge indeed.

She trotted along at the head of the children's crusade, undulating in her saddle with the supple, unconscious grace of the accomplished rider. The fact that she was guiding them to their destination made her an accomplice; it was all very well to sneer at the members of Philadelphia Meeting or feel exasperated at the rural Friends' adulation of the man and his symbolic black daughter; what about herself, who led the lambs to slaughter knowing what lay ahead for them? If anything happened to them, she would be at least as guilty as the canny merchants who had bought peace of mind with the paltry shekels they had dropped on the altar at the auction. So it was with more eagerness than usual that she listened to Joe Woodhouse's jeremiad. He turned up on the fourth day, riding a stunning Arabian mare, ostensibly to say goodbye to Becky before they entered the mountains, but it became apparent that he wanted a heart-to-heart talk with his aunt.

Becky, hurt and indignant, sulked in the wagon with her bored little sister and that implacable black jungle cat while Joe, riding ahead of

the train, unburdened himself to his aunt. He had, as representative of
Philadelphia Meeting, made a rash promise of Quaker assistance to
Chief Running Bull if the Delawares would remove themselves from
the scene without resorting to warfare. Of course, the Meeting had
disavowed him. "Look, Joe," she said, after he had blurted out his
story, "thee knew very well that a Meeting can never be expected
to approve a concern without having agonized over it in endless meditation. A concern is never a corporate affair; all any Meeting will
do is to give the individual or group of individuals a minute of approval, maybe a gift of money to help them realize their concern.
But in that case they must, first of all, convince the Meeting that
they really are acting in the power of the Lord. Now if thee had come
to the Meeting and said, 'Friends, I am called to strike out into the
wilderness with the Delawares and help start a school for their children,' thee would have had a much more sympathetic reception. They
would not have done a thing, at least not straightaway, but they
might have given thee a minute of support. To promise Running Bull
money and supplies on behalf of the Meeting was indeed an un-
Quakerly thing for thee to do. I'm sorry to agree with them, because
I think they are a bunch of procrastinators in Indian affairs, but in
this case they are right."

"But I cannot go back on my promise!" Joe cried petulantly. "I must
do something! I must!"

"Because of the Indians, or because of thy self-esteem?"

He gave it a moment of honest thought. "Both, I suppose. But it
really *is* in the interest of the Indians to move away." He looked at her
warily. "Isn't it?"

"I'm not so sure about that. Indians are much more tied to the
land than thee thinks."

"But surely it's better than to stay and have themselves massacred?"

She did not reply. The whole question of the Indians and the irresistible tide of white colonization was an insoluble one. Joe's suggestion to Running Bull had a lot to be said for it, but it was in effect
a form of surrender. How far could the Indians retreat before the
tide and keep their self-esteem? "How did thee fare with him?" she
asked.

"Who?"

"Running Bull."

"Oh, very well indeed. Which was surprising, considering that I told
him I was thy nephew. He seems to bear some grudge against thee."

"That he does." She grinned. "He was at one time the most sought-
after young Indian chief around. He was sent to England, visited at
Court, mingled with the aristocracy; at that time he was still young
and slender. Then, after he had convinced everybody that he was at
least as civilized as they, he came home and tried to poison his
uncle, who had usurped his place during his absence. The uncle, an
old man, called me in for consultation; I gave him an antidote and
went out on the lake with Running Bull in his canoe. Once we were
out of earshot, I told him to stop that nonsense or I would tell his

uncle the truth. He did stop, although the old man was killed in a hunting accident soon afterward. He has never forgiven me. Did he say he would follow thy advice?"

"Not exactly. But he gave me to understand as much."

"Don't believe it. He may in the end, but he will certainly wait and see if he can't get some money out of the Quakers first. Chances are he will."

"But thee said thyself a moment ago—"

"Not from the Meeting. But before I left I had a word with thy father, and I have the impression that he is contemplating a loan to Running Bull in exchange for trading privileges. So it would seem that, apart from being morally upstanding, thy suggestion has some commercial value."

"But he never spoke of it to me!" the poor boy exclaimed. "I tried to talk to him, but he was so preoccupied I simply gave up!"

"Come, come," she said mischievously. "Surely thee knows him by now? I know that dreamy look on his face, as though he were not paying any attention to what you are saying. I wouldn't be surprised if thee were sent back to Running Bull, this time as a representative of the house of Woodhouse, with the Quakerly message, 'We will help you settle west of the Ohio in exchange for a monopoly on your pelts for the next fifty years.' That would be the kind of arrangement my dear brother would have in mind."

"No," the boy said somberly. "I know what is behind it. Altar Rock."

"Thee means the idea of blowing it up?"

"Abe at least had the honesty to say he didn't want to spend money on the Delawares, as they had decided to leave anyhow. What I don't understand is why Father didn't say so, frankly. Why pretend he didn't know what I was talking about?"

"Thee would understand," she said, "if thee had played pinochle with him for as many years as I have." There was a long silence, during which he brooded. Then she asked casually, "How about that school? Wouldn't that be something for thee and Himsha?"

He looked at her as if she had struck him in the face. "And—and *who?*"

"Come, come! Thee is quite heart-smitten with her. And, for thy information, it is mutual."

"It is?" he asked eagerly. Ah, the innocence of youth! And its cruelty, she thought as she remembered poor Becky. Of all the family, Becky was the one who had made the most telling sacrifice for her father's testimony: she had lost her fiancé, her place in Philadelphia society, and she could have no illusions as to what lay in wait for her in the wilderness. Maybe it was just beginning to dawn on her. She should have a talk with the girl that night, try to prevail upon her to return to Philadelphia with this boy, even though she must realize she would never recapture him. A woman had a way of sensing those things, even an inexperienced one like Becky.

But that night, as they were setting up camp in the meadow in the foothills where she had stayed with George and Himsha last time, there suddenly was the sound of hoofbeats and in the light of their freshly started campfire loomed the massive bulk of Buffalo McHair on his mustang, surrounded by his cronies like Attila by his Huns. When Gulielma asked him what the devil he was doing there, he said, "Loudwater is going to be rough on you, so I thought I'd see you through." She asked flippantly, "In that case, why doesn't thee take them all the way and let me get back to my patients?" To her astonishment, he replied calmly, "All right, I will."

He meant what he said. The next morning, after bidding farewell to them all, she watched the wagon train draw out of sight, up the winding track on the mountainside. She waited until they were gone before turning her old mare and the balky mule with the dispensary heading north. It was time she took a look at the Delawares herself, despite that old rogue Running Bull. The more she thought about it, the more the boy's idea attracted her. The Iroquois would like nothing better than to exterminate them, man, woman and child; the French would not trust them enough to believe in any sudden change of heart on their part. By the look of things, Isaac had got himself a replica in young Joe. Poor Becky! The moment she chose to accompany her father instead of merely paying lip service and staying put like crafty old Beulah, the Woodhouses, father and son, had obviously written her off as a future bride because she was "unstable," a word Friends were particularly fond of. Odd that everyone professed to revere the Quaker saints of the glorious past, but the moment somebody set out to emulate their example, he was considered unstable. She remembered she was to have had a talk with the girl, to try to change her mind. But after a moment's reflection she shrugged her shoulders and continued on her way. If life had taught her one thing, it was that no one was responsible for the fate of another, not really.

*   *   *

To Abby Baker, the long journey through the wilderness was an adventure. At first, when there had been only Aunt Gulie and Cousin George to accompany them, she had been afraid; the night before Uncle Buffalo and his men turned up, she had actually been thinking of running away to one of the Quaker farm families and asking them to take her back to her mother. The idea of having to move in with Aunt Grizzle was unattractive, as was the knowledge that she would have to go to school, but it seemed preferable to being dragged through a dark forest full of wolves and bears and eagles that stole babies, with only Aunt Gulie and her clumsy Indian gun to defend her; she was sure that her father, when it came to the point, would be unable to fire his rifle or, if he did, hit anything. But when with frightening yells and a thunder of hoofs her favorite uncle came crashing out of the forest with his grinning friends, she changed her mind. She had known Uncle Buffalo for only a short while, but the disrespect with which he treated everybody except old Aunt Hannah had completely captivated her. And the nice thing was that he seemed to like her too; the moment he saw her he cried, "Well, if it isn't little Mary!" He picked her up, lifted her high, kissed her on both cheeks, and there was such a wonderful sense of security in the way he tossed her in the air, despite its scariness, that she did not mind he had forgotten her name. "Thee and I are going to see this sorry lot safely to the sea of grass," he said. "Thee had better ride out front with me, from time to time, to keep me awake."

"She has to have her lessons every day," Becky said in a merry voice but with cold eyes.

"Lessons?" Uncle Buffalo's eyes were round with mock astonishment. "What could thee teach a child that would be any use out here? French? We hope to give 'em a wide berth, believe me."

"She has her books and she has to learn. And so has Cleo." When Abby stuck out her tongue at her, Becky showed her true feelings, and snapped, "Now, don't be saucy with me, young woman! Not these days!"

"Days?" Uncle Buffalo shook his head. "Has thee any idea how far it is, my pretty lass?"

"Well . . ." For some reason, Becky flushed; it was a fascinating sight.

"Show me thy wagon, so I can put a guard around it," Uncle Buffalo said, putting an arm around Becky's shoulders. "Overnight I'll sleep on thy tailboard myself. How's that?"

"Oh, that won't be necessary . . ." Becky said as she was being led away, but she did not sound very convincing. Becky had met her match this time.

So, it turned out, had everybody else. Uncle Buffalo took command as a matter of course, and no one protested. The only one with whom he did not seem at ease was Cleo. He had never had any slaves, so he did not know black people. He tried to talk to her in his jolly, joshing way, but it got him nowhere, as Abby could have told him. Cleo was a nasty, hateful creature; she was, as a matter of fact, the only shadow in a wonderful adventure. Not just because of the way she behaved but because of her smell in the small coop of the wagon; it was not something that could be washed away. On the evening of the third day after Loudwater, Cleo vanished when they camped for the night in a little glen by a brook. Becky was the first one to notice her absence and went to tell Uncle Buffalo; he began to call, "Cleo! Cleo!" flushing a covey of quail with a flutter of wings. Someone called, 'She's here, Buffler! Here! Skinny-dippin' in the creek!" That made Uncle Buffalo very angry. "You come right back, Jake! Hear?!" Jake, who had no teeth and shaved very seldom, came loping back through the clover on his bow legs; like the others, he spent so much time on his horse, even sleeping on it occasionally, that his legs were bent to its shape. "Oooh!" he said as he joined them. "She sure is a sight for sore eyes, that one!" Uncle Buffalo was not in a joking mood. "If I catch thee spying on that woman once more, thee and I are going into the bush," he said. Abby did not know what it meant, but it was enough to make Jake protest with such outraged innocence that even Uncle Buffalo had to turn away from such purity. Jake gave her a wink behind the big man's back; although she frowned at him reprovingly, it made her feel proud and grown up and important. That night she began a new diary, headed, *"Abigail Baker, a pioneer of 10¾ years old"* in the back of her English exercise book. Her first entry was, *"Tonight Cleo took a swim in a brook with no clothes on. Jake, a friend of mine, saw her and told everybody who had sore eyes to follow her example. But Uncle Buffalo did not want any of the men to see anybody naked, any girl that is, so she went on splashing around until Becky went to fetch her. She came, but although she looked clean, her . . ."* That was as far as it went, for she did not have a lock on this diary, and she could not think of a word for "smell" that would not make Cleo mad should she stumble upon it. Not that there was much danger of that; although Becky tried every evening to teach her to read and write, Cleo just sat there chewing sunflower seeds, spitting the husks at the men who always hung around the wagon. The only person for whom Cleo had any respect at all was Father; sometimes, when Becky became exasperated by her lack of attention and complained to Papa, he took Cleo aside and they walked up and down for a while out of earshot, talking earnestly. Cleo obviously minded what he was saying and for a few days she would pretend to learn something of what Becky tried to stamp into her stupid head. But all she really wanted, as far as Abby could see, was to sit on the tailboard by herself, one leg dangling, the other pulled up, hanging on to the chain when the wagon was in motion so as not to be tossed off by its lurching, which became worse as they penetrated more deeply into the forest.

Apart from Cleo, there was nothing to mar the glorious journey for Abby. She had the fright of her life when she fell into the water half way across a foaming river, but Uncle Buffalo grabbed her as she was being dragged down the rapids, screaming, lifted her onto his shoulders, and she grabbed his ears in panic. Every day brought new excitement. She was given a baby groundhog by Jake that she tried to tame, but one night it ran away; she was bitten by a snake and yelled like a banshee and Becky frantically sucked her leg, until Uncle Buffalo turned up and told them it was a blacksnake that probably had been more frightened than she. She stayed awake nights to listen to the stories the men told around the campfire, wild stories about horses and Indians and buffaloes and squaws that fascinated her more than the testimonies of the Quaker saints her mother used to recite to her at bedtime; yet those were the only times she missed her mother. The food was delicious; although the cutting up of dead animals by the fireside was a horrible business, the smell of roasting meat that wafted through the evening air in thin gray layers was something she would never forget, as long as she lived. The forest was gloomy and sometimes frightening, with dark, dripping caves where things rustled as the wagons creaked past; but there was always someone else between her and the menace, one of Uncle Buffalo's riders, quite often Uncle Buffalo himself. Those were the times he would pick her off the tailboard without stopping, put her athwart his horse's neck and, one arm around her, start a long, grown-up conversation about whom she was going to marry, where she was going to live, what color she liked best in flowers, and whether she preferred duck to wild turkey. And when they ran out of things to talk about, they would play games, which she would always win because Uncle Buffalo, although he was the nicest man she knew, was rather stupid. Even a simple game like "Guess what I'm thinking about?" was too much for him; when, for instance, she said, "Mineral," he would ask, "Does it have feathers?" As far as real danger went, nobody would have known they were traveling through the virgin forest, even when they began to approach the French. Although Uncle Buffalo made them talk in whispers for a day or so, they never saw one. The spies he sent ahead never reported seeing one either, at least not as far as she knew.

Only when she fell sick, toward the end of the journey, did she begin to get fretful. For days on end, while the wagon bounced and lurched, she lay seasick on her palliasse underneath the cover. Branches scratched and streaked on it, bird droppings landed with a loud "tock," yellow and gray splashes on the canvas that looked interesting seen from below, for lack of anything else to look at. And, all the time, there sat Cleo on the tailboard, shutting out the air, clinging to the frame like a monkey, chewing seeds and spitting the husks at the head of the horse behind them.

Finally they reached their journey's end. It was a spot not much different from many others where they had camped for the night: at the foot of a hill, overlooking a lake with a little island in it. Only when Abby climbed to the top of the hill with Uncle Buffalo could she see the boundless expanse of the prairie in the distance, a sea of billowing grass, as far as her eye could reach, under a big sky full of white clouds. That evening, during meeting, her father ministered, said they would call it Pendle Hill, in memory of George Fox's vision of a great people to be gathered, and prayed to God to bless all those who dwelt here.

The next day Uncle Buffalo and his men went to work. First they dug a storm cellar, for this, Uncle Buffalo said, was whirlycane country. Whenever they saw one bearing down on them, like a big elephant's trunk from a black sky, they should run for that cellar as fast as their legs would carry them and bolt the door behind them. It would also serve to store firewood during the winter months; the chute that was meant to relieve the pressure inside the cellar during the storm so the door would not be sucked out of its hinges was dug at a slant so they could slide the logs down on it. Abby was given the task of keeping the men supplied with cool water while they chopped down trees and sawed logs and dug the storm cellar; they drank buckets of it, which she carried down from the spring in the hillside. It was all very exciting, but very tiring.

The second night in Pendle Hill, while the men swapped stories around the fire and Becky and Cleo tended the mules, Abby used the few precious minutes in which she had the wagon to herself by writing in her diary.

"I think I am going to like it here. I expeshily like the birds that sing on the little ileand in the lake. They sound like niteingales but uncle B. says they are called Veeries. Veerees. Veereys. I also like not traveling any longer. I cannot wait for my own bed. Uncle B. says he will carve a doll for me as soon as he finds a nice soft log. I would like a picaniny better but there are no slaves any more. I miss them and Becky does too I bet. She has to drive a mulecart herself now and all she has left from when she considdered herself a queen is the blue ribbon in her hair that she irons over the kettle each night. She has blisters. She has started to smell too. I like the fronteer but it is smelly. Cleo still swims naked for all the good it does, despite the cold lake. I saw her. She looks like an otter. Goodnight. P.S. God bless thee when thee reads this."

*   *   *

The rutted cart track between the cabin and the forest, where the men were chopping trees and sawing logs, seemed to get longer and more impossible by the hour, Becky thought, as she tried in vain to whip her lazy, mean-tempered mule into motion. The miserable beast had been giving her trouble right from the beginning, now it seemed to have made up its mind that it had had enough.

It happened toward evening, her last load of the day. As she stood there slapping the dusty flank of the beast with puny flips of her reins, she saw from the corner of her eye the other wagon coming back from the house empty, with Cleo lounging in the driver's seat. Her mule was literally galloping back to the clearing, as if it were eager to haul what must be their twentieth load of the day. Becky's eyes filled with tears of rage and desperation and she did something which she had never done before: she picked up a heavy branch and started to lambast her miserable beast with such fury that clouds of dust exploded from its hide. After a whack that took all her strength, the branch broke. It was as if she had tried to chastise a tree: not only did the mule refuse to budge, it stood there, eyes closed, motionless, as if it had never noticed the chastisement.

Cleo's wagon bounced and clattered past her, her silly beast huffing and puffing with exertion, Cleo herself, relaxed and serene, draped decoratively on the seat, one leg dangling. Becky stood there, fists clenched, eyes tightly closed, feeling the tears run down her grimy face, knowing that they made her look even more bedraggled and disheveled. What ever had made her yearn for the freedom of the pioneer, the rustic peace of the farmer? Torture, slavery, that was what it was; broken shoes, filthy clothes, blisters, sandspurs, ticks, hair like a mop, nails black and broken, muscles so sore every night that she took hours to fall asleep. Yet she could have put up with the bleak, back-breaking misery if it had not been for that black viper, that snooty, haughty . . . Becky could not think of a word venomous enough to express what she felt about Cleo at that moment; all she could do was whip the damned mule and shriek at the top of her voice, "Git! Go! Go, damn thee! Go!"

The mule refused to acknowledge the pitiful squeak of her rage. It closed its eyes and stood there as if in meeting. She sat down, sobbing with fatigue, self-pity and helpless rage; then, with the sudden resolve that she was not going to let herself be dominated by a mule, she wiped her eyes with the hem of a petticoat and started to gather dead twigs from the side of the road by the armful. Carrying them over to the mule, she stacked them underneath its belly. With a feeling of triumph she took the tinderbox from under the seat of the buggy and set fire to the pyre. For a moment it looked as if the mule acknowledged defeat; as the first flames lapped at its underbelly, singeing the wisps of dirty hair, it started to move. Calmly it walked a few steps, managing with animal cunning to avoid the fire; then, to her horror, it stopped when the flames were right underneath the wagon.

"Oh, no!" she cried, aghast. "Please! Please, dear Barry, don't do that to me! Come on, move! Move, please, for God's sake, move!" But the mule closed its eyes again and centered down with an expression of devotion, oblivious to her desperate cries.

Barry did not hear them, but someone else did. There was a sound of hoofs, creaking springs and loose floorboards as Cleo came to her aid. She jumped off the driver's seat with the grace of a cat, went calmly toward the head of the meditating mule, took the bit and said languidly, "All right, Barry, let's go," without even raising her voice. Barry opened one eye, saw her, pursed his lips as if he were about to spit, then seemed to have second thoughts and moved slowly forward. Becky watched open-mouthed as the cart drew away from the fire in the nick of time.

It was too much. She knew it was childish, but she could no longer stand the sight of mules, carts or the mocking black female. She turned around, ran toward the water's edge and disappeared down the narrow path between the forest and the reeds that skirted the lake. She ran as far as she could go; when she found her way barred by a fallen tree, she fell into the grass, her face in her hands.

Never in her life had she had such a sense of failure. She was no good for anything in this primitive world; she was a caricature compared to her father, let alone compared to that black, sleek animal Cleo, who slunk through the jungle as if she owned it. Yes, Cleo enjoyed herself here, damn her, like a healthy young animal feeling at home, in harmony with the surrounding world. Becky lay there steeped in misery until presently she heard a crackling of twigs and lifted her head. Cleo must have left the unhitching and tethering of the mules to Jake, who would, as usual, have been falling over himself to oblige; now she was going to take her dip in the lake.

Becky was about to rise to confront her, but she could not carry it off tonight. She could not expose herself to that condescending stare. Exasperated with herself, she clambered over the trunk of the fallen tree, tearing her skirt in the process, and jumped down on the other side, realizing too late that she now had to wait until Cleo was through with her ablutions. There was a splash, the doglike snorts of an animal gamboling in the lake. Well, she would just have to sit it out. As she crouched there waiting, her thoughts returned to the mystery of Cleo. She was not pregnant, she had never been; yet she had come with them. She had, after her own cool fashion, been eager to come. Why? What was she after? What promise was there for her in this frightening, violent land? Something must have lured her; she had certainly not come with them out of loyalty, or gratitude, or the desire to help. Why? Why?

She remembered her starry-eyed notions the night the decision had been made; 'Go for that of God in Cleo. A new Holy Experiment.' How innocent she had been! And taking her along to face the Meeting, to show the Baker children's answer rather than speak it out loud! It had been utterly sincere, and yet: had she consulted Cleo, or even explained to her what she was about to do? No. Unforgivable for someone who prated about never using a man as a means; she had used Cleo to impress the Meeting. It had been well intentioned, maybe even divinely inspired, but she saw now she had acted not as a Friend but as a slave-owner's daughter. Yet all those people had risen in response, and Uncle Jeremiah had said to her afterward, cryptically, "Well, Becky, thee has done it. This may well mean the beginning of the end of our supremacy in worldly affairs." She intended to ask him what he meant, but had never got around to it in the hectic weeks that followed. But even if that what she had done was to prove later to have been of great importance, all she, Becky, the unique and irreplaceable person, should consider was whether, by her high-handed act, she had violated the integrity of another unique, irreplaceable person. Alas—the moment she had come to know that irreplaceable person, she had discovered that she detested her, that she was lazy, devious, man-crazy, full of black, implacable hatred . . .

'God,' she prayed, 'God, make me a better person, make me worthy of what I have done—whatever it may have been.'

A twig cracked nearby; she peered under the tree and saw a pair of legs with leggings. Dirty little Jake! For a moment she considered kicking his shins, then she realized she had better lie low. But, oh! What a bitch that Cleo was! What a miserable, conniving bitch! She must know that she was being spied on by the men while she bathed every evening; it was obviously the true reason for her sudden passion for cleanliness, which had seemed notably absent in the past. The icy lake must be freezing cold—what a price to pay for driving some poor old buffalo hunter crazy! What satisfaction did it give her?

There was that same question again: Why had Cleo come? Why, why had she come? What was she after?

* * *

On a cool autumn morning, before sunrise, Buffalo McHair and his men left them to face the winter alone in their newly finished log cabin. The pungent scent of the banked peat fire gave a feeling of winter, but the early sunlight shining through the parchment window at the foot of the bed looked full of the promise of spring.

Boniface, his hands under his head, gazed at the particles of dust dancing in the beam of light and decided he would get up as soon as it shone into his eyes. Happy laziness filled him with intense well-being, a sense of fulfillment. He marveled at the way the hazardous adventure had worked out after so many people, himself included, had feared disaster. A fifty-year-old man? He doubted whether anyone had believed he would be able to adjust, even survive. What no one had foreseen was the miraculous rejuvenating effect nature had on a man in the virgin wilderness.

He had had the first intimation of this a few days after crossing the mountains, at the beginning of the trek along the erratic Indian trails that criss-crossed the forest between the Alleghenies and the great prairie. Until then he had hated the food, the cramped quarters, the swaying on the driver's seat of the miserable wagon. His boots had pinched, the rifle across his back had hurt him, he had sweated profusely in his leather jerkin; after the first rain shower had soaked it, he had been certain he would catch swamp fever and die in the dank, dark forest that echoed with eerie shrieks and rustlings, especially after dark. The nights had been the worst; on his back in his wagon, holding his breath, mortally afraid, he had been plagued by doubts, convinced he had been insane to embark upon this reckless venture.

One night the stifling prison of the wagon had become so filled with visions of murderous Indians that he crawled out into the open and lay on the tailboard gazing at the sky, a furrow of dark, translucent blue between the black walls of the forest. Orion and Canis Minor were embedded like jewels in the gold dust of distant stars. The immensity of the night awakened in him the awareness that he was surrounded not by ghouls and faceless horrors in the darkness, but by a world of living things like himself, asleep, afoot or on the wing, each after its own nature. Slowly he began to feel part of the forest, the soil, the sky, not an extraneous entity traversing this world of interlocking forms of life like a bullet. It filled him with curiosity, an eagerness to become acquainted with the life of which he was part, in all its variety and profusion. The next day he accepted the discomfort and began to feel at home in his trapper's outfit, which no longer seemed a disguise.

The ultimate acceptance of himself as part of the life of the wilderness came one evening, after they had made camp in a meadow beside a brook, when he wandered off to enjoy the silence and the peace. Birds warbled in the reeds; as he strayed farther away from the voices, the chopping, the laughter, the whinnying of horses on the campsite, their song became louder. Overhead, among the white clouds of summer, a bald eagle soared, indifferent to the dartings and flutterings of the small birds that tried to chase him away. A squirrel chittered in the dark arbor of an Indian chestnut tree; in the distance, beyond the fragile tufts of a row of birches on the crest of a rise, the *"hoo-arr"* of a cougar sounded. He sat down by the brook and listened to the tinkling and splashing of the water that curdled among the rocks; once again he was overcome by a sense of kinship, of unity with the life that surrounded him. Then he saw, downstream, beyond the screen of a young weeping willow trailing its branches in the water, a glistening black animal splashing and gamboling in the brook. It took a moment before he recognized Cleo, so artless was her sensuous enjoyment of the water as she lay there, black and shining, half submerged in the rippling brook. His first impulse was to walk away; but there was something so innocent, so gay about her uninhibited cavorting that he stayed where he was; not out of unhealthy curiosity, but because it was beautiful. Through the trailing fronds of the willow tree he watched her play. There could be no doubt; Cleo was part of nature, like the eagle soaring overhead, the red glory of the chestnut tree, the tender birches on the horizon.

That night, before going to sleep, he opened his Bible as usual and found himself reading the Song of Solomon. *"I am black but comely, O ye daughters of Jerusalem, as the tents of Kedar, as the curtains of Solomon."* It had not occurred to him before that the King's beloved had been a Negro. As he read on, the ancient words seemed to describe the image of beauty and joy he had seen that evening. *"Behold, thou art fair, my love; thou hast doves' eyes within thy locks, thy hair is as a flock of goats that appear from Mount Gilead, Thy neck is like the tower of David, Thy two breasts are like two young roes that are twins . . ."* He believed it now. He and the wilderness and all its creatures were one. He and Cleo and the squirrel and the chestnut tree, the eagle, the willow, the brook and the cougar were all part of one life.

Life, life—the word seemed to sing in his thoughts during the days that followed, as they penetrated more and more deeply into the virgin forest, farther away from the man he had been: narrow-minded, half-alive Boniface Baker of Eden Island. When finally they arrived at their destination, the transformation in himself almost frightened him. For with the joy, the vigor, the vitality a new personality seemed to have emerged with new values, a new concept of good and evil. The man who had rowed around his island had nothing in common with the man who now rowed in a skiff on the misty expanse of the lake in the wilderness. To the old Boniface Baker it would have been sinful to spy on a girl bathing in the lake; to the new Boniface, the one who had built his own cabin, bared to the waist, the woodsman who hunted elk and spread their skins in the sun to dry, there was only joy and beauty in the spectacle. He felt a surge of youth and strength at the sight of her, black Primavera rising from the evening sky mirrored in the lake; the thought of wanting to possess that vision of youth and beauty never occurred to him. The first turgid dream took him completely by surprise.

He was watching Cleo swimming in the lake, yet it was not the lake but another stretch of water; he recognized the Delaware River only when she waded ashore. Then he realized he was not sitting on the riverbank but lying on a bed, looking up at the red canopy of a chestnut tree. She smiled down on him and put one foot on the side of his bed. Suddenly he was choked by violent desire; then he realized that it was not a bed but a coffin, and that the tree was one of the chestnuts in the graveyard of Eden Island. The realization shocked him awake, his body covered with sweat; it took a while before the images of the dream dropped away. What remained was the desire he had felt when she stood looking down at him.

Now day was breaking, and he lay staring at the shaft of sunlight full of dancing dust. In the joy of resurrection which daybreak brought him, the dream seemed to have a place in the harmonious world of nature of which he was now part. Carnal desire was a natural emotion, as natural as the squirrels chasing one another in the trees and the elk trumpeting its mating call in the canyons of the forest. He was not responsible for his dreams; conscious thoughts of the same nature would be sinful, but not a dream. In any case, Beulah was about to join him; he had grown children who were even now under the same roof. He heard small sounds behind the partition of pelts that separated him from the rest of the cabin; one of them must be making breakfast. He heard the clatter of the kettle, the blowing of someone kindling the peat fire back to life. He dozed, eyes closed, listening to the sound of water coming to the boil, of steps going to the door.

But they did not go to the door. One of the pelts was lifted; he knew it was Cleo even before he saw her come toward him, a white bowl in her hands. His throat went tight and his heart thumped in his chest as all of his newly rejuvenated virility responded to the sight of the slender body, now chastely clothed, that he knew so intimately. She bent over him to hand him the bowl, and at that moment he knew with irrevocable certainty that he lusted after Cleo, that she aroused him more than any woman had ever done, that, whatever his conscience, his faith, his love for his wife or his children might tell him, his body, the new body, would not rest until the call of the elk had been answered.

He was in such terrible need to be alone with himself, with God, that instead of setting out with George as usual to hunt the day's food, he said to the youth as he saddled up, "George, I'd rather thee went alone this morning. I'll take the skiff and see if I can catch us some fish."

"Sure, Uncle Bonny. I'll snatch a succulent beastie or two. Thee go and see if thee can fool a fish."

The white, blinding disk of the autumn sun had not yet risen high enough above the rim of the forest to burn the mist off the lake when Boniface set out. It took him but a few strokes to find himself gliding into the same translucent cloud in which he had so often rested his oars on the Delaware to commune with that of God within him. But this morning he could not center down. The stillness and the isolation of the mist did not bring the awareness of the presence of God, but the awareness of Cleo. His loins ached for her lithe, young body. He sat, his head in his hands, lost in the fog with a feeling of damnation. Somewhere in the cloud the nightingales on the little island started their tremulous song, *"Veero, veery, veery, veery."*

Because of the fog, he did not see the two Indians on ponies, ghosting along the water's edge. The fragile song of the veeries was louder than the soft padding of the ponies' hoofs. They entered the clearing where the cabin stood, the smoke from its chimney mingling with the mist.

*   *   *

Becky was carrying a bucket of water from the spring to the cabin when she saw Cleo and Abby run across the clearing, hand in hand. At first she thought it was a game, then she saw Abby's distraught face. When the child stumbled, Cleo went on dragging her cruelly toward the storm cellar and ripped open the door; Abby's frantic shriek, "Becky! Come!" was muffled as Cleo pulled her inside. Becky looked around at the lake, where the girls had been doing the laundry, and froze. Indians! Two of them, naked, brown-skinned men, their bodies covered with paint, their horses without saddles, gray and white. They each carried a weapon, which they held away from their horses, as if ready to strike. They stood motionless as statues at the edge of the clearing, staring at the cellar. Then slowly they advanced toward the cabin.

Becky stood petrified, bucket in hand. Her muscles were taut with terror, she could not move. One of the Indians looked in her direction, and at that moment a voice cried, "Becky! Quick!" It was Cleo, standing in the entrance to the cellar, her hand on the bolt. The cry broke the spell; Becky dropped the bucket and with a burst of strength she had not known she possessed she raced toward the open cellar door. But even as she did so, her mind worked coolly, with detachment. She was running headlong into disaster; if they barricaded themselves in that cellar, the Indians would get in somehow; even if the door was bolted, there was the chute. The fact that Cleo had run away from them in terror, dragging Abby along, gave the Indians the notion that their very appearance filled them with fear and revulsion. But they would have to live with these people, share their land; she must not let fear run away with her, she must appeal to that of God in them, confront them in the power of the Lord.

Only as she reached the door did her reason get her body under its control. All that was primitive and blindly emotional in her cried out for her to dive into the darkness of the cellar and bolt the door behind her, but she managed to stop herself from doing so and turned around to face the Indians. Behind her, Cleo's voice cried with a terrible urgency, "No, no! Come!" But despite her pounding heart, the giddiness of her exertion, a great calm came over her. The Indians approached slowly on their horses, their clubs, or whatever they were, held away from them in that peculiar fashion. Just to stand there was not enough; if she wanted to convince them that she was not afraid, she should go to meet them. 'Like a dog that comes toward thee, barking,' she thought resolutely. 'Thee must show them thee is not afraid. Show them . . .'

She took a few steps toward them; the strange, detached calm pervaded her more fully. "Welcome, friends," she said, her voice high and cheerful. "We are happy to see you. We are Quakers. We are your friends." She hoped they did not hear how unnatural her voice sounded. But did they speak English? A small, quavering panic started in the pit of her stomach, she prayed to God to help her get through to the unique, irreplaceable individuals behind the lurid paint, the expressionless, closed faces, the black eyes staring at her fixedly, as if they were approaching a coiled snake.

"Won't you get down and wait until my father and his men return?" she asked, with a shrillness in her voice that she could not suppress, for the panic in the pit of her stomach grew under their scrutiny. "They are just around the corner, they will be here any moment . . . Welcome, friends . . . C-come, sit down . . ."

She no longer knew what she was saying. Something had unnerved her: a sound behind her back. It took her a few seconds before she realized that it had been the sound of the bolt on the cellar door. The two Indians slid off their horses with a swift, unexpected movement that made her gasp. She felt the urge to run, but her detachment remained in control. The Indians came toward her on foot. If she went on looking from one to the other, she could not hope to reach that of God in either of them; she must concentrate on the one most likely to respond. She smiled tremulously at the one on the left, for he had lowered his weapon as if reassured. It was a primitive ax, attached to a string around his waist from which it now dangled. His hands, small and alien as a monkey's, hung limply by his sides as he came. The paint on his face made it difficult to concentrate on his eyes, but she did so, bravely. She smiled and said, "Welcome, friend, welcome. We are Quakers. We are your friends. Won't you sit down?"

The eyes, staring at her from circles of yellow paint, did not respond. There seemed to be no depth to them; they gazed at her with the vacant idiocy of a goat. Her eyes pleaded with his, black little doors behind which that of God in him was hidden. Then she knew: I was wrong. I should have trusted Cleo. She knows the wilderness, I did not. Now I am facing it.

She knew what would happen before he raised his hand. It was
not she who knew, it was her body, as if it possessed a knowledge of
its own. She whispered, "No, no, please, no, no . . ." A finger hooked
into the top of her dress and she cried out at the wanton destructive-
ness of it. Her dress was ripped with sudden, vicious violence, and
she screamed, "Daddy! Daddy, help!"

Then her detachment left her. She struggled, screaming, screaming,
as the wilderness overwhelmed her.

* * *

At the first scream Abby made a dash for the door, but Cleo
pounced on her in the darkness and held her back. Outside, the
terrible screams mounted to such desperate shrillness that Abby sank
to her knees, sobbing, and covered her ears with her hands.

Even so, she could not shut them out. She tried to pray for Becky,
to plead with God to help her; then suddenly there were no screams
any more, even when she took her hands down and listened. She
dived at the door in a last, desperate effort to do something, to come
to her sister's aid instead of just sitting there, her hands on her ears,
praying. But again Cleo grabbed her and jerked her back; when she
protested, Cleo clapped a hand over her mouth, clammy and cold,
suffocating her. Abby struggled to free herself, but Cleo held her
securely and whispered in her ear, "Hush! If they hear thee, they'll
come for us!"

Come for them? How could they? The door was bolted; Uncle
Buffalo had said that even the strongest storm couldn't open it. Who
were they, anyway? She had caught only a fleeting glimpse of two
horses before Cleo had grabbed her and started to run for the cellar.
Who were they? French? Indians? Robbers? All she knew was that
they were men. Why had Becky fallen silent? Had they abducted her?
She struggled once more to get free, but Cleo tightened her grip and
whispered, "Hush! Here they come!"

For some reason, this was the moment Cleo released her. Abby
did not understand why; then, in the faint light from the chute, she
saw Cleo pick up something in the corner of the cellar: the ax with
which she split the logs. Then she heard voices, very close. She heard
them giggle; someone rattled the door. Cleo lifted the ax and Abby
froze with fright. Would she start chopping at them with the ax when
they came in? What would the Indians do to them if she failed? The
rattling stopped. The voices went away. Abby was about to lunge at
the door once more when suddenly the cellar went dark.

At first she could not understand why, then she realized with
horror that they must have found the chute. Someone was peering
down it, trying to look inside. There was a slithering sound, as of a
big log being shoved down the chute; it came down slowly, stopping
from time to time.

Someone was sliding down the chute, coming for them! Abby stifled a scream and closed her eyes in terror; then there was a loud, crunching thud. In the sudden silence she heard a rhythmic splashing.

The splashing made her open her eyes, she could not understand where it came from. Suddenly it became light again and she saw Cleo drag something away from the mouth of the chute, a body with paint on its legs. Then it went dark again.

A voice called down the chute questioningly, she could not understand the words. The other Indian must be calling to the first one. There came the same sound once more, as of a log slithering down haltingly. Abby pressed her hands on her mouth and prayed, 'God, God, help us, God, save me, save me . . .' There was another crunch and, once again, that rhythmic splashing.

As Cleo dragged the body out of the chute, the light came back and Abby saw it lying across the first. "What did thee do to them?" she whispered; then, in the shaft of light from the chute, she saw something attached to the belt of the second body: a tress of blond hair, with a blue bow in it. It was Becky's.

She was not conscious of hitting the ground.

* * *

George McHair was in high spirits. He had been able to stalk a small herd of moose, the first he had seen coming down from the north ahead of winter; they obviously had had no experience of man, for he had been able to get very close, under the wind, and fell a young buck with one clean shot that made it pitch forward instantly, dead before it hit the ground. He came riding home awkwardly, for the limp body of the moose took most of the room.

He was startled to see two horses skitter and gallop back into the woods at his approach; they must be wild mustangs. Overcome by the madcap desire to go after them, lasso one of them and break it in, he spurred his poor horse, which buckled at the knees under its heavy load, and came cantering into the clearing ready to dump the moose at the cabin door and race off in pursuit of the mustangs. Then he saw Boniface Baker.

He was squatting by the entrance of the cellar, cradling one of the girls, who must have fainted or something. He jumped down, hurried over, saw Uncle Bonny's chalk-white face and looked down at Becky's body. At the sight of her gruesome bald skull, her bloodied face, her torn dress, her nakedness, he turned away with a groan of horror and embarrassment. Where were the others? What had happened to Abby and Cleo?

As if in answer, the door to the storm cellar swung open and Cleo came out, holding an ax. She looked shocked, like Uncle Bonny; the ax was spattered with blood. Had she gone mad? Where was Abby? Grabbing the ax from her and shoving her aside, George rushed into the cellar.

At first he could not see a hand in front of his eyes. But when he bent to put down the ax, a shaft of sunlight shone on Abby's childish legs, her rumpled skirt; she lay on her side. He bent over her fearfully and picked her up; at least she still had her hair. He carried her outside and laid her gently in the grass, his back to Uncle Bonny, as if to protect him from the sight. She moaned, her lips moved, her eyes opened and filled with tears. He turned around and cried joyously, "Uncle Bonny! She's all right! Don't worry, she's fine! She is alive!"

Uncle Bonny slowly turned his head, looked at him and nodded, then he turned away again to gaze down at Becky's horrendous face, her hand in his.

George felt ashamed. What on earth had made him shout, 'Don't worry'? Suddenly he felt arms around his neck, looked down and there was Abby's face, lips parted, eyes half closed, hair dangling. "Yes," she whispered, "she is dead," pulled herself up and kissed him on the mouth before slumping back into unconsciousness.

He was so confused that he dusted his hands. He stood up, looked around for Cleo and saw her sitting a little way off, staring at the cellar. Maybe he should take another look there.

He found the two bodies and saw they were Indians. Only after he had dragged the first one into the open did he discover it was headless. He stood staring at it for a moment, aghast; in a daze, he went back for the other, which proved to be headless also. He went back a third time and emerged with the two heads, holding them by the hair. Then he heard a cry.

Abby was sitting upright in the grass where he had left her unconscious a few moments before. She stared at the heads, her hands on her mouth, her eyes round with horror. He tried to hide the heads behind his back, expecting her to faint again, but she lowered her hands, her body sagged with weariness, and she said, "I saw it."

"Yes . . . I'm sorry," he mumbled foolishly, wishing she would look away and give him a chance to get rid of them.

Then she said, "The night thee came across the lawn."

"The lawn . . . ?"

"The night thee swam across the river." She covered her face with her hands.

He turned to find a place for the heads and saw Cleo had covered Becky with a blanket and was now wrapping a kerchief around her skull. Uncle Bonny did not seem to notice what she was doing; he was still staring at Becky's face, holding her hand.

The way the black girl was bandaging Becky's head, or maybe just the fact that she was doing so, evoked in George a deep gratitude. Then it occurred to him that it had been she who beheaded the Indians.

It seemed in such contrast to what she was doing for Becky that he suddenly felt as if it were all a dream. He stood in total confusion when Cleo rose and went into the cellar. He heard the clanking of metal; she appeared again, holding out a shovel. In the dream, he went to take it from her; as he lifted his hand he dropped one of the heads. She turned away and beckoned him; he followed her, for she seemed to know exactly where she was going.

Only as she began to stake them out did he realize she wanted him to dig the graves.

*   *   *

That afternoon, as meeting for burial was about to start, Buffalo McHair and his men returned. Their arrival was totally unexpected; both George and Abby greeted them with unseemly joy. They had returned because their scouts had sighted Indians, and they were stunned by the news. Buffalo, tears running down his beard, stood grief-stricken beside Becky's body. Then, pulling himself together, he beckoned his men and they lined up behind Boniface Baker, Abby, Cleo and George. Together they entered the silence.

To Boniface Baker their arrival meant little. He seemed to be moving, numbed and speechless, in a strange indifference. He had not yet come to grips with reality; some instinctive protection had dulled his consciousness the moment he found Becky. What had happened since had not really penetrated to him; he had arranged for the burial calmly, with apparent tranquillity. He had ordered the Indians to be buried on each side of her, he himself had covered her body with a blanket and placed her bonnet on it. Now silence settled over the mourners facing the dead.

Boniface stood motionless and empty, waiting to be filled with the awareness of the presence of God. Never before had he felt so devoid of feeling, so stripped of all wishes, hopes, prayers. Suddenly, as they stood there, a host of Indians came out of the forest, shrieking, with a thunder of hoofs. They swamped the clearing with their milling mass; a voice behind Boniface shouted, "Kneel!" and he heard the clicking of rifles. Then the power of the Lord washed over him, made him swing around, lift his arms and cry with a voice that sounded above the shouting, *"Stop!"*

As if time itself had stopped, the Indians, Buffalo McHair, his men all stood motionless; only the horses snorted and pawed. Then a huge Indian slowly rode toward the graves, dismounted, lifted the blanket of one of the Indians, then Becky's, then the other. After that he slapped his horse on the rump; it galloped off toward the lake; he waddled, belly swaying, toward Boniface, but not to confront him: he came to stand by his side. He gestured to his Indians, there was a hushed sound of men dismounting, the multitudinous hoofbeats of horses scattering, then silence settled over the clearing once more. Awestruck, Boniface realized that all those present in the clearing were joined in meeting.

He stood there, vacant, utterly spent. Even when, finally, Buffalo and George walked toward the graves to bury the dead, he felt no emotion. With detachment he watched Buffalo and George lift Becky's body and lower it clumsily into the grave. When they took the spades and began to shovel earth into it, some Indians joined them and picked up the other bodies. They dumped them into the graves and started to shovel earth on top of them with their hands. When Buffalo and George had finished, they gave the spades to the Indians.

After all three bodies had been buried, Boniface was given Becky's bonnet, and they stood once more in silent worship. Birds sang, horses neighed on the water's edge, the evening breeze began to wash through the trees. The Indian chief broke meeting by holding out his hand; Boniface shook it, wondering how the chief knew that this was the way to end Quaker worship. Buffalo McHair said, "Well, Running Bull, where does thee spring from?"

The fat Indian answered in English, pointing at the cabin, "Is this the school we have been promised?"

Buffalo did not answer the question. "So thee now sends thy braves to slaughter the innocent?"

"Those were not my braves, those were Miamis," the chief replied. "You did well by sending them headless to the other world. They are nothing but savages, mad coyotes. But we have crushed them. Those two must have been all that was left of their murderous pack." Then he turned to Boniface Baker. "I am Running Bull, chief of the Unamis. We will build our village on the lake and send our children to thy school. Was the dead woman one of the teachers?"

Before Boniface could answer, Buffalo said, "Yes. She was his daughter." Then he took Bonny's arm and led him to the edge of the lake, through the nervous herd of grazing Indian horses that stared at them warily as they passed. As they stood looking out over the water, he said, "Sorry about the lie. But I know Running Bull, he is as vicious as a rattlesnake. For the time being, just say yes to anything he says. Tomorrow we'll start for Philadelphia."

"I am not leaving," Bonny said.

"Thee doesn't want to stay with those Indians, does thee?"

"I cannot leave Becky."

Buffalo looked at him. "All right," he said. "But does thee realize that thee will have to start a school for their children?"

Boniface did not answer. He stared at the little island in the distance, image of tranquillity.

"Look," Buffalo continued, "I'll leave some of my men with thee. I'll come back myself as soon as I have taken the girls to Philadelphia. Surely thee does not want to keep them here after what happened? In any case, don't let the Indians set up their village around thy cabin. Tell them to move to the other side of the lake. Tell them thee needs the space for a Quaker settlement, with cabins for the teachers and a store and a Meeting House. Running Bull will accept that, as long as it is understood that the settlement will serve his people. Is thee prepared to do that? If thee isn't, Friend, thee will soon join the three we buried today."

Boniface said nothing.

Buffalo put an arm around his shoulders. "Look, Bonny, when thee stopped us firing at those Indians, thee was truly in the power of the Lord. I want to talk to thee about that. I have a proposition to make."

Boniface gazed at the little island.

"I have been asking Philadelphia for years to send us a minister. Not a tame crow without fire or conviction, but a real man of God who would ennoble us by his conduct. Will thee be our minister, Bonny?"

Boniface closed his eyes and whispered, "Excuse me, I—I must be alone. Just for a few moments."

"I understand. I'll not press thee." Buffalo took his arm away. "I think George and I should be on our way. Would it be agreeable to thee if we left tonight? We should not hang around here, not with those two girls."

Boniface nodded. After the other had walked away, he went to the skiff, pushed it into the water, climbed in and rowed out onto the lake.

Halfway to the little island, when the sounds of horses and men had receded, the delicate song of the veeries could be heard in the distance. He gazed up at the sky, where the first stars now shimmered in the green of the evening, then he pulled in his oars, put them beside him, folded his hands and confronted his guilt.

It was he who had brought Becky out here. Lust for Cleo had driven him to leave his children that morning and row to the island to dream. It was he who had murdered Becky. His sin was beyond forgiveness.

He heard a cheering of many voices; as he looked at the shore, he saw a mass of naked Indians plunge into the water, squealing. They leaped about near the shore, splashing one another, gamboling, shouting; their voices echoed eerily in the forest. Only as they started to wash themselves, rubbing their chests, their arms, their faces, did he realize what they were doing. They were washing off the paint. It was peace.

He rowed back to the shore. They splashed him in their exuberance as his boat glided through their throng. An hour later he said farewell to Abby, George and Cleo, and they left. When at last he lay down on his bed, he was so exhausted that he fell asleep at once.

He woke in the middle of the night. He had not moved since he closed his eyes. He wondered what had wakened him; then he heard it again. A soft, short whinny, close by. He lay listening breathlessly; then there was the squeak of a door. He groped for the tinderbox at his bedside and lit the candle. Its timid light grew, bobbing.

"Who is there?"

He heard his heartbeat in his throat as he lay listening. Then the curtain of pelts at the foot of his bed was slowly moved aside.

"Oh, my God," he said.

It was Cleo.

CHAPTER TWO

OUTSIDE the high windows of the First Day classroom in the Meeting House in Philadelphia the first snow of winter was falling, covering the courtyard and the gravestones with a white mantle of silence. Inside the classroom all was silence too, although fourteen people sat in the narrow benches, in some discomfort, as they were meant for children. They were people of all ages, from all walks of life, none of them Friends. The only thing they had in common was that they were deaf mutes.

They were staring intently at their teacher, Beulah Baker, who, tall and dignified in her Quaker garb, stood by the blackboard. On it were drawn the first five letters of the alphabet and the corresponding finger positions in sign language. Slowly, with pontifical gestures as if she were bestowing a blessing upon them, she spelled out a series of words composed of the letters behind her, waiting after each one until every one of her pupils had repeated it.

A-B-E.

B-A-B-E.

B-A-D.

B-E-D.

An old German woman from Frankford was the slowest; a little Jewish boy the quickest. She was very fond of the boy; he watched her with such intense delight, such joy at having the world of the living unlocked for him. Again this morning she was tempted to race ahead with him, ahead of the others who sat there worried, frowning, their hands trying to form the words they were unable to speak. In the end she could resist him no longer; she beckoned young Abraham and gestured to him to compose a sentence for the class with the words on the board. There he stood, small and radiant with his ringlets and his long coat, and his long, graceful fingers formed the words without hesitation. "BAD ABE . . ."

She tapped him on the shoulder and indicated he should go slowly . . . *slowly*.

He grinned with a twinkle in his eye and gestured slowly: BAD ABE and BAD BABE in BED.

It was outrageous, but she had to turn away to hide her laughter. The class, eyeing them with worried incomprehension, obviously had not caught the scandalous sentence, thank heaven. It *was* scandalous, but the snow outside, the hope that radiated almost tangibly from the poor, calamity-stricken creatures in the room, the irrepressible, mischievous joy of young Abraham all added up to a marvelous sense of fulfillment. She was about to berate her favorite student when, behind the glass door to the passage, she saw Jeremiah's face peering at her. Was it time yet? It seemed they had just started. But there he was, beckoning her, so she invited the class to fold their hands in their laps and bend their heads for the customary few minutes of silent worship with which she opened and closed her lessons. It was gratifying to see how readily they had adopted that Quaker practice; all of them seemed eager to join her in a silent prayer of thanks. She had never thought of it before, but silent worship was the only one in which deaf mutes could fully participate.

Presently she shook hands with Abraham; his slender, sensitive hand felt nervous and fragile, like a bird. 'Oh,' she thought, 'thank Thee, God, thank Thee for allowing me to turn what was my curse into a blessing for others.' She smiled at her pupils, who smiled back, and went to join Jeremiah, leaving it to Abraham to wipe the words off the blackboard and rearrange the benches for First Day school tomorrow. She stepped from the bright room into the gloom of the corridor with a feeling of joy, eager to tell Jeremiah about young Abraham's joke, knowing he would love it, for they had designed the alphabet in sign language together.

But the moment he took her arm and put his hand on hers, she knew that something was wrong. With the sensitiveness to others' moods she had developed over the years because of her affliction, she sensed that he was terribly distressed; whatever had happened must be serious. As he led her, gently but with urgency, down the dark corridor, she asked herself, full of apprehension, what on earth it could be. War? Bonny? The children? Grizzle? Maybe the Meeting had decided to end her classes? No, that was inconceivable.

To her surprise, he guided her not to the courtyard, but to the large meeting hall. It was empty and the partition was raised; the white light of the snow, shadowless and all-pervading, made the empty rows of benches starker, the whitewashed walls bleaker. She turned and looked at him. "What is it, Jerry? Please, what is it?"

He took her to the front row of the benches, sat her down, looked behind them to see if they were alone, then he took both her hands, his eyes gazed into hers and he said, slowly and distinctly, "Be brave, dear heart. Becky is dead."

"Becky?"

He nodded and held her hands tightly. "She died of a sudden illness. A month ago. She did not suffer." He bent and kissed her hands; as he looked up, tears were running down his face. He took her in his arms and pressed her head against his shoulder.

She was overcome by the need to break away from his suffocating proximity, his excessive sorrow. The fact that he was more grief-stricken than she exasperated her, for she herself felt nothing, nothing at all. She must shake him off, be alone, face the truth by herself; she struggled free, as gently as she could; he gazed at her, his face haggard and streaked with tears. She said, "Please, Jerry, leave me for a moment, please. I'll join thee later. Leave me here, please. Just for a moment."

"Oh, God, oh, God," he muttered. "I wish I could take it from thee, I wish I could . . ."

She was incensed by his anguish. Didn't he see that she could not stand any more of this, that he must leave her alone to face the truth? But she managed to control herself, to smile and nod, trying to express gratitude, or whatever it was he wanted of her, until at last he rose to his feet and went up the aisle.

He was gone. She sat waiting for the grief to overwhelm her, the sudden realization of the truth that would devastate any normal mother. Becky was dead. Becky had died a month ago in the wilderness. She had not suffered. Well, that was fortunate. She was grateful that she had not suffered. Was that the way to react? 'Well, that was fortunate'? She could not understand herself. What *was* she feeling right now? She looked at the empty benches, the high windows with the snow falling outside. Becky was dead. Becky, little Becky, her child, had been dead for a month. While she herself had been teaching deaf mutes to speak in sign language, finding a fulfillment and happiness she had never known before, her child had died in the wilderness and was buried somewhere in a dark hole, to become part of the damp soil of the forest. Tentatively, ready to withdraw, she tried to imagine Becky, her Becky lying there. Under the ground. Worms . . . She covered her face and shrank from that vision. She shook it off and there was that indifference again, that eerie calm. It was the auction all over again: one by one, the petals fall. House gone, furniture gone, husband gone, child gone. The children had been gone for months now. For all she knew, Joshua might be dead too, and Abby. Maybe Jeremiah had not dared tell her all of it. Maybe Abby was dead too.

She tried to visualize it, but it remained abstract. She felt no sorrow. Maybe she was more concerned with young Abraham now than she was with her children. Abraham was here, Abraham depended on her, Abraham was learning to speak under her guidance. It was more fulfilling than teaching her own children had been. She remembered Becky's first sounds: "Baba, baba." She conjured up the image of the little child toddling toward her, saying, "Baba, baba." A toddler with drooping diapers, grimy little feet. Becky was dead. A child she had borne under her heart was dead. It was very sad. Any moment now she would weep, she would wail; but right now, staring at the windows, she could not grieve for the child who had deserted her. What a scandalous thought for a mother! No one had deserted anyone. Becky would have stayed with her if she had been able to hold her; instead she had gone with her father. They had not shed a tear when they left her behind. Little Abraham would be destroyed, should she desert him now.

Little Abraham! Dear God, was it possible that she loved a little Jew with ringlets more than she loved her own flesh and blood? Was it wrong? It probably was; she would have to face it, for there was nothing she could do about it. She would simulate the proper feelings in front of others, but she could not deceive God. Gazing at the windows, the snow, she realized that she could even face damnation with equanimity as long as God allowed her to teach her deaf mutes.

She rose and walked up the aisle. She felt unsteady, as if her body had been shocked while her emotions remained unaffected. She had to support herself as she walked slowly from bench to bench, a little frightened, for something was going on within her that she could not understand. As she came out the door, Jerry rushed toward her and she was grateful for his support. They stood for a moment close together, his arms around her, alone in the empty lobby. She looked at his tragic face, his dear, harrowed eyes; but she discerned a reticence in them, an evasiveness. As he opened the door to the white world outside, she asked, "Jerry? Tell me, tell me truthfully, is there more? Is—is Abby . . . ?"

"No, no!" he replied hastily. "Abby is well! As a matter of fact, that is the good news: she is here."

"Here?"

"Yes, at home. George McHair brought her. She wanted to come with me, but I thought it better . . ."

The thought that Abby was here suddenly filled her with the overwhelming need to hold her in her arms, to feel her living body. Abby back! Abby was back! She broke away from him and rushed toward the carriage and the horse, blurred by the tumbling snow.

When, with a cry, Abby threw herself upon her as she entered the hall of Grizzle's house and she held the trembling little body against her, the first impact hit her. Becky was gone. Never would she hold her in her arms again the way she now held the distraught, sobbing child. "Oh, Mama, Mama!" Abby wailed, her high, childish voice hoarse with pent-up grief. "Mama, Mama . . ."

Somehow, it was all in those words. As she pressed the sobbing child against her, she knew that Becky had not died of an illness. She knew it before Abby told her in whispers that night in bed, close to her, as close as she could get.

When finally Abby was asleep in her arms, it became reality to her at last. Her tears flashed in the candlelight as she lay staring at the ceiling, thinking, 'Love, dear love, dear little love . . . what have they done to thee?'

*   *   *

Joe Woodhouse came home late that night from the warehouse and he was shattered to learn that Becky had died of a fever. All night he tossed and turned, haunted by her image; it was the first time death had touched someone close to him. Toward morning he finally fell into a fitful sleep.

Breakfast was a somber meal, with everyone steeped in gloom.

Finally his mother said, "Joe, I think thee should go next door and present thy condolences to Aunt Beulah and little Abby. After all, thee was rather close to them."

"Yes, Mother," he said dutifully; but this was what he had been dreading. Condolences were difficult enough, to have to shout them at the top of your voice to someone who was deaf was lugubrious, and he was terrified that Aunt Beulah would break down and weep all over him. But he dutifully went next door when the meal was over.

He was kissed wetly on both cheeks by Aunt Grizzle the moment she opened the door. "Oh, poor boy, poor boy!" She pressed him against her and rubbed her moist face against his. "How heartbroken thee must be! How—how—oh!" She obviously could not think of a word that would not sound like an anti-climax. Joe was overcome by a feeling of distaste; it grew into loathing when she took his arm and dragged him along the passage, snottering, "Poor Beulah has taken to bed, Dr. Moremen has been to see her and given her a potion, but Abby is downstairs, poor little thing, poor, suffering, tortured little thing . . ." She threw open the door to the dining room almost with pride, as if to show him a new piece of furniture she had acquired. "I'll leave the two of you," she whispered. "I won't intrude—" and she hurried away.

Joe entered the dining room with the long face and the slow gait appropriate to the occasion. The child was sitting alone at the dining-room table, stuffing herself. She eyed him coldly as he came toward her; then she said, her mouth full of half-chewed bread, "Hello."

"I—I have come to present my condolences at the death of thy sister," Joe said. It sounded preposterously formal.

"Thank thee," she said nonchalantly, scooping chocolate ants off her plate with a spoon. The bread she was chewing must have been heaped high with them; under normal circumstances, Joe knew, Aunt Grizzle would have hit the ceiling at such extravagance. Obviously, the little monster was cashing in on the occasion as much as she could.

"It—it must have been a great shock to thee," he said coolly.

"It was." She rose in her chair, reached across the table, grabbed another piece of bread and started to butter it as if she were slapping mortar onto a brick.

"Was thee with her when she died?"

"No, all I heard were the screams."

"Screams?" He had not realized that to die of a fever must be an agonizing process. It disturbed him; he had imagined Becky passing away in her sleep, pale and emaciated, in an atmosphere of hushed awe.

"Yes," the child continued, heaping the slice of bread with chocolate ants. "It happened just outside the door of the cellar. I wanted to open it, but Cleo wouldn't let me. She was right, of course. If I had, the Indians would have got us too."

He went cold. "Indians . . . ?"

She frowned. "Didn't they tell thee?"

"But she died of fever!"

"She surely did not." She took a bite of the sandwich, spilling chocolate ants. She tried to catch them in her cupped hand, but they showered onto her plate and the tablecloth.

"Then how did she?" he cried. "What happened?"

She held up a finger, indicating her full mouth; she pushed most of it into her cheeks and mumbled, "She was—scalped—by Miamis." The final *s* resulted in a spray of chocolate ants.

He rose. "Don't tell that story to anyone else," he said, with a mixture of horror and rage.

"But it's true!" she cried. "Ask George! He saw her too! Her head—"

"George had the sense to stick to the story that thy sister died of a fever." He put his chair back at the table. "If I find out that thee has told this story to anybody else, anybody at all, I will, personally, wring thy neck!"

"Pooh!" she said, spewing chocolate ants; but he knew he had put fear into her.

He let himself out. Aunt Grizzle was hovering in the passage; he hastily assumed an expression of mourning.

"How is she?" It was an almost greedy whisper.

"She seems to be recovering," he replied.

"Oh, God!" Aunt Grizzle sobbed with alarming intensity. "I'd do *anything* to help the child forget . . ." Tears were running down her face.

He could take no more. "Excuse me," he muttered, and he made a dash for the front door with unbecoming abruptness.

* * *

Abby, the half-eaten sandwich in her hand, sat staring at the nightmare slowly rising: the headless brown body, Becky's hair hanging from its belt, the blue ribbon. She had thought that at last she could talk about it without breaking down; Joe's anger had shattered her tenuous self-confidence. With a cry she collapsed, her head on her arms, and sobbed, all alone in a terrifying darkness. The door opened, a gown rustled, sheltering arms embraced her and Aunt Grizzle's voice whispered, "Sweeting, sweeting! Abby, my lovey, lovey! What is the matter? What is it, my child, my baby, what is it?"

Mother had never talked to her like this; she lifted her tear-streaked face and gazed at the gray eyes full of tears. "Ow . . . Ow . . ." She heaved, trying to speak.

"Hush, baby, there, there, hush, Aunt Grizzle's here, all is well . . ."

She felt herself being pressed against Aunt Grizzle's unfamiliar bosom; after a soothing hand had patted her shoulder for a long time, she finally managed to gasp, "Oh, Aunt Grizzle . . . I'm so sorry, I spilled chocolate ants all over thy tablecloth . . ." She let herself go in wild, despairing sobs; only this time they were different.

"Never mind, never mind, my love, my lovey!" Aunt Grizzle said, kissing her hair, "eat as many as thee likes, spill them all over the place, I love thee, I love thee, I don't care . . ."

Their arms tightly wound around each other, they dissolved in tears.

*   *   *

Joe, in the brightness of the snow-covered street, turned right, to go home, but as he passed the first window of his father's house, he saw a face at the curtain. He could not confront anyone, not yet; he must first take in what Abby had told him. He did not doubt it was the truth; it explained the evasive way George McHair had talked about Becky's illness the night before.

Suddenly the full hideousness hit him. In a flash of hallucinatory vividness he saw Becky struggling, her dress torn, one naked Indian holding her pinned down while the other . . . God, dear God! The vision made him break into a run, jogging through the soft, powdery snow. He could not shake the screams, the struggle, what had happened to her beautiful blond hair . . .

He looked around and found he was standing on the bank of the Delaware. The white quayside with its black skeletal trees was empty except for the hooded shape of a woman standing on the corner of Water Street, feeding sparrows in the snow. He walked toward the forest of masts in the distance. How was it possible that a gentle, kind, vulnerable girl, someone who, despite her temper, had been so sensitive, so fastidious, so proud of her beautiful hair . . .

Oh, my God! He broke into a run again, but remembered the woman on the corner. He slowed down and walked, just short of a run, to the Meeting House; a panicky flight to God. He pushed open the gate; the stern façade with the tall windows staring down at him made him turn away and wander off among the tombstones. He pushed the snow off the seat of one of the benches and sat down, his head in his hands, staring at his feet buried in the snow. He heard the gate and saw someone come in, the same woman whose presence had driven him away before. Damn her! He was about to strike a tragic pose that would keep the busybody away when he recognized the tall, slender silhouette. "Himsha!" he cried, and something inside him seemed to break.

She came toward him, a vision of tender concern; when she stood by his side and her black eyes looked down at him, he grabbed her hand and cried, "Himsha, oh, Himsha! Thank God!"

He burst into tears, his head on her lap; his hat fell into the snow.

*   *   *

Himsha sat stroking Joe's hair. His face was buried in her lap, he lay there helpless as a child, in uncontrollable sorrow. But she could not help it, she was cursed with a lack of faith, an ingrained suspicion. All her love, her tenderness went out to him, yet at the same time odd, detached thoughts rose in her mind which she could not suppress. 'He comes up for air, like an otter—I wonder if he knew me the first time—I wonder if he ever lay in her lap like this.'

How could she think of the dead girl like that at this moment? She wished she had resisted the urge to go after him at the sight of his haggard face from the window. It was indelicate to run after a boy, even to console him. But there had been something strange in his eyes as he glanced up at the window. He had already heard about Becky's death, the night before. "Tell me, Joe," she said gently. "What has upset thee? What happened?"

"I cannot tell thee," he mumbled, his face in her lap.

With a return of the certainty that had made her run after him, she urged, "Try, Joe. It will help thee."

He lay silent for so long that her certainty withered; then suddenly he said, "Becky was killed by Indians and—and scalped. Abby heard her screams."

She sat motionless, staring at the back of his head, as the memory rose within her. Again she sat among the dead. Everybody was dead, even her little dog. The wigwams were burning; motionless, she stared at her mother, her sisters. She heard the shouts of the white men dancing around, swinging long tresses of black hair, spraying blood.

He lifted his head and looked at her. "Himsha?"

Part of her cried out to him, a desperate cry for help, but the other part, the part she trusted, had withdrawn, even from her own body, as when Petesey Paisley had attacked her.

"Himsha?"

She looked at his eyes, his innocence.

"What is the matter?"

He must not know. "I saw it happen to others," she whispered. It cost a great effort.

"Oh, dearest . . ." He sat up, took her hands and gazed into her eyes with such kindness that she slowly turned toward him, away from that memory. "I am so sorry . . . So terribly sorry . . ."

His gentleness made her feel as if she were rushing toward him from the burning wigwams, the screaming men, the horrible dolls with the pink bald heads. She wanted to halt her headlong rush, suppress the cry swelling within her; then he said, "Dearest . . ."

"Joe!" she cried, and she fell forward into his arms.

* * *

"Well, colleague," Gulielma Woodhouse asked, smiling, as she buttoned up her city dress. "What's the verdict?"

Dr. Moremen returned her smile with a look of bland reserve. She knew what the answer would be; she had known it for months. As she fumbled with the unfamiliar buttons on her cuffs, she wondered why she had not stayed with her own diagnosis. Had she expected him to prove her wrong? He was a good doctor, as doctors went in Philadelphia, but he knew less than she did in these matters.

"Well . . ." he said cautiously. "What is thy own diagnosis, Friend Gulielma?"

She felt her smile turn into a scowl; fortunately, she realized in time she was making the man the scapegoat for her own inner turmoil. "Never mind," she said. "I am sure we concur." Why should she not say it outright? For the same reason as he, obviously: to spare the patient's feelings. And why not? Why spare other people's feelings and brutalize her own? She did not have to spell it out, all she needed to do was make some necessary arrangements.

"Could thee help me with these miserable buttons, Friend?" she asked, holding out her cuff to him.

Dr. Moremen was happy to oblige. He fumbled with the minuscle buttons with alacrity, as if to make up for the death sentence.

"I have some important business in the far west," she said. "I was planning to stay in town until spring; would thee, in view of thy present findings, suggest that I should leave somewhat earlier?"

"I would," he said, preoccupied with the buttons.

"The sooner the better?"

"I would say so." He patted her wrist. "There. That has done it."

"Thank thee." She made a ritual gesture of rearranging her hair, what was left of it. Well, at least she could stop worrying about going bald. "It is thy opinion that the discomfort of a journey on horseback in the heart of winter is preferable to—well, the postponement?"

He was a little bemused by this, and no wonder. Why this infernal delicacy? She wanted to blurt out, 'Let's stop beating about the bush!' but could not bring herself to do it.

"I would say so," he replied vaguely.

"Whatever I may mean?"

Poor man, she had him completely bewildered. She should really stop this childish game.

"Sad business, poor Becky Baker," he said, escaping. "There's a lot of it around on the frontier, I gather. I hope it won't get to this city."

He obviously shared the common conviction that Becky Baker had died of swamp fever. "I doubt it," she said. "It's primarily endemic to outlying areas. Mainly isolated homesteads."

"What is it, in thy opinion? The diet? Vapors?"

She thought it over, then said, poker-faced, "The diet, I would say. Too much meat, and too much of it salted."

"Ah?" He perked up. "That would make an interesting paper, Gulielma Woodhouse. The Friends' Medical Society has a meeting between Christmas and New Year; would thee be prepared to address us on the subject?"

"I would have done so gladly, if thy advice had not been for me to leave without delay," she replied uncharitably.

"Yes—quite, quite." He preoccupied himself with his instruments, in unprofessional but rather endearing embarrassment. She wondered how he handled other fatal diagnoses. In her practice she had had few opportunities to cultivate a bedside manner; good thing she was not let loose to practice medicine on this sensitive, overcultured community with her frontier manners. "Well," she said, stopping herself in the nick of time from slapping her thighs before getting up. "Time I was going. Thank thee, Friend Moremen, for a delicately handled diagnosis."

He reacted with bashful humility. "Oh, come, come, dear colleague! I fail to understand why thee thought it necessary to consult me."

She did not say 'So do I.' She held out her hand and he made as if to kiss it; at the sight of it, he merely shook it gingerly.

"Well, I don't expect I'll be seeing thee again," she said theatrically. "I wish thee a happy, peaceable life."

"Thank thee," he said, unmoved. Her pathos seemed to have come as a relief.

Outside, she found the snow-covered city with its gay Christmas decorations darker than she had left it. Sleighs jangled past, full of cheerful, red-cheeked people bundled up in furs and wraps, the hoofbeat of the horses was muffled by the snow. A lamplighter was putting up his ladder against a lamppost, behind him a string of stars stretched to the Delaware, a black cavern underneath the blue evening sky; a Turkish moon rose over the New Jersey forest. She turned her back on it and started to walk back to her brother's house, for the last thing she wanted was to indulge in morose musings about the beauty of the earth. She would do well to get herself to the Huni Indians as fast as she could; who could tell?—she might be cured by one of their magic potions. There could be no doubt that Indian shamans had an uncanny skill; they were aware that the body's controlling agent was the soul. Despite his pious Quakerism, Friend Moremen would scoff at the idea that physical ailments might be induced by spiritual ills; to him and his Medical Society, man was a machine consisting of separate parts, some of which could be mended when they broke down; if they could not, the apparatus was condemned.

Isaac's mansion was decorated with a pagan Christmas wreath which had of late become acceptable to the Society, and also with some white-and-blue bunting around the fanlight heralding the forthcoming wedding and announcing that the future groom and bride were both living under this roof. In the world, such an arrangement would be considered indecent; the moment a couple announced their wedding plans, the groom was expected to seek lodgings elsewhere. Friends were inclined to trust the chastity of their young more readily than the Anglicans; however, she judged that some hefty bundling was going on in Isaac's staid abode at dead of night. Joe was a lucky boy to have roped in such a ravishing creature; compared to Becky, Himsha McHair was a swan compared to a goose. Poor Becky! Gulielma wondered whether Becky had been killed or died of fright. Indians rarely killed the women they raped; they scalped only the ones with fair hair. They were attracted by blond hair, like magpies by a mirror; once they got their hands on long blond tresses, they were unable to resist the temptation to make them dangle from their belts. It was possible that the girl had died of heart failure; she had always looked predisposed to it, with her bulging eyes, her slightly bluish pallor and the ease and frequency of her blush. Probably the double shock of the sexual assault and the scalping had brought it about. In a sense, she had been lucky.

After supper the Woodhouse family gathered in the candlelit parlor in the company of their neighbors. Abe's little daughters, Prudence and Charity, arrived; together with their young Aunt Caroline they sang Christmas carols and a few part songs that in less sophisticated circles would have been considered worldly. It was a happy occasion, full of nostalgia; feelings stirred in Gulielma that she did not want to encourage, so she started to observe the others. Behind the official young lovers Joe and Himsha, sitting hand in hand, another couple was obviously united by tender feelings: Jeremiah Best and his sister Beulah. Gulielma wondered if they realized the true nature of their lifelong attachment to each other; it seemed strange that at their age they could still sit holding hands in such innocence. By the grace of God, Grizzle Best was so addicted to spying on others that she never noticed what was going on under her very nose.

After the jolly evening was over, Gulielma was about to open the door to her bedroom when Beulah accosted her in the dark passage; she must have been waiting there. "Gulielma," she said, "on thy way to the Territory, would thee be passing by Pendle Hill?"

"Pendle Hill? Oh, Bonny? Yes, I might. Why?" She took care to raise her voice.

Beulah swallowed, her lips were trembling. "I would like thee to take him a letter," she said finally.

"Certainly, I'll be glad to." That seemed to be all there was to it; but Beulah's face was so distraught and tormented that Gulielma could not help asking, "Anything wrong?" It was a pity she had to shout it; she hoped no one would turn up to investigate.

For a moment it looked as if Beulah would blurt out what it was that filled her with such obvious distress. But she kept a tight hold on herself; she was, in some ways, a regal woman. "I am afraid I must tell him that I shall not join him this spring. Much as I would like to, my place is with Abby and—and my students."

Oh, yes, her students. Gulielma had heard about the work she and her brother Jeremiah were doing with the deaf mutes of the city. Very commendable. "I am sure he will be disappointed!" she cried.

"He will be desperate," Beulah Baker said calmly. "But after laboring over it for weeks, I decided this was my duty. Jeremiah agrees."

Gulielma gave her a searching look. "I'm sure he does." Then she added louder, "So do I!"

"Thank thee. I'll let thee have the letter tomorrow." Beulah gave her an oddly condescending smile, turned away and swept off.

Later that night Gulielma's stoic acceptance of her fate broke down. Pacing up and down in her bedroom, her shadow swelling and shrinking on the wall in the candlelight, she went through despair and torment in unbearable loneliness. If only Buffalo had been there, or even

Boniface Baker, anyone at all who shared with her the reality of the wilderness! In the unfamiliar and bewildering despair with which she found herself stricken, she thought of calling on Isaac, who, after all, was her brother, but he would try to persuade her to stay, have herself looked after, become an invalid, a burden. He would be unable to understand her desire to die, like any old sick animal in the wilderness, in the stillness of the forest, terrified, going through the green and white hell of pain, yet sustained by the thought that she was part of the life that surrounded her and would remain so after her consciousness had been snuffed out. In Philadelphia the rest of her days would be spent in fear and misery, out there she would remain active, leading a nearly normal life despite the pain. It would be a matter of how long she could keep her food down; when she could no longer take in sustenance, her life would come to an end. As she paced up and down in the cage of her room, the prospect seemed unbearable and yet seductive: to die of starvation in the snow-covered forest, alone at the foot of a tree, gazing up at the stars through the barren branches, her mule and her old mare dozing nearby. What would become of them, left to fend for themselves in the wilderness at dead of winter?

But now she was carrying things too far. There was plenty of time for all that. She undressed and crawled into the unhealthily soft, springy bed, forgetting about the warming pan and burning her feet with a shriek. She yanked the brazier out, checked the impulse to lay about her with it, whacking at the overstuffed furniture, the petulant portrait of George Fox scowling down at her. She put it on its tray in the corner of the room and came upon her musket.

It was like turning a corner in a strange city and meeting a friend. She took the old blunderbuss in her hands and caressed it with maudlin sentimentality. At that moment it symbolized the Hunis: freedom, peace, the courage to face the end with serenity. To die gazing at the stars through dead branches was terrifying, however natural and organic it might be; to die gazing at a deep blue sky, surrounded by soaring orange towers, was infinitely soothing. Yes—she would return to the Hunis to die, as she had promised them, smoke peyote, and all pain and anxiety would be gone; she would float into that sky like diving into a deep blue lake, watched by her Stone Age people to whom birth, death and eternity were simple mysteries, not complicated and awesome ones. Their concept of immortality was the continuation of life; on the eve of the end of Man a single, tall white cloud would appear in an empty blue sky beyond the snow-capped mountains; until that cloud appeared, their children were their immortality.

If only she had a child! She shrugged off the thought and the self-pity it provoked; but it gave her an idea. The next morning, before she went shopping for clay pipes, beads, pots and pans and the rest of the stores the Huni chief had jotted down for her on a bat's wing last time she left, she called Joe and Himsha into her room. She would have to leave before their wedding, she told them, and wanted to give them their gift now: an antique gun that had belonged to a Spanish conquistador, given to her by the head of a tribe of Indians in the mountains near Mexico. It was their passport to a secret land that no other white man could penetrate alive. She knew about Joe's plans for a school in Pendle Hill, to be built by his father in exchange for economic privileges; it was a noble plan, and with their aid it could become a solid school indeed. "But the real need is not among the Delawares," she said. "Boniface Baker will be capable of running that school once you get it started. But the Hunis! They are a different story. To start a Quaker school for Huni children would be a worthy concern indeed, and this gun is your key to their kingdom. God bless you, until we meet again."

It was a solemn moment. The two innocent children were deeply impressed; they never suspected it to be a childless woman's desperate stratagem to obtain some illusory sense of immortality.

After that, there was nothing left to do but to buy the stores and a second mule to carry them and to say farewell to everybody. On the fifteenth of December 1754, during a blizzard, Gulielma Woodhouse rode out toward the west, a huddled figure atop a gaunt gray mare, trailing two mules, one with an angular edifice on its back, the other loaded with pots, pans, shovels, axes and sundry bundles and boxes. The few pedestrians who saw her, blinded by the snow, took her to be a peddler going home for Christmas.

CHAPTER THREE

WHEN Joe Woodhouse was called into his father's office for an urgent conference with his brother Abe, he hated the idea. In the past he would have been excited and honored to be included in the family council, but his impending marriage had put him in a state of high spirits that bordered on euphoria; the call came just when he was about to leave with Himsha and his sister Carrie for a secret visit to Obadiah Best to discuss the school expedition.

He found his father and Abe closeted in the study; from the expression on his father's face he gathered that whatever it was Abe had told him had not improved his mood. He soon found out the reason.

In behalf of the house of Woodhouse and a few other interested parties, Abe had visited Eden Island to discuss the sale of Altar Rock with the new owners. "I must say," he said, "I did not expect to find a well-run establishment; it never was, not even under the Bakers, but even so I was unprepared." He smiled. Joe knew that smile; it usually meant that Abe was up to no good. "To cut a long story short, I found the place in complete chaos. I asked to be taken to their leader, who turned out to be Medea."

"Medea?" Joe asked.

"The fat old house slave who always loitered in the kitchen."

"Oh, Mammy. Did she quote a price for the rock?"

"Certainly," Abe replied derisively. "She asked what we were willing to offer; when I told her, she replied, 'Multiply that by ten, then we might talk.'"

"How much did thee tell her?"

"Five hundred."

"That was not exactly generous, was it?"

"For a piece of rock, of no use to anybody? If it had been left to me, I would not have offered them anything. I would simply have gone ahead and blown up the rock, and if they didn't like it they could have sued us in court."

"Needless to say," their father remarked, "I did not agree to that."

"No, thee did not," Abe continued with that unpleasant smile. "And look where it leaves us. I don't know what the Hendersons think about this, but I say: not in five thousand years."

"Are they open to bargaining?" Joe ventured.

"I doubt it. In my opinion, it is a sort of revenge. I don't think they care about the rock. I'm convinced that even if we were to agree to pay their price, they would think of some other way to sabotage the project. As far as I'm concerned, it's a waste of time. Let them rot."

His quiet viciousness chilled Joe. "And what about the harvest?" he asked. "Did thee discuss that at all?"

Abe shrugged his shoulders. "I discussed it with the owners of some neighboring plantations whom I met at the inn."

"I don't understand," Joe said. "What did thee discuss?"

"Well, the harvest!" Abe seemed irritated by his insistence. "Everybody agrees that they won't be able to harvest the indigo properly, and if they do, the quality of it is certain to be very poor. As I told Father, it's time we cast about for another source of indigo, or we may find ourselves out of the market."

"In other words, the plan is to boycott their harvest?"

"I did not say that."

"Who else is in on this?"

Abe shot him a hostile glance. "Now don't thee start going Quakerly on me too!" he said unpleasantly.

"How about thee, Father?"

Their father looked up unhappily. "I don't like this at all," he said. "I told Abe so. That is why I wanted this family meeting. It is my feeling—"

Abe would not let him finish. "Listen, you two," he said roughly. "I agreed to discuss this, but first let's get one thing straight: We cannot run a business the size of ours on unworldly principles. Since Father is now to all intents and purposes retired, I am the one who has to make the decisions, and it is my considered opinion—"

"To start with, I am not retired," his father interrupted with quiet anger. "And Joe is a full partner."

"But Joe is about to leave for the Northwest Territory to set up a trading post! I'll be the one who stays here, I'll have to make the decisions. I'd like to point out that in the matter of Eden Island every single merchant I have talked to in the city feels the way I do. We will not buy their harvest unless they agree to sell the rock at a reasonable price. We won't be held to ransom by a bunch of niggers who now find they have a stranglehold on the city. That is all there is to it. I don't care what this family council decides—we must abandon unworldly notions, or we'll find ourselves without a penny to our names. As long as I am running this business, that is not the way it is going to be."

There was an uncomfortable silence. Then their father said, "Abraham, in my long experience I have learned that the Quakerly principles are not only spiritually right but—"

"Oh, Father! We've gone over this a thousand times!"

"I know! And I want to go over it once again! Thee and thy cronies do not believe in the testimonies, you will not see that by adhering to them everybody concerned will be better off in the end. To bring those Negroes to their knees by a boycott flies in the face of everything Friends have stood for ever since they first landed on the banks of this river, and as a consequence you will not only lose virtue, but money as well."

"At least that's honest," Abe said. "I never heard thee say in so many words that thee adheres to the testimonies on commercial considerations."

If he had intended to provoke his father, he did not succeed. The old man said with quiet authority, "Friends have never considered virtuous only those principles which turn out to be unprofitable."

Abe sighed. "Very well, Father, think it over and let me know when thee has a better suggestion." With that, he rose, winked at his younger brother and left.

Joe and his father remained behind in acute discomfort. The old man said ruefully, "It's a great pity. If only he were not so *impatient.*"

Joe was overcome by despondency. He had the distinct feeling that his father, despite his apparent self-assurance, had no alternative to offer. "What is thee going to do?" he asked.

The old man shrugged his shoulders wearily. "I don't know yet. I have to think it over. Way will open."

"What about the Meeting?"

"The Meeting?"

"Isn't it responsible for the Negroes on Eden Island?"

"Why should it be?"

"Didn't the Meeting support Boniface Baker's testimony? The Negroes are now being preyed upon by other slave-owners, waiting for them to fall in their laps when they can't sell their harvest. Isn't the Meeting responsible for them, now that Uncle Bonny is no longer here?"

His father looked at him through narrowed eyes; Joe had the feeling that the old man was disturbed by his words. Finally he could stand his father's scrutiny no longer and said, "Thee looks at me as if I talked nonsense."

"No, no, not at all." The old man turned away and walked to the window. Then he said, looking out, "Let me think it over."

"Yes, Father." Joe rose. "Is there anything else?"

"Not for the moment."

Joe left the room with a feeling of failure.

* * *

"But what does thee want me to *do?*" Peleg Martin asked crossly.

Isaac Woodhouse shrugged his shoulders. "Just go there," he said, "find out what the situation is. If thee thinks it warrants intervention by the Meeting, let's bring it up."

Behind them in the little gazebo the pigeons which Peleg had been feeding cooed and rustled in their cages. Isaac gazed out of the dusty little window at the winter garden, luminous with snow.

"What's stopping thee?" Peleg asked.

"From what?"

"Telling that young fool that if he boycotts their harvest, whether alone or with others, the Meeting is going to throw him out on his ear. I need not tell thee that the house of Woodhouse without the Meeting would have a hard time surviving."

"I do not intend to let him do it," Isaac replied. "But it must not look as if I were forcing him."

Peleg snorted. "Well," he said, "he's thy son. If he were mine . . ."

"He is not," Isaac said tartly.

There was silence, in which the pigeons cooed, a sound of contentment and security.

"All right, I'll go and have a look." Peleg scooped a cupful of birdseed out of the bucket. Isaac watched him open the door of the cage and shake the seed into a feed bin. The pigeons, glinting blue and silver in the diffused light, rushed to it, pushing one another aside, and started pecking greedily. He touched Peleg's shoulder self-consciously. "Take my sleigh," he said. "I'll have it made ready for thee." Then he turned away and left.

*   *   *

Peleg Martin was surprised to find the taproom of the inn opposite the island crowded with young men, shouting and laughing at the counter. A row of muskets was propped up against the gaming table; a log fire roared at the far end of the room; the air was pungent with smoke. The innkeeper, when he saw him come in, hurried from behind the counter to greet him.

"Welcome, sir, welcome! We've been expecting you! Did Jacob take your horse, sir?"

"I didn't see anybody," Peleg grunted, blowing in his hands, wondering who the man mistook him for.

"Ah, that damn nigger!" the innkeeper cried. "I'll go then myself!"

"He's probably across the water, knocking up one of the wenches!" one of the youths at the counter cried; the others bellowed with laughter.

"It's a curse, that's what it is," the innkeeper muttered. At the door he stepped out of his slippers and stamped his feet into a pair of snow boots. He said to Peleg, "Sit down, sir, sit down! I'll be right back and serve you some hot toddy! You look as if you needed it."

Peleg sat down at the table; the heat of the taproom had made him giddy. He had had no idea when he set out that it would be so cold in the open sleigh, once outside the city. He sat there vaguely aware of the young men shouting and joking at the counter; the warmth slowly penetrated to his bones. By the time the innkeeper came back, lugging his valise, he felt better. He drank with relish the hot, sweet liquid that was put in front of him; the innkeeper sat down with him and began to prate endlessly. It took a while before he realized that the taproom had fallen silent and that the young men were listening attentively. The man was bewailing the hardships that had been imposed upon the inn since the niggers had taken over the island. One of the youths joshed, "Careful, Larry! That's no way to talk about your landlords!"

But the innkeeper's jeremiad could not be stopped. It all came pouring forth from the flabby, flustered man: the resentment, the anxiety, the hatred of the niggers who had turned what once was one of the most beautiful and fertile plantations of the valley into a jungle full of savages, where satanic rites were performed on moonlit nights, with banging drums and shrieks and potshots fired into the air . . .

"Potshots?" a youth at the counter said scathingly. "They're shooting one another!"

"Hold your tongue now," someone cried. "Let Larry talk! The tax assessor should know what to expect when he goes there on the morrow. Go ahead, Larry, tell him."

The innkeeper resumed his description of what had happened to the island and its inhabitants, and Peleg suddenly realized that the man did not know he was a Quaker; he had left his hat in the sleigh. The youths were obviously the sons of the owners of surrounding plantations and their friends, part of a volunteer brigade of self-appointed militia keeping a close watch on the island; they were spoiling for a fight with the Negroes. Another dozen youths arrived, armed with muskets; they reported no movement, all seemed to be quiet over there. They trooped to the counter to help themselves to hot toddy and pipes of tobacco, which they took across to the hearth, where they thawed out their limbs.

Finally, the innkeeper took him up to his room. The moment they were inside, the man listened at the door for a moment, then whispered, "Sorry, sir, for playing that little game with you. I know you're not a tax assessor. But I don't know what they would have done, sir, had they discovered who you are. Quakers are not very popular with them right now, since you gave the island to the niggers. And I understand how they feel. It's intolerable, sir, it really is. You are on your way over there, aren't you?"

"Yes."

"May I ask, sir, do you represent the Meeting?"

"Why?"

"I think the Quakers should know about this, sir. This cannot go on, sir, it is going to end in bloodshed . . ." His voice never rose above a whisper, he went on glancing nervously at the door.

"Why should it?"

"These boys are not going to rest until they have provoked the niggers into firing at them, sir. I can see it coming, sir, I hear their talk every day, and it's getting worse. It's getting so I wake up thinking I hear the sound of muskets and screams from across the water, sir."

"But surely their fathers know better than that? The Negroes are the legal owners of the island now."

"I know, sir, I know . . ." Again the man glanced at the door. "It's not a matter of what's legal, sir, it's a matter of what these people are going to stand for. You must see their point, sir; they have plantations of their own, full of slaves. They've got trouble keeping them in line as it is; now, with an island full of their own kind, liberated . . . Already, sir, they are escaping in droves and fleeing to the island—at least, that's the story I hear downstairs . . ."

"But does thee believe that story?"

"I don't know, sir. I swear I don't know. And it matters little whether it's true; it is an excuse for them to raid the island. All it needs is a couple of witnesses to swear that they saw a runaway slave swim across the river to the island and they will send a posse across. And then the fat's in the fire, sir. For the niggers have sentries posted in the trees all along the shore of the island. They are armed with rifles. You can see them through the spyglass the moment the fog lifts. What do you think is going to happen when a posse of armed men with hounds tries to land on the island? Who is going to fire the first shot? It doesn't matter who, but it's going to be a massacre. The owners are not going to rest, sir, until they have wiped them out, the lot of them. And I don't care what the government says or the law says; no one is going to stop them."

"Thank thee," Peleg said, tired.

"Thank you, sir. And please, sir, tell the Quakers. Maybe they can do something to prevent it. Mr. Baker was a gentleman, a real gentleman, and what he did was a Christian thing, but it wasn't practical, sir. All he really did was set them up for slaughter. And those that aren't slaughtered—well, I needn't tell you, sir. They'll be rounded up and sold back into slavery."

"I suppose thee is right."

"Yes, sir. Thank you, sir . . ." The man lighted the candle by the side of the bed. "Good night, sir, and forgive me for playing that little game. It was for your own good, sir; I don't want any trouble. Live and let live, that's my motto, sir."

"Good night."

"Good night, sir . . ."

The man left, and Peleg undressed, deep in thought. When finally he lay on his back, gazing at the shadows on the ceiling, he was beset by a sense of encroaching disaster. How was it possible that no one in the Meeting had realized that the neighboring owners were not going to stand for it? Of course they would provoke a showdown, and any man could see that the Negroes could not win. But what could the Meeting do? How could the Negroes, now running wild on the island, be protected? He saw no way out; the menace of the impending massacre became so oppressive that he folded his hands and prayed, beseeching God for guidance.

The prayer remained unanswered; but it brought a momentary peace in which he slept. When he awoke, the candle had burned itself out, the window was a pale gray square in the darkness, touched by the first hint of dawn. He rose to look out; fog, blue with the daybreak, obscured the view of the river; all he could see were the barren branches of a tree outside the window, draped with writhing shrouds of mist. He dressed and made his way downstairs; when he opened the glass door to the taproom, he found it empty. The only living thing was the fire, glaring at him with orange eyes. He put up the collar of his coat, pulled the woolen bonnet over his ears and opened the door to the yard.

It was not as cold as he had expected. The fog smelled of smoke and burning leaves, the soft sound of drops raining down from the trees made him wonder whether a sudden thaw had set in. Then he remembered the warm springs around the island that created this unnatural, temperate weather.

At the dock he rang the bell for the ferry. The rings of sound spiraled out into the fog. He stood listening awhile before a small sound at his feet caught his attention. He looked down and saw it was the chain; it had been lifted, dripping, from the water and now reached quivering into the fog, causing the wood of the jetty to creak. The ferry had set out from the other shore and was on its way toward him.

Presently a voice hailed him from the water. "Who's there?!"

"Peleg Martin!"

"What's ya business?" The voice sounded hostile.

"I'm Caleb Martin's father! I want to visit my son's grave! And talk to Medea!"

The silence lasted so long that when the chain at his feet began to stir again, he assumed the ferry was on its way back to the island. But there was the voice again, closer now.

"Are you alone?"

"Yes."

The chain crunched; the jetty creaked; suddenly, there was the ferry, black and angular, looming in the fog. He saw it was full of people standing in closed ranks. They were armed with rifles.

The bow of the clumsy vessel crunched against the dock. "Quick!" the voice snapped.

He hastily stepped on board and had to grope for support. As he stood there holding on to the rail, the boat backed off; in a few moments the bank disappeared in the mist. Nobody spoke, nobody moved; he was surrounded by hostility. They were all young Negro bucks dressed in multi-colored, homemade cloaks. It was an outlandish sight, as if he were on his way to a foreign country. Slowly the ferry made its way across, pushed by the current, then a soft gurgling approached in the fog; the massive shadow of Altar Rock moved past them with water curdling around it. There followed another long, silent passage through emptiness until finally the ferry landed with a jarring crunch.

The voice said, close by, "Follow me."

It was one of the young men, who now grouped themselves around him. Obediently he stepped ashore. From the fog a pack of dogs came bounding toward them, five, six skinny scavengers, barking shrilly, to be driven off by the young men.

There was a faint echo now of their footsteps on the gravel and a smell, the spicy, exotic smell of slave cooking; they must be nearing the house. With the same suddenness as the appearance of the dogs, there sounded an angry, multitudinous chorus of bleats and deep-throated bellows, as if they had disturbed a herd of browsing sheep. But there was the house; the towering pillars of its façade made it look like a pagan temple in the mist. He realized that the bleating came from inside; one of the young Negroes opened the door, the sound doubled in volume and a few four-legged shapes ran out into the fog.

He entered and stood aghast. In the light of the dawn he saw that the ground floor of the mansion had been turned into a stable. The black and white marble tiles were covered with straw; goats were everywhere, running in and out of the rooms, scrambling up and down the stairs, standing on the landing peering down, bleating with eerie, almost human voices.

"This way." The young Negro in the red cloak preceded him up the stairs, brushing the goats aside as he went. He led him down an empty passage toward an open door; Peleg realized it was Ann Traylor's room, the one on the northeast corner, overlooking the river. The tall, empty windows looked blindly into the mist; the floor was covered with skins. On a low, thronelike elevation sat Medea, cross-legged, enormous, her huge black bulk swathed in a white robe. She looked like the priestess of the temple. She smiled at him and said, "Well, well! Peleg Martin! Sit down. Make thyself comfortable." She waved her hand toward the pelts spread about the floor.

He hesitated, then lowered himself with difficulty. It was uncomfortable to sit so low to the ground; she loomed over him. The young Negro in the red cloak said something to her, in a foreign language. He had not known they still had a language of their own; the punishment for using their native tongue had been so severe that he had thought it long dead. For some reason, it enhanced his feeling of encroaching disaster.

Someone entered the room behind him. He looked around and saw a huge Negro with only one ear, dressed in one of those cloaks; it was the head driver who used to follow Caleb like a shadow. Medea said, "Thee knows Scipio, does thee not, Peleg?"

"Oh, yes—certainly." In his confusion, he tried to rise to his feet.

"Don't bother," the Negro said; then he addressed Medea in their own language.

What he said seemed to amuse her. "Of course not," she replied in English. Then she looked at Peleg with a grin. "Thee has not come to visit Caleb's grave, has thee?"

He looked at her for a moment, then said, "No."

"So why did you come?" the Negro giant asked rudely.

Medea's voice, high and melodious, spoke in that incomprehensible language. There was an angry retort from the giant, but after a few more lilting phrases of Medea's, spoken with an authority which even he could sense, Scipio and the young Negro in the red cloak left the room. The moment they were gone, she looked at him with

a sly smile and said, "Thee looks cold, Peleg. Would thee like a glass
of brandy?"

"I came to warn thee, Medea," he said.

She chuckled; it set the layers of her huge body rippling. "Peleg,
Peleg," she said, in a tone that dropped forty years out of his life.
"Thee is priceless."

Things were indeed changed. If he wanted to labor with her, he
would have to do so on a basis of equality, which was not going to
be easy after forty years. "It's about the rock," he said. "Abe Woodhouse came to ask thy price—"

"He came to tell me *his* price," she corrected, still watching him
with those mischievous eyes. It was the way she had looked at him
whenever he had come swaggering toward her, to bestow upon her
the priceless gift of his white maleness. She had been lithe, seductive;
now all that was left were the eyes.

"We must have a serious—" he began, but she clapped her hands,
cutting him short. A young girl came in, carrying a tray with a large
plate of roast meat and corn balls. She curtsied to Medea, who took
the plate, put it down by her side and waved the cowed creature out
of the room.

"Who sent thee?" She popped a corn ball into her mouth and
started to masticate messily.

"Nobody. I heard of it from Isaac Woodhouse and felt moved to
come and labor with thee. Five thousand pounds is outrageous. To
insist on that price will cost thee the sympathy of all those who now
support you. Thee cannot hold a whole city to ransom, simply out
of a spirit of rebellion or revenge or whatever it is."

"Cost me their sympathy?" she said. "That would be terrible."

"Medea! Make no mistake! This is serious!"

Suddenly her mood changed. Her smiling, jolly rotundity seemed to
tauten in the sinewy fury with which she had confronted him as a
girl, like a panther about to pounce. "What does thee take us for?"
she asked harshly. "Why does thee think we have sentries posted
around the island? What does thee think those white boys are up to
on yonder shore, with their rifles and their bloodhounds? How long
does thee think it will be before they invade? And thee comes to wag
a finger at me and tell me that if I do not behave like a slave I will
lose sympathy!"

"Thee would lose more than just sympathy," he said coldly. "Abe
Woodhouse is planning to join with the other merchants in a boycott
of thy harvest next year."

She frowned.

He realized she did not understand. "They have agreed among
themselves not to buy thy indigo."

She shrugged her shoulders. "So I'll sell it to someone else."

"Thee will not be able to sell it to anyone. Every single merchant
on the Atlantic seaboard will honor that boycott."

"So?" she asked.

"It is my suggestion that thee sell not only the rock, but the entire island, while there is still time."

"For five hundred pounds?"

"Not at all. I would propose to the Meeting that it take the island under its care, to serve notice on those trigger-happy boys ashore, and that it appoint a committee to arbitrate its sale."

"Who would buy it? Abe Woodhouse?"

"I don't know who. Somebody will. There are enough landowners who have their eye on it. One of them will pay a fair price."

"And then?"

"The money would be shared out among you, enabling you to buy land elsewhere, out of harm's way."

She picked up another corn ball and popped it into her mouth. "Peleg, Peleg," she said, "how little thee knows thy own race."

"But I assure thee—"

"There is no land for us to buy; nobody will sell their land to a nigger. They will take our money, all right, but then they will turn around and say, 'Who are you? I never saw you before!' Surely thee knows that, doesn't thee?"

"But if they are Quakers . . ."

"I can tell thee what Quakers will do. They will hire us as servants, gardeners, stableboys. They will pay us a little and have slavery without having to call it by its name. No, Peleg. There is only one Quaker I would trust, and that is Boniface Baker. But he's gone. As to the rest of you . . ." She grinned.

He knew it was hopeless. Not because she was unshakable, but because she was right. Mary Woodhouse had already asked him to inquire whether Medea would be interested in working for her, once the island was sold. Yet he continued doggedly. "What would the alternative be?"

"For the government to send troops to protect us."

He shook his head. "The Governor would not send troops to protect the Indians who came to us for shelter. Does thee think he would send—"

A goat stuck its head around the door and went away again.

"If you decide to try and stay here," he continued, "it would amount to suicide."

"Of course it would," she said flatly. "But what else can we do? Go back into slavery?"

He rose painfully to his feet. "Appeal to the Meeting to sell the island for you at a fair price, and get out while the going is good. You will have to act fast."

"Thank thee, Peleg, I'll think it over." She clapped her hands; this time the young Negro in the red cloak entered. She spoke to him in that musical, lilting voice; the boy nodded and left. After he was gone she held out her hand and said, "Thee'll have to help me up, Peleg. I'm not as nimble as I used to be."

He helped her to her feet, with difficulty, for she was very heavy.

When they emerged on the landing, the goats bleated and mewed; a few bobbed noisily down the stairs ahead of·them, to wait at the bottom, gazing up at them. Downstairs, the dogs came running, teeth bared, snarling; the palace guard chased them away.

Outside the old chaise was waiting in the fog, with the red-cloaked young man in the driver's seat. To Peleg's surprise, she climbed awkwardly into the chaise, pulled up by the young Negro and pushed by him. He joined her, expecting to be taken to the ferry; only when the young Negro flicked the reins and the mule turned the chaise around did he realize that they were on their way to the graveyard.

During the drive neither of them spoke. The seat was narrow; her huge body wallowed against him each time the buggy lurched, pressing him into the corner. At last the graveyard trees loomed above them, vague and formless in the mist. The young Negro helped them descend; when they stood side by side in the gray void, she took his arm and said, "This way."

The fog was thick. Small, low headstones appeared and disappeared as they shuffled past them. At last she said, "Here."

It was a headstone like the others, so blurred by the writhing fog that he could not discern its inscription. There was a seat next to the grave; she cleared off he snow and lowered her huge body onto it, groaning. Then she breathed, "Come, sit down," patting the seat with her black hand. He obeyed.

There was no sound other than her labored breathing; as it gradually died down, he heard the lapping of small waves in reeds nearby. There they sat, side by side, at the end of their lives, gazing at the grave of their son. Poor Caleb; he was better off where he was. What sort of future would he have had to face? The same future as the rest of them.

He imagined Caleb asking him, "Father, what must I do?" What advice could he have given him? What advice was there to give? There was one thing he could have done, rather than get himself killed by the raiders: vanish in the wilderness and start another life. But where? He could not have gone alone; there should have been others with whom to share the new life. Boniface Baker. Of course! He would have counseled him: Caleb, go and join Boniface Baker, now, before it is too late...

Suddenly, he put his hand on hers. "Medea," he said, "I think God gave me the answer."

*   *   *

As the Meeting listened in a deep hush to the croaking, dry voice of old Peleg Martin, Joe Woodhouse was struck with awe, as were the few hundred men in somber clothes, gathered together in the high-ceilinged room with the tall windows.

Presently Peleg sat down; after a moment Jeremiah Best said slowly, "The proposal before the Meeting is that it shall take the inhabitants of Eden Island under its care, oversee the sale of the property, and assist those who want to join the expedition to the Northwest Territory now being prepared by the school committee."

The silence in the room seemed to deepen; Joe realized that they had gone into worship. They sat motionless, in utter silence, for what seemed an unbearably long time; finally Uncle Jeremiah's quiet voice asked, "May I have the sense of the Meeting?"

Joe could not help himself; he was so afraid that the Meeting would back away from this crucial issue that he rose and cried, his voice shrill with pent-up emotion, "I unite!" He sat down, scarlet in the face; then someone else rose a few benches away.

It was Israel Henderson. "I am moved to say, after our young Friend's passionate response, that this may be the moment for us older Friends to realize that his was the voice of the future. If the next generation feels that this witness should be made, I can only say: So be it." He sat down ponderously.

"I unite with Friend Israel," a new voice said somewhere in the back. Joe craned his neck, as did the others, and saw it was Obadiah Best, tall, gangling, self-conscious. This was the first time Obadiah had raised his voice in Meeting. "I feel that this decision speaks to my condition, and I offer to serve on the evaluation committee, or on any other committee that may be formed to execute the sense of the Meeting, and—or—yes . . ." He sat down awkwardly.

There was another silence; finally Uncle Jeremiah asked, "Do Friends wish to present any other comments or recommendations?" When there was no reply, he concluded evenly, "The Meeting unites with the concern presented by Peleg Martin. Philip Howgill, would thee write a minute to that effect?"

The Meeting waited in silence until the recording clerk had finished scribbling: finally he read in his precise, pedantic voice, *"Minute number fifty-three. Peleg Martin reports on the siege suffered by the inhabitants of Eden Island, erstwhile slaves of Boniface Baker. In view of the threat of violence, Peleg Martin suggests that the inhabitants of the island be placed under the care of the Meeting, that the property be put up for sale at a price to be determined by the Meeting and that the proceeds be shared among the inhabitants in equal parts. A number of them have expressed the desire to join the school expedition to Pendle Hill; the Meeting will offer them assistance."*

"Is this minute approved?" Uncle Jeremiah asked. Several voices replied, "I approve." He continued, "In that case, may I have suggestions as to which committees shall be formed to serve this concern?"

When finally meeting broke, Joe Woodhouse went outside with the others into the blinding light of the sun on the snow. He sought out his brother, eager to discuss with him the new development. To his dismay, Abe said derisively, "It's all very well to decide these things in a state of spiritual inebriation, but would it not have been fitting to find out how Boniface Baker will feel at the sight of his new neighbors?

If I were he and saw that lot stampede toward me in the wilderness, I would bolt."

Joe felt outraged. How was it possible, after the spiritual experience of that morning, to come up with so snide a remark? But then, he reflected, Abe was not a true Quaker, but a wet one.

CHAPTER FOUR

I T was a brutal journey, worse than Gulielma had foreseen. Not because of the snow and the frost, she was prepared for those; she even enjoyed that part of it, once the blizzard was behind her. The world was of an extraordinary peace and radiance; there was no sense of farewell at all, no melancholy, no nostalgia. On the contrary, the farther she penetrated into the silent white wilderness west of Philadelphia, the more she was filled with serenity and peace.

But she had forgotten about the war. The snow and the frost had interrupted the hostilities between the Indians and the settlers, but not erased their traces. The moment she entered the region beyond Loudwater, grisly signs of past violence began to appear. The frost in the mountains had preserved the dead in eerie attitudes of agony and torment; horsemen crushed into the bracken with their mounts; broken-down carts, their contents spilled across the bridle path, covered with drifts of snow; hoofs and hands sticking out of the virginal whiteness; the naked body of a raped woman, frozen in wide-legged obscenity, head and torso buried in the snow. In the valley, the bodies of lynched Indians dangled from tree after tree, swinging spectrally in the wind that came whirling down the slopes, raising white spirals of powdered snow among the dead. Never had she seen the horrors of war so starkly caught in mid-madness.

She began to pass through Indian villages, Miamis, Potawatamis, small clusters of teepees with smoke rising from inside where the Indians were hibernating, huddled close together underneath their pelts, while outside the childless widows roamed. She knew the cruel, prehistoric practice, common to all nomadic Indian tribes, of destroying the teepee of a widow who had lost her last son and leaving her to die in the open; as a young doctor she had tried to save the sad, crazed old crones wandering aimlessly around the villages, wailing. But they did not want to be saved; to the Indians and to themselves, these women were already dead; their eerie, reedy lament in the frosty night was part of the spirit world, as were the whistling of the wind in the trees, the tinkling of icicles falling, the distant thunder of an avalanche rumbling down the mountainside. But this time it was not just one solitary, wandering soul keening her lament in the frosty night; this time she came across whole groups of them keeping one another cruelly alive by huddling together in the open, stretching out pleading hands to her as she passed, crying, *"Ayee! Ayee!"*—a sound that had nothing human left to it.

The braves she encountered were all on the warpath, but every Indian between the Delaware and the Pecos knew her. She doled out the usual powders and potions, careful not to antagonize the medicine men, whom she plied, in ecclesiastic privacy, with brandy. Everywhere she went the story was the same; all the tribes of the region were at war, with the British and among themselves. It transpired that only the Unami tribe of the Delawares, under their chief Running Bull, had migrated westward through the territory of the Miamis. They had razed whole villages on their way, raped women, tortured prisoners until they collapsed in unconsciousness and then set them free with their eyes gouged out. It was those poor blind wretches that she pitied most. She tried to restore the will to live in a few of them, but, like the widows whose eerie wailing haunted the night, they were doomed by their own resolve. Suicide was unknown among the Indians; but they could wish themselves to death, squatting motionless in their teepees, staring with sightless eyes, while around them underneath heaving pelts new life was sown with secretive cooings, suckings and giggles, to be born when the summer trees would turn into fiery glory, a sight they would never see again.

The melancholy of the war-ravaged Indians became so oppressive that she avoided their settlements as much as she could, confining herself to the summer trails that ran through the forest, now wiped out by the snow. She could still follow them, however; she had crisscrossed this wilderness at all seasons for forty years.

It took her twice as long as usual to reach Nightingale Lake, east of the Wabash, where Boniface Baker had settled on a hill that she knew as Bald Man's Head and he had christened Pendle Hill. She knew from George that Running Bull and his tribe and Buffalo and his scrawny hunters had pitched camp there for the winter; even so, it nearly gave her heart failure when she suddenly found her way barred by a huge, hairy beast atop a toy horse who yelled, "Gulielma! Blessed virgin! Where in blazes does thee spring from?!"

"Well, well, if it isn't Buffalo McHair!" She tried to feign composure, but after all those speechless days and nights her voice sounded like those of the keening old squaws.

"What is thee doing here?!" With his great beard and mane, his body indistinguishable from that of his horse, both of them spouting steam, he looked like a monster from mythology. He swung his little mustang alongside her, sending snow flying, put his arm around her, pulled her toward him and kissed her cheek. She nearly lost her balance and cried out angrily, but her chest swelled with joy. His smell was overpowering, a pungent mixture of rum, months of perspiration and the bad breath that came with the winter diet. "Buffalo McHair, thee stinks a mile in the wind," she said waspishly. "Next time, before embracing a woman, pray take a bath."

But he was undismayed. "Gulie, thee snarling bobcat!" he cried fondly, his beard and mustache turning white as his breath froze in them. "If I'd cracked a wishbone, I'd have wished to see thee right now. Why is thee here at this time of year? Has thee heard me in thy dreams?"

"Oh, pickle the gallantry!" But she was unable to hide her delight. "How is Boniface Baker?"

"Ah, thee has come to see *him?*"

Despite the banter, she sensed that something was wrong. "How is he?" she repeated.

"He has never recovered from the death of his daughter."

"I should say not. How long ago is it, three months? He is not like thee! He had only two of them, not hundreds sprinkled all over the territory."

"Gulie, listen to me." He took her hand in his as he rode along beside her. It was rather touching. "The man's in trouble, I don't know what to do with him. I've tried telling him stories. I've tried feeding him booze, I have taken him out to hunt, I even tried to make him our preacher. But nothing worked."

"Preacher? Hireling priest, thee means? No wonder thee did not cheer him up! That would be putting him in a state of damnation!"

"Nonsense. That may be so in Philadelphia, out here a man taking time to tell his friends about Jesus and the Inner Light is fed for it; he does the talking, we the hunting. What's wrong with that?"

"Friend, damnation is a personal matter, as thee well knows. If Boniface Baker feels damned, he is."

He let go of her hand to guide his horse around a root sticking out of the snow. "He does feel damned, that's for sure. But not because I turned him into a priest. He just sits there praying, with a face a foot long. Not very cheering, but my men go for that kind of gloom; they mistake it for religion."

"All right," she said, "I'll have a look at him."

"Maybe thee has something in thy pharmacy that will pep him up?"

"If he wanted to be pepped up, even mint tea would do it," she replied. "Like damnation, it's all in the mind."

"If mint tea did the trick, he should be turning cartwheels by now; that's what his black hussy plies him with. Whenever he prays aloud, which isn't often, you can smell mint 'way across the fire."

She had forgotten about the Negro girl; Bonny's state of damnation might have something to do with her. The answer was obvious almost as soon as she entered the cabin. The first thing she noticed was a smell like that of the slave quarters, an indefinable odor made up of Negro cooking, sweat and who knew what else? There could be no doubt that this was the lair of the black girl who rose to meet her when she stooped through the narrow doorway, not of the morose man she found lying on a bed behind a curtain of pelts, fully dressed, a mug on a little stool beside him.

"Good morning, Bonny, how is thee?" she said quietly, trying not to startle him.

If he was surprised by her arrival, he did not show it. He opened his eyes and looked at her. It was a look of such utter melancholy that her heart sank. This was a very sick man.

"I bring thee greetings of thy family and all Friends in Philadelphia," she said, sitting down on the edge of his bed. She took his hand; it was hot and moist. She checked his pulse as she went on talking. "Thee'll be pleased to hear that the Meeting has heard about thy plan to start a school for Indian children and made it their official concern. Come spring, a wagon train will set out from Philadelphia carrying all that is necessary to build a schoolhouse and a trading post. Joe Woodhouse and Himsha McHair have passed Meeting; they will come as teachers. How does thee like that?" His pulse was rapid and erratic. She looked at his eyes. There was a dilation, definitely.

"And Beulah?" By the sound of it, he was the same slightly pompous old Bonny she had known all his life.

"She's very well indeed. She's conducting a class for deaf mutes in the Meeting House. She and Jeremiah have invented a sign-language alphabet—very cunning, I must say, and a great boon to those poor people. She gave me a letter for thee. Would thee like to have it now?"

"Please."

She produced the letter from her haversack. She had read it, with regrettable indiscretion; in it Beulah told him that she could not join him, giving him all the reasons except the true one, that she had been reunited with her brother, with whom she had been in love ever since childhood.

He unfolded the paper with a loud crackling that seemed to deepen the silence and started to read. She should have looked away while he was being gored by his spouse; but she stayed where she was, for his reactions while reading were disturbing. His eyes filled with tears, his face slackened into that of a frightened boy; when he came to the end, he sobbed, "Oh, my God!" covered his face with his hands, and his shoulders started to heave with almost feminine abandon. She had a mild sedative in her apothecary that would calm him; as she got up and lifted the curtain of pelts, she caught a furtive movement from the corner of her eye. It was the Negro girl flitting back to the pile of skins in front of the fire. There was something puzzling about her stealthiness; Gulielma mulled it over while she fetched the medicine and walked back to the cabin. She sat down on the edge of Bonny's bed again, took the mug off the stool and sniffed its contents. It was mint tea, all right, but there was something else that she could not identify.

"Here," she said kindly. "Take this powder, with some water. It will calm thee down." She went to fetch some water and a beaker; when she came back, he was lying with his hands on his face, moaning, "I'm lost, I'm lost, now I'm really lost . . ."

"Come," she said briskly. "After taking this powder, thee'll see things much more clearly."

He heaved a shuddering sigh. "Damned . . . I am damned!" His voice broke. Despite its pathos, it had nothing theatrical about it; if ever she had observed a man in hell, it was he.

She put her arm under his shoulders, forced him to sit up and coaxed him into taking the potion. He drank it down, then he gave another deep, shuddering sigh and said, in the voice of Boniface Baker

of Eden Island again, "I am to blame for Becky's death. Now Beulah
has forsaken me, I am lost."

"Why, Bonny?" She asked it casually, but observed him sharply.
What was the matter with the man? He was in better shape physically
than she had ever known him to be. He had lost his paunch, his
face was no longer puffed up and flaccid, his muscle tone was that of
a much younger man. Then why this deathly melancholy? The rapid
pulse? The dilation of the pupils? Was he smoking peyote? Impossible; only the Huni Indians knew about that. Yet his symptoms
could only be explained by some artificial stimulation, either smoke,
or Indian snuff, a poison . . . Poison. She looked at the mug on the
little stool—'*If it were mint tea, he should be turning cartwheels by
now, for that is what his black hussy plies him with.*'

"Tell me, Bonny, why is thee lost without Beulah?"

He opened his eyes; the dilated pupils stared at her with the fixity
of shock. "Because I am consumed by carnal desire." He closed his
eyes; his face again became a mask of indifference.

She rose and lifted the curtain; this time the girl did not bother to
flee. "I wonder whether thee would be kind enough to unload and
corral my horse and my mules for me?" Gulielma asked. "I have to
occupy myself with Boniface Baker for a while."

The girl gazed at her with admirable self-possession, considering the
situation. For a moment it looked as if she were going to refuse;
then she turned away and went out, somehow managing to express
disdain with her posterior.

When Gulielma returned to Bonny's side, she found him sitting with
his hands in his lap, eyes closed, frozen in that immutable indifference.

"All right," she said. "The girl has gone to look after my horse.
We can talk freely, if thee wants to. It is she, isn't it?"

He opened his eyes and stared at her with those dilated pupils.
"It is not she. It is I. I cannot fathom the will of God. I have been
able to hold out as long as His will seemed clear. All these months
I have been able to withstand that of the devil in me because there
was hope, a future toward which I could live, Beulah's arrival. Now
there is no future. There is no longer anything to hold on to."

"Could thee tell me about thy symptoms, Boniface? Remember, I
am a physician."

"Symptoms?"

"How does thy lust express itself? Dreams? Daydreams?"

The indifference of his face was relieved by a rueful smile. "Dreams,
daydreams, day and night. Even if my mind forgets her for a moment,
my body never does."

Suddenly the whole thing fell into place. Heaven knew what Cleo
put in the mint tea she served so profusely, but it must be an aphrodisiac. No man, however saintly, was a match for the wiles of Salome.
What could the girl be using? Must be some plant or root. Fascinating.

He sighed, a sigh of utter exhaustion. No wonder; it was amazing
that he could still sit there in comparative sanity, exuding robust health;

he must be doing something right to emerge from this with nothing worse than an accelerated pulse, dilated pupils and excessive perspiration.

"I have tried everything," he said, still in that mournful voice. "I have rolled in the snow, bathed in a hole in the ice, run through the forest for miles, but nothing, nothing can take the devil away from me."

She resisted the impulse to cry, "Excellent!" No wonder he was in such good condition; the whole thing became somewhat less tragic. She would have to watch herself or she might become flippant. "Look, Boniface," she said earnestly, "I can give thee powders that will guarantee thee undisturbed sleep and relieve thee of thy symptoms during the day. But the problem is thy state of mind. Much as I unite with thy sense of sinfulness, there comes a point when it becomes morbid. In my opinion, thee has passed that point."

It revived him sufficiently to say, "Thee does not know what thee is talking about, Gulielma! Thee is not guilty of the death of thy child!"

"Come now, come now! As I heard it, thee was away when it happened."

"I was away because I wanted to be alone."

"What's wrong with that?"

"So I might indulge in lascivious daydreams," he added grimly.

There was something about his self-condemnation that did not sound right; he was punishing himself with relish. "Has it ever occurred to thee, Boniface, that thy guilt may be self-indulgent?"

He frowned.

"Thee may tell thyself that thee has carried on a titanic struggle with damnation all these months, but what thee has actually done, apart from living an extremely healthy life, is to turn thyself into a monument of self-centeredness."

He looked at her, astounded.

"What has thee achieved with thy wallowing in guilt?" she continued. "Started a school for Indian children? Occupied thyself with Buffalo and his men, who want a preacher? Thee has either been running through the forest, rolling in the snow, swimming in a hole in the ice, or lying on thy bed thinking about Boniface Baker in a state of damnation. What if thee is damned? What if thy soul will roast in hell for all eternity? Thee should forget about thy soul and try to give some sense to Becky's martyrdom. How about loving her, instead of hating her?"

"Hating her?" he cried. "How can thee say such a thing?"

"If thee has been wasting thy life because of a feeling of guilt, thee must be hating her. Hate is death. Turn away from thy guilt and give life."

"How?"

"By teaching the children, preaching to the men. Even loving Cleo would be giving life, if it were really love."

Now she had gone too far. She should have had more sense. It was not necessary for him to say, "Thank thee, Gulielma, I'll think it over," for her to know she had bungled it. And suddenly she knew why: she had been treating him as if he were exactly what he appeared to be, a pompous little man. Yet what he had done was a deed of such momentousness that, had he been anyone else, she would have approached him with a respect akin to devotion. "Bonny," she said, "I'm sorry. I have not been frank with thee. I think thee should know the cause of thy carnal excitement, or at least a strongly contributing factor to it. Cleo has been putting some potion into thy tea. I don't know what it is or where she got it, but I am certain that it is an aphrodisiac."

He looked at her fixedly with his pale, slightly bulging eyes, but said nothing.

"I don't know what thee is trying to do or prove," she continued, "but remember thee is dealing with a different race, a different mentality, almost a different species. Does thee not think thee has done enough for thy slaves? Let them find their own salvation."

"I don't know what thee is talking about," he said. "All I am trying to do is to remain alive and free myself of sin."

"Very well." She sighed and rose. "I'll get thee some more medicine. Take two powders a day, one on rising, one before going to bed. And take them in pure spring water, avoid tea or broth or any kind of brew she prepares."

"Very well," he said stiffly.

He was an odd little man. Could it be that he did not know what he was doing? As she turned to lift the curtain, she added, "By the way, I don't think I have more than two weeks' supply. Thee had better solve thy problem one way or another before the powders run out."

He looked at her so gloomily that she left with a feeling of defeat.

Outside, she found Buffalo McHair waiting for her. "Well?" he asked. "How is he?"

"I want a word with thee." She took him by the arm and led him toward the lake. There they sat down on an upturned skiff, after he had brushed the snow away.

"He is being drugged," she said matter-of-factly. "Cleo has been lacing his tea with some herb or mineral which turns him into a stallion in rut."

"Good Lord!" he said with a marked lack of commiseration.

"Don't let it put any ideas into thy head, my friend; the effects are not pleasurable. What's more, thee doesn't need it."

He chuckled.

"I'm giving him a sedative to neutralize it, but that won't get at the root of the problem. There's more to this than meets the eye. Maybe slavery is not finished by manumission. Maybe she will not feel free until she has made him her lover."

"Feel free by submitting to her master?"

"She would not be the once to submit, he would."

"Well, as long as he enjoys himself . . ."

"That's just the point," she said. "He is not enjoying himself. He is —well, I don't know what he is up to, or what his real problem is. He has me stumped, for the simple reason, I suppose, that I have never freed any slaves, or given away my possessions; all I have ever done is observe man and his antics with scientific detachment." She gazed at the frozen lake, the lonely, cold little island. Then she became aware that he was looking at her in a way that made her feel uncomfortable. "What is it?" she asked.

"Thee has changed, Gulie," he said gently. "Is thee unwell?"

Her sense of detachment collapsed.

"Gulie?"

She looked at him; his eyes were shrewd and perspicacious. She could hide nothing from this man. "I'm on my way to my Hunis," she said, trying to sound casual.

"At this time of year? Why?"

"Because I am dying."

Once it was out, she regretted it. It was as if she had let go of something that she could control only so long as she kept it to herself. But that was ridiculous; Moremen knew about it, why not he?

"Of what is thee dying?" He asked it kindly, but without commiseration. Somehow he had managed to find exactly the right tone, bless him. He was, indeed, the most tactful man she knew. Yet part of her yearned for something else.

"A cancer in the stomach." She strained to control her sudden, desperate need for sympathy. If she let herself go now, nothing could come of it but disaster. "Well, I had better be going." She stood up and dusted the snow off the seat of her breeches. "I would like to get there."

"I understand." He rose and held out his hand. "Good luck, Gulie. Take care."

She wanted to cry, 'Help me, for God's sake, hold me, protect me!' for suddenly the future looked full of menace. She must have been on a pilgrimage to him, without knowing it.

"Goodbye, Buffalo," she said. "Thee has been a real friend. My only one, as a matter of fact." She turned away. What a passion for play-acting she had! What incurable hunger for drama! The sooner she got away from here, the better. She should have stayed and made camp, if only for her horses' sake; but she would do so a mile or two down the trail.

One of his little runts came hopping toward her as she was saddling up her beasts. "Gulie Woodhouse!" he cried. "I have sprained my ankle, could thee wrap me up?"

"No," she said. "Binding it will make it worse. Go and stick thy foot in the snow, or in the lake, until it goes numb with cold. Then lie on thy back with thy hind leg strung up in the air. And lie alone, or thee'll sprain worse than thy ankle." She was about to climb into the saddle when she remembered Bonny's medicine. "Before thee does," she said to the little hop-along, "take this medicine

to Boniface Baker. Two powders a day, as prescribed, and kiss him
on the snoot for me." She took the powders out of drawer twenty-four,
marked SED. "Here, don't drop any. Peace to thee."

"Thee's leaving already?"

"I've got work to do." She swung into the saddle. "Do me a favor
and open the gate, there's a good boy."

The man obeyed, with a great show of lameness. Another actor.
How God could stand watching these perpetual histrionics was beyond
her comprehension; He must indeed be all love.

Love. There she stood at the gate, the black temptress. What a
superb specimen she was. "Goodbye, Cleo. Leave the man alone,
there's a good girl."

Cleo looked up at her without flinching. The black jewels stared
at her without passion or even recognition. With a sigh, she urged
her tired beasts through the gate and into the open. A dirty track
in the snow led into the forest; where it joined the bridle path
to the Wabash would be a good place to camp. The Wabash was a
two-day ride away under the best of circumstances; now it would
take twice that time. She should indeed have spent the night in the
settlement and started in the morning, but she could not bear to set
eyes on Buffalo again.

She forced herself not to think about him as she rode away. She
concentrated instead on Bonny Baker and his damnation. Pity she
had been unable to do anything for him. Could it be that she had
tackled the problem from the wrong end? Maybe the one she should
have worked on was the girl; she should have gone for that of God in
her. It must be there, behind those black jewels, that implacable
hatred. If it was there, it could be reached somehow.

Well, she had bungled what was probably her last professional
assignment. It hurt her pride, and she felt sorry for Bonny. Now that
his wife was not going to join him, he would probably end, once
the month was over, in the embrace of the black predator. And, like
the blinded Indian braves gazing unseeingly at the fire, he would die
of shame.

She wished, as she bent down to avoid a branch across the bridle
path, that God had granted her this last small triumph before calling
her bluff.

*   *   *

When Boniface Baker awakened from a deep, dreamless sleep
hours later, the little window at the foot of his bed was dark, the
curtain of pelts looped up. Cleo was squatting on her bed of
hides, sewing in the firelight, looking demure and domestic in her
gray Quaker dress. The scene was tranquil, the soft sounds of the
burning logs were homely; for the first time in months, he was at
peace. For the first time, his throat did not tighten at the sight of
her; it was as if he had shed an evil double who had strangled all that
was kind and compassionate in him with carnal desire. Now he

knew that it had been something she had put in his tea. He had yet to confront that revelation.

He rose to join her; she looked up. Her black eyes, speckled with the reflection of the fire, scrutinized him. He knew that look, as though she were waiting. Now he knew what she had been waiting for.

"Thee slept well," she said.

"Yes. I don't know what it was Gulielma gave me, but it worked."

"Would thee like some venison?"

"No, thank thee. I'm not hungry. Has thee eaten?"

"Yes. Shall I make thee some tea?"

"It is against doctor's orders." He said it casually, watching her.

She gave him that searching look again. "Did she say thee should not drink tea?"

"She said I should stay with pure water while I take the medicine."

"Thee has to take it for long?"

"Two weeks." He sat down on the floor by the fireside. She resumed her sewing. There was a tension between them now, despite the peaceable scene.

"What is thee doing?" he asked.

"Darning thy socks."

"But what is that inside?"

"A bowl. Has thee never seen a woman darn socks before?"

"I suppose so." He did not understand it; there was about her a serenity that seemed at odds with her duplicity as it now stood revealed. Could it be that Gulielma had been mistaken? It seemed impossible that this placid creature should have deliberately set out to cripple him with lust.

What sort of person was she, really? A girl born into slavery, whom Caleb had ordered raped by a stranger to break her spirit. Here she was in the wilderness, alone with her erstwhile owner, darning his socks. What had brought her here? She had not been pregnant; she had pretended to be, to prevail upon him to take her with him. Why? He could not begin to guess at the answer. It belonged to another world, the world of slavery. He remembered her as she had appeared before him, after Caleb had accused her of wanting to seduce Joshua: sullen, arms dangling, slack-jawed, so different from the girl she was now that she must have deliberately tried to make herself look stupid and ugly. He remembered the next time he had seen her: on the floor of Caleb's cottage, her black arms and legs encircling Joshua's frenzied white body. That had been the moment when he knew at last that slavery was totally evil. Then, her black naked body in the brook that day west of the Alleghenies. Had she already started then to give him her potion? Was that why he had been so struck by her beauty? Or had his desire been aroused of its own accord?

A profound uneasiness stirred within him. It seemed as if the bedrock of his life, his basic concept of himself began to crumble. He closed his eyes and prayed, for suddenly he realized how easily he could be lost, helpless in the throes of this desire, which had been assuaged only temporarily by Gulielma's powder. Suddenly he found himself thinking, 'Mercy; God, have mercy on her.' It did not make sense; it was *he* who was in need of mercy. He opened his eyes and looked at her dark face, her pale-palmed hands, the bowl with the sock, and suddenly he felt deeply moved, for there was about her something he had never realized before: a terrible loneliness. Here she was, hundreds of miles away from her people, probably the only Negro in the Northwest Territory. Her people always moved in groups or pairs, never alone. What was she seeking? What mysterious spirit, what secret power had enabled her to do this alone? Well, she had shown one power even as a slave: the power to drive men wild. That was why Caleb had sought to breed her. Could it be that she had tried to tempt him because that was the only power she had? But why him, who had set her free? There must be something she wanted, another goal; in order to reach it, she had found it necessary to assail him with the only power she possessed. But what could she want? She was free now, wasn't she? Or was there more to freedom? Must he do more? What else could he do? Educate her? Make her share not only his daily life but the world of the mind he lived in? The world of the spirit? Should he try to give her humanity? The mere thought was a denial of that of God in her. To assume that humanity was for him to bestow upon her was a terrible arrogance. Despite his sacrifice, he obviously was still a slave-owner at heart. To set her free, he must first free himself of that arrogance of seeing himself as one of the chosen, more precious to God than she. He must strip himself of his white skin, his white God, the ultimate presumption of exclusive revelation.

How could he? To start with: by making her his equal instead of his servant.

"How about starting that school for Indian children, thee and I?" he asked.

She looked up, startled.

"Thee knows how to read and write, does thee not?"

She shrugged her shoulders and looked away.

"Look—anyone can be a teacher as long as he stays one page ahead of the class. How much does thee know?"

"Nothing." She took up her darning again.

"Nothing? But thee went to classes! Didn't my wife teach thee to read and write when thee was little?"

"No." She said it flatly, a statement of fact.

"But I don't understand . . ." That had been one of the things he had been proudest of: other owners refused to teach their slaves anything, seeing it as either dangerous or a waste of time; Quakers taught their slaves' children to read and to write. "I *know* thee went to classes! Thee must have!"

"I did."

"Then how is it thee did not learn anything?"

"I did not wish to."

"Thee did not want to *learn?!*" He gazed at her, perplexed. There she sat, serene and relaxed, calmly stating that she had refused the gift of learning. "Why not?" he asked.

She shrugged her shoulders.

"But there must have been a reason! Why did thee not want to learn to read and write?"

She took the bowl out of the sock.

"Why, Cleo, why?" It was a cry of anguish.

She put the bowl inside another sock, pulled a length of wool from the ball, bit it off, threaded her needle.

He watched her, his mind a turmoil. The powerlessness of the slave. To refuse to learn anything might have been an act of independence. "And now?" he asked. "Would thee let me teach thee how to read and write now?"

She looked up. The inscrutable gaze of her black eyes rested upon him. "Why?" she asked.

"So that thee may teach Indian children."

"Why me?"

"Because thee is *here*. All they have is thee." He got up and went to the shelf where he kept his few books, to look for the hornbook he had brought from Philadelphia. It was not there; then he remembered that, of course, Abby had taken it back with her. What could he use? His hand went to the Bible, then, at an afterthought, to the first volume of Ann Traylor's diaries; he seemed to remember some child's writing at the end of it.

He took it down and opened it by the light of the fire. *"I think she is asleep at last, poor woman . . ."* He turned the book around and opened it from the other end. There it was! *"Adam ate the apple that Eve picked for him."* He had remembered rightly: it *was* an exercise book.

"Come, sit over here." He patted the floor by his side. "I have something here that we can use for a start; tomorrow I'll make up a hornbook. Come."

She hesitated a moment, then she put down her darning, crawled toward him and sat down by his side.

"Thee knows about letters, doesn't thee? Their function, I mean? Each letter is a sign standing for a sound. *A—Adam*. Does thee understand that?"

She slowly turned her head toward him. Her black, gold-flecked eyes, which he had never seen so close, looked at his mouth. Then she said calmly, "Yes."

For a moment his determination faltered as, from the depths of his body, a surging desire responded to that look. But something rallied to his aid, the knowledge that she knew no better than to assail him with the only power she had. He must guide the two of them through the morass of carnal desire until, with divine assistance, they reached the other shore where, in some mysterious manner, she would at last be free.

"Cleo," he said firmly, "stop looking at me as if thee were a lioness and I a lamb. People who want to learn do not eat their teachers."

He did not know if she had a sense of humor, he did not know her at all. Obviously, she hadn't. After a cold look from those gold-flecked eyes, she looked down at the book. "A," she said. "I know 'A.' That's all."

"Well," he said, in the tone of a schoolmaster already, "let's be thankful for small blessings. Let's go on from there." He started to spell, slowly: "A-D-A-M."

The logs hissed in the fireplace. Outside, a loon called mournfully on the frozen lake. Somewhere in the forest, a snow owl hooted in response. It was a cold, dark night out there.

* * *

The next morning, Gulielma rode slowly onto the prairie with her asthmatic old mare, the two mules huffing and clanking behind her. It was a relief to be out of the forest; the sea of grass, white and gray with hoarfrost which had turned its myriad stalks to tinsel, gave her a feeling of immensity and freedom that was intoxicating. But as the day wore on, the loneliness won out. Toward nightfall she began to feel afraid. Never before had she been afraid in the wilderness. She had long since discovered that the wolf packs which roamed the frozen wastes in winter were no more than earthbound buzzards, attacking only the feeble, the diseased, the dying. The Indians knew she was a medicine man and that she carried no money or valuables, only poison in the little drawers of her pharmacy. She would probably lose a few pots and pans to them, but she had taken that into account. The only real danger she was likely to encounter would be her own growing weakness. She did not regurgitate her food yet, she simply was no longer hungry. She could eat no more than a few mouthfuls each day, and had to force herself to do that. The moment was not far off in which she would have to face the truth about her condition. But the odd, crawly sensation she felt as night began to fall was not self-generated. She was alerted by an instinct which must date back to man's earliest roamings across the prairie: she was being observed.

Were there Indians about—out here? She knew that as she rode down the trails through the woods her progress was followed and reported from the moment she saddled up in the morning until she made camp at night. It had never troubled her; on the contrary, it gave her a feeling of companionship; at least, if her horse ditched her or she knocked herself out on a branch after falling asleep in the saddle, she would be picked up, were it only because of their insatiable curiosity. But here on this frozen prairie?

Boundless, bleak emptiness stretched out around her. Any Indian brave, however adept at stalking, would find it impossible to ghost along with her unobserved; that would take a legendary creature like Lone Seeing Eagle. But those were so rare that after forty years she could count them on the fingers of one hand; and why would a legendary creature like that be shadowing her? If she had been a wagon train, or some other delectable prey—but old Pissing Gulie, the man-woman with the blunderbuss and the horse pills? No Indian, despite their compulsive addiction to stalking, would go in for such an exercise in futility.

She looked up at the sky. Turkey buzzards were circling overhead. They had done so for hours; they were waiting for her to shoot some game for supper and let them have the spoils. She reined her horse; the stupid new mule bumped into the mare, it probably had been asleep on its feet. "Hush, Annie," she said, patting her huffed old horse's neck. "Stupid Patsy didn't do it on purpose. Easy now." Her hat tilted forward to shield her eyes from the setting sun, she scanned the horizon. There was nothing in sight; only the prairie, white and endless, overhead the buzzards. A snow owl swooped from a cluster of shrubs and winged away, low to the ground. There must be a prairie-dog town nearby, full of hibernating little critters; snow owls always found it hard to believe that their succulent little friends slept all winter. She slowly scanned the horizon with the unfocused look that would register any discrepancy in the skyline better than concentrated staring, and she caught a sign. It was infinitesimal, not more than a speck in the sky above the horizon. Her eyes came back to it, held it and she saw another, and another: buzzards, circling. That meant either an animal in the throes of death, or lonely riders, like herself.

She unloaded the mules, unsaddled the horse and let them forage for themselves on the frozen prairie, good luck to them. She put her shelter up against the cluster of shrubs from which the owl had swooped; that meant one angry bird, but the windbreak was too good to miss; toward morning it would be bitterly cold. What with her meager appetite, her resistance to cold was dropping. Yet, if truth be told, she had rarely felt better in her life. Well, let's see what tempting tidbits we can cook up tonight.

She busied herself like a child playing with a toy kitchen; but, tempting as the little meal was, she could down only a few mouthfuls. The fire, dwarfed at first by the world-large conflagration of the sunset, became a source of comfort and warmth as darkness descended. Merely to gaze at it, wrapped in her blanket, her chin on her knees, was a joy. One of the bonuses of old age was the return of innocence, this time the result not of ignorance but of a sense of proportion. *Sub specie aeternitatis,* Bonny's tormented sense of guilt was myopic. The only real sin, in love, was lovelessness. She smiled wryly at the fire; for a professional virgin, this was an abstract thought, to say the least. Poor Bonny, though. If only he had not been a Friend! The Quaker concept of the relationship between God and man put a terrible strain on the individual. Bonny was like Atlas, condemned to shoulder the responsibility for the fate of his own soul. Had he been an Anglican, a Papist or a Calvinist, he would have accepted his corruption as the outcome of man's original sin, turned to the atonement of Christ as his only hope for salvation, and proceeded to steam it up with his Nubian paramour until exhaustion forced on him a brief interval for somber reflection, after which he could start

all over again, as long as he threw himself onto the mercy of the
Son of Man. How simple, and how effective! Instead of which, as a
result of the notion that he had the devil within as well as God, and
that the choice was always his, he had rolled in the snow, tried to
freeze his sinful parts into submission by immersing them in a hole
in the ice and loped for miles through the forest. To tell him to
lower his sights, to coin a phrase, was futile; he considered himself
solely responsible for his own damnation, and therefore he was doomed,
unless Salome could be deflected from her cold-blooded determination.
His only hope, really, was to debilitate her with love. But she must
have been assaulted and brutalized so often in her short life that she
had no capacity left for a loving relationship with a white man, or
any man, for that matter. The moment she had a child of her own, of
course, love would assert itself with a vengeance; but by that time—

Beyond the horizon, now narrowed to the edge of the firelight, a
horse whinnied. She listened, without breathing, staring at the fire.
All her awareness was concentrated in her hearing, but she heard
nothing else. One short, nervous whinny; that was all. Had it been
Annie? Annie would only whinny at the scent of another horse. If it
was an Indian mustang, the other horse would not respond.

Whatever it was, there was nothing she could do about it. She
no longer had her blunderbuss with her, only her hunting rifle, which
was not nearly so effective as a threat. Well, she would know soon
enough. The only disturbing possibility was that it might be a rogue
Indian, cast out by his tribe. They did that as punishment for crimes
that did not warrant death. They would leave a condemned man his
horse, his bow and a quiver of arrows, and send him onto the prairie
to fend for himself. It was cruel punishment; most criminals did not
have enough intelligence to survive, that was why they had become
criminals in the first place. Usually, those banished were peeping Toms
or child violators. That, of course, was an interesting thought. She
might have the priceless experience of womanhood, after all; it depended on how long the poor brute had been roaming the frozen
prairie. If it had been long enough to render him hallucinatory, he
might conceivably be aroused by the mere fact that she was a female.

She lay down, her feet to the fire, rolled herself in her blanket
and wondered what it was like to be raped, as so many women
had been since the beginning of the war. Judging by the cases she
had seen, it depended on the individual. Becky had been destroyed
by it; some of the others had given her the impression, despite their
lamentations, that it had not been such a tragic ordeal. Scalping, of
course, was different; but there she could rest easy. Only an out-and-out
lunatic would ogle her mousy, moth-eaten coiffure.

She managed to catch a wink or two, but alertness never left her.
The slightest crackle of the fire, the faintest snap of a twig as frost
descended upon the prairie made her stare into the darkness, wide
awake. At one moment she was absolutely sure that she was being
observed, but no deluded male came prancing out of the darkness,
not even a coyote was sufficiently interested to investigate the bizarre

old animal curled up at the foot of the owl's juniper bush. Sunrise found her unravished, irritated by her own nocturnal fantasies.

The mules and the mare had stayed nearby, resigned to have themselves burdened with an old woman's incongruous junk for another day on the road to nowhere. The only effect of her long night was cold feet, which she could not get warm, even though she sat rubbing them in the saddle while Annie, with the rolling gait of a fishing boat, stayed on course, long since resigned to the incomprehensible.

*   *   *

It took Gulielma three days to reach the Wabash, and throughout that time she felt herself under observation. The second night she decided that an attack was unlikely, or the creature would have done so by now. The third night she wished her secret shadow would join her by the fireside for a chat. It was bitterly cold, the prairie was always much colder than the forest. She hoped she would be spared even a minor blizzard, for she wondered whether her feet would be able to withstand it. They refused to warm up; she took to slapping them and talking to them as if to a recalcitrant pair of twins. It was with mixed feelings that she stumbled upon a camp of French *voyageurs* when she reached the Wabash.

The six men, all of them undersized, hirsute and extremely voluble in French, had moored their flatboat loaded with pelts to four iron stakes driven into the frozen ground; two poles kept the vessel away from the bank. They were roasting the hind legs of a moose when she turned up at their campfire, saying, "Good evening, gentlemen. How do you do?"

Their instinctive reaction was to locate their rifles with a sidelong glance before they greeted her chivalrously and invited her to join them in their repast. She began by saying, as usual, "I'm a doctor. Any of you need mending?" Without waiting for an answer, she slapped Annie and the mules on the rump and sent them foraging. She would unload and rub them down later; being French, the men might do it for her. That was the thing about the Frogs: they were incurably gallant, treating even a scarecrow such as herself as if she were a beautiful, rich young widow.

She spent a pleasant evening in their company, first attending to their scratches and then catching up with the gossip of the river. Her French was atrocious, but so was their English; between them they managed to get the essentials across. There were the usual stories of buffalo felled with a single shot, impregnable chief's daughters crumbling at a kiss; they had the swaggering innocence of the young human male in the wilderness. There were also scathing comments on the inexperienced immigrants swarming west in their clumsy wagons without any notion of where they were going or what to expect. Usually they came in droves, but of late there had been an influx of solitary families separated from the others by the war. One wagon was camped a mile upstream, with a yoke of oxen, a man and wife, speaking

German, and a pregnant girl. What did those people think the chances
were for a baby to survive the winter out here? Where did they think
they were going? They had no idea of how to get across the Wabash,
nom de Dieu! What were they going to do? Camp there all winter?
Either that or be eaten by wolves, robbed by the Miamis, or frozen to
death. *Des fous furieux!* The *voyageurs* were angry because when
they had hailed the lonely wagon in passing, a volley of buckshot
and a barrage of German curses had been the reply. Why those people
should feel they had to defend a two-hundred-pound daughter with
a mustache and eight months pregnant to boot against six courteous,
civilized gentlemen was beyond understanding.

She slept more soundly than she had since leaving Philadelphia; it
was with a feeling of outrage that she found herself shaken awake
in the small hours by a frantic little Frenchman babbling nonsense.
Only after another frantic Frenchman had come to her aid with his
particular brand of river English did she understand they were talking
about the wagon upstream. The one who had shaken her awake
had heard a woman shriek at the top of her voice and gone to
investigate. The screams had been terrible; he thought one of the
women was being murdered until the flap of the wagon had opened
and the man had stumbled out; the Frenchman had caught a glimpse
of what was going on in there: the daughter was having her child.
So, although it would be a merciful thing to let them exterminate one
another before someone else did so, Christian duty compelled him to
tell her about it because she was a doctor.

Gulielma reached the wagon ten minutes later, escorted by all
six *voyageurs,* who stayed discreetly out of sight. The screams were
shrieks of unbearable torture; on the canvas, dimly lit by the lantern
inside, grotesque shadows were grappling in demented fury. She dismounted, walked toward the wagon and knocked on the tailboard.
She had to slam it with her fists before the flap was opened and
the silhouette of a bearded man loomed in the horseshoe of light.
"*Raus! Raus!*" he screamed; the shrieks rose in pitch behind him. As
he seemed to be about to leap on her, she took off her hat and
said in German, "Take it easy, friend, I'm a doctor. Let me have a
look at that girl."

"A doctor?!" he yelled. "We don't need a doctor, you interfering old
bitch!"

Behind him a woman's voice cried, *"Vaterchen! Vaterchen! Komm
doch! Komm schnell!"*

The man turned away; Gulielma, realizing that she was taking her
life in her hands, climbed onto the tailboard and stooped inside.

The sight was pitiful. A young woman, her stark white, bulging
belly quivering with the effort, lay bleeding profusely on a blood-
soaked mattress. An older woman, obviously her mother, was trying
to hold the girl's shoulders down as she struggled and thrashed, screaming in the agony of parturition. Most pitiful of all was the sight
of the poor girl's head; her skull was bald and pink with healing
skin, now broken in places.

"Let me at her," Gulielma said in German, pushing the man aside.

"Raus, raus!" he bellowed; his crazy eyes were glazed with shock; the only thing to do with people in his condition, especially males, was to ignore them.

"I'm a doctor!" she shouted to the woman, above the girl's screams. "Let me help her!"

The woman did not reply; she was not given the chance by the girl, who must be as strong as an ox. As Gulielma had hoped, the man collapsed, muttering, in a corner; she rolled up her sleeves, washed her hands in a bucket, sent the woman to boil some water and went to work, expertly, with the deftness acquired by forty years of dealing with childbirth in wigwams and cabins in the wilderness. This was a breech birth, but every time it astounded her anew how nature managed to right its wrongs when it came to sustaining new life. It was a bloody, brutal business, but in the end, with a shriek of crucifixion from the mother, the slippery little beastie was dragged into the world and induced to produce its first birdlike squeal, upside down in the lantern light. It was a little boy, a sturdy one; the moment he had asserted himself, she handed him over to the old woman, for the mother was going into shock. As she bent over the unconscious girl, a scream made her swing around. *"Nein! Nicht tun!"* It was the woman; Gulielma saw the man leap out of the wagon into the night with the newborn child.

With the instinctive choice of the new life over the old, she jumped after him, crying, "Stop him! Stop him!" The man, bellowing like a mad bull, rushed toward the river; suddenly he doubled back and headed for a tree looming in the darkness. Taking the baby by the legs, he swung it out to smash its head against the tree. Gulielma never knew how she did it, but somehow she found herself between the tree and the little body at the moment of impact. He hit her in the stomach with it, a staggering blow; she managed to grab hold of the child despite the searing pain that shot through her body. She knew she would be forced to give up the struggle, for the man in his demented state had the force of a lunatic; then two, three, six assailants jumped him from the darkness. He roared with rage, but let go of the child to fight them.

It was, despite their numbers, an unequal struggle; the berserk man hurled his attackers, one by one, into the darkness as if they were sacks of flour. She saw him coming for the child again, yelled, "Catch!" at a vague shape nearby and threw the baby. It was terribly reckless of her, but she had no choice, for there was the madman, right on top of her, screaming, *"Das Kind muss kaputt! Das Kind muss kaputt!"* pummeling her mercilessly, pinned against the tree. It was a strange, disembodied experience, she did not feel the blows, she felt a lightheaded serenity come over her that seemed joyful. She was amazed at the unconcern in which she lived her last moments; there was no terror, only amazement.

She came to at the thin, desperate crying of a child. She found herself lying on the ground beside the campfire, with the *voyageurs* kneeling around her. "Where is he?" she asked, managing to say it in French.

"Ah, lui, le taureau enragé? He knocked out Fonfon and Pierrot, but his wife got him: *Vlan!* With an ax handle."

"The child! Where is the child?" She rose on an elbow.

"Le voilà!" She was handed a squalling little bundle, wrapped messily in somebody's jerkin. The baby looked filthy and desperate and terrified out of its wits; and no wonder. The wonder was that it had survived at all.

"I—I'll have to go and see the girl . . ." She handed the baby back and tried to get up, for she remembered the stark white face of the mother in shock. The *voyageurs* tried to dissuade her, but she staggered to her feet. "Keep the child warm, I'll be right back," she said, and tried to hoist herself into the saddle. She could not make it, the pain in her stomach was paralyzing; a dozen hands helped her to mount. When she rode off in the direction of the wagon, she had trouble focusing, but it was not necessary, for she was being escorted again, two of them leading Annie by the bit.

When they arrived at the wagon, she was helped down and virtually carried to the tailboard; but that was as far as their chivalry went. At the first moan from the monster, whose boots stuck out under the canvas, they dissolved in the darkness.

The girl had recovered. At least, her eyes were open and she was gazing around her. Like her baby, she must be made of durable material. Her mother, slight and frail, must equal them; to lay out a rabid man with an ax handle needed considerable force. Gulielma, despite the excruciating pain in her stomach, helped the girl expel the afterbirth. She should really suture the rupture, but enough was enough; it was not extensive enough to make stitches mandatory. Furthermore, the father was awakening from his stupor and beginning to warm up for a repeat performance. She asked, "What about the child?"

"Nein, nein!" the woman replied in a whisper. "We don't want the child; you keep him!"

"My thanks," she said, "but that's impossible. It's your daughter's child, she'll be asking for him soon."

"Oh, no, she won't," the woman said. "Ask her yourself."

The man behind her back began to growl; Gulielma asked the sad, scalped girl, "Would thee like to see thy son, *Liebchen?"*

The girl shook her head, weak but determined.

"He's a bonny little boy, a lovely boy . . ."

"Nein, nein," the girl whispered thickly. Her lips were pale, there was blood in her mouth; she must have bitten her tongue.

"Thee cannot turn away from thy own child, *mein Kind,"* Gulielma insisted. "He is thy own flesh and blood—"

"He is not!" the woman cried, with chilling vehemence. "He is the seed of the devil! *Der Teufel! Der Teufel!* He should be drowned, for the good of mankind!"

"Was it rape?" Gulielma asked matter-of-factly.

"Ja! She was *vergewaltigt!* By the Indians! Seventeen times!"

Despite the anguish in the woman's voice, Gulielma could not help reflecting that the number was inhumanly precise. This did not make sense; the birth had been a struggle, but it had not been premature; nine months ago the Indians had been at peace. "Who is the father?" she asked.

"Der Teufel!" the woman shrieked, suddenly as demented as her husband had been. *"Ersäufe Ihn!* Throw him in *den Wabash!"*

The father, behind her, reared his ugly head, bellowing, *"Raus! Raus!"*

Gulielma tried one last time before the man could pounce. She took the girl's cold, limp hand and asked, "Does thee really not want thy own child?"

The girl looked at her with huge blue eyes. There was in them, despite all that must have happened to her, a heartbreaking innocence. *"Nein,"* she whispered, thickly because of her swollen tongue. "Let him die; he is bad, very bad." Then her face suddenly contorted in a grimace of grief; she burst into tears.

"Raus!" the madman grabbed Gulielma by the scruff of the neck. She managed to wrench herself free and, despite her precarious condition, to escape from him with a leap that would have made her gasp with admiration had someone else performed the feat. She landed on all fours in the darkness; inside the wagon the berserk man could be heard scrambling. She staggered into the night, blindly; at once helpful hands supported her and carried her to her horse.

When at last she let herself down by the fireside again and was handed the squalling bundle, she realized that she found herself with child. She eyed the creature almost with anger, but the screwed-up little face, the minute fists waving about in misery mollified her to the point where she cradled him, trying to pacify him. She looked up at the circle of faces around her and asked, "Anybody want a baby?"

There was a sentimental French *"Oooh . . ."* but no bidders.

"Look," she said reasonably, "I cannot keep this child. I am on my way to Mexico, two months across the desert. The poor little brute would be dead within a week."

Again there was a long *"Oooh"* but no takers. They had a most melodious way of turning her down.

"Well," she said with a sigh, "I might as well give him something that will shut him up or he'll yell himself to death. Know where my pharmacy is? That thing with the drawers, off my first mule?"

The faces nodded.

"Get me one of the bottles in drawer number seventeen. Remember that? Seventeen. One bottle."

One of the men scurried away helpfully. She remembered the seventeen times the Indians had raped the girl. Physically, she must have been able to withstand the shock, but mentally? What future was there for a German peasant girl with innocent blue eyes and no hair left, whose experience of love had been a gang rape by seventeen Indians? What monstrous degradation of all that made people human!

Now here was another beastie faced with the task of acquiring humanity. It would be infinitely more difficult in times to come than it had been during the gentle years of the Holy Experiment. She gazed at the little creature on her lap, the flailing tiny fists, the red mouth gaping with terror. 'Dear God,' she thought, 'what is the meaning of it all?'

There was the *voyageur* with the little bottle. She tried to read the label by the flickering firelight, but it was too dark to see. She took the cork out and sniffed the contents. "Yes, that's right. Now I need a piece of cloth—clean, if you have it."

"This do?" A helpful soul proffered a kerchief.

"That's fine. Mind if I tear it?" She did not wait for his answer; this was the least they could contribute to the welfare of the child. She made a crude pacifier out of the cloth and soaked the end in the sweet, syrupy sedative that she carried specially for babies. An Indian woman who found herself saddled with an orphan of suckling age smeared it on her nipples to pacify the screaming child; there was no nutritive value in the syrup, but even the most ravenous little papoose did not seem to mind. It was mysterious, for it tasted foul, like rotting leaves.

Here, for once, was a new arrival who had more sense. The pacifier, though dripping with the irresistible goo, was rejected with strangled fury. The way the child knocked it away suddenly gave her the idea that it might be the madman himself who had fathered it. His show of rage might have been an elaborate performance, put on, with peasant cunning, to keep the truth from his wife. 'Stop it,' she thought. 'Thee is an old woman with a dirty mind.'

Old or no, she was a woman. When the little boy refused to be pacified and began to show signs of going into shock, there was only one thing left to do. "Gentlemen," she said, "you would do me a favor if you would turn away. I have to feed this baby."

They did not understand, not even when she started to pull her jerkin over her head. She did it with a casualness that would have been convincing if she had not forgotten to take off her hat first; it landed on top of the baby, and although it was nothing compared to being bounced back and forth and used as a club, he shrieked like a stuck pig. Only when she bared one of her unappetizing breasts did the men watching her realize why she had requested privacy; they performed once more their magic trick of dissolving in the darkness. When she smeared a nipple with the syrup, there was not a *voyageur* in sight.

"Here, old feller," she said to the choking infant. "Let's see if thee will fall for this."

He did. The moment she put his little body against her chest and managed to make the huge red mouth clamp down on her nipple, his trembling ceased. The little fists, which had been fighting off demons for the first hour of his life, began to knead her breast like a kitten feeding. She winced, for, despite his size, he exerted the suction of a pump. Fascinated, almost disgusted, she observed the sucking little animal with curiosity, mixed with professional satisfaction at the success of her ruse.

That night she did not sleep much. The baby rested, but she did not. What was she going to do with him? Who could take in this pathetic little thing and feed it? The child needed mother's milk; she could keep him alive with the Indian syrup for only a few days; if she did not find a wet-nurse, he would die. Where could she find such a person out here? She sat staring at the dying fire, holding the baby, filled with anger toward the crazy family in the wagon. The girl was flowing with milk, she would have trouble stopping it; here was her child, her own flesh and blood, starving to death. Why? The more she thought about it, the more convinced she became that the brute with the beard was the father. To take the child back and force it on them would only result in its death the moment her back was turned. Where in the world could she take the little boy? An Indian tribe? The nearest one was Running Bull and his Unamis, back at Pendle Hill. She might be able to find a wet-nurse there, but the child should not be left with Indians. Of all sad, disoriented creatures, white children captured or adopted by the Indians were the saddest. They were never fully accepted by the tribe, forever yearned for their own race, but if they managed to return to white society, they found themselves ostracized and were forced to eke out a melancholy living between the two worlds as scouts, petty traders, gun runners or rum peddlers; most of the girls ended up as soiled doves in the forts on the frontier.

But what alternative was there? She gazed down at the babyish face, its utter weariness. If only she weren't a dying old crone! If only she still had some years ahead of her in which to set him on his way to becoming a human being! Or were these just the maudlin thoughts of sly old Gulie, who ran no risk of being taken at her word and therefore could safely indulge in daydreams? She grimaced and concentrated on how to save the little creature's life. Go all the way back across the Alleghenies to the first Friend's farm? She would inevitably arrive with a little corpse. Then what?

Suddenly she sat bolt upright, making the baby grunt with displeasure. Cleo! Margaret Fell, in Lancaster Castle, had written: *"The way to that of God in any woman, even the most hardened and disabused, is through a helpless, suffering child."* Why not dump this helpless, motherless infant in the black panther's lap and let that of God in her do its own work? Or would she be so embittered by the unimaginable degradation of slavery that to have her erstwhile master all to herself was essential for her survival? God only knew. But maybe the time had come for Gulielma Woodhouse to trust God for a change, rather than her own intelligence.

She left the next morning, at daybreak, after a voluble farewell from the *voyageurs*. To get to Pendle Hill in time to save the baby's life, she would have to make a forced ride. But old Annie and the two mules were already tired; the only way of prevailing upon the old mare to do anything strenuous was to make her believe she

was going home. Heading west, north or south, Annie was always
slow and obnoxious, but going east filled her with zest. Something in
the animal's brain equated "east" with "stable."

It worked once again. Annie surpassed herself in vigor and crotchety
skittishness when she was headed back east to cross the barren, bleak
immensity of the sea of grass. After the few nights of frost, with
a brisk, erratic wind in the early morning, the landscape had become
even more desolate and dismal. The wind had whisked bare patches
in the snow, dead grass had been whirled into giant nests. The bushes
and shrubs that, earlier, had looked peaceful with their snowy load
glistening in the sun had been turned into stark skeletons frozen in
writhing torment. Again there were patient buzzards circling overhead
and on the far horizon the specks of other buzzards, coasting along
with another lonely traveler.

That night, after she had lit her fire, she again had the eerie sensation of being observed at close range in the darkness. This time it
did not disturb her; the presence of the baby protected her against
whoever it was that approached them silently in the night and stood
there, invisible, watching. It was probably one of Running Bull's
scouts. The Unamis must be trying to establish a new territory for
themselves; pointless excursions like this were part of that procedure.
She sat, legs stretched out wide, leaning against her pack, as close to
the fire as she could, feeding the baby. He did not have any experience yet, poor thing; although his failure to draw any sustenance
despite his frantic efforts began to distress him, he did not blame her
arid breasts and turn away. The Indian syrup not only created the
illusion of feeding, it also sedated him; after ten minutes or so he
was bound to become drowsy, which would be the moment to spoon
some water into him to prevent dehydration. He would not enjoy it,
but his senses would be too dulled by then for him to protest.

She went through an elaborate mystification to heighten his illusion
of being fed. After a while she moved him from one breast to the
other; when he was through, she put him up against her shoulder and
patted his back to burp him. As the poor beastie took in nothing
but air, he belched with resonance. She sat cradling him, hugging and
kissing him for a while to induce a sense of security, and found herself thinking about Margaret Fell and what she had said about that
of God in women. If what the baby evoked in her was indeed that
of God, He was different from what she had imagined Him to be
all her life, more earthy, almost lighthearted. Ah, if He had been
really a God of love in the earthy sense, how much closer would she
have felt to Him all those long, barren years!

During their drowsy hours of closeness by the fireside, the idea of
having to part with this little companion filled her with regret. During
the day it was easier. The baby bounced on her back in his sling,
snoozing the hours away until the horse slowed down for the noonday rest. Then he started to squeal like a bird in the immensity of
the frozen prairie. They would rest for a while, she would feed him,
going through the whole performance of changing nipples, burping him

and changing his diaper, which, poor thing, became drier as the hours went by. His need for nourishment was desperate. Two more days to Pendle Hill, if all went well and the mules didn't become fed up with Annie's persistent tugging as she trotted toward her private mirage.

On the second day Henry, the mule carrying the apothecary, decided he had had enough. He suddenly stopped dead in his tracks, yanking old Annie backward and nearly throwing Gulielma out of the saddle, as she had been half asleep. He had done this before, and after years of experience she had adapted her pharmacy to just this eventuality. All mules had some peculiar personal trait, their only claim to individuality; Henry's was that he reacted to the size of a load rather than to its weight. If he believed that something was taken off his back, he was good for another bout of trotting. A carpenter in Philadelphia, bewildered but resigned, had sawed in half the edifice in which she carried her pills, powders and potions. The two halves, top and bottom, could also be lashed one behind the other. It did not change the weight of the load, if anything it made it more uncomfortable; but the profile was lowered, which to Henry's mulish mind gave the illusion that he was carrying less. Resignedly she dismounted, strolled over to Henry, patted his head and said, "Poor boy, thee is absolutely right, it is too much for a self-respecting mule. Let me throw half of it away." She rearranged the pharmacy, as she had done many times before, went back to the mule's head and pulled it around.

"How's that? Better? I should say so! Imagine, suddenly being rid of half your load! Look!"

He gave the angular object on his back a baleful glare, but it worked. He set out again, if not with renewed vigor, at least with moody resignation.

Her mind was so preoccupied with the child's steadily deteriorating condition that when at last the dark, wooded hill came in sight she had not yet planned how to go about leaving the baby with Bonny Baker without arousing the black girl's suspicion that this was merely part of a stratagem to save poor besotted Bonny from her clutches. But never mind; she should first go to Running Bull to see about a wet-nurse anyhow.

She did not relish the idea of going to see Running Bull. He was unpleasant, devious, and detested her. But her guess was that, under the circumstances, he would cooperate if he thought it would help the establishment of the school he wanted. It was rather endearing, the fierceness with which he clung to that school; although he was one of the most sophisticated and shrewdest Indians she knew, he still had a primitive, childish streak in him. The school had nothing to do with concern for the education of his children, it merely would be something no other tribe had. His braves had defeated the Miamis in what must have been the usual heinous, cruel manner; now he would seal their humiliation by establishing a school on their erstwhile territory, with white teachers, slaves to his tribe. Good thing Philadelphia Yearly Meeting did not realize what interpretation the Indians would give to the institute of learning with which they were about to be blessed. The only one who was a match for Running Bull was her brother Isaac, who undoubtedly would use the school to wrest from the Unamis a monopoly on their pelts.

She rode with some apprehension into Running Bull's newly established village on the far side of Nightingale Lake. The first timber wolves howled their mournful call in the caverns of the darkening forest; there were few people about. It was cold; thin smoke crinkled into the green sky from the tops of the wigwams. Outside the chief's teepee two sentinels sat huddled in their furs like big, cold birds that had settled down for the night. One went in to announce her, with indifference. She had not expected any commotion; everybody knew her and she was considered harmless, yet it reinforced her conviction that the mysterious presence on the horizon had been one of Running Bull's scouts. The sentry stuck his head out of the triangular entrance of the teepee and beckoned her inside. She dismounted and tethered old Annie.

"Thank thee, Friend." She stooped to go in, forgetting about the baby on her back; the man brusquely pushed her down. Good thing he did; it must be obvious that she had no experience of motherhood. "Greetings, mighty Friend," she said as she entered.

Running Bull, huge, smooth and shapeless like a beached whale, was lying on his side on a stack of skins, dressed only in a bead-embroidered clout which accentuated his nakedness. The temperature inside the tent was stifling; a brazier filled with glowing charcoal, large enough for a hall, stood in its center, and its heat hit her like a blast from a furnace. Perspiration sprang from her forehead and trickled down her nose and into her eyebrows.

"Well, well," the fat man said peevishly. He said it in his falsetto voice, which meant he was going to be unpleasant. His being a pederast did not help; he hated not only her but all women. She doubted whether he would be moved by the baby; for all she knew, it might arouse his appetite. "What gives us the pleasure of your visit?" he squeaked. "I thought you were on your way west."

"Indeed I was," she replied, sitting down on a pile of coonskins, hoping in vain that this would take some of the heat off her face. "Some urgent business forced me to return and I would like to discuss it with thee."

"With me?" The malevolent little eyes in the huge, perspiring face narrowed. As he lay there, the pendulous bulges of his fat drooping downward, his body gave a curiously distorted impression; his belly lay in front of him as if it were separate, a saurian egg laid by a monster from mythology. She remembered him as he had been when they first met: young, slender, effeminate, vulnerable. He had been a pretty boy; pity his affliction had prevented his flirting with the ladies in London during his visit. In some ways English aristocratic society was more primitive than his own; it was a matriarchy if ever there was one, and the only thing the women respected in a man was virility. No wonder he had returned full of hate and turned fat and repulsive; the Court of St. James's was not the proper place for a mincing Indian pansy.

"Yes," she said, undoing the sling in which she carried the baby. "I'd like to talk to thee about this creature." She put the child on her lap, leaning him against her stomach. His little head, weak with starvation, lolled to one side; he was oblivious of the whale gazing at him through the quivering column of hot air rising from the brazier.

"What is that?" Running Bull asked nastily.

"A baby boy."

"Thine, Pissing Gulie? Tchk, tchk!"

"That is a poor joke even for thee, friend," she said equably. "I rescued him when his family wanted to drown him in the Wabash."

"From what I see, that would have been a sensible idea." His hatred seemed to fill the hot little room. He had all the time in the world, he was going to take his time pulling the legs and the wings from this fly.

"Look," she said matter-of-factly, "I want this baby adopted by Boniface Baker and the black girl. But in order to bring that about I must go in for a little flim-flam. They must not know it was I who foisted the child upon them. He will have to be a foundling put on their doorstep by the Miamis."

His huge body seemed to freeze. He gazed at her with those slitted black pebbles without betraying what his reaction was. "Why?" The question was innocuous, but he had asked it in his own voice. He was beginning to take this seriously.

"I don't have to explain to thee the situation in the Baker cabin," she said. "Without going into lengthy detail, I do not have the impression that Boniface Baker is eager to start thy school."

The fat man chuckled. It was not a pleasant sound, it had nothing to do with good humor. "I have decided to give the Quakers another month to live up to the terms of our contract," he said in a manner that made her suspect he had rehearsed the phrase. "If by that time nothing has been done, Boniface Baker and his squaw will no longer be welcome in the land of the Unamis."

It was a distortion of the facts; there was no contract between the Quakers and himself, only the rash promise of an inexperienced boy. But she saw her chance. "That would be understandable but unwise," she replied. "All it would achieve is to chase the Quakers off thy territory, and with them all hope for a school. I am confident that once this child has been accepted by them, they will start a school before the spring."

"How so?"

"I can even foresee," she continued, ignoring the question, "that additional teachers might be forthcoming from Philadelphia." She looked at him with innocent eyes, hoping his spies had not already told him about the wagon train that was in preparation.

"Thee seems to foresee a great many things," he said listlessly, but he had slipped from "you" into "thee."

"It's worth a try, I would say. If it doesn't work, thee can always throw them out, all three of them."

He gazed at her with lazy perception. Then he produced what must be a smile, a brief rearrangement of the creases at the corners of his wet-lipped mouth. The Emperor Nero must have had a mouth like that. "What would thee have me do? Capture a Miami squaw and have her deliver the child?"

So he would go along with her. "Not exactly," she replied, blinking, as sweat ran into her eyes. "Have one of thy own squaws put the child in a basket on their doorstep tonight. We'll put some trinkets with it that will indicate it was done by the Miamis."

"And that my braves would have let the Miamis roam around our village undetected?" He feigned indignation.

"I thought thee had humiliated them sufficiently to allow their squaws to gather firewood without riddling them with arrows."

He appeared to mull it over, but in reality he was observing her. "And what trinkets did thee have in mind? A note saying 'We the Miamis present thee with this baby, please accept it with our regards'?"

"Not exactly, but something of the kind, yes."

"But the Miamis, dear friend, being stupid savages, do not read or write. They do not have an alphabet. They are like the beasts in the field. They shout, gesture and run. The only thing that distinguishes them from the coyotes is that they can make smoke."

"That is why I need thy advice," she said, deciding to lay it on with a trowel. "I thought thee might have a better idea."

He pursed his lips, which did not enhance his appearance. Nero must have looked that way when considering a new, obscene variation of torture. "Put something with it that no one can read," he said finally. "Something mysterious. Do not have them say at once, 'This is the work of the Miamis.' Let them come to thee to ask where this baby came from."

"But I won't be here. The moment I leave this child with thee, I go west once more."

"Then they will come to me, and I will tell them." He frowned thoughtfully. It gave her a feeling of relief. Somewhere inside that repulsive mass of bulging fat and sagging muscle was a little boy yearning to play games. "I'll have one of my squaws put the basket down, the sentries will see her and make so much noise outside the cabin that thy friends will open the door and see the baby."

"Perfect."

"And inside the basket we will put a puzzle. Stones with strange markings. An unfamiliar totem. Beads. Maybe a dead mouse."

"Why a dead mouse? Does it mean anything?"

"No. Just a dead mouse. Mystery."

"I see." Then a thought struck her. "What about a bat's wing with some Indian writing on it?"

"I have no bat's wing," he said disparagingly.

"I have one with me, writing and all." She rummaged in her haversack and produced the leathery membrane with long, thin toebones on which the Huni chief had written down the things he wanted her to bring, and a pendant made of stone in two colors, orange and blue, that she had taken along when she left last time because the colors reminded her of the ramparts in the sky.

"Where did thee get those?"

"Oh, I pick stuff up here and there." Before he was able to press for more, she continued, "We need a basket for him, and also, I'm afraid, a wet-nurse. This child has had no food since he was born, four days ago."

"Wet-nurse?" His English was very good, but there were limits.

"Nursing mother. Someone who just had a child of her own and has milk to spare."

His face expressed fatigue. "I'll find one. Show me those things."

She got to her feet, clumsily because of the baby, circled the infernal brazier and handed him the bat's wing and the trinket. She went back to her seat of coonskins while he studied the objects with curiosity, especially the bat's wing. He tried to decipher the hieroglyphs. "What does it say?"

"What should it say?" She was not going to tell him if she could help it; the less he knew about the existence of the Hunis, the better. They were hundreds of miles away, but if his interest were sufficiently aroused, he might conceivably take it into his head to go and have a look. A visit from Running Bull and his bloodthirsty braves was something the Hunis could do without.

He let it ride. "I assume it should say something like 'We present thee with this child in exchange for the daughter we killed,' " he said. "Or something of that nature, no?"

"Very good. What if we make it a little more emotional? Say, 'We leave this baby on your doorstep because only in this house is there a promise of love.' "

He smiled with a hint of lechery, but made no comment. Then he put the bat's wing down in front of his glistening belly and said, "All right, so be it. Goodbye."

"I'd like to put him in his basket myself. Could thee send for one?" It was not only caution that moved her; the idea of parting from the poor little mite was unexpectedly grievous. He slapped his thigh three times. One of the sentries stuck his head in. The man's teeth chattered, the frost must be bitter outside. Running Bull gave a rapid order, the head was withdrawn.

They waited for the man's return without speaking. It was not Running Bull's style to ease the silence with chit-chat. The baby, with tiny beads of sweat on his waxy forehead, whimpered weakly. She took him in her arms and hugged him and whispered in his ear, forgetting for a moment the huge Indian watching her with fascination. When their eyes met again, he asked maliciously, "Why not keep him thyself, Pissing Gulie? Thee needs a little dog at thy age."

"Oh, I don't know," she said carelessly. "There are plenty more where he came from."

For some reason, that seemed to amuse him; his repulsive body shook with laughter, in sections. Then the man came back with a basket.

It was the kind of basket in which Indian women gathered berries or roots; it had an oddly unfinished look. When she put the baby inside, gently, she suddenly felt she could take no more. Rising, she said, "Peace be with thee, Running Bull. Please arrange for that wet-nurse."

"But will thy friends ask for one? How will they know that is what it needs?"

"Trust the girl," she said. "She'll know. I don't think there's a single plantation where the lady of the house feeds her own children. It ruins the shape of the breast."

She turned to leave. The child was safe now; Running Bull, whatever his character, was an Indian. He would never harm a helpless child, unless he were stricken with the lunacy of war.

* * *

Boniface Baker was awakened from a deep, drugged sleep by shouts, yells, the stampede of running feet and the shrill, terrified shrieking of a hurt animal. He swung his feet out of bed and, supporting himself as the world reeled about him in his stupor, he stumbled to the door.

Outside, the snow lay still and luminous in the moonlight. Black shapes were scurrying away across the clearing toward the dark tangle of the forest; the shrieking little animal lay at his feet, in front of the door. He bent over it to see what it was, found a basket, and realized it was a baby.

Candlelight approached behind him from the cabin. It was Cleo; when she looked down and saw the basket, she seemed to recoil.

"It—it's a child," he said, bewildered by her reaction.

She did not seem to hear him. Her eyes, as she looked down at the child crying in its basket were so fierce that he turned away, alarmed. She looked like a cougar about to pounce. He bent down to pick up the basket, but she held him back.

"Cleo . . ."

She handed him the candle, her eyes on the child; then she knelt and picked it up. Its thin, high shrieks became muffled as she pressed it against her chest. She rose and carried it inside. "Close the door," she said.

He brought the basket inside and watched her as she put the baby on the stack of hides in front of the fire. She looked down at the child as it lay there, waving its puny arms; the black look of violence seemed to leave her eyes. She stretched out her hands toward it and took off its rags.

The baby she took out of the swaddling clothes was very small, very white. The head seemed extraordinarily large and bony, with sunken cheeks and hollow eyes; the big, wide mouth, screaming in agony, looked old and harrowed. It was a boy. She lifted him up, one hand under his wobbly, skeletal head, and put him against her breast. Nestling his head against her shoulder, she looked up.

"This baby is dying," she said. "He is starving. Go to the Indian village and ask for a woman who has lately had a child. Ask her to come here, quick."

"But what . . . ?"

She turned away from him, unbuttoned the top of her dress, took out a breast and pressed the child to it.

Those were the breasts that had haunted his dreams. He was suddenly overcome by a terrible sense of desolation.

"Quick, quick," she said over her shoulder, "does thee not understand? I have no milk and he knows it!"

On his way to the door he tripped over the basket and realized he was barefooted. He could not run to the Indian village like this; he must put on some clothes. He went behind the curtain; while he dressed hurriedly, he listened to the desperate sucking of the child, loud in the silence. As he came out from behind the curtain, scuffing his feet into his boots, Cleo looked up. "Hurry!" she said.

"I will . . ."

Outside, the snow was blue and luminous in the moonlight. The cold air tautened the skin on his face. 'Dear God,' he thought, 'Thy will be done, whatever it may be.'

Then he ran toward the village, his steps soft in the snow.

CHAPTER FIVE

A H, Beulah Baker thought, if only moral issues were clear-cut, the way she had assumed as a young girl! If only human impulses were black or white, good or evil!

There was, for instance, the matter of the slaves of Eden Island. The Meeting had taken them under its care, sold the island for them at a fair price and shared out the proceeds among them. Could any moral issue be more noble? Yet the results had, in some cases at least, been clearly evil. The moment the poor Negroes had been handed what must seem to them a staggering sum of money in gold coin, some had blown it all in one riotous week of drunken carousing in the alehouses on the waterfront, to end up, dead to the world, in the gutter, where they were promptly picked up and carried off to be resold into slavery. Others had gone into a morose decline, not knowing what to do with the money, pining dumbly for the security of the world they had left behind, until in the end, to the incredulous dismay of the Meeting, they asked to be taken back to the island, preferring to serve the new owner as slaves rather than to be separated from what they considered their home. The majority, after weeks of dithering and moping, had hired themselves out as house servants or gardeners to members of the Meeting at nominal salaries, seeking protection. Most affluent Friends who had thus far hesitated to join in the common practice of hiring Negro house servants to avoid the stigma of slavery, now found themselves in a quandary. Nobody came to ask Beulah for advice as to whom they should hire; no one seemed to remember that she had once owned them and thus knew them all. Jeremiah would have ended up with Scipio, for instance, if she had not managed to dissuade him in the nick of time. Every Quaker family in town who could afford it radiantly pulled in a Trojan horse, nobody had the sense to realize that these were the lazy ones, who now had enough money of their own to work only when the mood took them, and whose only concern was to be protected from slave-hunters.

The only ones who benefited fully from their newfound freedom were the few who decided to go with the school expedition to homestead tracts of wilderness in the Northwest Territory. They were the industrious and sober ones, with the exception of fat old Mammy, who, for some reason, had made up her mind to accompany them. But what could these people expect, once they arrived at their destination? How long would it be before white settlers overwhelmed them and their small holdings, to chase them off their hard-won property? Already a surprising number of members of the Meeting had decided to go, mainly young people who had yet to make their mark in the world, such as Joseph Woodhouse and his Himsha, George McHair, the idol of her daughter Abby, Ezekiel Henderson, Nathaniel Norris. What possessed these young people to give up the privileges and the secure future they had as scions of the leading families in the city? What gave them the idea that they could carve a new destiny for themselves out of the wilderness? Did no one remember Becky? Had she died in vain? It had become an insane fad, to go west with that miserable school to start rustic enterprises like smithies, carpenter shops, trading posts. Madness, that's what it was, youthful madness; it expressed itself in a rash of wild parties, so-called farewell celebrations but in truth cavortings and bundlings in sleighs and hunting lodges in the forest. Their sober elders, stunned and bewildered, remained behind in a city that suddenly seemed deserted by its youth, as if a plague had taken the young, the flower of the future. Anything was a pretext for a celebration, however far-fetched; the latest was the blowing up of Altar Rock that very morning. Scores of young folk had left yesterday to spend the night at the inn on the river: a jingling parade of sleighs and buggies, sulkies and phaetons, full of red-cheeked, bright-eyed youths and girls wrapped in furs and shawls, covered with buffalo hides, each horse worth a fortune, each contraption the fruit of the labor of their parents. Not one among them seemed to realize that the very splendor of their procession as it whooshed and jingled out of the city demonstrated the unworldliness of their notion that they would be suited by either temperament or education for the harsh existence of a pioneer in the wilderness. How were their children to be born without midwives or mothers to assist them? What lay ahead for gentle, fragile creatures like Himsha Woodhouse? Or Agnes Norris, who had been delicate since childhood and whose anguished, consumptive cough regularly disturbed the silence of the Women's Meeting? Madness, that's what it was; it all seemed to be summed up by the shuddering earthquake that rattled the windows of Philadelphia that morning, which, after a moment of stunned terror, they realized must have been "Ben's Bang." Any time now the revelers would come jingling back, flushed with excitement, full of breathless stories she would not believe, convinced that what had gone on in the inn last night had nothing to do with Ben's Bang. She would not say so aloud, but it seemed to her that it was her slaves who had sown the seeds of amorality, irresponsibility and rebellion all over the town.

How could she possibly join that expedition? She asked herself the question for the thousandth time as she walked home after classes. The mere thought of having to share in the madness of it all, the pointlessness, was more than she could bear. Yet she had to go. Her husband was out there; unless she wished to sever all ties with him, she must do her duty. She could no longer use Abby's education as an excuse, for the very purpose of the expedition was to found a school. She could not plead hardship, as several demented old crones like Bathsheba Moremen and Millie Clutterbuck had decided to go.

She had explored all possibilities, there simply was no way out. Even though it would be the death of her, she would have to join in the madness and leave behind all that gave her life meaning. The thought of having to say farewell forever to little Abraham, to Jerry, made her accelerate her pace and run the rest of the way home at an undignified trot, breathless and anguished.

She could not face Grizzle or even Jerry; she excused herself from the evening meal, feigning a headache. Locked in her room, she sank on her knees beside the bed to beseech God to take this cup away from her, knowing all the time that her duty was obvious and undoubtedly God's will. What she should be doing was asking Him for fortitude so she might do that duty with dignity and resignation.

Yet, as she knelt there praying, tears streaming down her face, it was as if she began to feel a small reassurance, a faint flicker of hope. It had nothing to do with reason; there was no earthly cause that would justify her shirking her duty. Yet, maybe because of the passion of her prayer, there seemed to rise within her a promise, a hope that clearly emanated from God.

In her deafness, she did not hear the jingling of the sleighbells, the shouts and the laughter in the street outside as the young ones returned from the blowing up of Altar Rock. She knelt there, passionately concentrating on the faint light of hope that dimmed and grew within her. It took a while before she became conscious even of a banging on her door, a rattling of the knob, a voice calling, "Beulah, Beulah, is thee there? Beulah! Beulah!" It was not the volume of the voice that finally got through to her, but its despair. It was Jerry.

She rushed to the door and opened it. There he stood in the hallway, his face a mask of incredulous horror.

Her first thought was an accident, somebody was dead. Her heart faltered. Abby; something had happened to Abby! "Jerry, what is it?"

He said tearfully, "Obadiah, Obadiah . . ." His mouth was drawn into a grimace that suddenly made him look completely helpless.

She threw her arms around him. "Jerry, what's the matter? What happened?"

"Obadiah—Obadiah's going to marry Carrie Woodhouse! He's getting out of the business! They want to go west! With the school!" Sobbing, he dropped his head on her shoulder.

She put her arms around him and stroked his hair, whispering, "Sweeting, sweeting, it's all right, it's all right . . . Calm down, love, calm down . . ." Then suddenly the faint light within her blazed into a sunrise. He needed her! Now he needed her more than Bonny did! With Obadiah gone, he would have to take on the shipyard again, all alone; she could not possibly desert him!

It was only in the small hours that at last the candles were snuffed in the Woodhouse parlor, where everybody of the older generation of the two families had gathered to discuss the disaster: Grizzle in tears, Mary Woodhouse majestically outraged, Isaac cantankerous with shock, Jeremiah feebly resigned to the inevitable. They had pleaded in vain with that impossible nincompoop Obadiah, who stammered like a child despite his thirty-four years, and with the defiant Carrie, looking much younger than her true age of eighteen. For that unhealthy, bald coot to make off with this fragile, pampered creature! It was even more irresponsible than leaving his old father to shoulder the yard all alone.

Beulah and Grizzle put Jerry to bed, like a patient; then Beulah left the two of them to face the bleak night alone. Finally she could go back to her room, where, after a prayer of inexpressible gratitude, she sat down to write to her husband. She had plenty of time yet, the expedition was not due to leave for another month, but she wanted to put her thoughts down while the basic issue was still clear in her mind. She tried to make it a loving, conciliatory letter, but, to her surprise and dismay, found herself becoming vindictive instead. She had given the matter much thought and brought it before God in many prayers, she wrote, and she had come to the conclusion that to bury herself in the wilderness and live on a footing of equality with her slaves did not speak to her condition. To set the slaves free, with all that that entailed, had been his witness, not hers, and she had discovered that she could not, out of a mere sense of duty, take on a testimony that was basically repugnant to her. It would violate that of God in her as surely as to keep slaves and lead a civilized life had violated that of God in him. After all, she was a person in her own right, despite her conjugal duties. To traipse about the wilderness in men's clothes and hobnob with the Indians might be to the taste of warped women like Gulielma Woodhouse . . .

She stopped, bemused. This was not at all how she felt, this had nothing to do with the issue . . . Ah, if only moral issues were clear-cut, the way they had been when she was a young girl . . .

* * *

Gulielma made camp on the open prairie. Only after she had unloaded the mules and taken the saddle off the old mare and sat leaning against it on her blanket, gazing at the fire, did she realize how exhausted she was. She was so tired that she could not bring herself to get up again to fetch the moosehide off the pack, although it was only a few feet away. She could no longer even lift her head when it sagged, her chin on her chest. This was nonsense; it was not yet cold enough for her to freeze to death, but just to sit there without cover would mean that the next morning she would be as stiff as a board. With an effort of will, she roused herself, staggered to the pack, pulled out the heavy hide and dragged it back to the blanket and the saddle. She lay down, heaved the ice-cold hide on top of her and settled down to sleep.

She never knew whether she actually slept; she must have, for at a given moment the dawn was there. But she felt as if she had not really rested; she must be more tired than she had known. The task of loading up the mules again seemed insurmountable, but finally it was all strapped on top of the beasts once more, Annie was saddled

and ready to give her pantomime of a dying camel. When she went
to hoist herself into the saddle, she found she did not have the
strength to do so; it took her ten minutes before she finally had
clawed her way up and found herself dangling limply across the
saddle. She had quite a bit of talent for the drama herself; her exhaustion was not nearly so tragic as she made it seem, but some
inner urge for play-acting got the better of her. "Oh, my God!" she
moaned, clinging spread-eagled on the saddle, "I can't make it, God,
I can't make it!" And all this although there was not a spectator in
sight, not even the mules, who were too wrapped up in their own
theatre to have eyes for anyone else's. They stood there, heads drooping, eyes closed, heaving sighs, steam spurting from their nostrils,
like dragons; the only one aware of her antics was Annie, who did
her best to match them. Together they went through an orgy of
huffing and puffing, moaning and staggering, before she managed to
haul herself upright in the saddle and tug the reins. "All right, old
girl," she panted, "that's it for now. Let's move."

But the old beast was loath to let go of her soul-satisfying performance; she set one wobbly foot in front of the other, stopped
in bewildered confusion, as if she could not remember which one to
move next, and nearly knelt down in a final flourish.

"Move!"

Annie left the stage reluctantly, but she moved, the mules, gloom-
sodden but resigned, in tow.

It became a curious day. On the one hand, Gulielma felt detached,
almost in high spirits; on the other, there was that irresistible temptation to dramatize, out of sheer boredom. "Oh, God . . ." she sighed
at intervals, reeling in the saddle. "I can't go on, God, I can't, I
can't . . ." It was, for some reason, gratifying; she had always
refrained from talking to herself, thinking it a sign of encroaching
senility, now she discovered why so many lonely people did so. It did
indeed give satisfaction. "Ha ha!" she cried, in a sudden change of
mood, addressing the mysterious presence beyond the horizon. "I see
thee, old spyglass! Won't thee join me? Doesn't thee like company?"
But there was nothing to be seen except for those specks of distant
buzzards, circling. "Yoo-hoo!" she hooted. "Who is thee, Friend? Come
on, show thyself, be sociable!" What rapturous gratification it gave
to holler at the top of her lungs, with sweeping, grandiose gestures at
the turkey vultures overhead. "Come down, let's have a word! Let's
visit with . . . oops!" She was too giddy to ride looking up, she had
almost turned turtle. "Well, let's see if there's anybody lower down . . .
Yoo-hoo! Anybody here?!"

She enjoyed herself hugely, while the three animals, weary and
disgusted, shambled along at a snail's pace. But at least they moved;
they did not do badly either, for toward sunset she recognized the
cluster of juniper bushes where she had camped before. She halted
the mare, slid out of the saddle, missed her footing and crashed
on her back in the snow. She was not hurt, but it gave her quite a
shock. It had not happened to her since she had broken in her first

horse. His name had been Apache, a beautiful chestnut mustang. Apache, that was a long, long time ago . . . Come on, old girl, on thy feet! She managed to hoist herself up by the stirrup, took the reins and guided Annie toward the campsite. To her amazement, the juniper bush was gone.

Now, that was idiotic. Where was it? She gazed around her; the prairie was empty. Not a shrub in sight. What could have happened to it? Her eye was caught by a rock half buried in the snow, shaped like an anvil. She knew that rock, it was at least three hours' ride this side of the juniper bush. How could she have made such a stupid mistake? "Don't tell me thee is hallucinating!" she said, grinning at herself. Three hours was too long to go; the sun was low, soon the night wind would whip up the powdered snow and send it into their noses and eyes. She had better make camp, although she would have liked a little more shelter. There was no firewood either; she would have to make a fire with sawgrass; but to go on feeding it was too much trouble. What did she want a fire for, anyhow? She didn't want to cook anything, she wasn't hungry. All she wanted was a piece of pemmican.

It was then she realized that she hadn't eaten for days. She had simply forgotten about it; the baby had absorbed all her attention. That was probably why she felt so lightheaded and had gone in for those melodramatics all day. She had better eat something or she might get entirely out of hand tomorrow. That's what it had been, of course: the euphoria of starvation. Fascinating. Quite pleasurable, really; if people knew how pleasant it was, they would not eat so much.

She managed to prevail upon the mules to lie down so she could slide their packs off. There was not much grazing anyhow, they might as well stay down; together they made a nice little shelter, if she covered them. It would mean going without a bottom blanket, but the hide was large enough to wrap around her. She felt so lightheaded and pleasantly tipsy when she lay down that she couldn't be bothered to pull out a piece of pemmican and go to the trouble of chewing it. She'd eat tomorrow. Promise? Promise. First thing, pemmican. Cross my heart. Good night, old girl. Call me if there's anything interesting. Giggling, she fell asleep.

This time she really did sleep. She even dreamed, pleasant flitting dreams without substance, airy, playful nonsense that made her laugh in her sleep. The sun woke her; it shone right in her eyes. She had no idea it was that late; if she wanted to get to the next shelter after the juniper bush, the snow-owl shrub near the prairie-dog town, they would have to move faster than they had yesterday. She felt refreshed and in high spirits, the long night's rest had done her a world of good. She got up, unsteadily. Patsy, good old mule, had not budged all night. Henry had, of course, he was an independent old cuss. He stood nearby, looking sorry for himself. "Come on, old girl, let's get up. Up, Patsy!" She slapped the gaunt, coarse flank of the mule whose body had sheltered her all night. When the animal did not move, she slapped her again; only when she walked around to her head and saw the glazed eyes staring sightlessly at the sky did she realize that the mule was dead.

Dead? She stood staring down at the lifeless beast in bafflement. Had she driven her too hard? Possibly; but it was more likely that Patsy simply had made up her mind she did not want to go all the way back again. Mules were like Indians; once they made up their minds to die, they died. Well, she was sorry. Patsy had been nice enough, although they had not had the time to really get to know each other. *Requiescat,* old girl. If mules go to heaven, I'll be around before long to see how thee is getting on. In the meantime, may thy angels bray thee to sleep.

It had been a splendid little speech, she had even managed to bring tears to her eyes, which in her present dehydrated state was not bad for an amateur mummer. So pleased, so pleased was she, the queen of Larabie, that she didn't realize she would have to ditch half of her load until she stood facing the jumble of packs, pots and pans and the two halves of her pharmacy cantilevered one on top of the other in the snow. Well, there was no choice, really. She was not going to practice any more medicine. She was a private citizen now, member of the Huni tribe, on her way home with presents for the family. She whistled to Henry, who refused to come, went to fetch him, and when he refused to budge, she clouted him on the snout. He snarled at her and muttered something, but she said, "Shut thy mouth!"

Realizing she meant business, he came. She loaded on him the packs, pots, pans and other junk that the late, lamented Patsy had carried so faithfully; he was in luck, for it weighed less than the pharmacy. When despite that pleasant surprise he would not move, she looked at the load again and realized it was higher than the two halves of the pharmacy. "Oh dear, oh dear," she muttered, "what it is to live with mules!"

She rearranged the load to his liking, slinging the utensils around his belly; after he had satisfied himself with a backward look, he deigned to proceed. Now, with the constant clanking of pots and pans, she sounded like an itinerant tinker; what little game there was would hear her coming a mile away. Well, she was not going to shoot game anyhow. She had enough pemmican to last her until she reached the Mississippi. She rode on, slower than she wished but as fast as the poor beasts would go. She was no longer frivolous but quite detached and pleasantly disposed. She could think of her own imminent demise, a term she decided to use from henceforth, with equanimity. It obviously was not nearly as imminent as she had thought; she felt she could go on like this, floating peaceably toward her goal, bobbing like a boat, virtually forever. She didn't really need any food, as she wasn't using up any energy; she was merely letting herself be carried from Nightingale Lake to the Huni Mountains. It seemed as far as the moon.

But then, the same was true of the clump of shrubs by the

prairie-dog town; it seemed almost unattainable. Yet the buzzards up there must be seeing it right now. "Hello, there!" she called, her head thrown back. "How are you toda—"

Minutes later, maybe half an hour later, maybe an hour, she slowly came to. She was lying on her back in the snow, stunned, terrified. She had no idea where she was or what had happened; then she saw Annie and Henry grazing nearby and realized she must have crashed off her horse. It gave her a sick, bilious qualm of fear. She had broken something. Or suffered a concussion. Cautiously she raised herself on one elbow, expecting jabs of pain in her legs or her back; but she felt nothing, just that sick taste of fear. She could not remember falling; she remembered looking up at the buzzards and shouting something, after that nothing until she came around. She stood up shakily and staggered over to Annie. To her surprise, the saddle felt warm. The sun was too weak to have done that; the reins and bridle were cold. There was only one explanation: her stupid buttocks could not have left that saddle more than thirty seconds ago, if that. Well, well, the enigma of the mind. Let's go.

She had some trouble mounting, but managed; here they went again, back on the treadmill of the trail. But something had happened in those few seconds of unconsciousness. Her high spirits were gone, her pleasurable equanimity, her self-confidence. In their stead she felt a shivery fear in the pit of her stomach, small and inarticulate. She didn't have a thought in her mind, only that vague, formless apprehension, until she saw the house.

It was such a surprise that she reined in her mare and stood stock still, staring at it, open-mouthed. She had never known there was a house anywhere near, nobody lived west of the forest other than the roaming Miamis. That someone had homesteaded here was the best-kept secret of the century. It was not a log cabin or a mud hut, but a proper house, built of stone with white stuccoed walls; it had windows with green shutters and a black tiled roof. How in the world had they managed to lug all that across the prairie?

"Hey, there!" she croaked, hearing how unprepossessing her voice must sound to strangers. "Anybody home?"

Her voice was echoed by the white façade, then, suddenly, something burst out of one of the windows: a giant white bird that winged away, hooting. A snow owl. She was gazing at the juniper bush where she had camped twice before.

She said out loud, quite calmly, "Gulielma, friend, thee is hallucinating. Get off that horse and review the situation. This is no good. No good at all." The day wasn't nearly done yet, but she had better stop here. She dismounted, freed old Annie of her saddle and Henry of his jangling load and sent them both off to forage with a slap on their haunches. But they would not go; they were not hungry either. "Annie, old girl," she said admonishingly, "don't start starving thyself, for thee sees what happens to those who do." She wondered if horses hallucinated too; for some reason, she was sure mules did not.

The fear in the pit of her stomach had grown tighter. From now on she would have to check everything she saw or thought she saw to make sure it was real. Unless she got some food inside her, the hallucinations would intensify. Soon the world would be peopled with monsters, she would be talking to stones, shouting at the sky, and falling off her horse all the time. Instead of giving that gun to Joe and Himsha, she should have blown her brains out with it. What had given her the idea that she would be able to make the mountains? She was a good doctor, she should have known that was nonsense. She didn't have a ghost of a chance; she would never reach the Mississippi. It would not be an unpleasant death, as far as death could ever be pleasant; if only she could keep that fear at bay, she would get more and more lightheaded, lurching across the prairie, to finally curl up somewhere in her moose skin and fall asleep. Next thing she'd know would be the other world, or nothing. Whichever way it worked out, she was prepared.

Was she? Was anyone, ever? What about that fear in her stomach? Come on, old mummer, be honest with thyself. Thee is scared out of thy wits. Suddenly, without warning, she found herself on her knees, her face in her hands, whispering, "God, help me, God, God, for Jesus' sake, help me, please, God, God, please, please . . ."

But God, if He had any sense, would see through those histrionics. She did herself. True, she was desperate; yet there was that infernal sense of the drama, the temptation to let herself go, to make a performance of it. With a sigh, she got to her feet and went to hack some branches off the inside of the bush, where it was dry. She made a fire, spread out her bottom blanket, dragged her saddle and the moose skin to her lair and sat, hunched up, her chin on her knees, staring at the sickly little flames among the frozen twigs. As she sat there, aware only of the flames, she suddenly had that sensation again of being observed. She looked around as far as she could without moving her head. There was no one to be seen, only the specks of the distant buzzards circling above her secret companion. Who could it be? Running Bull had not seemed interested in her movements. He had known she was coming, of course. It would have been shameful if his scouts had not told him that at least half a day ahead of her arrival. But this far out? Could it be that she was hallucinating, that the distant buzzards were not really there and never had been? She scanned the horizon, but saw no buzzards. The only real buzzards were the ones overhead, the ones that had caused her to lose her balance.

She lay down on her back and gazed at them, at her ease. "Friends," she said, "you're going to have a treat soon. Oh, not me! I'm going to be as tough and leathery as this moosehide: but Henry, he's going to be succulent. Yum-yum!" 'Shut up,' she thought. 'Hysterical bitch, shut up.'

She pulled herself up into a sitting position and gazed at the fire again, expecting it at any moment to turn into a palace full of white mice. She wondered what sort of night lay ahead.

Well, it was bad. The fear writhed within her until it could be ignored no longer; the darkness closed in and became so stifling that she got up, cursing, yet unable to help herself. She began to pace up and down in the snow, the way she had paced in the guest room in Isaac's house the night after seeing Moremen. The same terror, the same loneliness assailed her, but this time she could not shake them off. She knew that she was hallucinating when she thought she saw someone approaching in the night, yet, dimly aware of her own play-acting, she cried, "I know thee! Of course I do! I knew it was thee all along! Come on, show thyself! Come! Come, I'm waiting for thee!"

There was no answer. Her voice, shrill and hysterical, trailed away in the vast silence of the prairie.

"Death!" she yelled in the direction of those distant buzzards. "Death, come and sit with me! Come, I can't hold out any longer! I'm lonely, I'm scared! Does thee hear me . . . ? Oh, God, God," she moaned, covering her face with her hands, "what has become of me?" It was a cry of abject self-pity, yet it was real. She could not help it that her spirit was incarcerated in the body of a woman.

"Greetings, Gulie."

The voice was so real that she froze. That was the trouble with hallucinations: she would soon fall for them entirely.

"Thanks for singing out," the voice said. "I had some trouble finding thee. Thy fire is near gone."

Annie whinnied. That had not been a hallucination. She slowly lowered her hands and looked.

He stood on the edge of the night, his horse behind him. "Is thee all right, Gulie?" It was Buffalo McHair.

For a moment she did not believe her eyes; then she saw Annie wander toward the little horse. "Where the devil did thee spring from?" she asked shakily.

"I was sent to catch up with thee," he said, stepping closer. "Bonny Baker wants thee to translate this for him. They put a foundling on his doorstep, and this came with it." It was the bat's wing.

"Well, well," she said, swallowing. "Welcome into my parlor." She turned away, trying to get hold of herself. She did not know yet how she was feeling; one thing was manifest, though: the fear was gone. Suddenly she felt embarrassed. Had he heard her? Oh, my God, what a shameful exhibition! He *must* have, he had been well within earshot or he would not have appeared a second later, out of thin air, like an Indian.

Indian . . . "Was it thee?" she asked sharply.

"Excuse me?" His guileless, blue-eyed innocence gave him away. No virgin could ever look as innocent as Buffalo McHair with a guilty conscience.

"Has thee been following me for over a week now?"

He seemed to change from a guilty boy into the man who had rescued her from the bolting buggy the night Bonny Baker freed his slaves. "Yes," he said calmly. He sat down, cross-legged, by the fire.

"Why?"

"Look, Gulie, I'm not going to take any nonsense from thee on this. Thee is sick, thee told me so thyself; I am not about to let a sick friend come to grief, all by herself, out here on the prairie."

"Aha!" she sneered. "I see! Thee has it in thy stupid head that thee can take me back?"

"I don't want to take thee back. I know what it means to thee to get to thy Indians. I have come to take thee there."

"Thee has *what?*"

"Take thee there," he said calmly. "Thee knows full well thee'll never make it alone. Thee has already lost one mule; how far did thee think thee would get with those two old nags and all that junk thee is carrying? But now thee'll get there, leave it to me."

She stood staring at him, feeling the way she had felt when she had collapsed in his arms in the buggy; but with an effort of will she said, "Buffalo McHair, thee doesn't know what thee is talking about. I am very sick indeed. I don't think I'm going to make it. It will be a miracle if I get as far as the Mississippi. Let's put an end to this foolishness. Take me back to Pendle Hill, give me a bed in one of thy hovels and I'll die there in an orderly fashion. Thee can even sit by me as I go."

"No, Gulie," he replied, kindly but with calm authority, "it is not foolishness. It is what thee wants to do with thy life. Let's saddle up and do it. But first, let's have something to eat."

"I can't eat," she said, feeling herself weaken. "I can't keep any food down. That's why I am hallucinating."

He gave her a questioning look.

"Seeing things that aren't there. I set up camp here this afternon be-cause I took this damn bush to be a cottage with green shutters, of all things. Until a snow owl burst out of one of the windows."

"How about a swig of this?" He put his hand inside his jerkin and brought out the flat bottle. She remembered the delicious warmth the firewater had spread through her body after the first shock.

"If I have any of that, I'll be unmanageable," she said. She still had not recovered; she still did not know how she felt about his offer, his discreet surveillance all this time. But for the buzzards, she would never have known.

"I'll manage thee," he said, holding out the bottle.

She took it; it was warm with the heat of his body. "Listen, Buffalo," she said, "I'm serious. God knows what state I might be in before it's over. Don't embarrass me by taking on the nursing of a crazy woman; I would be mortified, in my more lucid moments."

"Thee would not." He said it without sentiment. "I have handled women all my life. Whatever thee does, it'll be all right with me."

"Thee is an old fool," she said. "Let's drown our sorrows. Bottoms up!" She lifted the bottle and was about to drink when she hesitated. "What we really should do is go into meeting," she said.

He grinned. "Thee looks as if thee needed something else but prayer right now. Bottoms up."

"On thy head be it." She tilted the bottle and took a mouthful. It

seared the back of her throat; when she swallowed, she felt the
burning heat go down; then it hit her stomach and she exploded,
shrieking, with excruciating pain. Blinded, shocked into terror, she
screamed, holding her stomach, rolling on the ground, "Help! Help!
Buffalo, God, help!" Then his arms were around her, he lifted her
cramped, trembling body and cradled her, saying, "It's all right, Gulie,
it's all right. I'm sorry, Gulie, I'm a bungling jackass. I'm sorry, it's
all right, it'll pass, it'll pass. Take it easy, now, easy . . ."

Despite the pain, despite the terror, despite this final proof that
her diagnosis had been right and that there was no hope for her,
the comfort of his proximity was inexpressible. His huge, coarse body
exuded such power and security that, with a shameless, feminine
wail, she gave in to the pain and the fear.

He cradled her until she was at peace. Nearby, in the firelight,
the old mare nuzzled the little mustang. On the edge of the night
Henry the mule stood sleeping, alone.

*   *   *

Buffalo watched over her as she lay fitfully sleeping, and it seemed
obvious to him that she would not last the week. But, to his amazement,
the woman who rose from her moosehide at the first light of dawn
was the Gulielma he had known all his life: tough, witty and possessed
by a driving energy.

They set out side by side, the moody mule with the clanking pots
and pans behind them. They joked and chatted all the way; only
when she dismounted for their noon rest did she betray her condition.
She was so weak that she fell as she slid out of the saddle; he went
to help her up, but she angrily rebuked him and struggled to her feet
by herself.

That night, at the campfire, she told hilarious stories until tears
of laughter ran down his face. She looked so young, so gay in
the firelight in that vast, icy cavern of the winter night that he
wondered whether she might not be getting better rather than worse.
She translated the note scribbled on the bat wing that, he knew,
she must have put with the baby herself, for he had seen her lug the
child all the way across the plains to Pendle Hill. But although he
knew she knew, he played his part, that obviously was the way
she wanted it. He promised to take the bat wing and her translation
back to the Bakers; then he tried to get some food into her by
brewing a stew of herbs and jackrabbit that would pacify even the
most angry stomach. She tried, but after a couple of mouthfuls he saw
her suddenly grow old before his eyes. A few moments earlier she
had been gay, high-spirited, full of drolleries; after a few spoonfuls
of his stew, her face went haggard, the lines became crevices and
she slumped, her hands on her stomach, against her saddle, eerily
transformed into a skeletal old woman racked with pain. He sat
down beside her, put his arms around her shoulders and felt her

shivering; he pulled the moosehide over her, but she went on trembling piteously. Only hours later did she finally relax; she fell asleep slumped against him, her old, wispy hair, spread out on his chest, turning white with the hoarfrost of his breath.

She could not last much longer; no one could survive without food for more than ten days at the utmost and God only knew how long it was since she had last eaten. But, miraculously, she rose again the next morning, tough and joking and wiry, full of the mysterious energy that drove her west toward her promised land. He had lived with wild animals long enough to know that in all living creatures there were reserves of energy that defied reason. He had known a lame bull moose that he had wanted to shoot but taken pity on at the last moment and left to die the natural way; six months later, four hundred miles away, he had spotted the same crippled bull again, still lurching along on his long journey. What had kept the game-legged moose alive? How had he fended off wolves, coyotes, his own vicious young bulls? It seemed impossible, yet there he was: limping on toward his mysterious goal. Here was the same enigma again: something in the woman's emaciated, pain-racked body gave her the strength to survive, because there was a goal she had set herself. He began to worry about the journey ahead of them. He had never ventured beyond the Missouri River, for there lived the Osage Indians, whose language he did not speak and who were too ferocious to fool with. The territory between the Alleghenies and the Missouri was half a world wide; he had never felt the urge to go farther. Now they would have to cross the territory of the Osages and other tribes beyond, of whom he only knew the names: Cheyenne, Kiowa, Comanche, Apache. They would have to ford rivers he did not know, cross the Llano Estacado desert, of which he had heard fearful rumors all his life. Even if the rumors were exaggerated and the Osages friendly, it would be a harsh, hazardous journey even for him; to go through that trial of strength with a dying woman was insane.

He took care to make light of it. He wanted to give her a sense of steady movement, for that was all she wanted; to move, to move. Every night she seemed more exhausted by pain and weariness; but in the morning she was the first to rise, kicking him awake before the dawn streaked the sky. Off they went, bobbing along at the uncomfortable trot with which she had roamed the wilderness for years. She knew no better than to bounce up and down sixty times a minute; her tailbone must be iron-clad by now, her buttocks as tough as mule skin. To him this peddler's trot was more wearying than if he cantered all day. The clanking of the pots and pans behind them began to grate on his nerves; the wheezing and coughing of the old nag she rode became depressing.

But as time went by he began to take her condition for granted. During the first week, until they reached the Mississippi River, he rode beside her in constant anxiety, expecting her to gasp and pitch forward any moment. But after a week of miraculous resurrections

each morning he gave up waiting for her sudden collapse; instead he
began to worry about the unfamiliar surroundings.

Ten days later they reached the Missouri at Pierre Louchant's
crossing. The squinting French trader warned them that the Kansas
and Osages were at war; anyone venturing into their territory was
bound to run into trouble. They decided to wait until next morning
before having themselves ferried across; he discussed the danger with
her that night at the campfire. He did not try to dissuade her, but
he could not help showing his apprehension.

"Don't worry, Buffalo," she said, looking at him with those twinkling
blue eyes that read every secret in a man's mind. "I know those
Indians. I've been gadding about among them for over forty years.
They can be mean, and if they're at war they're apt to be meaner
than ever; but even so they'll let us through, for they know me.
Once they see who it is, they'll calm down." She said it without
vanity; it was a statement of fact. She was a wonderful woman,
and once she was gone life would be a lot more dreary. She somehow
managed to make it seem a little better, more hopeful and basically
kind than it really was. Why did people like her have to die this
way? To watch her go through torture every time she tried to eat
a little made him question the nature of God. Was He indeed a God
of love, full of mercy and compassion, as the city Friends would
have it? Seeing Gulielma suffer like a dog, holding her shivering,
tortured body in his arms until it went limp with exhaustion, made
him wonder whether the love and the gaiety and the hope within
her were not the true divinity in this cruel world. When his time
to die came and he lay on his back on the prairie gazing at the
sky, he would try to think of Gulie. He would not cry out to the
Creator of these snow-decked plains where distant herds of buffalo
stampeded out of sight like distant thunder, but to the tenderness,
the mercy, the understanding in her heart. Where would her soul go
after she was gone? Where would that miracle of gentleness and
compassion, of simple human goodness go, once the light in those
mischievous, wise eyes was extinguished? Would it simply dissolve
in the frosty night of the prairie? What a waste, what a terrible
loss for everybody, not just for the Indians and himself and people
like Boniface Baker, but also crooks like Squinting Pete, who ferried
them across the next morning at a cutthroat price plus an extra louis,
so-called danger money. She paid the ransom with a smile, patted his
shoulder and said, "Friend Pete, thee is the noblest swindler I know.
I admire a man who robs me on principle rather than mere greed.
God bless thee, and may thy madness bring thee happiness." The
cross-eyed skunk gazed at her open-mouthed, and something in his
face made him look almost human. Then he said, *"Au revoir, Gulie
Pissante! Bon voyage, et bonne chance."*
As she had predicted, neither the Osages nor the Kansa Indians
harmed them. There was one ugly moment toward the end of the
second day when suddenly a swarm of shrieking Indians on war-

maddened ponies came thundering over the crest of a hill, a heart-stopping wave of violence sweeping down upon them. She put a hand on his arm, preventing him from reaching for his rifle; they sat motionless until they were surrounded. He closed his eyes at their approach, in spite of himself. The noise was deafening, their stench overpowering as they milled around them, shrieking, covering them with snow kicked up by their ponies. Then, all of a sudden, there was silence, in which only the tortured panting of their horses betrayed their presence. He opened his eyes and there they were: faces covered with war paint, tomahawks bloodied, fresh scalps hanging from their belts, stinking of death and butchery. Gulielma, her voice the same as ever, chatted with them in their language; she was asking them something that seemed to arouse their curiosity. At a given moment she lifted her jerkin, pulled out her undershirt, showed them her bare stomach and pointed at it, wincing. He had no idea what she was up to, but the effect was that at a yell of command from their chief, they turned and thundered off, the lot of them, to vanish, cheering, over the hill.

"What the devil was all that about?" he asked.

She replied, tucking her vest back into her breeches, "I told them that I'm sick and want to consult a colleague."

He knew her well enough not to press for more; that night, after they had settled down by the fire, the horses and the mule suddenly went berserk as, without warning, they found themselves surrounded by a silent mass of Indians, many more than there had been earlier. This time they did not arrive shrieking on war-crazed ponies; they surrounded the camp eerily, magically, as if they had materialized out of thin air. A grotesque creature came waddling from their midst into the light of the fire, an ancient Indian weighed down by a buffalo robe, with horns on his head, amulets dangling from his ears and in his hand a totem with cats' paws, dead lizards and the dried-out head of a beaver. Buffalo rose to his feet at the approach of the sorcerer; although the man's eyes were pitch black and as alien as an iguana's, something in them reminded him of Gulie.

Gulie herself did not rise. She sat cross-legged on her blanket, the moosehide over her knees. It was the hour when she suffered most; she was too weak and in too much pain to get to her feet. The shaman stepped in front of her, made what looked like the sign of the cross with his grisly totem, then he knelt by her side, took her hand, opened his mouth, stuck her fingers in it and bit them. She squealed; Buffalo could not help crying, "What the devil is he doing?!"

She replied, a little shaken, "Don't ask me, he's a specialist. Maybe he wants to find out whether I'm still alive." In spite of her banter, she seemed nervous.

The old Indian put his hand in his robe, produced a cowhorn with a stopper on it, went to the fire and emptied its contents into the flames. They flared up, white with a bluish fringe; as if it had been a signal, all the Indians around them slid off their ponies and knelt down in the snow, forming a low wall of staring faces around them.

The shaman began to chant. Jogging around her at an elderly trot, he howled and wailed, tossing his head, brandishing his totem with amulets, treading a ring of trampled snow around her. She lay on her back, her eyes closed, her face still and sad. The Indians stared, there was no sound except the eerie chanting of the shaman and in the background the snorting of horses. He seemed to chant and howl for hours; finally he poured another hornful of powder into the fire, which this time produced an explosion of billowing red smoke, then he knelt by her side again and took her hand. But instead of biting it, he helped her to her feet. She rose with difficulty; it was surprising she managed at all. She bowed to the shaman; he bowed back. They gingerly shook hands, first the right hand, then the left; she whispered something to him to which he listened intently, then he bowed once more, turned around and jogged to the other side of the fire. There he made a sign of the cross again with his amulets and backed away, bowing, through a gap in the wall of faces. He backed off, tossing his head, snorting; he seemed to change into a buffalo as he did so. By the time he vanished, the illusion was complete; it was as if they had been visited by a supernatural being, half god, half bison. The Indians vanished as quietly as they had come; there was a brief whinnying and trampling of ponies in the darkness, then they were gone. After the sound had died away in the silence, he asked, "Well? Did he do thee any good?"

She was sitting with her head on her knees, her arms around her legs. Without looking up, she said, "Of course not."

"I am sorry." It was all he could find to say.

She lifted her head. Her eyes were unfocused, as if they saw him only as a vague shape in the night. But her voice was unchanged when she said, "It really was a farewell ceremony, for both of us. I have known him for years. He is much better at his job than I am, but there's no point in asking God to suspend the laws of nature for my sake. 'Why me?' is a pointless question; the obvious answer is, 'Why not?' "

"But didn't he help thee at all?"

"He did." She smiled, her eyes seemed to rekindle their old mischief. "He filled me with a feeling of tenderness."

"By biting thy fingers?"

"By not charging me for his consultation. He is one of the most expensive specialists this side of the Llano Estacado. His normal fee in a case like this would be at least twenty louis."

"He charges money?"

"Of course he does. He's too smart to be palmed off with pelts or wampum. He wants money, and he spends it too."

"On what?"

"The rumor is that he goes to New Orleans every year, in clothes of the world, to visit the brothels." Suddenly she gazed at him again with that odd, unfocused look, as if she were looking at something behind him. "Buffalo, this is as good a moment as any to settle a few basic matters. I don't know why I have lasted this long. Scientifically speaking, I should have been dead a week ago. However, here I am, and I can't say I object. But chances are that it will be over any moment now. I want thee to know what to do when it happens."

He searched for words, but failed.

"First of all, I want thee to shoot old Annie. She is in pretty bad shape, and I don't want her to suffer. She's not like us, she has no means of gilding the pill by telling herself there may be a sense to it all."

"Very well. What else?"

"The stores I promised the Hunis. I'd rather those pots and pans got to them than my mortal remains, if thee sees my point." Her eyes had that mischievous twinkle again. She looked very much alive. "Just don't get it into thy head to start lugging my corpse along for sentimental reasons. That is apt to be an unsavory business, especially once we get to the Llano Estacado. Just dig a hole and put me in it, on my back. But do take those stores to the Hunis. I promised them."

"All right." He turned away and poked the fire. This was almost unbearable. "But how do I find them? I have never been this far."

"It's simple. Just follow the setting sun, as the saying goes." She reached out and touched his hand. "Don't worry, old friend. The moment I'm gone, thee will have a guide."

"An Indian?"

"Maybe several Indians. It depends where we are at that time. From now on they won't let us out of their sight. Don't worry, they know. I told the old shaman who thee is and where we are going. They'll see to it that thee gets there."

"All right," he said. "Now, how about some rest?"

"I should eat something first."

He had never thought she would say this. "Have one good night's rest, for a change."

She looked at him with sad fondness. "Buffalo," she said quietly, "thee and I should have married long ago."

He smiled at her. "As if thee would ever have stayed still long enough."

"Pity," she said, turning toward the fire. "But there we are."

"There we are," he said. Then he added, "Let's have meeting."

Without further words, they closed their eyes, bent their heads and entered the silence.

*   *   *

Only as they reached the Llano Estacado did Buffalo begin to grasp how far this incredible woman had roamed during the forty years of her ministry to the Indians. The distance they had covered since crossing the Missouri seemed unimaginable. He had lost count of the days; one was exactly like another and the landscape never changed, day after day of gray, arid plain covered with tasteless grass that the animals ate with repugnance.

Gradually Gulielma began to doze off at intervals during the day. There seemed to be no cause for concern; on the contrary, it seemed a good sign. She was not likely to fall off her horse; like himself, she could sleep while riding, her body was attuned to the slow, rolling gait of her old mare. She still suffered agonies every night, and she would go to great lengths to hide it from him. But gradually she began to lose contact with reality. Her humor sparkled less often; the odd, unfocused look in her eyes became common. Sometimes, while riding by his side, she would gaze at him with a faint smile, and her eyes would look as if they were focused on something on the horizon. "Gulie?" he would ask; and she would address someone behind him, "Is that Maggie?" So compelling became the suggestion of an invisible companion that he would turn around to assure himself there was no one there.

He himself began to see things, mirages, hallucinations, whatever they were. He would get a sudden glimpse of water shimmering on the horizon and wake up from his stupor, thinking it was a lake. A few seconds later it would be gone; there would be nothing on the distant skyline but the barren hills, the endless dead plain, so unlike the prairie. The prairie, in summer, was a luscious meadow the size of an ocean, teeming with life, color, motion, a rioting garden where the bees got drunk on the flowers and the birds swarmed in shifting black clouds. Toward fall the sawgrass, higher than a man, would turn it into a billowing sea of ever shifting colors, majestic, magnificent, filling him with reverence. But this endless desert was without life or movement, except for the weightless balls of the ghostly tumbleweed, bouncing eerily from horizon to horizon, and the spirals of dust that arose out of nothing, danced about for a while and then vanished, as did the imaginary lakes and mountain ranges and the little Indians on distant ridges: there one moment, gone the next. Yet, to Gulie, unfocused as her eyes might be, it was familiar country. "Ah," she said, catching sight of a hillock in no way different from the thousand others they had passed, "there's Hanioro's grave." She looked at it fondly as she slowly undulated past, slumped in the saddle. "Goodbye, Hanioro, little friend! Hope to see thee soon!" Turning toward him, she added, "Poor little mite. He was five years old." There were times when she seemed to have completely forgotten about him plodding wearily by her side, aware only of ghostly people whom she alone could see. At night by the campfire she would gaze, sometimes for as long as an hour, at the bright little flames that seemed to spurt and dart more restlessly here than they did on the prairie, as if fed by the same febrile energy that drove her.

"Buffalo," she suddenly said one night, staring at the fire, "don't take my antics too seriously. I wouldn't go in for all that play-acting if I didn't feel safe with thee."

He looked at her, startled, but said casually, "I don't know what thee's talking about."

She smiled at the fire. "Of course thee does."

She made him wonder whether she was indeed aware of what she was doing, or knew in lucid moments like these that she was hallucinating and had merely wanted to put him at his ease.

There could be no doubt that she was getting steadily weaker. She was now taking no food at all; she could not keep even a mouthful of broth down. She dozed for longer and longer periods on her horse; at night, the moment he unrolled her blanket and spread the moosehide over her, she would fall asleep at once, especially if he lay down beside her and she could put her head on his shoulder.

One morning he could not wake her. She seemed drugged; he had to lift her into the saddle. As he did so, he was shocked by her weight; she was as light as a child. At first he held on to her as they rode, their long shadows ahead of them shortening gradually as the sun rose. But it was not necessary; even in unconsciousness her body managed to maintain its balance as it swayed to and fro on the back of the gaunt old mare.

Meanwhile they were no longer alone. The small equestrian statues of three or four Indians, side by side on a distant ridge, appeared more frequently for brief moments. It was almost as if they knew how far her eyes could see, for they seemed to come gradually closer. As whole days passed without her being conscious of her whereabouts at all, they approached almost to within hailing distance for minutes at a time. It was as if they drew closer as the flame of her consciousness flickered lower.

One night, as he stopped to make camp, she woke up when he halted her horse. "Where are we?" she asked, confused.

"It's time to rest. Let me help thee down." But when he went to lift her out of the saddle, she stopped him and said, "Ride on."

"But, Gulie, it's going to be dark soon! The horses—"

"Ride on, Buffalo," she said, her eyes closed. "We are nearly there." She dozed off again.

He hesitated. The land was bleak and featureless. The setting sun blinded him as he tried to gaze ahead. The trail they were following stretched ahead endlessly, it seemed. There would be a moon; if it meant that much to her, they could ride on for a couple of hours after nightfall. He climbed back into the saddle, assured his little mustang Fury that there would be a long rest soon but not quite yet, and they resumed their dreamlike amble along the trail, Gulie asleep in the saddle. The sun went down behind a ridge of black cloud; the moon rose; in its shadowless light the landscape seemed different, full of ghostly life. After a while he began to lose his sense of direction; he was about to stop and make camp when he heard a soft neighing. In the moonlight five Indian horsemen appeared, a stone's throw away to his left. When they realized that he had seen them, they moved; close together, they rode slowly ahead, abreast.

Indian fashion, they were guiding him by riding alongside at a distance. Somehow they had known that this was what he needed; he had the feeling that he was being guided through a world of which he had no comprehension. After an hour or so, for no reason, it seemed, they stopped. He patted Fury's cold, wet neck; when he looked up, they were gone. He dismounted and went to help her down; when he touched her hand and found it to be cold, he was sure she was gone. But she woke up, dazedly. "God," she said. That was all.

He lifted her out of the saddle and gently put her down. He unrolled her blanket, but when he came to lift her onto it she was asleep. As he was very tired and the horses too, he did not bother to make a fire. He rubbed down Fury, who was wet with sweat; the other two were dry but shaky with exhaustion, especially Annie. He freed her of the saddle and Henry of his clanking load; he slapped their rumps to send them grazing. They walked only a few paces, stood still and fell asleep on their feet, each facing in a different direction, their heads hanging down. He went back to her, lay down beside her, pulled the moosehide over them both and gently put his arm under her head.

So they lay until daybreak. He was very tired, yet he could not sleep. With her head on his shoulder he gazed at the stars, wondering about God, and where the souls of those who died went. When dawn came, it did not cheer him the way it used to. He disengaged himself, gently, so as not to wake her; when he got to his feet and looked around for the horses, he saw an incredible sight.

To the west, where the night still lingered low over the desert, there soared out of the darkness the bright orange peaks of a mountain range, touched by the rays of the rising sun. The sky beyond them was cobalt blue; the orange peaks looked like towers and ramparts fashioned by a race of giants. He knew now why she had insisted they ride on last night; she wanted to see her mountains at sunrise. "Gulie!" he cried and ran toward her. "Gulie, look! Look!"

She did not wake up; he knelt beside her to shake her, gently. "Gulie . . ."

She slowly rolled onto her back. As he looked up, he saw the five horsemen a few paces away.

There was no question at all; she was dead. Although he had been expecting it for weeks, he stood staring down at her in stunned disbelief. It seemed impossible that the woman he had known so well and who had been so alive should now have turned into a thing.

In spite of what she had told him, he was not going to bury her here, alone on the empty plain. He could not put her back on her horse unless he lashed her across the saddle and he could not face that; he put her in front of him on Fury; her head resting on his shoulder the way it had rested every night as she slept. So they rode on toward the mountains.

Surprisingly, the day was not one of mourning or loneliness. The five Indians who rode alongside them were joined by others after each crest of a hill. At noon there were hundreds of them on both sides, all riding abreast of the small cortege, fanned out over the desert. There was about their vast numbers and the silence in which they rode in line with her, as far as the eye could reach, a great solemnity. It was the most impressive farewell he had ever known anyone to be given by Indians. It filled him with awe and at the same time with an overwhelming sorrow; he wept as they rode on toward the mountains with the muffled rumble of a thousand hoofs.

When the sun was about to set behind the orange ramparts now towering above them, the Indians halted as at a signal. In the distance, on the crest of a rise where the trail dropped away behind a massive boulder, stood a small figure with a parasol or a flag. Buffalo slowly rode toward it, pressing her against him. As he drew closer, he saw that the parasol was a canopy made of bright orange cloth, held aloft over the figure of a middle-aged Indian without headdress, clad in a short white robe. Something about him expressed power and authority; he must be the chief, the blood-brother Gulie had told about. The Indian's features were different from other tribes; his cheekbones were wider, his forehead narrower.

At the top of the rise Buffalo halted. The moment he did so, there appeared above the boulder and higher along the trail rows of faces; the whole mountainside was alive with people. He slid out of the saddle with Gulie in his arms; she was so light that he barely noticed the difference as he jumped to the ground. He stood for a moment in doubt, then, at a gesture of the chief, some men emerged from behind the boulder and went toward Henry the mule. They took off the jangling load, and one of them threw a blanket over the mule's back. It was white and red and embroidered with black figures. Then the chief came toward him and held out his arms to take her.

He did not want to let her go. He did not trust them; he suddenly wished he had buried her that morning. But this was the goal toward which she had journeyed, the purpose of her pilgrimage; he should not take it away from her. He put her body in the other man's arms.

The chief carried her to the mule and was helped onto its back by his men. Then the canopy was put up behind him, and the Indian holding the mule's head tugged the rope to set him in motion. But Henry refused to budge. The Indian tugged harder; the beast stood like a rock. Buffalo realized what the trouble was: the canopy, it was too high. He took it down; the chief looked menacing, as if he had committed an insult, but the mule started to move. Slowly, at the same trot with which he had jogged along with her all his life, Henry started up the trail and vanished behind the crest of the rise. The Indians ran after him, carrying the orange canopy; Buffalo saw it sink behind the boulder, swaying like a flower.

He waited until he saw it emerge again, climbing the trail, past all those waiting, silent people; he watched it grow smaller and smaller, a bright speck in the vastness of the mountainside; finally it vanished, to emerge no more. He turned around; on his way back to the horses he met a small group of Indians carrying the pots and pans.

Fury and Annie stood waiting for him. The old mare was exhausted; when, after he had swung himself into Fury's saddle, he tried to lead her along, she staggered. This was the end of the trail for her; he should not drag her any farther. He dismounted, took his rifle and gently led her to a spot where he would have made camp had he decided to stay. There he patted her neck and scratched her forehead and tugged her ear and whispered to her all the things Gulie would have whispered. Then he stepped back, bent his head, his rifle under his arm, and closed his eyes for meeting. He stood like that for a long time, facing the horse, who swayed wearily on her legs, her head hanging down. Then he slowly raised the rifle and shot her through the head.

She crumbled; there was a clatter of stirrups and a heavy thud as her body hit the ground. With a shuddering moan she heaved a sigh, but it was only the air being forced from her lungs. She had been dead when she fell.

He went back to Fury, who stood waiting fretfully, alarmed by the shot. "Don't worry, beastie," he said, patting the little horse's neck. "It's all right. This is what they wanted."

He rode back into the Llano Estacado.

CHAPTER SIX

H USH," Boniface Baker whispered, "hush, Moses. Be quiet . . ." The baby became interested in his mouth, stretched out a small pudgy hand and touched his lips. "Ook!" it said. "Hawa!"

Again Boniface whispered, "Hush!" The movement of his lips now fascinated the baby, who squealed again, more piercingly this time, and sent the two Indian girls nearest to them into a snotty explosion of merriment. Cleo, sitting in the center of the half circle of children, was undisturbed. She looked sternly at the girls and said, ' Lark Eye! Little Deer! Stop that foolishness! My, a person would say you girls had never seen a baby before!"

Subdued, the little girls fell silent.

"Now, then," Cleo continued, "let's hear the books of the New Testament, each of you in turn. Lark Eye, thee begin."

"Acts," one of the little girls said in a high, clear voice.

"Nonsense. What comes first, Little Deer?"

"St. Matthew," the other one chirruped.

"Very good. Lark Eye, what's next?"

"St. Mark!"

The girls continued calling the books of the New Testament with the zest that had struck Boniface in Indian children the moment he had started the outdoor school. He marveled at Cleo's composure; nobody seeing her there, squatting in front of her small class, would think that three months earlier she had been as illiterate as they, as purely instinctive. They were like little animals, full of vitality and irrepressible fun; like the birds, the budding trees, the scudding clouds overhead, they seemed part of spring. He remembered his own schooldays; at the first promise of spring outside he had been overcome by restlessness, as if his young body, still linked to nature, had awakened from hibernation. Now, here in the wilderness, the squirrels and the gophers, the owls and the bears were stirring back to life; the trees of the forest, shaken by the first warm wind, were showing a flush of green.

"Hawa!" little Moses shouted at the top of his lungs, bouncing up and down, waving his pudgy hands, delighted with something he had seen, maybe a reflection of the light, maybe a bird. "Woosh! Hawa-hawa-hawa!"

The noise the child made was such that the children lost track at Philemon. There was only one solution; but as Boniface rose to take the little screamer away, there was Cleo by his side, saying, "Give him to me."

"But thee still has half an hour to go!"

"It doesn't matter. He'll be quiet." She took the little boy from him, put him on her arm with a practiced gesture and went back to the front of the class. "Now let's let the baby hear how well we can count," she said, sitting down and putting him firmly on her lap. "All together now! Can you go to thirty?"

"Ye-es!" the children shouted in unison.

"All right, then, here we go: One . . ."

"Two! Three! Four!" the high, shrill voices shouted with the zest of spring's awakening. The baby sat on Cleo's lap, mouth open, an expression of delight on his face. His little hands began to wave with excitement and his bow legs to trample, until he bounced up and down, beside himself with joy. To see his innocent delight, safe in the protection of her strong black hands, flooded Boniface with tenderness. He closed his eyes and stood there for a moment in the cacophony of children's voices, overcome by a sudden awareness of the Presence. Then he heard shouting in the distance; a hand touched his arm and a voice said, "You'd better come! They're here!"

He looked around and saw it was Jake, in a state of excitement. "Who?"

"The wagon train! They are coming, up the lake!"

In the corral, Buffalo's men were saddling their horses, yodeling, yoo-hooing; far away, across the shimmering expanse of the lake, he saw a long, thin procession of toy wagons. He ran to his horse; as he was saddling up, he heard a joyous shout, "Uncle!" and there, huge on a sweat-streaked mustang, was George McHair. The youth jumped down, ambled toward him, arms outstretched, caught him in a bear hug that squeezed the breath out of him and cried, "Uncle Bonny! Bless thee!" overpowering him with a stench of unwashed body. He was kissed on both cheeks and slammed between the shoulder blades with a violence that made him pitch forward.

"For God's sake!" he cried; but the young ruffian grabbed his arms and hollered, shaking him, "Uncle! How wonderful to see thee! Come and meet the others! Where's thy horse?"

"I—here . . ."

Before he knew what was happening, he was lifted into the saddle by the young giant, who leaped onto his own horse and galloped off toward the lake. Stunned, he cantered after him.

As they approached the lead wagon of the train, pitching and rolling toward them, drawn by two teams of oxen, there came another yell, "Uncle!" On the driver's seat he saw young Joseph Woodhouse, nut brown, unshaven like a woodsman; next to him sat little Himsha, exquisite and delicate. As he was shaking the young man by the hand and muttering a bemused greeting, someone else hollered, "Uncle!" On the driver's seat of the next wagon he discovered Obadiah Best and Carrie Woodhouse, both lean and tanned, waving at him boisterously. He trotted toward them and asked, "What in the world are you doing here?"

"We're married!" Obadiah bellowed, as if he were fifty yards away. "We passed Meeting just before we left, and here we are! Has the school been built yet?"

"No, we—" His mouth fell open, for there, on the next wagon lumbering toward him, sat two of his slaves, Simeon and his wife, Clarissa. Behind them, under the looped-up front flap, peered the little black faces of their brood. He sat thunderstruck as the wagon swayed toward him. He saw a look of concern cross the young Negro's face and hastily put out his hand. "Simeon," he said, "Clarissa . . . what is this? Why aren't you on the island?"

"We had to sell it," the young Negro replied. "The other owners wouldn't let us be. So we decided to seek our fortune here."

"Well, I—" Then he saw on the next wagon two more of his slaves, Balthazar and Ruby. It looked as if all of the wagons that came lumbering toward him were filled with his former slaves. But as he went to welcome them, he discovered others, young white couples from Philadelphia, most of whom he knew. He went down the train, shaking hands, feeling it must be a dream: scores of children, black and white, dozens of oxen pulling flatbed carts loaded with plows, barrels, school benches, bedsteads, even a sitz bath filled with valises. He gaped at it. Who in the world would have lugged this incongruous thing hundreds of miles through the forest, in the teeth of a war? Then he heard a high, shrill voice scream, "Well! If it isn't Boniface Baker!" So strident was the cry that his horse shied under him; on the driver's seat of the last wagon of the train he recognized Bathsheba Moremen and Millicent Clutterbuck, the recording clerk of the Women's Meeting. He shook them gingerly by the hand, inquired after their health and felt that any moment he would wake up, drenched with perspiration. He rode along with them, listening to their genteel recital of the hardships they had suffered, the colics, the vapors, the Indians, the loss of two wagons through the ice of a treacherous river, the death of poor old Mammy, whom they had buried in the forest, a beautiful ceremony, beautiful; and not a *sign* of the French, thank God. Finally he asked, "But what are you Friends doing here?"

It was a reasonable question. Both spinsters must be in their late fifties; whatever happened, it was unlikely they would ever return to Philadelphia. "Well," Bathsheba Moremen said tartly, "we saw there were a lot of young children going, and young wives likely to have babies, so we asked ourselves, 'Why stay in Philadelphia where nobody needs us? Why not go along and take care of sufferings?'"

"Good thing we did!" Millie Clutterbuck said smugly. "We have had a lot of sickness among the children; our wagon has never been without at least two of them. Look!" She lifted the flap behind her. "One chickenpox, one whooping cough, and two sprained ankles."

His glance was met by the bored gaze of four small faces, three black and one white.

"Then we had old Mammy, of course, very, very sick, poor dear, and —wait! I have a letter for thee!" Millicent groped behind her for an incongruous-looking reticule, which she heaved onto her lap; after some noisy rummaging, she unearthed a letter addressed to him in Beulah's writing.

"Thank thee, Friend," he said, putting it in his pocket. "Well —I think I'd better ride ahead and see what needs to be done."

"Aren't we going to have meeting first?" Bathsheba Moremen asked. "Surely, after arriving safely at our destination, God deserves a prayer of thanks?"

"Surely, surely . . . Of course . . . See you later." He spurred his horse and escaped.

The arrival of the wagon train was surprisingly orderly; the wagons were arranged alongside one another with practiced precision. Hundreds of people milled around among lowing oxen, mules, horses, goats, swarms of children; Indians from the village turned up on their nervous mustangs to stare at the newcomers, especially at the Negroes. Children came running and squaws arrived with bouncing papooses on their backs; when the Indian and Negro children met, they gaped in a moment of disbelief, then began to chase one another, emitting high-pitched shrieks. Boniface was besieged by greetings, by information about Eden Island, about slaves who had stayed behind, and suddenly he felt he had had enough. He slipped away to the water's edge, pushed off the skiff and rowed out onto the lake as fast as he could.

Twenty minutes later the warbling of the veeries on the little island fell silent as the bow of the skiff slithered into the reeds. He jumped out, waded ashore and sat down at the foot of a tree. Leaning against it, eyes closed, he let the tension and the confusion drain out of him. After a while the first of the veeries hesitantly started up again; he opened his eyes and gazed out over the lake. In the distance the white-covered wagons stood clustered in the clearing. He could not distinguish individual people; all he saw was the dark blotch of their mass. Then he thought: Cleo. Where was she? How had she taken to this invasion? He had not seen her since Jake had come to warn him that the wagons were arriving. All those people, oxen, horses, goats, the sitz bath, Bathsheba Moremen and Millie Clutterbuck. . . . He closed his eyes with a feeling of despondency. What had he done to God, to find himself pounced upon by those women? Was it a sign? What did God want of him? Should he take Cleo and the baby and flee toward the Wabash? Then he remembered the letter.

He took it out of his pocket, opened it and read. There was Beulah's voice, calm and unemotional, telling him about Abby, about Obadiah Best and young Carrie Woodhouse deciding to get married and join the wagon train, about Jeremiah, who now was burdened with the yard; because of Jeremiah's plight, she could not join him as she had planned, but would stay on in Philadelphia indefinitely. She realized that by doing so she failed her duty as a wife . . .

He lowered the letter, for suddenly he knew: 'I must go back. This is madness. I belong with my wife and daughter.'

It was as if a darkness had been removed from his soul. There could be no doubt, this was what God wanted of him. He should not allow this poor woman, sickly and as deaf as a post, to destroy herself with a sense of guilt for not joining her husband in the wilderness.

He put the letter in his pocket and went back to the skiff. Only after he had rowed halfway back across the lake did his thoughts return to Cleo. If anyone were emotionally equipped to stand this blow, it was she. He deliberately did not think about the baby.

As he approached the shore, he was struck by the silence. He had left the clearing a noisy chaos; now it was empty; all was still. He pulled the skiff ashore and saw a large crowd of people sitting in silence on the ground behind the wagons; they had gone into meeting.

He made his way quietly toward them and scanned the faces, looking for Cleo. She was not there. He was struck by sudden anxiety. Where was she?

Common sense told him that there was no reason to fly into a panic; but instinct warned him that something was wrong. What could she have done? Run away? Why should she? Where could she run to? It did not make sense, but suddenly he was certain that she had run off into the forest with the baby. She must have been thrown into confusion by the arrival of her own people; she had run off blindly into the wilderness, taking the child with her.

Several of the worshipers began to watch him curiously; to wander about during meeting was a bad beginning, but he had to find out where she was.

The cabin? She might be there. He walked across to it, looked inside, called her name; she was not there. He was about to start into the forest when he spotted a row of diapers on the laundry line at the back of the cabin. Surely she would have taken them? She could not have made off into the woods. She was all right. Then it occurred to him where she must be. Of course. She had gone back to her people. She was in some wagon, chatting with friends, showing off the baby.

Suddenly he had an agonizing sense of loss. He could not understand it. Half an hour ago, on the island, he had been certain that God wanted him to go back to Beulah and Abby, he had even felt a sense of liberation at the idea. Now he was beset by the mad impulse to find Cleo and little Moses and to flee with them in the opposite direction. His inner turmoil was such that he walked over to Becky's grave, on the edge of the forest. On it lay a posy of wild flowers that he had placed there the day before. As he stood looking down on the small mound, tears came to his eyes. He closed them, lifted his face and prayed, 'Oh, God what must I do? What does Thee want of me?' Then, from somewhere close by, came a sound: the muffled crying of a baby.

He looked about him. The sound stopped. Where had it come from? His eyes roamed along the wall of the forest, looking for a place where she could be hidden. But there was no place; the brambles and the cat-briars had woven an impenetrable thicket between the trees. Then he saw it. The storm cellar. Its door stood ajar.

He glanced at the people in the distance, still in worship; then he walked over to the cellar and opened the door. It was pitch dark and chilly inside; there was a clammy, moldy odor.

"Cleo?"

No reply.

"Cleo . . ."

Then the baby cried, a few steps away from him.

He went toward the sound, groping in the darkness. He touched someone. "Cleo? Is that thee?"

"Yes." The baby fell silent.

He felt so relieved that he asked angrily, "Why did thee not reply? Why is thee hiding here? What ails thee?"

"Nothing."

"Thee would not be hiding here, away from everybody, if there were not something the matter! Is it all those people?"

After a silence the voice asked, "Are the white people all teachers?"

"Good heavens, no!" He laughed, relieved. "Just the two girls, Himsha and Carrie. Is that why thee hid? Don't fret, nobody is going to replace thee. But look how many more children have arrived! Thee will need help."

She said nothing.

"Come. Come with me, let us join meeting for worship. Come."

"I don't want to."

"Why not? Thee knows almost everybody there!"

"Thee join them. I want to stay here."

Though her voice sounded unemotional, he sensed a great distress in her. Why? What was she afraid of? It made him ask, at last, "Cleo? Why did thee come with me?"

There was a silence; then she said dispassionately, "Because I wanted revenge."

"For what?"

"For Harry."

"But it was Caleb who killed him . . ."

"Thee gave Harry to Joshua when he was little, as a toy to do with as he pleased."

"That's not true! Harry came to us as Joshua's friend!"

"And after he had played with him and enjoyed his body, he threw Harry away. I swore I would avenge him. I loved him. He was my brother." For the first time her voice betrayed emotion.

His heart went out to her. "Cleo, I—"

"I began with Joshua. But thee sent him away. So I turned on thee."

Suddenly he realized that he had lived in a world of make-believe. It was frightening. "Believe me," he said. "Harry—"

"And Ruth?"

"Who?"

"Thee does not remember little Ruth?"

"No. Was she—was she one of my slaves?"

"She was my sister. She was not like anyone else. She drew beautiful pictures of animals and people. She always made us laugh. Everyone loved her. Then she was sold. Together with eighteen other children. Does thee not remember?"

"Oh . . . yes . . ." It had been years ago, Caleb's idea. There had been too many children, too many mouths to feed without any work in return, so he had agreed, reluctantly, to sell a number of them. Humanely, to neighboring Friends. "But I made it a condition that they should be orphans! I told Caleb not to break up any families!"

"She screamed when they came for her. She hid in a corner, and we all tried to protect her; but she was grabbed and dragged away, screaming. I have never seen such eyes. She stretched out her hands toward us, then she was pulled out the door. I wanted to throw myself on them, but all I could do was sit there and look and hate."

"Who were they?"

"Caleb and Scipio."

"But the children were sold only to Quakers who would be kind and humane to them . . ."

"Think of thy own children. Think of Abby. Two men come and drag her away, and she screams and stretches out her hands toward thee, but thee can do nothing, and thee knows thee will never see her again."

He was filled with a sense of damnation. It was more than guilt, it was the awareness of something evil he had done that could never be undone, never forgiven. To have set his slaves free, to have given them his land had not been enough; it had not redeemed the horror of what he and Grandmother had done. Despite their conviction that they were humane, they had been monsters of cruelty.

He knew that he was pleading with her for something she could not give, but he could not help himself. "Thee must believe me, Cleo! I did not know! I—I did not realize . . . You were not real people to me! But you are now. I swear to thee, thee is as real and as precious to me as myself. Thee is my equal, my friend, we have a child together . . . Forgive me, for God's sake, forgive me! I did not know, I swear to thee, I did not know that thee was human!"

"To me thee was a monster," she said dispassionately. "I wanted to destroy thee. If that woman had not come, I would have succeeded."

"Which woman?"

"The one who gave thee the powders."

He wanted to disentangle himself from the cruelty, the violence. He said, "Moses is quiet now . . ."

"He always is, the moment he hears thy voice. He loves thee."

"Oh, but he loves *thee!*" It was a foolish thing to say, but he felt the desperate need to show her tenderness.

"That's right," she said. "He loves us both. He loves a monster and a slave."

For the first time he sensed an element of dramatization in what she said. It gave him back some of his self-confidence. "I will never be able to make good what I did, to thee or any of the others," he said, "but I want us to try and forget, to start again—" 'But what about

Beulah?' he thought. 'What about Abby?' Yet something forced him to say, "I do not want to lose thee. Thee and the baby are more important to me than—than anything else in my life. Thee must believe that."

She was silent for a while; then she said, "I believe it."

He waited for some inner assurance of the rightness of his decision, but all he felt was an indiscriminate tenderness that reached out to her, to the baby, to all those people out there who had traveled so far and so hazardously to join him, despite the fact that at one time he had considered himself their owner. He was moved to say, "This is the first time we have really talked to each other."

"Yes," she said. After a moment, she added, "That is because of the dark."

He stretched out his hand and touched her arm in the darkness; and suddenly there it was, all about them—the indefinable, unmistakable presence of God.

* * *

Buffalo McHair had intended to go straight to Pendle Hill, but he was sidetracked on the way by the Indian tribes, to whom he was now a familiar and respected personage. He found himself rounding up mustangs with the Apaches, getting drunk during a celebration of spring's arrival and becoming a Comanche in the process; he hunted buffalo with the Cheyennes and traded hides with the Osages. Finally he arrived at Pierre Louchant's landing, where he had himself ferried across for a bride's dowry plus one louis danger money, although the first dangerous man he had come across between the Llano Estacado and the Missouri was Pierre Louchant himself. The Frenchman asked, "Well? Did she get there?"

"Yes," he said. "She got there."

The prairie was in full flower. The air was filled with birdsong, chirrups, cries; the night before he reached the forest beyond the Wabash, he heard the call of the timber wolf welcoming him home. He was full of sentimental longing for his men, even for solemn little Boniface Baker, bless his heart. He rode on longer than usual and toward nightfall arrived at the beginning of the trail through the forest. It was unwise to approach an Indian settlement after dark, but he was so looking forward to embracing everybody and telling the story of his long, incredible journey that he decided to risk it.

The first odd thing he noticed was that halfway through the forest he knew, he suddenly found himself in open country again. The woods had been recently cleared, the soil plowed into a square field; at the far end he discerned a cabin in the dusk. Obviously, somebody had settled here since he left. He rode along the edge of the field; the trail veered back into the forest, but after a mere hundred yards or so there was another field, with a cabin. Who the devil were these people? Could it be that his own men had settled down with a squaw to grow runner beans? It seemed unlikely. They must be new settlers, from the east. But who had told them about this place, hundreds of miles from anywhere?

By the time he arrived at the lake, he had passed many new farms, all with brand-new cabins; strangely enough, none of them showed a light or a sign of life. Night had fallen; in the moonlight the deserted cabins in their neat little fields looked sinister, as if the inhabitants had been massacred in a raid.

At last, there was the Indian village. A passel of dogs ran to welcome him, barking furiously, shying his horse; but no human being was visible. Where was everybody? He pulled his rifle out of its holster and ghosted along the edge of the lake toward the clearing where the Baker cabin stood. Suddenly his little mustang whinnied. From the darkness came the muted, secretive reply of many horses. He rode cautiously up the bank and found a corral full of them, gazing curiously in his direction, snorting and pawing. Beyond them he saw a sight that made his mouth fall open.

Where six months ago there had been only a cabin and a storm cellar, now an entire village was starkly outlined in the moonlight. But it too seemed deserted; not a sound, not a light. He hushed Fury once again and rode slowly, cautiously, into a street of large, solid-looking buildings, the largest obviously a trading post, with a row of plows and wagon wheels outside. On its façade he read, painted in large black lettering clearly visible in the moonlight, WOODHOUSE & SONS, GENERAL MERCHANDISE. The street curved back toward the lake; he passed what he thought looked like a schoolhouse, then another corral full of curious, snorting horses. The adjoining house had a sign, GEORGE MCHAIR, HORSES TRADED AND TRAINED. Where was everybody? He rode on warily, his finger on the trigger.

Then he came upon the largest building of all, on the bank of the lake. It was surrounded by a porch and had tall, narrow windows; it looked like a Meeting House. It too was dark. He slid off his horse, gun in hand; around him he discovered more horses, tethered in the darkness under the trees.

He tiptoed up the steps to the porch. The doors were open; as he stood in the entrance, he discerned vague shapes sitting on benches. There must be over a hundred people gathered there; he even could distinguish, ghostlike at the far end of the hall, a row of silhouettes on a facing bench.

Nobody seemed to notice his entrance; he tiptoed to the last bench, across loudly creaking floorboards, and sat down beside a shadowy figure in the darkness, his rifle between his knees.

Who were all these people? Where in the world had they come from? Then he remembered: the school expedition. A lot of Pennsylvania Friends must have joined it. But why the darkness?

He asked the figure next to him, in a whisper, "Why no lights?"

As in reply, it rose to its feet and began to minister; he discovered it was a woman. She spoke about her children, who had got into a fight with someone else's children, and how distressed she had been until she realized that they were fighting each other not because of what they were, but who they were; even as she separated the fighters she had been filled with joy, for it was as if she had seen the dawning of the day when the lights would go on in Pendle Hill Meeting.

It was all rather confused, but her voice, husky and warm, was one of the most sensuous voices he had heard for a long time. It made him yearn for the company of women of his own kind instead of Comanche squaws. It put an entirely new aspect on his homecoming. He was grinning in the darkness, filled with un-Quakerly thoughts, when meeting broke. He groped for the hand of the woman, shook it warmly and said, "That was powerful ministry, Friend, powerful ministry."

She answered, "Thank thee"; then all around him lanterns were lit. He turned to his neighbor with his most roguish grin and froze; the woman was a Negro. She gave him a charming smile and said, "That's why."

He looked about him and saw, to his bafflement, that the Meeting was made up of Negroes, Indians, white people, all mixed together; there seemed to be no separation between the men and the women either. On the facing bench he recognized Obadiah Best, Boniface Baker, Cleo and Running Bull, his enormous belly glistening in the lantern light. Before he had a chance to recover, there was a shout, "Father!" and a young man came running toward him. It was George; and there were young Joe Woodhouse and Himsha, radiant with surprise and delight; within minutes he found himself the center of a crowd of people, white, black, Indian, begging for news of the outside world. Presently they all went outside, where somebody had started a fire and set up a roasting spit, and throughout the barbecue by moonlight the questioning and probing continued. He talked of where he had been, what he had seen, told stories, took an occasional swig from his flask, astounded by the free manner in which the Negroes mingled with the Indians and the whites.

Well—here it was, the Holy Experiment: a community in which people of all races lived together in equality and trust, like the beasts in the Peaceable Kingdom; a sight to gladden the heart of any Friend. He wondered why he felt so uncomfortable.

Finally, he found himself sitting at a table in his son's cabin in a circle of lamplight with George, Himsha and young Joe Woodhouse, now a member of his family. Himsha asked after Gulielma; when he told them about the end of her journey, and how he'd had to shoot her old horse, there were tears in Himsha's eyes and his own. Then, out of the blue, young Joe asked, "Would thee take us there?"

He had been about to take a swig; the bottle stopped in mid-air. "What's that?"

"Aunt Gulie suggested that Himsha and I go to the Hunis to start a Quaker school. She gave us an old gun which she said would serve as a passport, should we ever decide to go. We would like to, but we don't know how to get there. Would thee take us?"

"But—but I thought I saw thy name on the trading post as I came riding in?"

"Oh, that's all arranged," the boy replied. "Obadiah Best will take over. We never intended to stay here. The moment Aunt Gulie mentioned the Hunis to us, Himsha and I felt that was where we wanted to go."

"But it's very far," he protested, "and they are totally uncivilized, they don't need a school."

"All Indian children need a school," Himsha said firmly. She looked beautiful in the lamplight; she must be happy with the boy. He took the swig from his bottle and saw, in the jumbled images of a distant memory, a burning village, mutilated bodies, a tiny child sitting in their midst, frozen in horror. At the time, people had told him she would never recover, what she had seen was too much for her mind to bear. Now there she sat, talking about traveling to the other end of the world to start a school for Huni children. Again he had that odd feeling of discomfort. He should have been delighted at her courage, her independence. But there was about her a dreamlike quality that disturbed him, just as the entire settlement did.

"Look," he said, slapping the cork back into the bottle, "it is not only very far and a very hazardous journey, I don't think you can isolate yourselves among those Indians and—and remain yourselves." He knew he put it badly, but he did not know yet what exactly it was that troubled him so.

Joe Woodhouse reacted with indignation. "But, Father! Thee has seen with thy own eyes that people of all races can live together in harmony. Here: take Himsha and me. To me she's not an Indian, to her I'm not a white man, we think of each other as Himsha and Joe."

"Yes," he said. "But she's an Indian in a Quaker dress. Several of the Unamis are now wearing pants and shirts, no doubt sold to them by thee. Don't tell me they are not trying to look like thee. Behave like thee, think like thee. They'll end up by losing themselves. And that's what would happen to thee and her among the Hunis."

"Oh, Father!" Himsha cried incredulously. "Surely thee doesn't mean that? I haven't changed! Joe knows it! I even told him . . ." Suddenly she looked bashful.

"Go ahead, tell him," Joe urged. The boy was good to her. He liked the look of them together.

"Well," she continued bravely, "I told Joe that I am not really a Quaker. To me the prairie is the home of the Great Spirit."

"Who taught thee that?!" George asked, shocked. "Uncle Ellis?" She nodded.

"That old—!" George gazed at him, his eyes wide with outrage. *"That's* what he was doing every time he went to see her when I was gone!"

"Boy," he said, "don't be a jackass."

"But the sneaky way in which that old buzzard—!"

"George!" His authority was such that the boy shut up like a clam. "Thee has been telling me how beautifully everybody lives together in this place, how everyone is allowed to think as he pleases. Now here's a girl who confesses that she not only looks like an Indian but believes like one, and thee throws a tantrum. In other words, thee wants thy Indians and thy Negroes the way thee wants thy horses: tame, in pants."

Himsha giggled. The gay sound deflated him. "Well," he grunted, bringing out his flask again, "I'm just an old buffalo hunter who likes people the way God made them: wild." He took a swig. He must be getting jug-bitten, for his eyes filled with tears at the thought of how Gulie had drunk from this very bottle in the graveyard on the island, and by the campfire on the prairie when it had hit her like a bullet in her guts. Oh, my God, how he missed her! Where was she? Where the devil was she? Would he ever see her again? "What was that?" he asked, conscious of somebody holding forth at him.

"I said, thee can have my bed." It was George. "I'll sleep in the stable. Among my horses with pants."

He grunted and winked at Himsha, who gazed upon him with such tenderness that he felt like bursting into tears. "Never mind, child," he said. "There is no difference between thy belief and that of the Quakers. All it amounts to is that thee thinks of God as a prairie of light and love instead of as an ocean."

He discovered he liked the idea.

He got to talk to Boniface Baker and Cleo only the next morning, after Himsha had shown him the village: George's horse shop, Obadiah's smithy, Joe's trading post and the Rebekah Baker School, where Himsha, Carrie Best and Cleo were teachers.

The change that had come over the black girl since he had seen her last was astounding. He remembered her as a temptress who had bathed naked in brooks with less than six inches of water, setting his men howling like coyotes. He remembered her later, looking chaste and meek, darning Bonny Baker's socks and lacing his tea with a poison that drove him out of his mind. Now, there she sat, beside him on a log on the bank of the lake, cool and beautiful, with on her lap a fat little boy. She looked even less approachable than before, yet from the way Boniface Baker talked to her, there was obviously great tenderness between them. They talked for a while about Millie Clutterbuck, Running Bull and Obadiah Best; then they sat listening to the veeries, with the little boy on her lap stretching out his hands toward the island from whence the music came.

He said, "I brought the bat's wing you gave me for Gulie to look at, and her translation."

Cleo asked, "What does it say?"

"I have the piece of paper in my saddle bag, but it says something like, *'We deposit this fatherless child on your doorstep because in your house there is a promise of love.'*"

After a silence Boniface said, "Well, let's hope that this world of beauty and gentleness will not be destroyed the way the other was."

"Which one?"

"Eden Island. Has thee not heard about Altar Rock? They thought of a way to blow it up, and within a month after they did so, all the indigo plants on the island froze to death: the explosion had closed up the warm springs. Hawkins of Septiva, who bought the island, lost a lot of money. But the real loss cannot be measured in money," he added ruefully. "It was truly a heavenly place."

Buffalo looked at Cleo. She met his gaze, but did not betray whether she was thinking the same: heavenly, except to the slaves. The ordinary little man by his side had done a wonderful thing and stayed an ordinary little man in the process. It somehow seemed to hold a greater promise for mankind than if he had become a saint.

They sat there for a while, listening to the veeries and the baby's squeals of response. Then Buffalo asked, "What will happen to you all, once they catch up with you?"

"Who?"

"People like Parson Paisley and Pierre Louchant. They're bound to turn up sooner or later. What will you do then?"

"Way will open," Boniface said.

He had heard those words all his life. He still did not know whether they were the Friends' greatest strength or sanctimonious procrastination.

"It's not our survival which is important," Boniface continued, "it's the fact that we showed it can be done."

"Yes," he said, "I suppose so."

"We will hold out," the girl said in that curious flat voice.

He remembered Gulie holding out, against all rational expectations. For a few moments he felt as if she had joined them as they sat there, listening to the veeries, gazing at the lake. Then a bell sounded in the village and Boniface said, "Will thee join us for worship?"

He did so, declining the invitation to sit on the facing bench. Again he sat in the back row; not beside the handsome Negro woman of the night before, but beside Himsha, who put her arm through his as they entered the silence.

He tried to experience the presence of God, but felt a yearning for the prairie: the clouds, the birds, the vast, incandescent sea of grass. Although full of admiration for what these people had done, he was overcome by the urge to flee.

Suddenly a man's voice began to minister, intruding upon his thoughts. It was the voice of all weighty overseers, the same singsong, the same humble self-satisfaction. "When I was a boy on the banks of the Delaware . . ." It was Running Bull.

He stared at the fat, smug Indian on the facing bench; then he kissed his daughter's cheek, whispered in her ear, "Tell Jake to meet me at the Wabash" and, with loud creakings, despite the fact that he went on tiptoe, escaped into the sunlight. In the corral little Fury, who must have been watching out for him, whinnied. "Hush, beastie, hush . . ." He patted the hard, flat forehead, guided the little horse out the gate, closed it softly behind him, saddled up well out of earshot of the Meeting and trotted off down the village street.

GEORGE MCHAIR, HORSES TRADED AND TRAINED—WOODHOUSE &

SONS, GENERAL MERCHANDISE—REBEKAH BAKER SCHOOL—then the freshly plowed fields, the new cabins and, finally, the forest.

It was high noon when he reached the crest of the hill where the prairie began. "Ah!" he said as he saw it. For a moment he stood still, dazzled by its vastness; then he flicked the reins and cantered down the slope into the man-high sawgrass, flushing a cloud of birds as Fury plunged into the waves.

The sky was clear and bright, the wind swept spinning whorls across the shimmering plain.

The red speck of the feathers on his Quaker hat was the last of him to vanish in the infinite prairie of light and love.

Here ends Volume One of
The Peaceable Kingdom.
It is to be followed, and
completed, by Volume Two,
containing Part Three,
"The Peculiar People (Indiana, 1833),"
and Part Four, "The Lamb's War
(New Mexico, 1945)."

JAN DE HARTOG

JAN DE HARTOG was born in Haarlem, Holland, in 1914, the son of a Calvinist father and a Quaker mother. He ran off to sea at an early age. In 1940, just after the Germans occupied Holland, his novel *Holland's Glory* was published, a story of the Dutch ocean-going tugboats on which he had served. Although it mentioned neither the war nor the Germans, it became a symbol of Dutch defiance and was banned by the Nazis, but not until 300,000 copies had been sold. In 1943 the author escaped to England.

Since then Mr. de Hartog has written a number of books: *The Lost Sea, The Distant Shore, A Sailor's Life* (these three are now collected in the volume entitled *The Call of the Sea*), *The Little Ark, The Spiral Road, The Inspector, Waters of the New World, The Artist, The Hospital, The Captain* and *The Children*.

Mr. de Hartog's name has gained added familiarity through the popularity of his plays *Skipper Next to God* and *The Fourposter* (both of which became films, and *The Fourposter* was adapted for the musical stage as *I Do! I Do!*). Four of his novels have also been made into films: *The Distant Shore* as *The Key, The Inspector* as *Lisa, The Spiral Road* and *The Little Ark*.

Both Mr. de Hartog and his wife, Marjorie, are active in the Religious Society of Friends.